Thou Shalt Not

By

Rob Gibson

Other books by Rob Gibson
Tortured Souls

Western Books Written as Robin Gibson

The Ruination of Dan Becker
Ma Calhoun's Boys
Riders of Black Dawn
Tucker's Treasure
The Sherriff of Whiskey City
The Bandits of Whiskey City
The Legend of Whiskey City
The Doctor of Whiskey City
The Duchess of Whiskey City
The Warriors of Whiskey City
Diamonds and Dust

Cover art by Austin Allison

To
My little family:
My wife Kay
My daughter Paige
My boys
Danny and Dallas

CHAPTER ONE

Washington DC March 6th 2004 Thursday Night

Justine Salters sighed. So this is what happiness felt like. Clutching her tea mug, she leaned back into the thin cushions of her thread-bare couch. So much to do. An overflowing basket of laundry awaited her attention. Water from a leaky faucet dripped on dirty dishes in the kitchen sink. Her checkbook, which contained no money, sat atop a stack of unpaid bills.

Her books were open on the coffee table in front of her. She had a paper on investment theory due next week, and an accounting test she desperately needed to study for. The paper on theory she was somewhat excited about, but the accounting on the other hand, was sheer torture.

She sighed again, loosening her robe, as a wave of warmth washed over her. Whew! Jake Carter.

A smile stole across her face. Who would have ever thought? Justine reflected back to when she first met Jake. So long ago in the fourth grade city-wide spelling bee.

He was the rich kid, representing a snobby, private school. He'd looked so handsome in his pressed, immaculate uniform. She was the little black girl, nervous in her new to her, second-hand skirt. In the end it had come down to the two of them. After a long battle, she won. Sipping her tea, Justine allowed herself a guilty little smile. Man, he had been so mad.

Justine sighed; even back then, he was so cute.

The phone ringing startled her, and she sloshed tea on her robe. Dabbing at the tea, she smiled again. It would be Jake. They had a ritual of leaving each other messages at night. She had already left him a message on his voice mail.

"Hey girl, I know you are busy studying," Jake's voice said, sounding dreamy even through the crappy answering machine speaker. "I just wanted to call and wish you sweet dreams."

Ignoring the rule they had of not picking up, Justine jumped across the room and snatched the phone from the cradle, but too late Jake had already disconnected. Feeling a twinge of sadness, she wandered to the window. Pulling back the curtain she saw a light rain was falling. Not a soft spring rain, but a gray, cold rain with the ugly edge of winter. It would freeze tonight, Justine thought. She would have to wear her boots in the morning. She hated the boots. Gray and clumping they had about as much style and grace as a hippo in mud. In fact they reminded her so much of a hippo that she had drawn eyes on the toes with a yellow marker.

She thought about calling Jake back, but he had classes in the morning and she knew he needed to study. With a sigh, she sat down, dragging her books to her. Soon she was lost in the fascinating world of free markets and the theories of Milton Freidman. Her professor hated Freidman, but Justine found his views on economics fascinating. Twenty minutes later the doorbell rang, startling her out of her review of investment theory. For a second, she smiled, thinking it might be Jake. A frown crept onto her face, blotting out her earlier good mood like clouds blocking the sun. Of course, it wouldn't be Jake. It was far too late and he had an early class. No, likely it would be Rodney. Justine frowned. He would be wanting money.

Justine wasn't sure just what her brother was into, but she guessed it was not good. Rodney thought Jake's family had money and lately he had been pressuring his sister to borrow some. Justine knew that Jake's family did have money. His father was in construction or something. Jake had this little black sports car. Justine wasn't sure of the make, but she knew it went fast enough to take her breath away. He liked to speed around the beltway, scarring her half to death. As she walked to the door a picture of Jake driving flashed through her mind. His head thrown back, his teeth shining and his hair curling around his ears.

At the door, Justine paused, the vision of Jake fleeing from her mind. A dark sense of dread crept up her spine. She always got the chills when she had to answer the door after dark. The apartment she rented was close to school, but it was also cheap. Her front door had no peephole. Justine had complained to the manager several times. Each time, the manager had smiled at her around his ever-present cigar and promised to put one in. But to date, no peephole had been installed.

Checking to make sure the chain was hooked, she threw the deadbolt. As soon as she unlocked and twisted the doorknob, the door exploded inward, snapping the flimsy chain like it wasn't even there.

Bright lights flashed in Justine's head and she tasted blood in her mouth. She hit the floor with a thud, jarring her to the core. Stunned and out of breath, she was only vaguely aware of a large figure dropping astride of her.

"Nooo," she groaned, as she felt her robe being ripped away.

A stabbing pain ripped through her side, as she realized, he'd hit her. "Shut up, bitch," he hissed in a guttural whisper.

She tried to curl into a ball, but he slapped her, forcing her hands up over her head. She groaned again, slapping feebly as he ripped her panties away.

Frazier CO June 10th 2018 Sunday Mid-Morning

William Forsyth twisted the coffee cup in his hands, wishing he hadn't come. He hadn't been ready. Not ready for the grief pushing across the living room at him. Nor was he ready for the feelings welling up inside him. He thought he had put this all behind him.

He and Jared Morris had become friends their freshman year at college. Chance had thrust them together when they had been assigned to share a dorm room. Over the next four years of college and two years of grad school, they had formed a bond tighter than most brothers. Together they were going to rule the world. Jared's sudden death had shocked and shaken William.

"I'm sorry I haven't come out sooner to pay my respects," William found himself saying. Jared had been dead for almost a year. William spread his hands. "I guess I didn't want to face the fact that he was really gone."

Jared's mother, a woman who was considerably grayer and much more tired than the last time William had seen her, smiled. "I know, dear. It's hard. I know how close the two of you were."

"I gotta go," Jared's father said suddenly. He thrust out a hand awkwardly. "Good to see you, boy," he said.

William nodded, rising to his feet as he took the hand. "I'm sorry, sir."

Jack Morris mumbled something about work and hurried from the room. "He doesn't feel comfortable talking about Jared," Helen Morris said, a wistful note playing on her words. Helen shook her head. "We were so worried when you boys took those jobs in Washington DC. We heard how bad the crime is and worried day and night that one of you would be murdered." She laughed a bitter little laugh. "Then this."

"What happened?" William asked, finally getting to the real reason for his visit. "I mean, Jared was such a good skier. How could he ski into a tree?"

Helen shrugged her thin shoulders, smoothing her well-worn dress. William remembered Mrs. Morris always being so impeccably dressed always in stylish clothing. To see her in this thing, which William suspected was a robe and not a dress shocked him. "Accidents happen," Helen said, dabbing at her nose with a tissue. "The sheriff said Jared was on drugs. Is that true?"

William was taken back. Not by the accusing tone, but by the words. "The sheriff said Jared had drugs in his system when he died?" he asked, not sure he had heard right.

Helen nodded, dabbing with the tissue. William shook his head firmly. "Mrs. Morris, you must know that isn't true," William protested. "Jared was a fanatic about what he put into his body. Everything he ate had to be organic. He didn't even eat eggs. He used to lecture me for hours when he found out I had a hamburger."

That much was true. William felt a cold hand grip his spine. Jared Morris had been a fitness fanatic. He ran every day, went to the gym three times a week. He would never take drugs. Never. "Are you sure about that? I can't believe Jared would ever take drugs."

"That's what the sheriff's office told us."

Suddenly the room seemed to close in on William. It was so hot in here. He could feel the sweat breaking out on his brow. "Let me ask a few questions. Maybe there was some mistake."

William mumbled a few more excuses. He had to get out of there. Almost sprinting, William hurried to his rental car, cranking the AC on high. As he drove away from the house, William rolled it through his mind. Jared hadn't really been coming to Denver to ski. He'd been laying over on his way to Arizona. There had been no plan for him to stop and ski or see his parents. He'd been going to Arizona to check on a private business deal he and William had going.

Rolling down the window, William had to get some air. He had to think. At the time, William thought the idea of sneaking off to catch a few runs down the mountain sounded just like Jared. It had been November and Jared hadn't been skiing that season. That he would figure out a way to sneak in a few runs was more than possible, but taking drugs, that just wasn't him.

Sonoran Desert South of Tucson AZ June 10th 2018
Sunday Noon

Fred and Gloria Dooley were happy. Less than a year ago, neither of them thought they would be, or even could be, but here they were. Of all things. Happy.

Gloria shook her head, smiling to herself. Who would have thought? They certainly hadn't been the most popular kids in high school. They hadn't even been the most popular kids within their own clique. Somehow through that mess of confusion, heartbreak and hormones, they had found each other.

And damn it, they were happy.

Two days ago, they had become Mr. and Mrs. Fred Dooley. Next week they would move into their tiny, run-down apartment just north of the University. The next day, they would start summer school at the University of Arizona.

It was all planned out.

Gloria was going to study veterinary science. She was going to be vet. Fred was going to be an engineer. He had agonized over the decision for months, before picking his major. Since he'd been a kid, Fred had harbored an interest in archeology, but in the end he'd chosen engineering.

As much as the past and history intrigued him, the numbers of engineering captured him. But it was the news that Gloria was pregnant that made the decision for him. He gave up the thought of being an archeologist for the money of engineering.

Which was why they were hiking along the Arizona-Mexican border.

Fred might have chosen engineering for the money, but he wasn't about to turn his back on his first passion, archeology. Fred had heard a rumor that spear points had been found in the region, which dated back over a thousand years. Now, he was determined to find one.

In the spring, Fred had introduced Gloria to hiking, and to her surprise, she loved it. Gloria had always been an indoor person, lying in her room reading while the other kids were out playing. She'd never been invited out to play, but at the time she hadn't felt like she missed anything.

That was until Fred had taken her to Sedona. They had hiked the slick rock and had watched a sunset while sitting on the shoulder of Bell Rock. Something in the ancient stillness spoke to her. She felt a connection to the Earth. Now as they hiked, it felt like Christmas morning. Each time they topped a ridge it was like opening a new present, to see the wonders spread out before them.

Gloria had also become addicted to photography. At first she had simply wanted to take pictures of the places they had been to share with her friends, but that had changed. Nature, she found, was very hard to capture. Distance and definition had a tendency to blur together.

She hated when the pictures didn't truly capture what she saw. The washed out photos didn't convey what she felt. She was going to fix that. She was teaching herself advanced photography. It was a challenge she was relishing.

Gloria had several cameras. She was experimenting with different brands, lenses and exposure settings, learning which ones worked well with each different environment. Today, as they walked along a trail that had probably been there for centuries, she was fiddling with a Kodak, listening to Fred's voice as he talked of an ancient race that roamed these hills in some distant past. He was explaining why he thought, contrary to popular belief that these people had made bronze tools.

Gloria wasn't really listening. She didn't share his passion for archeology, but she did love the sound of his voice. Her husband.

She liked that. It had such a nice ring to it. She reached out, rubbing the back of his arm.

Fred stopped in mid-sentence. He glanced back at her, and she could see the adoration in his eyes. A warmth spread through her, as he gave her a clumsy hug. Gloria leaned into him, laying her head against his chest.

Walking arm and arm wasn't an easy thing to do while wearing backpacks, but they stumbled along, gazing into each other's eyes. The sun was shining upon them, bright and warm. All was right in the world.

Then it wasn't.

They were so wrapped up in their own little world, that the cry startled them.

Fred and Gloria were city kids, but they recognized the sound. An animal in distress.

The trail had crossed up out of the canon through a small saddle. From there, it opened into a small clearing. In the saddle, they lurched to a stop. For a second they were disorientated. Fred and Gloria had chosen this region for its remoteness. No one came here. Fred and Gloria had been sure they were alone; the sight of the group of men in front of them was confusing. Apparently the group of men in the small clearing were feeling the same confusion as they simply stared up at Fred and Gloria.

One man didn't stare, though. He couldn't. He was on his knees, stripped naked with a hood over his head and his hands tied behind his back. Another man stood behind the kneeling man, while two others leaned against two four wheelers.

For a second the two groups stared at each other, while Gloria unconsciously snapped pictures. Surprisingly it was Fred who reacted first. He'd seen enough movies to know what the little tableau spread out before them meant.

"Run!"

Fred stepped in front of Gloria, pushing her back in the direction from which they had come.

Gloria ran a couple of steps before the shots crashed down upon her. She glanced back as the bullets tore through her husband. His body jerked under each shot and almost seemed to rise up. "No!" she screamed as his body wilted to the ground.

For a second she stared at him, lying twisted and broken, big tears rolling down her face. A giant sob racked her thin body as she took a step, reaching out to him. A shout from the clearing snapped her back to the present, and a bolt of fear tore through her.

Spinning on her heel, she ran. Gloria was young and thanks to all the hiking, in good shape. She had on good hiking shoes while her pursuers wore heavy biker boots and were older. They were smokers and beer drinkers, and for a minute she thought she might out distance them. She could hear their grunts and cursing as they scrambled to catch her.

The trail was a narrow sliver, clinging to the side of the canyon, with a long drop off to the left. Gloria was small and able to run, while her larger pursuers were forced to step sideways sucking up against the canyon face.

Gloria was starting to pull away, when fate slapped her in the face. Her pack caught on a jagged out-cropping of rock, spinning her around. Waving her hands for balance, Gloria lost her hold on the camera and it flew from her hands and bounced over the edge.

For an awful second, Gloria thought she was going to follow it over. Terror knifing through her, she twisted her body away from the edge, even as she was falling. She hit on the edge of the trail, landing across a large rock. Pain ripped through her body, taking her breath away.

She lay still for a second; trying to get her breath each gasp feeling like a dagger was being plunged into her chest. She tried to crawl, then felt the hands grab her.

Washington DC March 7th 2004 Friday Early Morning

The drizzle had turned uglier. Now it was a blowing mist with stinging sleet mixed in. The temperatures had dropped and now the mist was freezing to the windshield of the car. The car belonged to the DC Metro police, so the heater didn't work worth a shit. When it was cold you had to choose between keeping the windshield clear, or keeping your feet half-assed warm. Detective Harley was trying to split the difference, with so-so results. As Harley watched the ice creep down the windshield, he cursed under his breath. 'Jeez, I hate this fucking weather," he complained, easing the sagging Crown Vic to the curb.

His partner, Len Dykes, laughed with genuine humor. "Shit, you bitch even more when it's hot."

"Naw, I hate the fucking rain. We should move down to Miami. Don't see those fellows on Miami Vice getting called out on a night like this." Recently divorced, Harley had just sprung for cable, and spent most of his time watching reruns.

Dykes laughed again, making a few notations of the time in his notebook. "Rains all the fucking time in Miami." Dykes opened his door, ending the discussion. It was a familiar conversation. One they'd had at dozens of murder scenes. They stepped out into a surreal world. It seemed as if they were stepping into an ocean of blue and red. The lights from the various emergency and police vehicles were reflecting off the wet pavement and all the moisture in the air, enveloping them.

Both men straightened slowly, rubbing their backs. "Dead end street," Harley observed. "Car would stick out like a whore in church."

"Bet nobody saw nothing."

"Still have to do a canvass," Harley said.

"Oh yeah," Dykes agreed, leading the way up the cracked sidewalk to the door. "Chain's broken."

Harley stooped looking closely at the lock and jamb. "Lock's okay. No sign of scratches. She opened the door for him. Maybe she knew him."

"Maybe not," Dykes said waving his notebook at the door. "No peephole. Maybe wasn't who she expected. Or she had to open the door a crack to see who it was."

Harley felt a flash of rage. He could see her, expecting her boyfriend or maybe just a girlfriend and getting some predator. "Should have had a peephole," he said, showing none of the rage he felt.

"Easy," Dykes muttered. He knew his partner well enough to read that dead pan.

"Hey, fellas, miserable night," Marty Wills said, as they pushed into the house. Wills was the assistant coroner. "Looks like a bad one," he commented, working the joints on the dead woman's fingers.

"What have we got, Marty?" Dykes asked.

"Dead girl, about twenty. Raped and strangled, I'd say."

"Happened right here?" Harley said, as much a statement as a question.

"No doubt about it," Wills answered. "See the long bruise on the side of her face? That was from the door. Traces of hair and tissue on the door."

"Anything stand out to you?" Dykes asked making a notation in his notebook.

"Lots of rage here. She didn't put up much of a fight. After the blow from the door, I doubt if she was able to resist much, but he beat her anyway. Pretty vicious."

"She probably knew her killer," Harley commented, more to himself than anyone.

"Hard to get that mad at a stranger," Marty answered.

"It happens, though," Dykes commented. "Got a time of death?"

Marty shrugged. "Been a while, I'd say less than twenty-four hours. Door was partly open and it was cold in here, that'll throw the temps off. Rigor is just starting to settle in." Marty scratched the point of his chin with a pen. "If I were to guess, I'd say late last night. I'll need a few markers to narrow it down."

Both detectives nodded. They knew he wanted a time for when she had last eaten. Her stomach contents could be analyzed to help establish a time of death. "Guy left behind some semen. I'll be able to get you a blood type."

"Thanks," Dykes said, glancing over at his partner. "I don't suppose you want to do the neighborhood?"

"I took it last time."

"It was sunny, and almost warm," Dykes said, but he was already buttoning his parka.

"Life sucks sometimes."

Harley walked into the kitchen. In the kitchen, he began to get a picture of Justine Salters. He saw a young woman who ate cheap, trying to eat healthy on a nothing budget. She didn't have a lot of money, he thought. On the table, he saw a checkbook and a stack of bills. A quick look at the checkbook confirmed her financial status. She was squeaking by. Looking at the bills, Harley saw she didn't have nearly enough in the account to cover the bills. He saw a pay stub from the University and another one from a convenience store. She had been going to school full time and working two jobs. Harley could feel his anger rising. She didn't deserve what happened to her.

He looked around, she kept a neat house. In the sink were two miss-matched plates and two glasses. A bowl sat on the other side of the sink. They had been rinsed, but not washed. Drying on a rack was a small skillet and a pot.

Harley used his foot to open the trashcan lid. Inside, he could see some lettuce scraps, and some carrot and cucumber peelings. Harley let the lid fall back into place.

She'd had company. A date? They'd had a salad and whatever else she could cook up in that skillet and pot. Some kind of casserole and she'd served it in the glass bowl.

Harley liked the fact that she had served it in a bowl instead of out of the pans. Harley's ex-wife had always served out of the pans, complaining that dishing it up just made another bowl to wash.

Harley liked the girl for taking the extra effort. On a hunch, he opened the frig. On the center shelf was a cottage cheese cartoon covered with cellophane. Leaning in he saw it was some kind of rice dish, with chicken strips mixed in. Behind the rice stood a bottle of wine, mostly empty. Harley studied the wine, but did not touch it. A beer man himself, Harley didn't know much about wine, but his instincts told him this wasn't the cheap stuff.

He walked back into the living room. He glanced at the phone saw the message light blinking on the machine beside the phone. He saw the black finger print dust on the phone but still asked Peter Long the print tech. "Pete, okay to look at the phone and the answering machine?"

"Go ahead, I'm done with it."

"You getting anything?"

"Quite a few prints. Nothing on the door, though."

"Bottle of wine in the frig, and a couple of glasses in the sink. Might check them." Harley said, slipping on a pair of reading glasses, as he studied the answering machine. He played the message. Sounded like it was from a boyfriend.

Harley played the message again. So they had a date ate some dinner, and then the boyfriend went home. Then he called and left a message. Somehow, that didn't make sense to Harley. Take a look at the boyfriend, he thought. The call was an alibi call. He nodded to himself. Yeah, take a long, hard look at the boyfriend, Harley thought.

Tucson City Jail Tucson AZ June 10th 2018 Sunday Late Night

He leaned back against the wall of the cell, a man totally at ease with his surroundings. His demeanor gave the appearance of a man used to jail. His dress, however was not that of a man who'd spent time behind bars. He wore a white golf shirt with the insignia of Augusta National Golf Club. Over the shirt he wore a Brooks Brothers black blazer. Faded jeans and black, pointed-toed boots completed the outfit.

He sat totally unmoving, his eyes closed. The jailor, who looked in from time to time thought he might even be asleep. He wasn't, he sensed the jailor looking and opened his eyes. For a minute, he simply stared at the jailor, then winked. With a smile, he closed his eyes again.

The jailor stared. His name was Bill, and he'd been handling prisoners for over ten years and he had never seen one act this way. He tried to put his finger on it. The man wasn't scared. Bill could always spot that, even when the prisoner tried to hide it. The others in the tank could always tell too.

None of the other prisoners were approaching or talking to this fellow. He simply sat there like he didn't have a care in the world. He wasn't angry about being arrested, which was the other dominate emotion that Bill usually saw.

Bill looked at the arrest sheet. Justin Carter was his name, and he'd been picked up down town on a D and D. Bill laughed as he read the report. Seems this fellow had pissed in Jeff Crowley's patrol car.

Jeff had left the windows cracked, and now he had a damp seat. Bill chuckled again. Crowley was an ass. There would be some who would want to buy this guy Carter a beer.

Bill glanced at the prisoner again. Funny, the guy didn't seem drunk. Curious, Bill checked the report. Carter had blown a point zero eight, barely enough to be arrested.

It hit Bill; Carter looked like a man who was exactly where he wanted to be. Strange. Very strange.

Sonoran Desert South of Tucson AZ June 11th 2018 Monday Morning

Sam Logan eased his Explorer up the fire road. He drove slowly, partly because the road was shit, washed out and rutted to the point it was barely passable. But mostly he drove slow because he knew what waited for him. More bodies. Coming up on the cop convention, he parked at the back of the line of cars. There were several sheriff cars and another state cruiser. Sam set for a minute, readying his mind, another dead body, and Sam had already seen too many.

Sam had served twenty-five years in the Marines doing two tours in Vietnam. In that time, Sam had seen his share of dead and dying. And now, after twenty some years as an Arizona Ranger, Sam had seen more than his share. Way more.

All the dead weighed upon him, stooping his shoulders and bending his back.

In Nam, Sam saw Kip Carlson, a young kid from Wisconsin torn apart by a machine gun burst. He once saw a sailor scalded to death when a steam line ruptured aboard a destroyer. He saw two cops gunned down in the streets of Tucson. The young kids, too many to count scattered on the highway, like so many broken bowling pins.

The accidents, Sam could deal with. Whether they were simple stupidity or part of God's plan, accidents no matter how tragic were a part of life.

It was the killings, which were eating on his soul. The things that humans did to each other. Sam felt like he lost a little bit of himself, every time he looked at one.

He was nearing the end. He could feel it.

Something was going on with Sam, he was changing inside. Last week he watched a story on the news about dog fighting and how the animals were being abused. A rage welled up inside him and had the men responsible for hurting the dogs been within reach he would have killed them. Then later, thinking about the animals, he had almost cried.

Sam took a deep breath, and then a nip from the vodka bottle he had taken to carrying. His hand shook a little, as he screwed the top back on. Damn, these were just kids. Kids on their honeymoon. Fuck it. He took another long pull from the bottle, and then slid it under the seat.

He poked a dip of Skoal in his mouth to cover the smell of alcohol, and then wearily got out of his vehicle. As a detective and with his seniority Sam was entitled to wear plain clothes, but he didn't. He wore the full uniform. He straightened his gun belt, and placed the flat-brimmed hat on his head. With another deep breath, he braced himself for what he would see. He slipped the stern look of a drill sergeant on his face and started out. Like the hat, the look fit his craggy features.

Sam walked slowly, scanning the terrain. Word was the kids were out here hiking on their honeymoon. Which made no darned since, if you asked Sam. Sam had hiked over half the world in his days in the Corps, and not one second of it compared to what he and his wife had done on their honeymoon.

Sam laughed a little, thinking of his honeymoon. He and Maureen had gone down to Rocky Point. Dang! They'd had themselves a time. But they never went hiking. Truth was they hardly left the room.

Sam recognized why the crazy thoughts were racing through his head. It was his mind's way of avoiding what was waiting for him. But he couldn't put it off no longer. It was time to work.

Sam tried to put himself in the place of the two kids, seeing what they would've seen. Nothing jumped out at him, as he marched along.

"Hey, Sam, up here."

If Sam had been the type to show his emotions, a flash of irritation would've exploded on his face. But since he wasn't, nothing showed as he glanced at Brett George. If you asked Sam, and not many did, Brett was everything that was wrong with the world these days.

He was young, which wouldn't be all bad, but he had a triple dose of smartass. And oh hell, that haircut. Honestly, Sam didn't know whether to be amused that a kid would pay seventy-five bucks for a haircut that made you look like you just got out of bed, or to just slap the supreme shit out of the kid. In the end, Sam grunted a greeting and jerked his head in the direction of the crime scene tape. "What we got?"

Brett popped some kind of fancy mint in his mouth, sucking on it as he answered. "Three down. First one, the naked guy, he's a junkie. No doubt about that, old hype marks on both arms and fresh ones on his legs."

Sam nodded absently. "Trying to hide his use."

"That's what we think. We think he was probably a mule or dealing, for who we don't know. We figure he got caught using or fucked up somehow and got brought out here."

"Makes sense," Sam said nodding. "Might check arrest reports. He could've been picked up."

"Yeah, that works," Brett agreed. "Guy's using and gets picked up in some narc sweep. That would be enough to earn a ride to the desert. For whatever reason, we figure they brought him out here to do him and looks like the newlyweds walked right into it."

Sam nodded, that made sense with what he was seeing. Sam was reading the ground and purposely not looking at the bodies. He'd get to see them soon enough. Squatting on his heels, Sam thought it over. He had assumed the kids came in along the fire road, but they hadn't. They had hiked in from the north. The druggies, and Sam knew this was about drugs; they had come in from the southwest using the same fire road Sam was now parked on.

"We figure the druggies put a gun on them. They shot the man, and then brought her down."

Now, Sam looked at the bodies. Bullets had ripped Fred's body to shreds. Sam could see the blood splattered on the rocks. No doubt but what the young man had been killed right there. Sam also saw something, which if he had any tears left, would've brought one to his eye. The couple had been walking side-by-side, but at the last instant, Fred had stepped in front of his wife. He'd tried to protect her. In Sam's mind, that made him a man.

Feeling sadness way down upon him, Sam looked down at the other two bodies. Both were stripped naked.

Sam barely glanced at the man. It was clear as day what had happened to him. The man's head had tipped forward and was resting in a thickening pool of blood and brain matter.

He'd been marched to that spot, forced to kneel, and a bullet put through his head. Sam shook his head. Cold.

Very cold.

Sam turned his eyes to the dead girl, and again felt his insides melt. She too was naked, but she lay on her side almost in the fetal position. In the last seconds of her life, she'd try to cover herself but they had robbed her of even that.

"Raped?" Sam asked his voice hard as ice.

"Yeah," Brett said, popping another mint. "They had their fun with her, and then pop." Brett said, and punctuated it by putting his finger to his temple. "Bang."

"You're wrong about one thing, though."

"Oh yeah," Brett said, the doubt sounding in his voice. "What's that?"

Sam tipped his head at the body. "Her, she didn't go down there willingly." Sam pointed at the ground. "He stepped in front and took the bullets while she ran." Sam pointed at some scuffs in the dirt. "That's where they drug her back."

"Huh," Brett grunted, sounding unimpressed. He shrugged. "That shit doesn't matter. What matters is that they left DNA behind. If they are in the system, we got them."

"Yeah, maybe. But if they ain't in the system, you won't get shit." Sam shook his head. Damn kids didn't want to work anymore; they just wanted to depend on technology.

Sam turned his back and started following the trail where Gloria had fled. It irked Sam that nobody was doing this. Sam didn't really expect to find anything, but it was a stone. You didn't leave it unturned. And it wasn't like you had to be Daniel Boone to follow the tracks. They were plain as the lines on a highway.

Right away, Sam felt a melancholy. Damn, she had run hard. Sam could see where her toes had dug in the ground. She had made it a hundred yards, and Sam's heart cried for her. She had made it just far enough to gain a glimmer of hope. Sam knew that's when the real fear would set in.

Even though, he knew the outcome, Sam couldn't help but root for her. He was crushed when he saw where she fell. Sam knelt beside the spot where she fell. His throat burned and an acrid, nasty taste came to his mouth. He saw where her hands had skidded across the ground and he saw the huge boot prints straddling where she fell.

"Damn," Sam said softly, feeling a slow anger. He felt a quick wish that he could've known them. The scrawny, young man who put his skinny body between his wife and the bullets. And the young lady he had loved, and who had fought so hard for her own life.

A rough, racking cough tour from his body, and the tears he didn't think he had rolled down his wrinkled face. Right then, he made a promise to the young couple. He would find the man who did this and they would, by God, they would pay. They would pay dearly.

Sam slowly stood with his knees cracking as he straightened up. Reaching down to rub an aching knee, Sam saw a flash of color. Working slowly, Sam dropped over the edge, sliding down ten feet to a huge boulder wedged on the canyon wall. The strap of a camera was caught against the boulder.

Even if he couldn't see her name printed on the camera strap, he would have known it was hers. Bracing his feet against another boulder, Sam reached out, hooking the strap with his finger. Sam pulled the camera to him, turning it in his hands. As he gazed at the camera, another tear traced slowly down his face.

Sam raised his head, staring into the sky that was so blue it reminded him of water. For the first time in his life, Sam felt the touch of God.

Sam grinned a savage smile, as he stared at the camera in his hands. In the whole world, there was one kind of digital camera he knew how to work. It was a Kodak. This very model.

Maureen had bought one when they heard Sarah was pregnant. Sam hadn't been close to his kids, and he didn't want to make the same mistake with his grandkids. Desperate to be a part of the process, Sam had mastered the camera. He was going to take the pictures. But then in one awful night, Sarah the unborn baby and Sam's son Sammy were taken from him.

Now, Sam knew it was God's work that it was the very same kind of camera that he now held. Sam turned on the camera, somewhat surprised to find it still worked. He switched from capture to view and immediately the little clearing jumped to life on the screen. But this time there were five men and two trucks crowded into the small clearing.

Except for the man on his knees, they were all looking up at the camera. Sam stared at their images for a long time. Burning the faces into his memory. One by one, Sam studied them. He couldn't put a name to any of them, but one looked familiar. Somewhere, Sam had seen him before.

He flipped open the cover door, and withdrew the memory card. Holding the camera by the strap, he rolled it couple of times like he was roping a steer, then let it go. He watched as the camera lifted off into the canyon. It winked once in the sun then was gone replaced by a lazy, little dust cloud.

Sam watched it for a minute, then scrambled back up to the trail. Walking back, Sam's mind was churning. If he could ID one of the men in the photo, he would learn the rest of them. Sam was trying to place the man in the photo when Dave Dunkowski came up the fire road carrying a blanket. "Hey, jarhead."

"Got your security blanket there, Army?" Sam asked, smiling. Despite the fact that Dave had served in the Army and then for no good fucking reason decided to become a lowly Sheriff's deputy, Sam liked him.

"I'm going to cover that girl up. It ain't right, her laying out like that."

"I'll help you." Sam said then glanced sideways at Dave. "Brett ain't gonna like that. Messin' with the crime scene."

"Fuck him," Dave said, then chuckled a little. "Don't worry about Brett, he ain't so bad."

"Nothing wrong with him that a few hundred trips up the reaper wouldn't cure."

Dunkowski snorted, rolling his eyes. "Oh crap, you leathernecks and that fucking hill. I tell you what, while you boys were playing grab ass running up and down that hill, us Army men, we were learning to shoot."

"My ass!" Sam snorted. "Shit, we washed out pricks that could outshoot any of you army guys."

"Yeah, right." Dave said, turning serious as he grabbed Sam and pulled him to a stop to a stop. "What was on that camera?"

Sam shot a look at his old friend, then gazed off into the distance. "You saw that, huh?"

"I did, and I'm guessing you don't plan on sharing what you found with Brett?"

"I wasn't," Sam replied. "I don't know what I was thinking."

"You were thinking, you might handle this one on your own." Dave looked his friend in the eye. "You know if we hook them up for this, they might get twelve years and be out in five. You were thinking you might want to do a little better than that."

"Shit, I was thinking I might just kill them."

"Figured that," Dave said. "Anything on that camera, we can use?"

Sam chuckled a little. "Damn straight, she took their picture big as life."

"No woofin'?" Dave said grinning broadly. "You recognize any of them?"

"Maybe. I've seen one of them around but I can't put a name to him."

Sam looked off across the brown hills toward Mexico. "You know, if a person were to be at the Cactus tonight, I might buy him a beer. We might look at some pictures together."

"I know a few the older guys who like beer. Guys who were getting tired of watching assholes walk away from this kind shit."

"Maybe guys who would like to change some of that?"

"I believe they would." Dave said nodding seriously. "I would."

Sam cocked his head, looking at his old friend. "You sure? I ain't talking about slapping a few wrists here. God may have mercy, but I'm fresh out."

Dave leaned back against a rock, looking over his shoulder to make sure no one was listening. "You been thinking on this?"

Sam nodded. "It's been coming on. You sure you want to buy into this?"

"You been thinking on it, well so have I." Scowling, Dave spat on the ground. "Last guy I arrested, robbed a convenience store and beat the lady behind the counter, broke her jaw. We caught him coming out, still had her blood on his knuckles. He was laughing when I hooked him up." Dave looked off into the distance. "Little fucker made bail and was out before I finished my shift and wrote the report."

"That shit ain't right."

"No. It ain't," Dave said slowly. "So if you want some help, I'm in and like I said, I know some fellas that would buy in."

Sam nodded slowly. "If they are people we can trust, then they would be welcome."

Denver International Airport Denver Co June 11th 2018 Monday Morning

William Forsyth tugged his tie loose, swearing under his breath. He paced the concourse, clutching his cell phone. He glanced at the watch on his wrist to the cell phone screen, then down the concourse. This was a routine he'd developed over the last twenty minutes. Every little bit he would pull the ticket out of his jacket pocket and check the boarding time.

Pacing again, he glanced at his cell phone. "Fuck!" he said, drawing a look of ire from a lady with two young kids.

"Sorry," he muttered, looking past the woman and down the concourse.

The woman ignored him, making a face as she dragged her kids a few seats away.

Feeling like an asshole, Forsyth turned away. From the inside pocket of his jacket, Forsyth pulled out a rolled up paper. It was a police report. The conclusions of the report were that Jared Morris had died in a skiing accident. Just reading the report gave William Forsyth a chill. Like a cold hand had been placed on his back.

Jared had grown up on skis. He was the best skier Forsyth had ever seen, barely missed qualifying for the US National Team. That he had skied into a tree on an easy run was hard to believe. What really bothered William was the toxicology report stapled to the back.

William had gotten the report from the sheriff's office on the pretext of being a family friend and lawyer. William had bluffed that he might challenge the surprising toxicology as it could prevent the parents from collecting the life insurance. He hadn't made any friends, but he had gotten a copy of the reports.

Feeling a trickle of sweat roll down his back, Forsyth stabbed the redial button. Turning to the window, he muttered while the phone rang. When the voice mail came on, he hurriedly whispered a message. "Brody, it's me. We got trouble. They know. I'm coming into town. I'll call you when I land."

Snapping the phone closed, Forsyth wiped the sweat from his brow and looked at his watch again. He glanced down the concourse, half expecting to see that psycho Carter stalking him. What the hell had he gotten himself into?

It seemed so innocent at the time. A chance to make some extra money. A smart, hard business deal. Now, he'd give every dollar he had to be clear of this. Dread settling heavily into the pit of his stomach, he opened his cell phone again. He opened the phone book and scrolled down to

Kathy Reynolds. He stared at the number for a long minute. He should warn her. Hating himself, he flipped the phone closed just as the boarding call was announced. Fucking Brody, he thought as he walked down the jet way.

Washington DC Asst. DA Geena Dixon's Office March 10th 2004 Monday Afternoon

Geena looked up from the file she was reading when the phone buzzed on her desk. She pressed the button connecting her to the secretary she shared with four other prosecutors. "Yes," she said, leaning forward towards the phone.

"Detectives Harley and Dykes to see you," a disembodied answer warbled over the cheap speaker.

Geena frowned, even though she liked both detectives. They had always treated her with respect and listened when she gave her opinion. It was the fact that they were here that gave her pause. Geena couldn't think of a scenario where that would be a good thing. "Send them in," she said, and the door opened immediately. Geena smiled. This must be important, they had been standing with a hand on the door. Harley came through first, and he wore a troubled expression. Geena was struck by how much they resembled each other. Dykes was black and Harley was white, but they still looked alike. Both were overweight with the rundown, sloping shoulders of men who had seen too many dead bodies. "What can I do for you, gentlemen?" Geena asked, motioning them towards the chairs at her desk.

"We need to ask some advice," Dykes said, somewhat reluctantly.

"You want my advice? I must tell you I'm flattered," Geena said, feeling somewhat better about the interview. "What can I help you with?"

"You heard about the Salters' case?" Harley asked.

"Just what I've been reading in the paper. Black girl raped and strangled. You've got a lot of press on that one."

The detectives exchanged a couple of quick smirks. "That was Harley's idea, using the press" Dykes said. "We got a couple of hits off that."

"I also read you have a suspect. Jacob Carter?" She looked at the two men. "Is he good for it?"

"We know the son of a bitch did it!" Harley exploded.

Dykes put a hand on his partner's arm. "We do know who did it. The thing is, we can't really prove it. At this point we would normally pull the punk in and put him in the room and sweat it out of him."

"So what's the difference here?"

"The thing is this is a rich kid. We figure the minute we go near him, he'll lawyer up."

Geena shrugged. "Standard practice. What's the problem?"

"Well, we think we got him, but a good lawyer can knock down everything we have," Dykes said. "And you can bet he'll have a damn good lawyer."

"Are you sure it's him? This Carter kid?"

"Fuck yes! It's him alright!" Harley said, his face turning redder as he rose half out of his seat.

"Alright," Geena said, taking out a fresh legal pad. She wrote the name Salters across the top. "Lay it out for me. What do you have? Any physical evidence?"

The detectives nodded. They both knew that lawyers loved physical evidence. It was hard to argue with or impeach. "We got tons that tie him to the scene," Dykes replied.

"That's good," Geena said, then stopped as both men shook their heads.

"He was dating the girl. They had a date that night. He admits he was there earlier. Claims he left around ten. He called her from his place around ten-thirty and left a message."

"So they were dating? We have confirmation of that?"

Both men nodded. "We confirmed it through witnesses and through reading her journal."

"What was the time of death?"

"Coroner puts it between nine and two-thirty."

"That's a wide window," Geena commented.

Dykes shrugged, but Harley hitched his chair closer. "This is either a smart little piece of shit or he got lucky. Door was partially open, and it was cold that night. Cold messes up the liver temps and the lividity. Throws off the whole shooting match. My guess is he knew that."

"We have a match on his DNA from the rape kit," Dykes said quietly.

"If they were dating of course he's going to claim they had consensual sex earlier that night," Geena observed.

"Of course, but the coroner didn't find any other semen in her body. Just his," Harley said, quickly. Geena could tell the two men had debated this many times already.

"Killer could have worn a condom. That would be the smart thing to do."

"Doesn't look like that kind of killing," Dykes replied. "Lots of anger, and violence. Not a lot of planning."

"But on the other hand you are going to argue that the killer left the door open to throw off the time of death. That he made a phone call to help set up an alibi. That does speak of planning."

The detectives shrugged again. They had already been down that road. "Okay was the call an alibi call?" Both men nodded immediately. "Was she already dead at that time?"

"We don't think so," Dykes said. "Marty thinks the time of death was after eleven. Eleven to twelve somewhere in there is his best guess."

"Okay so she's alive when the call comes in. Why doesn't she answer?"

"Her girlfriend said she and Carter had a system. They would call and say good night, but not pick up if they were studying. The girl was studying; her books were still open on the couch."

"The way we see it, they have their date, Carter goes to his condo and calls. That says he was home. Then he jumps in his car and goes back. He kicks in the door and kills her."

"We may have caught a break on the door. Some fibers match a coat...." Harley dug out his notebook, consulting it. "Northface was the coat brand. Witness say Carter has a coat like that and he was wearing it that night. Before their date, he stopped and bought a bottle of wine. We have him on video. He's wearing the coat."

"He could have left the fibers on the door when he was there for his date."

Harley shook his head hard enough to make Geena's neck hurt. "No way. It took some force to transfer those fibers. They got there when he shoved the door open."

"That's an argument," Geena said, looking down at her notes. "Okay let's back up a sec. You said, his DNA matched the semen found in Ms. Salters' body. Did he consent to a sample?"

"No. Like we said, we haven't talked to him yet. We got it out of his trash. Found a toothbrush he was throwing away," Dykes replied.

"So we would need to confirm that?"

"Yeah, but it's solid. Guy lives alone. It's a good match."

Geena placed her pen carefully on the desk, choosing her words with even more care. She liked these guys and the last thing she wanted to do was insult them. They had been in the game a lot longer than she. "Look guys, if you say he's the man, I want to believe you, but I have to be honest. I'm not quite there with him. I need something more. What about motive?"

They looked at each other, and it was Harley who answered. "It's a little thin," he said, somewhat sheepishly. He sighed heavily, shooting a look at his partner. "She beat him in a grade school spelling bee."

"That's thin. That's the definition of thin. Bulimic even"

"Yeah, for now it's the best we got but who knows, maybe she dumped him? We don't know when the sex happened or if it was consensual. Maybe she wouldn't put out for him? Shit, we're working on it," Harley said, his voice heavy with defeat.

"The way we figure it, he decides to kill her, for what reason, who knows. He goes over for a date, maybe she dumps him, maybe they fight cause she won't put out. Maybe he just wants to do it, doesn't matter, he decides to kill her."

Harley took over the story from his partner. "He goes home, talks to a neighbor."

"That's important," Dykes interrupted, nodding vigorously. "Neighbor said he never even looked at her before, now he goes out of his way to chat her up."

"That's right," Harley said, growing excited. "She's leaving the laundry, and he goes to get his mail. Shit it's ten-thirty. Who waits to get their mail till ten-thirty?"

"That's right," Dykes put in. "We think he waited for a chance when somebody was down there. Then he talks to the neighbor. She's forty, married with three kids, by the way."

"So he wasn't trying to pick her up," Geena observed.

"Nope," Harley said. "She said normally, he don't talk to anyone at the apartment complex, but that night he was real chatty. She said he was in a good mood."

"That could be a problem," Geena said cutting in. "Hard to make the jump from him being in a good mood, to a killing rage in just a matter of minutes."

"Yeah, but he was just setting up his alibi. Went out of his way to talk to someone he normally wouldn't give the time of day," Dykes argued.

"That is something, but to a jury it might not stack up against the fact that she will say he was in a good mood." Geena spread her hands in an apology. "Sorry. What else have you got?"

"Okay after he talks to the neighbor, he goes to his apartment makes the call to Salters."

"Setting up the alibi," Geena said nodding.

"Right," Harley said, taking up the story. "So he watches out his window, making sure the coast is clear, then drives back over to her place."

"Risky," Geena observed, making a note of it. "If a neighbor saw him, his alibi would be shot."

"Not so risky as you would think," Dykes told her. "His apartment is in the back corner. There is an entrance off the alley to the complex. His garage faces it. If he was backed into his garage he could pull straight out into the alley. Thirty feet at the most. Ten feet down the alley and he is out of sight. Take maybe ten seconds at the most."

"Door shut behind him and nobody knows he's gone," Harley growled, hitching his chair an inch closer.

"Plus he disabled the light in the garage," Dykes put in. "We got a picture through the garage window. The cover and light bulb from the garage door opener are lying on a bench."

"So he goes over, kills her and comes back," Harley said. "We timed it. Takes twenty minutes to get to her place, you could do it in fifteen if you were hustling."

"Which you wouldn't be, not if you had just committed murder."

"Exactly. If you think it takes twenty minutes over and twenty minutes back and twenty minutes to do the girl, that's an hour. At eleven-thirty he's back home, studying. He then makes a call to a classmate with a question about a lesson."

"That's pretty standard. When I was in law school, I called my friends all the time," Geena said.

"Yeah but the thing is, Carter never did that. This is the first time he ever called. You look at his grades and he ain't been doing much studying. He's real close to flunking out."

Geena shrugged, enjoying this. "If I was his lawyer, I would simply claim that's why he's busting his ass at midnight, so he doesn't flunk out."

Dykes shook his head. "That boy ain't never busted his ass. Not once in his whole life."

Harley was nodding along with his partner. "Look at the times. Just enough time for him to leave his house and go kill that girl and get back between the two phone calls. That is one hell of a coincidence if you ask me. The other thing is look at what Marty gave us for a time of death. He's right there, at eleven-thirty."

"Okay, I'm starting to believe you, but there's no way we could even think about going to trial with what you've got."

"We have a couple of wits. They put Carter's car at her house after eleven."

Geena sat up. "Okay. Now we're talking. How reliable are they?"

Again the two detectives shared a look. "Not the greatest," Dykes said, somewhat reluctantly. "First one is a Geraldine Carver. She lives half a block down the street from Salters. She said she saw a car which looked like Carter's. It was parked down the street a little from Salters' apartment. She said it was definitely there at eleven-thirty." Dykes blew out a sigh. "She's real clear on the time. She has a sixteen year old son and he was due home at eleven. She was watching out the window. He got home a few minutes after eleven-thirty. She says she didn't get a real clear look at the car, and wasn't really paying attention. Says she can't swear it was Carters car."

"What about the son? Did he see it?"

"Nope," Dykes said. "He said it wasn't there when he got home."

Geena leaned back thinking. "Okay, as witnesses go, Geraldine doesn't completely suck. If your other witness is good, then she will be great backing him up. If she has to stand on her own?" Geena left the thought unfinished.

"The other witness is Salters' brother Rodney."

"Tell me he's good."

"He's a piece of shit gangbanger," Dykes said, his voice seething. "He says he was waiting for Carter to leave. Rodney says he is into Reggie Red for thirty thousand and his sister was supposed to ask Carter for some money."

"That sounds promising. Maybe that is what they fought about," Geena said, her interest piquing.

"Not really," Harley corrected. "I want to believe him, but he just doesn't come across. He's just looking to make a buck. Little fucker already has a lawyer. He's just waiting to sue Carter in civil court."

"So how much of what he said is true?"

Harley and Dykes exchanged a look. "He does owe Reggie the money," Dykes said. "I imagine he was hoping his sister could pry some money out of Carter, but the rest is bullshit."

"Was he the one who found the body?"

"Nope and that don't fit with his story. He shoulda been there right after Carter left. It was after four when she was found."

"What's his version why he wasn't there?" Geena asked.

"He claims he got tired of waiting around and went to a party." Dykes shrugged his heavy shoulders. "Doesn't sound right if he really needs the money. Word around is Reggie is running out of patience with the boy."

"So he's selling a bill of goods to make his civil suit work?"

Harley nodded. "His story isn't even any good. He knew the plate number of the car, but he had it parked right in front of the apartment."

"And the Carver lady had it up the street," Geena said. "What about knowing the plate number?"

"He got it from watching Carter. He didn't come forward until after the article in the paper."

"Tell me it was a vanity plate or at least an easy number to remember," Geena said.

"Nope, just an ordinary number."

Geena took her time. The two detectives waited patiently while she read back through her notes. "I'm sorry gentlemen. Unless you come up with something more, I have to agree with your assessment. You're in trouble." Geena looked back down at her notes. "May have to let this one go."

"No fucking way!" Harley said, slapping her desk with his hand. "This girl didn't deserve to die!"

"Well give me one piece of hard evidence that can't be torn down, and we'll get this guy. You got anything else?"

"No," Dykes said quietly. "We're scraping the bottom of the barrel, but we ain't finding anything."

Geena spread her hands. "I can't see anything we can do. We couldn't indict with what you have now. Give me one thing, and we'll make a go of it."

Harley handed her a file he had been carrying. "Read this. Get to know Justine Salters. Then tell me we have to walk away." Harley placed the file carefully on her desk. "Don't worry we'll get something on this little piece of shit."

Tucson Airport Tucson AZ June 11th 2018 Monday
Noon

William Forsyth stepped off the plane feeling much better. It wasn't possible that Jared had been murdered. Things like that just didn't happen. Not in the business world. Killing was for thugs in the streets, not brokers, lawyers and accountants.

For a fleeting second, William thought of Carter. That man scared him. Rumor around the office was that Carter had killed a girl in college and Van Zandt had gotten him off.

Forsyth shook his head. That was crazy. William knew you couldn't believe office rumors, they were never right. Besides, Van Zandt was a well-respected lawyer and businessman. Certainly not the kind of man who would have someone killed. Preposterous.

So he and Jared had decided to take a small bite out of Van Zandt's deal? So what? The deal was worth billions. Van Zandt wouldn't risk blowing it squabbling over a couple of million.

Of course he wouldn't. Forsyth thought about it. Van Zandt might bluster and threaten, but in the end he would go along. He certainly wouldn't kill anyone.

What he needed to do, William decided was find Brody and Kathy as quickly as possible. Get the deal done. He stood to walk away with a couple of million. He would leave DC. Do what he wanted. Travel maybe.

William was feeling pretty good as he waited on his bags. A whisper of doubt swirled in the back of his mind. The thing with Jared and the drugs, that wasn't right.

Of course, Jared drank all that weird tea. Maybe he got some that had peyote or some crap in it. Wondering about it, Forsyth watched the bags pass in front of him. Was that possible? It sounded possible. He should get on the internet and do some research. Jared was always ordering that health tea from all sorts of weird places. The Himalayas, Cambodia, Indonesia, places like that. They grew opium in those places. Maybe he got a contaminated batch?

Of course. That was probably it.

William Forsyth smiled a silly little grin. Jesus, he was such a girl. Scared that Mister Van Zandt might have him killed. How ridicules was that? While most people wouldn't call Mister Van Zandt a nice man, he surely wasn't a killer.

William laughed a little. Just get the deal done and collect the payoff. It would work out,

William thought as he pulled his bag off the carousel. He was almost smiling when his phone rang. Thinking it might be Kathy or Brody, he frantically dug out the cell. "Yes," he said, fumbling to hold onto his bags and bring the phone to his ear.

"Billy," a smooth voice said. "You've been a bad boy, Billy."

William dropped his bags. "What? Who is this?" he asked, but deep inside he knew; Carter.

"Billy, you've been snooping around where you shouldn't."

William felt a catch in his throat. "No," he squawked.

"Oh yes you have. You've been talking to cops."

"No I swear."

"Is it hot in Tucson?"

The walls seemed to rush in, like a special effect from a movie. "Uh, what," William sputtered, his mind racing.

"I'll be seeing you soon."

**Saguaro Bar and Grill Tucson AZ June 11th 2018
Monday Evening**

Feeling a little like a teenager sneaking out of the house, Sam Logan turned into the parking lot of the Saguaro Bar and Grill. The place had been there forever and it had always been called the Cactus. Sam was driving his wife's car, but even so he parked in the back. He took a moment, sitting in the car watching the front of the bar. If he went through with this, things were going to change. And once this was started, there would be no going back

Sam slipped into the bar, pausing just inside the door, as he studied the group at the back table. Sam knew them all by site. All were ex-military and Sam was sure that they had all served in Vietnam.

There were a couple of Sheriff's deputies, one guy from the state police, one from Tucson Police Department. A couple was retired, some were still active.

Sam stopped at the bar and ordered two more pitchers. After paying, he drifted back to the table pulling up a chair. "Fellas," he grunted. "We all know what we're doing here?"

"We do. We're taking some back." Dave said. "Gonna put some assholes down."

"That we are," Sam growled, pulling out the pictures he had printed up. He passed the pictures around. "Anyone recognize these guys?"

A guy who Sam knew was a patrol sergeant with TPD, tapped the center picture. "This guy," he said pointing to the man Sam had recognized. "I know this dude."

Sam nodded "Yeah, me too. I've seen him around, but I couldn't put a name to him."

"Damn, me neither," a deputy named Clint said. He pushed the picture at the other deputy whose name Sam couldn't place. "Richie, you know this guy? He was running stolen bike parts down in your neck of the woods."

Richie Odell, the name clicked into Sam's brain. Richie picked up the picture turning it in his hands. "Yeah, shit, his name is Hector something. Ran with Chappy Miers some."

"Chappy fucking Miers, now there's an ass hole we should take out," a retired cop named Ted said. Dead silence followed his words and he looked across the table shaking his head. "Shit, ain't that what this is about, taking some assholes outta the mix?"

"It is," Sam said quietly. "Anybody got a problem with that?" His face grim his death, Sam looked around the table, letting his gaze fall on each man.

"How many times have we talked about something just like this?" Ted asked, looking around the group. "If Chappy Miers ain't number one on that list, tell me, who would be?"

"I heard Chappy was out in Cali, riding with one of those big MC gangs out there," Dave said.

"Was, he's back," the Tucson cop said. "I saw the fucker couple of days ago."

"There you go," Ted said, slapping the table. "I say we do Chappy, and that fucking Dell while we're at it."

"Take a fucking elephant gun to take down that fucking Dell," Dave said. "He's always been big, but I think the fucker's been doing steroids or something."

"I'd sure want to do him from a distance," Ted said, then looked at Sam. "What do you think?"

"In good time, but I want these guys first," Sam said, picking up one of the photos. He held it staring at the images, then realized they were all looking at him. "They killed some kids. They were newlyweds," he said, his voice cracking. "He was a scrawny, little fucker. But he stepped in front of the bullets, he tried to protect her."

Silence settled on the table, and one by one they nodded. These men at this table had seen a lot of death, and they knew how sometimes one could stick with you.

They could see this one in particular was eating at Sam. "All right," Dave said, his voice heavy. "We do these first."

"How do we track them?"

The Tucson cop nodded his head at the pictures "That one, in the black T-shirt, he ain't wearing a cut, but he's MC."

"You recognize him?" Sam demanded.

"No, but that tat on his neck. That's straight up gangland."

"Out of SoCal," Ted agreed.

"You know who could ID this guy for us?" The Tucson cop said looking around the table. "Johnny Mitchell."

"Mitch?" Sam wondered, raising an eyebrow. "You think? Damn it, the last time I saw that boy, he tried to sell me part interest in a farm for big-assed birds."

"How much did he talk you out of?" Dave asked, openly laughing.

"Hundred bucks, from my wife" Sam growled. "Little prick. You think he would know these guys?"

"Hell yes," Richie agreed. "I swear that boy must know everybody in the whole damn state."

"Everything female anyway" Dave agreed. "That boy does better in real life than I did in my fantasies. When I still had fantasies."

"Shit, that's because most of your fantasies were about food not pussy," Ritchie said.

"Yeah," Dave said, patting his belly. "But you gotta admit, women come and go but a good cheeseburger will stay with you forever."

"When did you ever have women coming?" Clint asked, smiling over his beer.

"Hey, I satisfied every woman I was with," Dave said seriously. He looked at the disbelieving faces and smiled. "I musta, because none of them ever came back for seconds."

For just a second there was silence around the table and then interrupted with laughter. "Pretty fucking hard to argue with that," Sam said.

"Hey," the Tucson cop said. "I just got one of them." He stabbed the picture with a bent, scarred finger. "Ain't that John Kittles kid? What the hell was his name?"

The eyeglasses all went back on as everybody stared at the pictures. "Shit, maybe." Sam said.

"Naw, it's him." Richie said looking around the table. "Hell, anybody surprised he became a piece of shit?"

"Bill Jack, that was his name," the Tucson cop said shaking his head. "I swear you name a kid Bill Jack and you're just garan-fucking-teed he will grow up to be a dip shit."

"I'd say," Ted agreed. "But I'm sure he's inside. Did a liquor store year or so back. Pistol whipped the owner, then got caught because he stopped and was raping the guy's wife."

"Hell yes, I remember that," Sam said. "But that was at least two years back. He could be out now. I'd almost bet he is." Sam pulled out a second pair of glasses and slipped over the first, gazing intently at the picture. "But you're right it's him, Bill Jack, dumbass."

"Let's run the fucker down," Clint said.

"We'll need a place to talk to him. A nice private place," Ted said.

"I've got a place, out east of Oracle," Sam said. "It's pretty desolate and I've got a shop building."

"Good spot?" Richie asked.

"It'll do."

"He ain't gonna want to talk," Dave observed.

Richie had an idea. "I heard about this dude, when he wanted to get a guy to talk, he would staple a feller's nut sack to a stump. Then he would ask his question. If he didn't get the answer he wanted, he'd take a meat tenderizing hammer and smash ol' left nut flat."

Every man at the table winced and shifted in their seat. "Hurts just thinking about it," Ritchie said shaking his head. "Anyway, after that he'd ask again. Way I heard it, he never had to ask a third time."

"Shit," Clint said a grimace on his face. "I guess not."

"Anybody got a problem with that?" Sam asked, looking at the faces suddenly gone hard.

Ted picked up the picture of Fred and Gloria. "Skinny fucker," he commented. "What did you say his name was?"

"Fred," Sam croaked, not sure he could get anymore out. All of a sudden his throat felt dry as the desert.

"Took some balls," Ted said, raising his glass. "To Fred, rest easy brother, we got your back."

With a few drinks and a clinking of sunglasses, a pact was born.

People were going to die.

Garage Northwest Tucson AZ June 11 2018 Monday Late Night

I may be in deep shit. The thought sprang suddenly into Detective John Mitchell's mind. Mitch, as he was called remained impassive, as his mind raced to access the situation. Looking for an edge.

"Come on, pretty boy, do it. If you got the balls," a biker called Jersey Joe taunted.

Mitch glanced across the table at the biker, trying to find a crack into the other man's thoughts. "Ain't got the balls," Joe sneered.

Mitch ignored the insult, glancing down at the cards in front of him. A nice pair of nines. Another nine had come on the river, giving him three of a kind. What worried Mitch was the jack that came on fourth street, and the pair of fours that came early on the flop. Mitch rechecked the community cards the jack, his nine, the pair of fours and a deuce. No way to get a straight. The suits were scattered so a flush was out. Only thing that could beat him would be a pair of fours or a pair of jacks.

There was a grand in the pot already and over two hundred of it was Mitch's. Still a monster hand to win. Right now Mitch was ahead four hundred, he could let go of the two hundred in the pot, fold and walk away two hundred heavy.

He wasn't going to do that.

Mitch smiled across the table, "You're bluffing, buddy."

"Cost you to find out."

"Maybe," Mitch grunted, looking down at his stack. Just over six hundred. Not enough to break Joe, but enough to hamstring the biker. Mitch was going to bet, the odds were overwhelmingly in his favor, he was just fidgeting trying to draw Joe out.

"Fuck it," Mitch said, blowing out a heavy sigh. "I'm all in," he added, shoving his chips in the middle.

"God damn it, Mitch. You are one rotten cocksucker," Joe groaned, but he was happy. He had wanted Mitch to bet. Mitch could tell.

One of us is in for a big surprise, Mitch thought, watching as Joe played with his chips. "Fuck you," he grunted, still fondling his chips. A slow grin split Joe's face. "You are a sly fucker, but I think I got you beat."

"Cost you to find out," Mitch said, throwing the line right back at Joe.

Joe shook his head. "I got you. You might have jacks, but I don't think so, I seen Sally muck one," he said, waving a hand to Sally Rose, who used to anchor the nine o'clock news.

"Could have nines," Mitch offered.

"Shit no," Joe shot back, which made Mitch think, he's holding a nine. Betting two pair of some kind. "I'll call," Joe said, flipping over his cards. "Two pair nines and deuces."

"Three nines," Mitch countered, turning his own cards.

Joe stared at the cards for a long minute, then shook his head. "You fucker," he griped counting out the chips to cover Mitch's bet. "Bastard. You bout cleaned me out."

Mitch grinned, pulling in the chips. "Hurts a little, don't it?"

"Crap, who dealt that mess?" Joe moaned.

"You did," Sally said, taking the button from him, and gathering the cards. "My deal now,"

"So deal," Joe grumbled, tossing in his ante. He scowled at Mitch "Hey, asshole, shouldn't you be out making the streets safe?"

"Hell, the biggest crooks are probably right here in this room," Mitch said, tossing in his own ante, the twenty extra since he had the small blind.

"You got that right," Bill Jenkins said sourly. Besides Joe, Bill was the big loser tonight. Bill owned a string of appliance stores, and he might not like it, but Mitch knew he could afford his losses. But he was still going to bitch about it. "Much more of this and I will be eating a PBJ for lunch all week."

"Oh, hell, Bill you'll screw some little old lady on a washer-dryer set before noon tomorrow, make twice what you dumped here tonight," Sally said, dealing out the cards. She glared at him. "You got the big blind."

"Oh yeah," Bill said, tossing another forty into the pot.

Sally glanced at Richard Chatfield, whose garage they were playing in. "Hey Rick, you in?"

Chatfield looked up from the sandwich he was making. "Naw, deal me out this time."

Sally dealt quickly flipping the cards like a professional dealer. Mitch ignored his cards watching the other players as they checked their hands. He saw the quick scrunch of Bill's eyebrows. He doesn't have anything, but since he's already in for forty, he's hoping no one will raise so he can see the flop.

Joe peaked at his cards, a crafty look sneaking onto his face. He's got something; he's going to make a play.

Sally took a quick look at her hand, then leaned back in her chair. She'll fold, Mitch thought. "Bet's to you, Mitch," Sally said.

Mitch glanced at his cards. Nine and ten of hearts. A good hand to start with. Lots of possibilities. Might as well get rid of Bill and Sally now. "I'll raise," he said, measuring Joe's stack. "Two hundred," he added figuring that would almost put Joe all in.

Bill tossed his cards in, heading to the cooler for a beer.

"Trying to buy the pot huh?" Joe said, grinning. "I'll call."

Sally tossed her hand in. "Here's the flop," she said, dealing three cards face up in front of her.

Again, Mitch ignored the cards, watching his opponent. The crafty look stayed and a smile tugged at Joe's lips. Whatever came helped him. Mitch glanced at the flop. Ace of hearts, eight of clubs and jack of hearts. Mitch glanced at Joe, who had plastered a blank look on his face. He had pocket aces, and now he's got three of them and thinks he's unbeatable.

"You only got, what, twenty chips left, might as well push 'em in the middle," Mitch taunted.

The crafty look stole back across Joe's broad features. "Sure. Unless you want to have some real fun."

"What did you have in mind?"

"I know you always do table stakes, but since it's just you and me on this hand we might do something else."

"You got more money, fine with me."

"I got these," Joe said, turning sideways, grabbing his saddle bags. He took three cigar boxes from them. "Havana Cubans."

"Bullshit!" Bill said.

"No, they are the real deal."

"Where would you get Cubans?" Sally demanded.

"Shit, I get around. I got friends."

Mitch looked at the boxes surprised to see they were indeed Cuban cigars. "These are illegal," Mitch said.

"Yeah, says who?"

"The feds," Chatfield said, picking up the box. "Shit, I think these are real. I saw some when I was in Puerto Rico."

"Damn right they're real," Joe said. "So what do you say Mitch? These three boxes gotta be worth more than your whole stack. What you say we push the whole mess in the middle and have some real fun."

Mitch glanced at the flop cards. He had a lot of outs to win this hand. Any heart would do it or a queen or seven. Course he would have to dodge the other ace or anything that paired the board. Still the odds were in his favor. And he wanted those cigars.

"Shit," he said, grinning at Joe. "It's only money. You're on."

Grinning impishly, Joe pounded the table. "Hot damn, Mitch. That's why I like you. You're one crazy bastard." He flipped his cards with gusto. "Pocket aces. Gives me three. Beat that!"

Mitch turned his cards slowly, watching Joe frown at them. "Not bad, but that straight will be a bitch to draw."

"Yeah, flush is more likely," Mitch replied, gravely.

"Yeah, shit, flush," Joe said, rubbing the back of his neck. "Damn, didn't see that one"

"Here comes the turn," Sally said, turning the next card. "Three of spades," she said.

"No help there," Joe said gleefully. "Down to one card buddy."

"Yeah," Mitch said, starting to sweat a little.

Sally paused a bit, looking around the table. Even Chatfield was watching the action as he munched on his sandwich. Sally slid the card from the deck and placed it carefully next to the others.

Joe stared at it for a long second, the look of joy frozen on his face. "Mother fucker," he said, the look sliding into a scowl. "Mother fucker!" he yelled, slamming his fist down on the table hard enough to make the chips jump. Joe seemed to swell up, and looked to be on the verge of exploding.

Without a word he grabbed his bags and stormed from the garage. For a second a heavy silence pressed down upon them. When they heard Joe's Harley fire up and scream up the street, Chatfield blew out a big sigh. "Fuck me, that was intense."

"I thought he might lose it and go nuts," Jenkins added, sweat beading on his forehead.

"Naw, Joe's alright," Mitch said opening a box and offering it around.

"Maybe," Sally said, in a grave voice as she took a cigar from the box. "But that fuckin' Chappy Miers is a psycho."

Mitch shrugged stacking the boxes. "He's in LA."

Sally shook his head. "Nope, he's back."

Tucson Daily News AZ June 12th 2018 Tuesday Early Morning

Jackson Pyle sat at his desk, typing methodically into his computer. Stifling a yawn, he took a drink of his coffee. It was a story Jackson had written many times. Bunch of rich young assholes had wrapped their shiny sports car around a utility pole. Racing out on Sandario Road. All of them drunk. Stupid little shits never learned, Jackson thought as he wrote.

Of course, that wasn't the way he wrote it. He played up the sympathy angle. He down played the part about the drinking, but mentioned several times that none of them were wearing seatbelts. Pyle didn't wear a seatbelt himself. You see as many wrecks as Jackson had, and you began to realize, it didn't matter. If you were meant to walk away, you would. If not, then you were meat on a slab.

Take this wreck for instance. Four kids in a little Nissan, hit a pole at seventy. Three dead, but the girl in the front passenger's seat walked away without a scratch. Figure that. Logically, she had the least chance of survival, the pole hit almost right in front of her, but she walked away clean. Hardly a scratch on her pretty face.

She was pretty too. Jackson closed his eyes. Nice rack too. Firm and round. For a second, Jackson pictured her naked. For some reason in his vision she was walking across a field of flowers. Like there was anything like that around here.

Jackson came out of his daydream with a snort. Shit, he had to get the article done. He glanced at his screen, finding his place. Oh yeah, seatbelts. The paper wanted to stress seatbelts, so he mentioned it.

He was just finishing the story when his phone rang. "Tucson Daily News, Jackson Pyle speaking," he said, tucking the phone under his chin, as he started the spell check.

"Jackson, old buddy," came the syrupy voice of Darby Collins.

"What do you want, Darby?"

"Gonna do you a favor," Darby replied smoothly.

"Yeah, what would that be?" the doubt Jackson felt coming through in his tone.

"Give a you a lead on a good story," Darby replied. "Just got a hit from my source in the department. Guy offed himself over at the Kings Palace Inn. You know the place?"

"Sure," Jackson replied, tiredly. The King was a dump off Stone Road. "No story there, probably some junkie stuck a hot load up his arm."

"Sure, sure, but hey, we gotta cover it. The thing is I'm kinda tied up this morning. I know it's time for you to get out of there, but I was hoping you could go cover for me. You never know, it might work into a good story."

As the senior reporter, Darby worked days, and Jackson covered the graveyard. If there was any kind of story, no way would Darby want to hand it off. "It's been a long night," Jackson said. He was winning and he knew it. Hated himself for the winning. Just tell him straight up to take a hike, he thought.

"Won't take too long. I know you. You work fast. You can knock this out in no time. Besides, you are much better at this kind of a story than me. You got the right touch for these."

Jackson knew he was being bullshitted, but it felt good all the same. "Alright," he said, blowing out a sigh. "Soon as I file my story, I'll head over there."

"Hey, thanks, partner. I owe you one," Darby said, hanging up before Jackson could reply.

Tucson AZ June 12th 2018 Tuesday Early Morning

Mitch stopped beside his dented Isuzu Trooper. He leaned against the vehicle, puffing on the Cuban as he enjoyed the night. "It's beautiful at this time of night," Sally said, coming up to lean beside him. "That's one reason I enjoyed doing the broadcast. We'd get out of the studio at this time and nights would be just like this."

"Why did you give it up?"

"Getting old," she said like she was in her fifties instead of thirties. "Saw the writing on the wall. A male anchor, he becomes distinguished and can hold on forever, but a female, she's just too old."

"That's gotta suck."

Sally shrugged taking a puff from her cigar. "Lots of things suck. Whatcha gonna do?"

Mitch laughed. "Words to live by."

"It isn't all bad, I like the producing."

They stood in silence, puffing on the cigars. Mitch had the feeling that despite her words, Sally longed to be back on TV. "Wish you could go back?" he asked.

"I'd give my left nut," she replied seriously.

"I'll bet," Mitch said, laughing. He'd forgotten that Sally could embarrass a room full of teamsters.

"Don't get me wrong, the producing is interesting, and I actually feel like an adult, but God help me I miss being on TV. It's like a drug."

She turned to face him. "So, Mitchell, how come you never asked me out on a date or even asked me over to your house some late night?"

"Shit," Mitch said, suddenly coughing on his cigar. "What?"

Sally laughed rubbing his back. She reached down and grabbed his butt. "You should have asked; I just might have went."

Mitch was coughing, trying to get his breath and trying to think of something to say, when his phone rang. He snatched like a drowning man grabbing as life preserver. "Work," he croaked. "I'll have to take this," he said.

"Saved by the bell," Sally said. She tossed the half smoked Cuban in the street and then kissed Mitch's cheek. "Think about it. I still might go."

"Sure," Mitch said, fumbling with his phone. "Hello," he squawked as Sally waved.

"See you next week, Mitch," she said, throwing a look over her shoulder, that could have stopped freeway traffic.

"Mitch, you there. Damn it, you there?" Mitch could here Sam Logan shouting into the phone.

"Uh, yeah, I'm here."

"Shit, you drunk? You sound funny."

"Oh, no. I'm fine. What do you need?"

"Had a question. I'm looking for a guy thought you might know him."

"Shoot," Mitch said. "This have to do about that thing out in the desert."

"Yeah," Sam said, feeling wary all of a sudden. He'd hoped maybe Mitch hadn't heard about it. Might have been a mistake calling him.

"I heard it was a bad deal."

"Ain't they all?" Sam said. "Anyway, I was going to ask you, if you remembered this wanna be biker named Hector something? Used to run around with Chappy some."

"Hector Flores, came here from Cali several years ago, rode that rice grinder he painted with a roller. That the guy, you were thinking of?"

"Flores, yeah, damn it, could place his last name to save my ass."

"Happens when you get old and the Alzheimer's sets in."

"Blow me, it ain't the Alzheimer's I got, it's the incontinence. I'm due for a change; you wanna come and change my diaper." Sam waited a beat then asked. "You heard anything of Flores? Got a line on where he might be crashing these days?"

"Naw, hadn't heard of him in a while, thought he went back to Cali." Mitch said. "You think he's involved in that deal out in the desert?"

"Not really," Sam said, being careful what he said. Mitch was as sharp as they came and Sam didn't want him thinking too much about this conversation. "Heard he was mulling for some new outfit. Looks like these kids stumbled on some drug deal. Thought maybe Flores might know who's the new player running things across the border out that way."

"I haven't seen Flores for a long time. I can ask around if you want?"

"Naw, lets hold off. Too many people asking might spook him."

"Hey, did you think about that steak thing. I talked to Maureen about it."

Sam groaned into the phone. "Damn, Mitch, I'm an old man. I want to retire someday. I can't afford to be investing in your half-assed, hair-brained schemes."

"No, this is the real deal, man," Mitch said. "Did you even look at the prospectus?"

"Oh hell," Sam moaned. "Didn't you already fleece my wife out of some money on this?"

"Sure, Maureen invested," Mitch said smoothly. "But I thought you might want to double down on it. It's a good deal."

Perry Van Zandt's Office Washington DC March 13th 2002 Thursday Evening

"Let's get one thing straight right now. I don't care if you spend the rest of your life in jail."

Perry Van Zandt said this without the slightest bit of emotion. He leaned across a desk which cost more than many DC families made in a year. He tapped a cheap pen against the gleaming top of the desk, all the while his eyes bored holes into the young man who sat across from him. Jacob Simon Carter III. Accused of murder.

"For all the money I'm paying you, you damn well better start caring!"

Becket shifted his gaze a fraction, centered it on the older of the two men in his office. Van Zandt dropped the pen, wondering how the man could make a three thousand dollar custom made suit look like a Wal-Mart special. Distaste puckered the corner of Van Zandt's mouth and contempt leaked into his tone. "Your fee is inconsequential to me."

"I wouldn't call a flat million dollar fee inconsequential," Jacob Carter II said, sweat tracking down his jowls and soaking into the collar of his shirt. "Anyway you look at it, that's a hunk of money."

Van Zandt shrugged, amusement playing on his tanned face. Van Zandt was a man who liked his golf and his sailing. He wore the year around tan of an outdoorsman. He smiled at the elder Carter, but the smile didn't reach Van Zandt's ice-cold, blue eyes. When he spoke his tone was precise and focused as a laser. "This case will last a minimum of one month, and could conceivably last as long as two years. In the amount of time I will spend preparing this case, I could easily surpass one million dollars in earnings."

Jacob the second or Big Jake as he liked to be called, dearly wanted to call bullshit, but he had a sneaky suspicion that Van Zandt was telling the truth. Van Zandt might be a slick, slimy bastard, but from what Big Jake had heard, the man could make money faster than the Philadelphia mint.

Little Jake sneered, a practiced, condescending expression. "Then why are you representing me?'

"Let me assure you, it's not because I believe you are innocent," Van Zandt said bluntly. He picked up the pen again. "Frankly I don't care. I rather imagine society would be better served with you getting fucked in some prison shower for the next twenty years."

"You arrogant prick!" Little Jake spat him.

Big Jake squirmed in his chair. He was known at the club for telling some of the nastiest jokes, but the cold profanity coming from Van Zandt's cultured mouth made him uncomfortable. "Shut up, boy. This is the man who is going to save your life."

Junior sneered again, looking away. He wandered how his old man could make so much money and still be such a sniffling twit.

Van Zandt watched the exchange, a smiling tugging at his thin lips. "You don't think you need me?" he asked mildly, directing his question at the younger Carter.

Junior met his gaze unflinchingly. "Frankly, no. I don't see why we need to pay you so much money."

"You need me because you raped and murdered a young back lady. And you did it in DC which means there will be several black faces sitting in judgment of you."

Junior shrugged. "We simply go for a change of venue," he said with the confidence of a young man who has never been denied anything in his life.

"On what grounds?" Van Zandt asked surprised that he was actually interested in hearing the young man's answer.

"Too much publicity," Junior replied promptly. "With all the media coverage, I couldn't possibly get a fair hearing in this town."

Van Zandt dismissed the argument with a quick flip of his hand. "Be denied faster than we could file it."

"Why?"

"Yeah, why?" Big Jake sputtered. "Christ on a crutch, the media has done everything but declare him guilty."

Van Zandt shook his head. "No, this is DC. Everything is political. No judge is going to rule to let you take this case out of here. He'd be crucified for playing favorites because you are white." Van Zandt glanced at Junior. "I would

expect better from a second year law student from GW."
He smiled, Van Zandt's degree was from Columbia.

"So I take it we won't be asking for a change of venue?"

Van Zandt eyed Junior. Perhaps there was something to this young man. Of the two, the son was the stronger, but Van Zandt had suspected that from his research. "No, we won't."

"How do you plan to attack these charges? I've got a few ideas. It's important that we prove Junior's innocence." Big Jake grunted heavily, hitching his chair closer to the desk. "Now, the way I see it, we need..."

Van Zandt held up his hand, cutting Big Jake off. "First of all, if I take this case there are a few stipulations. First of all, I am in complete control of Junior's defense. I won't have you getting together with your corporate lawyer and coming in here with suggestions."

"Well, hey, now, I have a law degree myself," Big Jake huffed, more sweat popping out on his forehead.

Van Zandt shrugged. "Be that as it may, all I will require from you is the retainer." Van Zandt paused letting that sink in. "Now, Mister Carter, if you would step outside, Mrs. Reynolds will help you arrange payment."

"Okay, but it might take me a few days to scrape together that much."

"Nonsense," Van Zandt said. "You have two point one million in the Royal Cayman Bank. As it happens, I also have an account with that establishment. Mrs. Reynolds will help you arrange the transfer."

Big Jake's mouth fell open, and Van Zandt could smell the sausage he'd had for breakfast that morning. The man was an oaf. How did such a man manage to make so much money?

Of course Van Zandt knew the answer without even asking. Carter had inherited a company which manufactured toilet parts. While Big Jake was far from a genius, he was just sharp enough to keep things running smoothly. His real strength was in networking. Big Jake played an acceptable game of golf and a lousy game of poker. He was a good loser though. He knew how to glad hand, spread money around. Big Jake had a good feel for who to threaten, whose ass to kiss and who to buy off.

With all that, Big Jake knew instantly he wouldn't get anywhere arguing with Van Zandt. He nodded, heaving his bulk up out of his chair. He squeezed his son's shoulder, glared at Van Zandt, before stepping out of the office.

Van Zandt waited until the door closed, then opened the file in front of him. The file contained everything that was known about one Jacob Simon Carter III. Van Zandt opened the file, but did not look at it. He knew what it said. It said that Junior was a highly intelligent, athletic young man, who if he put his mind to it, could do anything. The problem, according to the file, was that Junior didn't often put his mind to anything.

Van Zandt studied the young man across from him. The elder Carter might be an oaf, barely smart enough to keep a successful company functioning, but the son was something different.

The son was something hard and shiny. Slick and sharp, like a scalpel. He reminded Van Zandt of a big cat. Dangerous and at times lazy, but quick to pounce.

"The first thing I want is for you to get back into school."

"I've been suspended."

"Don't worry about that, it's been taken care of. You can resume your studies on Monday. Mrs. Reynolds has your books and the assignment you missed. One of my associates is waiting in the conference room to help you get caught up. As soon as we finish here I want you to meet with him and start on your school work."

"I don't see the point, right now."

Van Zandt ignored that, tapping the file with his finger. "I see you are currently ranked in the lower third of your class at law school. Not exactly stellar work."

Junior shrugged insolently. "It's not important to me," he said. "What's that got to do with my case?"

"Not a damn thing," Van Zandt said shortly. "But it has everything to do with your future."

Junior smiled. "We don't win and I won't have a future."

"You don't seem to be particularly worried about it."

"It's out of my hands," Junior said, still smiling. "Besides, they say you are the best."

"I am that. When I get you off, I want something from you."

Junior leaned in, a look of curiosity on his handsome face. "My old man is paying you a million dollars."

Van Zandt ignored the jab. "Tell me, what are you plans? Where do you see yourself in ten years?"

Junior shrugged. "I haven't given much thought about it."

"Lower third of your class? Obviously not." Van Zandt closed the file, leaning his elbows on top of it. Steepling his fingers, he studied the young man. "I suppose you will inherit the family business. Good money, but do you really want to spend your life making shitters?"

"Not hardly."

"Chasing ambulances?" Van Zandt fired back. Junior shook his head, straightening up in his chair. He sensed something important was about to happen.

Van Zandt tapped the file. "This says you are an intelligent young fellow who can think on his feet. Prove it to me. Give an assessment of your job prospects. Keep in mind that even after you're acquitted, many people will assume that you are guilty."

Junior was silent for a long time, his face knitted up. Van Zandt waited, giving the young man a chance to think.

"Exactly," Van Zandt said after a few moments of silence. "You won't have many options. Of course, there is always your father's company. I hear it makes a ton of money. You could work there."

Junior frowned, turning his head to look out the window, as if looking away would fix his problems. Van Zandt pressed the younger man. "But that would be terribly boring, wouldn't it." Van Zandt straightened the file "Is that why you murdered that young woman? You were bored?"

"Who says I killed her."

Van Zandt smiled, Junior had avoided the simple trap. "But you did. We can dispense with the other. Why did you kill her?"

"I hated her," Junior said, then cocked his head, thinking. "Yeah, I guess I was bored too."

"Which brings us back to the other thing. Once you are acquitted, how would you like to come to work for me?"

"Are you offering me a job?"

"No, I'm offering you the opportunity for a job."

"In what capacity?" Junior asked. Briggs, Downey and Van Zandt wasn't the largest firm in Washington, but they were the most prestigious. Junior wasn't sure exactly what they did, but he knew it had something to do with taxes. Van Zandt as the Senior Partner defended the occasional murder case as a hobby. His hobby had earned him National acclaim.

Going to work for Briggs, Downey and Van Zandt would be a coup. Junior knew some of his classmates who would kill for such an opportunity. But he hesitated. Junior had no interest in becoming a tax lawyer. Junior chose his words carefully. "I don't particularly care for tax law."

"You wouldn't be working for Briggs, Downey and Van Zandt, if that's what you were thinking."

"I wondered. My question still stands. What would I be doing?"

"You would become a member of Van Zandt and Associates, but you really wouldn't be practicing law."

Junior frowned. "Then why bother finishing law school?"

"Consider it a test. I want to see if you can start something and see it through to fruition."

Van Zandt stood up crossing around in front of the desk. "A law degree will open some doors for you, but the real reason is the nature of your work…," Van Zandt paused, choosing his words carefully. "You will be working right up to the boundaries of the law. I want you to know exactly where those boundaries are."

King's Palace Inn Tucson AZ June 12th 2018 Tuesday Early Morning

Jackson Pyle stopped just short of the threshold of the motel room door. Poking his head inside, he glanced quickly about. A man in a rumpled suit, sat on the bed, slumped back against the wall. Jackson couldn't see any visible wounds, from his angle, but he could see the gore splattered on the wall. Even without the blood and brains on the wall, Jackson would have known the man was dead. He had that slumping, empty sack look that Jackson knew from many long years of looking at dead bodies, meant death. Cocking his head Jackson saw the chrome-plated revolver, just beyond the dead man's outstretched fingers. From Jackson's point of view, it almost looked like the man was straining to pick it up.

A bottle of Glenn Fiddich sat on the bedside table. The bottle was almost empty. A glass which was empty, sat on top of a laptop. Craning his neck, Jackson could see a piece of paper and an unmarked bottle of pills.

A burly man in frayed slacks and a plaid sport coat that would take an act of God to button came out of the bathroom. He was reading from a small pocket notebook, and either didn't see Jackson or was pretending that he didn't. Which Jackson knew was a distinct possibility.

"Anything interesting?" Jackson asked.

Harvey Jenkins looked up from the notes he was writing. "You're not supposed to be in here."

"Sorry," Jackson mumbled, backing up to the point he was no longer touching the crime scene tape. "Suicide?"

Jenkins shot Jackson a scathing look, and then pointedly turned his back. Jackson felt the rage. He wanted to step into the room, snatch up that 357 and splatter what little brains Jenkins had across the wall. Jackson slowly smoothed the edges off his rage. He'd been getting the blinding rages since he was a kid and over the years, he had learned to control them, let them smolder, until time came when he could get even.

"Come on, I've been up all night and I have to file a story here," Jackson said, keeping his rage out of his voice. "It was suicide, wasn't it?"

Jenkins partner came out of the bathroom. "Looks that way, Jackie," Jones said. All of the cops called Jackson Jackie, but only Jones made it sound sorta friendly.

"Is that a note?"

Jones nodded gravely. "Looks like it. It's under the bottle, which makes it hard to read, but could be a note."

"Any chance of getting a copy, when you can move it?" Jackson asked, and instantly knew he'd went too far.

Both detectives turned their backs, while Jackson stood with his hands in his pockets. His nemesis Darby Collins would have smiled made a joke, smoothing things over. Darby would have at least gotten a look at the note.

Jackson was hating himself and his own ineptitude, when it dawned on him; there were plenty of things here that just didn't add up. The suit the dead man was wearing, while rumpled, was a good suit. Jackson squinted, probably a very good suit. Not the type of suit often seen in the King's Palace Inn. The small leather overnight bag at the foot of the bed spoke of quality as well. The shoes in the cedar stretchers looked very pricey. Besides who bothered putting their shoes in stretchers if they were fixing to off themselves?

His interest growing Jackson slowly surveyed the room. This guy used a glass for the scotch instead of drinking from the bottle. Most people Jackson knew wouldn't have bothered. Jackson didn't know a lot about scotch, but he was sure Glenn Fiddich was top shelf.

Jackson did know about laptops, and the one on the night stand was the latest and greatest. Ultra-thin, with a touch screen and converted to a tablet, a first rate machine. At least two grand, probably three. And the gun. That wasn't no cheap Saturday night special. It was a chrome-plated Smith and Wesson 357. At least five bills for that gun. This had been a man of some means.

"Any ID, yet?" Jackson asked, and was ignored. "Come on guys, give me something," Jackson pleaded, knowing he was whining, and hating himself for it.

Jones looked up. "No wallet in the jacket. Probably in the pants, but we have to wait on the coroner before we can move him to see. He paid cash for the room and gave the name Clay Kershaw. Could be his real name, but I bet he was just a baseball fan."

Jackson nodded scribbling in his own notebook. "Any drugs, besides the ones on the table?"

"No signs of it. Motel clerk said he was half bagged when he checked in."

"Suicide, then?"

"Looks that way," Jones said.

"He have any company?" Jackson asked.

Jackson felt a nudge and turned to see Linda Fang. For a second, Jackson stared at Linda. He'd never had an oriental, and her exotic beauty drew him in. She had a camera around her neck and carried a finger print case. "Excuse me," she said.

"Jackie, get you skinny butt outta here. We got work to do," Jenkins growled.

Rage flashed through Jackson like lightening. Had been holding a gun, he might very well have shot Jenkins. "Sorry," Linda said as she eased past him, ducking under the crime tape.

"Sure," Jackson muttered hurriedly holding up the tape so she could cross under. "I'll call you later to see if you get an ID," Jackson said, trying to save face. He didn't have Jenkins cell, but he knew Darby did.

The cops ignored him, and Jackson stood scuffing his toe, trying to think of something to say. Finally, he turned away a red haze dancing before his eyes. He'd deal with Jenkins one of these days. As he looked across the parking lot, it occurred to him that the lot was mostly empty. Other than the cops cars there was only one vehicle in the lot. At the far end sat an older 4-Runner. The vehicle had a wrinkled look, like wrapping paper the day after Christmas. Obviously not the dead man's car

Jackson started to ask how the dead man got to the motel, but then stopped. Jenkins and Jones had already made up their minds. They were already calling this a suicide, and now just going through the motions. Jackson knew they should be canvassing the neighborhood, talking to people. There should be cops scouring the parking lot.

They had made up their minds, but something wasn't right. Jackson had the fantasy of proving this was a murder and bringing in the killer himself. That might impress Linda. A scoop like that would get him off the night shift. No more writing about the mishaps of spoiled rich kids, and bar fights between grown men who should know better.

As Jackson wandered away, he heard Jenkins mention four am as a time of death. Jackson paused. Where were they getting that? The computer maybe? Four was a reasonable time for a suicide. Drinking all afternoon and night working up the nerve, then just before dawn, pulling the trigger. Jackson knew from seeing countless sunrises from the wrong side, that the hours just before dawn was the witch hour. The times when his emotions could gang up on a man.

Jackson looked around the parking lot for something, but there was nothing. How did the man get there? Maybe a cab? He could call some cab companies. Jackson kicked a cup out into the street. Fuck it, just write the story and get some sleep. The cops wouldn't release the ID until after the next of kin was notified.

Maybe it was a better story without it. Play up the suicide angle. Speculate on what could drive a man to such desperate straits. Maybe use the unrequited love angle.

It didn't bother Jackson that it might very well turn out be a murder and not suicide. He had a motto. Never let the truth get in the way of a good story. Besides it would be a chance to stick it to Jenkins. Writing the story in his head, Jackson shambled to his car parked on the street. Didn't matter anyway, if this story turned out to be anything, it would be passed on to Darby.

Jackson could feel the familiar red haze building in front of his eyes. Someday he would deal with Darby. He could picture it, Darby strapped to a table….

Jackson was jarred out of his thoughts by a gleeful shout. Startled Jackson glanced up to see a homeless man holding something aloft. From the distance, Jackson couldn't see what it was the man had found. He wrinkled his nose as the bum sang and danced a little jig. Damn bums.

Jackson started to dismiss the incident, but then changed his mind. "Whatcha got there?" he called walking down the street.

The bum took a step back half turning away and clutching the object to his chest. "It's mine; I found it fair and square!"

"Easy old timer," Jackson said, seeing it was a wallet, clutched in those grimy fingers. "It's okay; I don't want to take it. I just want to see it."

The bum held it up, then yanked it back to his chest. "There, you seen it, now git."

With just that brief look, Jackson could tell it was a good wallet. Soft and supple with deep, rich colors. Calfskin, maybe. It was one of those long wallets, designed to be carried in a suit coat pocket, not in the hip pocket. "Just let me look at it for a second."

"Stay back," he growled, yanking a rusty knife from his pocket.

"Easy," Jackson cooed. "I don't want to take it; I just need to look at It for a minute.

"Ha, I wasn't born yesterday, asshole," the bum said opening the wallet. Jackson took an involuntary step forward, straining to see inside the wallet. "Hey, I said stay back!" the bum shouted slashing the air with the knife.

"Yeowee," he shouted snatching some cash out of the wallet. He stuffed the cash into his pocket. Jackson saw some hundreds before the cash disappeared into the tattered jeans. The bum pulled out a receipt, glanced at it then let it fall.

Jackson scooped up the receipt. Kinko's. The receipt was date stamped for 8:10 pm the day before. There was a note guaranteeing the order would be complete by nine am today. Jackson glanced at his watch, almost eight.

The bum dumped the rest of the stuff out of the wallet. An airline ticket a couple of credit cards, a photo and a driver's license. "You can have that junk, I'm taking the rest."

Jackson waited until the bum shambled away. Knowing there would be more cops coming; Jackson quickly raked the stuff into a pile and scooped it up. Holding the stuff to his chest, much like the bum had done, Jackson hurried to his car.

Once inside the car, Jackson spread the stuff over the passenger seat. There was a photo of very attractive young woman and a girl. On the back it said, Kathy and Josie. Next he looked at the driver's license. Issued from the State of Virginia to a William Joseph Forsyth. Bet they didn't call him Billy Joe, Jackson thought as he copied all the information from the driver's license. He got Billy Joe's social security number from the license. The address was unfamiliar to Jackson, but he would be willing to bet it was a suburb of Washington.

Jackson quickly rifled through the cards. American Express, Neiman Marcus, a gold Visa, and a Saks. No gas card. Maybe he used the Visa for gas, or maybe he didn't drive. Jackson knew people in New York didn't drive but he wasn't sure about Washington.

Holding the cards in his right hand, Jackson tapped them against his left palm. He'd planned to take the stuff back to Jones and Jenkins, but now he hesitated.

The fact that the wallet was several blocks down the street in a trash can intrigued him. Also made suicide improbable. Murder then.

But why would the killer dump them in the trash can. Jackson tapped the cards faster. This was obviously a planned affair. If it was murder, someone had taken a lot of trouble to make it appear like a suicide. If the wallet was left in the room, then the suicide was solid.

"Fuck Jenkins," Jackson muttered, slipping the cards in his pocket. He started the car, heading back to his office, writing the story in his mind. Let it out a little at a time. He could hold onto the story because he would be the only one with the information. He could shove the story right up Darby's ass, and burn Jenkins along the way.

Mitch's House Tucson AZ June 12th 2018 Tuesday Morning

Detective John Mitchell was in a good mood. The sun was shining and the temps were only supposed to be in the low hundreds. No showers in the forecast at all. Which was good since Mitch had a four o'clock tee time.

Best of all, he finally had his car running. For a year, Mitch had been working on a sixty-eight Mustang. Yesterday, he had finally gotten the newly rebuilt 428 back in. That motor had cost him over three grand, but at last it was ready.

Feeling good Mitch headed for the garage. He was a tall man with easy graceful movements. He wore his hair longer than most cops.

Munching on a bagel, Mitch grabbed the keys to the Mustang. The bagels were unusual. His normal breakfast was pop tarts and toaster strudel. But, since he had turned thirty over the winter, as of today, he was turning over a new leaf. He was going to eat healthier.

Of course, eating healthier didn't include cigars. At the door, Mitch dug several cigars from his cheap humidor, stuffing them into his jacket pocket. The cigars were good ones. Illegal Cubans. Mitch smiled, man you just had to love people that thought pocket aces were unbeatable.

It was going to be a good day.

Mitch stepped into his garage, hitting the door opener with his left hand. For a second, he stood and admired the car. It wasn't really pretty. It looked like a beat up junkyard dog. Powerful, with a nasty streak. It needed paint. The back half of the car was the original blue, and the front half was primer gray.

Still it was his baby. Mitch had put over a year into the car. Working nights and hunting parts on the internet. Feeling a sense of pride, Mitch opened the driver's door, which screeched like the gates of hell. Gonna have to fix that, Mitch thought as he slid into the seat. The outside of the car might need work, but the inside was immaculate. Over the winter, Mitch had completely redone the inside.

Mitch slid the key into the ignition, feeling a thrill surge through him. He turned the key, expecting to hear the motor roar to life. Nothing. Not even a click. "What the hell?' he muttered, wiggling the gearshift, as he tried the key again. Still nothing. "Son of a bitch!"

Mitch smacked the steering wheel, still muttering under his breath. He switched on the headlights looking at the wall in front of him. Nothing. Battery was stone dead.

Jumping out, Mitch pulled the clips on the hood pins. Opening the hood, he connected his battery charger. Immediately, the needle jumped to the peg. The battery was completely dead. "Damn," Mitch muttered, taking the charger off. Rummaging around on his work bench, Mitch found a wrench and removed the battery cable. After reconnecting the charger, he regretfully lowered the hood.

Pursing his lips, Mitch glanced across the garage. A dented Trooper sat beside the Mustang. In front of the Trooper was a Honda Shadow. It was such a nice day, he should take the Shadow. Grabbing the keys from the hook beside the door, Mitch fired the bike up. Straddling the bike, he walked it out of the garage. Sitting in the driveway as the garage door rolled down, Mitch enjoyed the coolness of the morning.

"You're gonna kill yourself on that damn thing one of these days."

Mitch glanced over at his neighbor, Judge Harlan Sanderson. The judge was backing his seventy-eight, Lincoln Mark four out of the garage. "Hey, judge, we still on for this afternoon?" Mitch called.

"If you got the money to lose, I can always find the time to take it," the judge grumbled.

"I'll have plenty of money tonight. I'll be eating Red Lobster on you."

The judge stabbed a bony finger at him. "Only thing you will be eating is a big ol' shitburger."

"We'll see."

"See you at four," the judge called, roaring away in a cloud of smoke.

Mitch smiled, waving away the smoke. If things worked the way they usually did, he'd be paying the judge five bucks. Mitch waited a few seconds to let the smoke clear. Damn the judge should get that thing fixed, Mitch thought as he took off down the street. The Shadow was a nice bike, easy to ride, with enough snap to get your heart pumping.

Mitch was sitting at a light, admiring the view of two women jogging through the crosswalk, when his phone rang. Glancing at the light to see that it was still red, Mitch dug out the phone. He glanced at the screen, recognizing the chief's private line. "Huh?" Mitch grunted, easing the bike up on the sidewalk before answering.

"Mitch, its Andy. I need to speak to you." '

"I can be in your office in ten minutes," Mitch said, knowing the ten minutes was a stretch.

"Don't bother. On second thought, just get your ass over to the U."

"What have we got?" Mitch asked, digging out his notebook.

"College girl got snatched right off the street. Nasty business. Way we are hearing it, a guy jumped out of a van, smacked the girl, knocked her down then pitched her into the van."

"Where at?"

"Off Anklin. Right in front of her apartment."

"That's a ways from the University."

"So, you are wondering if she was targeted specifically?"

Mitch smiled. The chief was new, and he didn't have a lot of experience in police work, but he caught on very fast. "That was my thought. Of course Pima College is right there. Maybe that's where she's going."

"My information is she is enrolled at the U of A," the chief answered, and Mitch could tell he was eating. The chief was a whip thin business man, but he could put doughnuts away with the best beat cop.

"Do we know who she is?" Mitch asked.

"Local girl. Angie Brody."

"That Brad Brody's kid?"

"That's being double-checked, but it looks that way. What does that mean to you?"

Mitch shrugged, even though the chief couldn't see it. "I don't know, I've heard a few things about Brody though."

"What kind of things?"

"Just that his books might not always add up. Some of the materials on his jobs might walk away. I heard his own house was built completely with materials that walked away from his other jobsites."

"Anything that would bring on something like this?"

"I wouldn't think so, but you never know. He did some work on the Casinos. Some of those Indian boys can get kinda rough. I would have expected to hear that he got drug out in the desert and beat within an inch of his life. Not this."

"Pretty cold to go after a guy's kid," the chief noted.

"Yeah, probably a long shot," Mitch agreed. "Still worth taking a look at down the line. Maybe a psycho or maybe a ransom. What about Brody? Do you know him? He got the kind of money to pay a big ransom?" Mitch asked, knowing the chief had run a bank for years and likely would know Brody.

"I know him a little. Seen him around the club, played a few rounds with him. Kinda pushy, and arrogant. Lousy golfer, good poker player." The chief paused, considering the other question. "About the money. Maybe. I never dealt with him directly, but Brad always seemed to be scrambling, right on the verge of being over extended. He could probably scrape together a million. Maybe two if he was really desperate."

"Somebody has your kid. That would be a pretty good motivator."

"You'd think so," the chief said, dryly. "Well, get your ass over there. Keep me posted. I'll call Brad once it's established it's his daughter."

"Please don't do that," Mitch said quietly. "Let me know when it's verified. I'll send someone over to tell him in person."

The chief chuckled without humor. "You got a nasty suspicious streak in you. You want to see how he reacts. You think he's involved?"

"Never know. He likes to gamble. Maybe he is over extended? Who knows? Might be desperate."

"Really desperate, but it's a good thought. I'll let you know." Mitch started to hang up when he heard the chief speak again. "Oh, and Mitch, this is the exact reason we created your unit. To handle big stuff just like this. I guess I don't have to tell you, not everyone agreed with creating your unit, or with putting you in charge." The chief paused. "Make us look good. People are watching."

"Yes, sir."

Tucson Daily News Office Tucson AZ June 12th 2018 Tuesday Mid-Morning

Back at the office Jackson typed up the story, writing it as a suicide. Quoting the cops, Jenkins in particular, on that. He kept the story short and to the point. It was an easy write, taking only a few minutes.

After filing the story, he ran Forsyth through Lex and Nex. Not much there. Using Forsyth's social, he ran a credit report. Forsyth ran a lot of money through his accounts each month, but very seldom carried a balance. He leased a Mercedes, one year old.

This was a man who had a lot to live for.

The plane ticket said Forsyth arrived in Tucson from Denver at twelve-seventeen. Jackson leaned back in his chair. Why from Denver? So, Mister Forsyth gets here at quarter after noon, gets out of the airport around one, arrives at the King Palace Inn at two, and then kills himself around four am.

What was he doing all that time?

Better yet, where did the gun come from? You couldn't fly with a gun. At least Jackson always had the impression you couldn't. Perhaps a person could make arrangements. Jackson shook his head, dismissing the thought. Not likely.

So he got the gun here.

Who does he know in town?

No, wait. That was all wrong. If he were murdered, the killer would have brought the gun. Another reason to believe Forsyth was murdered.

Jackson picked up the receipt from Kinko's. Forsyth had dropped off a computer disk at eight that evening. He'd paid in advance, for two printed hard copies and an extra disk. The order wasn't going to be ready until this morning. That didn't sound like a man who was planning to be dead. He had an order to pick up.

Why stay at the King? There were nicer places right out at the airport. The Kinko's was on Speedway, which was close to the King; perhaps that was why he chose the King. Jackson Pulled up the yellow pages on his computer and the Kinko's on Speedway was the closest to the airport. Still why the King? It was such a dump.

He's hiding, Jackson thought suddenly. He's on the run and thinks he will be safe in a dump like the King. Jackson drummed his fingers on the armrest, as he leaned back in his chair. That made some sense. He should have been safe at the King. Most of the people who lived Tucson couldn't tell you were the King was. The question was if Forsyth had been murdered, how did the killer know Forsyth was at the King? He'd been followed, Jackson thought.

What had he left at Kinko's?

Jackson smoothed the receipt on his desk. What was this about? Jackson had seen enough people die that he knew, the receipt didn't have to mean a damn thing. Murder had a way of interrupting people's lives. He could have been making invitations to the family barbeque.

Still Jackson didn't think so. Forsyth was running. Running for his life. He flew, or drove to Denver, then to Tucson. Why Tucson? That could be important, or maybe it just could have been the first flight out.

Jackson glanced down at the receipt. That was the key. A man on the run wouldn't stop to make copies of the family recipes. Forsyth came into some information he shouldn't have. He was making copies to protect himself.

Jackson snorted at himself; he'd been watching too many movies. Things like that didn't really happen. Did they?

Jackson leaned back in his chair, scratching the patchy stubble on his cheeks. His eyes kept drifting back to the receipt, like it was a snake in the tall grass. Jackson flicked his tongue, lizard-like, licking his lips. Suppose it was something.

Jackson leaned back, closing his eyes. Suppose, just suppose it was the reason Forsyth was killed. Jackson could see himself, cracking the case. Writing a new story each day, slowly letting the facts out. A week of above the fold, front page stories.

Jackson could see it, almost taste it. Maybe Forsyth would have a widow. Maybe the woman in the photo. She was a chesty thing, with shinning green eyes and blonde hair. Maybe she couldn't collect on the million dollar life insurance, because of course, Forsyth took his own life. Jackson could see himself riding in on a headline like some kind of knight. His stories, proving that Forsyth was murdered. Jackson smiled, that meant double indemnity.

Jackson groaned slightly, his mind drifting away. He could see the grateful widow expressing her gratitude.

"Jackie,"

Jackson woke with a start, banging his knee on the desk. "Shit," he muttered trying to get his bearings. The sight of Forsyth's naked widow was rudely replaced by the beaming face of Darby Lewis.

"Hey, buddy, you better go home and get some sleep." Darby shook Jackson on the shoulder. "We wouldn't want to have an accident."

Embarrassed, Jackson slid his chair under the desk, hiding the bulge in his pants. "I dozed off, I guess."

"I guess," Darby laughed. "What happened over at the King? I looked at the story you filed. Didn't look like much?"

Anger flared inside Jackson. He could see the handwriting on the wall. If there was a story, Darby was gonna try and snake it from him. "Naw, not much there.

Some stock broker took the big train. I was kinda hoping there might be some love triangle or something like that."

"Wasn't much then," Darby grunted, already losing interest.

"Not unless this guy was handling Jimmy Hoffa's money," Jackson said, trying to sound casual. "Cops are thinking he just had enough and decided to check out. I thought if it's slow tonight I might check with the cops to see if there was enough to do a follow up."

"I wouldn't bother."

"You're right, but if I need some filler, I could do something on it, tie in the rising suicide rate. That sort of thing."

"Waste of time," Darby said, stooping down.

"Maybe the guy was leveraged deep into those sub-prime loans. Might make some kind of story out of that."

"Be a dog," Darby replied straightening up. "You dropped something," he said, holding up the receipt from Kinko's.

Fuck! Jackson thought. Panicked, he snatched at it, but Darby quickly pulled it back. Holding his hand out to keep Jackson at bay, Darby looked at the receipt. "Kinko's? What are you doing? Writing a book?" Darby laughed like that was the funniest thing he had ever heard of.

"Maybe," Jackson admitted, not waning Darby to figure out what the receipt really meant. "Can I have it back? I need to go pick up my order."

Sure," Darby said, letting the receipt flutter back down to the floor. "Big waste of time and money, if you ask me."

"Why?" Jackson said, letting the flash of anger he felt show in his voice. "You are always talking of writing a book. Why is it stupid for me to try?" Jackson demanded, really angry and forgetting for a second that he wasn't actually writing a book.

"Cause I have talent," Darby replied arrogantly.

"And I don't?"

"Fuck no." Darby laughed and leaned in so close, Jackson could smell the mints he was always sucking on. "Jackson, you couldn't write your way out of a wet paper bag."

"Yeah, we'll see about that."

"I'm sure we will," Darby replied, turning his back on Jackson.

For a second, Jackson wanted to rush Darby, but then he smoothed down his anger. He could wait. He would cram this story up Darby's lily-white ass. Grabbing the receipt, Jackson stalked to the door. He'd show Darby, he'd show them all.

By the time he got to his car, Jackson was thinking rationally again. He would have to be very careful. Once the story broke big, Darby would for sure try to skank it out from underneath him. Darby had the ear of Donnie Cruz, the editor. Which was an amazing feat of body contortion, sense Darby's lips rarely left Cruz's ass.

What he needed to do was get the story wrapped up tight. He would have to stay one step ahead and never let Darby get a foothold on the story.

As he drove, Jackson planned. He would write the story in stages. Try and always have the next stage nailed down. By the time he reached Kinko's, Jackson had a plan. He might have to set on the story for a day. Or maybe do some generic fluff piece about it tomorrow. That would be the best. He could screw Jenkins that way. Jackson smiled, as he got out of the car. He could get a quote from Jenkins today, confirming the suicide.

The smile was still on his lips as he pushed through the glass doors of the Kinko's. A small bird-like woman behind the counter returned the smile. "Welcome to Kinko's. How may I help you?"

"Yes you may, Marcy" Jackson said, looking at her name tag. Jackson knew he should have been nervous. He was committing a crime, probably. Obstruction at the very least. But Jackson wasn't particularly nervous. In fact, he was feeling more confidence than ever. "I'm here to pick up an order my boss dropped off yesterday." He smiled pushing the receipt across the counter. "Is it by chance ready?"

Marcy fumbled for some glasses hanging by a small gold chain from her neck. Placing the glasses on her nose, she peered at the receipt. "Just finished it up," she announced, turning to a rack containing several file folders. "Here it is."

"Thank you," Jackson said, snatching it from her hand. "Do I owe you anything?"

"No, Mister Morris paid in full."

"Thanks." Jackson started to turn away, but the name stopped him. Morris? What was that about? "Is the original CD that Mister Morris brought in here?"

"Yes, we also made a copy of the CD as well as printing out two hard copies."

"Well, that should do it then," Jackson said tapping the edge of the envelope against the counter. He wanted to ask for a description of Morris, but couldn't think of a plausible explanation. "You have a nice day," he said finally.

Jackson caressed the envelope as he forced himself to walk slowly to his car. He wanted to give the impression of a bored employee, running a tiresome errand. Sprinting to his car ripping the envelope open as he ran certainly wouldn't give that impression.

If the cops ever got around to coming over here and asking questions, Jackson didn't want Marcy to remember much about him. Walking like he hadn't a care in the world, Jackson sauntered across the parking lot to his car. He could feel the envelope burning his fingers. This was an important moment in his life. Jackson could feel it.

His car was still in sight of the store, so he tossed the envelope in the seat as he slid into the car. He backed out slowly and turning onto Speedway. A few blocks down he pulled into a McDonalds. It was too hot to sit in the car, so he went into McDonalds. At the counter, he ordered a large black coffee and an Egg McMuffin.

When his order came, he carried to a table in the back. The McMuffin, he tossed aside. He was too keyed up to eat. Tearing the tab off the envelope, he dumped the contents on the table. The two CDs, he merely glanced at. They were labeled with the name Morris only. Two files were also on the table. A quick glance told him they were merely copies of each other. Well that was what he expected.

Snapping the lid off his coffee, Jackson took a quick sip, before spreading the file out. At first Jackson was disappointed. It was simply the last will and testament of one William Joseph Forsyth. Jackson felt something sink inside. Suicide meant no story and a will made suicide more plausible.

Made sense. Guy was gonna off himself, he'd want to set things straight

Jackson scratched his chin. Course a will that wasn't witnessed, that wasn't legal. Forsyth looked like the type of person who would know that. Besides, why make a will and do yourself while it was sitting down town at Kinko's?

A thrill jetting through him, Jackson picked up the file. There was something going on here. Forsyth had known he was in danger. He was taking precautions.

Drinking his coffee as he read, Jackson started on the will. After a few minutes, the coffee was forgotten. The will deteriorated into some kind of rambling confession and accusation. As he read, Jackson didn't notice the looks he was drawing. He didn't even realize he was muttering to himself, exclaiming ever few minutes.

When he finished, Jackson leaned back in his seat, sweating profusely and his hands shaking. He took a sip of the coffee, surprised to see it had cooled. Checking his watch, Jackson saw he had been reading for an hour. Sipping the cool coffee, Jackson tried to digest what he had just read.

It was clear that Forsyth had been murdered. Jackson realized the same people wouldn't hesitate to kill him as well.

From his reading, Jackson knew that Forsyth wasn't the first person that had been killed. A man named Jared Morris had been killed as well. Jackson thought about it. At least now he knew where the name Morris came from.

Jackson wondered how much money was at stake here. Millions, probably billions. The money wouldn't be the important thing, Jackson figured. The power, that was what, was really at stake here.

After all they were talking about the most powerful position on the face of the earth.

President of the United States of America.

Now that was a prize worth killing for.

CHAPTER TWO

Angie Brody's Apartment Tucson AZ June 12th 2018 Tuesday Morning

Mitch roared up to the crime scene, guided in by the flashing lights. The apartment complex was a non-descript collection of stucco buildings. The buildings were arranged in a sprawling U shape. On the south side of the U, a dozen uniformed cops were gathered. So many it looked like a cop convention.

Mitch smiled, he could tell how far along the investigation was just by looking at the cops. Jerry Hartek and Oscar Olshan were talking to the uniforms. That told Mitch they had been there about five minutes. Carly Parker another member of Mitch's team was just arriving. Like Mitch, she was coming from home. Mitch saw her park her Jeep Wrangler on the street.

Linda Fang, the crime scene tech was taking a picture of something under a parked car. Mitch shot the bike up into the parking lot, leaving it sitting on the sidewalk.

Jerry Hartek broke away from the uniform he was talking to, heading towards Mitch. "What do we have?" Mitch asked.

Jerry was already shaking his head. "Not much. Guy didn't leave us much."

"What's Linda shooting?"

"Cell phone," Oscar Olshan grunted. "Belonged to the victim. Looks like it might have blood on it."

"How sure are we of the victim's ID?" Mitch asked.

Hartek and Olshan exchanged a quick glance and a nod. "Pretty sure, three witnesses saw it go down. They all knew her, and they all agreed, Angie Brody," Hartek said.

"Okay, word from downtown is she's Brad Brody's daughter."

Jerry and Ollie exchanged another glance. "We were wondering about that," Ollie said. "How does that change things?"

"I'm not quite sure at this point, but once we know for sure she's Brody's daughter, I want you to track him down and do the notification personally."

Ollie nodded, shooting Mitch a serious look. "You think the old man might be involved?"

Mitch shrugged. "Wouldn't be unheard of. Some of the things I've heard of Brody makes me wonder."

Ollie nodded. "Okay, I'll head out now. Give me a shout on the cell once you get the ID nailed down."

"Soon as we hear," Mitch said, and then added. "Take Carly with you."

Ollie had already started to walk away. "Parker? You sure about that?" he asked, turning back.

"You got a problem with Parker?" Mitch asked. Surprised at the thought. Ollie wasn't that type of person.

Ollie had been on the force a long time, he had mentored Mitch when Mitch first made detective. Ollie had always been more than willing to help the younger guys coming up. When Mitch had been tasked to form this team, Ollie had been the first one he thought of. Jerry Hartek and his partner Wade Nichols, who was out on a medical leave were the second.

Ollie squirmed a little at the question. "Shit, Mitch I don't know. She seems alright, I guess."

"But you do have a problem with her?" Mitch asked, surprised at the conflict. "Is it because we brought her up so quick? You don't think she paid her dues?"

"Hell, no. I don't care about that shit. If you think she's up to the job, then she is."

"Is it because she's a woman?"

"Well, yeah, I guess." Ollie's face began to turn red. "When Wade gets back you are going to put him and Jerry together. As you should, they work well together. But that's gonna leave me with Parker."

"And you don't like that?"

"Yeah, I mean I don't want to have to watch what I say. Is she gonna go whining to HR every time I say fuck."

"You got a problem with HR?"

"Oh, hate them ass wipes. Can't smoke in the car. I seen it before, they come up with all kinds of things; hostile work place and such shit." Ollie paused, looking about like a hunted man, an edge of desperation in his voice. "If I slip and say fuck, they gonna haul me in there."

"Do you have to say fuck?" Mitch asked trying to hide a smile.

"Fuck yes," Ollie shot back. "Damn it, Mitch this ain't funny. I just don't want to have to worry about everything I say or do. What if I need to fart in the car?"

Mitch was openly laughing now. "When did you ever worry about that? That night we were watching that club over off Congress for Jimmy Cruz, you almost killed me."

Ollie let out a satisfied chuckle. "Those chili cheese fries will do that. But you see what I'm saying. I mean who cares about you dickweeds, but in front of a girl?'"

Mitch laughed. "I guess you'll just have to work things out."

"And to think I recommended you for this job. I wouldn't have done it if I knew you were gonna turn into such a prick."

"Yeah, I'm a prick. I'm making you ride with a gorgeous twenty-six year old blonde. You poor bastard."

"That's another thing, how the hell am supposed to look her in the eye with some of those shirts she wears?"

"I don't know," Mitch replied honestly. He'd had that problem himself. Nature had been kind to Carly Parker, and she liked to wear button-up shirts under black blazers. Mitch knew he should tell her to button up a couple of more buttons. But damn. That seemed wrong on general principles. If a girl wanted to show some cleavage, who was he to stop it? Mitch plastered a serious look on his face. "But guess what old man; you're going to have to deal with it."

"Thanks," Ollie grumbled, as Carly came up. "Come on, kid, you're with me."

"You got a problem with Parker?" Mitch asked as soon as Ollie and Carly were out of earshot.

Hartek had been trying to hide a smile, now he let out a full-fledged laugh. "Hell if she can keep Ollie from farting in the car, she's alright with me."

Mitch laughed. "That's a tall order, I don't think she can pull it off." He turned serious. "Really, you got a problem with Parker?"

"Not really. She seems to know her stuff."

"Okay, so what are we picking up here on the physical side?"

"Nada," Hartek replied promptly. He popped a piece of gum into his mouth. "No tire tracks, no footprints, nothing."

"How about the wits?"

"Well that gets better, but I don't know how it's going to help us. White van, they all agreed on that, but we got a Chevy, a Toyota and a don't know for the make."

"Plate number?" Mitch asked, not really expecting anything.

"We got a number. Lady wrote it down," Hartek said, handing Mitch a note. "I ran it already."

"Tell me it belongs to someone who is good for this."

"Not really. Plate is registered to a ninety-eight Ford Taurus. Car belongs to a Melvin and Delores Sampson of Ajo. The town, not the street. According to their licenses, Melvin and Delores are sixty-six and sixty-three respectively."

"Shit, you think she got the plate wrong?"

Hartek shrugged. "She seemed pretty sure. Wrote it down even."

"Plate stolen then?"

"Unless you think Melvin and Delores came up here and snatched that girl." Jerry grinned. "Might happen. Older couple wanting a little sex toy to spice things up."

"Yeah, right, but we need to check it out. I'll make a couple of calls; see if the plate was stolen."

"Damn, there doesn't seem to be anything to do here. No physical evidence and the witnesses didn't give us anything we can use."

Mitch frowned, looking off to the south. "So, was this thing planned out, or did this guy just get lucky?"

Hartek shrugged again. "Beats the hell outta me. Feels like the guy just drove up and snatched her."

"He thought it out enough to switch plates."

Jerry nodded. "Means he's thinking ahead. If this is some guy out on the prowl, there's gonna be more."

"Fuck, I hope not. That's the last thing we need." Mitch ran his fingers through his hair. "Alright, we need to go back through it with the witnesses. Let's pull all the surveillance tapes from the area. Check every ATM, convenience store, gas station, and bank. Go back a week."

"Shit that'll take forever."

"I know, for now I want to look at this morning, maybe the guy stopped for coffee. We can come back to the rest later. If this guy planned it out, he's been around here."

Hartek nodded. "If he targeted her, maybe he's been following her. Might see if we can nail down her schedule. Might be a few more cameras we can pull."

"Good thinking, get on her schedule as soon as we finish up here."

"I've already got a couple of uniforms doing a canvass; I'll get a couple started on the cameras in this area."

"Double up on the canvasses. If this guy has been hanging around, maybe someone saw him. Which one of the witnesses got the tag number?"

"That one, the older lady. Darla Pringle is the name." Mitch's eyes followed the pointing finger to a lady in a pink jogging suit. "She lives in an apartment behind Brody. She was just heading out for a walk when it went down."

"Okay, I'll talk to her first." As Mitch walked away, he dug out his cell phone. Scrolling through the memory, he found the number for Sam Logan. Sam was a member of the State Police. Now a special investigator, Sam had spent years patrolling the highways of southern Arizona. He knew everyone.

Mitch punched the speed dial for Sam's number, bringing the cell to his ear. "Damn it, Mitch I ain't got any money to invest in your hair-brained schemes," Sam said, as a way of greeting.

Mitch laughed, surprised that Sam had caller ID. Usually Sam didn't go for anything like that wasn't made before nineteen-seventy. "Good morning to you too. I do have a good deal lined up, but I ain't sharing it with a tight, old ratchet ass like you. Besides, that isn't why I called you."

"What's up," Logan asked, sounding more alert.

"We got a girl snatched off the street. Witness got a plate number, but it came back as a Ford Taurus, out in Ajo."

"I take it your guy wasn't driving a Taurus?"

"Nope, white van."

"Think the plate was stolen?"

"That was my thought. I was wondering if you knew the sheriff or chief of police out in Ajo. I need to check this out pretty quick."

"I know the sheriff out there pretty good. Give me the number, I'll run it down for you."

"Thanks," Mitch said, then read the plate number to him. "Car it goes to is registered to a Melvin and Delores Sampson."

"Shit. I'll check it out, but I can tell you right now, Mel or his wife ain't involved in this."

"You know them?"

"Better than twenty years. Been deer hunting a few times with Mel. He was in the corps."

Mitch knew that Sam had been in the Marines, that made him and Sampson buddies. "What about kids? They got a son who might be good for something like this?"

"They have a son. Good boy. Bout broke Mel's heart when he joined the Air Force. Right now the kid's over in the Gulf somewhere flying jets. Mel can't stop talking about the boy."

"Shit. Okay, I guess this isn't going to be simple."

Logan chuckled, without a trace of humor. "They never are. Hate the ones like this. I'll call the sheriff out there; get him to check it out for you."

"Thanks, Let him know, I'll be calling later. What's his name?"

"Herb Willard. Good man, but not much of a police officer. "

Mitch frowned. "You mean I can't trust him."

"No, no. Herb is honest as the day is long, but he's never been a cop before. He got elected a few years back, and he does a great job handling the local kids and the speeders, but he's never done any kind of an investigation. If you want, I can run down there this morning, ask around for you."

Mitch hesitated. He wanted someone he could trust to know what to ask and what to follow up on, but he hated to ask." Well, how busy are you? I know you got that thing out in the desert. How is that going?"

Sam chuckled, but there was no humor in it. In fact Mitch could hear a hard edge of anger riding on the laugh. "I'm off that. Wonder boy, Brett George is on it."

"Well, fuck," Mitch said for lack of anything better to say. "That's gotta suck."

"Yeah," Sam said, sounding like he was biting through a two by four. "Don't that make you feel safe, knowing wonder boy is out there?"

"Aw, Brett ain't so bad."

Sam laughed again. "You know, that's what everybody says when you mention him, he ain't so bad."

"What happened with Flores? You ever able to run him down?"

"Naw, never even got a whiff of him."

"Well, maybe Brett will have better luck."

"Doubt it, he's gone." Sam replied, and then added. "It was a long shot anyway."

"So you ain't busy then?"

Sam laughed. "Not too. Chasing some rumor about a Mex trying to horn in on the drug trade. Supposed to be tying up with a local. Can't run it down, but a lot of people are talking about it. You want me to run out to Ajo?"

"If you got the time, I sure would appreciate it. If the plate was stolen, find out if they have been in Tucson lately and where they went."

Logan chuckled again. "Thanks for the tip. Geez, I wouldn't have thought of asking that."

"Sorry," Mitch said. "I know you know what to do, I just got a bad feeling about this."

"No problem."

"Our guy was driving a white van. I guess there's a chance he might be from out there. You might keep your eyes open for that."

"I'll do that."

"Once we get some better descriptions of the vehicle and the guy, I'll call you."

"Give me a couple of hours. Cell reception after you get past Kit Peak is kinda iffy."

"You got it," Mitch said, punching off his phone. He walked up to where Darla Pringle was sitting on a wrought iron bench. "Good morning, ma'am. My name is Detective Mitchell. I have a few questions for you."

"Do we have to go downtown?"

Mitch smiled. A TV watcher. "I don't think that will be necessary at this time. We may need you to look at some pictures later."

"Oh," she said, and Mitch could tell, she was disappointed.

"It may become necessary for you to give a formal statement, but for now, can you just tell me what happened? Do you mind if I record our conversation?" Mitch asked showing her a small digital recorder.

"No." Darla sat up straighter, adjusting her glasses. "Well, it was early. I was just going out for my morning walk. I walk every morning. I have to stay in shape for my square dancing. I go every week, sometimes we drive up to Phoenix. Do you square dance, Detective?'

"No, ma'am, that's something I've never tried," Mitch replied, then gently steered the conversation back to the matter at hand. "So, you were going out for your morning walk."

"Yes, that's when I saw Angie coming out of her apartment. She walked out towards her car. She was just getting out to the parking lot when her phone rang."

Mitch made a note to ask a question about the phone, but didn't interrupt. She was rolling, picturing it in her mind. Mitch wanted to keep that going.

"Angie was getting her cell out of her purse when that van pulled up and stopped right in front of her. This guy gets out and walks around the van. He opened the side door and took out a box. I didn't think nothing about it. Just another damn delivery. Then all of a sudden, he smacked her. Looked like he was going to walk by, then he just turned and popped her hard. Real hard. She went down and quick as a wink, he pitched her into the van. Then he drove away."

"You say her phone rang?"

"Yep, she was just answering it when he punched her."

"You said, that at first you didn't think anything was wrong. The guy didn't come screaming up?"

Darla scowled. "No, he kinda just eased up in the van. I swear, I thought he was a delivery man."

"What do you remember about the van? Did it have any signs or markings on it?"

"No, it was plain white."

"Are you sure about the plate number?"

Darla nodded her head vigorously. "Yes, I'm sure. Soon as I saw him driving away, I looked at it. The tag was right in front of me. I wrote it down, then dialed nine-one-one."

"That was quick thinking," Mitch said, not wanting to tell her the plate probably meant nothing. "It would have been pretty early for a college girl to be up. Did you think it was odd to see Angie out and about so early?"

"No. I think she had an early class this summer, or maybe she had a part time job, because I would see her most mornings on Tuesdays and Thursdays."

"So she was on schedule this morning?"

Darla nodded. "I think so. I go for my walk at the same time every day, and like I said, it's not unusual to see her on Tuesdays and Thursday."

"Okay," Mitch said, making a note to find out where Angie was heading this morning. "Did you see the van earlier this morning? Was it waiting on her?"

Darla's face scrunched up, a habit she had when concentrating. "I don't really know where it came from. I had the impression it came from the street, but I really didn't see it."

"The driver, what do you remember about him?"

"He wasn't a big man, but he was strong. He picked her up and put her in the van easy."

"Anything else?"

"He was good looking in a hard sort of way."

"What do you mean by that?" Mitch asked.

"Like he could be mean if he decided to."

Mitch went over it again with her several times, but didn't come with anything new. "Would you have time to come in this morning and look at some pictures? You could go through the mug shot books and we have some pictures of vans you could look. It would be very important if you could nail down what type of van it was."

Darla hesitated, a beat before nodding. "If you think it would help Angie, I'll do it."

"Thank you. It might save her life," Mitch said, not really sure it would help, but it damn sure wouldn't hurt. These kinds of things always came down to the details. "I'll get one of the patrol units to give you a ride in."

"Go right now?"

"In about ten minutes. Is that okay?' Mitch asked and she nodded, as Mitch's cell phone rang. "Excuse me."

Mitch turned his back a little as he dug out the phone. "Mitch, its Andy."

"Yeah, chief. What did you find out? Is she Brad Brody's daughter?"

"Yes. Daughter with his first wife."

"Okay, I've got Ollie and Parker running him down. I'll give them a call and tell them to deliver the news once they track him down. What about the girl's mom? Do we know where she is?"

"No, we need to track that down."

"Don't worry about it. We can get that from this end. If the daughter's friend doesn't know, we can get it from Brody."

"Very good," the chief replied briskly. "What's going on out there? Anything usable from the crime scene?"

"Not a thing from the physical side of things. We have some good witnesses, we're sorting through it all now."

"Keep me posted. And, Mitch, you need anything on this, all you have to do is ask."

"Thank you, sir. There is one thing. We will have some witnesses coming in. If you could get someone to set them up with the books; that would help." Mitch called them books, even though the photos were on computer now. They had been called books for years, and probably always would be.

"Sounds like a good job for Harris," the chief said, then laughed nervously. "Don't worry about it. I'll get him rolling on that."

After thanking the chief, Mitch closed the phone and turned back to Darla. "If you would have asked, I could have told you that she's Brad Brody's daughter."

Mitch glanced at her in surprise. "You know Brody?"

Darla colored a little. "I talked to him a few times when he would come over."

"He come to see his daughter a lot?"

"Some," Darla said, coloring a little more. "I shouldn't say this," she started and Mitch knew, even if she shouldn't, she was going to. "It seemed like he came over more when Angie was gone."

"You think he was having an affair with the roommate?"

Darla redness had blossomed into a full-blown blush. "I don't know, but he'd stop by when Angie was gone. I mean, I hate to say anything bad about Lindsey, but when Brody would stop by, he'd stay a while."

"Huh?" Mitch grunted, thinking it over.

"Does that mean anything?"

"Honestly, I don't know," Mitch replied, shaking his head. "But everything helps. I'll send someone to pick you up."

As he walked away, Mitch dismissed the idea of Brody having an affair with his daughter's roommate as unimportant. It was just one of those bizarre little twists that came up on every case. It always amazed Mitch to find out how twisted and messed up most people's lives were.

The cell phone call, now that could be vital. The fact that she got the call, did that mean the kidnapper had an accomplice?"

Mitch ran the sequence through in his mind. The kidnapper could have had Angie's number on speed dial. He hits the button when she comes out of her apartment. He could just leave his cell in the seat when he got out.

The timing on that would have been tricky. Suppose she answered the phone quickly? A thought occurred to Mitch and he spun back to Darla Pringle. "Did Angie answer the call? Could you tell if there was someone on the other end?"

"She answered. I heard her say hello. I don't know if anyone answered. Do you think the call was part of it? Something to distract her?"

"Maybe. I need to go check on it," Mitch said, hurrying to catch Linda Fang. "Linda," he called, as she was loading her gear into the back of her van. "Are you done with the cell phone?"

"Sure, I don't think there is too much use in dusting it for prints. The surfaces aren't very receptive to holding prints."

"She was getting a call when the attack went down. I'm wondering if the call was part of it."

"You want to see who called?"

"Yes, that okay?"

"Sure," Linda replied, digging the phone out of an evidence box. It was the only item in the box, a testament to how efficient the kidnapper had been. "Here," she said, holding out the phone, still encased in a heavy plastic bag.

Mitch didn't take the phone out of the bag; instead, he worked the touch screen through the plastic. After a couple of wrong buttons, he found the main menu. Punching up the recent calls, he located the last received call.

Mitch copied the number down in his notebook, also noting the time the call came in, as well as the duration of the call. Surprisingly, the call lasted almost three minutes. That was strange; Mitch had been expecting the call to be shorter. Mitch knew from experience that even though the telling of the attack made it sound longer, the attack probably lasted less than a minute.

Hartek came up, smacking his gum. "You got something?"

Mitch shrugged. "She got a call. I'm thinking it was to distract her."

Hartek shrugged. "Makes some sense I guess. She wasn't a tiny thing and she was in shape. It wouldn't have been easy to take her quick."

"That's what I'm thinking. He calls her, or an accomplice does, then while she's distracted, he gets close. She never sees the punch coming."

"You gonna call the number?"

"I don't know, I'm thinking about it. But if it's a cell and it's turned on, we might be able to track it from the signal."

Hartek was nodding. "You call, he thinks about that and turns it off and we're screwed."

"Yeah," Mitch agreed sourly. He dearly wanted to dial the number and talk to the kidnapper, threaten him. "We should wait," he decided.

"First thing, we need to find out if it's a cell or a land line. If it's a land line, we need to get there now. If it's a cell, maybe we can track it."

"Be nice to track the fucker right to his house."

"Ain't gonna be that easy," Mitch predicted. "This is going to be a grind."

"You want me to get on the phone?" Hartek asked.

"Yeah, I'll talk to the chief. If you get a location, I'll have some ERU guys ready to go."

"I'm on it," Jerry said, taking down the number.

"You get anything from the roommate?"

"Not really. She saw it, but she wasn't really paying attention. I kinda got the feeling if it didn't happen on American Idol or Survivor, she wouldn't notice."

"I'm gonna make a run at the roommate. Story going around is she's polishing Brody's apple."

Jerry grinned, smacking his gum and raising an eyebrow. "No shit?" he grunted.

"That's what I heard."

"Lucky bastard. That girl looks like she could suck start a B-52."

Mitch laughed. "I'll keep that in mind. Get going on that phone."

"Suck start a B-52?" Mitch turned to see Linda Fang. He'd forgotten that she was there.

"Oh shit, I'm sorry," Mitch said, as she laughed.

"Don't worry about it, I hadn't heard that one. I may use it myself. You about done with the phone."

"Oh yeah, sure," Mitch said, hurriedly handing it to her.

"Is there anything else, I can do here?"

"I don't think so," Mitch said, rubbing his jaw. "There just isn't much here."

"Okay, I'll get headed back in. I'm sorry, it doesn't seem like I was much help today."

"Yeah," Mitch replied. "Well if there isn't anything to find, there isn't much you can do."

"I took some samples from the sand in the parking lot. If we find the girl, maybe we can match it. I also shot a couple hundred pictures."

"Sounds good," Mitch said, nodding to her.

"After she left, Mitch made a quick call to the chief, arranging for some storm troopers in case Jerry had any luck with the phone. After ringing off with the chief, Mitch crossed over to Angie and Lindsey's apartment. He knocked lightly, checking the battery on his cell phone while he waited.

Lindsey answered the door, a pained expression marring what was otherwise a very beautiful face. "What more questions?'

Mitch gave her a quick smile. "I'm afraid so. My name is Detective John Mitchell. I need to go over with you exactly what you saw."

"Oh, crap. I already told the other cops everything I saw."

Mitch cocked his head, studying her. This wasn't the reaction he had been expecting. She should be worried about her friend, willing to do anything to help out. "I'm sorry, I know this is an imposition, but we are trying to do everything we can to help Angie," he said, watching for a reaction. His comment went right over her head. She didn't realize she was supposed to be worried.

"Okay, you can come in," she said stepping back. She took a seat on a round chair. Making a motion for Mitch to sit on a brown futon.

Mitch took a seat studying her. "I'd like to ask you a few questions about yourself to get some background."

Mitch had been expecting some resistance, but now she brightened. "Okay," she said, with a touch of eagerness.

She likes talking about herself, Mitch thought. "Okay, first of all, what is your full name?"

"Lindsey Jane Meredith."

"Do you work, or are you a student?"

"I'm taking some acting classes, but I work part time at the restaurant at Star Pass."

"Nice place," Mitch commented, then deliberately switched the conversation. "What can you tell me about Angie? Has anyone been bothering her? Any strange phone calls?"

Lindsey screwed up her face, and seemed to be thinking about the question, even though Mitch knew, Jerry Hartek would have already asked. After a long pause, she gave a slow seductive shrug. "No, I don't think so."

"Do you know if she had any change in her schedule recently? A new job, new class, or maybe a new place to work out?"

Again the long pause. "Not really. Summer classes started at the end of May."

"Okay," Mitch said, writing it down. Classes started about a month ago, could be the place where she picked up a stalker. Something to check out.

"What about you and Angie? How long have you known each other?"

"We met in a dance class a couple of years ago," she said, then thought about the question. "Why are you asking about me?"

"It's just routine," Mitch said easily. "I'm hearing that you and Brody are having an affair. Is that true?"

A quick look of surprise shot across her face. "Where did you hear that?"

"It doesn't matter where I heard it," Mitch said, letting a little steel creep into his voice. "Is it true?"

"Mister Brody is a great man. He is helping me."

Mitch nodded, not in agreement with her statement, but in confirmation that she was sleeping with Brody. "How exactly is he helping you?"

"He helped me get the job at the golf course, and he's paying for a vocal coach."

"Is he paying for this apartment?"

"He helps sometimes," Lindsey answered, turning sullen. "I don't see what this has to do with Angie getting kidnapped. How is all of this going to help you get her back?"

"Right now, we are just gathering information. We don't know at this point if this is someone Angie knows, or if it was a stranger."

Lindsey registered surprise. "You don't think that this was actually someone she knows?"

Mitch nodded. Statistically, that would be the most likely. But if it was a stranger, they needed to figure out where he saw her first. "What about Angie? Is she seeing anybody?"

"No, not really. There's a guy she sees from time to time. That's been going on since I have known her."

Hmm, Mitch thought. Might be something here. "Is there any violence there? The guy smack her around?"

Lindsey shook her head quickly. "No, I don't think so, Tim wouldn't hit her. He kinda drifts away."

"Drifts away?"

"Yeah, he's a drummer. He gets gigs or a chance to do some session work and he doesn't call or come around. That used to infuriate Angie. But then he'd be back. She didn't seem to be able to resist him."

"Mitch caught the twang of distaste in her voice. "You don't like him?"

Lindsey frowned. "He's alright, I guess. I think she could have done so much better. I mean Tim's a guy who's going nowhere."

"Do you think he could have anything to do with this?"

Lindsey laughed, a harsh barking laugh. "Tim, no, first of all I think Angie could have beat him up, besides I can't see him having enough ambition to do anything."

Mitch made note to speak with Tim. "Okay, how about this morning. What exactly happened?"

"I didn't see it all. I was doing my Pilates." She stated waving an arm at the TV. "I heard something and went to look out the window. I saw him throwing Angie into the van."

"What about the van? What can you tell me about it?"

"It was white. I don't know what kind."

"Did you see any signs? Any major dents or scratches?"

"I didn't see any."

"How about the inside of the van? You see anything?"

"It was like a police van. It was screened off between the back and the driver's seat."

Mitch made a note of that, even though it didn't surprise him. He figured there had been something. There wouldn't be time for him to restrain her and he couldn't count on the punch incapacitating her long enough.

"What about the guy?"

"He was dressed nice. I did notice that."

What was he wearing?"

"Jeans, they were Calvin's, I think. A nice button up shirt and a really nice jacket."

"What color was the shirt and jacket?" Mitch knew it had already been asked, but he wanted to pull her back into the moment.

"Dark jacket, light colored shirt."

"What did he look like?"

"He wasn't all that big, but he was in good shape." She screwed up her face, seeming to think about it. "He had a dark complexion and dark hair."

"Has she been getting any calls? People hanging up?"

"No."

Mitch noted the quick decision answer. He'd been deliberately jumping around with his questions, hoping to jar something out of her. Every question had been answered slowly, but with the phone, Lindsey had answered quickly.

Something to think about.

Brad Brody's Construction Site Tucson AZ June 12th 2018 Tuesday Mid-Morning

Carly Parker shifted in her seat. She could feel an attitude pushing across the car at her. Tugging on her seatbelt, she glanced over at Ollie. Jerry Hartek and Wade Nichols seemed to accept her, but so far Ollie had kept his distance. Now as they sat across from Brad Brody's construction site, the silence began to grate on her.

"Does Mitch think that Brody had something to do with his daughter's abduction?" she asked, unable to take the silence any longer.

"I don't know. I guess so."

"Do you?"

Ollie shrugged. "Something to do. Got to cover all the bases."

"You don't like me."

"No, that ain't true," Ollie grunted. "I like you okay."

Carly laughed, trying to sound merry, but it came out more of a nervous squeak. "Oh no you don't. I can tell. Remember, I'm supposed to be a detective."

Ollie looked out his side window, concentrating on the construction shack. He grunted, shifting in his seat, and clearing his throat.

"Have I done something wrong?"

Carly smiled as she watched the dark red color climb up Ollie's neck. He shifted again, clearing his throat. "You ain't done anything," he said, his voice gruff.

"Is it because I'm new? I've heard the talk around. People are saying that I got this assignment because I slept with Mitch. Or maybe because he wants to sleep with me."

"I don't pay no attention to that shit!" Ollie exploded. "If Mitch didn't think you were up to the job, he wouldn't have put you in it."

"So what's your problem with me?" Carly asked a curious frown on her face. "Oh, my God! It's because I'm a girl."

Ollie became silent, his face growing redder by the minute, as he looked out the window. "Oh man, that's it."

"No it ain't," Ollie protested.

"Oh yes, it is," Carly accused, sounding more amused than angry. "So what do you have against women?"

"Nothing," Ollie said, fiddling with the blinkers. "Aw shit," he muttered. "It's not you; I just don't want to be riding all the time with a woman. I don't want to have to watch every little thing I say. I'm too old to change."

"Fuck you, you old bastard," Carly said, trying to hide a smile. "You honestly think that I would go crying to the chief every time you cuss. I oughta kick your wrinkled, old butt."

For a second, Ollie stared at her, then the hint of a smile tugged at his lips. "So, I can say whatever I want."

Carly shrugged. "Sure."

"So, if I were to say that Senator Jillian Braxton is a liberal bitch who should be gagged and rode like a Mexican donkey? That would be alright?"

"Sure, I don't know who you would find to sign up for that job, but I agree it needs to be done."

"Hell, Mitch would do it." Ollie was smiling openly now. "So if I see an attractive young female walking down the street in a low-cut shirt?"

"You can say whatever," Carly replied, then held up a hand. "As long as I can. If we see some young guy in a tight pair of jeans."

"Oh hell no!" Ollie roared. "I ain't gonna have you commenting on some guy's butt."

"Who said I would be looking in the butt. Jeans can be tight in the front."

Ollie's face which had almost returned to its normal color was flaming now. "Oh, hell no!"

They sat in silence for a few minutes, Carly chuckling to herself. "What about gas?" Ollie started. "Sometimes we like to stop by Filbritos for breakfast burritos. Sometimes they give me gas."

"Oh hell no!" Carly said, mimicking his earlier tone.

They laughed together for a second, and then Carly turned serious. "So what exactly are we looking for?"

Ollie shrugged relieved to be talking about something else. "Something out of the ordinary about the way he reacts. I don't know, it's a feelin' you get just watching him."

Carly nodded. "I'm not sure I know what would be out of the ordinary. How would one react if they just found their daughter had been kidnapped?"

Ollie shifted in his seat thinking about it. "Look for a big first reaction. It's been my experience that news like this comes on people slowly. Takes a minute to soak in or at least for them to accept it. It builds on them, after a few minutes it really gets on top of them. If they know it's coming and are trying to fake it, they react big right off the bat, then they kinda back away from it."

"So if he throws his hands in the air and starts crying right off?"

"Then he knew it was coming," Ollie said. "If he just looks at you with a dumb look, then he had no idea." Ollie's cell rang, and he scooped if off the dash. He spoke into it then listened for a few seconds. Closing the phone with a snap, he glanced over at Carly. "Okay, that was Mitch. We're on."

Angie Brody's Apartment Tucson AZ June 12th 2018 Tuesday Mid-Morning

Mitch pulled away from the crime scene, thinking there was something here that didn't add up. The attack had a spontaneous feel to it, but the cell phone call, that spoke of planning? Or was it just a trick the guy had used before. Maybe this wasn't planned, just rehearsed and perfected on several other victims. Have to check and see if any other abductions fit this profile.

And what about the girl? Had she brought this on herself? Did she flirt around? Use drugs? Had she picked up a stalker? Or was it something deeper, something sinister involving her old man?

Mitch didn't know Brad Brody, but he'd heard of him. Mitch didn't like what he had heard and knew that could be clouding his judgment. Nothing from the crime scene pointed to Brody being involved, but Mitch could hear a tiny voice in the back of his head whispering that Brody was involved.

Mitch gunned the Shadow, turning west on Speedway. Maybe a quick ride up through Gates Pass while he thought it over.

He was roaring through the pass, when his cell went off. Hitting the blinker, Mitch cut into the parking lot at the top. Coasting the bike across the empty lot, he dug out his cell, glancing at the screen, smiling as he tapped the touch screen. "Frankie, what's up?"

"Mitch, you rotten son of a bitch!" Frankie snarled. Mitch grinned. Francine O'Hare, part Irish part Mexican, and part something that was really mean. A pit bull with world class tits, that's what Ollie, had called her. Mitch smiled again, with all of that; she could be a lot of fun. She could drink tequila like a pipefitter and dance like a stripper. She liked wearing skin tight black tank tops and had the body for it. Mitch shook his head. He'd always had a little thing for her.

"Geez, Frankie, who pissed in your Wheaties? It's way too early to be this pissed off."

"Don't sweet talk me, you sorry son of a bitch," she snapped, really cranked for this early in the morning. "I heard you scored some cigars at a poker game the other night?"

"Yeah."

"You try them yet?"

"Hell yes. I had one on the way home."

"Shit!" Frankie growled, and then smoothed down her anger. "You like them?'

"Oh yeah, they were sweet," Mitch answered wondering where this was heading.

"They should be, they were mine."

Mitch laughed. "Then you should be talking to Jersey Joe."

"If I could find the cocksucker, I would." Mitch could hear her take a long breath. "Look, I got a pipeline to get them direct from Cuba. You interested?"

Mitch frowned, seeing the hook behind the bait and wondering where this was going. "How much?"

"That depends. You think you could move some of them for me?"

"Frankie. What the hell are you talking about?"

"I'm talking about fifty maybe a hundred boxes a week. Like I said, I got a pipeline."

"Shit, Frankie, those things are illegal. I can't be hocking illegal Cuban cigars, I'm a cop."

It was Frankie's turn to laugh. "When did that ever stop you?"

"Frankie."

"God damn it, Mitch I know you're a cop. I'll do the selling, I just need you to pass out some free samples, and make a few introductions. I bet you know everybody in town that sucks on those damn things."

"Why would I want to do that?"

"Cause you got all my free samples. Cause you owe me."

"Bullshit, I owe you. You should have been smarter than to trust Joe."

"I didn't have time to do it myself, and he was handy and cheap."

"Does he seem cheap now?"

"I know," Frankie sighed. "Pass out some free cigars, I though even that moron could do that." She sighed again, and Mitch could feel her playing him. "Look I'm in a bind, man. You could help me out. I could give a free box every month."

Mitch smiled at a couple of attractive women sweating furiously as they pedaled by. Mitch watched the women as they disappeared over the crest of the hill, waiting. "Damn it," Frankie growled. "Okay, I get it, you want a piece, how 'bout one percent of the profit."

"And two boxes a month."

"Done."

District Attorney's Office Washington DC April 5th 2004 Monday Afternoon

Van Zandt escorted Junior quietly in the back door of the District Attorney's office. Just inside the back door, he stopped, turning to face his client. "When we go in here, I don't want you to say a word. Even if they ask you a question, let me do all the talking."

"What about all the rehearsal time we put in? What was that for?"

Van Zandt smiled. "We may have to end up telling our story today. But if we don't have to we won't. It's not that I don't trust you to remember what to say, I do. Right now, we don't know for sure what they know. So, we say nothing. Today, we will learn what they know."

Junior frowned. Van Zandt smiled at the frown and let the young man think. "As you pointed out, I am inexperienced in these matters, but it seems to me they won't volunteer anything. They'll hold back until discovery. That's after I'm booked and charged."

"Very good. I see you've been paying attention in law school," Van Zandt replied, flashing his white teeth in a wolf-like grin. "You're right, they won't volunteer any information, but if we listen carefully, they will reveal more than they know."

The frown slowly melted off Junior's face, replaced by a look of enlightenment. "The questions they ask!"

"That's right, so we listen, but we do not speak."

Van Zandt led the way to the elevator, then up and through a maze of hallways. He stopped in front of a battered wooden desk, with a prim-faced receptionist. "Mister Van Zandt," she said, and Junior's ear was keen enough to catch the hint of wariness in her tone. "What can we do for you this morning?"

"I'd like to see Ms. Dixon."

"What is this regarding?"

"Regarding the Salters' case," Van Zandt replied in a clipped business-like tone. "I'm bringing my client in for an interview."

"Who is your client?" the receptionist asked, trying to sound bored as she jotted it all down.

"This is Mister Carter."

Her expression told Van Zandt that Junior's name had been discussed. She quickly buzzed the inner office. Van Zandt could hear Geena Dixon's harried voice on the tinny sounding speaker. "Mister Van Zandt is here with Jacob Carter."

Geena Dixon came out of her office. She was trying to hide her excitement, but it was there. "Am I to understand that you are representing Mister Carter and he is here to surrender to us?"

Van Zandt laughed. "To the first part of your question, yes, Mister Carter has retained me as his council. As to the second part of your question," Van Zandt paused, smiling deliberately. "No fucking way!"

"Then, may I ask, why are you here?"

"We wish to set the record straight. My client will agree to an interview. We are certain that after interviewing Mister Carter, you will see that he is completely innocent. Perhaps then you can call off this witch-hunt against my client and move on to catching the man who really killed that lovely young lady."

"Save it for the jury, counselor," Dixon grunted, turning to her secretary. "Call Detectives Harley and Dykes, ask them to join us in the interview room. Also ask Mister North to join us."

She turned back to Van Zandt and Junior. "After you gentlemen."

"If you don't mind, I'd like a few words in private with my client. Perhaps we could get some coffee and meet you there."

Dixon grimaced. "I'm sure you've had more than enough time to get your stories straight. I'll have coffee brought in."

Van Zandt showed her his hungry-shark smile. "We can leave."

"And I can slap your client in cuffs and have his ass hauled over to lock-up. We can have this little meeting after he's spent a few nights in jail."

Van Zandt shook his head gravely. "Do that and you won't get a word out of him."

"I bet he'll get to know his cellmates, though."

"I've already spoken with Judge Hamilton. I can have him out on bond in time for dinner."

Dixon frowned, realizing she had been baited into an argument she couldn't win. "Alright, you can use the small conference room until the detectives arrive."

"Thank you, Ms. Dixon. I trust there are no recording devices in that room."

Red color shot up her neck. "Fuck you, counselor," she snapped. "I'm sure you know the way."

Van Zandt gave her a mock salute, chuckling as she spun away. "Don't forget the coffee.

" I thought you were going to get me thrown in jail," Carter said mildly.

When they were in the room, Van Zandt tossed his briefcase on the table. "What did you learn from that?"

"You were trying to get her mad. Throw her off."

"Very good. I also wanted to show her up a little. Maybe she will give something away trying to get even with me."

Junior nodded processing the information. He felt a surge of confidence. Van Zandt was indeed the best. He didn't miss even the smallest of tricks.

Van Zandt opened his briefcase. "Now remember don't say a word. Remember; watch your facial expressions and body language. This is a poker game. You'll have four pairs of eyes on you. Do not underestimate those detectives, they might not look like much, but they have been doing this a long time."

After that, they waited in silence for twenty minutes.

Geena Dixon came in with a rush, armed with a stack of files. Behind her came Lance North, also carrying a stack of folders. Van Zandt took a second to study young North.

North wore an off the rack suit and properly serious scowl. He sat down and Van Zandt promptly dismissed him. North was too wet behind the ears. He was here to take notes and learn.

The two cops were a different story. They both wore thread- bare, stained jackets, but they were sharp-eyed and alert. They each carried battered briefcase and oversized coffee cups. They refilled their cups before dropping into chairs.

Geena took out a tape recorder and set it on the table. "I don't suppose you mind if we tape now?" she asked raising an eyebrow.

"Certainly not, Van Zandt replied, pulling out a digital recorder of his own. "Just so there's no mistake."

"Of course," Geena added with a sweet smile. The black detective pulled out a battered cheap Casio and placed it besides the others. "Since we are already recording, I assume we are ready to begin." She looked around the table receiving nods from everyone except Junior who stared straight ahead. He's scared, she thought.

Junior was scared, despite his confidence in Van Zandt; he couldn't help but feel a quiver deep in his stomach. He tried to control it and met Geena Dixon's gaze. She looked away first, clearing her throat as she glanced down at her files.

"This is a formal interview with Jacob Carter the III. This interview is regarding the death and apparent murder of Justine Salters. Present are the afore mentioned Mr. Carter, his counsel, Perry Van Zandt, Assistant Deputy District Attorney, Lance North, myself, Deputy District Attorney Geena Dixon, Detectives Dykes and Harley from D.C. Metro. I'll now turn the questioning over to the detectives."

"Excuse me, Ms. Dixon; I'd like it on the record that my client came forth voluntarily for this interview."

"Duly noted councilor," Geena Dixon said in a clipped tone.

Detective Harley took the lead, after getting a nod from Dixon.

Van Zandt watched the exchange; they'd decided before hand the detectives would handle the questioning. Still, Van Zandt had the sense they weren't as prepared as they would have liked to be.

"Can Mr. Carter give us an alibi for the time of Justine Salters' death?" Harley asked, his tone sneering.

"I'm sure we could if we knew what time frame you were talking about," Van Zandt said calmly.

Harley didn't even show a flicker of disappointment that his simple trap failed. With a shark like Van Zandt, he didn't expect it to work. He slowly took out his notebook, even though he knew the time of death. He fumbled through the book, letting time grind down upon Junior. Most suspects couldn't stand the silence, they had to say something.

Junior didn't crack, he simply watched as Harley reviewed his notes. "Coroner puts the time of death between 10 p.m. and 1 a.m. Tuesday night."

"Tuesday?" Van Zandt asked. "Let me confer with my client." Without waiting for approval, he pulled Junior aside. "Are you sure there is no paper trail on you that night?" he whispered. "You didn't use a credit card, get cash from an ATM? Stop at a convenience store where they might catch you on a surveillance camera?"

"No sir, I went straight home."

"Okay, I checked, there are no traffic cameras on your route home." He led the way back to the table. He reached across the table and flicked on his recorder. "We're back on record," he said after all three recorders were rolling. "Unfortunately, my client was home alone. He was studying for an exam in contractual law."

"You were studying?" Dykes sneered, leaning across the table. "You aren't exactly student of the year."

Harley leaned eagerly across the table. "That's right. Our records show you are almost flunked out of GW."

"My client is aware of his precarious position at school," Van Zandt answered smoothly. "That is precisely why he was home studying."

"How does he explain the fact we found his prints in her apartment?"

Van Zandt ignored the question, asking one of his own. "Is that why you are prosecuting my client? Because his prints were found in the apartment? Are you aware that Ms. Salters and my client were schoolmates and remained friends?"

"We know they went to school together, but not that they were friends."

Geena Dixon stepped in. "Is it not true that you and Justine Salters were rivals in school?" she paused a beat, but Junior stared impassively at her. "Is it also true that she bested you on numerous occasions and you hated her?"

"You hated her. You stalked her, you ripped her clothes off, you raped her, and then you killed her?" Harley snapped.

"No," Junior said speaking for the first time. "None of that is true."

"Shit, you're lying piece of shit," Harley roared, slapping the table.

Dykes stood up. "Look son, we know you killed her. We found some hair with the rape kit. We do a DNA match against you and I bet it's going to be a dead ringer." Dykes walked around then sat on the table. "Now son, I don't think you meant to kill her, I think maybe things got outta hand."

"Save your tired routine," Van Zandt said in a bored tone. "Ask your questions and get this over with."

"When was the last time you saw Justine Salters?" Harley asked.

"That night," Junior said after receiving a brief nod from Van Zandt.

Van Zandt enjoyed the confused looks around the table. "So, you admit you were with her the night she died?" Dixon asked. Junior nodded. "What time was that?"

"I left about six I guess. I wasn't watching the clock."

"What were you doing?"

Junior squirmed, looking away from Ms. Dixon. "We were having sex."

"Let me get this straight. You had sex with Justine Salters on the night she was killed?" Harley asked, and Junior nodded.

"Did you love her? Dykes asked.

Junior cocked his head, pretending to consider the question. "I don't know, our relationship hadn't preceded that far."

"But you were fucking her?" Harley sneered.

Junior let his head fall, pretending to be embarrassed, but in fact he was amazed at how well Van Zandt has scripted this conversation. "I wouldn't use those words, but we had a physical relationship."

Harley leaned across the table "So, were you into kinky shit? Ropes, choking, that sort of shit.

"No of course not."

Dykes again tried to step in with the soft approach. "Are you sure, son? Cause if you guys were experimenting and things got out of hand and you fucked up. That'd probably be accidental death. Not your fault, but it would give her folks some closure. To know what happened.

"She was alive when I left her."

"And that was around nine?" Dykes asked casually.

"No, as I said around six."

"You go straight home? Didn't stop anywhere?" Harley asked.

"No, after I left her I drove straight home."

"What time you get home?"

Junior shrugged. "I'm not sure."

"You don't know." Harley snapped. "Looks like you would know. It's mighty important to your alibi."

Junior shrugged. "If I had any idea I would need an alibi I would have watched the clock closer. I guess it was between six thirty and seven. I didn't turn my lights on while driving but it was getting dark."

"So, you're saying the last time you spoke with Justine Salters was around six?"

"No that is incorrect."

Junior wanted to smile as he watched the four of them perk up, like hunting dogs picking up the scent. They were thinking at last something to pick at.

"So, you saw her later?"

"No, I spoke with her. She called me later that evening."

"What time was that?"

"Around ten-thirty, I guess."

"How long did you talk?"

"Not long. She knew I was studying. She just called to say goodnight."

"So, she was going to bed?"

Junior frowned. "I'm not sure, I guess I assumed so because she said she called to wish me goodnight."

For a second there was silence. The others knew they had nothing but Harley wouldn't give it up. He kept the questions up for two more hours, doubling back trying to increase the rapid fire questions, Junior slowed the pace by stopping to think before answering.

At the end it was Van Zandt who called an end to the questions.

Harley tried to bluster, but Van Zandt held up his hand. "You are asking the same questions over and over."

"And I'll keep asking them until I get a straight answer."

"May I suggest that instead of badgering and bullying an innocent man you would be better served pursuing other avenues of the investigation."

Junior smiled, he could almost see Harley's' blood pressure rising, but Van Zandt wasn't done yet. "My client has given you vital new evidence."

"He didn't give us shit."

"That's incorrect." Van Zandt replied smoothly. "He narrowed the time of death until after ten-thirty."

"Yeah, if he's telling the truth." Dykes pointed out.

"You can verify that by obtaining Ms. Salter's phone records. They should give an exact time of the call.'

"We requested her phone records; we're still waiting on them." Dykes said. "We should be getting them this afternoon."

"Good." Van Zandt said, closing his leather-bound note pad. "The records should solidify my clients alibi."

"How do you figure that?" Harley demanded.

"If my client was at home at ten-thirty, that backs up his claim that he was home studying. It's a stretch that he drove over there and killed her in the time frame."

"Shit he had plenty of time. He already admitted he drove from her place earlier in less than an hour."

"Puts him at the very end of the coroner's time frame."

"Maybe the call set him off." Harley snapped, seizing the idea. "Maybe she called and broke it off. That woulda pissed off Mister College boy stud. A lowly, nigger chick throwing him over. She pissed him off and he went over and killed her."

"That's weak." Van Zandt replied smoothly, he'd been expecting this argument. "You're talking fit of rage."

"That's right." Harley sneered at Junior. "Pissed you off, didn't it? Little, black bitch shitting on you. Tell me punk, did it feel good doing her."

"Don't answer that." Van Zandt said unruffled. "Can we dispense with the theatrics?" He asked calmly, looking at Geena Dixon. She was the one he had to convince. "You don't believe any of this."

She shrugged. "Dissolution of a romance has been a motive for murder in the past"

"So you would try and convince a jury that a few hours after making love to this woman that my client killed her?" Van Zandt paused smiling at her. "I would point out to the jury that most people who kill in a fit of rage either beat their victims or stabs them. In that fit of rage if a killer strangles their victims, they do it with their bare hands, not with a cheap extension cord."

"We only have your word that they made love." Dykes points out.

"The phone call supports that." Van Zandt countered.

"No." Geena Dixon said. "It fits in with the story your client is telling. I can think of several scenarios that would fit with the facts we know now."

Van Zandt smiled, the smile of a shark closing in on his prey. "So can I, but I don't have to prove our story to a jury."

Geena Dixon sighed. God she hated Van Zandt. She hated backing down to him, but he was right. Junior Carter didn't have to prove his story. They'd name fifty people who could be the killer."

"I understand her brother has been arraigned for possession with intent to sell. Maybe you should look at him and his friends." Van Zandt said driving his point home.

"Thank you for coming in, Mister Jacobs. If we have any questions we'll be in touch.

"Please direct any such inquiries through my office." Van Zandt said, packing his notes into his briefcase.

"Of course." Geena said. "Speaking of requests we would like a sample of Mister Jacob's pubic hair for comparisons.

"Do you have a warrant?"

"No." Geena Dixon said. "I can get one."

"No need." Van Zandt replied. "I assume you don't want Mister Jacobs to drop his trousers right here."

"No, the metro crime lab will be sufficient."

Van Zandt and Jacobs walked out of the building in silence. They didn't speak until they were seated in Van Zandt's Lexus. "Now what happens?" Carter asked.

"In a few days I'll have a chat with the lovely little Ms. Dixon. She'll bluster a little, but unless they find somewhere you fucked up, you'll be off the hook. In a couple of weeks there will be twenty new murders for them to worry about. They won't waste time on a case that isn't going anywhere."

"I don't know." Junior worried. "That Harley seemed pissed"

Van Zandt pulled the car into gear. "Don't worry. In a month you'll be a free man." Van Zandt stopped the car at the end of the parking ramp. "Tell me what did it feel like?"

Junior smiled knowing immediately what Van Zandt meant. He licked his lips. "It felt good. Really good."

Van Zandt pulled two expensive cigars from the humidor plugged into the lighter. He passed one to Junior. "I knew it." He said reverently.

Brad Brody's Construction Site Tucson AZ June 12th 2018 Tuesday Late Morning

Ollie stared out the windshield at the construction site, but not really seeing it. "What you thinking?" Carly asked, breaking the silence.

Ollie shook his head, glancing sideways at his partner. "Nothing, really. I was just thinking how to do this. How I want to break it to him."

"Is that so important?"

Ollie shrugged a slow, heavy movement which rocked the car. "I think so. It's one of those little things, but sometimes you can learn a lot."

"Sure, I get that," Carly agreed eagerly. "So, how do we play it with Brody?"

"Slow," Ollie decided. "I want to give it to him slow. A little bit at a time, see how he reacts."

"So, I keep out of it?"

"No, I want you to press him. Don't say anything; just act mad and kinda lean into him."

"Get into his personal space a little?"

Ollie chuckled, picturing her backing him up in a corner. "Yeah, but not a lot."

Carly nodded her face serious. "Distract him?"

"That's it. Let him know you disapprove, maybe he'll be wondering why and let something show."

"You think he's involved?"

Ollie pursed his lips, blowing out a sigh. "Statistics say he might be. But yeah, I kinda think he is. Sure, she's a young woman, probably cute, so it could be something sexual, but with what I've heard about Brody, I think it's a good bet he's in on it."

"What do you know about him?"

"I know you wouldn't want to buy a house he built. I heard he screwed over more than one partner."

"How would that work? Him being involved?"

Ollie shrugged; he hadn't worked that all out just yet. "I ain't sure, but he's a scumbag, and he's close to it, in my world that makes him a suspect."

"Should I write that down? Is that one of your rules?"

Ollie laughed. "Naw, nothing like that. Just watch the bastard. He might be trying to pull some kind of insurance scam."

"Then would she be a willing victim in this?"

Ollie shrugged. "Maybe. Let's go find out. You ready?"

Carly nodded grimly. "So, I just stand there looking mad?"

"Think you can handle it?"

"Shut up!"

Ollie was still chuckling, when his cell phone started spewing a light breezy song. Carly smirked, digging an elbow into his side. "Justin Bieber?"

"Aw, shit, my kid put that on there. Damned if I can figure out how to get it off." He punched a button quickly silencing the music. "Call her back later."

Carly nodded, a smirk coming to her face. She had a sneaky feeling that if Ollie wanted the song off, he could change it. "Are we ready?"

"Let's go jack him up," Ollie grunted slipping the phone into his pocket. "Okay, we start subtle like, but we push him a little."

They got out of the car, Ollie stretching his back. They marched across the street, which was covered with dust and dried mud, almost obscuring the asphalt beneath. Construction debris lined the curb, blown up against the rickety chain-link fence which circled the property.

"Somebody should make them clean this up," Carly fumed.

"Good luck with that," Ollie said, then shot her a grin. "Hold onto that though, that's the perfect attitude."

Ollie led the way through the gate and as they approached the trailer, a tall, whip-thin man stepped out of the trailer. Aggression boiling off the man; he took a drag from his cigarette, looking them over coldly. "Can I help you?"

"Tucson PD," Ollie replied, flipping his badge out in one smooth, practiced motion. "We need to speak to Mister Brody."

"He's busy, you can tell me."

Carly watched the transformation sweep across Ollie's broad face. Gone in an instant were the friendly laugh lines, replaced by a cold, mean look. "And who might you be?"

"Cal Pierson. I'm Mister Brody's foreman."

"Well, mister foreman, we need to speak to Mister Brody."

"What about?"

"We'll tell him that."

Pierson shrugged, flipping his cigarette away. "He's inside," he said, opening the trailer door and stepping inside.

Carly followed behind Ollie, wrinkling her nose as they stepped inside. The trailer was a pig sty, smelling of old coffee, cigarettes, stale food and sweat. The floor was filthy, covered with muddy footprints, spilt coffee and various other substances which Carly decided she was better off not know what they were.

Two large folding tables sat against the far wall. Both tables were littered with maps, plans and assorted debris. On a small cart in the corner, sat a coffee pot which looked like it hadn't been washed since it came out of the box.

Brody sat behind a desk at the far end of the trailer, looking intently at a laptop. As they approached he shut the lid of the laptop, leaning forward over it, as he shot a quick glance at Cal.

"Cops," Cal said with a shrug. "They want to see you."

A quick look flitted across Brody's face, then it was gone. "What can I do for you, officers?" Brody was a short, chubby man, but his voice was a rich deep voice of a much larger man.

"I'm afraid we have some disturbing news for you," Ollie said, his voice grave as midnight.

This time, not even a flicker registered with Brody, he simply leaned another notch forward, placing his elbows on the laptop. "What?"

Watching Brody, Carly edged around Ollie, crossing her arms as she planted herself beside Brody's desk. Ollie ignored her, watching Brody intently. "This concerns your daughter," Ollie supplied in an undertaker's voice.

Ollie paused, giving Brody a chance to speak. He would have expected some kind of question from him. Ask what had happened, or at least what she had done. But Brody didn't. He just sat looking up at Ollie.

Ollie let the silence build, until it was grating on Carly's nerves. She saw Cal pull out a pack of smokes, shooting a glance at Brody. Finally, Ollie dug out his notebook and slipped on a pair of reading glasses. "Is your daughter Angie Brody?" he asked and got a curt nod from Brody. "And she lives in Palo Rancho Apartments off of Anklin?"

Again, Ollie got a nod from Brody, but nothing more. Ollie shifted his feet, feigning being uncomfortable, while Cal fired up his cigarette. "We have reason to believe that she has been abducted."

"Abducted?" Brody asked finally finding his voice. He scrunched up his eyebrows. "You mean kidnapped?"

"I'm afraid, so," Ollie replied, with a small nod as he removed his glasses, returning them to his shirt pocket. "Witnesses saw her being forced into a van."

Brody blew out a sigh and wrung his hands. "Are you sure it was her?"

"No doubt about it. Three people saw it go down. They all agreed, it was your daughter. Do you know anyone who might want to harm your daughter?"

"No."

Ollie paused, giving Brody a chance to elaborate. Ollie glanced down at his notebook. "Has your daughter been receiving any strange calls? Problems with guys? Any unwanted attention? A stalker, maybe?"

"Like I said, no." Brody said, shifting in his seat. "My daughter and I haven't been close for the last few years. We're both busy and just seem to have grown apart. I haven't seen Angie in a month."

Ollie nodded writing it down. "Yeah, it happens. I take it you haven't received any ransom demands?"

"No."

"Okay. I can have a tech come out and wire up your phones."

Now Brody flinched, shooting a look at Cal. For the first time, Brody seemed to be uncomfortable. "I don't think that will be necessary," he said.

"You need to think this through, Mr. Brody," Ollie prodded gently. "We would just record the demands, none of your other calls, but we would have tracking equipment we might be able to use that to track her."

Brody was already shaking his head. "No."

"That's your call," Ollie replied softly. "We certainly can't force you to let us tap your phones, but you need to think about this. It might help us get Angie back."

"This is your daughter we're talking about," Carly said leaning into Brody a little, a hard edge riding in her tone. "I would think that you would want to do everything you could to help."

Brody snorted. "Give me a break. You aren't going to track anybody. Everybody has a cell, and you can buy a throw away phone anywhere. That's what he would use, if he's gonna call."

"He?" Ollie said, raising an eyebrow.

For a second, Brody looked confused, and then waved a hand in the air. "He, her, they, them. I don't know, but if they call, you can bet it'll be on a pre-paid cell. Good luck tracking that."

"Probably," Ollie admitted. "But it is still an avenue to pursue."

"Waste of time." Brody grunted, waving it away. "I'd say your time would be far better spent trying to find her."

Ollie held Brody's gaze until the contractor looked away. "It's your call," Ollie replied, glancing down at his notebook. "We have a few more questions."

Brody scowled, and then flipped his hand at the detective. "Go ahead,"

"Do you think this might have anything to do with your business? Can you think of anybody that might go after her to hurt you?"

"No," Brody replied quickly, but his eyes flicked to Cal, then back to Ollie.

"You sure?"

"Damn right I'm sure," Brody snapped his face burning. "And I resent the hell out of the inference. I'm a contractor, Detective, that's it. I build homes, neighborhoods. Who would have a problem with that?"

Ollie shrugged. "Maybe tree huggers? Maybe you been killing owls or rats or some shit? You ever have trouble with those folks?"

Brody let go of a tight little smile. "They're all pussies."

"Okay," Ollie said, letting it go. "What about Angie's mom? I understand you two are divorced."

"That's right."

"Do you know where we could reach her?"

"No idea. My advice is start checking all the bars between here and LA. I'm sure you'll run across her in one of them."

Ollie nodded, flipping his notebook closed. The interview was over. "If you are contacted with demands, you will let us know."

"You will be my first call," Brody said, barely masking his contempt

Ollie and Carly walked silently to the car. "What did you think?" Ollie asked as soon as they were in the car.

Carly frowned, looking up at the roof of the car. "He's hiding something. He knows more than he was telling us."

"Yup," Ollie grunted, starting the car and flipping the ac on high. "He did seem surprised at first, but I think he already knew about Angie. I think he was surprised to see us so fast."

"He's a dick," Carly said, turning her vent on her face. "He sure didn't want us to see what he was looking at on that laptop."

"Really," Ollie said innocently. "I musta missed that."

"Bullshit," Carly snorted, drawing a chuckle from her partner. "And he didn't want to give us access to his phones."

"Yup," Ollie agreed pulling the car into gear. He glanced sideways at her. "You notice anything about Pierson?"

"Other than the fact that he is a complete ass?" Carly closed her eyes, tipping her head back. "He seemed a little…, I don't know something."

"Out of place?"

"Yeah, maybe."

"Good," Ollie said, nodding to her. "You're right. I bet that fucker wouldn't know a hammer from a skill saw."

"His boots were new," Carly said, opening her eyes.

"Yup, and that cap was mighty clean. And I noticed his hands; they didn't look like the hands of somebody who works for a living."

"So we check him out?"

"Yup, we crawl right up his ass."

Gates Pass Tucson AZ June 12th 2018 Tuesday Late Morning

Leaning back on his bike, enjoying the feeling of the sun, Mitch smiled; he might make a nice profit from the cigars. He looked across the valley falling away to the west. What about Angie? He should take a look at the boyfriend. When a woman met with violence, statistically it was one of the men in her life who was responsible. Ollie and Parker were checking out the dad, he should take the boyfriend.

Of course it could be a predator. Some chance encounter with the wrong person that they would never track down.

If it were a predator, they probably wouldn't catch him in time to save Angie Brody. Might not catch him in time to save the next one. If it was somebody she knew, they had a chance. Maybe the boyfriend.

Mitch checked his notes. Tim Siebert lived in Vail. Huh, Vail? Seemed odd. Vail was an older suburb east of Tucson. Lately it had become very trendy. Mitch had looked out in Vail when he had bought his house, but couldn't afford to buy out there.

Seemed out of place that a young musician would live there. Mitch would have expected Siebert to live downtown close to the University where the action was.

Mitch was still pondering it, when his phone rang. Glancing at the screen, he saw it was Sam Logan. "Sam."

"Got some news, don't know how it helps you."

"What you got?"

"Mel's car is missing the plate, he didn't even know, we had to go look."

"Have they been in Tucson lately?" Mitch asked.

"Once in the last few weeks. That was Wednesday. Mel had an appointment over at the VA hospital and then they went to that camper place over off Irvington, then stopped at Wal-Mart."

"Okay, Sam, thanks. I owe you one."

"Probably be a cold day in hell before I ever collect," Sam said, chuckling as he hung up.

Mitch idly tapped the phone on the handle bars. Sam's news was pretty much what he expected. What did it tell him?

Mitch swiped the slider on his phone, and tapped the icon with Jerry's picture. "Jerry any luck with the phone?"

"Nothing good," Jerry grunted, and Mitch could hear him shuffling papers. "It is a Trac-phone, purchased by a Justin Carter at a Wal-Mart last week."

"When, which Wal-Mart?"

"Wednesday, the Wal-Mart on Valencia."

"Shit, that is where he picked up the license plate. Melvin and Delores Sampson were at that Wal-Mart on Wednesday."

"You want me to go check it out?"

"Naw, Ollie and Carly are still out that way, I'll get them to do it. I want you to look at Brody. Get in the computer and find out everything you can about him, and his company. While you're at it run Justin Carter, probably an alias, but see what you can find."

"Okay."

"I'm going to jack up the boyfriend, see if there is anything there."

Mitch hung up, immediately dialing Ollie's number. "You guys still down south?"

"Yeah, just finished up with Brody."

"How did that go? Anything there?"

"I'm not sure, but it went." Ollie hesitated. "My gut tells me he's involved."

"Oh yeah?" Mitch said, a little surprised. He'd checked out Brody as a matter of course, and because the man had a reputation of being a sleeze ball, but hadn't really expected anything to come of it. "How so?"

Ollie paused, trying to put his suspicions into words. "First off, he seemed more worried about giving us the bum's rush outta the place than finding out what happened to his girl."

"Maybe he already knew."

"That's what we're thinking," Ollie agreed.

"Anything else?"

"He declined the tap on his phone and he's got this goon hanging around. We didn't like the feel of him."

"Got a name?"

"Cal Pierson. We were gonna run him through the box."

"Jerry's back at the office, running Brody and getting the book started. Have him do it. I need you guys to swing by the Wal-Mart on Valencia. The phone used to call Angie at the time of the attack came from there."

"Pre-paid?"

"You know it. Bought by a Justin Carter last Wednesday. Same day coincidently that Melvin Sampson was there. And Melvin is missing the plate off his Taurus."

"Let me guess that is the number Darla Pringle wrote down?"

"You got it," Mitch said. "So check it out and if Jerry comes up with something from the computer, you guys can run it down."

"Sure," Ollie said, "I was thinking, I might try and pick up that Pierson jasper later, follow him and see what he's about."

"Sounds good, if you guys get a chance, go over to U of A and start running down her friends, teachers and schedule."

"Yeah, we got it, mother," Ollie drawled.

"I know, just get it done."

Tucson Daily News Offices Tucson AZ June 12th 2018
Tuesday Noon

Jackson Pyle sat at his desk, a sheen of sweat on his fore head. A four page article he had just finished glowed from his computer screen. On the desk in front of him, sat a fat manila file. The file contained everything he had been able to dig up using Forsyth's manifesto as a guide. The article he had written from the file glowed from the computer.

Beside the file was a scratch pad with a number written on it. The number was the public number for Jillian Braxton's campaign headquarters in Phoenix.

Jackson had taken what Forsyth had written and expanded on it. The work had been surprisingly easy. With his experience as a reporter, Jackson had quickly been able to verify what William Forsyth had claimed.

Senator Braxton and a DC lawyer named Van Zandt had quite a little scam going. While their tracks were pretty well hidden, once you had the key, it unraveled pretty easily. Jackson believed Forsyth wasn't the first one they had killed.

While proving they killed Jared Morris might be impossible, exposing the rest of their deal would be easy. Jackson scrolled down the screen quickly scanning his story. He probably didn't have enough to send anyone to jail, but he had enough to kill the deal. He sure had enough to ruin Braxton's bid for the Presidency.

The question was; what to do with what he had?

The way Jackson saw it, he had three choices. The safest was to simply hit delete on the computer and toss the file in the shredder. Walk away and forget the whole thing. That was what he should do.

Lizard-like, Jackson flicked his tongue across his dry lips.

He wasn't going to do that.

He could hit send and the story would go to his editor. He could easily do several follow ups. Maybe get a week on the front page. He might end up with a book deal.

The problem was, once his story hit, every report in the country would be after the story. They would be on it like jackals over a downed carcass. With his head start,

Jackson could keep ahead of them for a few days, but they would soon overtake him. He'd be swallowed up in the crowd.

In the end, what would he gain? A few days on the front page of a second rate paper. That's if Darby didn't find a way to snake the story from him. What would that get him? Maybe a book deal? A move to the Citizen? A move to one of the bigger papers in Phoenix?

Jackson frowned. A few short days ago, he would have jumped at the chance for any of that. Now it didn't hardly seem like enough.

Jackson leaned back in his chair, running his hand through his greasy black hair. He had a feeling of destiny. There was a reason he had found this stuff. There was a reason Braxton was in Phoenix at this very moment. It was fate. This was his one chance at the brass ring

If Braxton wanted to be President, she would have to pay up. Jackson knew he should stay away from Van Zandt. Van Zandt didn't have as much to lose. Van Zandt might just kill him.

But Braxton couldn't afford even the hint of a scandal. She would pay up. Maybe, if she became President, he could be her personal press secretary. He could see it in his mind. Rubbing elbows with the world's most powerful people. He would get a nice apartment in DC. Get a convertible. A baby beamer.

On the other hand, he could just take the money. Get a place in Mexico. At Rocky Point, or maybe Cabo. Yeah Cabo. He could hang out at Sammy Hagar's place.

How much to ask for? A million sounded good. He wrote the figure below Braxton's phone number. Was that too much? No not enough. He could always come down. Five mil was a good starting point.

Five million? A man could live like a God in Mexico on the interest.

No more hot dusty days, sweltering in his crappy house. No more long nights waiting on cops to release information. He would be done with all of that.

The thought gave him courage and he snatched up his phone. Stabbing the buttons, he dialed the Senator's number. His throat went dry as the phone rang. This was it!

"Headquarters for a new and better America," a pleasant sounding lady said. "Would you like to make a contribution for a better tomorrow?"

"No thanks," Jackson squawked, having trouble with his voice. He cleared his throat, trying again. "My name is Jackson Pyle, with the Tucson Daily News. I was hoping to schedule a few moments with the Senator."

"I'm sorry. All inquiries need to go through Ms. Schroeder's office."

"I see. Could you transfer me to her office?"

Jackson fidgeted, his nerve bleeding away. Finally a woman came on the line. "This is Tamera Schroeder. How may I help you?"

"My name is Jackson Pyle, with the Tucson Daily News. I was hoping to schedule a few moments with the Senator."

"I'm sorry; the Senator's schedule is very tight. She simply doesn't have time to meet with anyone privately. Perhaps I could arrange a pass to her press conference tonight."

Jackson had been expecting this. His last chance to back out. He waited a heartbeat, before plunging in. "That would not be quick enough. I'm just preparing to file a story which concerns the Senator and I was hoping to check a few facts with her before the story goes out."

"That will not be possible."

"The story concerns Peyton Holdings and could be potentially damaging to the Senator. Perhaps you want to run it by the Senator. I can hold."

"I'm sorry, the Senator is very busy."

So Schroeder wasn't in the inner circle. Interesting. "Okay, but can I say in the story that I tried to reach the Senator for comment, and she had none? Could I use your name in the story?"

Jackson waited, picturing the girl squirming. They both knew Jackson could do just what he asked. He didn't need to ask. Finally, Jackson heard a sigh. "Please hold. I will ask the Senator if she wishes to make a comment."

"Thank you, Ms. Schroeder."

Jackson waited for ten minutes, listening to a mantra of campaign promises. Jackson was about to think they were blowing him off, when a shrill voice came on the line. "What do you want?"

"Senator Braxton?"

"Yes, now get to the point."

"I'm Jackson...."

"I already know that!" she snapped. "Either get to the point or hang up."

"I have a story about to go out that I thought you might want to comment on. It concerns Peyton Holdings."

"Never heard of it," Braxton snapped.

"Really? The straw company you and Perry Van Zandt are using to pull your little scam here in Arizona? Have you heard of William Forsyth? My story concerns him as well."

Jackson paused, but only silence greeted him. "Are you there? "

"What do you want?"

I don't think this is something we should discuss over the phone. I was hoping we could meet and discuss this privately."

Jackson held his breath. This was it.

"Eight o'clock tonight. My hotel. Don't be late."

Tim Siebert's House Vail AZ June 12th 2018 Tuesday Afternoon

Tim Siebert's house in Vail wasn't what Mitch had been expecting. He'd expected a trailer on a dirt lot or an older home. This was a nice new home, built in one of the subdivisions that had sprung up out here in the last few years.

"Huh," Mitch grunted as he swung the bike into the driveway, parking beside a Scion. Wrinkling his nose at the Scion, Mitch put the kickstand down and swung off the bike. On the wide front porch a young man lay sprawled in a lawn chair, clutching a bong to his chest.

The young man raised his head slightly, taking in Mitch with bleary eyes. "Dude, nice bike."

"Thanks," Mitch replied, stepping up onto the porch. "You Tim Siebert?"

The kid stared at him with stoned eyes, then shook his head. "No, man, he's inside." He licked his lips, a little craftiness sneaking through the slackness in his face. "Are you the dude, man?"

"No, man," Mitch said pulling his badge out and dropping his voice to a whisper. "I'm the cops, man."

The kid simply stared for a moment, and then shot a quick glance at the stuff on the table. "Oh, shit."

"Is it alright if I go on in?"

"Uh, sure dude."

Mitch turned opening the door. "Thanks," he said, laughing as he heard the sound of breaking glass and an anguished cry. Once inside, Mitch took in the house in one sweeping glance. The house continued to surprise him. The inside looked like any suburban home. Probably cleaner than Mitch's own house.

In the living room was a large flat screen with a couch and matching chairs grouped around it. A nice throw rug covered the tile floor between the couch and TV. As he walked through the spotless kitchen, Mitch became aware of a weird thumping sound.

Mitch came through the kitchen and into a large room. He saw a young man wearing headphones, thumping out a song on an electric keyboard. As the young man played, oblivious to Mitch's presence, Mitch took stock of the room.

Originally, the room had been designed to be a dining room and family room together. Now it was crowded with musical instruments, a huge drum set dominating the far side of the room. Despite the clean appearance of the place Mitch could smell old cigarette smoke, stale beer and pot.

The man at the keyboard glanced up, slowly pulling the headphones down around his neck. "What do you want? You looking for Derek?"

Mitch shook his head. "No I'm looking for Tim Siebert. I'm a cop."

The young man glanced at the joint burning in the ashtray, then back at Mitch. Holding Mitch's gaze, he picked up the joint, taking a long drag, before stubbing it out in the ashtray. "What you want?" he croaked, emitting a cloud of smoke.

"You Siebert?"

"Yeah, and I'm busy."

Mitch paused, rethinking how he would come at the kid. This wasn't the young man he had expected. The dope, he'd expected, but despite the dope, this young man exuded intensity. Not the type to wander away as Lindsey had put it.

"Thought you were a drummer?" Mitch commented, waving a hand at the piano.

Siebert shrugged. "Writing."

Mitch nodded, still trying to get a read on the man. "You play all of these?"

Siebert offered the same shrug. "Sure."

"Do you know Angie Brody?" Mitch asked, deciding on the straight ahead approach.

A look rolled across his face. A shadow of fear. "What happened to her?" he asked slowly.

Mitch recognized the catch in Siebert's voice. He'd heard it from thousands of parents asking about their kids. They knew it was going to be bad news. They didn't want to hear the answer, but couldn't help asking the question.

"What makes you think something happened to her?"

"Angie's not the type to get into trouble. You're a cop asking about her…," Siebert's words trailed off into a shrug. "What happened to her?" he demanded, his voice a raw, desperate whisper.

"She was kidnapped."

"Shit!" Siebert said a knee-jerk reaction. He snapped up straight and very still. Mitch waited, letting the silence work on the man. After a second Siebert slumped, seeming to melt in on himself. "Oh, no."

"When was the last time you saw her?"

Siebert didn't react to the question. He sank a little lower, his fingers playing with the headphones around his neck. "When did you see her last?" Mitch repeated, letting a little cop steel creep into his voice.

"Huh?" Siebert said, his head jerking up. "Uh, what day is this?"

"Tuesday."

"Sorry, I've been writing. I sometimes lose track of time when I'm writing." Siebert scratched his goatee. "Week ago Sunday. We went to her old man's for a cookout."

"Over a week? That's a long time to go without seeing your girlfriend."

"I was writing." He said it apologetically; probably the way he'd said it to Angie a thousand times.

"Angie and her dad get a long?"

"Sure, I guess."

The answer came a little too quickly and was a little too pat. "How about you? You get along with Brody?"

"I don't think he likes me much. I know he told Angie she could do better," Siebert whined a little as he said it, like he might suspect it to be true.

"How 'bout you? You like Brody?"

"He's a dick!" Siebert laughed a little. "You know the type. Way too uptight and way too concerned about making money. No time for what really matters."

"What matters to you, Tim?" Mitch asked. "Smoking dope?"

"No," Tim said, shaking his head. "The weed helps smooth things out. Makes the writing come easier. That's all."

"So, what is important?"

"Music, family, friends and enjoying the things you love. Your dreams, that's what matters. Not building cookie cutter houses for corporate drones."

"What if your dream is to build houses for people?"

"Huh?" Siebert grunted as if the concept was foreign to him.

"You know a guy named Justin Carter?"

Siebert paused, and Mitch could see him thinking it over. "No, I don't think so. Is he the guy who took Angie?"

"No," Mitch replied. "Just a name that came up." Mitch paused to see if Siebert would add something. "Who's the guy on the porch?"

"My brother Derek."

Mitch waved a hand at the instruments. "He play too?"

Siebert laughed. "Shit, all he does is smoke dope and he can't even suck on a bong with any rhythm."

"This is a nice place," Mitch commented looking around like he just noticed the house.

"Our parents left it to us."

Mitch raised an eyebrow. "They both dead?"

"Yeah," came the dull answer. Siebert laughed with no humor. "Dad was a tax lawyer, worked his butt off for years, then one day he buys this huge camper and some fancy diesel pickup. He and mom were going to travel. In his whole life, Dad never drove anything bigger than an Audi station wagon." Siebert shook his head and Mitch could see the pain still there. "First day out he wrapped it around a guard rail over by Payson."

"Aw man, that sucks."

"Yeah," Siebert glanced at the joint. "My dad and I didn't get along. There was a time I thought I hated him." Tim glanced up and Mitch could see the tears forming in his eyes. "I'd give anything to see him and mom walk through that door."

"So, write a song about that."

His whole face looking like a raw, red wound, Siebert raised his eyes, meeting Mitch's. "I will someday. When I'm ready."

"You guys expecting your dealer?"

"Yeah," Tim answered his mind still in the past.

"What you expecting?"

Siebert jerked back, remembering he was talking to a cop. "Aw man, just some reefer."

"Angie use?"

"Not really. She'd do a bowl every once in a while."

"Who's your dealer?"

"Aw, man."

"You can tell me or I can wait until he shows up."

"Aw man," Siebert repeated and Mitch could see the fear on his face. "C'mon dude."

"Who?" Mitch snapped.

"Biker dude, I don't know his name. Everybody calls him Horsy."

"I know Horsy," Mitch said feeling better. He'd been wondering about the dealer. There were some of those guys out there you wouldn't want to leave alone with a female pit bull. But Mitch knew Horsey.

"Angie say anything about a guy bothering her, calling her, following her?"

"No, but I haven't talked to her."

"Okay," Mitch said putting his notebook away.

"What can I do to help?"

"Talk to her friends. Find out if she's met any new men, had any trouble."

"You should check out her Facebook page. She put everything about her life on there."

"Shit," Mitch grumbled, kicking himself for not thinking about it. People put their whole world on Facebook. "Okay, good idea. I'll get somebody checking on that."

"You going to find her?" Siebert squawked.

"Yes, I will." Mitch left the young man staring at his piano.

Mitch was walking out the front door, when he saw a Harley round the corner. Smiling grimly, Mitch stepped back against the wall. He waited until the bike stopped.

"Hey, Horsy," he said stepping out of the shadows. "How's it going?"

Horsy did a quick double take, and then smiled broadly. "Mitch, fancy seeing you here."

"Small world," Mitch agreed. "Heard you were out in Cali, riding with Chappy."

"Came back," Horsy said, hesitating a beat. "So did Chappy."

"So, I heard."

"Oh yeah, the poker game," Horsy laughed, leaning. "Joe was pissed, but that ain't nothing compared to Frankie."

"She called me this morning, seemed a little put out about it."

Horsy laughed. "Be careful, brother, that girl will cut your nuts off."

"He's a cop!" Derek blurted out.

Horsy shot a look at the boy. "Shit, I know that. I've known Mitch since you were in diapers." Horsy turned his smile back on. "So, what brings you out to Vail? If I recall right, there ain't a Dunkin Doughnuts for miles."

Ignoring the jab, Mitch matched his grin. "I got a tip. I heard there was a biker dealing weed out here."

The grin never flickered, but Mitch saw the tightening around his eyes. "Well, shit, that sounds pretty fucking serious. You better go get that fucker fast. You sure you don't need back up?"

"I'm good." Mitch crossed to Horsy's bike. "If I was to look in those saddle bags, I bet I'd find some dope."

Mitch saw Horsy's body tense. "I'd say you best have a warrant in that pocket."

Mitch grinned at Horsy. He'd known the biker for years. "What are you gonna do Elliot? Kick my ass?"

Horsy's face burned red at the use of his given name. "I just might, Johnny."

Mitch grinned at the older man. "You sure you can? You're getting up in years. I'm thinking you're too old for that kind of stuff. You might break a hip."

Horsy relaxed, laughing a little. "Shit, Mitchell, you're becoming a real horse's ass." He leaned back against the bike shaking a cigarette out of its pack. "So what are you really doing out here?"

"You hear about that girl who got snatched this morning?"

"Sure, heard about it on the news." Horsy lit his smoke, took a deep drag, and then waved the cigarette at the house. "And you think these whistle dicks had something to do with it?"

"No," Mitch said. "One of them was dating the girl."

"Aw shit man, so why you hassling me?"

"We're gonna need some help on this one. You hear anything; I need to know about it, like right now."

"Shit yeah," Horsy agreed. He rubbed his head. "Man, that sucks, young girl like that. Crap, Candi's girls are getting to be teenagers now. I'd kill anybody that messed with them."

Mitch smiled; Horsy had a couple of step daughters. When Mitch was on patrol he'd been called to a Chucky Cheese when Horsy and some of his biker buddies took the girls to the restaurant. Mitch chuckled, shaking his head. "I was remembering when you took them to Chucky Cheese."

Horsy laughed, snorting a little. "Scared the hell outta them soccer moms."

"Yeah. So you'll ask around? I'm scared for this girl."

Horsy nodded running a meaty hand along his beard. "Uh, Mitch, uh, like I said, Chappy's back."

"I know, I heard. Witness said the guy who grabbed her was small."

"Shit, wasn't him. Only thing small about Chappy is his dick."

"Yeah, heard about that too," Mitch said.

"Well I gotta shove off, but I'll ask around about that girl," Horsy said, flicking his smoke into the street and swinging on his bike.

Mitch stepped up to the bike. "You know anything about Brad Brody? Hear any rumors?"

"Brody? The contractor?" Horsey asked and Mitch nodded. "Only thing I heard about him was if he built a house for you, you best count the building materials every night."

"Okay, what about Cal Pierson or Justin Carter? You know either of them?"

Horsey rubbed his jaw, cocking his head. "No, don't think so," he said slowly.

"Okay," Mitch said, patting the gas tank. "Let me know if you hear anything," he added, stepping back as Horsey fired up the bike.

Mitch smiled as the biker roared away. He knew Horsy would wait a few minutes then be back.

Tucson Police Department Tucson AZ June 12th 2018 Tuesday Afternoon

Mitch entered his team's offices to see Jerry Hartek hunched over his computer. "How's it coming," Mitch asked.

Hartek looked up, scowling at his boss. "Shit, I don't know. You should get someone else to do this. I wish Wade was here. He understands this crap."

"You will be okay. You're good with the computer."

"Fuck that. Parksy is better, 'specially on the financial stuff."

"She's helping Ollie run down Angie's friends, but if you need her I can get in here," Mitch offered.

"Aw, I'm alright, she can go with Ollie," Jerry said, mollified by the offer. Scratching his head, Hartek turned back to the computer. "You're supposed to be a financial wizard; maybe you can make sense of it."

"What are you getting?"

Jerry picked a yellow legal pad covered with scrawled notes. "I did a real quick sneak peak, and there he looks really good. His wife's Nordstrom's card will be past due if they don't receive a payment in a couple of days. Other than that, he's easily current on everything else."

"So, he isn't over extended?"

"No, and that's the problem. It looks to me like he should be. He's got two major projects going. He should be borrowing more and he should be running short. His cash flow doesn't support what he has to be spending. But somehow, he's still got money in his account."

"Where's it coming from?" Mitch asked leaning in to look.

"Beats the hell outta me. But it keeps coming in."

"Can you find out where the money is coming from?"

"Not without a warrant, or somebody that can hack into his bank records. Course that would be illegal."

"Course it would be," Mitch agreed, and then looked at Hartek. "You know anybody that could do it?"

"Wade probably could or maybe that kid, Smitty on patrol. I hear he can make a computer do anything. You want me to call him?"

Mitch mulled it over, as he headed over to the coffee machine. Such a move would be illegal; nothing they found could be used in court. On the other hand, they were trying to save the life of a young girl. "Let's wait. I'll run it by Sanderson, see if we can get a blind warrant."

"If he turns you down, it might get back to Brody. He might start covering up."

"I know. I'll think it over. Maybe we can think of something. You find anything else?"

"There's one thing. I don't know if it means anything, but Brody has been buying land out east of Casa Grande."

"Huh?" Mitch grunted. "Land development?"

"I don't know. I suppose so, that's his business, but this land is flat out in the middle of nowhere. Quite a ways from the Interstate even."

"Some kind of commercial development then?"

"That would be my guess. It sure would be a crappy place to live. But why would you want to put a business out there?" Hartek leaned back in his chair, lacing his fingers behind his head. "A funny thing is, there's been a lot of land bought up out there. Brody has bought a lot of it, but somebody else is buying land in the same area."

"Maybe he's trying to horn in on somebody's deal. Might be why the girl was snatched. Who else is buying land?"

"That's the question. Except for the land Brody bought, the rest of it has all been purchased by corporations. Of course that could still be Brody, buying it under cover."

"Could be," Mitch admitted, still not quite buying that. "Why would he buy some of it out in the open and try and hide the other? How about the dates? Was he hiding it early?"

"Nope, the stuff he bought is scattered all through."

"Doesn't make any sense, unless he is trying to horn in on someone else's deal. Keep at it. If you need some help I'll get Parksy in to help you. Try and track down the ownership of those companies. I have a feeling this is going to come down to money."

Mitch paused in the hall. After a second he punched the speed dial. His call was answered after eleven rings. "Hey Mitch."

"Wade, how's the knee?"

"Stiffer than my dick."

"So it's loosening up nicely."

"Yeah, pretty much. What's going on?"

"You hear about the Angie Brody thing?"

"Yeah, I was wondering if you would call."

"You up for some work?"

"Sure, I was cleared last week to come back on light duty."

"Last week?" Mitch asked, almost hearing Wade's grin over the phone.

"Didn't I tell you? Shit thought I sent you an email. You saying you didn't get my email? Cause I sent it, you might want to check with your internet provider."

"Yeah, right."

"Anyway, I didn't hear back so I figured I was good to slide down to Rocky Point for a little extended therapy."

"What's her name?"

"Carrie something or other."

"College girl?"

"Naw, older, she's almost thirty."

"Damn, you better be careful, she'll be dragging your ass down the aisle."

"Never happen, buddy," Wade said cheerfully.

"Happened three times already," Mitch shot back.

"Never again. Don't take me all day to learn."

"So three times was enough?" Mitch said with a smile.

"More than enough. So, what do you need me to do?"

Mitch quickly laid out the case. "I want you to help with the computer work and get started on a book."

"I'll see you in an hour."

"I'll be gone, but you can help Jerry. He's looking into Brody's finances."

"You got it."

Vail AZ June 12th 2018 Tuesday Afternoon

Horsey pulled away from Tim Siebert's house, gunning the bike down the street. "Damn it!" he yelled, letting go of the throttle. He wrenched the bike to the curb, jamming on the rear break. He grabbed his pre-paid, cell, stabbing the numbers. "What's this shit about Brody's girl getting pinched?" he snarled.

"What?" a hoarse voice came back "Are you sure?"

"Fucking well right I'm sure. I just got jacked up by Johnny Mitchell, asking me about it. You remember Mitch?"

"He came looking for you?"

"I don't think so, he was out at Siebert's when I showed up to make a delivery. He was just wanting me to ask around."

"So he don't know shit, then."

"Don't bet on it, buddy. He was asking me about Brody. And about Cal Pierson."

"Shit!"

"Tell me that we didn't have anything to do with this?" Horsey asked his voice grim as an approaching storm.

"No way."

"You better not be lying to me Chappy."

Outside Ajo AZ June 12th 2018 Tuesday Afternoon

Sam drove with the window down. He drove slowly, breathing deep, taking in the smells of the desert. Most people thought the desert was just heat and dust, but Sam knew better.

All those years on patrol, Sam learned to love driving slow with the windows down. It was better than therapy. It cleansed your soul. If you listened, the desert could save you. Listen to the wind, step back and hear the cries of generations gone by.

Sam loved the road.

When the promotion was offered to move off the road, Sam took it without thinking. It was just what you did. Sam had been brought up with the philosophy that you worked hard. You showed up every day, and you moved up. That was the reward.

But Sam had been too long out of the desert. Today, though he couldn't enjoy the solitude. Today impatience was riding him. After a few minutes, he rolled up the windows and flipped the AC on.

He dropped the hammer on the Explorer and headed for Tucson. He had the radio, but didn't even notice when he lost the station and static oozed from the speakers. The static was white noise, calming noise, soothing the back of his mind, while the rest of his brain churned like an angry sea. It had been that way for weeks; Sam could find no peace in his own mind.

Today was especially bad.

First as a Marine and then as a Trooper, Sam had pledge to defend and uphold the laws of the United States of America. A duty he did not take lightly.

Now, he was fixing to break a bunch of those laws. More than that, he had already broken the law. When he took that memory card out of the camera he'd crossed a line. Committed a crime. Probably for the first time in his life.

Sam had no illusions how this was going to end. They couldn't win. Not in his lifetime. They would be caught. Sam pounded the steering wheel, and made himself a promise. He wouldn't be taken alive.

He wouldn't go to jail, and he certainly wouldn't put Maureen through the spectacle of a public trial. If he was going to be caught, he'd end it himself.

But they would take out some assholes along the way.

It bothered Sam that he wasn't being totally honest with the men helping him. He told himself that it was for their own good, but part of it was, if they really knew what he was planning, they might try and stop him.

Sam was crunching through it in his mind, trying to reconcile what he was doing with the oaths he had sworn, when the phone rang. Sam glanced at the screen and grinned savagely. "You got him?"

"Spotted him about five minutes ago," Ted replied. "He's at that park south of Broadway out by Old Spanish Trail."

Sam nodded, he knew the park. "What's he doing?"

"Watching some women work out," Ted said, disgust dripping from his voice.

"Anyway, you could grab him without too much fuss?"

Ted chuckled. "Hell, man, I'm a cop."

"Yeah, I just don't think it would be good if anyone remembered him getting snatched."

"Hell, who's going to miss him? I say it'd be best if he was just gone."

"Alright," Sam said. "Get him. I'll meet you at my place."

Rancho Vistoso Golf Club Tucson AZ June 12th 2018 Tuesday Early Evening

Mitch grimaced, grabbing onto the side of the golf cart as the judge took a corner way to fast then slammed on the brakes barely avoiding the two carts already parked at the tee box. Mitch grinned to himself. The judge was a fast player, he hated having to wait. "Hole fourteen," Mitch said, feigning seriousness. "Two shots back. That's a lot to make up in such a short time. I think I got you this time."

"You got shit!" the judge fumed.

Mitch grinned some more. This was the latest in a round he had ever been up on the judge. If he kept the pressure up, he might just beat the old fucker. "I hope you brought your checkbook."

"All I need is a deposit slip," the judge said, pulling out his hybrid wood. "You can't handle this hole. We'll be even when we leave."

Mitch grinned, but he knew the judge was right. Over the years, this hole had flat kicked his butt. The hole was named Risky and it required a delicate touch. There was three ways to play the hole. The hole was an L-shaped hole, doglegged to the left. You could hit a long iron straight out, then turn and hit a hundred yard shot into the green. As long as the first shot was hit the right distance, the hole was easy. The other way was to angle left with a short iron, then another short iron over the desert to the green. The last way was to tee it up, and let the driver go. One good smash with the driver and you were on the green.

As they waited, Mitch noted that all four of the men in the group ahead of them had drivers in their hands. They were going to take the risk. "You know Brad Brody?" Mitch asked, digging a couple of the Cubans out of his bag.

"A little. Pompous ass," the judge said. "That his girl that was abducted today?" he asked and Mitch nodded. The judge accepted the cigar Mitch offered, biting the end off. "I take it you are thinking he might be involved?"

"I don't know," Mitch said, and then shook his head. "What I really think is maybe somebody is using her to force Brody into line."

"God damn it, that pisses me off," the judge said, really fuming. "Damn people ought to leave kids out of this kind of shit!"

"What I need to know is why." Mitch lit his cigar, then held the lighter to the judge's. They puffed in silence, enjoying the moment. "So you know anything about Brody?"

The judge shrugged, studying the ash at the end of his cigar. "Not really. I heard a rumor that he's tied in with the Mafia back east. I didn't think it was true, but who knows."

They fell silent as the group ahead hit their shots. "I did hear something about Brody being sued. Something about a land deal up north. Didn't sound like much, but you never know."

"I'll check into it," Mitch said, as they waited, watching the group ahead of them.

"Damn, this is good cigar," the judge said, studying the ash on the end of his cigar.

"Cuban," Mitch said. "I got a friend who gets them. You interested?"

"Damn boy, these things are illegal."

"So how many do you want?"

"I'll try a box." The judge grinned at Mitch, waving a hand at the now empty tee box. "Well, big hitter. You have the honors, pull out that driver and put it on," the judge said as the group in front of them cleared the hole.

Mitch grinned pulling a four iron. "You'd like that wouldn't you old man?" Mitch teed up his ball. Every time he played this hole he went for the green and had only hit it once. Today he would play it safe. He would play the judge's game.

"It ain't gonna work. Easy and smart ain't your game. Best play it like you always do, long and dumb," the judge teased.

"Watch and learn," Mitch said, taking a smooth practice swing. He addressed the ball and then hit a smooth shot straight right down the middle.

"Good shot," the judge said. "Might be long."

Mitch grimaced as the ball soared. Damn the judge might be right. The ball was really going. "Shit," Mitch said as it hit and bounced through the fairway and into the desert.

"Damned unlucky" the judge said, with a cackle. He teed up his ball, giving Mitch a smirk, before he hit it. "That'll work," he said as his ball came to rest in the middle. "Going to get interesting now."

Somewhere Outside Tucson AZ June 12th 2018
Tuesday Dark

Angie Brody woke slowly. At first, she tried to pull the blanket up and snuggle in her bed. But the blanket was rough and the bed very hard. She felt the cold, hard concrete beneath her. Then it came back, the man with the delivery. He'd hit her! She touched her face, which was very sore. Vaguely, like something from a dream, she remembered the attack, the van, and the needle. The needle. She'd been drugged. She rubbed the spot on the inside of her arm, and could feel a knot where the needle went in.

Angie opened her eyes, but it was very dark. "Hello," she called out unable to see.

She waited, but no answer came. As she waited, Angie became aware of how quiet it was, like a tomb. A bolt of panic shot through her. My God! She was buried alive, for a second, the panic kept her frozen in place, her body rigid, as if she were being electrocuted.

Slowly the panic dissipated, and she was able to move. Stiffly she reached out, but only touched darkness. Moving like an infirmed person, she sat up. Feeling outward, she slowly stood up.

Moving unsteadily, she took a hesitant step forward. Immediately something touched her neck. Screaming, she jumped back, batting with her hands. As her hands hit the object, she realized it was a string, hanging from the ceiling. A light!

Waving her hands frantically, she felt about for the string, grabbing at it like a drowning man reaching for a life line. Whimpering in frustration, she clawed the empty air. Finally, her hands found the string, and she jerked it savagely, breaking a foot of string off.

The light came on, a weird yellowish light. The light seemed to battle with the darkness, only causing the shadows to retreat, but not go away.

Turning slowly, Angie took in her surroundings. She was in a small concrete room, perhaps ten feet square. As she turned, Angie realized, there was no door, she was sealed in. Taking a step back, she began to scream.

Mitch's House Tucson AZ June 12th 2018 Tuesday
Late Evening

At home, Mitch grabbed a beer, twisting the top off as he went to his laptop sitting on the dining room table. Mitch pulled up Angie Brody's Facebook page and was immediately impressed. This was a busy young lady.

He saw pictures of parties and night clubs. She was also into hiking. There were pictures of Angie on Push Ridge and other places Mitch didn't recognize. Besides a full load at U of A, Angie still found time to volunteer. He studied her picture. She was a very pretty young lady. She had a smile that filed up the camera, lighting up the pictures. She was athletically built with an exciting body. Mitch could see how she would attract a predator.

Scrolling down, Mitch saw she owned two houses. From what he gathered they were wrecks that she was hoping to fix up and flip. There was a photo of her standing in the middle of a wrecked kitchen, with an excited smile on her face.

Mitch leaned back in his chair. That could be where she picked up a predator. Construction jobs drew all types. All though the industry was changing, most companies still didn't require drug screening, so they attracted some pretty shady guys.

On impulse, Mitch picked up the phone and dialed Brad Brody's number. "Mister Brody, this is Detective Mitchell."

"Yeah," Brody grunted.

Mitch paused, a little taken back by the response. He'd expected questions about his daughter and the investigation.

"Uh, yeah, I was going to ask if you knew your daughter was buying houses to flip?"

"Of course I knew, I helped her secure her financing and cosigned her note."

"Okay, do you know if she has been hiring anybody to start rehabbing the houses?"

"No, I really don't know. It was her deal to run and I let her do it. She could have done the work herself. She grew up on my job sites."

"Okay. If you could ask around, see if she was hiring?"

"Yeah, I guess."

Mitch hung up staring at the wall. "Shit," he said. There was definitely something wrong with Brody's reaction to the whole thing.

Damn, maybe they were wasting time looking for a predator. Ollie had been right! Something was definitely going on with Brody. Brody wasn't asking questions about the investigation, and what was going on with his daughter. That told Mitch that maybe he already knew. Everything Mitch knew, was telling him to drop the predator angle and crawl up Brody's ass.

The thing was, Mitch knew he couldn't do that. Even if a predator had picked up Angie there was a chance she was still alive. And there was a better chance, if there was a predator, Angie wouldn't be his last victim. They had to keep pushing that angle, be ready if there was another victim, but it bothered Mitch. Mitch was feeling what Ollie saw. There was something wrong with Brody's reaction to the whole situation.

Mitch snatched up the phone. "Wade, did we get through the list of Brody's employees?"

"Just finishing now."

"Good, tell me there is somebody we know on that list."

Wade chuckled, a deep, merry sound. "How about Bennie Peoples?"

"No shit, Bennie?" Mitch said, rubbing his chin. "I heard he got clean."

Wade snorted. "No way. Bennie likes it too much. Me and him, we go way back. He's been good for some tips through the years."

"I don't suppose you have an address on him?"

"You bet, a trailer up off Ruthrath. You wanna take a ride out there?"

"You up to it?"

"Shit yes, I'm getting bored in the office. I need to do some walking to loosen up the knee, and like I said, me and Bennie are old pals."

"I'm at home; you could swing by and pick me up."

"You got it, boss. See you in half an hour."

Mitch was waiting out in front of his house, sipping a coke, when he heard what sounded like an M-80 going off in a toilet. Aw shit. Mitch groaned at the sound, knowing what it meant. Wade had an old Cadillac convertible that should have went on the scrap heap years ago, but Wade loved the old car. Not enough to actually fix anything on it, but he liked driving it He claimed it was a babe magnet, but Mitch secretly wondered how he could get any self-respecting female to go into that car without first applying a chloroform soaked rag. Mitch had personally seen fish taco wrappers in the back seat from a place that had went out of business years ago.

Mitch grimaced as he heard the car backfire again, and amid a cloud of smoke, the caddy rounded the corner swaying sideways on the worn out suspension. The tires howled in protest as the big car bucked around the corner. The sight of those tires gave Mitch a physical pain. Wade Nichols was the only guy in the world who would put mud grips on a Caddy.

As usual, Wade wore shorts, a Hawaiian shirt and flip-flops. Wade was known for his sandals and flip-flops. Today, he had the top down and two fishing poles extended from the back of the car. Shaking his head, Mitch finished his Coke tossing the can in the trash, before stepping down to the curb.

"Driving the Caddy?"

"Hate that fucking Rover," Wade answered.

Mitch smiled. Wade had a new Range Rover with all the bells and whistles, but still he drove the caddy. "You find anything on Brody?" Mitch asked, sliding into the car.

Wade pursed his lips, cutting off a car as he pulled out before answering. "Not really, but there's something there. Brody should be hurting, but he ain't."

"That's what Jerry thought. How do we unravel it?"

Wade shrugged. "Squeeze him."

"With what?"

"I'd suggest a pair of vice grips. I like Craftsman's. Clamp 'em on his nuts and squeeze."

"Really, Craftsman? I kinda prefer Snap-Ons."

"Snap-Ons?" Wade glanced sideways at Mitch. " Fuckin' rich bastard."

"Yeah, I wish," Mitch said grimacing as they bounced across Ina Street at fifty-five, the caddy's bumper shooting sparks as it scraped the asphalt.

"I heard Ollie was pitching a bitch about being paired with Parker?" Wade commented. "If you want I could run with her. Show her the ropes a little."

"Oh hell no. You'd be trying to get her into bed."

Wade shot a lopsided grin at Mitch. "Gonna try that either way."

"We got anything on Bennie?" Mitch asked, grabbing onto the dash, the tires howling in protest as Wade took a corner about ten miles an hour too fast.

"Not really. But it's Bennie. We shouldn't need anything."

They screeched to a halt in front of a rundown trailer house. A rail-thin man stood under a yard light, cooking burgers on a homemade grill. "Detectives, how's it hangin'?" he asked, trying to sound cheerful, but an undercurrent of wariness cut through his voice.

"Bennie, how the hell are you?" Wade asked cheerfully.

Bennie actually considered the question, scratching his chin with a big, square spatula. "Alright I guess, been working."

"You still on the shit?" Wade asked.

"No man, I swear."

Mitch and Wade exchanged a look; both of them caught the quick furtive glance away before Bennie answered. "You sure?" Mitch asked softly.

"Aw shit, man I'm clean. Just a little weed."

"That's illegal."

Bennie glanced skeptically at Mitch. "You sure? Man, I thought they changed all that."

Mitch shook his head. Bennie was serious. "I hear you're working for Brad Brody?"

Bennie took a small step back, looking away again. "Yeah, pay's ok, but it's just plain stuff."

"No fancy work?" Wade asked. Bennie was a tile layer and when he was high, he could lay down tile in geometrical patterns that were simply beautiful.

"Hell no, Brody's got no imagination. Every house the same, basic stuff."

"What about Brody?" Mitch asked. "He keeping you busy?"

Again, the hesitation. "Naw, fucker's got us working six hour days."

"How's Brody to work for?"

"I didn't have nothing to do with that girl getting pinched. I don't know nothin' about it."

Mitch took a step forward, crowding the smaller man just a little. "How do you know that's why we're here?" he asked a nasty edge riding on his tone.

"Aw shit man, why else would you be here?" Bennie whined.

"You know her?" Wade asked taking the spatula from Bennie and flipping the burgers.

"Not really. I used to see her out at the jobsites every once in a while, but I never really talked to her."

"Has she been trying to get guys to help her flip houses?"

"Huh?"

"She bought two repos to flip. She'll need guys to do the work."

This time Bennie held Mitch's gaze. "I hadn't heard about it. I woulda hit her up for some work."

"You know anybody who talked about her too much? Somebody who mighta grabbed her?"

Bennie shook his head as he thought. "No, I don't think....., hey I did hear Chappy Miers was back in town. You should take a look at that crazy mother fucker."

"Wasn't him. Witness said guy was small."

"Shit, nothing small about Chappy."

"You're a small guy," Mitch suggested. "Where were you on Tuesday morning?"

"He was with me."

Mitch looked up to see a woman in her thirties standing in the door of the trailer, a long neck beer dangling from her fingers. "Sandy," Mitch said. Sandy was attractive in a redneck trailer trash sort of way. She waited tables at a bar on the edge of downtown.

"Really," Wade asked, a note of doubt in his voice.

"Yeah, I bought the bar from Tony and hired Bennie to do some work."

"Saw the bathrooms," Wade commented, glancing at Bennie. "Thought it looked like your work. Pretty nice." Wade let his gaze slid casually to Sandy "Bought the bar, huh?"

"Yeah," she said, sullenly and crossing her arms across her chest.

"Good place, you should do well there," Wade said. "Why did Tony sell anyway? I thought he would die in that place."

"Prostate cancer," Sandy replied simply. "When it came right down to the nut cutting he didn't want to die behind that bar."

"So Bennie was with you? That early in the morning?"

"We've been seeing each other," Sandy provided sounding a little defensive.

"Nice," Wade said sincerely.

"Witness said this guy was small and wiry. Dark haired and dressed nice," Mitch said steering the conversation back to the investigation. "Either of you know anybody like that?"

"No," Bennie said and Sandy shook her head.

"Ask around the job site," Mitch instructed.

Bennie twisted his hands, looking down the street, "Ah man!"

"What?" Mitch demanded. "Be something good in it for you."

"Man, Brody's getting paranoid. Anybody asking questions is gonna get run off or worse."

"What about that dude, Cal?" Wade asked. "What's his story?"

"Dunno, he showed up a couple of weeks ago."

"Is he like a foreman or something?"

Bennie shrugged. "Beats me, guy never leaves the trailer."

Mitch and Wade exchanged a quick glance, "Keeping an eye on Brody," Wade commented.

"Yeah," Mitch grunted, looking back at Bennie. Sandy had come up beside him, sliding an arm around his waist. "You hear anything, you give me a call."

"Sure Mitch," Bennie replied.

"Hey, Mitch, we should go partners flipping houses like that girl was gonna do. You put up the cash, Bennie does the work, split it fifty-fifty."

Mitch glanced at her, funny how she jumped on the idea. He'd been rolling the idea buying a house to flip around in his own mind. "Maybe," he said. "Let me think about it."

"Do that."

"He'd have to be straight," Mitch said waving a hand at Bennie.

Sandy grinned pulling Bennie close. "Don't worry," she promised, a genuine smile dancing across her lips. The smile quickly twisted into a grimace, "Aw shit, Bennie you burned the burgers."

"I thought he was watching them," Bennie said, gesturing to Wade who still held the spatula.

"Aw crap, you're all worthless," Sandy griped, snatching the spatula from Wade. She pulled the burgers off the grill, which looked like lumps of charcoal. "Ruined."

She glanced at the three men, and then turned back into the trailer. She stomped inside.

"Damn, sorry man," Mitch said sincerely.

Bennie glanced nervously at the trailer. "Aw, it's alright. She'll cool down."

"I don't know," Wade said laughing and shaking his head. "She's hotter than the grill."

"Yeah," Bennie agreed, slinging another worried glance at the trailer.

Sandy emerged, carrying a box of burgers. "Well shit, since we're starting over, you boys want a burger?"

"Thanks but we gotta fly," Mitch said. He started to turn away, then stopped, looking back at the box of burgers. "Where did you get them?"

Sandy shrugged, looking at Bennie. "Some dude came in the bar. Said he'd missed his delivery at a restaurant. Offered a whole box to me at half price if I paid cash." She tipped the box so they could see inside. "I got burgers and a shitload of steaks."

"Son of a bitch!" Mitch exploded.

"What?" Wade asked.

"You remember that steak deal I got into a month or so back? Those are my steaks!"

"Bullshit!" Sandy said firmly. "I paid cash."

"Yeah," Mitch grunted waving the box away.

Wade was openly laughing. "I told you that you couldn't trust Stansford. Fucker's ripping you off, man."

"Gonna wring his fat neck," Mitch grumbled, turning toward the car.

Sandy said, "Hey Mitch, don't forget about those houses. We could make some money."

"Yeah, yeah," Mitch muttered, waving her off.

"You really got the money to buy houses?" Wade asked, as they piled into the car.

Mitch shrugged. "Maybe one. If I had to I could probably scrape up enough to do two."

"Shit, you are rich."

"Not really, but I've put a little back."

Biltmore Hotel, Phoenix AZ June 12th 2018 Tuesday Night

Jackson stepped out of the elevator, feeling more than a little nervous. These people had already killed twice to protect themselves. They surely wouldn't hesitate to make it three.

Two burly men with coiled cords coming from their ears stood on either side of the door. One was black, the other white, but they looked oddly similar. They were dressed alike, same close cropped hair and both wore the same expression. As Jackson approached the black one stepped out blocking Jackson's path. "Can I help you, sir," the man asked politely. The white one pulled back his coat, letting Jackson get a good look at the gun which hung from a shoulder rig inside his coat.

"Jackson Pyle. I have an appointment with the Senator."

"Can I see some ID, please."

"Sure," Jackson replied, fumbling for his driver's license and press card. The agent, whom Jackson assumed was with the Secret Service, took the cards. He glanced at them, then passed them to his white associate. The agent took them, turning his back, Jackson could hear him talking.

"Would you please open the case."

"Sure," Jackson said, trying to hear what the other agent was saying. The black agent rifled through the printout, probed the top and bottom of the case. From his belt he took a wand and passed it over the case. Apparently, the wand made the appropriate number of squawks and warbles because the agent passed it back with a curt thank you.

"Please raise your hands over your head." Jackson complied, holding his arms straight out as the agent passed the wand over his body. "Turn around." Jackson's arms were growing tired, as he heard the wand chirping and complaining. The chirping stopped, and Jackson felt the agent's hands on his body. The pat down was quick, professional, and firm enough that Jackson could feel the muscles behind those hands.

"Thank you, Mister Pyle. You may go in now." The agent said, opening the door for him.

As Jackson passed by them, the other agent passed him his cards. Jackson had to admire their team work. No signal had passed between them that Jackson saw or heard. Still they had both finished their clearings at the same time.

As Jackson passed through the door, one of the agents reached inside and pulled the door closed. Stuffing the cards into his pocket, Jackson approached the huge desk which dominated the entry room. A blazingly attractive young woman sat behind the desk, typing into a hand held tablet. As Jackson approached, she stood, laying the tablet face down on the desk. "Good afternoon, Mister Pyle. Please come with me." Without looking to see if Jackson was following, she led the way to a huge set of double doors. As they walked, Jackson admired the curve of her ass and the seductive swish of the skirt. Pretty short skirt for a liberal, Jackson thought.

She opened the door, stepping aside so Jackson could pass. "The Senator will be with you in a moment."

"Sure, thanks," Jackson said, taking the room in. It was a room obviously set up for staffers. A table with coolers of ice, water and soft drinks sat along the back wall. A huge urn of what Jackson assumed was coffee rested on the end of the table. Another long table held sandwiches and snacks. Several chairs were scattered haphazardly out in front.

The message was subtle, but it was there. The good Senator might stoop to receive him, but he wasn't going to get close to her inner circle.

"There's coffee, soft drinks and snacks. Feel free to help yourself. I will let the Senator know you are here."

"Thank you, ah...."

"Schroeder. Tamera Schroeder."

"Thank you, Tamera."

Alone in the room, Jackson glanced around. He idly picked up a campaign folder from a table. Even though he had expected to be kept waiting, he felt his nerves going. A burning sensation settled into the pit of his stomach.

It was too late to back out now. Just the mention of Forsyth and Morris was enough to get him killed. It was all or nothing now. Jackson ran through what he was going to say through his mind. He knew a lot, but he didn't know it all.

Jackson lit a cigarette, prowling the room. He was going to have to bluff part of it. He picked up a campaign button twirling it in his fingers. "This is a non-smoking room." Jackson turned and saw Senator Braxton standing hand on hips in the doorway. "You can keep the button though."

"No thanks," Jackson said tossing it on the table. He ground his cigarette out on the table. For a long second, they stared at each other, sizing one another up. Jackson knew from his research that she was fifty-four, but looked at least ten years older. She had probably never been a handsome woman at any age, but now the miles showed on her. Jackson looked away flicking the cigarette in the general direction of a trash can.

"Are you going to spit on the floor, next?'

"I might," Jackson said, actually thinking of doing it.

A deep silence grew between them. Jackson felt uncomfortable, his brain scrambling for an opening. All of the quick witty questions he'd rehearsed had flown right from his mind. He shifted his feet, and immediately knew it was wrong.

A quick spark flashed in her eyes. The first round had gone to the Senator. "Okay, I haven't got all day. Ask your questions."

Jackson cleared his throat. His mouth was dry and his armpits sweat furiously, while the Senator looked cool and composed. He was definitely out of his league here. Still there was no going back now. He shifted his feet again. "Would you care to comment on the death of one William Joseph Forsyth?"

Senator Braxton smiled, baring her teeth. "I hear he was a very troubled young man, who unfortunately saw fit to take his own life. It's a tragic thing. I plan to create legislation to help our troubled youth find counseling."

"Save it for the campaign trail," Jackson said, surprising himself with the strength of his tone. "Did you know him?'

The Senator's smile never flickered. "I knew of him. I don't know as I ever met him. He worked for a law firm I do business with." She walked past him to the water bottles. "Are these the questions that you really want to ask? I have a really busy schedule."

She was ready to blow him off. Jackson knew he was losing. "Do you know he wrote some kind of manifesto before he died? Were you aware that his death wasn't a suicide? That he was murdered. Oh, but of course I bet you already knew that."

The bottle paused half way to her lips, the hesitation was fleeting, but Jackson caught it. He'd caught her with a heavy body blow. "For someone you barely knew, William Joseph Forsyth certainly knew a lot about your business. Does the name Peyton Holdings LTD mean anything to you?"

Braxton covered any reaction she might have by taking a drink. "Doesn't ring any bells," she said around the bottle.

"How about Jared Morris?"

This time the bottle came away from her lips slowly, and she shook her head, her movements wooden. "I don't believe so."

"Funny, I would have thought you would remember the man you had killed. Have you had so many killed that they don't tend to stand out? He was from Denver. Did you know that? Do you get to Denver much?"

For a second, the fire snapped in Braxton's eyes and Jackson thought she would hurl the bottle at him. Instead of throwing the bottle, she set it on the table very gently. "Perhaps you should come back to my office."

As Jackson followed her, he tried to organize his thoughts. He'd fired his best shots. Now, all he had left was guesses and suppositions. The good Senator had been ready for him, but Jackson didn't think she had been ready for all that he knew.

She took a seat behind a huge cherry desk, waving him into a chair. "First of all, Mister Pyle, I will not make any statements for the record. I want to make that very clear."

"So, you did know Jared Morris?" Jackson pushed, hoping she would let something slip. "What about Peyton Holdings?"

Braxton spun her chair; with her back to him she walked to the window. "What do you want?"

"So, you confirm that you knew Jared Morris?"

"No, God damn it!" she snapped, spinning around. "If you print anything, I will sue your ass." She placed her hands on her hips, looking down her nose at him. "I'll ask again. What do you want from me?"

So, here it is. What did he want? As he considered, Braxton stepped up. "You understand, of course, this is in no way an admission of anything. But as you must also realize, even the hint of scandal right now would be disastrous to my campaign."

"So, you think you can just buy me off? Pay me to kill the story?"

Braxton snorted rather indelicately. "You damn right. That's exactly what I think. If you weren't wanting to be bought off you wouldn't be here with your hand out. You would have blind-sided me."

"I was thinking two million bucks," Jackson said, surprising himself with the confidence he felt.

Braxton didn't bat an eye. "That can be arranged. I'll want all the copies of Forsyth's manuscript."

"When I get the money."

"Of course." Braxton sat back down. "That will take some time. I'll get back to you tomorrow."

After Jackson left, Braxton swiveled her chair, staring out the window. Pyle was going to be a problem. Fucking Forsyth! Fuckin' greedy little snot. Why couldn't he just hold it together a few more months?

Braxton sighed. She didn't have time for this shit. She had a speech to give in an hour. Tomorrow, she would be in Denver.

Denver.

Just the thought brought her up short. Did Pyle know about Denver? Good question. Braxton looked up at the ceiling and closed her eyes. This was supposed to be a simple arraignment. In, out, make a little cash. Nothing to it.

Sighing again, she turned back to the desk and flipped open her laptop. Logging in, she typed a quick message, hesitating before she pressed send. The Senator didn't like using the email. She didn't like written records.

Her people assured her it was the most private form of communication. With the new encryption packages, the email was virtually impenetrable. She had her own server and the laptop was hers, so the emails couldn't be considered government property. But still, there was a written record. She didn't like that on general principle. A feeling of dread dogging her, she pressed send. Drinking the water, she paced, working on her speech, waiting for the reply.

It came quickly. Announced with a silly, annoying bong. The message was short. "Pyle must be dealt with."

"Well, no shit," Braxton muttered. "What are you suggesting?" she typed.

The reply was fast. "Does he know about Denver?"

Braxton considered the question. Did he? Pyle made a couple of references to Denver. Did that mean he knew? Not likely. If he actually knew, he would have been more direct. He had been fishing, she decided.

"No," Braxton typed, praying it was true. If Pyle knew about Denver, and had talked to anyone, they were all fucked.

"Find out what he knows, and get rid of him."

CHAPTER THREE

**Sam Logan's Property North of Oracle Junction AZ
June 12th 2018 Tuesday Night**

Bill Jack was crying, slobbering down his shirt, when Sam walked into his shop building. For an instant, a hopeful expression blossomed on Bill Jack's face, but it quickly wilted as he read Sam's grim expression. "You start, already?" Sam grunted.

"Nope," Ted replied, taking a sip from his beer bottle. "Me and Bill Jack just been getting acquainted. We had a couple of beers and I explained things."

"Yeah, see you found my beer," Sam grunted, crossing to the fridge.

"Wasn't like it was well hid," Ted said with a shrug.

"Huh," Sam said grabbing himself a beer. He twisted the top off and threw it at Bill Jack. "Hey, pussy. Quit your blubbering and man up for a second. We got some talking to do."

Bill Jack turned his head slowly to look at Sam. "Why, you're gonna kill me anyway."

"Maybe," Sam grunted, hating to lie at a time like this. "But one thing is for sure, you don't tell us what we want to know, we are going to cause you some serious pain."

Sam got a refill for Ted and another one for Bill Jack. "Let's drink a beer and think about things." He threw a hard look at Bill Jack. "I'd be contemplating the error in my ways, if I was you."

"If it was me I'd be concentrating about how much pain we could cause you," Ted suggested

They drank without speaking, the only sound in the metal building was Bill Jack's sniffling. "Tell me what happened out there in the desert," Sam asked softly.

"What?" Bill Jack sputtered. "What desert?"

Sam looked across at Ted. "How'd that go? Smash his nuts with a hammer?"

"Supposed to staple his nut sack to a stump first, but fuck it. I don't see no stump and I'm tired of fucking around."

Ted picked up a shotgun, calmly racked a shell in the chamber and then poked the barrel into Bill Jack's crotch. "Now, Sam is gonna ask you some questions. If I think you are lying or holding back, I'm just gonna pull the trigger."

"Like I said, what happened out there?" Sam asked.

"That dude, Jimmy, he was using, so we took 'em out there to kill 'em. Henry don't allow no using."

"Who's Henry?"

"Biker dude."

"Henry got a last name?"

"Aw man, come on. They will kill me for sure," Bill Jack whined, wiping his nose with the back of his hand.

"Hey, dipshit," Ted growled given the shotgun a goose. "I'd be more worried about what we are gonna do. I'm fixing to blow your nuts out your asshole."

"Flores!" Bill Jack screamed. "Henry Flores."

Sam glanced at Ted who shrugged. "Is Henry local?"

"No, man, I think he's outta Cali. San Diego maybe."

"How did you get hooked up with him?"

"Fucking Chappy Miers."

Sam leaned in close, speaking softly. "So, what is the deal?"

"Chappy and Henry are hooking up with some big shot down in Mexico. He's got a tunnel or something, they bring it to us, and then we run it into Cali."

"That Henry Flores, he related to Hector?" Ted asked.

"Yeah man, cousins or some such shit."

"What happened out there with those two kids?" Sam asked, his voice hardly a whisper now. This was the question he'd been waiting to ask.

"They just stumbled upon us, when we were fixing to do Jimmy."

"So, just wrong place, wrong time?" Sam asked, trying to sound friendly.

"Yeah, yeah man, that was it!" Bill Jack said, seizing on the friendly sound like a drowning man hugging a life preserver. "Just bad damn luck, that's all."

"You in on raping that girl?"

"No, man," Bill Jack declared, licking his lips, a sweaty, hungry look crawling onto his face. "No way, I didn't have nothing to do with that."

"You sure?" Ted asked with a wink and nudge at Bill Jack. "She sure was a tasty looking number."

"Yeah man, you a homo or something?" Sam asked.

"No, I ain't!"

"But you didn't go after that girl?" Ted demanded, kicking Bill Jack's leg. "What's the matter? Your pecker don't work right?"

"No," Bill Jack replied, pouting.

"Come on," Sam encouraged. "She was a right fine number and you didn't touch her?" He shot a look at Ted. "Gotta be a homo."

Bill Jack looked from one to the other, a wolfish look on his face. His face was flushed and his eyes became glassy, as he licked his lips. "Well, yeah, maybe I did a little." Bill Jack let out a little giggle. "She didn't like it at first, but..."

While Bill Jack was talking, Sam pulled out a small twenty-two pistol he'd picked up several years ago. He pressed the pistol against a roll of shop towels, leaned in and shot Bill Jack in the temple.

Bill Jack stopped talking, his head tipped forward and he slumped over, falling to the floor. Sam stared at the body for a second, fighting a queasy feeling. The killing unnerved him a bit. It was like he flipped a switch and the man was gone forever. "You okay with this?" he asked, his voice sounding like he had been chewing on gravel.

"No problem," Ted replied, his own voice very rough. "I sure as hell didn't want to hear him brag about raping that girl."

"Nope," Sam said getting a heavy trash bag off the shelf. "Fucker got off easy."

"We probably saved a good half-dozen rapes over the next few years," Ted said, helping pull the trash bag over Bill Jack's head.

"Yup," Sam agreed. "And at least that many robberies and muggings."

They were just talking, trying to make the guilt go away. It worked, after a fashion. Reminding themselves of the crimes Bill Jack had committed and probably would commit did make it a bit easier.

"Now what?" Ted asked.

"I got a cheap tarp over there," Sam said, waving his hand at the back corner of the shop. "We'll roll him up in that. I know just the spot to dump him."

"Shit, let's get it done. I'm tired all of a sudden," Ted said.

"It's the stress," Sam said, as they rolled Bill Jack onto the open tarp. "Kicks your ass every time."

"I guess," Ted agreed.

Together, they carried Bill Jack outside. "Better put him in my truck," Ted said, pointing to his Durango.

"You think?"

"Yeah," Ted said, jerking his head at Sam's Explorer. "That comes from the State. Never know, they might have it Lo Jacked or some such shit."

"Shit, good thought," Sam admitted.

By the time they had Bill Jack's body rolled into the back of the Durango, both men were breathing hard. "Aw crap, gettin old," Sam complained.

"Yeah," Ted agreed, looking around. "Nice place. How come you and Maureen never built out here?"

"Was gonna. Figured on starting this year sometime. But now, after the accident, we just said fuck it."

Tucson Police Headquarters Tucson AZ June 113th 2018 Wednesday Morning

Detective John Mitchell swung into the parking lot. He gave a little gas to the Mustang, smiling as the tires spun and barked. He'd been restoring his sixty-eight Mustang for over a year. This was the first time he'd been able to drive it to work. He'd spent the better part of two hours chasing down a short in the wiring.

The car was running fine, but the air conditioner was out. This was going to be a day for the AC. Already warm; it was going to be brutally hot.

Leaving the car idling, Mitch got out, and pulled the hood pins. "Finally, got her running?" Ray Jimenez asked, wandering up to the car, as Mitch raised the hood.

"Yeah, got the motor back a couple a days ago."

"She giving you trouble?"

"Damn AC isn't working," Mitch grunted

Ray laughed. "Ain't that a bitch? You're going to need AC. I heard it might get up to one fifteen today."

"Yeah, I heard that too," Mitch grunted, as they both bent over the hood looking at the motor.

"Compressor's turning. Car set for a long time. Bet it's out of Freon."

"Hopefully. That would be an easy fix."

"Sounds good, though" Ray commented.

"I'm thinking of upping the cam."

"Idles rough when you do that."

Mitch grinned running a hand along the fender. "Yeah, but it'll run like a striped-assed ape."

"How's it run now?"

Mitch laughed, shaking his head. "Don't know. I just got it out last night. Still breaking it in. I drove around half the night, just easing around, putting miles on."

"You should get out on the Interstate. Head towards El Paso. Put some miles on her."

"Thought about it. I really was tempted, but I knew I couldn't keep my foot out of it."

"Shit, I always heard break 'em in the way you're gonna drive," Ray's partner, Dick Wylie said. "Put your foot in it, and keep it there. Won't hurt it."

"Yeah, right," Mitch grunted. "I got three grand in this motor. I'm gonna listen to you. What's that you're driving? A Chevette?"

Wylie shrugged, ignoring the jab. "Suit yourself, but I'm telling you. Just drive it."

"You guys hear anything on the Angie Brody thing?"

Both officers shook their heads. "We did some looking," Wylie said, running his hand through his gray crew-cut. "Man nobody knows nothing. We even squeezed Ronnie T. Stupid fuck, was setting on the curb smoking a doobie, holding a rock. We offered to let him keep his stash if he knew anything."

"Did he know anything?"

Wylie shook his head. "Naw, but we let him off. He's supposed to come up with something for us tonight."

"Believe that when pigs fly," Mitch said.

Wylie ran his hand through his hair again. "I know, I shouldn't have let him keep his stuff. I was just hoping... you know."

Mitch nodded. "I'm not saying you did wrong. You're right. Any chance we got to take to find that girl. She's running out of time."

"We'll keep looking. I keep trying to think of somebody we could really squeeze," Wylie said, his voice troubled.

"I tell you what, you find somebody to squeeze, go ahead and pull their nuts off. I'll back you up on it."

Wylie nodded and wandered away, an aimless look to him. "The Brody thing is really getting to him. Tonya starts to college this year. She's going out to San Diego State this fall."

"Yeah, you like to think your kids are safe at college." Mitch shut the hood. "How's the world treating you? You like working nights?"

"Didn't think I would, but yeah, I do. Dick's a good guy to learn from. Get to spend a lot of time with Lucas, and it sure saves on daycare."

"Gotta spend time with the kids. Specially when they're little like Lucas."

Ray grinned. "Yeah, I missed a lot of that with Taylor. Seemed like I was working all the time when she was real little." He grinned, patting the hood of the car. "Course, if I didn't have kids, I could afford one of these babies."

Mitch laughed. "Costs more than kids and twice the trouble. What grade is Taylor in?"

"She's in second this coming year."

"She still playing the piano?" Mitch asked as they headed up to the station.

"Yeah, she's getting pretty good. Her music school is selling candy bars to raise money."

"How much?"

"Dollar a bar."

Mitch pulled some cash from his pocket, and peeled off a twenty. "Give me twenty."

"I'll bring them up to your office soon as I get checked out."

"Naw," Mitch said, waving his hand. "Pass them out at roll call tomorrow."

"Thanks," Jimenez replied, stuffing the twenty in his pocket. "You said you were out last night, you pick anything up on the girl?" he asked, and Mitch knew he was referring to Angie Brody.

"Not a word. I must have talked to a hundred people last night. Nobody knows anything."

"Psycho, probably," Ray said. "Makes you sick. Young girl like that."

"Yeah. Jesus, I hope it's not a psycho." Mitch frowned, shaking his head. "We've been lucky in that respect. When I was out in LA last year for training, they had two serials working."

"Speaking of LA and psychos, we heard last night that Chappy and Dell Miers was back in town."

"Heard that. Shit, I was sure hoping they would like it out in LA."

"Guess not. They're back. I tell you what, though, if you were to ask me who I thought might be a serial killer; that fucking Chappy would be the first person I thought of."

Mitch nodded. "Doesn't fit the description. Two witnesses said the guy was small and wiry."

"Only thing small about Chappy is his brain."

"You know it," Mitch said as they reached the door. "Aw, shit, I brought Monte some cigars and I forgot them in the car."

"Hopefully those cigars will cheer him up, he's getting grumpy."

"Happens when you get old and feeble."

"Yeah, tell him that."

They parted laughing. Mitch liked the young patrolman. Ray Jimenez would be a good candidate if Mitch were able to expand his department. Mitch was the head of the newly formed Special Crimes Unit. Right now, Mitch had four people, Carly Parker, Wade Nichols, Oscar Olshan, and Jerry Hartek. Be nice to have another body or two. Course, if they didn't find Angie Brody soon, he might not have a unit to expand, Mitch thought to himself.

Grabbing the cigars off the seat, Mitch headed back inside. He stopped, chatting with the patrolmen coming in from their shift. To an outsider, Mitch might look like a man without a care. But Mitch wasn't just smoozing, he was listening. Patrol cops talked to a lot of people during their night shift. By listening and asking the occasional question, Mitch was trying to pick up a scrap of something, anything that might give him a thread to pull.

Angie Brody was quickly running out of time.

Mitch had checked this morning. Brody hadn't received a ransom call. Mitch was still holding out hope that she had been picked up in a straight kidnapping for ransom, but that hope was dying a slow death. If she was being held for ransom, she still had a chance.

If it was some psycho as Ray Jimenez had suggested, she was probably dead already. Mitch kept up on the statistics. She'd been gone right at twenty-four hours, and the average time before a psycho killed their victims was under forty-eight. Mitch could hear the clock ticking in his head. That girl was running out of time.

Inside, Mitch made his way up front. He was looking for Monte Simms the night patrol watch commander. He spotted Monte looking over the arrest log. "Hey, Monte. I got something for you."

"Yeah, what's that? Your usual ration of shit?"

"Something better," Mitch replied gleefully, as he held the cigars over his head.

"Ah, stogies."

"Stogies my ass. These are Cubans."

"Mitch, you are so full of shit," Monte growled, then raised an eyebrow as Mitch shook his head. "Cubans? No shit? Where did you get Cubans?"

"Jersey Joe. Crazy fucker thought pocket aces were unbeatable."

"Aw shit. Where the hell would he get Cubans?"

"Frankie O'Hara."

"Where'd she get them?"

"Beats me, but they are good."

"Well, shit, worth trying I guess," Monte said, snatching the cigars. "Thanks, Mitch."

"Hey, how come Monte gets cigars?" Pete McElroy protested.

"Cause Monte puts out," Mitch replied.

"Damn right," Monte said grinning, as he stuffed the cigars in his uniform pocket.

"I might put out for Cubans," McElroy said, laughing.

"Sergeant Mitchell," Commander Tim Harris called his voice echoing across the squad room. "I need to speak with you."

Before Mitch could answer, Monte grabbed his sleeve. "Hey, Mitch, dispatch just took a call from Leroy Bell. Said he had a body in one of his rooms. Might be the Brody girl."

Mitch felt a sinking feeling in the pit of his stomach. Damn! He'd had hopes they would find her.

"Sergeant Mitchell," Harris called again.

"Yeah, hang on a sec," Mitch yelled back. "Any details from the motel?" he asked Monte.

"Not much. Leroy called it in, all he said was white, blonde chick, about twenty."

"You got anybody rolling?"

"Yeah, Smitty and Rosa were still out. Dispatch gave them the call."

"Good, Smitty will know what to do. Page my guys for me. See if Mickey's in, I'd like him on this." Mickey was Michael Chang, hands down the best Crime Scene Tech in the city. "Let's try and keep this off the radio. I'd like to keep it quiet as long as we can."

"You got it. Cell phones only. Parker is already in, I saw her a few minutes ago, I'll get started on the rest."

"You got time to do all that?" Mitch asked, knowing Monte was due to get off soon.

"Yeah, I got time, I'll get everybody rolling."

"Thanks," Mitch said, dragging his feet as he crossed to where Harris stood in the doorway. "Sorry, Tim, I don't have time to go over those overtime vouchers, I'm kinda running here."

Color shot up Harris's neck and for a second, Mitch thought he might blow a gasket. Harris jerked on his vest, a clear sign he was angry. "Those forms are important. People won't get paid for their overtime if you don't sign off on them."

"Don't worry about it Timmy, I'll get to them tonight. Like I said, I'm kinda running here. I think Angie Brody might have turned up."

Harris smoothed his hair and jerked down his jacket. "Is she alive?' he asked.

Mitch shrugged. "We got a call. Body in a motel room. Young blonde girl."

"Okay, the chief and I will need a report. I will alert him, be in his office in ten minutes."

Mitch snorted. "Shit, you already know what I know. I need to get out to the scene and start processing things."

Harris shot Mitch one of his trademark condescending looks. "Detective Mitchell, why must I always be forced to remind you of the chain of command? We will have to get a press release out, and the chief will want an update. Be in his office in five minutes. I'm sure your people can handle things for a few minutes."

Mitch started to argue, then shrugged. Fuck it. Let Harris dig his own grave. Instead Mitch gave a small nod then turned away. Muttering to himself, Mitch hurried to the office which housed his unit. The office had been divided in two parts. A very small office for Mitch and the larger part for the four detectives. Parker was at her desk, when he arrived. "You get the word?" he asked.

"Yeah, I was just waiting on you."

Mitch could sense the excitement radiating from her. To most people, the excitement might seem out of place. Wrong even, but Mitch understood, felt a little bit of it himself. The thrill of the hunt. "I'm going to be tied up here a few minutes. I want you to go ahead, take charge of the scene. Ollie and Jerry are on their way. Let's try to keep this quiet."

"I'll do what I can. "

"And Carly, this is your scene to run. When Ollie and Jerry get there, you are still in charge." Mitch smiled at her. "Of course, if they have a suggestion..."

"It would be good to listen to them."

Mitch smiled again. She would be alright. "You and Ollie get things worked out?"

She laughed. "He was afraid of saying fuck around me. I told him to fuck the hell off, and that I would kick his ass if he even thought about farting in the car."

"Good girl."

Mitch grabbed his cell as he headed down the hall to the chief's office. Once he saw he was out of earshot, he punched in Ollie's number. "You get the call from Monte?"

"Yeah, I'm on my way. Be there in twenty. You know any more than Monte told me?"

"No," Mitch said unconsciously shaking his head. "Look, I got to go brief the chief and Harris."

"Aw crap, you're kidding me."

"Nope," Mitch replied. "Harris thought they needed an update."

Ollie laughed harshly. "Tell him to fuck off. What can you tell him at this point?"

"Not a thing," Mitch replied cheerfully. "Let the chief see what a dumbass Harris really is."

Ollie chuckled. "You are a sly dog."

"Look, Ollie, I told Parker this was her scene to run, so let her do it, but keep an eye on things."

"You got it, boss. I'll make sure she doesn't miss anything. But she's pretty good, catches on quick."

Jacob Carter's Apartment Washington DC May 2th 2010 Wednesday Evening

Jake Carter glanced out the window, cursing as he saw the dirty brown car parked across the street. "Fuck!" he shouted. He took a quick angry drink of bourbon. That asshole Harley!

Shit it had been years. Why couldn't that asshole give up?

Carter stormed around the apartment, stopping every little bit to stare out the window. Once he saw Harley clearly as the detective lit a cigarette. "Motherfucker," Carter mumbled, resuming his pacing. That God damn Harley. He was going to ruin everything. Carter had a job to do for Van Zandt. He couldn't afford to have Harley show up at the wrong time.

He should just go down and kill the bastard. Carter glanced down at his watch. He had a date coming, but she wasn't due for an hour. He should just kill the fat prick. Carter idly swirled the bourbon in his glass, considering it. He had a clean gun.

He could circle the block, come out of the alley right across from Harley's car. He'd be right on top of the car. Just walk up, and shoot. It would be over in seconds. He could be back in his apartment in a minute, certainly less than two.

Carter took a sip of his drink, figuring the angles. He would be left with the gun. That would be bad. Cops would certainly search his apartment. And the GSR. Carter knew cops could test his hands for gunshot residue, and know if he'd fired a gun. How to get that off his hands? Could he use his date as an alibi? The timing on that would be tricky. If she was late? Or early. Early could be real bad.

Doing Harley would be unlike any killing he had ever done. It could easily be made to look like a robbery. This was a safe neighborhood, but this was also DC, crime was everywhere. He could use a silencer. He had one.

The silencer would give him a chance to take Harley's gun and wallet. Of course, he would have to get rid of that stuff, along with his own gun. And he would still have the GSR on his hands to contend with. That was going to be a problem.

Could it be washed off? Carter wasn't sure. Maybe with some kind of industrial cleaner? If he could wash it off, that would be almost as good as an alibi. Maybe he could find out. Lost in thought, Carter wandered back to the window.

The gun and silencer were for the job for Van Zandt in Colorado. If he used them to kill Harley, he would have to get another set. That was always a pain. But did he really need a clean gun out in Colorado? He wasn't going to shoot anyone, the gun was for persuasion. Still, if things went bad and he had to shoot?

He needed a clean gun.

As inviting as killing Harley sounded, it just wouldn't work. Not tonight. He pulled back the curtain, looking down at the car. It was too dark to see, but Carter knew, Harley was watching. He flipped the bird, smiled as he let the curtain fall back. Fuck you Harley. You're a dead man.

This would take some planning. Not tonight, but one night soon.

Tucson Police Headquarters Tucson AZ June 10 2015 Wednesday Morning

Mitch took his time heading down to the chief's office. He made a detour by the coffee machine, grabbing a cup. "Morning, Louise," he said, as he came up to the chief's office.

Louise who had been the secretary to three different chiefs smiled up at Mitch. "Go on in Detective, they are waiting for you."

"Thanks."

"Mitch, I was wondering. How we are doing on the emu farm. Is it going good?" Louise asked, as Mitch headed to the door.

Mitch had talked Louise and several cops into an emu farm he and a partner were trying to get going. So far the going had been tough. They had bought eggs, built pens, but so far, none of them had hatched.

"Uh... yeah sure, good," Mitch said, quickly.

"Do we have any birds yet? Roy and I can't wait to see them. If this works out, it will really help our retirement."

"We should see some birds any day now," Mitch assured, spilling the scalding coffee across the back of his hand as he hurriedly pushed through the door. Licking coffee off his hand, Mitch closed the door behind him. The chief sat behind his desk, munching on a powdered doughnut. He held up a finger as he chewed, and swallowed. "Good morning, Mitch," the chief said pleasantly.

"Morning, chief," Mitch said, dropping into a leather chair, that he knew from experience wasn't nearly as comfortable as it looked. "What can I do for you this morning?"

"I was hoping for an update on Angie Brody."

"Brody giving you a hard time?"

"No," the chief said shaking his head. "I've hardly talked to the man. It's the press I was thinking of. We are starting to get some very pointed questions." The chief pushed his doughnut aside, leaning forward and placing his elbows on the desk. "I formed your unit to handle things precisely like this."

Harris gave a little snort, stepping forward into the conversation. "A move which I opposed."

The chief shot a quick, hard glance at Harris. "Commander Harris! I am well aware of your feelings on the subject. You do not have to repeat them over and over." The chief held Harris' gaze until the other man looked down at the carpet. "The fact is, Mitch, we need some results. It may not be fair, but that's the way it is."

"We have a body. Call came from a motel off Sixth Ave."

The chief took the news without a change of expression, and Mitch couldn't tell if Harris had already told him the news. "Is it her? Angie Brody?"

Mitch shrugged. "Too early to tell, but it sounds like it could be."

"Let us know the minute you find out," Harris said.

"You want to get your name in the paper?" Mitch asked, turning a disgusted stare at Harris. "It'll be late this evening or morning before we know for sure."

"Make that a priority," Harris ordered.

"No" Mitch replied quietly. "There was a young woman murdered last night. We need to catch the guy who did this, whether it turns out she is Angie Brody or not. We will work the case in the correct order, not skip ahead trying to see if it is, just so you can get your name in the paper."

The chief had been watching the exchange with an amused expression. "You're right, Mitch. We need to catch this guy. Do what you think needs to be done."

Mitch nodded, climbing to his feet. "We're doing everything we can, but if he doesn't leave us anything, there ain't a helluva lot we can do."

"Understood," the chief replied, leaning back in his chair. "But there must be other avenues that can be pursued."

"We are looking hard at Angie Brody herself."

Harris snorted, shaking his head. "That's a big help. Investigate the victim."

Mitch turned a cold stare on Harris. "And what would you do, Commander?"

Harris backed up a step, fumbling with his vest. "I wouldn't be investigating the victim. I would be out there finding her."

Mitch laughed, waving his arm at the door. "Be my guest. Go start knocking on doors," he said, contempt practically dripping from his tone. "We are investigating Angie to see if someone would have a grudge against her. We are also trying to figure out where he might have picked her up."

"You're looking ahead to the next one. Trying to have things to compare," the chief said.

Mitch squirmed a little. "It's something to do. Chances are if it's a predator, there will be more."

"No, you're right. The best players are always looking ahead a move or two." The chief picked up a pencil, twirling it between his fingers. "Mitch, I know you're not a politician, but the fact is, we live in a political world. But that is my problem. You are by far the best investigator we have. Go do your thing. Don't run your investigation to suit the press. Do what needs to be done."

"Thanks," Mitch said, turning to the door. At the door he turned back. "But you need something to give them."

"Something would be nice."

Outside Jacob Carter's Apartment Washington DC
June 25th 2010 Friday Evening

Harley clipped the curb as he parked. The car's sagging suspension protested and rocked for several seconds. Throwing the car into park, Harley glanced up at Carter's window. A couple of lights were on and Harley saw a shadow move behind a curtain. So the little prick was home.

Harley had never stopped to fully examine exactly why he was doing this. He knew, he couldn't shoot the prick, so he settled for tormenting him. Wasn't quite the same, but Harley drew pleasure from it. And these days, Harley had so little pleasure in his life. And if Carter so much as jaywalked, Harley was going to haul his ass in.

Harley glanced back up at the window, reaching for a grease soaked bag on the passenger's seat. Harley smacked his lips. The great thing about coming over here was the deli a few blocks over. That deli served, in Harley's opinion, the best fried baloney sandwich anywhere.

Harley pulled the sandwich out of the bag with loving care. Crap, if his doctor could see this he'd shit a brick.

Harley wasn't worried. If his ex-wife couldn't kill him, cholesterol didn't have a chance. Harley was digging in the bag for the fries, when a shadow fell across his window.

A sense of alarm shot through Harley. Grabbing at his gun, Harley started to turn. He heard a boom, and a bright light flashed in front of him. The light seemed to spread, until it enveloped Harley.

Harley didn't feel it as his head slammed into the steering wheel. He didn't hear the horn of his car blaring.

Up in his apartment, Carter sipped his drink and smiled. Fucking with Harley had always been good for a laugh, but now, Carter was relieved that the fat slob was gone.

Still smiling, Carter picked up his phone, calmly punching in nine-one-one. "A man was just shot."

Starlight Motel Tucson AZ June 13th 2018
Wednesday Morning

Mitch pulled up to the hotel, surprised only to see a single cruiser. He got out wondering where all the cops were. He would have expected the parking lot to look like a cop convention. A single squad car sat in the motel parking lot. Mitch eased the Mustang to the curb, letting it idle for a minute before shutting it down.

The first person he saw was Ira Bolton. He stood on the balcony outside the motel room door. Mitch climbed out of his car, a scowl on his face. Bolton was Harris' snitch inside the department, but it was more than that. Bolton could piss off the Pope. Still scowling, Mitch stalked up the stairs, glaring the whole time up at Bolton.

"Bolton, what the fuck are you doing here?"

Bolton hooked his thumbs in his belt. "Somebody needs to keep an eye on your girl. I don't think she knows what she is doing."

"Shit, Bolton you're the one that doesn't know what you're doing. The last thing we need is another person traipsing through the crime scene." Mitch pushed past the fat patrol sergeant, and into the motel room.

Mitch stopped, just inside the door, forcing Bolton to stand outside. Slowly Mitch scanned the room, trying to soak in every detail and commit it to memory. The room seemed to be a normal motel room. If the victim had put up a fight, it hadn't happened here. There was no sign of a struggle.

Next he looked to the body on the bed. The body was completely wrapped in some kind of plastic. Only the top of her head and her feet were visible. "Who's got the log?" he asked, referring to the log of everyone who visited the crime scene.

"It's on my box," Mickey Chan called from the other side of the bed.

Mitch nodded to Linda Fang, who was filming the scene, and picked up the log. After scribbling his name in the log, Mitch drew on a pair of latex gloves. He leaned in looking at the body. The plastic was hard to see through and it was also smashing the victim's features. The hair was right, as was the size and build of the victim.

Even through the plastic, Mitch could see the blood on her chest and stomach. "Stabbed?" he muttered to himself.

"That's my guess," Mickey said, from the other side of the bed. "If you look close, you can see a big slash across her lower abdomen."

Mitch leaned closer, and imagined he could see the wound. The plastic distorted everything. "Find a weapon?"

"It's rolled up with her, I think. Look by her left leg."

Mitch could see what looked like a hunting knife by her leg. "You got something over there?" he asked Mickey, who was now examining the bed with a magnifying glass on a head set.

"Couple of hairs," Chang grunted. "Looks to be from the victim."

Mitch nodded. It was too much to hope for that they might get some usable DNA. Careful not to disturb anything, he squatted tilting his head to see her right ankle. A small rose tattoo was visible, protruding from the plastic.

"Damn it, Bolton, get your fat ass out of the way," Ollie said, shouldering into the room. "You see the tattoo?" he asked.

Mitch nodded, slowly straightening. "Yeah," he said tiredly. "Looks right."

"So it's her?" Bolton asked.

"Don't you have anything better to do?" Mitch snapped.

"Yeah, I bet Harris' ass is getting cold. Best go back and re-apply your lips before he comes down with a case of rectal chaffing," Ollie added.

"Fuck you Olshan. You guys are using my people; I got every right to be here."

"If you want to stay here, start helping with the canvas of the neighborhood. Or better yet, get your fat ass down in the parking lot. We need every piece of trash picked up and bagged. Gonna be hard though, some dumbass parked a squad right in the middle of the parking lot."

Bolton's face flamed bright red, but he couldn't hold Ollie's cold stare. "Don't tie up all my people here all day. Your dog and pony show aside, we got real work to do."

"Yeah, blow me," Ollie said, waiting until Bolton was gone to add. "You know he's going to run to Harris and tell him everything."

Mitch shrugged. "Where is everybody?"

Ollie chuckled, shaking his head. "Parker made everyone park around back. Said you wanted to keep it quiet, and a herd of cop cars might tip off the media.

Mitch raised an eyebrow. "Not bad," he said. "I wasn't worried about the cars. What I meant is, where is everybody?"

"Parker had Jerry get the patrol guys started on the canvas. She put me to talking to the maid, and she took on Leroy."

"No shit? Leroy?" Mitch chuckled. "That'll be an eye-opener."

Ollie nodded. "Leroy can be hard to take if you don't know him."

"He can be hard to take if you do know him," Mitch agreed. "How's she doing?"

"She's doing alright. She had me and Jerry do a quick walk through, then she sent us off. She wanted to get Jerry looking for witnesses before they wandered away, went to work or some shit like that."

Mitch pursed his lips, that was good thinking. "What did you get from the maid? Anything good?"

Ollie rubbed his face. "Man, I don't know," he grumbled pulling out his notebook. "She said the room was vacant last night."

"Really?" Mitch said, going to the door. The door was old and scarred, but no fresh scratches.

"Guy either had a key or he was real good with a set of picks."

"You thinking Leroy?"

"Damn, I don't know. This is a little raw for him, and all the witnesses agreed, the man who snatched Angie was white." Mitch thought about it. Leroy Bell was a peeper and there had been a couple of rapes over the years that he had been suspected of.

"Guys like Leroy, it ain't rare that they move up. Starts with peeping and flashing, then you get a rape, and then a killing. Happens all the time."

Ollie was right. It was a pattern they had seen before. "Shall we go see how she's doing with him?"

"Might as well."

"Hey, Mickey, we're going down to see Leroy. You need anything?"

Mickey rose up taking off a headset with a magnifying glass attached. "Not that I can think of."

"Anything jumping out at you?"

Mickey nodded. "Yeah, the room is clean."

"How clean?"

"Two sets of prints in the whole place."

"No shit? Two sets?" Ollie grunted.

"Yup. Found them side by side on the bathroom mirror."

"Planted for us to find?"

"Good guess," Chang replied. "They were pretty good."

"Aw shit, we got a psycho," Olshan groaned.

"What about the body?" Mitch asked.

"Hard to tell with the plastic."

"What's up with that?" Ollie asked.

Chang shrugged. "Off hand, I'd say it was an attempt to slow down decomposition. Or maybe he was hoping to hold in the smell. Either way, it didn't work since he left the door partially open."

"Maybe the plastic was to move the body," Mitch said, thinking out loud. "Maybe it got light, he saw the maid coming, or something spooked him and he ran."

"Maybe," Mickey said, a doubtful look on his face. "If he's going to move her, why clean the room? Why leave the two sets of prints?"

"Shit, why would he leave those prints anyway?" Ollie wanted to know.

"Who knows?" Mitch said, glancing across at Mickey. "What's your plan on removing the plastic?"

"I'm waiting on a call back from Larry Hall." Larry Hall was the coroner. "I haven't got hold of him, but I'm thinking we wait. Take it off in the morgue. I'm hoping to save any evidence that might be trapped in the plastic."

"Sounds good, if Larry agrees," Mitch said.

"It'll slow down things. Identifying the body, getting the autopsy done. Might throw off TOD calculations." Mickey warned.

"Do what you have to do. Plastic is probably going to raise hell with the time of death anyway."

Outside Jacob Carter's Apartment Washington DC
June 25th 2010 Friday Night

Dykes pulled up to the crime scene, parking behind a squad car. For a long time, he sat in the car, staring blindly through the windshield. Harley gone, he couldn't believe it.

Shit, how many crime scenes had they been to together? Hundreds? Maybe more. Dykes sighed. Maybe it was only fitting they should say goodbye like this. Suddenly, Dykes felt very old and tired.

Sighing again, he pushed open the door. Out of habit, he flipped open his badge, hanging it from the breast pocket of his jacket. Dragging his feet, he headed toward Harley's car. Scott Bender stood at the rear of Harley's car. Dykes nodded unconsciously. Harley was in good hands. Bender and his partner Casper Macaulay were very good.

"You guys catch the case?" Dykes asked.

Bender looked up, nodding his head. "Man, I'm sorry. I know you guys were tight."

"Yeah man, sorry," Marty Wills the coroner called from the front of the car.

"Yeah," Dykes said tightly. "Look, I don't want to step on you guys."

Bender snorted, waving a hand. "Don't worry about it. We know you are going to want to be in on bringing the little prick down."

"Thanks, Scotty," Dykes replied quietly. "So what happened?"

"Looks like he had just got here. He'd bought one of those nasty-assed sandwiches, but hadn't taken a bite."

They shared a quick laugh. "He hadn't been here long," Dykes agreed. "He loved those sandwiches, I thought they smelled like a duck's ass, but Harley loved them. I saw him eat six one right after the other." Dykes felt himself rambling, and stopped taking a deep breath. "How did it go down?"

"Looks like the shooter just walked up and stuck a gun in the window. One shot. He never saw it coming. I doubt if he even felt it."

"Thank God for that." Dykes jerked his head in the direction of Carter's apartment. "Any chance the little prick didn't do it?"

Bender shrugged. "His wallet, gun and badge are gone. Coulda been a robbery. You might know more than me. You guys have anything on the prick that might have him worried?"

"Not really, but Harley liked to call him. Jerk him around. Maybe he pushed a button. But I guarantee you, that little prick up there is the one who did this," Dykes shouted, jabbing a finger at Carter's window. "He just took the stuff to throw us off." Dykes paused, thinking about it. "Although, he might want to keep Harley's badge."

"If he did, then we got his little ass. We were on the scene less than thirty minutes after the shooting went down. He was home when we got here; we've had somebody watching him."

"You got people combing the neighborhood for Harley's shit?"

Bender nodded. "Twenty uniforms. The stuff can't be far. Carter made a nine-one-one call. Comparing his call to the two others that came in, he called in within seconds of the shooting."

Dykes looked up at the window, thinking it through. "Trying to build an alibi. He did that with Salters. Used the phone to set up some kind of a half-assed alibi."

"Won't work," Bender assured. "We got him sewed up. No kind of alibi is going to make GSR go away. Mac's getting a search warrant and an order to do a GSR test. Soon as he gets here, we're going in."

Dykes nodded, but he didn't share Bender's optimism. He and Harley had been chasing Carter a long time. It didn't seem right that it should be so easy. "We got anything from the scene?

Bender shook his head. "Naw, not much. I'm guessing the killer came out of the alley. Asphalt back there, so no foot prints. When he came out of the alley, he would have been almost on top of Harley's car. He walks up, fires, and grabs Harley's stuff. Wouldn't take but a few seconds."

"You said some witnesses called it in. They any good?"

Bender pursed his lips, looking down the street. "That's kind of funny. They all agreed. Tall man wearing a blue hooded sweatshirt. Hood was up, so we got no race or hair color. Funny thing is, Carter gave that exact same description on his nine-one-one call."

Dykes shrugged. "Well, Carter knew what he was wearing. And he didn't really give us anything. Of course, if he has a blue sweatshirt."

"And it tests positive for GSR nitrates, we got his ass," Bender agreed. "The tall bit worries me, though. Carter ain't exactly tall."

They were just talking, killing time. No case ever fit together perfectly. There were always problems, especially where witnesses were involved. It would be something for the lawyers to argue over. If Carter came back positive for the nitrates, he was gone.

Dykes looked to the front of the car. He heaved his shoulders. He had been dreading this part. He blew out a heavy sigh. "I got to see him."

"Yeah, I know," Bender said quietly. "It ain't bad."

Dykes tugged down his jacket, walking slowly to the front of the car.

"Sorry, man," Wills said, twisting a pair of gloves in his hands as he stepped back away from the car.

Dykes nodded, taking a deep breath. He glanced in at Harley slumped over the wheel. "Looks like he's just drunk," Dykes said, avoiding looking at the puckered hole behind Harley's left ear.

"Yeah, bet he's slept a few nights like this," Bender said.

Dykes chuckled. "You know, right now, where ever he's at; he's pissed about that sandwich."

They laughed. A little too loud and a little long. It was Bender who turned serious. He awkwardly squeezed Dykes' arm. "Harley was a good guy. Tonight we're gonna nail that little prick's ass to the wall and tomorrow night we are going to raise a glass to Harley."

"I'm buying the first round," Dykes said as Casper Macaulay screeched up to the crime scene.

He jumped out while the car was still rocking, waving a handful of paper over his head. "Got 'em. Search warrant for the apartment and his car."

"What about the GSR?" Bender asked, excitement riding into his voice.

"In the bag," Macaulay said holding the papers a little higher.

"Let's go jack that little fucker up."

Starlight Motel Tucson AZ June 13th 2018
Wednesday Mid-Morning

"So what do you make of this?" Ollie asked as they descended the stairs.

"Something seems wrong," Mitch answered, knowing Ollie was feeling the same thing.

Ollie nodded. "I thought we were on to something with the idea that she might have been grabbed to squeeze her old man." Ollie stopped at the bottom of the stairs. "This seems like something different. Like a psycho."

"Yeah. Maybe we were just hoping it had something to do with Brody. We knew all along if it was a psycho, she was as good as dead," Mitch replied, but he felt a tickle along the back of his neck. They were missing something.

"If it's a psycho, this won't be the end of it. You know there will be more."

"I know," Mitch said, not liking the thought.

They entered the office to a strange scene. Leroy Bell, a tall black man with a bullet-shaped bald head and huge, sloping shoulders was backed into a corner of the tiny office. Leroy had long arms and big hands. At the moment he was clutching his right hand to his stomach. From the door, Mitch could see the hand was swelling, an angry welt rising on the back of the hand.

Carly leaned against the counter, a satisfied smirk on her face as she tapped a telescoping baton in her hand. "What happened, Leroy?" Mitch asked cheerfully. "You get stung by a bee?"

"Bee my ass! Bitch hit me! That's police brutality."

"Yeah, and what did you do?" Olshan asked, a dangerous edge riding his voice.

"Nothin'," Leroy replied sullenly. "Maybe, I tried to grab her ass a little."

"You want to try again?" Carly asked, the smirk still on her face as she raised the baton.

Leroy actually seemed to be considering the question. "I dunno, it's a nice ass."

Mitch laughed, taking Leroy's hand. "I bet you will live," he said, looking at the hand. "Now, we need to know about the dead girl."

"Man, I don't know nothin' 'bout that!"

Mitch gave Leroy's hand a quick, hard squeeze. "Are you sure about that?" he asked softly, watching the bigger man wince. "You sure that wasn't one of your girls?"

Leroy jerked his hand away, trying to back away. "No way, man. I tell you, I don't know anything. Far as I knew, that room was empty."

"Are you sure?" Carly asked, pressing forward. "It seems highly unlikely that someone could break into that room without you knowing about it."

Leroy shrugged. "I was watching WWF."

"Don't give us that shit!" Ollie snapped. "You have to keep an eye on your girls."

As Leroy shrugged again, Mitch leaned back against a scarred coke machine. "Leroy, there is only two ways this is going to go down," he said, speaking very softly. "You keep jerking us around, and I will haul your ass in right now. You will be charged as an accessory."

"Never stick," Leroy said, unconcerned.

"Shit with your record, I can't hardly believe you weren't involved," Olshan said, his voice sounding like ice breaking. "I bet when a jury finds out that you like showing your dick to little girls at the bus stop, they will believe it too."

"I know the law. You can't say that shit in court about me." He circled behind the counter, waving them away. "I got work to do."

Mitch pushed away from the coke machine grabbing Leroy's shirt jerking him up against the counter. "If you do beat it, I will personally see that there is a squad car with two officers inside parked right outside. They will be there all night every night for a month. Let's see how much business your girls do then."

"Man, that ain't right," Leroy howled.

Now it was Mitch's turn to shrug. "Too bad. Of course, if you were to give us something we can use, I'd give you and your girls a free pass next time they get picked up."

Leroy licked his lips. "No shit? A free pass?"

Mitch nodded taking out one of his cards, holding it out. "All you have to do is call me."

Leroy took the card, staring at it a pained expression on his face. "Damn, Mitch, I keep telling you I don't know nothing. I ain't rented that room but once in a year."

"Really?" Carly sneered. "This place? I'm shocked that you aren't full every night." She glanced at Mitch. "He's lying."

"No, I ain't!" Leroy protested. "That wasn't one of my girls, they like the rooms close to the office, so's if they get in trouble they can yell and I will come running."

"What about travelers?" Ollie demanded. "Don't you get any of them?"

"Sure, we get a few, but they all got suitcases and shit. They want to be on the ground floor or close to the stairs. Nobody wants that back room. I tell you, I only rented it once in forever."

"When was the last time you rented that room?"

"Couple of nights ago. Dude requested it."

"This dude. What did he look like?"

A foxy look sprang to Leroy's face. "If I tell you what he looked like, that get me and the girls that free pass you was talking 'bout?"

Mitch tapped the card. "If the description is good, all you got to do is call me."

Leroy grinned, stuffing the card into his pocket. "I tell you one thing, now that I think about it, that mother fucker looked like a killer. Mother fucker looked like somebody that could cut your heart out and laugh while he done it."

"Okay," Mitch said, making a rolling motion with his hand. "What did he look like?"

"He wasn't tall, but he wasn't short neither. Bout medium, I guess. He wasn't a big feller, but he was solid. Looked like he worked out. Moved like he had some game. He'd be quick."

"What did he look like? What color was his hair?"

"Dark hair, and he looked like a white boy. Not some cracker, but a rich boy."

"How was he dressed?"

"Like a banker. Had a suit coat, but he had some style too. I thought he was a dealer."

Mitch nodded, that fit right in with what Darla Pringle and Lindsey Meredith had said. "What was he driving?"

"Black car. I don't know what kind."

"You got a check-in card?" Ollie asked.

Leroy sighed. "Mighta throwed it away."

"Yeah right," Ollie growled, smacking the counter with his palm. "Give us the damn card."

Shaking his head, Leroy dug in a cardboard box, grinning sheepishly, he passed the card over. Mitch smiled grimly. He knew Leroy had been hoping to hang onto the card and use it later to get a better deal. Mitch took the card, glancing down at it. "Justin Carter?" he said reading the name on the card. He glanced at Carly and Ollie, but they both shook their heads.

"He pay cash?" Mitch asked, and Leroy nodded. Mitch turned the card over in his hands. The card said black Nissan with Arizona plates. "Probably a rental, but we can check it out. Maybe the rental company keeps better records than Leroy."

"Hey, man, I gave you the dude's car."

"Yeah," Mitch said dryly. "You think of anything else or you hear anything, you call me. Pass the word, there's something good in it for anyone that can give us this dude."

Leroy was nodding as they left, but Mitch knew, he wouldn't pass the word. He wouldn't want word getting out he was friendly with cops. "He knows something more," Mitch observed.

"Maybe," Ollie agreed. "Be strange if this guy picked this place out of the blue. I bet he's been here before. Maybe he's been here with some of Leroy's girls."

"So Leroy is a pimp?" Carly asked.

"Not really," Ollie replied. "Some independents use this place. They give Leroy a kick back and probably some action on the side. For that he will come running if a john gets out of line."

Jerry Hartek wandered up, munching on an ice cream bar. "Let me guess, you got nothing," Ollie said.

Jerry finished his ice cream, flipping the stick in the direction of the trash can. "Less than that," he said around a mouthful of ice cream. "You guys get anything we can work?"

"Got a plate number and a name," Mitch said. "I want you and Carly to start working on the car. See where that leads. Maybe we can trace a credit card, if the car is a rental. Check with Linda, see if she got any hits from the prints they lifted from the room." Mitch turned to Ollie. "You want to babysit things here. See if anything else comes out of the room, maybe roust out Leroy's girls. See if they know anything."

"Sure thing boss."

"I've got some paperwork to do, and I want to see if the Feds have anything on a Justin Carter."

Jacob Carter's Apartment Washington DC June 26th 2010 Saturday After Midnight

After six hours of searching, they were calling it a night. Nobody wanted to give up, but they had to face facts. They weren't finding anything. They hadn't found anything in Carter's apartment or in the surrounding neighborhood.

Scott Bender leaned against his car, sighing as he stared up at Carter's apartment. "Maybe we got to face it. Maybe the little prick didn't do it."

"No," Dykes said, feeling tired as death. "He's too smug. He did it."

"I don't know," Casper Macaulay said. "He passed the GSR. Can't fake that. I hate to admit it, but I don't think he did it."

"Oh, he did it. He just had help."

Tucson AZ June 13th 2018 Wednesday Evening

Mitch pulled up to a small warehouse just off Tucson Boulevard. He screeched to a halt beside a Camry with temporary plates. "Son of a bitch!" he grunted slapping the steering wheel. "A fucking new car!"

Grinding his teeth and glaring at the new Toyota, Mitch climbed out of the Mustang. "Fucking, Stansford." Shaking his head and his hands balling into fists, Mitch stalked up to the door, kicking it open with his foot.

"Terry, you son of a bitch!"

"Mitch, that you?" a voice called from an office off to the left.

"Yeah, it's me," Mitch said, still yelling as he stormed into the office. He stopped short as he saw Stansford totaling up a stack of checks. Beside the calculator were several stacks of cash. The cash was divided into stacks of twenties, tens, and ones.

Terry pulled a hundred dollar bill out of the stack of checks, placing it in a new stack. "Hey Mitch, how's it going?"

Mitch slapped the desk. "Not very fucking good. Not with my partner stealing from me!"

Startled, Terry looked up. "Stealing from you? Shit Mitch, what are you talking about?"

Mitch flipped the money into Terry's lap with a savage sweep of his hand. "That's what the fuck I'm talking about!"

"The cash? Damn dude, that's just business."

"Business, my ass!" Mitch shouted. "Don't fuck with me. I know all about you sending guys out to sell the stuff out the back door."

Terry scooped the money off his lap, dumping it back on the desk. Leaning back in his chair, he ran a hand through his thinning hair and laughed. "Shit Mitch, that's how it's done."

"Don't shit me, man. I saw the new car you're driving."

"So I bought a new car, so what? Man, business is doing good."

"Not from my end. I haven't seen any money. That start-up money wasn't all mine. I have people to answer to."

"Well like I said, business is good. Damn good"

"For you!" Mitch sputtered. He stepped forward, putting on his cop face and crowding Stansford. "Don't fuck with me, Terry. I'm not in the mood to hear any of your bullshit. I know you got people out selling the stuff on the sly."

Terry chuckled. "Sit down man, have a beer," Terry said, swiveling to a small frig behind his desk. "Ok, man, let me explain how this works." He passed a beer to Mitch and opened one for himself.

Mitch twisted the top off his beer, tossing the lid forcibly at the trash can. "So, explain it to me," he said in a nasty sarcastic tone.

"Okay," Terry said, blowing out a sigh. "See, this is how it works. We got ten trucks. They go out every day."

"We bought ten trucks?"

"Oh, shit no, we leased 'em. Fleet lease, dirt cheap," Terry said, his tone that of a teacher explaining something simple to a dim child. "Okay, the trucks go out, two or three guys in a truck and they sell the meat.'

"You mean door to door?"

"Sure," Terry said, shrugging, and taking a big hit off his beer. "They make up some bullshit story like they missed a delivery at a restaurant. That the restaurant will only take deliveries between certain hours and they missed it."

"Is that true? About the restaurants?"

Terry took a quick angry drink. "How the fuck should I know? Who the fuck cares. Just listen. So they make up some bullshit story and offer the customer a really good deal."

"Why make up a story."

"Cause the deal sucks and if people thought about it, nobody would buy the meat." Terry finished his beer, launching the bottle in the direction of the trashcan before heaving himself up out of his chair. "Come back with me," he said. He pushed through a scarred door and into the warehouse bay. Scattered about the bay were several small pickups. In the back of each truck was a chest type freezer. A cord ran from each freezer to a rat's nest of cords plugged into one outlet.

"That up to fire code?" Mitch asked, pointing to the jumble.

"Blow me," Terry grumbled, climbing into the back of one of the trucks. He opened one of the freezers, pulling out a box. "These are the boxes," he said, holding it up.

"Yeah, I know. I've seen them, remember?"

Terry ignored Mitch's grumbling, running a hand over the box, as he balanced it on the edge of the pickup bed. "Our people go out and sell these. For each box they sell, we get one hundred and eighty dollars. Anything they get over that, they can keep."

"Okay," Mitch said, nodding. He'd heard all of this before, when he put up his money. "So why make up a bullshit story?"

Terry grinned, looking over his shoulder quickly. "Makes folks think they are getting a good deal." He paused looking around again, then slapped the box. "How much meat do you think is in here?"

Mitch shrugged, setting his beer down and stepping forward, as he eyed the box. "I don't know, sixty pounds."

Terry laughed, slapping the box again. "Shit no, twenty-two pounds!"

"Damn," Mitch grunted, doing a fast calculation. "That's over eight bucks a pound."

Terry nodded, still grinning. "Score one for the jock."

"How the hell do we sell it?"

"Hell man, they don't never mention anything about the pounds. They spread the meat out." Terry opened the box, pulling out a couple of pieces of meat. "See how it's individually wrapped, you spread it out, looks like a lot, and you just keep saying what a good deal they are getting."

"And that works?"

Terry grinned, nodding his head furiously. "Damn straight, make folks think they are screwing you, and they can't wait to hand over their money. First rule of business."

"What do you know about the rules of business? Closest you ever came to a college was when you were hustling those porno calendars."

"Hey we made money on those."

Mitch laughed, they had, and it'd been fun too. Terry might not have been to school, but Mitch was sure the man knew more about making money than most big time CEOs. "So all of this," Mitch said, waving his hand at the meat spread out. "This works?"

Terry was practically beaming now. "I guess it does. I got three or four guys who go out and sell three boxes every day. I got one girl who does five." Terry dropped his voice to a whisper. "I think she might be throwing in a hand job with each box."

"Aw, shit, really? You're kidding me?" Mitch asked, groaning.

Terry shrugged, and began tossing the meat back in the box. "Don't know and don't care. I don't think she is, but that is a rumor. Personally, I think she wears these low cut tank tops and shakes her tits a little and that's all it takes." Terry licked his lips, looking over his shoulder. "I swear, she's got a set of jugs that would give a boner to a statue."

Terry jumped down from the truck. "Anyway, I'm sending out fifteen, twenty guys a day, and they sell thirty to forty boxes every day. Business is good."

"So why do I have to hear about it on the street?"

"When was the last time you checked your email, dickhead?"

"You ever read the papers, asshole?" Mitch shot back, an easy smile slipping onto his face. "I been kinda busy. So what did you email me?"

"Come back to the office," Terry said, leading the way. "You want another beer?"

"Naw, soon as we finish here, I gotta get back at it."

"Gonna find that girl?" Terry asked, digging himself another beer out of the frig.

"That's the plan."

"Luck with that," Terry grunted, dropping heavily into his chair.

"Man you gotta get in shape," Mitch said, watching the sweat squeeze out of every pore on the big man's face.

"Kiss my ass, round is a shape." Terry took a long hit off his beer, smacking his lips. "Anyway, I been depositing the checks, and we are showing a small profit just off the checks, but the cash?" Terry fished out a key and opened a desk drawer. "This is what I emailed you about. We definitely need to talk about this."

"Holy shit!" Mitch exclaimed, gazing in at the drawer full of cash.

"Damn straight, holy shit," Terry said, licking his lips. "Now, we can deposit all this cash, pay the taxes on it or…."

"Or we what?"

"Well, we are showing a profit, just off the checks, course wouldn't look right if we didn't deposit some cash." Terry paused, licking his lips again. "I was thinking we deposit." More lip licking. "Maybe half the cash. Books would look real good and we could split the rest."

"What's the cut today?" Mitch asked, absently rubbing his chin.

"Not counting today's take almost ten grand. We put half of that in the bank; we could walk away with twenty-five hundred each."

"I've got a couple of investors to think of," Mitch said, thinking it over.

Terry shrugged his heavy shoulders. "It's off the books, so if you wanted, you could just slip it into your pocket." Terry grinned spreading his hands under Mitch's scowl. "Hey cut them in, it's up to you." Terry took a hit off his beer, licking his lips again. "So what do you want to do?"

"Let's do it," Mitch decided. "I better not find out your skimming the cash, though.

Terry shrugged spreading his hands again. "Hey, it's me, you can trust me."

"Yeah, 'bout as far as I can throw your ass," Mitch grumbled but with a good-natured smile, as he watched Terry count out the money. Taking the money, Mitch started to leave, then stopped. "You say you got people going door to door?"

"That's how it's done."

Looking out at the empty lot, Mitch banged the palm of his hand on the push bar of the door. He snapped his fingers, and then pointed at Terry. "What time do your people head out?"

"Eight, eight-thirty."

Mitch nodded. "Okay, I'll have some pictures brought by. You pass them out, tell your people to keep their eyes open. Be some good money in it for whoever gives us something we can use."

"This about that Brody girl?"

"Yeah, we need to find her. She's running out of time."

"Okay, but keep the money small. Make it too much and we'll have everybody driving around on our gas looking for her and nobody selling meat."

"Okay, on second thought, I think I'll send somebody over in the morning, give your people a briefing."

Perry Van Zandt's House Washington DC June 26th 2010 Saturday Morning

Perry Van Zandt needed a drink. He poured himself a snifter of cognac, his hand shaking, as he downed the brandy in one long drink.

The drink warmed his stomach, but Van Zandt still felt a chill. A part of Van Zandt recognized the fact that it was warm in the room. He knew, it was the stress and the adrenaline bleeding off which gave him the chill.

Despite the knowledge, he flipped the switch, turning on the gas fireplace and poured himself another drink. Backed up to the fire, Van Zandt sipped this drink and stared at the gun.

Ugly was the word that came to mind. Short and stubby, with the front sight protruding like a malformed buck tooth, the revolver looked ready to attack on its own. It seemed to pulsate energy, like a living, hating thing. Just sitting there, the gun looked like it wanted to kill something.

Van Zandt picked it up. Ugly in one way but strangely beautiful in another. Built for one purpose, to kill a man. Van Zandt rubbed the barrel against his cheek, replaying the incident in his mind. One minute the fat cop was there, then bang! He was gone forever.

The killing had been satisfying, but not in the way Van Zandt had imagined. Standing in the alley as the cop drove up, knowing he, Perry Van Zandt had the final decision whether this man lived or died, and that had been extremely satisfying. The thought that a person lived only on his whim, had given him an erection.

The killing itself had been somewhat of a disappointment. Van Zandt had defended killers for years, listened to them talk, and he had wondered. At the time somewhere in the back of his mind, Van Zandt had known that someday, he would kill someone, just to see what it was like. Van Zandt had seen no light leaving the body, felt nothing about it. No rapture. The man had simply died, expelling his bodily gasses in one long disgusting fart.

Van Zandt felt no revelation, no translucent moment, nothing. But Van Zandt did realize one thing. Killing was a handy tool. The fat cop had been making trouble for Carter, and now he was gone. Problem solved. Interesting.

Van Zandt glanced at the gun in his hand. He should get rid of it. If the cops found it here, he would be gone. "Shit!" Van Zandt exclaimed, spilling his drink on a two thousand dollar rug. He was handling the gun without his gloves.

He hurriedly picked up the cheap sweatshirt, wiping the gun down with quick vicious swipes. Stupid, he knew better. He should get rid of it, drop it in the river.

But he wasn't going to. There was more than one way to use a gun. This one might come in handy later.

Biltmore Hotel Phoenix AZ June 13th 2018
Wednesday Evening

Jackson was more comfortable this time. He had the good Senator. In the past few hours, he'd replayed their earlier meeting. Over and over he'd ran the encounter through his head. She'd postured and looked down on him, but in the end, she had caved.

The Senator had tried to control things and keep him in his place, but she'd had no choice but to give in. Jackson realized, now, that he had asked for too little. Now was his time. Jackson bounced on his toes as he rode the elevator up. Suddenly and for the first time in his life Jackson felt confident. He felt powerful.

Jackson thought about the Senator. She wasn't exactly a handsome woman. He licked his lips with a quick darting motion. He'd never bedded a powerful woman like the Senator. Jackson licked his lips again. Something to think about.

She'd be soft. Pale breasts, with dainty pink nipples. In his mind he could see it. She'd put perfume between her breasts. Something classy. Channel Number 5. Jackson closed his eyes. He could smell the perfume. He jumped as the elevator dinged, and the door slid open.

A very tan woman clutching a hairless dog stood in front of the elevator. "Excuse me," Jackson muttered, edging past her as she barged in. Momentarily disorientated, it took him a few seconds to realize, he had gotten off on the wrong floor. "Fuck," he muttered, stabbing the button to return the elevator car. Feeling stupid, he tapped his foot, looking around while he waited.

Once back in the car, he took a moment to gather himself. This was his day! Today was his future. What was that old line? This is the first day of the rest of your life. Jackson could feel it. The future was his. He had the power, after all. Darby Lewis could kiss his ass. In fact, all of them could kiss his ass.

Jackson strode out of the elevator with a purpose. This time the guards showed the proper respect. After a quick frisk, they opened the door. "Go on in, Mister Pyle. She's waiting on you."

"Thanks," Jackson said, then immediately regretted it. He didn't have to talk to them anymore.

The Senator was sitting behind a desk, looking at a file. She's waiting, Jackson thought. She doesn't want me to know it, but she has been waiting for me. Now Jackson wished he had taken more time. Let the bitch wait.

Glancing up, she held up her hand, and then looked back down at the file. Jackson smiled letting her have her moment. While she pretended to read, he studied her. She was dressed in a white, silk blouse, and a dark skirt with tiny pinstripes. The top two buttons of the shirt were open, affording Jackson a view of cleavage. Self-consciously, Jackson looked, wondering if it were deliberate. Maybe. He stared at her, his tongue snaking across his suddenly dry lips.

Senator Braxton looked up suddenly, catching Jackson staring. With a tisking sound of annoyance she leaned back, pulling the shirt together. Smiling at the scathing look she was branding him with, Jackson stepped up to the desk. "Good afternoon, Senator."

"Did you bring it?" she snapped.

Jackson surveyed the room before answering. While still far nicer than any room Jackson had ever stayed in, this was obviously a scaled down operation. "You're not going to offer me a drink or a snack this time?" he asked, enjoying the moment.

Without bothering to answer, Braxton pushed back from the desk. She stalked to the small frig in the corner. She pulled a bottle of water from the frig and tossed it to Jackson. "I'm waiting."

Jackson took a drink from the water then set it on the desk. The Senator stood, arms folded across her chest, tapping her foot. Jackson smiled at her. "Okay, then." He dug into his soft, leather briefcase. The briefcase was new, bought this very morning. Inside were two folders. Jackson chose the plain manila one. Drawing the folder out of the case slowly, Jackson showed it to her, then dropped it on the desk. She started forward, but Jackson slapped his hand down on the folder. "First things first. I showed you mine, now it's your turn to show me yours." Jackson let the innuendo hang in the air for a moment. "Where's the money?"

"Of course, the money," she said, contempt practically dripping from her words. She picked up a flat case, the kind used by architects and artists. The zipper was open and she pulled back the flap, revealing some papers. "Bearer bonds. Harder to trace than cash."

"Of course," Jackson said, like he used them every day. When in fact all he knew about them was what he had seen on TV. Taking the case, he used his finger to flick the file to her.

"I trust this is the only copy."

Jackson had been thumbing through the bonds, now he looked up and smiled. He'd practiced this part. "Might be."

Senator Braxton slammed the file down on the desk. Her teeth barred she took a step forward. She was close enough that Jackson caught the faint whiff of cigarette smoke on her breath. Funny, in her campaign she railed nonstop against the tobacco industry.

"Listen, you creepy little shit, if you think for a second that I'm going to continue paying you, you're crazy. I could snap my fingers and you'd be dead within the hour."

Jackson had been expecting the anger, but her condescension startled him. Pissed him off in fact. For a second he seriously considered killing her. Be so easy to snap her neck. The thought of killing her calmed him, and he managed a thin smile. He picked up his briefcase, pulling out the other folder. "You kill me and this will be what's on the front page of my paper tomorrow."

A pained frown shot across her face as she snatched the folder from him. "I've already filed that story in my email. It goes to my editor in about two hours. Of course, I could always stop it. Maybe replace it with a one on one interview with you."

Jackson waited while she scanned the article. He hadn't held back one bit. Normally Jackson would have parceled out the information, stretching out into two or three stories.

But for this, Jackson wanted the big bang. He needed to shock the Senator. Besides if the story was ever printed, that would mean he was dead. If that were the case, he wanted to make sure he took the bitch down hard.

Jackson watched her read. She was breathing hard, and her blouse had gaped open again. Jackson stepped up next to her. "Interesting read. Don't you think?" Jackson touched the lapel of her blouse, rolling the fabric between his fingers. Braxton flinched but didn't pull away as he pulled her blouse open a fraction wider. "People who work for you don't stick around long. Pretty high death rate."

"You swine," she spat at him, knocking his hand away. "Don't touch me."

"What's the matter, Senator? Don't you find me attractive?" Jackson grinned at her. "You might stay out of jail, but you can kiss the Presidency goodbye if this comes out."

"You're bluffing," Braxton sneered. "You don't have any real proof. Nothing that would stand up in court."

Jackson touched her blouse again, this time resting the edge of his hand on the top of her breast. "I don't know about that. I bet that nice lady in Kinko's would remember Forsyth. What do you think?"

Jackson caressed the top of her breast. "The question is; how bad do you want to be President."

CHAPTER FOUR

Mitch's House Tucson AZ June 14th 2018 Thursday Early Morning

Mitch picked up his phone, still feeling groggy. "Somebody better be dead," he snapped hoarsely.

"Mitch, we got big trouble," a harried voice which Mitch recognized but couldn't quite place said.

Mitch sat up finally placing the voice of Olshan. "Ollie, is that you?"

"Fuck yeah, it's me, but it ain't her."

"Isn't who? What the hell are you talking about?" Mitch asked, tucking the phone under his chin and rubbing his eyes. "It's too fucking early for playing games."

"The hotel chick. It ain't her. Angie Brody. It ain't her," Ollie said, his voice rising.

"Aw shit," Mitch said, swinging out of bed. "How sure are you?"

"Pretty near dead fucking certain. Larry Hall is doing the autopsy right now. We took finger prints off the body and compared them to the ones Angie Brody gave on her college dorm check in last year. I ain't an expert, but me and Larry both agree, it ain't her. Shit you saw her face, her own mother wouldn't recognize her, but it don't really look like her neither. Mickey is coming in to double check the prints, should be here in about an hour. Larry took some dental molds. I was thinking maybe I should run them over to her dentist?"

"Yeah, go," Mitch said, stumbling into the bathroom.

"It gets worse," Ollie said. "The Citizen has a big story plastered across the front page, saying it is her." Ollie paused to let that settle, before dropping the second half of his bomb. "They quote Harris directly on that."

"Aw shit. I told the stupid fucker to hold off. I had a feeling about this." Stifling a yawn, Mitch flipped on the coffee machine. "Alright the damage is done. Let's get going on the confirmation that it isn't her. Who else is there?"

"Hartek. I think maybe Wade is in."

"Okay, good. Have Jerry get the ball rolling on nailing down who she is. Run the prints through FBI, DOJ, State Police, everybody. We'll need some face shots of the body. Start going through missing persons reports. Hell you know the drill, just get it done."

"We're on it. Hartek is calling Parksy in right now. We figured we need to get this nailed down quick."

"Good thinking, anybody you need, grab them. I'm going to take a quick shower. Have someone call me when Larry is done with the autopsy."

"What about the press? Them fuckers are going to crucify us."

"Don't worry about them for now. Let's just get on top of this."

Mitch killed the phone. He stumbled outside in his boxers to grab the judge's paper. Looking both ways, he ran across the yard and snagged the paper. If the judge caught him, he'd ride Mitch about it forever. Carrying the paper inside, Mitch poured a cup of coffee. Digging through the frig, he found some lunch meat that he didn't remember buying, but didn't seem too old. Sipping his coffee and munching on the meat, Mitch quickly scanned the article. It was written by Tom Black. Tom was an old hand, and put together a compelling story. It bothered Mitch a little that he didn't come off to well in the story.

Mitch smiled at that. He would break it off in that little prick, Black. Fucking asshole should have called to confirm his story. It was Mitch's case after all. Mitch reread the story, thinking how to handle it. Black indeed quoted Harris on the identification of Angie Brody. As he showered, an idea beginning to form. He began rehearsing what he would say in his mind. Would be nice if they could ID the girl before he spoke with the press. Either way he'd stick it to both Black and Harris.

The phone was ringing when Mitch stepped out of the shower. Drying his hair with one hand, Mitch picked up the phone. "Yeah," he grunted, tossing the towel in the corner.

"You wanted us to call?" Parker said.

"Yeah, what else came out of the autopsy?"

"A couple of things." Mitch could hear paper rustling as she flipped through her notebook. "She was strangled, but that wasn't cause of death. Cause of death was…"

"Blood loss," Mitch guessed. "Probably from the stab wound."

"You got it," Parker confirmed. "Larry thinks she was strangled more than once."

"So he was torturing her?"

"That was Larry's thought, probably while he was raping her."

"Maybe not," Mitch said, thinking ahead. "We might want to be prepared for a video to show up. I don't think he would tape himself doing that."

"A tape," Parker said, and Mitch could hear her curse under her breath. "Why the hell would he do that?"

"I'm thinking about Angie Brody. I think this girl was a message to her old man."

"Step in line or this is what is going to happen to your little girl."

"That's what I'm thinking."

"So why the fuck doesn't he step in line?" Parker growled, and Mitch could feel her indignation over the phone.

He shrugged to himself, whishing he had the answer. "That's the question."

Thirty minutes later, Mitch eased the Mustang into the back of the station. Now, he was glad he hadn't driven the car much. None of the press parked out front gave it a second glance. Several TV trucks were parked in front of the station. Now that Harris had tied Angie Brody in with the motel case, they were circling.

As Mitch climbed out of the car, his cell chirped with a text for the third time. With a glance Mitch saw it was Harris' extension. Just as he had the last two, Mitch cleared the number off the screen.

Mitch barely stepped into the building before Bolton scurried up to him. "Commander Harris is waiting in the chief's office," he said, sounding like a parrot. "You better hurry. They've been waiting for quite some time. I texted you several times," he squawked as Mitch veered over towards the doughnuts.

Mitch ignored him, picking through the doughnuts. "Sergeant, they are waiting," Bolton said, tapping his foot.

"Sure," Mitch said, taking a cup of coffee and spearing a couple of doughnuts with the other hand. He started towards the chief's office, dragging along in Bolton's wake. When his cell rang, Mitch stopped, trying to balance the doughnuts and coffee in one hand while he dug out the cell with the other. "Tell them I'll be right in."

"But they are waiting."

"Bolton, they want a report on the motel killing. Right?" Mitch added, and Bolton nodded. "Well, if I take this call, I might have something to report."

Mitch answered his phone ignoring Bolton, who stood open-mouthed. "Go," Mitch said knowing it was Olshan. Apparently Bolton thought Mitch was talking to him, because he scurried away.

"Just leaving Doctor Weinstein's office now. Hotel chick definitely wasn't Angie Brody."

"Okay, get back here. Let's see if we can pin down who she was."

Killing the phone, Mitch headed to the chief's office. He entered munching on a doughnut. Harris was pacing the floor and he took a step towards Mitch. "Mitchell, where the hell have you been?"

Mitch ignored him, dropping into a chair across from the chief. Harris crossed to stand beside the chief, looking down on Mitch. "We've got half the press in town out there. Your guys have been running on this for over a day. Tell me you got something."

Mitch finished his doughnut, licking his fingers. When he spoke, he directed his words to the chief. "We got something, but it ain't good. Dead chick in the hotel wasn't Angie Brody."

Mitch ignored Harris, watching the red color of anger spread across the chief's face. "That wasn't what I read in the paper this morning," the chief said quietly.

Mitch shrugged, knowing the ball was in Harris' court. "You told me it was her," Harris said, meekly.

"No, you said it was her. I told said sure it looked like it could be Angie Brody and that we were operating under the assumption it was her. I never told you to go blabbing to the press it was her."

"We had to tell them something," Harris protested.

"I don't believe that we did," Mitch shot back.

The chief held up his hand. "Doesn't matter now, but for the record, I agree with Mitch. We didn't have to tell them something we weren't sure about." Harris started to protest, but the chief cut him off with a savage gesture. "The question is, how do we handle it?"

"I can handle the press," Mitch said. "I spoke with Brody, last night and again this morning. He knows that we were never certain it was his daughter."

"Do you think that was wise? We may be on shaky ground any way. There's a good chance he might sue."

"Sue for what?" Mitch countered. "Because the newspapers got it wrong? We can't be held responsible for that. Besides, trust me, he ain't gonna sue."

"And why is that?" Harris demanded with a sneer.

"Because he's involved," the chief said quietly. "That's what this is all about, isn't it?"

Mitch nodded. "I figure the girl in the motel was a message to him."

"If you don't step up, this is what's going to happen to your daughter."

Mitch grimly nodded again. "Something along those lines."

"So what are they wanting him to do?" the chief asked.

"I'm not sure. I've got my guys going through his finances right now. Maybe it's there."

"What about Brody himself. What's he saying?"

Mitch shrugged. "Right now he isn't saying anything."

"Anyway we can force him to talk?" Harris asked.

"I don't know," Mitch said, sipping his coffee. "Right now we don't have any leverage."

"His daughter isn't enough leverage?" Harris asked.

"Doesn't seem to be. Judging from the dead girl in the motel, he ain't giving them what they want." Mitch's phone rang as he finished speaking. "Maybe we have some news," he said opening the phone.

"This can't be good," the chief predicted, watching Mitch as he took the call.

"Sir, perhaps we need to re-think the direction of this investigation," Harris suggested.

"You think you could do better?" the chief asked mildly, as Mitch moved to the other side of the office.

"With all due respect, I believe I could. Detective Mitchell and his team seem to be spinning their wheels here. They should be out looking for the man who took Angie Brody, not investigating her father."

The chief sighed, digging in his humidor for a cigar. "Try one of these," Mitch said, extending a cigar as he shut his phone down with a practiced one handed swipe. "They're Havana's. Got them from a buddy."

"Thanks," the chief said, peeling off the label.

"Don't thank me; you're going to need it."

"Oh, shit," the chief muttered, biting off the end of the cigar, and spitting it forcibly in the trash.

Mitch offered a cigar to Harris, who declined, wrinkling his nose. "The chief and I were just discussing whether we should consider a change in direction of the investigation," Harris said, taking advantage of the silence while Mitch and the chief were lighting up. "I feel, and I think the chief would agree that the most important thing at this juncture is to ID the man who took Angie Brody."

Mitch took the cigar from his mouth, blowing smoke. "Already done. The man's name is Justin Carter. From the DC area," Mitch said, enjoying watching Harris' mouth drop open.

"No shit, well that's good news," the chief grunted around his cigar.

"Don't bet on it," Mitch replied. "Seems Mister Carter was a guest in our jail Sunday night. Booked in around ten on a D and D."

"Son of a bitch," the chief muttered. "How do we know it was him?"

"We only lifted two sets of prints out of that motel room. One was Angie Brody. One was his. We got the match straight out of our own computer. His prints were put in our system when he was arrested Sunday."

"Then he got out and killed that young girl," the chief said sourly.

"Yep, paid a two hundred dollar fine and walked."

"We better hope the press doesn't find out about that," Harris said, pulling at his collar.

"Shit, I bet they already know," Mitch said.

"Why would you say that?" Harris squeaked.

"Think about the way it went down. Jeff Crowley stopped at the McDonalds at Speedway and Campbell for dinner."

"Right by the University," the chief observed.

"Exactly. Well Jeff left the driver's window on the squad cracked a few inches. It was hot Sunday. He's inside getting his Big Mac when he looks out and sees our boy Carter pissing in his car window."

"Couldn't happen to a nicer guy," the chief said with a chortle. Station gossip said Jeff Crowley had given the chief a ticket for doing five over just a few months before the chief came on board. "Hope it was the driver's window."

"As a matter of fact, it was," Mitch said sharing a smile with the chief, and thinking maybe the rumors were true. Mitch shook his head, getting his mind back to the business at hand. "So Jeff hauls him in. He blew point 0 eight."

"So, why does it necessarily follow that the press knows."

"He wasn't drunk out of his mind. Hell, used to be legal to drive at that. This was calculated. Another message to Brody. I don't know who this Justin Carter is, but you can bet your ass Brody does. And I'm willing to bet Carter is somebody you wouldn't want your daughter anywhere near."

"I don't know. It doesn't sound right," Harris whined.

"Shit he leaves a perfect print at the scene. Mickey said it was a better print than on some of the print cards we get. The other print belonged to Angie Brody. He was sending a message. Hell, the whole deal with the D and D was probably just to get his prints in our system."

"Still doesn't stand up," Harris protested. "When we catch him we got him cold and even if we don't pick him up, he'll always be on the run. He'd get picked up sooner or later. When he does, he's going away for the murder."

"Oh hell no. All we got is his prints in the room. We've already checked, he rented that room a few days earlier. Place still has the old fashioned deadbolts, he probably made a key then. Goes to court, he can explain why his prints were in the room. He stayed in that room a few days earlier. The real killer wiped the room, just happened to miss that one set."

"Risky. How would he know the room would still be empty?" the chief wondered.

"Hell, the place is a dive. Place ain't never full. Course maybe he didn't care. Maybe he figured he'd just kill whoever was in the room and do what he wanted. Maybe...," Mitch stopped, a thought trying to push through the clutter in his brain.

"What?"

"Aw, I don't know," Mitch said, shaking his head, to clear the cobwebs. Damn it, he was missing something. "I was just thinking," he said slowly, trying to bring to the surface what his mind was trying to tell him. "We have been assuming that the hotel chick was a working girl. Maybe that was her room. Leroy Bell said she wasn't, but he could be lying." Mitch shook his head, trying to clear his mind. There was something there, just in the back of his mind. "I don't know about the hooker thing. I think there is something else."

"I like your first idea better, but check them out," the chief said.

"I'll talk to everyone who knows. We have to keep this from the press," Harris said.

"Don't bother," Mitch said. "He didn't go to all this trouble then hope we are dumb enough to talk to the press. I bet some reporter got an anonymous phone call already."

"How do we handle it?" the chief asked.

"Shit, we treat it like it's nothing, which is what it is. Most people who have committed a murder had been arrested before. It happens every day. Can't keep someone locked up for something they might be thinking of doing."

"You're right about that," the chief said, holding the cigar out and admiring the smoke. "We need to ID the dead girl. At least give the impression we're on top of things."

"We're working on it. Jerry is showing her picture around, see if she is a working girl. The tattoo may help…," Mitch trailed off. He looked up at the ceiling, and closed his eyes. The fog in his mind lifted and he saw a face. "Aw, man."

"What," the chief said, slamming forward in his chair, and sitting the cigar aside. "What just happened?"

"The tattoo," Mitch said. "Her roommate had one just like it."

"So?" Harris said. "Doesn't necessarily mean anything. All these chicks these days got tats."

"No, we have it on good account that Brody was doing the roommate. It was all part of the message."

The chief waved his hand at the door. "Go, check it out."

Tucson Daily News Offices Tucson AZ June 14 2018
Thursday Morning

Jackson Pyle sat at his desk, basking in the sweet glow of anticipation. His first front page, and above the fold story no less. Thursday wasn't the best day for his first front page story, but Thursday was what it was. Funny how excited he was. Especially since he had already decided to get out of the newspaper game.

He'd made a promise to get out of the country. It was a promise he had damn well better keep. Jackson had a slimy, uncomfortable feeling if he didn't he might end up like William Forsyth. Didn't matter, he was ready to leave.

He could buy a place just north of Cabo. Jackson had done some looking on the internet and places just a few miles north of Cabo were pretty reasonable.

Get a nice beach house, maybe a yacht too. Spend his days fishing. Hell, he might even take up golf. Jackson closed his eyes and he could picture it. Evenings in a nice restaurant in Cabo, nights in a club dancing with a variety of pretty girls. Parties on the yacht. The vision was so clear, he could almost taste the tequila.

A paper landed on his desk with a dull plop. Jackson opened his eyes to see Maria from the mail room pushing her cart as she delivered papers to all the reporter's cubes. He glanced down at the paper, seeing the sprawling headline with his name below it. Damn, it felt surprisingly good.

Jackson pulled the paper closer. One of the photos he had taken was beside the headline. It showed Braxton at her desk, pouring over a stack of papers. Not exactly inspired, but the quality was good.

Reverently, Jackson unfolded the paper, surprised to see his story covered the entire front page. Another picture was in the bottom right corner.

Jackson studied the picture, very pleased. This picture was inspired. It depicted a thoughtful Senator perched in the window sill of her hotel room, the lights of Phoenix spread out behind her. The picture softened the Senator giving her a more human look.

Jackson read the story and again was pleased. Even though, he had basically given the Senator a soapbox to climb on, the story was good. For some reason, unknown even to him, Jackson had sweated over the story. He had worked hard, pouring every ounce of skill he had into it.

The story carried over to the second page, which shocked Jackson. Normally the rest of the story would be back on the tenth page. Another photo would have been good, though.

Careful with the creases, Jackson refolded the paper and placed it in his briefcase. He should stop and get a few more copies. Maybe buy one from a newsstand. For some reason, that appealed to him. He spent the next hour cleaning out his desk, carrying his meager stack of belongings out to his car.

He should get a new car. A Land Rover. No, maybe a Porsche Cayenne. A luxury SUV would be the ticket, but something snappy that handled well. Leather seats, GPS, MP3, everything.

Still thinking about the car, Jackson wandered back to his cube. He glanced down at his watch, almost six. Working quickly, he typed a letter of resignation into his email account. He set it to go out at noon.

Glancing at his watch, he saw it was almost seven. Darby Lewis wouldn't be in until at least eight. Jackson told himself that he wasn't waiting for Darby, that he was waiting for the call from Braxton's people. Actually, he could set his office line to forward to his cell. He did that all the time.

Truthfully, he was waiting for Darby. He wanted to rub the son of a bitch's nose in it. Jackson's story had bumped Darby from the front page and Jackson was in a mood to gloat. Suddenly Jackson wanted to read Darby's story. See just what kind of trash he had relegated to the back page. Damn, he had already carried his copy down to the car.

Pushing back his chair, he went into Kelly Ramirez's cube. Kelly did the movie reviews and covered the social scene. She wouldn't miss it; she didn't come until after lunch. Snagging Kelly's paper, he went back to his cube, flipping through the paper until he found Darby's story on page four.

Jackson snorted to himself as he read. It was an interview with an old state cop named Sam Logan. Logan was worried that some Mexican drug runner was gearing up to use Tucson as his base of operations in the states. Jackson snorted again. Hardly news. A story like that came out every few months. Jackson pushed the paper away. What a crock.

Bored, Jackson went through his desk again, making sure he hadn't missed anything. All that remained was the flash drive he had loaded all the information he had gathered on the good Senator. Jackson picked up the drive, rubbing its shiny, smooth surface with his thumb. Amazing, something so small could be worth so much.

Jackson raised the drive to his lips, kissing it softly. Feeling silly, he glanced around, and shoved the drive into his pocket. He glanced at his watch. Five after eight. Where was Darby? Prick would be late today of all days. Leaning out of his cube, he looked down the row of cubicles to Darby's office. It was empty. Yeah, piece of shit, Darby Lewis had an office, Jackson thought for the thousandth time. Though it was only marginally bigger than a broom closet, but it was an office. Made Jackson's blood boil just thinking of it.

Leaning back in his chair, Jackson forced a chuckle at his anger. What did he care? In a couple of hours, he would walk out the front door of this dump and never come back. Then, while Darby was sweating it out in his tiny little office, Jackson would be on the beach feeling the cool Pacific breezes blowing over him.

Jackson glanced at his watch again. He should get a new watch. A Rolex. Jackson frowned. Was there something better than a Rolex? More stylish?

Jackson frowned. Seemed like he had heard that somewhere. One way to find out. Flicking on his computer monitor, Jackson brought up the internet, googling watches. Damn, there were a lot of watches.

"One story on the front page and you think you are big time."

Jackson turned to see Darby sneering at him over a cup of Starbucks. Jackson shrugged. "Just dreaming a little," Jackson said surprised that he no longer felt intimidated by Darby.

"Well, don't get used to it. It will be five more years before you hit the front page again."

Jackson shrugged again. "Might do it again tomorrow."

"Yeah, right," Darby sneered. "What really pisses me off is you pushed an important piece to the back with a fluff piece on some politician."

Jackson smiled at Darby's choice of words. It was even money that Jillian Braxton would be the next President of the United States and he was referring to her as some politician. Suddenly tired of it, Jackson leaned back in his chair. "Face it, man. Your piece was a dog. We hear those rumors all the time. My story was better."

"Whatever," Darby said, with a condescending flip of his hand. "So, what are you still doing here? Waiting to gloat?"

"No, I'm waiting for a call from the Senator's people. If they liked the piece, they might give some stuff for a follow up," Jackson said, hoping the last part was true. Be nice to get on the front page one more time.

Darby swore under his breath. "What I can't figure out is how you managed to get an interview with her. Word is she isn't granting one on one interviews."

Jackson shrugged, trying to make it casual. He and the Senator had discussed this very thing. It would be best for all concerned that they have a plausible explanation for the interview. After some time they had come up with a story. "You know Kathy Reynolds?"

Darby shook his head, which caused Jackson in turn to shake his. This man was supposed to be a reporter? The paper's so called number one reporter? Pathetic. "She's chair of the fund raising committee for the Senator here in Arizona."

Darby gave a shrug, sipping his coffee. "So?"

"Any way, Kathy owed me a favor. She got me in to see the Senator."

Darby's face lit up and he slapped his knee. "Shit! I knew it! Some sleazy deal. What is this Reynolds chick, some rich bitch who got drunk and wrecked her Lexus? You kept her name out of it and now she owes you?"

"No, it wasn't like that," Jackson said, hoping Darby would drop it.

"Bullshit! I bet it was exactly like that," Darby said. Finding a story he could live with he started to wander away. Jackson smiled, Darby would tell it just like that. Not that Jackson might be a good reporter, but that he had just got lucky. Oh well, fuck 'em, Jackson thought as his phone rang.

Jackson glanced at the caller ID and didn't recognize the number. Feeling a quickening in his heart, he picked up the receiver. "Jackson Pyle speaking."

"Mister Pyle, this is Tamera Schroeder, I am calling for the Senator."

"Good morning, Tamera" Jackson said, feeling a surge of lust crash through him. That woman stirred something in him. "I trust the Senator was pleased with the article?"

"Yes, sir. She was very pleased. We are hearing several of the wire services are going to pick up your story. Congratulations. Your story will go out nationwide.

"Thank you," Jackson replied, to stunned to say anything else.

"The Senator was wondering if you would consider doing another piece about her."

Jackson shook his head, trying to get some clear thoughts going. "Of course," he said, trying to figure out where this was going. Was the bitch going to try and double cross him? "The Senator had said she would have a packet of information for me. Is that coming today?"

"I'm afraid not. The Senator asked me to inform you that she would be a day or so putting the packet together for you, but she would send it to you by messenger tomorrow. I sent you an email with the stuff for your new article. It should be in your inbox as we speak."

Rubbing his chin, Jackson stared up at the ceiling, feeling the familiar, burning anger surge through him. Braxton had promised him the money today. Was she trying to fuck him?

"Mister Pyle?"

"Huh?" Jackson grunted, shaking his head.

"I asked if you received my email?" Tamera asked in a clipped, condescending tone.

Jackson's anger evaporated under her condescension, and he ducked his head, hunching his shoulders. "Hang on, let me check." Jackson logged into his email, pulling up the message from the Senator's office. "Yes, I have it." Jackson said, scrolling through the list.

"These are issues that directly affect voters in Arizona," Tamera explained. "The Senator said you two spoke of them last night."

"Sure," Jackson muttered, reading the list. Proposed Federal funding for a light rail commuter train between Tucson and Phoenix. Three wind farms to generate electricity. The designation of more land as National Parks. A proposal to bring water from San Diego to both Phoenix and Tucson. Jackson had heard rumors about this. Supposedly it could be done and be cost effective. Federal funds for a new airport. A state of the art facility that would serve both the Tucson and Phoenix metro areas. That might work if they got the light rail going. "Looks good, but if you want to get to the voters hearts here, you should talk about closing the border."

"No that is off limits."

Jackson chuckled. Of course not, that didn't fit with the Senator's national liberal message.

Tucson Police Headquarters Tucson AZ June 14th 2018 Thursday Morning

Mitch entered his team's offices to see Jerry and Wade huddled around Jerry's computer. "How's it coming?" Mitch asked.

"Okay, we've been looking into Brody. We were thinking about what you said, that Brody was horning into somebody's deal. And we thought; how does that work?" Jerry asked.

"With the kidnapping," Wade supplied.

"I don't know," Mitch said, shaking his head. "Somebody has a big deal going; Brody gets wind of it, buys a couple of tracks of land, so they grab Angie to force him to sell."

Wade was already shaking his head. "Naw, doesn't work if you really stop to think about it. See that's what we thought, but it doesn't track. If Brody was trying to horn in on somebody's deal, why would he do that?"

"Easy," Mitch replied. "To make money."

"Exactly," Wade said, snapping his fingers. "So no need to kidnap Angie."

"Because, Brody would already be looking to sell," Mitch said.

"Right you are, my boy," Wade said, grinning. "Sure Brody is going to jack the price up, but if you got a gigantic deal going you don't quibble over price, you just pucker your ass, pay up and move on. Come back and kick Brody's ass later if you need to."

"We had it backwards." Mitch leaned back in his chair, something clicking in his brain. "Somebody is horning in on Brody's deal."

"There you go, sonny boy" Wade said, snapping his fingers again, and pointing at Mitch.

"After we started thinking that way we found something very interesting," Jerry said, looking through the papers on the desk. "Brody's been buying equipment."

"Is he hiding it?"

"Maybe," Jerry said, looking at Wade, who shrugged. Jerry glanced down at his notes. "A company called Tucson Partners LLC., which Brody is listed as President, bought a concrete company that was going broke."

"Big fucker too," Wade added. "Batch plant, twenty some trucks."

"And now that concrete company is buying scrapers, loaders, dump trucks and track hoes."

"Good time to be buying," Mitch commented.

"He's been getting good deals. I checked with a buddy of mine, he's been getting the equipment for at least half off," Wade supplied.

"Great deals," Jerry agreed. "But why does he need all this heavy equipment? He builds houses. Why does he need ten huge track hoes?"

"Branching out," Wade wondered. "Good time to be buying, but not much work."

"Government job, has to be" Mitch said. "Brody has an in, some way to ensure he gets the bid. So he starts buying land to make a little extra on the side."

"Somebody gets wind of it and tries to muscle in." Wade shrugged, leaning back. "So what do you think?"

"Sounds like you boys are on the right track," Mitch said approvingly. "Run it down. See where it goes."

"How does this help us find Angie Brody?" Jerry asked.

"Shit, I don't know, but it's gotta help." Mitch leaned back in his chair, a nugget of an idea worrying his mind like a pebble in his shoe. "Good work, guys, but I'm seeing a problem."

"Why doesn't Brody cave in?" Jerry Hartek finished.

"That's the question we been kicking back and forth," Wade said, easing his leg up on the desk. "Shit, he wants to get his project going and surely he wants to get his daughter back. So just give them what they want."

"He can't give in," Jerry decided. "Question is why."

"I've got an idea about that," Mitch said, trying to pull the idea together. "Suppose, Brody has a partner, somebody he can't cross."

"Makes sense," Wade said. "He should be barely scraping by in this economy. No way should he have enough money to buy a Tonka truck, much less all the shit he's been snapping up."

"He took money from somebody." Mitch said. "Somebody who is going to want it back. Maybe somebody took a stake in this deal for payment."

"You're talking Mafia?" Jerry asked, frowning at the thought.

"Shit, maybe," Mitch said, frowning himself. "Could be a drug cartel, a dealer or even a loan shark. The thing is, he took their money." Mitch paced a little circle. "So, Brody takes the money from someone he doesn't dare cross, so he can't give in to whoever took his daughter." He glanced at the two detectives. "Is that how it would work?"

"Maybe," Jerry said. "But maybe who he took the money from is who grabbed the girl. Just making sure he keeps on the straight and narrow."

"Huh," Mitch grunted. "Could be."

"So, we keep digging," Wade said.

"Yeah, gotta be something there," Mitch replied. "Good work, keep at it."

"I'd rather be on the streets," Jerry complained.

"Maybe you want my job. I have to go talk to the press and see if I can clean up Harris's mess."

That brought a smile to Hartek's face. "What a dickhead. He really stepped in it this time."

"Yeah, with both feet," Mitch agreed. "Now, I have to go scrape his shoes."

"Good luck with that," Hartek said, smirking as he turned back to his computer.

"Find something. We need a break," Mitch told him as he walked out of the office. Mitch walked through the station, contemplating what he would say. He was half tempted to throw Harris under the bus. In the end, Mitch knew it would be better to have Harris owing him.

At the front door, Mitch stopped, looking outside. A group of reporters and camera people were milling about. Mitch wished he had called a regular press conference.

Outsides on the steps would look like he was hiding. Like they had to hunt him down. The last thing they need was to look like they had something to hide. Especially since they did.

Taking a deep breath, Mitch pushed through the doors. He made three steps before he was spotted. Ten questions flew at him. "I don't have a lot of time, so I'll only answer one question each. Who wants to go first?"

Not surprisingly, it was Starla Chavez. She was the newest, and thought going first was some kind of honor. The veterans, or the ones with their producer at hand waited, hoping someone else would ask one of their questions. Mitch knew they would dub in themselves asking the question later.

Starla Chavez smiled, taking a small step forward. Mitch smiled back, keeping his eyes on her forehead, which wasn't an easy feat.

"Detective Mitchell, in light of the recent developments, what would you say to all the people who opposed the formation of your unit?"

"I would say this is exactly the reason this unit was formed."

"But your handling of this case has been less than stellar. Wouldn't you agree?"

"No, Starla, I wouldn't agree with that statement. My team and I have been working very hard to locate Angie Brody. And we are getting closer. We are pursuing some very good leads into why she was abducted."

"Grant Peterson, Channel Seven News," Peterson said, cutting in front of his own reporter, Starla Chavez. "This wasn't the work of a sexual predator?"

"We don't believe so at this time," Mitch answered calmly.

"Then what was the motive for this attack?" Peterson shot back.

Mitch caught the use of the word attack, but decided to let it go. "Greed, money, power. The usual motives," he replied simply.

Peterson ignoring the one question rule, took another step forward. "But wasn't the dead girl in the motel the same type as Angie Body? So much so, that you identified her as Angie Brody?"

"Yes, she is similar to Angie Brody, and no, we didn't miss-identify her. As of now, we haven't been able to establish her identity."

"That's not what the paper said."

"I assume you are referring to Tom's article in the Citizen this morning. The quote attributed to Commander Harris was misleading. To begin with Commander Harris is not involved in this investigation, and is not privy to all the details." Mitch paused, struggling not to smile. He knew how Harris liked to portray himself as one of the department's top investigators, he'd have trouble getting anyone to believe that now. Keeping his tone solemn, Mitch continued. "Secondly, the commander did not realize he was speaking on the record. What Harris actually said was that the body looked like Angie Brody."

Mitch glanced over at Tom Black and he could see the reporter was seething. Fuck him, Mitch thought. Black shouldn't have printed the article until the family had been notified.

"So, you deny that it was assumed the body in the hotel was Angie Brody?" Black fired at Mitch.

"I would say assumed is a trifle strong. We considered it to be a strong possibility, and we immediately began to check it out. Our investigation had already led us to believe that Angie Brody was being held for a specific reason. Her death at that time did not make sense with what we knew. So while we considered it possible that the body was that of

Angie Brody, we had reservations. And as it turned out, it wasn't Angie Brody in that room."

"Who was the girl that was killed?"

"At this time, we don't know."

"Why was she killed?"

"Well as it was stated earlier, she resembled Angie Brody, physically. We believe she was killed to send a message."

"And what message was that?"

"This is what could happen to Angie."

"Does this mean that Brad Brody is involved?"

"I'm sorry, but I cannot comment on that part of our investigation at this time."

"There have been rumors of a possible mob involvement in Mister Brody's business. Especially with the Indian Gaming Casinos he is building. Do you suspect the mob in Miss Brody's disappearance?"

"As I said, I cannot comment on that part of the investigation."

"What about the rumor we heard that the man who killed that poor girl in the motel was actually in police custody the night before she was killed?"

"Fingerprints belonging to the man were found in the motel room. At this time, we believe that his arrest was planned as part of the message."

That was as far as Mitch wanted to go. Making a show of looking at his watch, Mitch then clapped his hands. "I appreciate you coming, but Detective Parker and I do have to run. Thanks, for coming today. If you see Detective Olshan, he has some pictures of Angie Brody and Justin Carter for you."

"Are you suggesting we do your work for you?" Tom Black demanded, still smarting from Mitch's assertion he got his facts wrong.

Mitch smiled his sweetest smile. "Not at all, Tom. You don't want to run them, then don't." Mitch smiled sweetly at the man. Everybody else would be running the pictures, and Black would have little choice but to do the same. "Good day." Mitch jerked his head for Carly to follow him, then headed back inside.

Deacons' Clubhouse South Tucson AZ June 14 2018
Thursday Mid-morning

Chappy Miers had a problem. He had too many fucking partners. He found himself whipsawed into a corner, and wasn't quite sure how to get out. Cursing under his breath he crossed behind the bar. As he drew himself a beer, Chappy shook his head. He should have known he couldn't trust Flores.

A part of his brain realized it was his own damn fault. He knew going in what kind of a dude Flores was. He knew from the first that Flores would try and take over. He never should have laid the whole thing out for Flores. A few too many tequilas and way too much bragging when he asked Flores for the money, that was the problem.

It seemed like such a sweet deal when Tanner approached him with it. Give Brody a few hundred thousand bucks to buy some land and collect a cool million in profits a few months later when the property sold. Easy money.

The thing was, at the time Chappy didn't have the few hundred thousand, so he went to Flores. He and Flores had just struck a partnership to move some Mexican drugs together, so it seemed like a natural place to get the money. Besides, Henry Flores was the president of the Southern California chapter of the Deacons Motorcycle Club. That chapter had twenty times the membership that Chappy's Tucson bunch had, and fifty times the ready cash.

Chappy took the money, and now that it was time to collect, Flores was getting greedy. He was forcing Brody to hold out for a bigger share. And of course, Van Zandt was balking.

The thing was, Flores could afford to wait, but Chappy could not. Flores and Chappy had a deal with the Mexican Cartels and they were expecting a huge shipment in the next few days. What Flores didn't know was that Chappy had a side deal with the Cartel to take another shipment a few days later. And Chappy didn't have the money. That money was supposed to come from the Brody deal.

Chappy began to sweat. The Mexican Cartels didn't look kindly on being stiffed. Chappy wasn't sure what they would do if he showed up to the meeting without the money, but he knew, it would not be an experience he would enjoy. He'd heard rumors of folks who short-changed the Cartels that were skinned alive. Chappy had no idea if the rumors were true and he wanted to keep it that way.

Chappy couldn't afford to cross Flores. They might all be Deacons but that wouldn't make any difference. Flores would want blood if he found out Chappy was dealing behind his back. Chappy knew if it came to a war with Flores, he would lose. The Cali Chapter had more men, more money and more guns. And they had more ambition, Chappy realized.

Chappy glanced around the empty clubhouse. It was almost eleven and not a soul was stirring. Chappy's guys were content to party half the night and sleep till noon. They worked just hard enough to keep themselves in beer and pussy.

And now Chappy's best man, and greatest earner was drifting away from the club. Tanner had always been a little different, but ever since he started dating that rich bitch, Tanner was pulling back even more.

Chappy rubbed his chin. Maybe he should do something about that bitch? An accident maybe? Chappy frowned to himself, pushing his beer around on the bar. It was an idea, but if Tanner ever found out? Chappy didn't even like to think about that. That fucking Tanner was a one-man wrecking crew.

Forget about Tanner and the bitch, Chappy told himself. Concentrate on the problem at hand. Flores.

Chappy considered just taking Flores out. In any kind of a fight, Chappy knew he could pound Flores into a grease stain. The problem was, Flores' men were extremely loyal. If he killed Flores, even in a fair fight, they just might rise up against him. And that would not be good

Chappy wondered about trying to squeeze Brody, but Brody was terrified of Flores. Flores had promised Brody that if he signed Van Zandt' papers, he would be dead before the ink dried. To punctuate that threat, Flores had placed one of his crew with Brody. Was in fact, making Brody pay the man a salary.

Chappy knew, he could threaten Brody but they would be hollow threats. Chappy was in the same boat as Van Zandt. They needed Brody to sign the papers. And until he did sign they couldn't kill him. And of course, Brody knew this as well. Which was why he wasn't signing.

Chappy finished his beer and set the glass under the tap. As the glass filled, Chappy wondered idly who might inherit if Brody did die.

An interesting thought, but it would take way too much time. He needed the money now. Chappy took a sip of the fresh beer. He damn well better think of something fast. If he showed up to that meeting with only his dick in his hand, he was a dead man.

There was one chance, maybe. Seemed like a long shot, but Chappy was getting desperate. With a sigh, he pulled out his cheap, prepaid, flip phone and dialed a number he had gotten from Brody. "Van Zandt and Associates," a smooth, slightly feminine voice answered.

"Give me Van Zandt."

"I'm sorry, Mister Van Zandt is very busy this morning. He isn't taking any calls. If you want to leave a message, I will see that he receives it."

"Oh, he'll take my call," Chappy said. "Tell him it's Brody from Arizona and I'm ready to deal."

"One moment."

Almost immediately, Chappy heard a click and then a cultured voice tinged with impatience sprang from the phone. "Yes."

"I've got a deal for you."

"You're not Brad Brody," Van Zandt observed, dispassionately.

"Nope," Chappy admitted. "But what if I was to tell you I was the man who could get Brody to sign your papers?"

"I'm listening."

"I'd need two hundred and fifty thousand up front."

Chappy no sooner utter the words when he felt the connection go dead. Pulling the phone from his ear, he saw call ended blinking from the screen.

"Shit!" he screamed at the top of his lungs. He was tempted to throw the phone across the bar but managed to control himself. He needed to think.

Think fast or he was a dead man.

Biltmore Hotel Phoenix AZ June 14 2018 Thursday Afternoon

Tamera Schroeder sat at her desk, her back rigid, and her whole body feeling like a block of wood. She felt like her heart was barely beating, but her palms were sweating, and sheen of perspiration covered her forehead. Her hair carefully styled that morning, now lay flat and lifeless on her head.

It couldn't be true. Simply could not be.

Tamera stared at the wall, her eyes unfocused. She didn't even notice Derrick Allisen until he spoke. "Tamera, are you alright? You don't look well."

Swiveling her head slowly, Tamera blinked a couple of times. "What?" she croaked.

"Are you feeling unwell?" Allisen repeated.

"Aw, no," Tamera squawked, her voice breaking, as she placed her hands on her desk, quickly covering the object there. "No, I'm fine."

Derrick shook his head, a look of empathy springing to his face. "Perhaps, you should go to your room and lie down. I can cover for you."

For a second, Tamera stared blankly at his soft face, then she nodded slowly. "Okay," she said dully. "Maybe that would be best." All of a sudden, Tamera did want to leave, but not to lie down.

"Super," Allisen said, nodding his head furiously. "I will just go tell the Senator that I will be taking over for you. Do you need anything? Some soup from the kitchen, perhaps?"

"No, I will be fine," she said, pretty sure she would never be fine again.

"I will be right back," Allisen said, giving her a comforting smile as he scurried from the room.

She felt a wave of nausea, and for a second thought she would throw up on her desk. Was this the start of it, she wondered. Too early for that, this was just nerves.

Angie and Lindsey's Apartment Tucson AZ June 14 2018 Thursday Afternoon

"Police! Open the door."

Mitch banged on the door with one hand, ringing the doorbell with the other. "Feels empty," Carly said, leaning over, trying to look in the window.

Mitch nodded, banging the door again. She was right, the apartment felt empty. On a beat, cops checked doors. Thousands of doors. After a few hundred, a cop got a feel for it. They could just tell. This place was empty.

"Shit," Mitch said, glancing around, a bad feeling creeping up his spine. For a second, they were alone. "Shit. Keep your eyes open. I'm going to slip the lock."

He started to turn away to go to the car for his picks, then thought, what the hell. Surprisingly, the doorknob turned easily under his hand. The door popped open a couple of inches. "Shit," Mitch said, pulling his gun. That wasn't good. He glanced at Parker who was also bringing out her pistol. Their eyes locked for a second, then Carly gave a small nod.

"I've got a bad feeling about this," she whispered, holding her gun with both hands.

"Yeah," Mitch grunted. Sliding off to the side of the door, he pushed it open with his toe, sweeping the living room with the barrel of his pistol. Seeing nothing, Mitch went through the door with a rush. He stepped left towards the small kitchen. As he glanced behind the breakfast bar, he saw Carly slide into the apartment, moving to the right.

Mitch moved quickly checking the bedroom on the left. "Clear over here," he said.

He saw Carly checked the one on the right. "Clear," she whispered.

"I got a bad feeling about this." Mitch said, checking the bathroom, and finding it empty.

"I already said that," Carly said, still whispering.

Mitch nodded absently. This place had a vibe, like a murder scene. "Aw fuck, I knew it."

"What is it?"

"You ever notice that Angie Brody and Lindsey Merideth look quite a bit alike."

"You mean blond perky and dumb?" Carly asked, with a small laugh. "Or do you mean over-sexed and over-indulged?"

Mitch ignored the comments, knowing it was just the stress bleeding off. "I was thinking about the girl in the motel." Mitch said looking around the living room. "Find something that might have Lindsey's finger prints on it?"

"Got a Sobee's bottle here."

"Good." Mitch grumbled, trying to think it through. He had no proof that a crime had even been committed. He pulled out his cell phone. He glanced over at Carly, as he stabbed a preset on his phone. "First time through a door?"

She nodded. "Yeah. What a fucking rush."

Mitch nodded, hearing the phone being answered. "Mickey, this is Mitch. Any luck on finding the identity of the dead girl?"

"No, whoever she is she isn't in the system. You're gonna have to come up with something on your end."

"I might have something for you." Mitch said. "We can't find Angie Brody's roommate. She fits the general description of the dead girl. "We got a bottle from the apartment."

"You want me to check it against the dead girl?"

"Yeah, that was my thought. If we can get a match I'd say it's about eighty five percent she's the one.

"You got a name, we could start looking for some other way to match prints or get an ID."

"Lindsey Jane Merideth." Mitch said. "I'll get Carly to checking it out. That may be an alias.

"Get me the bottle; I can have you a match today. It won't be good enough for court, but it'll be ninety percent."

"Thanks, Mickey. Quick as you can. I've got a bad feeling about this. If it's her, I'll see about getting a warrant, maybe you or Linda could come over to her apartment."

"You think that's where he got her?"

"Maybe. He'd have a key."

"Huh?" Mickey said, then quickly added. "Oh yeah, from the other girl, Angie Brody."

"You got it. I'm sending Parker now."

"You think it was her in the motel?" Parker asked.

Mitch nodded, feeling a wave of guilt snap through him. "Yeah, it's her." He said, rummaging around and finding a Wal-Mart bag. "It makes sense. They want to pressure Brody, he was doing her, that's a pretty good card." Mitch shook his head. "We should have seen this coming."

"I don't know. They have his daughter. No reason to think they would need any more leverage than that," Parker said, slipping the bottle into the bag.

"Yeah, but Brody still ain't giving them what they want. We were picking up on that. We shoulda been ready."

"Don't beat yourself up. We couldn't have predicted this. We don't even know if the dead girl is Lindsey."

"It's her," Mitch said grimly. He tossed her his keys. "Get this to Mickey. Then we will know."

"You're not going?"

"No. I want to do a little checking around here."

"You want me to come back and pick you up?"

Mitch shook his head. "No, I want you to get started digging into Lindsey's background. Find out if that is her real name. Call out to Starr Pass where she worked. I want to know everything there is to know about her. If Ollie or Jerry are free, have one of them come pick me up. Otherwise, I'll catch a ride in with a patrol."

After Parker left, Mitch took a quick look around the apartment, considering his options. He should back out immediately. He was probably okay with the initial entry. The door had been unlocked and they had a plausible reason to believe that Lindsey Merideth might be in danger.

That covered the entry, but Mitch knew; now, he should back out. But, he wanted to look around some first. As he paced the small living room, a nasty grin pulled his lips back.

As an officer of the law, he couldn't just go off and leave the apartment unsecured. The door had a deadbolt. It took a key to secure it. Walking through the apartment, Mitch pulled out his cell phone. He was in Angie's bedroom, when the internet came up on his phone. He googled the name of the apartment complex, looking under the bed as the number came up. He hit connect as he opened the closet.

"Good morning ma'am," Mitch said in response to the cheery greeting. He walked out of Angie's bedroom and back into the living room. "This is Detective John Mitchell of the Tucson Police Department. Could I have someone bring a key and meet me at apartment twelve-fourteen?"

"I'm sorry, Detective, but unless you have a warrant, I cannot let you in."

"I'm already in," Mitch replied. "I need someone to come lock up for me."

"Oh." There was a long pause. "Okay. I'll have someone from maintenance meet you there."

"Thanks," Mitch said. He killed the phone, opened the front door, leaving it standing open. Working fast, Mitch took a quick look in the kitchen. Nothing caught his eye as being out of place, so he moved to the living room.

A tall floor lamp was overturned, protruding from behind a chair. On the floor beside the lamp was a picture in a plastic frame. Mitch squatted beside the picture, but did not touch it. The photo was a picture of Angie and Lindsey in a night club. A man partially obscured by Lindsey's head had his arm around Angie. Mitch didn't recognize the man, but he was pretty sure it wasn't anyone he'd seen connected with the case. The club looked familiar, but Mitch couldn't place it.

Knowing he didn't have much time, Mitch moved on. The bathroom looked like a crime scene. To the casual eye, it might appear that a triple homicide had occurred in the small room. Mitch knew otherwise. From years of looking at people's private spaces, he knew this was a typical bathroom of two young women.

Lindsey's bedroom was a mess as well. Clothes were draped or piled on every object in the room. Mitch shook his head. This young lady had enough clothes to start a store. Shoes were littered across the floor and as far as Mitch could see, none of them matched.

Mitch turned a slow circle, taking in the room. No CDs. No books. Not even a magazine. This lady seemed to have no interests other than clothes. That didn't seem quite right. She was trying to break into showbiz. There should be trade magazines, books on acting singing or whatever she was trying to do.

There was a TV though. Mitch glanced at it. Forty-eight-inch flat screen, with a surround sound. A grand for that. Mitch opened the bottom of the TV cabinet. A few DVDs and behind them a small silver box. Mitch picked it up, sterling silver. Inside the box were several grams of coke.

Mitch replaced the box, closing the cabinet. He opened a free standing jewelry box. Mitch didn't know a lot about women's jewelry, but this stuff looked expensive. In the bottom drawer of the box was a small bundle of hundreds. Mitch rifled them, guessing there was a couple of thousand.

Feeling the clock ticking in his head, Mitch moved to the night stand, pulling open the top drawer. A cheap cell phone sat atop an assortment of batteries, lip stick and lotion. Mitch bent closer; this wasn't the cell phone of a party girl. It was your basic flip phone, no touch screen, not even a camera.

Mitch sat on the edge of the bed, pursing his lips. Could it be? Pulling out his own cell and his notebook, Mitch found where he had written down the number of the phone that called Angie Brody at the time of her attack. Holding the notebook in one hand and his cell in the other, Mitch dialed that number.

Punching send, he watched the phone in the drawer. After a few seconds, it began to vibrate and dance across the drawer.

Frowning, Mitch ended the call, killing the vibrating of the other cell. Did the killer plant it here, or was Lindsey Merideth a part of this? Good question. Mitch didn't know enough about the two girl's relationship, to even begin to answer that one. Were they close? Did they get along? One would normally assume that a roommate wouldn't do something like that. Mitch had seen enough to know that relationships can sour, jealousies can development, breeding all manners of resentment.

The real question was what to do with the phone. Should he take it? They knew it was a prepaid. What else could they learn from it? Mitch was still debating, when he heard a step behind him.

Sliding the drawer shut with his knee, Mitch turned to see an older black man standing in the living room. The man was dressed in gray work clothes that looked like they had been pressed within an inch of their lives. The creases on his pants looked sharp enough to cut grass. "Are you maintenance?"

The older man nodded, extending his hand. "Clyde Loftus."

Mitch stepped into the living room, taking the man's hand. "Detective John Mitchell. You heard what happened to Angie Brody?"

Clyde nodded again, bobbing his head. "I wasn't here that day. That's my day off but I heard about it. Folks ain't hardly been talking 'bout nothing else. I've already had ten people call wanting new locks on their doors."

"This isn't going to help then," Mitch said, already liking the older man. "I'm afraid something might have happened to Lindsey Merideth as well. She didn't show up for work, and we haven't been able to reach her. When I came over to check on her, my partner and I found the door open," Mitch explained, as Clyde nodded. Mitch noticed when Clyde nodded; he had a habit of rocking back on the balls of his feet. "I need you to lock up the apartment and not let anyone in. You have a key?" Clyde nodded and rocked some more.

"Good, well, let's lock it up. Don't let anyone in. I may have some officers come back later today, but they will have a warrant."

"I'm to let them in?"

"You got it," Mitch said, following Clyde out of the apartment. "Have you seen anybody strange hanging around? Maybe watching the two girls?"

Clyde chuckled, a deep merry sound. "I seen lots of fellas hanging around those two and some of them were mighty strange, but I think they were harmless."

"You know the girls very well?"

Clyde shrugged. "I talked to them from time to time. They were always friendly enough. Had to come over bout once a month to unclog their toilet. You wouldn't believe some of the things women will try and flush."

"You ever see anyone in a white van?"

"No, no vans. Mostly fast little cars, a fancy pickup or two. Mostly the fellas that came around were fancy boys. Nothing to them." Clyde frowned, running a hand over his graying hair. "You know, come to think about it, there was a fella who come by a couple of weeks ago. He was a bit older, but he was trouble. I saw that."

"Oh yeah," Mitch said interested. "How do you mean trouble?"

"The other ones, they were lambs. This jasper was a wolf. He had a mean streak. You know what I mean?"

"Yeah, I do," Mitch agreed. "You think you could pick his picture from a group?"

Clyde thought about, then shrugged. "Maybe. He was the kind of feller you'd remember."

"How many times did you see him?"

"Just the once. He was with Lindsey."

"You happen to see what he was driving?"

"It wasn't a van. Little, black car. One of those that looks like it's hauling ass sitting at a stoplight."

"You know what kind it was."

"Naw, foreign job I think. Out of my price range."

"Okay, I'll have somebody bring some pictures by for you to look at." Mitch glanced down at his watch. "You got time today?"

"Sure," Clyde replied. "I'm here all day."

"Thanks, Clyde," Mitch said, taking out a business card. "You think of anything, give me a call."

"Sure," Clyde said, locking the door and rattling the lock. "Don't let anybody in."

"No, don't. I have a bad feeling about this. I think something bad happened to Lindsey."

Clyde gave him a knowing look. "You'll be wanting to get a CSI crew in here. I know how it works. My wife watches all the shows."

"Then you know we need to keep the room sealed until they get here."

"I'll keep my eye on it."

"Thanks, Clyde," Mitch said, shaking the man's hand.

Mitch walked away, thinking it over. Lindsey with Carter? How does that happen? He uses her to get close to Angie Brody. Figure out her schedule. Then when Brody doesn't cave, he kills Lindsey to ratchet up the pressure. Cold as hell, unless Carter liked the killing.

Mitch dug out his cell and called Carly. "You drop the bottle off with Mickey?"

"Yes, he said, there were a couple of usable prints on the bottle. He should have something for us in an hour or so."

"Good."

"You want me to come back out there and pick you up?"

"No. Work on Lindsey. If Mickey matches up those prints, we are going to need to get her ID nailed down."

"She doesn't have a driver's license in Arizona under that name. There's a couple of hundred Lindsey Jane Merideth's in the system nationwide. You want me to start nailing them down?"

"No, I don't think that is her real name. Call out to Star Pass; get the social she used out there. Run that down and see what you get."

"I will probably need a warrant for that."

"Yeah, shit. You can draw one up and float it around. I doubt if we can get a judge to sign it. Course if Mickey can match the prints, that would help."

"I'll draw one up and go camp on his door until he gets the prints done."

"Good girl. Is Ollie or Jerry around?"

"Jerry is running something down on that phone, but Ollie is here. You want him to come pick you up?"

"Yeah but have him put together a six-pack with Carter's mug shot in the mix. Maintenance man here saw a strange man with Lindsey a few days before the kidnapping. Fits with the descriptions we've been getting of Carter."

"Shit," Carly sputtered. "We interviewed the maintenance men. Nobody said anything about it then."

"I know, this guy was off that day."

"Okay," Carly said and Mitch could hear the relief in her voice. "I'll tell Ollie."

Mitch closed his phone, thinking about it. The phone in Lindsey's drawer seemed to point that she had been involved in Angie's abduction. It made some sense now that Carter would want to get rid of her.

That stopped Mitch. What kind of life did he lead when the murder of a young girl made sense? He felt the twinge of guilt again. He should have seen this coming.

What to do now? He needed to get a warrant to get back into the apartment. He had no illusions that they would find anything that would help them find Angie Brody. What he wanted was that cell phone. It might hold in its memory a way to track Carter.

Mitch wondered about his decision to leave it. Had he taken it, anything they found on it wouldn't be used in court. On impulse, Mitch took out his cell phone and called the DA's office, asking for Lisa Johnson. "Mitch, how are you?" she asked.

"Good" Mitch replied. "I was needing some legal advice."

"My advice is to admit nothing, even if the kid looks like you, and get a DNA test."

"Very funny," Mitch replied. "I need some guidance on a case." Mitch quickly explained about the phone, Angie Brody, and Lindsey Merideth.

"You should be okay with the entry, but anything else you better have a warrant."

"What are the chances of getting one?"

"With what you got now? Bout as much chance as one of your investments paying off."

"God damn it, I'm being serious."

Lisa laughed. "I know. Look, you're not going to get a warrant unless the girl in the motel turns out to be Lindsey. Nail that down and you won't have any trouble with the warrant"

"The fact that she's missing isn't enough to get a warrant?" Mitch protested.

Lisa laughed again. "Oh shit, Mitch. Who's to say she's missing? Because she didn't show up for work? She's an adult, unless you can show some evidence that she's in danger or has been the victim of some crime, you aren't going to get a warrant."

"What about the phone? That could help us find Angie Brody."

"For God's sake, don't mention the phone to a judge. I wish you hadn't told me about it. You shouldn't have looked around after you established Lindsey Merideth wasn't there. You mention that to a judge and he might throw out everything you find at the apartment."

"Fuck, if I didn't look around I wouldn't even know about the phone."

"Well, that doesn't matter. You say Brody was boinking the roommate? Maybe he's paying the bills."

"If he's paying the bills, he can let us in," Mitch said, kicking himself for not thinking of that.

"As long as his name is on the lease."

"Okay, thanks for the advice."

Mitch thought about it for a second, then walked over to the leasing office. A cute brunette sat behind a desk. The office was made to look like a living room. "Good afternoon are you looking for an apartment?"

"No," Mitch replied, flashing his badge. "I'm Detective John Mitchell."

"Okay," she said, a note of caution sliding into her voice. "What can I do for you?"

"I'm investigating Angie Brody's disappearance."

"Oh yeah, that was a tragedy. How are you coming? Have you found her?"

"Not yet. What I need to know is who is on the lease for her apartment."

She bit her lip. "I'm sorry, I can't give you that. That's confidential information."

"I could come back with a subpoena."

She brightened, the smile back in place. "Then I would be able to help you."

Mitch was leaving when his phone rang. "Mitch, its Mickey."

"Tell me you have something good."

"I'd say it's about ninety percent that it's Lindsey Merideth in the motel room."

"Shit, okay."

"I thought you would be happy."

"I was kinda hoping it wouldn't be her. She was kinda flakey, but I liked her. You know."

"Yeah, sorry. Sometimes I tend to forget they're real people. It's easier that way."

"I've got Parker checking it out. We're not sure Lindsey Merideth is her real name."

"Makes sense. She's not in any of the data bases I have."

"Okay, I'll keep Parker on it." Mitch hung up, and immediately punched in Parker's number. "Carly, its official, the dead girl's prints match the ones on the bottle. How are you coming?"

"Just getting going on the warrants."

"What about a name change? Anything filed with the courts on that?"

"No, if she changed her name legally, she didn't do it here in Arizona."

"Okay, keep trying. Get the warrant ready, but hold on to it. I want to make a few calls first."

"You got it."

"Ollie get gone with the six-pack?"

"Yeah, he was just leaving."

Mitch hung up, wandering the area. He bought a diet coke, studying the layout of the apartment complex and the surrounding area. The one thing that struck Mitch was how difficult it would have been to watch Angie.

While the offices of the apartment complex were open to the street, the apartments were tucked and angled away from the street. There wasn't any parking on the street close to the complex. To effectively watch Angie Brody, Carter would have had to park in the complex parking lot. Sitting all day in a car would have drawn attention. Mitch had read the reports; nobody had seen anything like that.

What did that mean? It meant that Carter hadn't watched her. Unless he had rented an apartment in the complex. Lot of trouble and expense to go through.

It made more sense that Lindsey Merideth had helped. Whether she had knowingly helped or just been duped. If Mitch were to guess, he would say a little of both. Carter wouldn't have trusted Lindsey with too much. What would he have said to convince her to help him?

That was the question. Lindsey hadn't struck him as that cold. She was greedy though. Still setting your roommate up to be kidnapped was pretty brutal. That took a special kind of sociopath. Wasn't the vibe that Lindsey gave off.

Maybe Angie had been in on it. Didn't seem likely, but it wouldn't be unheard of. Maybe that drummer she was dating wanted to cut a record. That took money. Maybe she was trying to squeeze some money out of daddy so her boyfriend could be the next big rock star. Wouldn't hurt to do some checking on that end.

While they were at it, they definitely needed to look at Angie and Lindsey's relationship. See if there was any friction there. Turn Lindsey upside down. There might be some motivation there.

Mitch was still thinking about it, when he heard the barking squeal of tires. A few seconds later, Ollie raced into the parking lot, squealing the tires again.

"Hey old man, you want to buy me a set of tires?" he called as Ollie climbed out of the car.

"Aw shit, I had to do something to drown out that shit you had on the radio. Ain't you ever heard of Carrie Underwood?"

Mitch smiled. He had paid six hundred dollars for that MP3, CD player, with Sirius Satellite and Ollie called it a radio. "That was the Foo Fighters. You should listen, some people actually like them."

"Did you say Foo or poo, cause I know what that sounded like."

"Jeez you're a cranky old bastard."

Mitch's Office Tucson AZ June 14 2018 Thursday Late Afternoon

Mitch placed all the paper they had on the Angie Brody case in a small stack. He flipped through the rolodex until he came to the number for the FBI behavioral sciences department in Quantico Virginia. He pulled out the card, tapping it on the stack of paper, while he stared absently out the window.

"Shit," he muttered. They were already having trouble holding the Bureau out of the case. They were making noise about it being a kidnapping. Since no ransom had been asked for, Mitch had kept them out. If Mitch thought for a second that the Bureau would have a better chance of getting Angie Brody back, he would turn the case over to them in a heartbeat. The thing was, while the FBI was very good at what they did, they had absolutely no contacts on the street. That was how they were going to find Angie Brody. Some junkie or petty criminal was going to give her up.

"Shit," Mitch repeated. Calling the FBI might be a big mistake. The thing was, Mitch had a sneaky suspicion that this wasn't Carter's first rodeo. The whole thing was way too slick. Carter had done this before. And if he had done it before, he might be known to the Feds. The killing of Lindsey, that took a special kind of sickness. The Feds had a huge data base on that kind of thing. "Fuck it," he muttered grabbing the phone off the hook.

His call was answered immediately, by a proper sounding young man, who asked in a bored tone what Mitch's business might be.

Mitch identified himself and gave him a quick rundown of the case. He could tell that he wasn't getting anywhere. Not until he mentioned the name Carter.

"Did you say Jacob Carter?"

Even over the phone, Mitch felt the change in the man's attitude. All traces of boredom were gone from the man's voice. Now his tone carried a knife's edge of excitement. Wondering about it, Mitch leaned back in his chair. "He gave the name Justin Carter. We haven't been able to confirm that is his real name. What does the name Jacob Carter mean to you?"

The question was ignored, as the line was silent a long second. "Detective Mitchell, I am going to transfer you to Special Agent Dixon. Please hold."

While he waited, Mitch tucked the phone under his chin, leafing through the paper on his desk. Every mention of Carter, it was Justin, not Jacob. Whoever this Jacob Carter was, the FBI certainly had a hard on for him. Mitch felt a tickle in the back of neck. This was something. Enough of something that person manning the phones was contacting a Special Agent at home after hours. Mitch glanced at his watch, almost four. That would make it almost seven there, and still he transferred the call to the Special Agent's home. Interesting.

After several minutes on hold, a smooth feminine voice with just the hint of a sexy rasp came on the line. "May I help you?"

"I'm holding for Agent Dixon."

"This is Special Agent Dixon," she said, the rasp a little more pronounced, now that she was agitated.

"Pleased to meet you," Mitch said, trying to be smooth. "I'm Detective John Mitchell."

"I know all of that," she said, not quite snapping. "I'm interested in this Mister Carter, I understand you had him in custody and released him. Is that correct?"

"That is correct," Mitch answered, realizing the reason for the long wait on hold was the other agent had filled her in on the details

"Tell me Detective Mitchell; is the Tucson Police department in the habit of releasing murder suspects?"

Mitch chuckled. Despite the dressing down she was trying to give him, he already kinda liked her. "At the time we had Mister Carter in custody, we didn't know he was a suspect. Hell, we didn't even know we had a murder at that time."

There was a long pause. "I'm sorry, Detective. Obviously, I don't know all the facts of your case. Tell me what did this man Carter look like?"

"I never saw him, but like you said, we did have him in custody. I'm looking at his mug shot, right now."

"What does he look like?" Agent Dixon asked, a bit of hoarse desperation in her voice.

"Late twenties, early thirties. Dark colored hair, just looking at the picture; smart-ass is the word that comes to mind."

Mitch heard a quick intake of breath. "That describes Jacob Carter to a tee. Can you send me a copy of the mug shot?"

"Sure," Mitch said easily. "We are digital now. Give me an email and I'll shoot it right to you."

Mitch wrote down the address she gave him, then called up the net on his computer. "I understand you had a young girl kidnapped and murdered. Is that correct?"

"Not quite," Mitch said, waiting for his email page to open. "We had a kidnapping and a girl murdered, but it wasn't the same girl."

"Hmm, that's strange. Any chance the first girl is already dead, and you just haven't discovered the body?"

Mitch shrugged, even though she couldn't see him. "I guess anything is possible, but that would be two girls in forty-eight hours. Seems a little excessive to me."

"With Carter anything is possible. The normal rules don't apply to him. But you are right, that would be off the charts, even for him.""

"If you want I can send you all the paper we have on the case. We scan everything into the computer; I can forward it all to you."

"That would be good. I'll look it over tonight. Maybe I can have some conclusions for you in the morning."

"Thanks. You should be getting the mug shot anytime."

"It's here." There was a long pause. "Shit, it's him," Agent Dixon said quietly.

"Jacob Carter?"

"Yes, it's him. We have quite a file on that young man."

"Can you send it to me?"

"Yes. Give me a second and I'll send it straight out."

"Sounds like you know him personally?" Mitch observed.

"We crossed paths before."

"So, tell me. How do I catch him?"

"I don't think you do, Detective. Nobody else has."

Perry Van Zandt's Office Washington DC June 14 2018 Thursday Late Afternoon

Perry Van Zandt frowned, scowling down at the document on his desk. They go to trial in three days and his opening statement was not ready. There were problems. He was marking the document with a red pen, when his phone rang. This was the line that rang straight in the office, bypassing his secretary. Only a few people had that number.

Wondering what could be going wrong now, Van Zandt picked up the phone. "Yes," he said softly.

"Van Zandt, we need to meet!"

"What is the matter?" Van Zandt asked his voice mild as he pushed back in his chair and frowned at the far wall.

"No, not on the phone."

"Okay," Van Zandt said, his frown blossoming into a full blown scowl. "I'll meet you at the club in an hour."

"No, not at the club. We shouldn't be seen together. Be out in front in fifteen minutes, I'll pick you up."

Van Zandt didn't like the tone, or the fact that he was being ordered around. He was tempted to refuse, but let it go. Van Zandt had learned; never let pride get in the way of business. "I'll be there," he said, hanging up.

Van Zandt carefully finished the water on his desk, placing the empty crystal glass on a tray. In the morning when he arrived a new glass and fresh pitcher of water would be on his desk. He placed his pen in his desk, and gathered the document, placing it in a folder. Moving deliberately, he packed the folder and other essentials in his briefcase. Van Zandt locked his desk, slipped into his jacket, and then shut off the light.

As he stepped out of the office, the heat and humidity rushed over him, leaving the impression of being smothered in a wet blanket. Showing no signs of discomfort, Van Zandt waited patiently. It occurred to Van Zandt that it would have been better to have met at the club. If anyone were watching, they would see Braxton pick him up. After a few minutes a black Range Rover glided to the curb. Van Zandt didn't move for a second, simply holding his briefcase and frowning at the ridicules vehicle.

Carl Braxton owned land in New Hampshire and liked to portray himself as an outdoors man. Van Zandt had little time for such pretentions. He liked sailing and golf, but didn't care for hunting and the other outdoor activities.

None of this showed on his face as he opened the door and stepped up into the vehicle. Neither man spoke until Braxton merged back into traffic. "We have a problem." Braxton whined.

Van Zandt remained silent as he arranged the briefcase on the floor between his feet. "The reporter? Yes, I know, it's being taken care of."

"No, not the reporter, my wife's press secretary."

"Miss Schroeder?" Van Zandt asked, glancing at Braxton. There had been a rumor floating around that Braxton had been sleeping with Schroeder. "Is she pregnant?" he asked quietly.

"No! Christ no!" Braxton screeched, and Van Zandt knew immediately he was lying.

"She better not be," Van Zandt hissed, for no other reason other than he liked to see people squirm. Truthfully, he couldn't care less about Tamera Schroeder's maternal condition. Unless it could be used to his advantage? Suppose something happened to her? Who would get the blame? The seed of a plan germinating in his mind, Van Zandt glared at his companion. "Are you sure?"

"I said no," Braxton said, almost crying as he slapped on the brakes and screeched to a halt at a red light. "But she found out about the payoff to that reporter guy."

"Jackson Pyle," Van Zandt supplied, feeling a flash of irritation. He had an incredible memory for names and faces, and very little patience for those who didn't share his gift. "Is she going to make a problem out of this?" Van Zandt didn't care about Miss Schroeder, but this might be trouble. He might have to accelerate the plan forming in his mind.

Braxton flipped the air conditioning to high mopping sweat from his face. "Is she going to be a problem?" Van Zandt repeated his voice soft.

"I don't know." Braxton stared straight ahead, unable to look at Van Zandt. "Yes, maybe," he said finally. He eased the Range Rover from the light. "She called me all upset about it. I don't know what she might do."

"Hmm." Van Zandt lightly fingered his chin. "Maybe she should go."

Braxton wrenched the Range Rover to the curb, turning to face Van Zandt. "Fuck, I don't know. If even a hint of this blew back on Jillian, she could just kiss the Presidency goodbye."

Van Zandt shrugged. Jillian Braxton becoming President was a trivial matter to him. Secretly he thought her to be a dithering twit. Looking to make the world perfect, when anybody with sense knew that was unachievable. Van Zandt's face was calm, showing none of his distaste. "Maybe you should control Miss Schroeder."

"I don't know if I can." Braxton looked out the front of the Range Rover, unable to meet Van Zandt's gaze.

"Does she know about Arizona?" Van Zandt demanded his tone quiet and menacing.

"No," Braxton said, still looking out the windshield. "She might know something about Forsyth."

"What does she know?"

"I don't know, maybe nothing." Braxton continued to stare straight ahead playing with the steering wheel. "She was asking me about him and how he died. If he really took his own life."

"She has to go."

"What about Jillian and the Presidency?"

"Fuck that," Van Zandt said harshly, making Braxton jump in his seat. "We already have too much invested in Arizona to risk it. I spoke with Senator Moncrieff last night. We have the votes to get this out of committee."

A greedy light flashed in Braxton's eyes as he turned to face Van Zandt. "No shit?" He rubbed the side of his face. A greedy look swept across his face. "So, it is a done deal, then?"

"All we need is for Arizona to make a formal request""

"Do you think Reynolds and Brody can deliver that?"

"You and your wife assured me they could. If not, your wife may have to bring some pressure to bear on Governor Axelsen."

Braxton was rubbing his face again. "Yeah, she can do that. What about that fucking Brody?"

Van Zandt shrugged it away. "We have his daughter; he'll make sure we get what we need."

"Then what?" Braxton worried. "Christ, between Brody and those kids you had working for you this could end up costing us a bundle. You should be more careful who you hire."

Van Zandt shrugged, summing up his estimation of Braxton's opinion. "You hire the smartest people you can find. I would be very disappointed if they couldn't come up with a way to make a little extra on the side."

"Well hell, you sound like you are almost proud of them," Braxton said in exasperation. Unconcerned, Van Zandt shrugged again. "Christ, you had them killed. Why bother if you don't care."

"I never said I didn't care. I said I expected it." Van Zandt gave a smile that would have made a jack-o-lantern shiver. "I dealt with them as I did so the next smart person who thinks they can make extra off me, will think twice."

Braxton swallowed, mopping his face with a handkerchief. "What about Brody? He was right in on it with those kids."

"Don't worry about Brody, once Governor Axelsen submits the request to congress, we won't need Brody. Carter is out there, when the time comes, he will take care of Brody."

"Crap, Carter. Do you trust that little psychopath?"

"He is a very useful tool."

"Is any of this going to come back on Jillian?" Braxton demanded, his eyes narrowing as Van Zandt gave a casual shrug. "God damn it!" he exploded, pounding the steering wheel. "That was the arrangement when we brought you in on this deal. If Jillian delivered the votes in Congress and got Axelsen to sponsor the deal, you would see that she is the next President."

Van Zandt eyed the man impassively. When on the rare occasion he thought about them, he wondered about Carl and Jillian Braxton. Carl doted on the woman and had spent a good portion of his personal fortune financing her political career. On the other hand, according to Van

Zandt's information, Braxton had stuck his dick in every female he could get to open her legs for him. Van Zandt gave a small shrug. "Might not happen."

"You promised," Braxton accused.

"You still stand to make a good deal of money."

"Shit, fifteen or twenty million at the most," Braxton complained, whining.

Van Zandt smiled a nasty grin. A few years ago, Braxton could have pulled off the attitude that twenty million was nothing to him, but Van Zandt knew that was no longer the case. Braxton had made some foolish deals and spent a bloody fortune on this campaign, he needed the money. Van Zandt ignored the other man, pulling his phone and calling for his driver to come pick him up. After killing his phone, he placed it carefully in his pocket.

Van Zandt pinned the older man with a hard look. "Just see that you hold up your end. Can you manage that?" Braxton nodded, then shivered as he saw something dark and oily creep into Van Zandt's thin smile. "Don't worry," Van Zandt said softly, and licked his lips. "I will take care of Miss Schroeder."

CHAPTER FIVE

City Streets Tucson AZ June 14 2018 Thursday Night

Mitch was rolling around. After watching five minutes of the news he'd grabbed his coat and headed out. On every single station the reporters had crucified him and his team, second-guessing every move they have made. Even sweet looking Starla Chavez had taken shots at him.

Restless and pissed, he was out rolling around. He had the windows down, letting the cool night air wash over him. It felt good to be doing something, not that he was learning anything. He'd talked to a couple of hookers on Miracle Mile. They complained that some local kids were doing drive by shootings with paintball guns, but knew nothing about Angie Brody.

One of the girls who called herself Trixxxie, but Mitch knew her real name was Paula, leaned in smacking her gum. "Hey, Mitch, I heard you were the man to see if a girl had some extra money to invest," she whispered in Mitch's ear.

"Maybe," Mitch said. "How much are we talking?"

She smiled, looking over her shoulder to make sure the other girls weren't listening. They were already drifting away, knowing they wouldn't get any business while talking to Mitch. "Ten thousand, four hundred and sixty-seven dollars," she said with a wink.

"Holly shit!" Mitch exclaimed, not surprised that she knew exactly how much she had, but that it was so much. Most of these girls could count money quicker than a Wall Street broker and spend it just as fast. "Damn girl. What are you doing with that kind of money?"

She laughed. "Shit, I don't want to be doing this when I'm twenty-five like some of these skanks. I got plans."

"Gonna go to LA, be in the movies?"

"Ha," she laughed patting Mitch's arm. "I'm gonna buy me a ranch out by Sierra Vista and find me a cowboy with a nice smile and a big dick." She closed her eyes, picturing it. "We will drink wine at sunset, raise cows and kids." For a second she had a faraway look, then she snapped back. "Can you help me?"

"Paula that is too much money for me." Mitch dug out one of his cards, writing a number on the back. "This is a guy I use. His name is Lewis Philson. Call him, he will take care of you."

She touched his arm. "Thanks, dude," she said, lightly kissing his cheek. "You know anything about cows?"

"I know I like steak, that's about it," Mitch replied, with a smile.

"Well hell, what good are you then?" she said, pushing back from the car.

"Let me know if you hear anything about that girl," Mitch called as she walked away and received a thumb's up and an ass swish in return.

Smiling, Mitch moved on. After talking to the girls, he went in a pawn shop on Grant, looked at a couple of guns. There was a nice Sig .380. Mitch held the gun, sighting in on the security camera in the back. "That's a right nice gun," the owner Bruce said, smacking on a piece of Juicy Fruit. "A nice dress gun to wear when you're out on the town. Just what a young, single guy like you needs."

"Yeah, all I need is another gun," Mitch said, regretfully laying the gun back on the counter. He might not need it, but damn, he sure did want it.

"Shit, you show that gun to some young thing and she'll cream her jeans. Be on you like white on rice," Bruce said, with a hacking wheezing laugh. "Make you a good deal on it, too. Just cause it's you."

"Yeah, right," Mitch grunted. "Besides, I'm putting all my cash into the car.

"Sounded nice when you pulled up." Bruce hesitated, looking both ways to make sure they were alone. "I guess maybe, you heard that Dell and Chappy Miers was back in town."

Mitch nodded, absently picking the Sig back up. "Yeah, I heard," Mitch said, working the action on the pistol, liking the crisp feel of the slide. "I haven't seen them yet."

Bruce ran a hand over his bald head, looked both ways again, motioning for Mitch to lean closer. "I heard that Chappy was working a deal with some Mex drug dealer. Word is he is going to be bringing a big load of shit across the border." Bruce took another look over his shoulder. "Somebody might have mentioned that there is a meeting going down."

Mitch cocked his head, looking sideways at the older man, wondering how much he could believe. Mitch had long suspected that Bruce might deal a little shit out the back door. Was this a legit tip, or was Bruce trying to slow down the competition? "When?" he asked.

Bruce squirmed a little, checking again to make sure they were alone. "Sometime in the next couple of days. Way I hear it, Chappy has big plans. Gonna be big time."

"Is that a fact?"

"That's what I hear. What I hear is Chappy wants to be a big man. Run all of southern AZ," he said, pronouncing it hayzee. Coughing, Bruce launched his wad of Juicy Fruit towards a trash can behind the counter. The gum missed the can, sticking to the wall beside countless other pieces of gum. "Damn, I miss smoking," he complained, unwrapping a fresh piece. "You want the Sig or not?"

"Not today," Mitch said, running his hand along the slide. With a sigh of regret, he passed it to Bruce. "You hear anything about that girl, let me know."

Bruce shrugged his thin shoulders. "Like I said, Chappy Miers."

"Nope witnesses say the guy that grabbed her was small."

Bruce was nodding along. "And the only thing small about Chappy is his brain."

"You know it," Mitch replied, turning away.

Mitch stepped out into the night. Fucking Chappy Miers. That was all he needed. Mitch had known Chappy for years, since they were in school. Chappy had been a bully in school, and over the years had blossomed into a regular psychopath. With Chappy in town, it was only a matter of time before trouble happened.

Leaning against the fender of his car, Mitch dug out his cell, dialing Sam Logan's number. "Sam, its Mitch."

"Hey Mitch. Anything shake out with those plates?"

"Not much, might have figured out where they got lifted, but that's about it."

"Yeah, Mel didn't even know they were gone until we went out to the barn to look, I figure they lost them when they were in Tucson."

"Probably, our guy bought a pre-paid at that Wal-Mart same day your guy Mel was there," Mitch agreed. "Look the reason I called was you mentioned something about trying to run down a new local connection with Mexican drugs."

"Yeah," Sam said, and Mitch could hear the old man perking up, like a hunting dog catching the scent. "You got something for me on that?"

"Maybe. I heard tonight that Chappy Miers is setting up a big meeting with a Mexican dealer. He's supposed to be bringing a big shipment across."

"Aw shit. You sure know how to ruin a perfectly good night."

"Yeah," Mitch said, chuckling at his friend's misery. "You heard anything about Angie Brody?" Mitch asked, even though he knew, if Sam had heard anything, he would have called.

"No, not a damn thing," Sam rasped. "Which is weird by itself. I mean I shoulda heard something, even if it was just pure dee bullshit. But I ain't heard so much as peep."

"Me neither," Mitch said. "You're right, though. It is odd that we haven't heard something."

"Yeah, either nobody knows nothing, or they are too scared to say, but nobody is talking about it." Logan paused. "Shit if that damn Chappy Miers is back in town, you might want to jack his ass up. Snatching some pretty young thing off the street sounds just like him."

"Couple of wits saw it go down, they all agreed the guy was kinda small."

Logan sighed. "Well, the only thing small about Chappy is his IQ."

Thinking about that, Mitch hung up. Sam was right. There should be at least some gossip, some idle chatter about it on the streets. The news was full of it, but no one was talking about it on the street.

Mitch was still thinking about it when his phone rang in his hand. He glanced at the number, not recognizing it. "Yeah," he grunted into the phone.

"Detective Mitchell, this is Special Agent Dixon. We spoke earlier."

Mitch raised an eyebrow, it was after ten in Tucson, what time did that make it in DC? Late. Very Late. "What can I do for you, Agent Dixon?"

"I'm sorry to call so late. I hope I didn't wake you."

"No, I'm out chasing a few things down."

"Really," she said a glimmer of hope shinning in her tone. "You have new developments?"

"Naw, I'm just out trying to pick up a scrap of something. Any little thing we might be able to run down."

"Okay," she said, disappointment crushing down her earlier sparkle. "I was thinking I would come out there," Agent Dixon said, faltering just a little.

Mitch leaned back against the car frowning. He really didn't want a bunch of feds, trying to big-foot his case, but at this point he would take any help he could get. "Sure, right now we can use some new ideas."

"Thank you. My plane lands at one."

"I'll have someone pick you up."

"That really won't be necessary. I can manage my own way to your office."

"It's no problem. I'll pick you up."

"Thank you then."

Sam Logan's House Tucson AZ June 14 2018 Thursday Night

Sam hung up the phone, rubbing his chin as he stared out the back door and into the darkness. "Do you have to go back out?" his wife asked, ready to make some coffee.

"No," he replied, shaking his head. "That was just Mitch, passing along some info."

"Mitch," she repeated, a smile creeping onto her face. "He called yesterday; I'm going to get some money on that steak thing."

"You gave him money for those steaks? I thought you bought into the bird farm?"

Maureen smiled, giving him a swat. "I did. I did both."

"Oh hell," Sam said, rolling his eyes. "Well, you certainly prove the old adage that there is one born every minute."

"Ha, lot you know old man. I told you, I'm getting some money."

"Yeah," Sam grumbled, but he was smiling. "I'll believe it when I see the money in your hand."

Maureen gave him a not quite gentle cuff upside the head. "You hush old man. Mitch is a good boy."

"Yeah, he is," Sam agreed, pulling his wife into his lap. He held her, thinking about how many times they had sat at this very table. They had been sitting in this very spot, her on his lap, when Maureen told him she was pregnant with Sammy. They had been sitting here when they got the call about the accident.

Maureen leaned down and kissed the top of his head. "Tell you what; Mitch said he would drop the money by sometime next week. You keep Friday night open, and I will take you out to dinner. My treat." She pointed a finger down at him. "You write that down in your book, I don't want you claiming you forgot. I'll not have you using that excuse this early."

"Yeah," Sam grunted, still thinking back to the night when the call came in about the kids.

"You okay?"

"Yeah, yeah," Sam said, shaking his head. "I was just thinking about all the things that happened right here at this table."

Maureen's face softened with a wistful smile. "It does seem like our whole lives have been lived right here. Good and bad."

"We don't have to keep going with this? I can stop it right now?" Sam said, looking into her eyes.

Maureen shook her head. "Now, we've been through this. It's what must be done. It's the right thing to do. I just wish you would let me do more."

"You don't want to be in on this," Sam said, taking her hand in his. "I just worry that I'll be gone when you need me most."

"I'll get by," she said, leaning into his chest. "You just keep next Friday open."

"Where are you taking me?"

"I don't know. Where would you like to go?"

Sam grinned, wagging his eyebrows. "How about Hooters?"

"You better watch yourself old man. I still have a rolling pin and just because I don't get it out much anymore don't mean I don't know how to use it."

"Yes, ma'am," Sam said, pulling her close. "Ruby Tuesdays?"

"Sure," Maureen said, smiling because that is where they always went. Sam would grumble over the menu for ten minutes, then he would order a steak, baked potato and a Coors Light, hold the gravy and hold the damned salad.

Sam rubbed her back. "A lot of years," he said quietly.

"Good years," she agreed.

"I was thinking of all the things that happened here. I was thinking of the call."

"I know," Maureen croaked, her voice barely a whisper and a single tear tracking uncertainly down her face. "I was thinking about when the kids said they was pregnant."

"Yeah," Sam whispered, then let out a painful, barking laugh. "Remember when Sammy set us down here and told us about his plans to open up a lemonade stand?"

Maureen laughed a low, bittersweet chuckle. "What was he about seven or eight? I will never forget him explaining to us how he was going to be the lemonade king."

"Yup," Sam said, nodding. "He was gonna buy us a new car, and we should by God better go start looking for one."

They both laughed, picturing a freckle-faced boy in the striped shirt that he favored, seriously explaining how he was going to make enough to buy them a new car. "That was a long time ago," Maureen said.

"Damn dear, we're old," Sam said. "When did that happen?"

"Speak for yourself, buster," Maureen said, getting to her feet and dragging Sam with her. "Come with me and I'll show you who is old."

Tucson Police Headquarters Tucson AZ June 15th 2018 Friday Morning

Wade and Jerry were huddled around Wade's computer. As Mitch pushed through the door, he could feel an electric excitement boiling off the two men. "Tell me you got something."

They turned as one. "We got an ID on the dead girl," Jerry said.

"No, shit," Mitch said, dragging a chair up. "Who was she? Does it help us?"

"Fuck if I know," Wade said, running a hand through his curly blonde hair. "Her real name was Lindsey Meredith Humphries, originally from Boston."

"Where'd you get the match?"

"Straight out of the Metro DC data base." Jerry stopped, rubbing the point of his chin with a knuckle.

"Funny thing is, she's in the system, but no arrest reports, no record of charges ever being filed."

"So why is she in the system? Think she was on the corner?"

Both men shrugged. Wade sighed easing his leg out straight. "We called back there, talked to some flatfoot. He didn't know her, but said he would ask around and get back to us."

Jerry snorted. "He ain't gonna call."

"From DC, huh?" Mitch grunted, thinking it over. "I'm picking up that F.B.I. agent today, maybe she knows someone we can call; get a line on this girl."

Wade nodded slowly. "This Lindsey, you think she was part of this?"

Mitch shrugged. "Man, I don't know. She's from DC, so is Carter. Seems like a helluva coincidence."

"Damn, she's been working out at Star Pass for almost two years. Seems like a long time to have something in play," Jerry wondered.

"Two years," Wade said, loosening his knee brace and scratching his leg. "That is a long time."

"Maybe," Mitch admitted. "But two years ain't so long in real estate terms. If this really is a big deal, two years isn't an over long lead time for something like that."

"But they put this Lindsey chick with Angie two years ago, just so they could snatch Angie to bring Brody back in line?" Jerry said shaking his head. "I don't see it."

"Seems like a helluva stretch," Wade agreed.

"She was doing Brody," Mitch reminded them.

"So, you think they put Lindsey next to Brody to keep an eye on him?" Jerry asked.

"Man, I don't know," Mitch said, running a hand through his hair. "Maybe. Seems like they got in bed with Brody, but maybe they didn't think he could be trusted."

"With good reason, apparently," Wade commented dryly.

"Apparently," Mitch agreed. "So, if they don't trust Brody, maybe they put Lindsey with him just to keep track of what he's doing."

"You think she's a pro?" Wade wondered.

"That would explain why she's in the DC system," Jerry observed.

"She hasn't been busted, so more likely she has a sugar daddy," Mitch agreed.

"Still seems like a stretch to me," Wade argued. "They been paying her for two years? I don't see it. Be easier just to get rid of Brody"

"Maybe they need Brody," Mitch asked.

"That might be it," Jerry said. "But why? What is so special about Brody?"

Garage behind Deacon's Clubhouse Tucson AZ June 15th 2018 Friday Afternoon

Chappy sat on the garage floor, leaning back against the wall, his head pounding like an engine break on a big rig. For the first time in his life, Chappy felt despair. If he had just a little more time he might be able to raise the money.

He'd tried working on the '42 knuckle-head he was restoring but he couldn't concentrate. His mind kept returning to his problem. Not with any solutions, just the worry.

He'd tried getting drunk and had drank enough beer to float a battleship but that hadn't helped. He hadn't gotten drunk, just tired. Somewhere around dawn, he fell asleep or passed out, wasn't sure which. But now he had a full-blown hangover and he still had the worry dogging his mind.

He was considering getting up to take a piss when the phone rang. He glanced at the screen, which was blank, but the phone was still ringing. Curious, he flipped the phone open. "Yeah."

"I trust you know who this is," a smooth voice said.

"Yeah, I remember you, man."

"Good," Van Zandt said shortly. "If you are still interested in making some money. I might be able to help you. Two hundred and fifty thousand was the number if I remember correctly."

"What's the job?" Chappy barked, grabbing onto the lifeline like a drowning man.

"Not on the phone. Do you know a bar called The Bucket?"

"I've been there," Chappy said, thinking he'd only been there about a thousand times.

"Good, meet my associate Mister Carter there in one hour."

Tucson Airport Tucson AZ June 15 2018 Friday Afternoon

She came through the jet way, and Mitch recognized her, even though she didn't look anything like her voice suggested. She had a little bit of a cop's walk, and a little bit of a sex kitten's seductive swing. She paused a beat at the bottom of the jet way, tossing her hair, but Mitch saw her eyes sweep the concourse.

Mitch didn't step forward to meet her; instead, he leaned back, watching her. She walked like a cop, taking her own space. She didn't glide gracefully, but she moved athletically, like a quarterback coming up to the line. This was a woman that was used to taking care of herself.

She had dark hair, in a stylish mid-length cut, framing her face and bringing out her delicate features. Her eyes were large and round. She was wearing a silk blouse and a mid-length skirt. All in all a striking figure.

She glanced his way, a quick up and down measuring look, then away. Mitch smiled to himself, pleased that she hadn't made him as a cop. Mitch waited until she was even with him, before pushing away from the rail he was leaning against. "Agent Dixon," he said.

She swept him with that same up and down look. "Detective Mitchell?" she said, skepticism riding the edge of her voice.

"That's me," Mitch said, flashing his best smile. "Do you have any bags?"

"Just these," she said, shrugging her shoulders to indicate the laptop bag in her left hand and the small over-night bag slung over her left shoulder.

"Let me help you with those."

"Thanks," she grunted, passing him the over-night bag.

Mitch smiled again. He knew she would hang onto the laptop bag. Most women would have kept their clothes, or the lightest bag. But not this woman.

"I don't suppose you have him?"

Her tone was curt, but then Mitch suspected it might be most of the time. "Not yet. We're looking."

"Too much to hope for," she said, then gestured to a lady's room sign. "I need to make a stop in there."

"Sure, I'll hold your other bag."

"I got it."

"Sure," Mitch said, grinning, watching her walk away as he fished out his cell. "Wade, it's Mitch, anything new?"

"Nothing of note. Ollie and Parker are running down a tip that came in over the phone. I don't expect much to come of it."

"What was the tip?"

"Waitress from a dinner over off First called it in. Said a couple came in, acting strange, woman didn't act happy.

Ollie took a couple of six-packs of pictures over to see if she could pick out either Carter or Angie Brody."

"Okay, keep me posted. I just picked up Dixon."

"Yeah? What's she like?"

"Typical east coast. A little up tight, pretty tightly wound."

"Is she pretty?"

"Maybe," Mitch hedged, wondering why he didn't want to admit it. Geena Dixon was a very striking woman. Mitch would bet she would look dynamite in a pair of jeans.

"Aw shit, you're wanting to bang her already."

"Get back to work," Mitch snapped, killing the phone, as Dixon came out of the ladies' room.

"Okay," she said. "Where do we start?"

Mitch gave a small shrug. "Well, he didn't leave much at either of the crime scenes. Just the fingerprints."

"The finger print thing, that is new, but the rest of it does sound like him. He is a cocky son of a bitch."

"Wasn't much at either crime scene, no use going to either of them, unless you just want to. Maybe you could start by telling me everything you know about him. I want to get a better feel for him."

"What do you mean?"

"What kind of people will he be comfortable with? Is he into bikes? Cars? Drugs? Who would he go to for help?"

"He likes golf, poker, and fine foods. Doesn't have many friends."

Geena was still thinking when a loud voice cut across the concourse. "Mitch. Hey, Mitch," a tall, whip-thin black man called waving a hand over his head.

For a fleeting second, Mitch frowned, then an easy smile slipped onto his face. "Marcus, what are you doing out here?"

Now it was Marcus' turn to scowl, a dark, black look. "Shit, Heather's mom's coming back into town. I gotta pick her ass up."

"Ouch," Mitch said, grinning openly. "She staying with you?"

"You know it," Marcus said sourly. All of a sudden, his face turned on like a light bulb. "Say, I heard you were still looking for Mustang parts. Jimmy just got in a seventy-one."

"You and Jimmie haven't been doing some mid-night shopping?"

Marcus held up his hands, revealing grease stains. "Shit no, we came on it clean," he said, rolling out a cackling laugh. "Man, you ain't gonna believe it. This old grandma wrapped it around a signal pole off Speedway."

"No shit."

"Yeah, no shit" Marcus replied, still laughing. "I guess the old man bought it brand spanking new back in the day. He's been babying it all these years. Fucking thing only had thirty thousand miles on it. Wouldn't even let the wife drive it."

"Smart man."

"You'd think so, but see it didn't work out. He's seventy, and grandma sees him grabbing at the maid's ass. They got this little hot illegal helping out around the house." Marcus was openly laughing now. "So, grandma sees granddaddy grabbing a handful, and she gets pissed. She decides to take it out on the Mustang. She went to the grocery store, backed it into a light pole and scraped it along a cart. Then she goes to Wal-Mart. Guess it had more power than her Taurus. It ended up on the medium right there at Kolb and Speedway."

"You got to be kidding."

"I shit you not. The body of this car is toast. She musta hit everything there was to hit on the way, but the drive train is pure cherry."

"Tell Jimmie I will give him a call. I still need a few things. Trouble is, mine's a sixty-eight. I don't know how many parts will work."

"Shoulda bought a 'vette. Damn Chevy parts will exchange back to the beginning of time."

Mitch nodded absently. "Like them Mustangs, though," Mitch said, seeing Geena Dixon fidgeting. "You hear anything about a bunch of 4K TVs falling off a truck?"

A foxy look stole onto Marcus's face. "Maybe. Why do you want to know?"

"I need something to squeeze somebody with. I need to find out about a new bad boy in town."

"Oh, fuck. I can tell you about that. I heard that fuckin' Chappy Miers is back in town."

"I'm talking about that girl that got snatched the other day."

"Well, shit that sounds like Chappy. You remember what he done to Gypsy?"

Mitch nodded. Gypsy was a black girl a couple of years ahead of Mitch in school. She'd gotten a little too friendly with Chappy Miers at a party. They'd stolen away for a quickie. Somehow, things got out of hand and he beat her half to death. "Some of the brothers still want to kill that mother fucker over that," Marcus said, cutting across Mitch's memories.

"Yeah, but the guy who grabbed that girl, witnesses said he was smaller and wiry. That sound like Chappy?"

Marcus grinned. "Hell, only thing small about Chappy is his dick."

"Yeah, what do you know about those flat screens?"

Marcus looked both ways, taking a step closer. "What about her?' he asked, jerking his head in Geena's direction.

"Don't worry about her. She's a cop from back east."

"A cop? No way!" Marcus said, sending a leering look in Geena's direction. "You wanna cuff me? I might consent to a strip search."

"Shit, Marcus, shut the hell up," Mitch snapped. "What do you know about the TVs?"

"Alright, you don't have to get all up in my shit," Marcus said, sulking.

"Come on Marcus. We are on the clock on this one," Mitch said, taking out a fifty from his wallet. He wrote an email address on the bill. "This guy can help you with the parts for that spitfire."

Marcus snatched the bill, a look of glee spreading across his face. He and Jimmie had been restoring a spitfire convertible for years. "You didn't hear it from me, but Dealer Sam is running a special right now. Fifty-five-inch 4K flat screen for two hundred."

"Thanks," Mitch said, clapping Marcus on the back. "And don't forget to keep your ears open about the thing with that girl. Be worth some bucks if somebody could help us out."

"I ain't heard nothin', but I'll pass the word. Not that I'm likely to hear. I'm gonna be stuck at home with Heather's mom."

Mitch laughed. "Oh hell, get twenty rolls of quarters and drop her at Casino of the Sun."

Marcus brightened. "Shit, that there is an idea." He grinned at Mitch. "You know, you ain't quite as dumb as the papers said you was."

"I have my good days," Mitch admitted. "Spread the word. Anything we can get could be good for a free pass on something."

"Sure, Mitch," Marcus said, nodding his head. "You want that motor. It's in cherry condition. Be nice to have on hand if you ever track down a Mach-1. It'd slip right in. You think about it. I gotta go." Marcus slapped the side of his face and shook his head as if he were contemplating the wrath of the devil. "Lord help me if I'm late."

Mitch thought about the motor as Marcus shuffled off. Just before Marcus disappeared from sight, Mitch called out. "Tell Jimmie to call me. I might take that motor." Mitch turned to Geena, who standing one hand on her hip, glaring at him. "You ready?" he asked.

"Unless you want to go buy a new suit, or maybe shop for some shoes."

Mitch smiled, not at all bothered that she was angry. "I do have a few errands to run. We can compare notes while we're rolling around," Mitch said, as a blaze of anger swept across her face. She opened her mouth for an angry retort, but Mitch cut her off. "Look, I don't know what you expect here, but there ain't a lot to do. The crime scenes are shit. If you want to see them fine, but there's absolutely nothing to see there. I've got all the paper we've generated on this. You can look at it, and tell me what you know about Carter. If nothing shakes out of that," Mitch ended with a shrug.

"So, we just sit back and do nothing, until he kills another girl?" Geena asked, plenty of bite in her tone.

"No, we do what we are doing. We get the word out on the street. To guys like Marcus we offer something, other guys we are squeezing. Sooner or later, somebody will know something. Until then we study what we have. Here's our file," Mitch said, handing her the file.

Geena didn't say anything, taking the file and flipping it open. She paged through it quickly. "Not much here," she said, a bit of edge in her tone.

"Fuck you!" Mitch snapped, stepping in front of her. "You've been after this guy what almost ten years? We've only had a couple of days."

For a second they locked eyes, it was Geena looked away. "Sorry, I guess I deserved that."

For a second, Mitch held onto his anger, then he smiled, shaking his head. "Naw, forget it. Come on I'll buy you a cup of coffee."

"Okay," she said, as they walked up to a small coffee kiosk. Mitch held up two fingers digging in his pocket. "No offense, Mitchell," Geena said, looking around. "But this is a crappy, little airport."

"Yeah," Mitch agreed handing her a cup. "They keep talking about building a new one, but no one around here can agree on what to do, so nothing gets done."

"You are meaner than I thought," Geena said, abruptly changing the subject.

"Huh?" Mitch grunted, dropping his change into the tip jar.

"When I first saw you, I thought you were nothing more than a soft, pretty boy, but I see now. You got a mean streak."

"Thanks," Mitch said. "If that was intended to be a compliment."

Geena gave Mitch a short shrug, which struck Mitch as very back eastern. "Whatever," she said.

Shouldering her bag, Mitch slipped on a pair of sunglasses, leading her out the door. The Trooper stood at the end of the drop off lane. Geena made a face when she realized the Trooper was their destination. She cocked her head, glancing sideways at Mitch. "Don't tell me this is what passes for a police car out here?"

"Oh hell, no, this is what passes for a limo out here," Mitch said popping the door locks. He tossed her bag in the back atop a tent, his golf clubs and an old sleeping bag. "If you want to take a quick look at the file, I need to make a few calls."

Mitch started the Trooper, flipping the AC on high. "The file is everything we have on Angie Brody and Lindsey

Meredith," Mitch said, hitting the speed dial for Wade Nichols.

"Okay," Geena grunted already reading. "If you don't mind, I would still like to take a walk through the motel room where Meredith was killed."

"Sure," Mitch said, as Wade answered the phone. "How are you coming on Brody?" he asked.

He could hear the exasperation in the sigh Wade let out. "I don't know, Mitch. I think there is something here. I can feel it. I don't know enough about his business to see it."

"What have you found?"

"Well like Jerry said, Brody isn't making enough money on his projects to support his operation. He does a lot of business with holding companies. Jerry's trying to trace them down. Most of his money seems like it might come from back east, but we haven't been able to nail down to a person or company."

"Okay, keep at it."

"Mitch, we need someone who knows about business to look at this stuff. What about Kathy Reynolds? You know her pretty well from what I hear. She works in finance, she could help."

"No," Mitch snapped. "Keep looking."

"Trouble?" Geena asked, without looking up from her reading.

"No," Mitch said, punching a number on his cell. "Ollie, what are you doing?"

"Eating doughnuts and talking to dirt bags."

"How'd it go at the diner?"

"That was a bust. Waitress couldn't pick out either one of them. Her boyfriend is in jail. She was just hoping to spring him."

"Yeah," Mitch grunted. "You got time to take a run at Dealer Sam?"

"Sure thing, boss. You got something?"

"Marcus Haynes said Dealer was running a special on flat screens."

Mitch could almost hear Ollie smile. "Let me guess; those TVs are a little scratched from falling off a truck somewhere?"

"That'd be my guess. Jack him up. See what shakes out."

"I'm on it."

Mitch killed the phone, tossing it in a cubby in the dash. "Find anything we missed?" he asked, glancing over at Geena.

"Not really," she said, and Mitch couldn't tell if she was disappointed or happy. "I take it that you are crawling up Brody's ass?"

Mitch nodded. "We're trying to sort through his finances right now. Seems to be something there, we just haven't shaken it loose. It's getting pretty murky."

"I heard. Who is this Kathy Reynolds? An old flame of yours?"

"Something like that," Mitch grumbled.

"Okay," Geena said, letting out a rolling, musical laugh. "I won't pry, but if you want I can have a guy at the Bureau take a look. We have a couple of people who are whizzes at unraveling that type of thing."

"Something to think about. I want to give my guys another day," Mitch said, unwilling to give over his investigation to the Feds. "Tell me about Carter."

"His real name is Jacob Carter. The Justin thing maybe a slap at me."

"Really, we were wondering about the initials. JC, we thought it might be a Christ complex."

"Could be, but it doesn't fit with his profile," Geena said. "He may be taunting me. The first girl he killed was an

African-American girl named Justine Salters. I was involved with that case, so maybe he's just trying to get at me."

"Could be," Mitch admitted, pulling the Trooper into gear and easing away from the curb. "Seems like a stretch though. How would he even know we would call you about him?"

"He would know I would hear about this sooner or later." Geena gave a rueful shrug. "I've kinda made a hobby out of him since the Salters thing." Geena cocked her head, nibbling on her lip. "You never know with him. He does like jerking us around. The Christ thing could be coincidence or it could be his idea of a joke."

"What about him? Tell me about him," Mitch said.

"Rich kid. Grew up in the burbs of DC. Exclusive gated community. Spent summers on Long Island or up in the Hamptons. He went to Harvard. After Harvard, he went to GW Law. It's kind of murky why he left Harvard for GW. But his grades went from an almost four point to a two point five. He was at GW when Justine Salters was killed."

"So, he was smart enough to get by at GW Law School without really trying?"

"Apparently so. He is smart. Almost off the charts. After the Justine Salters thing, he transferred to Columbia and finished law school with respectable grades."

Mitch mulled it over as he wound out of the airport and onto Tucson Boulevard. "You said he left Harvard under murky circumstances. Was it sex or drugs?"

"Maybe both, but we think it was sex. There were rumors of date rape. Daddy paid off a couple of times. We heard there was one girl who was hurt pretty bad, but she wouldn't talk to us. No charges were filed, but he left the school."

"And of course, daddy paid off again."

"More than likely. He went to GW. That's where we crossed paths."

"You were on the force then? Doing sex crimes?"

"No, he had already graduated to murder by then."

"You were in homicide?"

Geena shook her head. "No, I wasn't on the force. I was a prosecutor with the DA's office." Geena shot him a frown as he turned east onto Valencia. "Aren't we going to the murder scene? We should have turned left," she said, then added. "I did a map search on the computer."

"Well, your computer doesn't live here. The interstate is just a few blocks, it'll be faster."

"Okay," Geena replied, sounding far from convinced. She took a sip of her coffee, studying the detective. He had a soft look about him, almost pretty. He had an easy smile, but he could be a prick. "You sound surprised that I might have been on a homicide table."

Mitch buzzed through a light at Palo Verde that was at least pink. "I was. You don't have that hard cop feel to you. I figured you were only on the job a year or so. Not long enough to make homicide."

She laughed, setting the coffee on the dash and clapping her hands. "Very good. You are a better detective than I thought. Right after law school, I went through the academy. I spent three months on a beat. Hated every minute of it. When the chance came to use my law degree at the prosecutor's office, I took it."

"Then on up to the feds?"

"Sure, I was a female with a law degree, and a minor in physiology, and a little street cop experience. Seemed like a natural move. It gave me a chance to stay after Carter. DCPD had already given up on him."

"You got it bad for him," Mitch observed, worried by that fact. Passion tended to ruin judgment.

"That girl he killed; Justine Salters. That got to me. Justine was a bright, young lady, working very hard for a future. He took that away. Every day, I feel like I let her down."

"Tell me about that," Mitch said, roaring up the on ramp and onto I-10. "The Salter's murder."

Geena nodded as if she approved of the question, or had been expecting it. "It was crude by his standards. I'm still not sure if he planned it out and it wasn't very refined, or it was just a spur of the moment deal. Either way, it seems to have set him off. Most of the other profilers think it was spur of the moment, but it gave him a taste and he liked it."

"You don't think so?"

"No," Geena said, sipping her coffee. "Like I said, it was crude by his standards today. He had some luck and a very good lawyer which got him off, but there were things that indicated planning. He managed to come up with a gas receipt and a couple of other things that helped his alibi. Seemed convenient. I kept coming back to the fact that he knew this girl since they were kids. She beat him in a city-wide grade school spelling bee."

"You think he waited all that time for revenge? For a spelling bee?"

"If anyone would, it would be Carter."

"And in the end, he walked on Salters. Then where did he go?"

"He graduated from law school a little over a year later, the next day he went to work for the lawyer that got him off."

"Then he started racking up the bodies?"

Geena shook her head. "Not right away. There was a lull. During the lull, we think maybe he killed a cop."

"Tell me about that."

Geena shrugged. "It was one of the original detectives from the Salters case. He used to park outside Carter's apartment."

"Just jacking with him," Mitch said, nodding. "You ever tie Carter to it? The cop killing?"

"No, it happened right out in front of Carter's apartment, but there was no physical evidence to tie him to it, and he passed a GSR. He hadn't fired a gun."

"Then the lull?"

"He was starting his career and traveling a lot. There could be a couple out on the road, but I've done a lot of checking and if there is, I haven't found them."

Mitch swung off the freeway and down onto Speedway. "So, he's working, pressure mounting. Any romantic attachments?"

"Nothing that stands out."

"But he starts killing. You find anything that was a trigger?"

"Nothing concrete. He was helping his boss on a murder trial. We think maybe that brought the Justine Salters memory back."

"Could be," Mitch agreed. "Pressure was building inside him anyway. Maybe the trial set him off, or maybe it was just as long as he could go. I understand that's how these guys work."

"Your grasp of this is impressive."

"I read a book or two," Mitch said. "So, he's working and pressures are building then he pops. He rapes and kills that woman in New Jersey? Was he ever a suspect?"

"No, he had no ties to the woman. It was several months later, after we got the note that we started looking at him."

"I was looking through the stuff you faxed me. You linked him through the notes?

"Yes. We would get a note, telling us where to find a body."

"Did you ever get any physical evidence tying Carter to the killings?"

Geena shook her head. "No. The bodies were months old when we found them. Not much chance to get any kind of evidence."

"Then, he's changing his method."

"Apparently. Although, I think you might get a note in a day or so."

"Maybe the prints are the note in this case. He left them so we couldn't miss them."

"I don't think so. He enjoys taunting us with the notes too much. The prints are a new thing. Probably just another way to taunt us."

"I don't know. The prints tie him to the scene." Mitch swung into the motel parking lot. "Why would he do that? Seems like he's been careful not to leave any direct ties to a scene."

"He could be dissimilating. The pressures that work on these guys are tremendous. None of them are able to stand up to them for long. Sometimes they completely freak out and other times deep down, they want to be caught."

"I don't think this guy wants to be caught. He's got something in play here."

Mitch led the way up the stairs. "We are about ready to release the room. Unless you see something, we'll probably let it go," Mitch said, pulling out a knife and slicing through the crime scene tape on the door.

The room was hot, with a wet, sticky feel to it as they stepped inside. "So why do you think he left the prints?" Geena asked, sweeping the room with her eyes.

"At first, I assumed he was sending a message to Brody. That's still my best guess. Somehow, I think Brody knows who this Carter is and what he is capable of."

"Could be," Geena grunted, looking under the bed. "You say Brody is a land developer. Carter works for Van Zandt and Associates."

Mitch shook his head; the name meant nothing to him. "That a law firm?"

Geena Dixon smiled. "You might say that. There are a couple of lawyers on staff, and a bunch of bankers and accountants. More accountants than lawyers."

Mitch frowned. "I thought they were the ones that handled Carter's defense on the Salter's case."

"They were," Geena replied, going into the bathroom. "The Senior partner, Perry Van Zandt likes to dabble in criminal law. Murder cases only. He is the Senior Partner at a firm called Briggs, Downey and Van Zandt. They are a very old, very prestigious firm. They have written most of the tax code, going back to the days when income tax was first written into law." Geena slid back the shower curtain, looking inside. "Like I said, this Van Zandt he likes to dabble in murder cases. He's very good. He started Van Zandt and Associates to do that, but over the years it has morphed into some kind of investment firm. I'm not sure exactly what they do, but the point is, Carter would have plenty of contacts in the business world. He might well know Brody."

"My people are thinking that Brody is getting a lot of his money from back east. Maybe through this Van Zandt and Associates."

"Could be," Geena said, turning a circle in the small room. "Alright, I'm done here," she said. "I don't know why I wanted to come here," she said, a bit of a sheepish note in her voice. "I always come, hoping for a flash of something."

"Know what you mean," Mitch said.

"Any thoughts on why he chose this place?"

"My guess is that it is cheap, and if you got cash, nobody asks any questions."

Geena nodded. "You know, except for the first one, Justine Salters, we were never able to find a murder sight. I was hoping for something."

"This guy is definitely changing his pattern," Mitch said, pulling the door closed. "We need to figure out why. Is he losing it, or is he sending a message to Brody? I lean towards the message theory."

Geena stepped up to the truck, frowning across the hood at Mitch. "I'm not sure I agree. You're assuming that just because we haven't found a body, that Angie Brody is still alive."

"You don't think so?"

Geena gave a small shrug. "Carter isn't known for keeping his victims alive. He hides the bodies, waiting months before sending a note with clues how to find it. As far as that goes, this fits right in with his established pattern. It was all in the stuff I sent."

"I haven't gotten all the way through it."

"It was in the summary I included. Surely you got through that."

"No, I put that back. I wanted to read through your report without any preconceived ideas."

Geena slid into the truck, looking out the side window. Mitch climbed in knowing he had hurt her feelings. "You don't think I'm a good investigator. You don't trust me."

"No, it wasn't that. I hadn't even met you. I just know how easy it is to get locked into a theory. Even if some of the evidence doesn't support it, it's hard to let go of your first theory."

Geena nodded, still looking out the window. Mitch sighed, knowing he had to make the peace. "Look we are assuming all of this is tied to Brad Brody, and we're having trouble seeing past that. You are right, we need to look harder at the fact it may have nothing to do with him."

Geena nodded. "What about the dad? You say he is having financial troubles. Any chance this is just an insurance scam?"

"Anything is possible. We looked at that, but he only has fifty grand on her. Not enough to really help him."

"Probably got double indemnity. That would kick it up to a hundred."

"Still wouldn't help him. He runs that much through his company in a month." Mitch paused. "We do have a new development," Mitch said as she read. "Something you might be able to help us with."

Geena looked up hopefully. "What is it?"

"The dead girl in the motel. We got an ID. Lindsey Humphries. That name mean anything to you?"

Geena placed the file in her lap, looking up at the roof of the Trooper. "No," she said slowly. "I don't think that name ever came up in regard to Carter."

"Okay, that was a long shot," Mitch said. "But there is something you still might help us with. We got the match right out of the DC Metro data base. You have anybody we could call to run it down for us? Ask a few questions, find out who she was?"

"Len Dykes," she said, already reaching for her purse. "He was one of the original detectives on the Salters case."

"That his partner that was killed?"

"Yes, so he will want to help." Geena pulled out her phone, scrolling through her contacts. "Here's his number."

Mitch dialed while she went back to the file. "Dykes," a gruff, harried voice said after the first ring.

"This is Detective John Mitchell with the Tucson Police Department. Geena Dixon gave me your number."

Mitch could sense a change in the man before he even spoke. "If Geena is involved this must be about Jacob Carter."

"Yes sir," Mitch said, giving the man a quick rundown of the case.

"Sounds like you're pretty sure our boy Carter is the one who snatched that girl?"

"Yeah, bout ninety-nine percent."

"I would agree, but I don't know how I can help you. Geena probably knows more about Carter and the way he thinks than I do. If she's helping you, I'd say you are in good hands."

"Sure, I was calling about Lindsey Humphries."

"That the girl killed in the motel?"

"Yeah, she's from back east, your neck of the woods. We ID'd her out of your data base."

"Name doesn't ring a bell, but I can ask around,"

"She was printed and in the system, but couldn't find any record of her ever being booked."

"Somebody reached down."

"She was on the corner then?"

Dykes laughed, a rich hearty sound, like a Santa chuckle on steroids. "Let me explain how it works here. You get some schmuck from Boise Indiana."

"Idaho," Mitch corrected, already liking the man.

Dykes snorted. "Indiana, Idaho, who the fuck cares, but they get themselves elected, and right away they think they are important. Got to have some high-class pussy hanging around. Some of these girls draw in ten grand a night. So, they ain't exactly on the corner."

"And if they get picked up, somebody makes sure they don't spend enough time in jail to talk."

"You got it."

"What about this guy Van Zandt that Geena was telling me about? He into anything like that?"

Dykes' tone darkened. "I don't know. Van Zandt is real careful in everything he does. Trying to get anything on him is like trying to grab smoke outta the air."

"Okay," Mitch said. "Whatever you can find out that would be a help."

"I'll get back to you in a couple days. Say hi to Geena for me."

"Sure," Mitch said, tossing the phone on the dash. "Dykes said hi," he said, watching her face soften, moving a bit in the direction of a smile.

"That's nice," she said, the beginnings of a grin still tugging at the corners of her mouth, but then her face hardened, sweeping the smile away. "Carter, how do we catch him?"

"We do what we're doing. He's moving around. People are seeing him. We keep talking to people. Showing the pictures around. Somebody has seen them. We just have to find that person."

"In time to save Angie Brody?"

Mitch shrugged looking out the window. "Maybe."

Tamera Schroeder's Room Biltmore Hotel, Phoenix AZ June 15th 2018 Friday Night

Tamera paced her room, clutching her cell phone as a drowning person might clutch a life line. She looked out the peephole, but was rewarded with only a distorted view of an empty hallway. Pacing again, she crossed in front of the bed. A single tear rolled down her face as she pulled back the curtains and glanced out the window, then. For the tenth time, she checked her phone, making sure she still had a good signal.

Relax, she told herself. She forced herself to take a deep breath. He would be here. He was only a little late. Just over an hour. That wasn't much, she told herself. Anything could have happened. His flight could have been delayed, trouble at the rental car agency. Even an accident on the freeway. Any number of things could have held him up.

They were in love. He was coming.

Finding meager comfort in her thoughts, she sat on the bed. Opening the Facebook app on her phone, she tried to lose herself in the babble. Normally, the mindlessness of scrolling through the timeline helped to relax her, but not tonight. Tonight, she found herself sitting at attention on the edge of the bed, stabbing the screen of her phone.

Why didn't he call?

Her hands trembling slightly, she shut down the Facebook app, checking the time. Almost seven, why didn't he call? Was he backing out?

Last night she had spoken with Carl for over an hour. He had promised that once the election was over, they would be together. He would quietly leave his wife. It had been decided, she would get a small house in San Diego, close to her parents. Once the election was over, Carl would quietly leave his wife and come live with her.

Of course, he had explained, she couldn't remain on the campaign. Not while she was pregnant. If that last part had been an attempt to convince her to get an abortion, it hadn't worked. Tamera had campaigned for abortion. She had fervently believed in abortion, right up until the moment she became pregnant.

Tamera smiled; a glowing look enveloped her entire face. She rubbed her stomach unconsciously. This baby was a blessing. It was special, she could feel it.

Her smile grew as a soft knock sounded at her door. On feet that barely seemed to touch the carpet, she flew to the door, throwing it open wide.

The warm smile melted into a cold look of terror, as a small scream tore past her lips.

CHAPTER SIX

**Saguaro Bar and Grill Tucson, AZ June 15th 2018
Friday Night**

Sam glanced over at Ted. "You sure you're okay with this?" he asked, watching intently as Ted shrugged. Sam leaned forward, pressing the matter. "Everybody else backed away when they saw we were actually going to kill people. Why not you? Why doesn't it bother you that we took a life and are going to take another?"

Ted stood up, taking a sip of his beer as he walked to the window. He looked out across the nearly empty parking lot. "Might ask you the same question," he said quietly. He turned back to their table. "Sure, I know about what happened to your boy and his wife, but is that really it?"

Sam laughed, a harsh barking sound that had no humor in it. "That was part of it, I gotta say after that accident my 'give a shit' just got up and walked away," he whispered. "But really, I'm just get tired of seeing these assholes walk. I signed up to stop them."

"Me too," Ted said, sliding back in the booth. "Before I picked him up, I did a little research on our late friend Bill Jack. He has a record going back forever. Started out petty, but if you've read as many of those things as we have you can see an undercurrent there."

"Yeah," Sam said nodding. "I've seen it lots of times. You read a file and see what they got caught at and you just know it's the tip of the iceberg compared to what they really did."

Ted sipped his beer, and looked seriously at Sam. "That Bill Jack, he walked a couple of times on technicalities. Once on a nasty sexual assault, had him dead to rights on DNA and everything, but chain of custody on the evidence got fucked up. Some idiot in the lab forgot to lock everything up when he went to lunch; so, Bill Jack walked." Ted stopped finishing his beer in one long gulp. His face looking like he was in pain, he held up the empty to the waitress and made a circling motion. Knowing the man had something on his mind; Sam kept quiet and sipped his own beer. Ted shook his head, his chin dipping down towards his chest, reminding Sam of a bull elk that had been shot. "That reminded me of something. Just after I got hired on, me and my partner, Dean Dewey, did you know him?"

"Dewey? Sure." Sam smiled. "Drank a lot of beer with him. We used to race sand buggies out in the desert."

Ted smiled, but it was more of a look of pain than joy. "Shit, yeah, I forgot about those damn buggies," Ted said, a quick grin darting across his face. "Anyway, me and Dean was out on patrol when the call comes over the radio, high school girl attacked. We were close, so we burned it that way. We were a couple of blocks away from where the attack took place, when it came over the radio that her attacker was driving a blue, Chevy pickup, with a scrape on the passenger side."

Ted paused as the waitress set their beers down. "And right then, we pull up to a red light beside a blue truck. Ford, but it has a scrape down the side so we are looking it over, and Dean recognizes the driver. One Jimmy Houston."

Sam nodded. "Aw shit, I remember Houston, real piece of crap right there."

"That's about word for word what Dean said about Jimmy at the time, so we pull him over. In a tool box we find a tee shirt with blood on it. The blood was later matched to the girl. We hauled his ass in and everybody is happy. This guy had a rep and everybody knew the whole world was better off with this asshole locked up."

"But some judge kicked the shirt because of your search," Sam said, knowing the answer without even hearing the story.

"Yep," Ted replied bitterly. "Said that the wit described a Chevy and he was in a Ford so we violated poor Mister Houston's rights with an illegal search. When I read that shit about Bill Jack brought all of that back. So, no, it don't bother me one fucking bit that he is in the ground."

"Me neither," Sam said, looking into his beer. "Coldest damn thing I ever done, shooting him. Thought it might bother me some, but so far it ain't."

"Don't lose a minutes' sleep over him. He ain't worth it."

"Who ain't?" Dave asked, sliding into the booth.

"Bill Jack," Sam grunted.

"Yeah, better for everybody that he's dead."

"Where is everybody else?" Ted asked.

"Aw man," Dave sputtered, squirming in his chair. "They ain't coming."

"The Bill Jack thing spooked them?" Ted wanted to know.

"Yeah," Dave acknowledge. "But they won't say anything."

"You sure?" Sam asked.

"Pretty sure," Dave replied. "Besides, what can we do if they don't keep quiet?"

For a second, Sam's face was grim as death, then like a stray dog hunting a treat a thin smile crept onto to his face. "Go to jail, or Mexico I guess," he decided.

"Shit of the two I might take jail," Ted said.

They waited as the waitress brought Dave a beer, then Sam glanced around the table. "We need to find that Hector feller."

"Already done," Dave said smugly. He took a long pull from his beer, smacking his lips. "He's at a rundown trailer out in the desert south of Three Points. Be the perfect place to talk to him."

"How the hell do you know that?" Ted demanded.

"Hell, I'm a cop. In fact, I'm like a super cop or something," Dave declared. "I went out and done some real police work, nothing you two would know about."

Sam snorted shaking his head. "No really, how did you find him?"

"He fell right into my lap," Dave admitted with a chuckle. "I was watching Tanner's shop, trying to pick up Chappy Miers when Hector came along. When he left I followed, that's why I was late."

"Tanner, huh?" Sam said, rubbing his chin. "You think he's involved with this? I always gave him credit for some brains."

"He's a Deacon and always been tight with Chappy," Dave said. "They go way back those two. Tanner might actually be the one person Chappy is afraid of."

"Shit, Tanner, I always kinda liked him. I'd hate to see him messed up in this shit," Ted said, shaking his head.

They were quiet for a minute, while Sam finished his beer in one long drink. "Fuck it. Let's go snag that asshole, Hector."

Mitch's House Tucson AZ June 16th 2018 Saturday
Early Morning

Day five of the search. Mitch woke early and was feeling grumpy. His body was telling him he needed more sleep, but his mind wouldn't shut down. Angie Brody. Each day that passed stacked the odds against her.

Chances were, she was already dead. It would really go against the profile if she was still alive. These psychos always had a pattern. They were driven to kill. Most times it was the killing which really cranked these guys up. More than the sex, it was the killing that got them off. They simply couldn't hold it back for days.

Still, Mitch was holding onto the hope that she had been snatched for a reason. That it wasn't some random psycho and that she was leverage against her father. What they wanted Mitch couldn't begin to guess. As far as Mitch knew they hadn't made demands, but then Brody hadn't been very forth coming.

Brody wasn't behaving as Mitch would have expected. He should be either cooperating with the investigation or giving in to the kidnapper's demands, if any. As far as Mitch could tell he was doing neither. Almost like he didn't care, or couldn't do anything. Mitch had tried to keep Brody up to date and involved with the case, but the contractor was hard to catch and didn't really seem interested when Mitch did get a hold of him.

Not right.

Brody should be calling him, bitching and screaming into the phone. Not hiding out. Unless, maybe he already knew what was happening to his daughter.

Mitch leaned back into the pillow, closing his eyes. There was something he was missing. A thread of something, he could almost see it. Frustrated, he punched the pillow. It was like trying to remember a name or something. It was right there, he just couldn't pull it up.

The phone rang, cutting across his thoughts. "Damn," he muttered, he'd been so close, now it was gone floating away like smoke in a high wind. Shaking his head, he snatched the cell from the nightstand, sliding the activator with an angry gesture. "Hey, boss, we got a problem," Ollie said, sounding way too cheerful for this hour of the morning. "You know Jackson Pyle?"

"Aw, shit. What did he write, now?"

"Nothing and he won't neither. Somebody went and blew a big hole right through him."

"Not exactly a tragedy."

"Yeah, but you better get over here just the same."

Mitch groaned. "We don't have time for this. Let CAPs handle it."

The Crimes Against Persons handled assaults, rapes and killings. Tucson wasn't large enough to have a dedicated homicide table. There had been a big stink when Mitch's division had been formed, many in the department had wanted a full time homicide unit instead of the special group. In the end the chief had went with the special unit.

"Naw, you better haul your ass over here."

"Look, Ollie, I suppose Jackson might qualify as a minor celebrity in this town, but even that's a stretch. The bottom line is with this Angie Brody thing, we just don't have the time or the resources. Jackson just ain't that big of a name."

"It ain't Pyle that I am worried about. I don't want to say anything over the cell, but you better get your ass over here. Fast!"

"Okay, I'm on my way," Mitch said, already hustling towards the door. Something about Ollie's attitude bothered Mitch. Ollie wasn't one to panic. Something big was in the wind. "Ollie, you do whatever you think is necessary."

"I've already lined up the respondents, and read them the riot act. They know they will be patrolling the dump if any of this gets out. I called Parks and Jerry, they're both on the way."

"I'll be there in twenty minutes," Mitch said, just catching Ollie's snort before the connection died.

It was a nice cool morning and Mitch was in a hurry. Good day to take the Mustang, Mitch decided.

The Mustang came to life with a roar. The sound always gave Mitch a small thrill, like the sight of a beautiful woman walking by.

Punching the garage door control, Mitch waited impatiently as the door rolled open. Once the door was open, he eased out of the garage. Out in the street, he stabbed the garage door control button, then pinned the accelerator to the floor.

The car spun for a second, then shot down the street. Almost as an afterthought, Mitch licked the suction cup, and stuck the flasher to the windshield. He flipped on the lights and siren as he came up to the corner. He took the turn on Naranja too fast and the back end broke loose. Letting off the gas for a second, Mitch over-steered the turn, then stepped back on the gas.

As the car straightened out, Mitch grabbed his cell, punching the speed dial for dispatch. The speedometer was rolling past sixty when the call went through. "Cindy, its Mitch."

"Hey, cutie, what can I do for you."

"Are your traffic cameras working today?"

"It ain't Monday, so there's always a shot."

"I need to get to Golf Links and Camino Seco. How's my best route today?"

"You coming from your house?"

"Yeah, I'm just coming up on Lambert now."

"Okay. Oracle's a mess. Cut over to La Canada," she said, and Mitch could hear her working the computer. "Ina's okay, but Orange Grove is heavy. River looks wide open. No wait, I heard there's some kind of construction today on River."

"So, Ina is my best bet?"

"Affirmative. Then Craycroft is your best way south."

"Naw, I'd get caught at the base this time of day."

"Yeah, you're right. At Speedway, go east. Both Kolb and Pantano look good from there."

"Okay, thanks, Cindy."

"You running down to that Jackson Pyle thing?"

"Yeah, what have you heard on that?"

"Not much. Just that somebody blew a big hole in him."

"Okay, try to keep it off the air."

"Will do, sweetie. And I'll keep an eye on traffic for you. I can hold the light at Oracle for you."

"Thanks, I knew I could count on you."

"Hey, Mitch, how are we doing on that steak thing? Am I going to be able to turn in my headset anytime soon?"

Mitch squirmed in the seat. "We're just getting off the ground. Got some money for you, it ain't much, but it's a start. Things should really be rolling in a week or so," Mitch said, coming up on the turn at Ina. The light was yellow and turning red as he got to the intersection. Leaning on the horn, Mitch swept around the corner, cutting off an Acura. He waved a hand at the driver and laughed as he got a one-finger salute in return.

"Okay, sounds like you're busy. Just let me know when I'm rich."

"Sure," Mitch replied, punching off the phone. Slicing the Mustang around an Explorer, Mitch pushed the speed dial for Ollie. It was ringing when he caught the light at Oracle. "Olshan, here. That you, Mitch?"

"Yeah, I'm still inbound, but I was thinking; do we need any more assets there?"

"No, we got lucky, Mickey is already here."

Mitch nodded, that was good, Mickey was the best. "That's good. How about bodies to do any canvassing?"

"We got a couple. I was thinking we might want to keep it small for a while."

"Whatever you say. I'll see you in ten minutes."

Twelve minutes later, Mitch slid to a stop in front of an old Spanish style house. The once red brick had faded to a dull orange. The yard was a mixture of wiry, tough-looking weeds and dust. A pathetic, scraggly tree fought for life in the center of the yard. Olshan was waiting under the tree.

Mitch parked behind a cruiser. "Nice paint job," the young patrolman said with a grin. "What shade is that; powder blue and crap gray?"

"Thanks, I like it," Mitch grunted, searching for a name, finally coming up with Neal. "Any witnesses, Neal?" Mitch asked, unable to recall whether Neal was his first or last name"

"Fuck that. Any doughnuts?" Ollie asked, ambling over.

"None that don't suck," Neal answered.

"See if you can round me up one that don't suck.'

"Witness or doughnut?" the young patrolman asked grinning widely.

"Both."

"You got it," Neal said, he started to turn away, then hesitated a second. "Hey, Mitch, you got any openings on your crew? I'd sure like to get out of patrol."

Mitch laughed. "If we don't catch somebody quick, we aren't going to need anybody. We're all gonna be walking a

beat. Now go find me somebody who saw something."
Mitch ducked under the crime scene tape.

Ollie was shaking his head. "Fucking rookies, getting ballsier every year."

"Yeah. Alright, what have we got here that is so important?"

"It ain't Pyle, and that is for fucking sure."

"Well what is it?"

"It's the dead girl in his bed."

"Aw shit."

"Damn right, aw shit," Ollie sputtered. "And that ain't the half of it."

"Oh shit. What's worse than a dead girl in his bed?"

"How about twenty nipples in a plastic baggie in the freezer?"

"Aw shit. You mean like…," Mitch rubbed his hand across his chest. "Like nipples?"

"Yup. Jerry found them. Right between a quart of rocky road and a bag of frozen peas."

"Aw shit." Mitch groaned. "For Christ sakes don't let that get out, about the ice cream. The press would just love it."

"Yeah, so what do you think, about the nipples?"

"Aw shit"

"Would you stop saying that. It creeps me out."

"Aw shit. Were they like all lefts or rights?'

Ollie scowled and shrugged. "Fuck if I know. They weren't labeled."

"So, we could have twenty dead women then?"

"Shit, I hope not. I'm hoping just ten. This boy obviously had a severe titty fetish. Hopefully, he had to get both of them."

"The girl in the bed, was she mutilated?"

"Nope, just dead. I think he got interrupted before he could finish."

"How'd he do her," Mitch asked.

"Strangled."

"Rope?"

"Yeah, I'd say so. Her neck was pretty marked up and there was a piece of that cheap yellow rope on the floor. That mean anything to you?"

"Maybe. I don't know. Any idea who she was?"

"Purse is inside. We haven't been through it yet. I wanted to wait until Mickey was done."

"Probably smart," Mitch agreed. "So, what's the story with Pyle? How did that go down?"

Olshan shook his head. "Fucking cowboy night at the OK shit hole was what it was. Looks like some yahoo walked up, rang the bell, and just opened up when Pyle answered the door. Eleven shots at least. Sprayed all over the place."

"Anything on the gun? I don't suppose he dropped any brass."

"All over the flowers. Nine mil. Mickey thinks we might get a print off of one of them."

They walked up the stairs; Mitch squatted next to the body. Pyle lay on his side, almost like he was sleeping. Ragged holes were torn in his back where the bullets ripped through his body. "Shooter didn't go inside?"

"Doesn't look that way. It was a hit and run."

"So, this was amateur night?" Mitch straightened up, dusting his hands.

"Or maybe somebody wanted it to look that way."

"There's that," Mitch agreed. He could hear the traffic rumbling down Golf Links. "Push Mickey. We need to ID that girl. Maybe we can find out where he picked her up."

"What about Pyle?"

"Fuck him. I'll handle that. For now, we need to track the girl. Maybe we can use this to take some of the heat off the Angie Brody thing."

"Sure, right after I skip down to Rocky Point with Pam Anderson," Ollie snorted, rolling his eyes.

"Pam Anderson? Jeez you are an old bastard," Mitch taunted. "But you are right, we need to get after it. Soon as Mickey's done, I want you and Jerry to tear this place apart. He's been dumping bodies. We need to find out where. I'll have Parker start sifting through the missing person's reports."

"Hey, Mitch," Neal called, hurrying a woman wearing a pink fuzzy robe up the street. In her ragged, pink slippers, she was having trouble keeping up. "I found a witness," Neal announced proudly.

"She saw it?"

Neal hesitated, his eyes drifting away. "Well, not exactly."

The woman stepped forward, sweeping Neal aside with a bony arm. Squaring off with Mitch, she used a gnarled finger to push up glasses that were at least forty years out of date. "I didn't see it, but I sure enough heard it. It was one of them damned motorcycles. Came roaring up the street right at five. Rattled my windows, it did."

"Did you see the motorcycle?"

"Hell no!" she snorted. "I've seen a motorcycle. Wasn't about to get out of bed just to look at another one."

"Are you sure it was a bike?"

"I said it was and it was. Asshole down the block has one. He's always ripping up and down the street." She stopped, poking Mitch in the chest with a bony finger. "You know how come that noise ordinance doesn't apply to them damn motorcycles? My grandson got a ticket for having his stereo too loud. Forty bucks can you believe that? Them pricks on those bikes tear around all the time, just like they own the place. Damn things are loud enough to wake the dead for Pete's sake. Don't see nobody giving them no tickets."

"Sorry about that ma'am," Mitch said, holding up his hand. He had the feeling she could ramble all day once she got going. "We don't write the laws. We just enforce them"

"Well go enforce them. Damn people are always running that stop sign at Stella. Damn sure never see any cops over there."

"Excuse us just a second." Mitch grabbed Neal and pulled him aside. "I told you to get me a witness who didn't suck."

Neal shot him a hurt look. "Sorry, man. She was all there was."

"Okay," Mitch grumbled. "When you guys leave, stop at Stella and write some tickets." Mitch shooed Neal away, turning back to the woman. "Okay, Inez, if we could get back to this morning. You heard the motorcycle, then what happened?"

"Then what?" she howled. "All hell broke loose, that's what happened. All them shots, then that motorcycle tore outta here."

"Hold on," Mitch said, hating to interrupt her, but he wanted to ask about the shots. "Can you tell me how many shots there were?"

She frowned, scrunching her whole face up. "I don't know but there was a bunch."

"Did they sound like a machine gun? A rolling sound?"

Inez was already shaking her head, couple of her curlers flapping. "No, it wasn't a machine gun. I've heard them on TV. The shots were fast, but not a machine gun."

A semi-auto, Mitch thought, nodding at her. That fit with the shell casings. "Okay you heard the shots, then the motorcycle left."

"Yeah. Those motorcycles are loud anytime but they are real loud when they are hustling."

"He was hurrying then?"

Inez rolled her eyes and shook her head, "Hell, yes! I mean he had just shot someone. He took out like his ass was on fire."

"Sure. Can you tell me what he looked like?"

For the first time, Inez hesitated. "Well, I really didn't see anything. I mostly just heard it."

Mitch raised an eyebrow. He'd bet a squirrel couldn't walk up the street without her knowing about it. "Are you sure you didn't go to the window for just a peek?"

Inez pulled her robe tighter, backing off a step. "Well, maybe," she admitted.

"Okay, good. Now take your time, think back. What color was the motorcycle?"

"It was basically black. The gas tank had a skeleton in a top hat smoking and playing cards."

"Very good, Inez. You are doing great. Now think. Did the skeleton have a red bandana?

"I think so," she said, nodding quickly. "I remember the bandana. I think the color was red"

Mitch nodded, writing it all down. "What about the man? Think back. What did he look like?"

"I don't recall much about him. I guess I didn't get much of a look at him."

Mitch looked down the street, purposely letting a frown cross his face. "You said he rode down the street. He went right by your house?" Mitch asked and Inez nodded meekly. He took her hand. "I know you are afraid."

"Am not," Inez declared, pulling away from him. "Assholes don't scare me!"

Mitch nodded, waiting. This was a woman that couldn't be pushed. He waited letting the silence get on top of her. "Well, he was kinda a big fella. Lots of tattoos."

Mitch smiled at her. "Okay, you're doing so good. Now when you say he was a big feller, was he fat?"

Inez shook her head. "Not fat, burly. Ripped is what the kids would say."

"So, he was muscular?"

"Yep, like a weight lifter."

"Good. Now about the tattoos. Do you remember any of them?'

Inez shook her head. "I just saw them. He didn't have any sleeves." She was warming to the task, snapping her fingers. "The jacket had a picture on the back. I remember that now. It was the same as the picture on the motorcycle." Inez stopped twisting her hands together as she frowned. "At least I think it was the same."

"It was close, anyway," Mitch offered.

"Yeah, I'm pretty sure."

"Good. You're doing well. Now back to the guy. Can you remember anything else about him?"

"Well, like I said, he was a big guy." She cocked her head, thinking hard. "He was kinda good looking, in a rough sort of way."

"He was good looking, then."

"I wouldn't kick him out of bed," she said, with a shrug. "But I bet he's got a mean streak. Nobody you'd want to meet in a dark alley."

"What about his hair?" Mitch asked. "Was it long, short? What color?"

"Blonde hair. Kinda short and spiky looking."

Mitch exchanged a quick look with Neal. Behind Neal, he saw Parker getting out of her car. "You know who it was?' Inez asked.

"Maybe," Mitch admitted, waving Parker over. "Sounds like a guy I know."

"But you can't tell me, huh?" Inez asked, already knowing the answer.

"Sorry," Mitch said, as Parker approached. "Inez, this is Detective Parker. I want you to go with her. She will ask you a bunch more questions. I want you to tell her everything you can remember. Can you do that?"

Inez nodded and Mitch turned to Parker. "This is Inez Perry. She saw the shooting go down. Take her downtown and get her story down. If you think it is worth the trouble, get her with Marcy Brown."

"Marcy Brown?" Parker asked.

"She's an artist. She does composites for us. Ollie should have her number."

After Parker led Inez away, Neal slid up next to Mitch. "Did I do good?"

Mitch laughed. "Yeah, I think you did. I have a feeling that once she gets started talking it's going to be hard to get her stopped." Mitch glanced around. "You riding with McElroy?"

"Yeah,"

"How do you like that?"

Neal shrugged. "He's alright. He just doesn't have any ambition. I think he likes chasing the radio all day long."

"Pete's a good man. You can learn a lot from him. I know you want to move up, but don't worry, it'll happen. Take your time and learn while you can."

"Yeah, sure," Neal grumbled, sounding like he had heard that a hundred times before. Which Mitch realized, he probably had.

"Anyway, I want you guys to keep up a presence in this area. Maybe bust a few speeders."

Neal smiled wolfishly. "Maybe keep an eye on that stop sign."

"You got it. We want to keep our witness happy, make her feel safe. You guys might want to make it a point to cruise this area for the next few days."

"We can do that."

"Good. While you guys are out here I want you to completely canvass the area. Check with anybody who might have seen anything. Check with the bums…."

"Transients."

"What?" Mitch asked, irritated at the interruption.

"Memo came out last week. We are supposed to call them transients," Neal explained.

"Whatever," Mitch said, waving it off. "Talk to them; see if anybody saw a motorcycle this morning. Free meal and a night in a hotel in it for them."

"You buying?"

"If I have to," Mitch replied. "Also, I want to know everything there is to know about Jackson Pyle. Talk to the neighbors. Talk to the stores around here. I want to know where he shopped. I want to know what convenience store he went to. I want to know if he was Coke or Pepsi. Did he eat out or cook at home? Was he Burger King or Macs? I'll see you guys get some pictures to show around."

Neal's' partner Pete McElroy had come up, hearing the last of it. "You want the full court press? High profile?"

"Very high. I want everyone to see you. Might take some of the heat off."

McElroy snorted out a laugh. "You really think so?"

Mitch shrugged. "Might buy us a day before they start calling for my nuts to be roasted on a spit."

'Well, shit, you know we're all about saving your nuts. Course they're so tiny, I think they would just burn, not roast." McElroy turned serious. "How about overtime?"

"All you need. Just put it on my tab."

"What about Bolton? He ain't gonna like you pulling us off our regular patrol."

Bolton, shit. Mitch grimaced at the thought of the fat sergeant who ran the day patrol shifts. "Don't worry about him. I'll take care of him."

McElroy grinned at that. "Alright, get us the pictures and we'll start working the immediate area."

"Tell you what, run over to the paper; they should have a picture of him on file. Use that," Mitch said, realizing he didn't have a picture of Pyle.

"We can do that," Pete said nodding. "We'll start the canvass when we get back. We can just spiral out as we go. How far out do you want us to go?"

"Keep going as long as you're picking stuff up. Go at least five blocks out after your last hit."

After they were gone, Mitch crossed the yard. At the front door he stopped, waiting on Ollie. "Hey Mickey, alright if we check the id?"

"Yeah, sure, just be careful."

"Anything stand out?" Mitch asked, while Ollie unpacked a video camera.

"Well, she was definitely raped. Looks like the doer had a pretty well regimented program."

"Anything we've seen before?"

"You're talking about the girl over in the motel?" Mickey asked, and Mitch nodded. "Good eye, there are some definite similarities. A couple of big differences though."

"What's that?' Mitch asked, making sure Ollie hadn't started filming. He didn't want their speculations on tape.

"The victims for starters. First girl was a party girl. This one, judging by her clothes, this was an upscale lady."

"She had a nice purse," Mitch agreed studying the bag without picking it up. "Big, though. I'd say this was a working girl."

"Hooker?" Ollie asked, still fiddling with the camera.

"Not according to her clothes. Too conservative," Mickey observed.

"I meant business woman," Mitch explained. "Purse is quality, but too big to be stylish. It's what's called functionally expensive."

"How the fuck you know that?" Ollie asked, laughing.

"I date high class women."

Ollie laughed. "I suppose that any woman who would date you would have to be high, but I doubt if they have any class."

"Kiss my butt," Mitch shot back, taking the rubber gloves that Ollie offered. After snapping them on, he waited until Ollie had the video camera up and running. Moving carefully, Mitch took the dead woman's purse. Holding it up in front of the camera, Mitch peered inside the purse. A set of keys were fastened by a clip to the inside of the purse. "She drove an Acura."

"Car would match the clothes," Ollie said quietly.

Mitch nodded. He'd been thinking the same thing. "She had an I-pad mini," Mitch announced drawing out a tablet.

"Bag it," Mickey said. "I can take a look at it later."

Ollie paused the camera. "We should get Wade to take look at it. Guy knows these things in and out."

Mitch nodded, as Ollie resumed taping. When it came to computers, everyone knew, Wade Nichols was the king. Taking an evidence bag from Ollie, he slipped the tablet into it.

"We got pills in the bag. Two bottles," Ollie said, pointing the camera into the bag.

"Let's leave them," Mitch decided.

"You think she was drugged?"

Mitch shrugged, no way to know until the autopsy was done. Still looking in the purse, he pulled out a small wallet, the type used to carry business cards. "You getting this?"

"I got it," Ollie answered, leaning closer with the camera.

Mitch opened the wallet, removing a driver's license. "Tamera Schroeder." Mitch looked at the picture. "It's her."

Mitch turned the license so Ollie could see. "I'd say so," he agreed. "It's her."

"She's got all the right cards," Mitch said looking through the little wallet. "Niemen Marcus, Visa Gold, and Amex."

Hartek came in from the other room. "Check this out,' he said, holding a scrap of paper sealed in an evidence bag. "Looks like Pyle had an appointment, yesterday at five-thirty."

On the paper was a phone number, a notation for the time and date. At the bottom was written JB. "Any idea who JB is?' Mitch asked and Hartek shrugged. "What about the number?'

"Biltmore in Phoenix."

"That might be good," Mitch decided. "I'll get Parker started on that end. She can find out if anyone was registered there with those initials. Maybe we can get a warrant."

Mitch flipped open his cell punching the speed dial for Parker. "Our vic had a California driver's license. Maybe that was who he was meeting."

"Her initials JB?"

"Good point. Course he still coulda picked her up there."

"Probably did," Hartek started, but Mitch waved him off as Parker came on the line.

"Parker, as soon as you're finished with Inez, I need you to start drawing up some warrants."

"Aw, shit," Parker groaned. "I knew I was going to get stuck with the shit work."

"I know it sucks, but that's just the way it worked out this time. We're gonna need a warrant for everything on Pyle. Office, car, safety deposit box, and anything else he might have. We also need a guest list from the Biltmore in Phoenix."

"Biltmore?" Parks asked. "Which one?"

"I'm not sure, but here is the number," Mitch said, giving her the number.

"What am I looking for?"

"Pyle apparently had a meeting with someone there. Someone whose initials are JB. Our vic's name is Tamera Schroeder. She had a California driver's license. We think he might have picked her up there. See if she was registered there. How are you doing with Inez?"

"Just got here. She's in with Marcy Brown."

"Good, go ahead and call the Biltmore. If you find out Schroeder was registered or anyone with the initials JB get those rooms sealed. If you need backup from there, call Rolando Wynn. He's with the PHD. Also run a quick check on Schroeder, nothing fancy, just fast."

"I could plug her into Lex and Nex. Should give an idea of who she was."

"Yeah, that's perfect. Let me know what you come up with," Mitch said, watching Geena Dixon poke her head in the room.

Braxton's Apartment New York, NY June 16th 2018
Saturday Late Morning

There are moments in a person's life, a single moment that changes everything. It changes everything they are and everything they will be. For most people, they don't even recognize those moments when they are happening. But they happen all the time; days that redefine an entire life.

Carl Braxton had one of those days. At the time, he certainly didn't realize it. Had no clue that this day would change his life forever. It all started simply enough. He was eating breakfast in his New York apartment. He wasn't alone, a young lady was sprawled on the couch, scrolling through her phone.

She was naked, but even so Carl wished she would go. He cleared his throat, trying a gentle nudge to get her started moving. "I'm just having bagels for breakfast, since I need to go into the office early this morning." A lie, he was planning to head up to his cabin in New Hampshire. "You want one?" he asked, holding out a bagel.

The girl, Braxton thought her name might be Zoey, barely looked up. "No, I'm good," she replied, showing absolutely no signs of leaving.

Braxton cursed under his breath, searching for a way to get her out of the apartment. Sweating a little, he checked his watch. The housekeeper was due any time, and Braxton had a feeling that the old shrew reported back to Jillian everything that went on.

For a second, Braxton thought of Tamera. She should be settled in the new place in San Diego. With Van Zandt's help he'd gotten her into a nice little house close to the beach in La Jolla. In time Braxton would purchase the house for her. A new Ford Escape, registered in her name should already be in the driveway. Van Zandt was handling it all, and said he could keep it quiet, but Braxton couldn't help but wonder what this was going to cost him. In the grand scheme of things, Braxton wondered just how far he could trust Van Zandt. Braxton felt safe as long as their interests were intertwined, but after that, he better watch himself.

"Huh, that is so weird."

Carl grunted, jerked out of his thoughts by Zoey's words. "What did you say?" he asked, hoping she was asking for a cab.

"I just got the weirdest text."

"What was that?" Braxton asked out of reflex, thinking he couldn't possibly care less about the answer.

"It says, *Tamera Schroeder is dead, she was killed last night.*" Zoey made a face. "Is that not the creepiest thing?"

For a second, Carl froze, his skin clammy and bile rising up his throat. He felt trapped and thought he could actually see the walls closing in on him. "That is strange," he said, sounding like a bad actor reading from a cue card. "Who's it from," he croaked, having trouble breathing.

"Oh, I don't know," Zoey replied, her breasts jiggling as she shrugged. "Who cares some weirdo."

"Do you even know a Tamera Schroeder?"

Zoey rolled her eyes as only a young pretty girl can do. "Oh, as if."

Carl felt a pounding in his chest, and the walls felt like they might crush him. Fuckin' Van Zandt! He knew he shouldn't trust the prick. Carl tried to catch his breath, Van Zandt texted her. Wait. How could he even know about Zoey? Braxton himself had just met the girl last night.

Drawing in a ragged breath, Braxton glanced wildly about. Was the apartment bugged? He glared at Zoey who was paying him no attention. Could she be a plant? Oh hell! In a flash, Braxton remembered Van Zandt bragging about how he had put a girl next to Brody to watch him and report back. Could Zoey be doing that?

In a flash, he knew she was!

"Get up, get dressed!" he shouted, "You've got to go."

"What? We haven't even had breakfast," she protested, pouting. "You said we could go shopping later."

"I said get your ass dressed!" Braxton roared, bounding across the room. He grabbed her wrist, dragging her off the couch and slinging her across the room.

She bounced off the wall, and into his arms. He slapped her face, then shoved her in the direction of the bedroom. "Get your shit and get your ass outta here!" he screamed, spittle flying from his mouth.

Rubbing the red spot on her cheek, Zoey opened her mouth like she might say something, but Braxton took a step towards her. With a small bleat, she scurried into the bedroom.

His heart racing and his palms sweating, Braxton stumbled to the liquor cabinet. "Fuck me," he growled, grabbing a bottle of scotch. He took a quick pull from the bottle, then a deep breath. As the shaking subsided, he started to think. Oh man, just how fucked was he?

Tamera had been pregnant. And of course, the father of her baby would be the natural suspect in her death. Braxton scrubbed the side of his face with a meaty palm. Could they pull DNA from a fetus? Oh hell, for sure they could. If they could pull DNA from a single hair, then certainly they could get it from an unborn fetus.

But would they? Well, that answer was as plain as a turd in the punchbowl. He'd said it himself, the father would be a prime suspect. The police would do everything they could to identify the father. Including getting samples from everyone who they might suspect being the father. They could very well ask him for a sample.

Would they have reason to look at him? He had been careful. As far as Braxton knew no one knew about the affair. He hadn't been around the campaign for a few weeks and definitely not while they had been in Arizona. Braxton breathed a sigh of relief.

He should be clear.

Still he should stay away from the campaign for a while. He had been planning to go to the cabin for a week or so, that was a good idea. Let things die down. If he gave the cops no reason to look at him, he would be okay. And in six months or so there would be a dozen new murders for them to worry about. Braxton took another small snort from the scotch and replaced the bottle. He began to breathe a little easier. It was going to be alright. Nobody knew about him and Tamera.

The smile which was starting to grow on his face froze when a horrible thought jumped into his mind.

Somebody knew!

Somebody sent that text to Zoey. Shit, it had to be Van Zandt. Braxton had told Van Zandt about the affair and the pregnancy, when enlisting the lawyer's help getting Tamera moved out of the way. And since Van Zandt knew about the affair, he would make sure everyone knew. Braxton looked wildly about, almost expecting the cops to break down his door any second.

It wasn't fair!

He was a good person. Braxton sniffled a little. It didn't matter, he would go to jail. He hadn't killed her. It wasn't fair. Braxton pounded his fist into the wall, cracking the plaster. It wasn't right.

Fucking Van Zandt.

On impulse, he grabbed his phone. He sat on the couch and was dialing, when he saw Zoey slinking along the wall, creeping towards the door.

With a roar, Braxton surged to his feet. To do what, he had no idea. A rage was boiling through him, almost obscuring his vision. He might have slapped her, or he might beat her to death.

What he might have done, never happened as Van Zandt's condescending voice spewed from the cell phone. "What?"

Braxton stopped, shaking his head, like an animal that has been wounded and doesn't know why. In his rage he forgot he had called. As he hesitated, Zoey scampered from the room. Braxton stopped in the center of the room, bowing his head like a bull about to charge.

"Braxton, what do you want?"

Immediately upon hearing Van Zandt's voice, Braxton's anger switched from Zoey to Van Zandt. "You killed her. You son of a bitch!"

"No, you did," came the mocking answer.

"What?"

This time Van Zandt openly laughed. "You killed her when you knocked her up, or when you couldn't control her."

"No, you killed her," Braxton hissed.

"Me?" Van Zandt asked, feigning innocence. "I never even met the lady. I would have no reason to kill her. You on the other hand. You knocked her up, so maybe you killed her." Van Zandt chuckled, obviously enjoying himself. "Could have been your wife, I guess. Now she had a motive!"

"You rotten cocksucker!" Braxton screamed, and had Van Zandt been in the room, he would have gladly beaten him to death. "You can forget that deal in Arizona. I will personally make sure it never goes through."

Van Zandt considered asking how Braxton thought he could do such a thing, but then thought better of it. "Don't worry, you and your wife are safe. Right now, the police think they know who killed Miss Schroeder." In an instant, Van Zandt's voice changed. His tone went from friendly to something vastly different, something hard, with an ugly edge. "One phone call could change that."

"What do you mean?" Braxton stammered.

"They think that reporter Jackson Pyle was a serial killer and that he killed Miss Schroeder to satisfy his own twisted needs." Van Zandt paused. "And at this time, your wife knows nothing about her being pregnant."

"I see no need for her to know that," Braxton squeaked.

"I agree," Van Zandt said heartily, but the nasty voice was right back. "And as long as you and I understand each other she won't." Van Zandt left the threat unsaid, but it hung in the air.

"What do you want me to do?" Braxton asked his anger gone, replied with a greasy, nervous feeling.

"Do?" Van Zandt sneered. "What I want you to do is keep your dick in your pants, suck it up and you and your bitch wife to hold up your end of the deal!"

Van Zandt killed the connection, tossing the phone on the table. He stared thoughtfully at the phone. It was a prepaid, but after that conversation it had better go away. He picked it up, crossing to the sink, he ran a bowl full of water and dropped the phone into it.

A smile broke across his face, as he watched the phone sink. He'd only been half truthful with Braxton. From his sources inside the Tucson Police Department, he knew the cops were thinking that Jackson Pyle killed Tamera Schroeder.

Van Zandt smiled again, very pleased with himself. As long as the cops thought the reporter had been a serial killer, they would look no farther to find her killer. They wouldn't even wonder why she had been killed. A motive was not needed. She was an attractive female, that would be enough.

But?

Van Zandt smile again, a truly evil grin.

But if they were at all competent, and Van Zandt's information told him they were. Then they would soon find out the nipples were fakes.

Once that happened, they would start looking for a motive. The pregnancy would lead them right to the Braxtons.

Crime Scene Jackson Pyle's House Tucson AZ June 16th 2018 Saturday Late Morning

"Come on in," Mitch said, waving Geena in. "Sorry about this morning, but we got a little sidetracked here."

Geena nodded, taking in the scene. "Is this tied to Angie Brody?"

"Naw, I don't see how it could be. This guy Pyle was just a local scumbag. Sort of a celebrity I guess. Give me a few minutes to wrap up here." Mitch started to turn away, then stopped. "Do serial killers ever communicate with each other?"

"It's rare, but not totally unheard of. Usually it's because they have something in common other than the killing. Why?"

Mitch shrugged. "Just a stray thought. Looks like maybe Pyle was a serial as well. I just wondered if he could have been tied up with Jacob Carter."

"Why would you think that?"

Mitch shrugged. "I don't know, it just seems weird that we would have two serials going at the same time. Thought that maybe they might be somehow connected."

Geena frowned, pursing her lips. "Anything is possible, of course, but it would be out of the profile parameters. Unless, they were connected in some other way."

"Huh?" Mitch grunted absorbing the information. "What other ways?"

"Family, work, something like that. Something they could bond over."

Mitch nodded. "Okay, it'll take me a few minutes to finish up here. Feel free to take a look around. Anything you can see to help us here would be appreciated." With Geena in tow, Mitch crossed to where Hartek and Ollie were working. "You see any loose ends we can start pulling?'

"Not really," Mickey replied with a shrug. "This guy was good at what he does. He had a system."

"Not his first rodeo then?"

"Nope."

"Most serials have some kind of system. It evolves over time, a balancing act between what they need from their victims and their need not to get caught," Geena offered.

"I'd say this guy had it down," Hartek muttered.

"Jackson fucking Pyle," Ollie grumbled. "Shit, looking back, you'd think we might have seen this coming. He always was a little squirrely."

Mitch shrugged. "Yeah, but he never really seemed dangerous. If I had to pick a crime I thought Pyle would do, I would have said, flasher."

"Yeah, maybe a peeper. I could see that," Ollie agreed reluctantly.

"Well, we were all wrong,"

"Don't take it too hard," Geena offered. "Most serials are never even suspected until they are caught. Often times they will go to great lengths to hide what they really are. It's nearly impossible to just pick one out of a crowd."

"So where are we on this?" Mitch asked.

Hartek pulled out his notebook. That was what made him and Wade such a good team. Wade flew by the seat of his pants, making leaps from hunches and instinct. Hartek operated solely on the details. Hartek read his notes a few seconds, then looked up.

"We got the brass, maybe a print on that. Mickey says he thinks he might be able to pull a print. We got the wit you talked to. Sounds like a drug hit."

"Yeah 'cept we ain't found shit," Ollie complained. "Never seen a dealer that didn't keep a stash around the house."

Hartek shrugged. "There's that. If you ask me, a person would have to be on something to do what he did to that girl."

"So maybe it wasn't drugs." Mitch paused. "Tear the place apart. Look at everything. If he was dealing there will be something here. If it was something else? Well, find it."

"Once Mickey's done, maybe, we could bring in a dog," Jerry wondered out loud.

"Yeah, good idea. Do it."

"You gonna talk to Tanner?" Jerry asked.

"Yeah, I'll go see him this afternoon. Can't really see him being good for this, though. He's too smart. "

"Naw, wouldn't be him. Some of his crew though." Ollie frowned. "Got to admit, that description she gave was dead nuts on for Tanner."

"I'll talk to him," Mitch promised, leading Geena out to his car. She waited until they were pulling away from the curb. "Do you think it is wise to be fragmenting your team? Angie Brody's life might very well hang in the balance."

"I know. I know," Mitch said, slamming the accelerator to the floor. The big car jumped forward, slamming them back in their seats.

"Man, for a thing that looks like a total piece of shit, this car kinda moves," Geena commented.

"It'll loosen your panty shields," Mitch said, backing out of it and moving to the center of the road, preparing to take a hard right. "The thing is, what if we drop this, then it turns out it is connected to the Angie Brody thing? What then?"

"Do you think they are?"

"Your dress shields loose? I wouldn't want to venture a guess."

Geena made a face at him. "Connected I mean."

"I don't really know," Mitch admitted, taking the corner too fast. "The thing is, Tucson just doesn't have this kind of thing. I'm not even sure if we have ever had a true serial killer here. And now to think there are two operating here at the same time. That seems a bit out there. And if they are connected maybe we can break something loose."

Geena pursed her lips. "It wouldn't be out of the realm of possibility, but the chances of a guy like Pyle being connected to Carter is slim. It's frustrating, we aren't getting anywhere."

"I know and I don't have any fucking ideas. I mean we can push Brody today, but if he holds firm? In the end there ain't much we can do to nudge him." Mitch ran the stop sign at Stella, glancing over at Geena. "Maybe your friends at the IRS could freeze his accounts. That might break some information out of him."

Geena shot Mitch a look and changed the subject. "So, who is this guy Tanner?"

"His real name is Roscoe Tannenbaum. He goes by Tanner, though."

"What's his story?"

"He belongs to this half-assed motorcycle gang called the Deacons and he runs a bike shop over off Palo Verde. He's an okay guy. Might run a few stolen bikes and parts through his shop, maybe a little weed and toot out the back door, but he's okay."

"You almost sound like you like the guy."

Mitch shrugged. "Yeah, maybe, I don't know. Known him forever. He's okay." Mitch's phone buzzed, interrupting his thoughts. "Yeah," he said connecting the call.

"Mitch, I got a few hits on Tamera Schroeder," Parks said, a little out of breath. "Get this shit, she works for Jillian Braxton!"

"As in Senator and Presidential Candidate Jillian Braxton?"

"The very same," Parks replied. "Tamera Schroeder is the Press Secretary for the Senator, and she was registered at the hotel."

"What about the good Senator?"

"The hotel wasn't very forthcoming about her. We'll need a warrant."

"Get one. I want both of those rooms sealed," Mitch snapped.

"Warrant's on the way. I told them no one was to go in any room associated with Tamera Schroeder. Like I said, they wouldn't tell me if the Senator was a guest of the hotel, but I did find out that earlier in the week when Braxton was in Phoenix, she stayed at the Biltmore."

"She was there," Mitch said, as Geena tugged his sleeve.

"How do you know that?" Parks asked, as Mitch switched his cell to speaker. "Another stop in Phoenix isn't in any of her published itineraries. Just because Schroeder was here doesn't mean Braxton was."

"Remember the meeting Pyle had."

"Ah, JB for Jillian Braxton!"

"You got it. If Pyle was trying to get an interview with Braxton, he would go through her press secretary."

"Okay I called your friend Rolando Brown; he's sending some people to seal the room." Parks hesitated. "You want me to go up there?'

"No, get back with Rollo. Tell him what we need. He can handle that better than we can. Go ahead and get the statement from Inez. Take your time with her. This is all connected back to Angie Brody."

"If you say so," Parks said, not quite sounding convinced. "Do you want me to show her a photo lineup? Maybe she could pick Tanner out."

Mitch thought about it, drumming the steering wheel. "No, hold off on that. Might hurt us if she couldn't pick him out."

Mitch punched off the phone. He glanced over at Geena. "Fuck Brody, let's go see Tanner."

"What makes you so certain this is tied in with Angie Brody all of a sudden?'

Mitch shrugged, slapping the car down into second gear, and taking a hard corner. "Look at it this way," he said, running the tach up near the redline. Mitch shifted into fourth, sliding into the left lane and blowing past a Grand Prix. "We got this Justin Carter...."

"Jacob Carter," Geena corrected, holding onto the dash and pushing back into her seat as Mitch darted into the oncoming lane, passing a truck.

"Huh?" Mitch grunted jerking the car back into his own lane.

"His real name is Jacob. The Justin is just an alias."

"Yeah, right, but like I said we got this Jacob Carter, big time crazy mother fucker from back east." At mother fucker, Mitch swept back into the right lane blowing past an Acura. "Now you come along telling me this crazy bastard is connected to a big time DC tax lawyer."

"Not just a big time tax lawyer. Van Zandt is *the* tax lawyer. He probably writes most of the tax codes himself."

"Okay, so you can bet your ass this Van Zandt knows the Senator?"

Mitch glanced over at Geena. She nodded, gripping the dash with one hand. "He would, and I'm guessing he would be a big contributor to her campaign," she admitted.

Mitch nodded, fuming as he was stuck behind a truck. "So, Van Zandt's in bed with the Senator, and through Carter, he's also putting the squeeze on our own local scumbag contractor, Brody." Mitch saw a break in the curb line, and took it, ramping up on the sidewalk. "Now enter Jackson Pyle. Now, most times Jackson couldn't get a meeting with the guy running for dog catcher, but all of a sudden, he gets a private interview with Braxton. Then the next thing, he turns up dead."

"Okay, I admit, it's a long string of coincidences. So, what do we do?" Geena asked bracing herself against the dash.

"I say we go jack up Tanner. Find out why he did Pyle."

"And you think this guy Tanner might die of a heart attack in the next few minutes?" Geena demanded as Mitch bounced the car off the sidewalk and down onto the street.

"Naw, I'm just in a hurry," Mitch said, killing the flasher and easing up to a red light. He grinned across at her. "God, love this shit!" he whooped, pounding the steering wheel with the palm of his hand. Grinning from ear to ear, Mitch glanced sideways at her. "But I do want to get on Tanner fast. Maybe catch him before he can set up an alibi."

"What do you mean?"

Mitch shot her a glance as he eased away from the light. He kept forgetting that she was an analyst and probably had very little in the way of street experience. "These assholes, they know a little about the law. One thing they really know about is reasonable doubt. Give him a few hours and Tanner will have a half dozen guys swearing he was nowhere near Jackson Pyle's house this morning."

"Wouldn't he do that before going to pay a visit on Mister Pyle?"

"He might have," Mitch admitted. "In which case we are fucked. But this has a spur of the moment feel to it." Mitch shook his head. "Shit, I'd hope if he actually thought about it, Tanner could come up with something smarter than just riding up and blasting away,"

"How are we going to do this?" Geena asked, and Mitch realized she had probably never done this before.

"We'll just go in and hit him with it. Start asking questions. If he gives us an alibi, I'll get someone to go run it down." With that thought, Mitch picked up his phone and called Olshan. "Ollie, how's it going over there? How long you think you'll be?"

"We could be here all day. What's up?"

"Geena and I are on our way to jack Tanner up. If he tries to float some bullshit alibi, I might need someone to run it before he has a chance to call his homies. Also check with Mickey. I might need to run a residue test."

Mitch could almost hear Ollie thinking. "If you want, either Hartek or I could grab a uniform and run the alibis."

"Okay, sounds good, if McElroy and Neal are still around, take Neal. He can use the experience."

"You got it, boss. Let us know when."

"Will do. You finding anything there?"

"Yeah, nothing that makes any sense yet."

"Keep at it." Mitch killed the connection, tossing the phone on the dash.

"Can you run a gunshot residue test without his consent?" Geena asked, as Mitch tossed the phone in the consol.

"If we arrest him."

"Why not do that? Just walk straight in and arrest him. Get him locked down before he even has a chance to do anything."

Mitch mulled it over. "Not a bad idea. Maybe sweat him a little then offer a deal." Mitch turned off the street and parked in front of a well-kept metal building. "Let's see how it goes."

"This is his shop?"

"This is the place."

"Huh. It's not what I was expecting. I was thinking it would be some seedy claptrap building, with weeds and a grease stain extending out to the street."

Mitch smiled, pushing his door open. "Tanner thinks if he keeps the place up and looking nice it will keep the cops from snooping around."

"Does that work?"

"Sure, until you shoot some reporter in broad daylight." Mitch laughed, then stopped, frowning at the building. "You know, it does work. We know he runs a few hot parts through here maybe a little weed and other shit out the back door, but we never come and roust him. Now, you take Sparky O'Neal, he runs a craphole like you just described and we are always over there."

Geena nodded. "What you are saying is Tanner is smart guy. Maybe, too smart to ride over and kill somebody in front of their house."

"You're right." Mitch scowled at the building. "What are we missing?"

Geena shrugged and slung her purse over her shoulder. "Let's go see what he has to say."

They stepped into the shop which smelled pleasantly of leather and oil, mixed with a hint of grease. Tanner sat behind a computer, the screen casting a blue shadow across his face. "Mitch," he said rising to his feet in a smooth, graceful motion. "I see you are finally driving the mustang. Too much car for you. You ain't got the swagger to pull it off, you should sell that too me."

"Fat chance."

"Well damn, at least grease the doors. Shit, I could hear them all the way in here." Tanner crossed to a shelf and grabbed an aerosol can. "Use this. It'll make them work smooth as a baby's butt," he said, tossing the can to Mitch. "How's that motor running."

"Not bad. Might go with a hotter cam."

"Make it idle rough," Tanner said, looking out the window at the car. "When are you going to get it ready to paint?"

"Soon I hope," Mitch said. "Haven't decided on a color yet."

"Red," Tanner said, promptly. "Maybe hard silver with black stripes. If you need somebody to paint it, call Toby Callahan's boy."

"Chad?" Mitch asked and Tanner nodded. "Shit, how old is he anyway?'

"Hell, Mitch. We're getting old. He's sixteen," Tanner said, pulling out a box of doughnuts from under the counter and placing them on top of the counter. "Help yourselves. Coffee's over there."

"No shit, you think Chad?"

"I tell you, the kid is good, better than Toby even." Tanner pointed to a bike. "He did that green bike. He feathered that in by hand."

Mitch looked at the bike which started as a peaceful, pale sea green and ended up an angry, dark green crashing wave. "Very nice," Mitch said, and meant it. "I hope he ain't painting cars for Toby."

"Well he is, but Toby's retired. He gave up boosting and opened this little shop rebuilding Camaros and Trans Ams."

"Commission work?" Mitch asked, scoring a cream filled long-john out of the doughnut box.

"Yeah, mostly. They'll buy the occasional car if they can find one in decent shape. They seem to be doing pretty good. Always a market for those old Chevys. The kid bought a Sportster from me the other day." Tanner snatched a cake doughnut from the box. "But hell, you didn't come all the way out here to talk to me about bikes and paint jobs. What can I do for Tucson's finest?"

"We need to ask where you were this morning."

Tanner was flicking sprinkles from his doughnut. "Hate these things," he muttered, stalling. "Well, I opened up this morning around nine, but I reckon you want to know about earlier."

"How about around five this morning?"

Tanner cocked his head, thinking it over. He sighed, dropping the doughnut in the trash. "I was down south of Golf Links. I shot that mother fucker Jackson Pyle."

"Whoa, whoa!" Mitch shouted. "Tanner, wait a minute. Don't say another word."

"Shit, Mitch. What does it matter now?"

"It matters," Mitch said, pulling a small recorder from his pocket. He turned it on, sitting it on the counter between them. "Is it okay if I record our conversation?"

"Sure," Tanner said, shrugging his heavy shoulders.

"Okay, I'm Detective John Mitchell. With me is Geena Dixon of the FBI. We are going to interview Roscoe Tannenbaum. First I'm going to read Mister Tannenbaum his rights."

"Aw, shit, Mitch, I've only heard them about a thousand times," Tanner complained.

"Make it a thousand and one," Mitch said, crisply. He read the rights slowly off the card. "Mister Tannenbaum, do you understand the rights I have just read you?"

"Yeah, sure."

"Do you wish to talk to us?'

"Yeah, I'm ready."

"Would you like a lawyer to be present while you speak to us? My advice would be to wait for a lawyer." Mitch had never in his life said that to a suspect, but something about Tanner's attitude didn't feel right.

"Naw, I'm good. Ask your questions."

"Did you kill Jackson Pyle?"

Tanner nodded, gravely. "Yeah, I shot that mother fucker alright. Can't say as I'm one bit sorry neither. He deserved it."

"Okay you shot Mister Pyle. What time was that?"

Tanner grinned at Mitch, holding up his hands. "Don't know exactly, I don't wear no watch, but I reckon it was early, maybe around five this morning."

Mitch grimaced; he'd give that one to Tanner. "How many times did you fire?"

Now, Tanner hesitated. He glanced from Mitch to Geena then back again. "Hell, I don't know. I was just shootin'."

"What kind of gun?"

"Ruger, nine."

"Is that gun here on the premises?"

"Naw, I dumped it," Tanner said easily.

"You got rid of the gun?"

"Yup."

"Where?"

Tanner took a long sip from his coffee. "I tossed it in the lake."

"Lake? What lake?' Mitch demanded.

Tanner sighed, scratching his goatee. He was frowning, and Mitch could almost see his mind turning, then all of a sudden, Tanner's his face smoothed out. "That pond at Golf Links and Camino Seco!"

"So, the gun isn't here?"

"Nope. It's at the bottom of that lake."

"Would you be willing to submit to a GSR test?"

Again, Tanner hesitated. "Aw, man, I don't know about that. Maybe I should wait until I talk to a lawyer about that."

"Okay," Mitch said, nodding. "We're going to stop right there. Mister Tannenbaum, we're going to take you into custody."

"You gonna haul me in the Mustang?" Tanner asked with a grin. "Be kind of crowded."

"We'll wait for a squad," Mitch said, then called on the cell for two squads and a pair of detectives. After hanging up, Mitch glanced at Tanner. "Do you want to lock up? We'll come back later with a warrant to do a search, but I guarantee everything will be put back the way it was."

Tanner shrugged. "Naw. Go ahead, do your search now. I don't care."

"That's okay. We'll wait for the warrant."

"Suit yourself." Tanner ran a hand over his stubby blonde hair. "You mind if I call Kathy Reynolds? She works for me sometimes. She can come over and take care of the shop after you guys leave."

"Kathy?" Mitch asked raising an eyebrow.

"Yeah, we been going out for a while," Tanner replied, with a small grin. "We was kinda talking of getting married. Guess that ain't gonna happen now. Still, you mind if I give her a call?"

"I'd rather you didn't, but I will call her, and make sure she is here before we leave," Mitch promised, and Tanner shrugged again. "You and Kathy. When did that happen?"

"Couple of months ago. She came by looking for one of those Vespas," Tanner said, his tone saying what he thought of the Vespas. "I talked her into a nice little bike. I gave her a few lessons on riding it. We kinda hit it off," he said, sounding a little sheepish at the end.

"She's nice," Mitch said, stepping away. "I will call Kathy now." He took a couple of steps away, his mind whirling. Tanner and Kathy? Wow. Mitch pulled Kathy's number from his contacts, and dialed the call. Mitch scowled. She didn't answer, of course she never answered, Mitch remembered that about her. Always drove him crazy.

Mitch left a quick message, then walked back to the counter. "Left her a message," he said, holding up the phone, then changed the subject. "You think I should go with the new cam?"

Tanner shrugged. "Might be better to look into converting it to fuel injected."

"Too much money and hassle," Mitch said. They talked cars and bikes. Mitch deliberately kept the recorder on. He wanted to be able to prove he didn't press the questioning after Tanner asked for a lawyer.

"Heard you were playing ball again," Tanner commented.

"Yeah been playing a little basketball over at the base. You ever play anymore?"

"Naw, miss it sometimes. Course football was more my game. We're all too old to play football." Tanner shook his head. "You know a good lawyer?"

"Terry Milton is who I'd call."

A patrolman, Don Reed pushed through the front door, he pointed at Mitch. "Boy, you better watch out, Parksy is pissed."

"Yeah, I figured," Mitch said. "Who you got coming."

"Jonsey and Jenkins," Reed answered. "What exactly are we looking for?

"Guns of any kind."

"Anything that would tie him to Senator Braxton or Brody," Geena said.

"Yeah, go through the books. Double check all the money."

"You got it boss," Reed said, then added. "How is all of this going to help us find Angie Brody?"

"I don't know, but it's all connected." Mitch watched as the two patrolmen who had accompanied Reed hooked the cuffs on Tanner. "Sorry about that, man."

Tanner tried to shrug, but with his hands cuffed behind his back, it didn't come off well. "It ain't the first time."

"Take him down; make sure he gets his call. I'll be along shortly to book him."

"What's the charge?"

Mitch looked squarely at Tanner. "Murder, first degree."

Mitch and Geena followed them out. "Reed is right," Geena said as they got in the car. "I fear we are losing focus on Angie."

"It's all tied together," Mitch insisted.

"I hope you're right, because that girl is running out of time."

"I know, but we just got to find a string to pull. We pull it long enough it will lead us to Angie Brody. Somebody knows where she is."

"Do you think this motorcycle gang, what are they called? Deacons? Do you think they could be helping Carter? Maybe hiding him and the girl?"

Mitch frowned. "I don't know. They ain't exactly a gang. They hang out together, got a kind of half-assed bar. Word is they run a little weed across the border, maybe some coke. They boost a few bikes, a car here and there, but maybe they are just a bunch of guys who'd rather ride bikes than work."

"So, we're spinning our wheels here?"

"No, we're making progress. We've established that Senator Braxton is involved. That brings us full circle back to Van Zandt. We're getting there."

"But are we going to get there in time to save Angie Brody? And how many people are going to have to die between now and then?"

"Well, you can't count Jackson Pyle. That fucker was involved somehow."

"You're right about that, but Jackson is the square peg in all of this. The rest of the players are out of his league. My quick take on him was he was a third-rate reporter at a second-rate paper."

"That would be our boy Jackson," Mitch agreed.

"Okay," Geena said. "Tell me, how does he get tied up with the heavy hitters? People like Van Zandt and Braxton are a little out of his social circle."

"Aw shit!" Mitch exclaimed, slamming his fist down on the roof of the car. "I'm so stupid," he said, leaning in the window to grab his cell. Mitch shook his head, while he stabbed the speed dial button, "Parksy, I need three things," he barked into the phone.

"Jesus, Mitch, my list is getting pretty long."

"I know, but this is important. I need you to get the number of the Tucson Daily News." Mitch waited, digging out his notebook while he heard the clacking of her keyboard. Mitch looked at Geena. "He was a reporter. He found something out."

A look flashed across Geena's face. "Blackmail?"

"That would be my guess," Mitch said, as Parker came back and gave him the number. "Okay, good, now I want you to call down to dispatch. Have them get somebody over to Pyle's desk. Nothing is to be touched, and I want them standing there five minutes ago."

"You want lights and sirens?"

"Hell, yes, shoot them out of a fucking cannon for all I care. I just want them there. Then I want you to draw up warrants for his office, cube, his desk, a locker if he had one. If he had a lunch box I want a warrant for it."

"Shit, Mitch the paper will protest."

"I know, but the man was just killed. We need to look at his desk."

"What do you want me to put in the warrant for PC?"

"Crap, probable cause?" Mitch thought about it. "We know he had a meeting with Braxton, work from there."

"Okay, what is the third thing?"

"Get warrants for Tanner's shop and home. He just confessed to shooting Pyle."

"Damn, Mitch, I 'm going to be stuck in here all day."

"I know, but I think you would be the best to get the statement from Inez. Besides you're good with the warrants, so get on it."

Mitch killed the phone tapping it in his palm. "Okay what did I miss?' Geena asked.

"Like you said, Jackson doesn't fit in with the group, so I'm guessing he found something out. Being a low life, he tried to blackmail them."

"And they used Tanner to eliminate him?" Geena asked, skeptically. "That's a stretch. Tanner doesn't fit in with that group either."

"That's true, but Tanner didn't kill Pyle."

"Okay maybe, but he's still taking the fall for whom ever did. Why would he do that?"

"I don't know," Mitch admitted. "I think the first thing we need to find out, is what Jackson Pyle had on the Senator."

"Then we can use that to find Angie Brody!"

"Hopefully," Mitch said. "The trouble is, I'm running out of bodies. I need to keep Olshan and Hartek on Pyle's house. Reed, Jenkins and Jones can do the search here and then Tanner's house. We need to interview Tanner, and Kathy Reynolds. We also need to search Jackson's office at the paper." Mitch ran his hand over the hood of the car, thinking. "Maybe we should jack up this guy Van Zandt?"

Geena scowled. "That wouldn't be like hauling in some junkie. Perry Van Zandt is one of the most powerful men in Washington. In the entire country. He's also a lawyer."

Mitch spread his hands and shrugged. Van Zandt didn't scare him. The man was guilty.

"What now?" Geena asked.

"I want to talk to Tanner. We need to speak with Kathy Reynolds as well." Mitch stopped, he also wanted to be in on the search of Jackson Pyle's office. "Fuck it; let's go over to the court house. I want to pick up the warrants and get going on the search of Pyle's office. See if we can find what he had on the Senator."

"I don't know. Doesn't it stand to reason, that if Braxton had Pyle killed, they would have made sure they had whatever he was using to blackmail them?"

Mitch frowned. He liked talking with Geena. She had a way of punching the holes in his thinking. "You're right, but Jackson was also a weasely little fucker. He might have been able to stash something they wouldn't find. Besides, I'm not sure they are the ones who had him killed."

"Why would you say that? Seems to make perfect sense to me."

"I know but the timing seems off. They just had a few hours to track down what he had on them. Besides, if they wanted to kill Pyle, why do it that way. Why not just have him disappear? They had to know this would come straight back to them. It's hard to cover the fact that the Senator met with him. Too many people might know about that. Hell, he did a story on the Senator."

"So why did Tanner kill him?'

"He didn't. That much I'm sure of."

Geena cocked her head raising an eyebrow. "Mitch, I know you like the guy, but he fits the description. He knew what caliber of gun was used, and he confessed. Face it, he's the shooter."

"I know he confessed, but it wasn't like any other confession I ever took. And why confess, then balk at the GSR?"

"Who knows? But what does it matter?"

Before Mitch could answer, a silver Lexus swung into the parking lot. An attractive thirtyish woman jumped from the car. Geena could see that the woman was agitated, but Geena also expected that this woman always moved quickly and was probably agitated most of the time. "Kathy Reynolds?" Geena guessed and Mitch nodded.

"Mitch, you son of a bitch! What the hell is going on? Where is Tanner?"

"He's been arrested."

Geena watched the exchange and quickly realized, there was more than just a little history between them. "God damn it Mitch, what the hell did you do?"

"We came over to question Tanner about a shooting," Mitch replied calmly. He made a quick gesture at Geena. "This is Agent Dixon of the FBI."

Kathy shot a quick, curt nod in Geena's direction, then flicked her eyes back on Mitch, branding him with a vicious stare. "A shooting? And you think Tanner is involved?"

"A witness gave a pretty good description of him. We came over to ask him about it and he confessed."

Kathy Reynolds staggered back a step, like she had taken a punch. "What do you mean he confessed? Who was shot?"

She knows what's coming, Geena realized. Whatever was happening, she was a part of it, or at least she knew about some of it. "Jackson Pyle," Mitch told her.

Kathy gave a quick odd jerk of her head; her hand flinched like she was going to cover her mouth, but then stopped suddenly. "Oh, no," she whispered.

Mitch shot a quick look at Geena, and got a small nod in return. Reynolds knew something. "Kathy, if you want to help Tanner, you better tell me what you know."

Kathy spread her hands. She was doing her best to look innocent, but the way she kept shifting her gaze was a dead giveaway. "I don't know what you are talking about," she said, sullenly.

Mitch smiled, and for the first time, Geena saw the steel in him. "Kathy, don't bullshit me," he said, softly, but reminding Geena of the low growl of a dog about to attack.

Fire snapped in Kathy's eyes. "Fuck you, Mitch!"

Uh, oh, Geena thought, here comes some of that history. Mitch grabbed her by the arm. "Damn it, Kathy I'm on your side here. Tanner is in a lot of trouble with this.

He's already confessed to one murder, and that is going to tie into kidnapping and maybe a couple more counts of murder. If he takes the fall for this, he won't ever get out."

A single tear rolled down Kathy's face, meandering on an uncertain path across her cheek. "Damn it, I don't know anything," she said her voice hoarse. She wiped the tear away with an angry gesture. "I know something has been troubling him the last week or so. I haven't been able to get him to open up, but he hasn't been sleeping."

Mitch nodded. "Okay, if you want to help him, get him to come clean with me. He needs to tell us what he knows."

Geena watched the two of them. It was obvious that Kathy was lying and it was equally obvious that Mitch wanted to believe her. He wanted to believe she wasn't involved, Geena realized. Geena stepped forward, crowding the other woman a little. "Ms. Reynolds, you're lying to us. You need to tell us what you know. Tanner needs your help."

Kathy looked at Geena. "I don't know what you are talking about," she said coldly. She glanced back at Mitch with a fawning look. "But what can I do?"

"Check the visitor's schedule out at the prison," Geena said coldly.

Mitch glanced sharply at Geena. "We need to find out what's going on," he said.

Geena stepped between them. "When you say Tanner wasn't sleeping, what was he on? Is he using?"

Kathy shook her head. "He wasn't on anything! Tanner hates drugs. Something was bothering him. He never said anything, but sometimes I would wake up and he would be sitting out on the deck."

Geena watched the pain flash across Mitch's face, as he realized they were living together. She took Reynolds' hand leading her away. Mitch stepped back, letting them talk. He leaned against the car, thinking. Tanner had been pushed into this. Mitch could feel an undercurrent of desperation coming from the big man.

Someone or something had pushed Roscoe Tannenbaum into a corner. Whatever it was it was heavy. Tanner was a tough man. Once Tanner had been stabbed by a broken pool cue. He had pulled the cue from his side and beat two guys half to death with it.

"Crap," Mitch growled. What scared that type of man?

As Mitch tried to figure it out a gray Taurus swung into the rapidly filling parking lot. Howard Jones was the first out of the car, he waved at Mitch. "Hey, Mitch. Working with you. So, I guess we finally made the big time?"

"Tells you how desperate I am," Mitch shot back.

"Do we kiss your ass now, or later?"

"Now is good. We can go around back if you're bashful."

"What are we looking for?" Jenkins asked, struggling to get out of the car.

"A gun for one thing."

"Shit, there's going to be tons of guns in there," Jenkins complained.

"I know. Tag and bag them all. Be on the lookout for a nine," Mitch said. "Also, go through the paper. Something is pushing and scaring him. We need to find out what that might be."

"Scaring Tanner? Shit." Jones shook his head. "You ever hear about him beating up half the crowd at Heck and Winks that time. I always figured he was the one who burned the place down."

"Might have been," Mitch said absently. "If you guys need some help get some more units in here." Mitch started to turn away, then stopped. "I know this place is going to be a bitch to search, but we can't afford to miss anything. This case is going to come down to the details."

Jones nodded and looked Mitch in the eye. "If there's anything here. We will find it."

"Good deal," Mitch said nodding. "We have a warrant on the way, hold back on the search until it gets here, but go ahead and seal up the place."

Geena came back, shaking her head. "She knows something."

"You get anything from Kathy?"

"Not much, sorry for butting in."

"No, you did the right thing." Mitch gestured to the Mustang. "Let's go see if we can hurry up the warrants."

They climbed into the car. "You two seem to have some history," she observed.

"It was a long time ago."

"She still holds some feelings for you, I think."

"Bullshit. Like I said, it was a long time ago."

"I think you still got a little thing for her as well."

"Shut up," Mitch growled, firing the car up. "She tell you anything we can use?"

Geena laughed, a rolling melody. "What's wrong Mitchell? Don't like talking about old flames?" she taunted, getting only a grunt in return. "Okay, she's worried about Tanner, that much is certain. She claims she has no idea why he might go after Pyle. Which is bullshit."

"You think she's holding back?"

"Oh yeah. She knew something was up. I don't think she was all that surprised to hear he took out Pyle. That's not quite right. She was expecting something bad, maybe not this but something involving Pyle."

"Shit," Mitch said, swerving onto the street. This was getting too complicated. "There's got to be a thread running through all of this."

"Are you sure? I mean I don't see it yet. Face it, these maybe just random acts."

"Can't be," Mitch grunted.

"Why? What makes you so sure?"

"Cause if it isn't all connected; we're fucked."

"We maybe fucked."

"Naw," Mitch said, heading up on the ramp. "Pyle is the key. He'd be the weak link. He wasn't part of this. I'd bet he stumbled onto something, somehow found what was going on. Being the weasel that he was he tried to blackmail them and they killed him."

"Do you think we will find anything at the paper?"

"Shit, I hope so. If Pyle was at all smart, he held something back for leverage."

"Surely they wouldn't have killed him until they secured all he had."

"I'm sure they thought they got it all, but Pyle always struck me as a sneaky fuck. Maybe not smart, but sneaky. I'm hoping they missed something."

"Don't bet on it. Think of the people Braxton would have access to. These people would be the best at what they do. They are very smart and very resourceful."

Mitch snorted. "Bullshit, we're already onto them. We'll get them eventually. I just pray it's in time to save Angie Brody."

Geena shook her head. "Don't under estimate them. You may know Jackson Pyle met with the Senator, but proving it may be another matter. And, even if you can prove they met, so what? The woman is running for President, she meets with reporters every day. So what if one of them happens to get killed. That's the genius of having someone like Tanner kill Pyle. Deniability."

"You're right, but now that we know, it'll be easier to run down the evidence."

Geena shook her head, pursing her lips. "Maybe, but I still say it's going to be hard to connect all the dots. How can you tie Tanner to the Senator?"

Mitch shrugged. "I may not have to. I'm still far from convinced that Tanner did the shooting."

"Look, I know you like the guy, but face it, he confessed."

Mitch nodded absently. "He wasn't giving it all to us. Why would he confess? We really didn't have anything on him. If he did dump the gun in that pond, we would likely never find it. Without the gun, it would be hard to make a case."

"You're forgetting about the print on the shell."

"Ain't gonna be Tanner's, I'd bet the farm on that. Besides, Tanner doesn't even know we have that." Mitch parked in a no parking spot in front of the court house. He set the brake, then turned to look at Geena. "Tell me, why would Tanner confess, then balk at the GSR?"

Geena shrugged. "Who knows? Maybe he was already having second thoughts about the confession. He might get around the confession, but the GSR would send him away."

"Maybe," Mitch admitted. He ran a hand across his face. "Or maybe, he knows he is gonna come up clean on the GSR."

"Admit it Mitchell. You like the guy. You want him to be innocent," Geena said, a teasing note creeping into her tone. "Which is a strange coincidence, considering that he is about to marry an old flame of yours."

"Hey, Kathy is still a friend. I can be happy for her," Mitch protested.

Geena nodded softly. "Yeah, I can see that about you."

Parker was coming up the sidewalk with a file as they got out of the car. "You finish with all the warrants for Pyle?"

"Just finished with the last one. I did what I could to establish a link to Angie Brody."

Mitch riffled through them, quickly scanning them. "How solid is that link from Van Zandt to Jillian Braxton's husband?"

"That much is solid," Carly said, smiling. "Part of public record. No doubt about it. Van Zandt handled the sale."

"Good work," Mitch said, nodding his head. "That should do it. It ain't like Pyle is going to protest."

"The paper might. Or the judge might balk at giving you carte blanch to search there."

Mitch shrugged. "We're not asking for carte blanch, we just want to search the places Pyle had access to. Besides I'm taking them to Judge Sanderson."

"He won't sign it just because you guys are friends and play golf together."

"I know, but he will sign them," Mitch said. "Where are you on everything else?"

"Getting ready to take a run at Inez."

"Okay, get on that." Mitch and Geena were walking up to the courthouse, when Mitch looked back and saw a meter maid heading towards his car. "Hang on a sec."

She was pulling out here ticket book when Mitch skidded to a stop in front of his car. "You can't park there," she said briskly, smiling when she saw Mitch. "Oh, hey, Mitch."

Mitch smiled and waved, searching for a name. "Beverly," he came up with, hoping it was right. "We're in a hurry to get some warrants signed."

"The Brody thing?" Beverly asked, flipping her ticket book closed with a practiced casual flip.

"Yeah, we're trying to see if the Jackson Pyle thing ties in."

"Alright, cutie, go ahead," she said, flashing Mitch a smile. Mitch was halfway up the steps, when he heard her call. "Hey, Mitch, with all that money you're making now, you could at least paint this jalopy."

"One day soon," Mitch said, waving his hand over his head. At the door, he stopped again. "Beverly, have you guys got any pictures of Jacob Carter?"

Beverly shook her head. "That's the guy from the Brody case?"

"Yeah, yeah, that's him. Look, I'm in a hurry, but who would I talk to about getting you guys the pictures?"

"Patty Seaver is our supervisor."

"Okay, I'll see you guys get the pictures."

"Hey, Mitch, we're all girls."

"Whatever," Mitch grunted, hurrying to catch up with Geena, who was standing in the doorway. "Meter maids?"

"Hey, they see a lot of people."

"I know, it's a good idea. Hard to believe it hasn't been thought of already." Geena paused as they passed through the door. "What do you think about giving some pictures to private security companies?"

Mitch frowned as they flashed their badges at the deputies manning the metal detectors. "I don't know," he said, as a deputy waved them through.

"It's like you said about the meter maids, they see a lot of people."

"You're right, but I don't see Carter going to a lot of places that has security. If he's smart he'll avoid those types of places."

"Can't avoid them all. Grocery stores usually have a security guard or two. I assume he's feeding her."

Mitch shrugged. "It's a thought," he admitted grudgingly. "No shit. They have security guards at supermarkets?"

"Most of them do, and they have cameras."

"Huh," Mitch grunted, as they stepped into the judge's outer office. "It's worth a shot I guess," he said, rapping on the judge's door.

A grunt sounded from inside. Mitch took that as an invitation and pushed the door open. "Good morning, Judge."

Dressed in Bermuda shorts and a golf shirt, Sanderson waved a hand towards the chairs. "Now, tell me dear boy. What is so important that you are holding up my Saturday tee time?" he asked without looking up from the faxed copies of the warrants.

Mitch waited until Geena had sat, then took a seat himself. "I need to get some warrants signed."

"Hell, I can see that," the judge grumbled, holding up the faxed copies and shaking them at Mitch. "Please, Johnny, tell me why I should grant you these warrants."

"Well, judge, we believe Jackson Pyle came into some information. Information he gathered in the course of his duties as a reporter for the Tucson Daily News. He then used that information to blackmail Senator Jillian Braxton."

The judge smiled steepling his fingers and leaning back in his chair. "And you can prove all of this of course."

"We can prove Pyle met with the Senator and as for the other...."

"Hold it, Johnny. Spare me the legal ease. I have to listen to lawyers all day." The judge dug a cigar out of his humidor. "And spare me all your usual bullshit. I just want to hear what you know. But first, introduce me to your lovely accomplice."

"Sorry, Judge, this is Geena Dixon. Ms. Dixon is an FBI agent." Mitch jerked his head at the judge. "Judge Harlan Sanderson."

"Pleased to meet you, your honor," Geena said rising gracefully to her feet and extending her hand.

"The pleasure is all mine," the judge said, taking her hand and kissing it lightly. "Dixon is an English name, but if I were to wager, I would say some of your ancestors were Italian."

"You'd win," Geena said brightly. "My mother was half Italian."

"Very good. Now, I'm old enough to be your father, so I am going to give you some fatherly advice. While you are hanging out with Johnnie keep one eye on your virtue and the other eye on your pocket book."

Geena smiled. "Thank you, sir, I will be sure to do that."

"Now, back to the nasty business at hand." The judge slapped his hands down on the warrant. "Okay, Johnny, tell me why I should let you go poking through that newspaper."

Mitch scooted his chair forward. "Well, first of all, Pyle obviously had something on Braxton."

The judge raised an eyebrow. "Really? And what would that be?"

"That we don't know for sure. That's one of the things we will be looking for."

"Providing you get the warrant. You haven't convinced me."

"We can link Braxton to the Angie Brody abduction."

Sanderson leaned back in his chair, looking very serious. "Tell me about that."

Mitch shot a glance at Geena. "Do you know of a man named Perry Van Zandt?"

Sanderson knitted his brow. "Lawyer back east, isn't he? Seems I remember him handling a few big murder trials."

Geena hitched her chair closer. "That's just his hobby. He's the Managing Senior Partner in Briggs, Downey and Van Zandt."

"The tax firm?"

"That's the one," replied, her voice raising a notch. "Jacob Carter works for the firm and he was once defended on a murder charge by Van Zandt himself."

"How sure are you about the connection from Carter to Van Zandt?"

"Very sure," Geena replied firmly. "I was the DA representing the state on the case. It never got to trial. But Carter was guilty."

"Okay, all very interesting, but how does this tie in to Braxton?"

"Braxton is a Senator and Van Zandt basically writes the tax code. They know each other," Geena insisted.

The judge pursed his lips, swiveling in his chair to gaze out the window. "I have no doubt they know each other, but that's a long way from what you are suggesting."

"We have a couple of more things," Mitch said, looking through the warrants. Damn, Parks had done a great job pulling in data. "We know that Van Zandt and Associates handled the sale of Joe Braxton's holdings in upstate New York."

"That strengthens the link," Sanderson admitted. "What else have you got?"

"If Jackson Pyle got something on Braxton, it had to come from right here in Tucson. As far as we can tell the man didn't leave the state for over a year. If he found out something here, it would have to tie in with the Angie Brody thing. That's just the only thing we got going big enough to involve someone like Braxton."

Judge Sanderson shook his head. "While I certainly see the logic in what you are saying, it just isn't strong enough for me to grant the warrants for you to tear apart that newspaper office."

The judge smiled, holding up his hand to cut off the explosion from Mitch. "Hold on, Johnnie. The good thing is,

I talked to Donnie Cruz over at the paper. They have no problems with you searching Pyle's area."

"What about the computers? Do we get a look at the computers?" Mitch demanded.

"To a point. Someone from the paper will do that for you."

"Shit, judge, they might miss it."

The judge smiled. "I wouldn't worry about it, Johnnie. Donnie seemed like a man ready to make a deal. They have no idea what Pyle had, but boy would they like to. I'm sure you can work something out with them." The judge signed the top warrant and passed it to Mitch. "You work something out and Donnie calls me and says they withdraw their objection to the phones and computers, then I'll sign the rest."

Mitch nodded, seeing through what the judge was saying. He stood and scooped up the signed warrant. "Hey, Johnnie," the judge called after them.

"Yeah, Judge," Mitch answered, one hand on the door.

"Find that girl."

CHAPTER SEVEN

Sonoran Desert Southwest of Tucson AZ June 16th 2018 Saturday Late Afternoon

A heavy stillness hung in the air. Not a breath of wind stirred. The desert was silent as a tomb, the heat keeping even the bugs quiet. The man who was stretched out in the nest of boulders ignored both the heat and the humidity. He wore a soaked bandana tied around his forehead and another one around his neck. He had a flat bag of water strapped to his back with a tube running up beside his mouth. From time to time he would take a sip of the water. A rifle rested on a sandbag in front of him.

The safety was on and the scope capped to protect the lens from fogging. The rifle looked old, with a dull pewter finish. The rifle didn't look new, but it was, in fact it was state of the art. A Patriot Arms rifle, it came with a five-round clip, but Sam had upgraded with a ten-round purchased off the internet. With one in the pipe that gave him eleven shots without reloading. Chambered at seven point six-two millimeters with a one hundred and seventy-five grain cartridge, the rifle was deadly accurate out to eight hundred yards.

Sam had test fired it to verify that fact. More than once.

Sam sighed, wondering for the thousandth time about what he was doing. He was a cop, sworn to protect people. What was he doing? He was about to massacre several men. It bothered Sam a little that he wasn't more upset. Sam realized he could call himself a cop no longer. He had crossed a line. The man he had been before was dead and gone now. Gone forever. Sam felt a pang at the loss of his former life. It had been a good life. But some things just had to be done. Sometimes they were a hard, and sometimes people had to die. Sam was here in this place to kill somebody. But he wasn't going to enjoy it. Not really.

A Bushnell spotting scope with a laser range finder and tripod sat on the sandbag beside the rifle. Sam had checked and double checked the range to the crossroads. Six hundred and fifty-five yards. From GPS readings taken earlier, he knew the nest of boulders was twenty-two feet higher than the crossroads.

The crossroads weren't much. Just the intersection of two jeep trails. A lonely spot in the desert to meet. Even though he hadn't been the one who picked this spot, Sam knew it had been chosen for exactly that reason. It's isolation, away from prying eyes. Sam might not have selected this, but it was perfect for his intentions.

Sam smiled grimly, it had taken some prodding, but Hector had spilled the beans on this meeting. It was funny, once Hector started talking, he almost didn't stop. Sam had learned a lot. He was still trying to figure out just how to use this newfound information. But the first step was to shut down this meeting.

Part of it was the drugs. Sam truly hated drugs. He knew that he couldn't stop the flow of drugs across the border, but he could stop this batch.

But it wasn't just the drugs. This bunch had killed Fred and Gloria Dooley. Just the thought of what happened to those youngsters was enough to make Sam's blood boil. These assholes were rabid animals and needed to be put down.

Sam ran a hand along the barrel of the rifle, almost a lover's caress. He smiled a grim smile. Yes siree, they needed to be put down. And Sam figured he was the man for the job.

Without moving his head, he flicked his eyes to the cheap watch strapped around his wrist. Getting close to the time. They should be coming. Theirs wasn't the type of meeting that one was late for. The meeting was between a Mexican drug runner named Sanchez and a couple of bikers named Chappy Miers and Henry Flores. Sanchez was looking to move up on the Mexican side of the border, and this was his first move. Sanchez wasn't his real name. Sam knew this and didn't care.

Sanchez and bikers were teaming up. Together, they were looking to carve themselves a niche in the drug trade in southern Arizona and California. Chappy had contacts on the streets of Tucson as well as Phoenix. Flores' gangs rode in So Cal. Sanchez could get the drugs to the border and Chappy could move them to Cali for Flores to sell.

After they got him talking, Hector told them that this was the first meeting. They were going to set up the pipeline and hammer out the details. After this, Chappy, Flores and Sanchez wouldn't be at the meetings. They would have underlings do this, the most dangerous part.

Sam ran through his plan in his head. He wouldn't have much choice when the time came. He'd have to take out the most heavily armed ones first.

Hector said four to eight men at the meeting. If it were seven or eight, he'd have to walk away. Get his man another day. If it was six, well, he'd just have to size it up and make that call on the fly. Besides the rifle, Sam carried a nine-millimeter, semi-automatic pistol belted around his waist. Besides the pistol, two extra clips were also fastened to the belt. The pistol was mainly from habit. If the situation deteriorated to the point where he needed the pistol, Sam was in trouble. Crap in the pants kind of trouble.

He also carried a small .556 caliber Bushmaster rifle. He had modified it to be fully automatic. He had a thirty-round clip inserted into the weapon and one more in each hip pocket. If he failed with the sniper rifle, and it became a firefight, he would take up the .556 and move forward, working down the slope. For the third time, he scanned the route he would take. It was steep and he would be moving fast. That was the bad part. The good news was, if he kept low, he would have some cover. Earlier, he had cleared the route of most of the loose rocks and debris.

At the bottom, he would have ten yards to cross with no cover. Hopefully, once he burst from cover and opened up with the Bushmaster rifle, he could catch them back on their heels. If not? If they were ready for him?

Sam knew very well that he could die in the next hour. He was prepared for that. Sam wasn't sure he wanted to die, but he lately wasn't sure he really cared either. It was better than a life of drooling down his chin, and crapping in his pants. Wasn't it?

As he pondered that question, Sam saw a dust cloud rolling in from the north. Chappy Miers. With a slow controlled movement, he brought the spotting scope to his eye. He could make out a rusted, silver Ford Bronco bouncing along the rutted trail. He looked, but the distance was too great and there was too much sun-glare to see how many people might be inside the Bronco.

Sam turned the scope from the Bronco. It didn't matter how many were inside. He'd know that soon enough. For now, he needed to know if they were alone. Slowly he scanned his surroundings, looking for movement or dust.

He was still looking when the Bronco slid to a stop twenty yards from the crossroads. Sam smiled. It would take at least three seconds to sprint from the crossroads to the truck. In that amount of time, he could fire ten shots.

Sam flicked the scope to the truck, but there was still too much sun to see in. Sam returned to scanning. A black BMW sedan was coming in from the west. It came fast ignoring what the rough trail was doing to the suspension of the car, braked hard at the crossroads and turned south. The trunk came open as the car slid to a stop.

Sam could see two men sitting in the front of the car. They stepped out, standing on either side of the car. The doors popped open on the Bronco. Flores slid from the driver's seat and Chappy Miers bounced out of the passenger's side. But it wasn't Chappy. Chappy was a big man, this man was tall but thinner. Sam grabbed the spotting scope training it on the man. Calvin Ramsey. Sam swore bitterly. He had wanted to kill Chappy. If there was ever a soul that needed to be dispatched from this world, it was Chappy fucking Miers.

Sam spat in the dust, thinking it over. Of course, Ramsey would be better. According to Hector, Ramsey was Flores' right-hand man and had been one of them out in the desert. Hell, this was better. Chappy could wait. Sam might find a use for Chappy.

Flores had a semi-automatic pistol tucked in his belt. Ramsey carried a saw-off shotgun angled towards the ground. Seeing the guns, the Mexicans pulled back their coats to reveal Mac tens, slung secret service style under their coats.

For a sweet second, Sam thought his job might get easier. But then Flores broke into a big smile. "Well, hell, we gonna kill each other or do some business?" he asked in a hearty voice.

For a second, Sam could feel the tension from where he was. Then Sanchez laughed. "We have a trunk full of merchandise. Do you have the money?"

"A bunch of it." Flores snapped his fingers and Ramsey stepped to the back of the Bronco and pulled out a bag designed to haul a deer carcass. Sanchez nodded to his companion, who pulled two huge gym bags from the trunk of the beamer.

Sam smiled. There was a lot of money and a lot of drugs down there. Hector had been right. This was a huge deal.

Slowly, Sam drew the rifle to him. He popped the cover off the far end of the scope. Afraid of his breath fogging the lens, he left the near end covered. As they conducted business, Sam reshot the distance. Six hundred and fifty-two yards. Soon, he would take the shot.

As the men talked, Sam could see their body language slowly begin to relax. He'd wait until they were done. That was the point where they would be the most off guard.

For a second, Sam wished he had his old bolt-action. It was slightly more accurate, and immensely more comfortable. Of course, at just under seven hundred yards it wouldn't matter. What was needed on this job was rate of fire. Sam could throw the bolt and fire as fast as anybody, but he was under no illusions, the semi–auto was faster.

Sam watched through the spotting scope as the meeting progressed. Flores was a natural at this. His wide grin and back-slapping humor had defused the tension. Sam couldn't hear the words, but he could read the body language. Sensing the meet was reaching a conclusion, he popped the rear scope cover. A plan began to form in his head. If he took out Sanchez first…. Pulling the rifle tight to his shoulder, Sam placed the crosshairs on Sanchez's head. Without thinking, he blew out a breath and squeezed the trigger. The bullet blew through Sanchez's head, exploding out the other side, spraying his companion with blood, bone and brains.

Sanchez's bodyguard was a tough man and the veteran of many gun battles, but now, covered with his boss' brains, he froze. Sam had been counting on that. It was why he took Sanchez first. He needed that man to hesitate if only for a couple of seconds.

Sam saw none of it. He was already swinging the rifle to cover Flores. Sam had thought out the sequence. He figured Ramsey would be the hardest to kill, but Flores would react the fastest. He was right, while Ramsey was fumbling, trying to unlimber the shotgun, which would be completely useless at this range, Flores spun for the truck. Sam caught him in the crosshairs as he turned. Sam snapped off two quick shots. The first smashed Flores' left shoulder. The second went under his arm clipping the bottom of his heart and blowing out through his lungs.

Knowing both shots were hits, Sam spun the rifle to Ramsey. The big man was firing the shotgun, when Sam shot him. A coffee cup would cover the two bullets that exploded through Ramsey's chest. His body went immediately limp and he melted to the ground.

Sam pivoted the rifle catching the Mexican in the sights as the man scrambled for cover behind the Beamer. Sam's first shot hit the body guard in the neck. The man stumbled falling to one knee. This time Sam took a second, centering the crosshairs on the man's back. He screamed as Sam fired, the bullet cutting the scream off.

Looking over the top of the scope, Sam surveyed the scene. He was sure each man was dead. After a second, Sam tucked the rifle under his chin and coldly fired a bullet into the head of each man. After the last shot, Sam punched the safety on. He calmly covered the scope, and slid the rifle into a desert camo, soft case. He zipped the bag closed, then picked up the eleven spent shells.

After a quick sip of the water, he placed the unused assault rifle into a bag, then the spotting scope went into a plastic case. Suddenly very tired, Sam blew out a sigh. He was getting too old for this kind of shit.

Sam climbed to his feet, gathering his gear. Walking slowly away from the crossroads, he crossed down into a wash where an ATV sat. Working steadily, he loaded his stuff on the ATV. Once the gear was safely strapped on the ATV, he walked back to the shooting nest. Methodically, he went over every inch of the sniper's nest. He wasn't worried about tracks, the wind would take care of that, he was looking for anything that could be tied to him. While the thought of dying didn't particularly worry him, Sam had a real fear of jail. The humiliation of a public trial scared him. What such a spectacle would do to Maureen.

Finally satisfied that he had left nothing behind, Sam returned to the ATV. Swinging aboard, he started the machine and drove down to the bodies. Ignoring the fallen men, he loaded the money and drugs. As he worked, Sam watched a bank of dark clouds rolling in from the southwest.

He smiled grimly. Wouldn't it be a bitch to get caught out here in a flash flood? The thought worried him, but still, he didn't hurry. The weather was something he couldn't control. What would happen, would happen. Sam would just have to ride with it.

But damn it, sure would suck big time to get caught in a flood.

**Cooper Designs Wilmot Road Tucson AZ June 16th
2018 Saturday Evening**

Rachael Cooper looked at her watch. Damn! It was almost six already. She glanced up at the clock on the wall, just in case the watch was wrong or she read it wrong the first time.

Crap, still six. She sighed, glared at her computer screen. The layout needed work. Rachael was an architect, and the house she was designing still needed work. She liked the rooms individually, but they had no flow. She needed to stay and work, but she had people coming over at eight.

It was just Randy's poker club, but she liked to have some stuff ready for them. Sighing again, she closed the laptop, pulled it from the docking station, and slipped it into a soft black case. Maybe she could get some work done at home tonight.

What to serve? Maybe some of those pizza rolls, the guys loved those things. That would necessitate a stop by Fry's, but if she hurried, she had time. Slinging the bag over her shoulder, she dumped her cup of tea in the sink and flipped off the lights. Rushing, she took the outside stairs two at a time down to the parking lot.

Rachael was a small woman, compactly built with a small waist. She'd been an athlete in high school, but when it became apparent that her small stature was going to hold her back, she switched to her other passion, art. Somehow art, over the years, had morphed into designing houses.

Now, as she neared thirty, Rachael found herself returning to physical things. Randy had introduced her to weights, which she liked and to kayaking which she truly loved.

They had a kayak trip to Mexico planned for next month. Rachael was thinking about the kayak trip when she hit the bottom of the stairs. They needed new life jackets. Randy hated them, but Rachael insisted. Maybe some new wetsuits. Randy had bought new wetsuits, but they were your basic black. Rachael shook her head. If she left it up to Randy, everything they owned would be black. Preoccupied, she hurried to her car.

Rachael was a striking woman, used to the stares of men. As a result, she barely noticed the man who openly gawked at her as she rushed to her car. She didn't notice his hot stare, the way he licked his lips as she slid into the car. As she whipped her Miata out of the parking lot, she never saw him get in his own car and follow.

He stayed back, following her Miata as she wove through the moderate traffic on Speedway. He stayed with her as she turned into the supermarket, parking a row over from her. The man licked his lips again. He dearly wanted to follow her into the store. He wanted to watch her walk, watch her bend over to get something from the lower shelf. In his mind, he could see it.

Feeling his body burn, he watched her disappear into the store. He wanted to follow, but it would be too easy to lose her in the store. He leaned back in the seat, feeling the fire smolder inside him. Oh man, she did something to him. She tugged at something deep inside him. He pulled out the knife, placing the cool metal against his cheek.

It was a western knife, a heavy hunting knife. Night after night, he'd honed the blade until it was sharp enough to shave with. Slowly he caressed his cheek with the flat side of the blade. The steel felt almost cold against his flushed skin.

Unaware of the danger lurking so close, Rachael hurried through the store, snatching items off the shelves and tossing them in her cart. She grabbed pizza rolls and jalapeno poppers. What else? Chips. Lots of chips.

Rachael had to smile. Randy trained hard and ate healthy, but when poker night rolled around, he ate like a pig. She grabbed bean dip and salsa. On impulse, she grabbed tortillas. She could make them quesadillas. Okay, she thought going through the list in her head. What else. Beer, they would need beer. She grabbed a thirty pack, pausing to peruse the wine.

Maybe a nice rosé for her.

It was hot in the car, and the sweat rolled down his cheeks in waves. He didn't even notice the heat, his eyes glued to the door. His breath caught as she came breezing through the door, her bags swinging from her arms. The beer was heavy, but she carried it easily. His chest began to ache. She was fantastic. Perfect.

He absently rubbed the sweat from his face as he tracked her with his eyes. His gaze lingered on the swing of her hips, picturing her without her clothes. Yes, she was perfect.

An electric shock surged through him. He couldn't wait any longer. He groaned a sound of both pleasure and pain. Tonight. He would do it tonight.

The drive to her house was sheer torture. She was so close. At one point, he pulled up beside her at a stop light. He didn't mean to look, but couldn't help himself.

She glanced over at him, flashing a quick smile. The smile burned right through him, igniting a fire inside. So, she knew. She knew they were meant for each other. The smile proved that. He stole another glance, then the light changed and she was gone.

He sat at the light until an angry horn sounded behind him. Furious and cursing wildly, he slammed the car into gear, pinning the accelerator to the floor.

After a few seconds the burning fury cooled, to a cold rage. He slapped the dash. It wasn't fair. She was his. They were meant for each other.

He didn't try to catch up, he knew where she lived. Lived with that prick!

He parked down the street, watching her house. The garage was open and he could see the back of her car. He could sense movement inside the garage, but couldn't quite see her. Maybe if he eased up a couple of houses.

He was thinking of moving up, had actually pulled the car into gear, when the black truck swung into the driveway, stopping with a bark from the tires.

"Shit!" he growled, smacking the steering wheel with his palm. The husband! Fuck him! God how he hated that little fucker. Look at him strut.

He picked up the knife, gazing at his own distorted reflection in the shiny steel. Strut now you fuck, this is going to be your last day on earth. He laid the knife aside, and picked up a wooden tee ball bat. It was all worked out.

Cold rage mixed with hot sexual passion, clouding his vision. Tonight. It'd be so easy.

They had good locks on the front door, but a cheap crappy one in the back. The house backed up to a wash, across the wash was a small park. He started his car, driving around to the park. From his parking spot, he could see the upper part of the house. Every once in a while, he'd catch a glimpse of her as she passed a window.

He would wait until they went to bed, then slip across the wash. He could slip the lock on the back door with a butter knife. That door led to the garage. From the garage he would enter the kitchen, then a set of stairs. The master bedroom was at the end of the hall.

He knew this because he had been inside before. Two days earlier while they were at work, he'd snuck in, prowling the house. He'd rolled around in the laundry room in a pile of her dirty clothes.

As he waited, he checked his inventory. The razor-sharp, hunting knife in a scabbard from his belt. The butter knife, the tee ball bat and a roll of gray tape. The tee ball bat was for the husband. Not too hard. Not enough to kill him, just enough so he could be handled. Get his hands and feet taped, then the woman. It'd be so easy.

A killing fire raging through his body, he leaned back closing his eyes. Mm mm…. The woman.

Tonight.

Mitch's House Tucson AZ June 16th 2018 Saturday Night

Mitch sat at home, a bottle of Fat Tire on the table beside him. He felt tired all of a sudden. The search of Jackson Pyle's office at the paper had been a bust. Obviously, the reporter had cleared his desk, or Braxton's goons had. The bottom line was, there was simply nothing to find in the office.

Yawning, Mitch called Wade Nichols. "Hey Wade, how's it going?"

"It's going," Wade grunted.

"You get anything off Schroeder's Ipad?" Mitch asked, not really expecting much.

"Naw, not really," Wade replied. "Braxton did meet with Pyle if that helps. Schroeder was keeping a schedule for the Senator, I seen an entry for the meeting in the notes on the Ipad."

Mitch shrugged. "Every little bit helps."

"I think you were right about the blackmail. Pyle had a few new things and brochures for cars and watches."

"Oh yeah, what did he buy?"

"A new MP3. A big fancy one."

"Thanks, that helps some," Mitch said, picking up his beer. "You still good to help us out a little more on this?"

"Sure, I was going crazy."

"Thanks," Mitch said, and killed the phone.

He took a drink, then set the beer on the counter. He idly watched the sweat beads roll down the bottle. Monsoons were coming; worst part of the summer. Every summer the monsoons marched in, the humidity shot up and Mitch would boil.

Thunderstorms rolled in every night. Made it damn hard to get around of golf in. Of course, with this Angie Brody thing, he would have a hard time getting a round in before Thanksgiving.

Funny thing was, he was thinking of golf when the phone rang. "Hey, Mitch, guess what?" Ollie barked, his voice betraying a little excitement.

"What's that?"

"You were right about Tanner. Seems our Mr. Tanner is a creature of habit. He stops at that Circle K at Country Club and Valencia every morning for some smokes and one of those energy drinks."

"Is that a fact?" Mitch asked picking up his beer. "If I were a gambling man, I'd bet my left nut they have him on video at the time of the shooting."

"Your tiny balls are safe. He walked in the store about ten minutes after."

Mitch took a swig from the bottle then frowned at it. "Ten minutes? I don't know. If he drove like a bat outta hell, he might make it from Pyle's in ten minutes. And if the surveillance clock is off a few minutes. Or if that old bat was wrong about the time."

"We checked, surveillance clock is dead on nuts. It's tied in with an alarm through the phone system. The time is set by the phones. It's right on."

"That helps." Mitch frowned at the ceiling, running it through his mind. "Still if Inez Perry was wrong about the time, by just a little bit?"

"Oh, I guess you didn't hear, but we got corroboration on her story. She was right on the time."

"Oh yeah," Mitch grunted. "Good witness?"

"Pretty good. Young Married couple, setting in their breakfast nook," Ollie said, his tone leaving no doubt what he thought about breakfast nooks. "They thought Inez's time was probably right, but they also said they were watching Channel 7 News and they remembered the motorcycle cause the news had a story on about a motorcycle cracking up on Mt Lemon last night. They thought it funny that a bike went tearing by while that story was playing."

"You called the station?"

"Yup," Ollie said with a trace of humor. "Story was just over two minutes long, and aired right on the time Inez Perry said it all went down."

"Shit, that is good work."

Ollie chuckled. "Wasn't me."

"Aw crap, you mean?"

"Yup, that little prick Neal found them. Little asshole is going to be hard to live with now."

"Yeah," Mitch grunted sourly. He finished his beer, mulling it over, picturing the drive in his mind. "Still might be possible. We should drive it to be sure."

"Already done, Jerry drove it twice both ways. Best time he got was twenty-seven minutes."

Mitch snorted, "Jerry, shit. My Grandma could out drive him. Did he at least take the car seats out?"

"No, he didn't," Ollie said with a laugh. "But it don't matter."

"Why's that?"

"Outside camera, shows Tanner pulling in that old jeep of his. No way he woulda had time to swing by his place and switch. Even that early, it would add at least forty-five minutes."

"At least. Course he coulda had the jeep stashed somewhere along the way. Switched vehicles."

"That'd take some time. Minute or two."

"If he were trying to set up an alibi, I could see something like that, but then why confess?"

Mitch could almost hear Ollie's shrug. "Who knows, maybe he realized we had his ass and just said fuck it."

"Shit, we barely showed up. I asked where he was and he just came out with it!"

"Beats me," Ollie said. "But it makes about as much sense as anything else about this case."

"No, it makes perfect sense. He's covering for somebody. He jerks us around as long as he can, then all of a sudden, he trots out this alibi. If he can string it out long enough, whoever really did the killing has time to cover his tracks."

"Or just get the hell outta dodge."

"You're right. You up for some OT?"

"Always."

"Call Parksy. I want you guys to start running every KA we got for Tanner. If we get an ID on any of Pyle's victims, we can run them against Tanner's known associates. Maybe there will be a connection."

"Maybe, but nailing down the vics may take some time. Even with DNA from the titties there's gonna be some we won't know about right away."

"You're right, but we might get lucky. If we have to, we can use missing persons. Somebody wanted Jackson Pyle dead, and that somebody knows Tanner."

"That'll take forever, but it's going to be a place to start. What are you going to be doing?"

"I'm gonna check a few things, then I'm gonna go jack up Tanner."

"You gonna bring that FBI lady into it?"

Mitch hesitated, "Yeah, I'll call her. I owe her that much."

"You gonna call her or just roll over and whisper in her ear?"

"Screw you, you dirty old man! I'm at home alone."

"If you say so," Ollie said, a rattling chuckle following his words. "But if you are alone, be sure to wash your hands."

"Better watch yourself old man or you'll be trying to squeeze your fat ass into your patrol uniform." Mitch stated then hung up the phone.

Digging in his pocket, he pulled out his cell phone. He should call Geena. Calling up his contacts, he started scrolling through for Geena's number. "Aw shit," Mitch exclaimed. Calls! There woulda been a call that morning. Cursing himself for not thinking of it earlier, he hit redial. "Ollie, before you guys get started on the lists, I want you to draw up a warrant for all of Tanner's phone records."

"You're thinking there was a call that morning?"

"Damn right."

"Shit Mitch, it woulda went to his cell."

"You're probably right, but get all his phones, I want to see who has been calling him."

"Yeah, yeah, but what I'm saying is we got Tanner's cell in evidence right now. He had it on him when he was booked. You could just look at it."

"I'll do that before I go to talk to him, but we still need the warrants. When you get them, fax them over to Judge Sanderson's office. I'll drop by and fill him in."

"Jerry's still here," Ollie suggested. "He could do the warrants. He's got a nice touch with that."

"That would be good. Get him started."

Hanging up the phone, Mitch called Geena as he walked out the door.

"Special Agent Dixon."

"Geena, its Mitch. We've got a couple of leads. We're running them now. If you want in, be out in front of your hotel in twenty minutes."

"Oh shit, what have you got?"

"A couple of threads, we're gonna pull them."

"You better be right. Give me a half hour."

"Half hour in front of your hotel."

Mitch swiped off the phone, as he stepped up to Judge Sanderson's porch. Before he could ring the bell, the door swung open.

"John Mitchell, you didn't just break a date with some sweet young thing to go chasing around all night?" Elizabeth Sanderson asked, a smile belying her stern tone.

"Actually, I was calling to see if a girl wanted to go with me."

"Oh," Mrs. Sanderson said a twinkle in her eye. "Is it that Detective Parker? Harlan says she's a real hottie."

"She is that," Mitch said nervously. "Wasn't her though. I'm chasing a lead with an FBI agent."

"This FBI lady, now, is she a hottie?"

Mitch smiled. "I would say she is, but we're just working together." Elizabeth arched her eyebrows, and gave him a knowing smile. "Is the Judge around?"

"Yes, he's downstairs. He's been watching for you. He...," Elizabeth stopped and seemed flustered, as she pushed back her hair. "I mean, he must have some new golf clubs, he's been wanting to talk to you." She took Mitch's arm and led him to the stairs. "You should think about settling down. You need a woman in your life. Especially now."

"What? Why now?"

Elizabeth smiled and patted his arm. "Harlan, Johnny's here!" she shouted. "Go on down, I'll get some coffee."

"None for me, I really can't stay long."

"I'll put yours in a travel mug. You can take it with you."

"OK, thank you," Mitch said, starting down the stairs. "Judge, you down here?"

"Johnny, get yourself down here," the judge called, sounding more angry than ever. At the bottom of the stairs was a large room covered in green carpet. Six little flags were placed in holes sunk into the floor. A cluster of Titlist golf balls were around one hole. "Geez, judge, did you get any in the cup?" Mitch kidded.

"Shut up and sit down," the judge muttered, pointing with his putter at a large black leather sofa. "Watch this, smart-ass." The judge lined a putt up at the farthest cup, about thirty feet away. He rapped the ball with an easy stroke. The ball tracked smoothly across the carpet, rimming out of the cup at the last second. "Crap!" The judge tossed the putter in the corner where it clattered off a stack of other clubs. "Damn thing! One hundred and fifty bucks for that damn thing and it doesn't put straight!"

Mitch smiled. Judge Sanderson was the best putter Mitch had ever seen. "Maybe it's the guy holding it."

The judge glared at him, then shook his head. "You don't return calls anymore? I've been trying to get a hold of you all week."

"Sorry, judge. I always like taking your money, but I've just been too busy this week."

"It's not about that. If you'd bother to check your mail, you'd see there's a summons to be in my court Monday at nine am. I damn well expect you to be there."

"Aw shit, judge, can't you post pone it? I'm right in the middle of this case and things are starting to percolate."

"No, normally I'd push it back, but this is too important." The judge pointed the putter at Mitch. "You be in my courtroom. Don't be late."

Mitch frowned. "What is this about? Am I in some kind of trouble? I mean if this is about that emu thing, I sure thought the guy was legit. And it ain't dead. We still might make some money off the deal anyway. Those eggs could still hatch."

"It's not about the birds. Forget about the damn birds."

"What then? Am I in trouble?"

The judge cackled, slapping his thigh. "Oh yeah, but not the kind you are thinking." The judge grabbed a scared old blade putter.

"What is this about?"

"Don't worry, just be there Wednesday at nine," the judge said, sinking a putt.

"You said Monday," Mitch protested.

"Huh? Did I? Well hell be there both days, and wear a damned tie."

"Did you tell him yet?" Elizabeth asked, practically beaming as she came down the stairs with a tray of coffee.

"I told him," the judge said, draining another putt.

"No, you didn't," Mitch protested. "All you said was to be in court Monday at nine. Maybe Wednesday."

"Harlan Sanderson," Elizabeth said, setting the tray down on the coffee table. She glared at her husband, shaking her head. "Alright, I won't spoil your surprise." She picked up two travel mugs. "One for the FBI lady friend."

"You got a date?" the judge asked, looking up from his putt.

"No, chasing a lead. I've got a warrant coming over."

"Warrant? You've got a new suspect?"

"No, not really. We're trying to exclude Roscoe Tannenbaum."

"The man who confessed to the Pyle killing?"

"Yeah, we got him on a surveillance camera across town shortly after the murder."

The judge frowned tapping his putter against the carpet. "You're thinking he is covering for someone?"

"That's the thought. We want to take a look at his cell phone."

"You want to see who he's been talking to?"

"Yeah, and we want to see who he talked to the morning of the murder. Seems like there would have been a call just before or shortly after the shooting."

"Unless it was all set up beforehand."

"Then we've got some work to do."

"Okay, do you need it tonight?"

"If we could. I want to hit Tanner with it tonight. We have his cell phone in lockup. I'd like to have the warrant signed before I look through the phone."

"Okay, I'll sign it tonight. I'll fax a copy to your office; you can pick up the original at court Monday."

"You're not going to tell me about it?"

"Nope, go back to work."

"Okay," Mitch said, taking the two coffees. "Elizabeth, thanks for the coffee."

Mitch left quickly. He thought about going up to his mailbox to see the summons, but then decided he didn't have the time. Instead he slid in the Mustang. He started it, listening to the motor as he watched the oil pressure build. Once the pressure was up, Mitch backed out of the driveway. He called Dispatch asking for two patrol cars to meet him at Pyle's house.

Running through the gears, he headed down Lambert. Touching 60 MPH at times, Mitch cut across to Cortaro Farms and then on to the Interstate. Running a red light, Mitch made a left and roared up the on ramp.

Hitting seventy at the merge lane, he blew past an Eclipse. Pushing the Mustang to eighty, Mitch held the speed for a few miles then dropped back to seventy.

Geena was waiting in front of the motel when Mitch slid in the parking lot. "Sorry I'm late. I had to get a warrant signed."

"What have you got going?"

"Tanner was across town at the time of the murder."

"How credible is the witness?"

"Pretty credible. Time stamped surveillance camera."

"Oh," Geena said, sliding into the car. "What's the warrant for?"

"Tanner's phones. Want to see if Tanner got a call."

"Covering for somebody," Geena agreed. "So, what are we doing?"

"We've got Tanner on video at a Circle K ten minutes after the shooting. I want to drive it to establish there's no way possible to make it in time."

"Then what?"

"We take a look at Tanner's cell phone, then we talk to him."

Geena cocked her head, pursing her lips. "Not much to squeeze him with. He's already confessed to the murder, so what you gonna use to keep him?"

"That depends on what we find in his phone. Might get lucky and find out who he's covering for. If not?" Mitch shrugged pursing his lips. "Maybe we just cut him loose."

Two patrol cars sat at the curb in front of Jackson Pyle's house. Mitch pulled up beside them. "Smitty," he said to a veteran officer. "Sorry to pull you guys away from your doughnuts, but this won't take long."

"Aw shit, don't worry. We always like to help out. What you got going?"

"Gonna make a speed run to the Circle K out on Valencia. We want you guys to block for us."

"Sure, the one on County Club?"

"That's the one. If you guys got a stop watch, you might give us an independent time."

"We can do that. I'll have Jimmy go block the intersection at Kolb."

Smith walked over to the other car and explained to Ray Jimenez, the driver, what they were doing. "Jimmy'll give us a call when they are ready."

"That's good," Mitch said. "Thought you were on days now."

"Yeah, but Chris is playing in a tournament all this week so I switched to nights for a week."

"How's Chris doing?" Mitch asked and Smith's partner Rosa Ibanez groaned. Chris was Smith's son and was going to be a senior in High School. He was a damn good shortstop.

"Oh, damn, Mitch, that's all I been hearing about. I don't mind doing a week of nights, but all this talk about baseball? Yuck," Rosa said, making a face.

Smitty grinned, ignoring his partner. "He had a 0 for the first night, but he bounced right back. He's batting 346 with a homer the next two games. Stole a base yesterday."

"That's good. That's a good tournament for him to shine."

"I'll say. I talked to scouts from U of A, ASU and UCLA. Word is a guy from Stanford will be there tomorrow."

"All good schools."

"They are that." Smith said as his radio beeped. "That's Jimmy."

"Okay, I'll let you get a couple of blocks ahead of me. You can block Valencia then I'll go from there."

"Cool."

As they got in his car, Geena asked "Is Chris his son?"

"Yeah, kid's a helluva baseball player."

"Better than you were?"

Mitch started the car, thinking it over. "I think he is. Kid's got some pop."

"What's an '0 for?" Geena asked.

Mitch dumped the clutch, squealing the tires as he took off. "An '0 for', even though it's pronounced 'oh for', it's really a 'zero'. It means he didn't get a hit." Mitch explained, grabbing second gear. "Like he went 0 for 3."

"Oh," Geena said pushing back against the dash, as the car roared down Escalante. The flashing red lights of the two cars reflected weirdly off the buildings and trees.

"God, I love this shit." Mitch said watching Smith take the corner onto Kolb. He could see Jimenez and his partner holding traffic. Just short of the corner he slapped the brakes hard, dropping the gear shift into second. As he went into the curve, Mitch let off the brake and the clutch. At the apex of the curve he leaned slowly into the accelerator.

The car seemed to leap forward. At forty he slammed it into third and pinned the accelerator. He was doing seventy and just going into fourth when he saw Smith's brake lights come on. "Hang on."

They took the turn onto Valencia, and Mitch slapped the shifter into second and floored it. The rear wheels spun, skidding the car sideways. Mitch laughed as Geena let out a little scream. Running through the gears, they were doing almost a hundred when they flew up the overpass, crossing over the railroad tracks. Coming up on the Interstate, Mitch let off the gas, liking the sound of the pipes rattling.

He let a car come off the ramp then went through the red light. He cut left passing the car in the turning lane. He hit the light green at Alvernon, the Mustang bouncing as they flew through the intersection.

The light caught him at Palo Verde. He had to stop and let a couple of cars clear. From there he roared the last few minutes to Country Club. He waited for a truck to go then shot across to the Circle K.

"What's the time?" he asked, sliding into a parking spot.

"Twelve minutes and eight seconds."

"No way Tanner could have made it any quicker."

"Not unless he was flying," Geena said dryly. She sighed, finally letting go of the dash. "Jesus, for an old heap, this thing can move."

"I told you it would knock your panty shields loose. You might want to go check them?"

Geena laughed, "I just might." She leaned in a little, her face flushed. "That was fun."

Mitch felt the tingle of something about to happen. The moment was broken by Smith pulling in beside them. "We got you at twelve and a half."

Mitch held Geena's gaze for a second. "Bullshit," he said turning to Smith. "Twelve – eight."

"Naw, I had to penalize you for that sloppy turn."

"Sloppy my ass," Mitch snapped, then smiled. "You guys want some coffee, maybe a doughnut?"

Rosa looked ready to agree but Smith shook his head. "Naw, thanks, Mitch. We just got a call, gotta run."

"Okay, thanks guys."

"Some of them doughnuts at role call would be nice."

"Count on it," Mitch said. "You want something?" he asked Geena as Smitty backed away.

"No, I'm fine," she said, picking up the cup from the cup holder.

"Let's go talk to Tanner," Mitch backed out then picked up his cell phone. "Jerry, Mitch," he said. "You done with the warrants?"

"All done, I even called to make sure they were signed."

"Good, get Tanner's phone out of lockup and see who he talked to Wednesday morning."

Mitch tossed the phone in the console. "Any thoughts on how we approach Tanner?"

"If he's covering for someone, we can use that."

Mitch had just asked out of courtesy. He knew Geena probably had little experience interviewing suspects, but she'd answered with some confidence. "What are you thinking?" he asked.

"I haven't had time to do much of a work up on him, but he does run to a type. He's protecting someone. That says he feels like that person needs protection. He thinks they are vulnerable. I'm not sure why, but if we can figure that out, we can squeeze him through that person."

"He's protecting someone for a reason. He's going to keep quiet."

"Possibly, but he might try to explain things."

"Okay, I see what you're saying; it's another way to bring pressure to bear. Get him started talking."

"You're right, he'll say more than he intends."

"Tonight, let's not give anything away."

They pulled in front of the gate then Mitch called Jerry. "What did you get off the phone?"

"He had two calls, both from Kathy. One approximately thirty minutes before and one just after."

"How long were the calls?"

"Short, first was two minutes and seventeen seconds the second was a minute forty-three."

"Delivering a message."

"Or just saying good morning," Jerry countered.

"Twice? That's a lot."

"Maybe, they're in love?" Jerry kidded, then turned. "There was a text. Came in twenty minutes after the shooting."

"A text? What did it say? Who was it from?"

"What it said was, 'It's done', who it was from, I don't know, the number was blocked."

"Could be the call on Pyle, or could be some paint job on a Harley is finished."

"Yeah, that's it."

"Any chance to find out who sent the text?"

"Sure, the company can give it to us in the morning. Bet you money it's gonna be a pre-paid."

"Yeah, shit." Mitch said. "Anything else?"

"Naw, I'm looking back through his calls and his phone book, I didn't see any surprises."

"Okay, you can knock off or if they need some help you can help Ollie and Parks."

"I'll help them, if it's all the same. I can use some overtime. The wife wants to take a trip 'back east'."

"Good, double check the phone. I still want to jack Tanner, but we're going in blind."

Mitch hung up, then glanced at Geena. "Nothing much from the phone."

"Yeah, I kinda got that. But you still want to go ahead and interview Tanner."

"I do, but I'm not sure it's the right thing to do. I want to look in his eyes, but I don't know if it's the right thing or just that I can't think of any other move to make."

"Why do you feel like you must make a move? We're picking up evidence, soon we'll have enough."

"Yeah, the thing is, I don't how much more evidence there is. We need to get something moving. If we rattle Tanner, I don't think he will give anything, he's too experienced for that. The thing is he'll have to contact the killer somehow, we can bet on that."

"Unless he goes through an intermediary."

"If we're on top of it, we can see through it."

"Do you think you can rattle him? He doesn't seem the type to panic. From what I can gather, Tanner's not a sociopath, but he's a tough man. Probably no stranger to jail."

"That's Tanner alright, but the thing is, he'll have to contact the killer to warn him."

"So, we go in and we talk, but we don't say anything."

"That's right, we play like we don't know anything."

They walked into the jail. An oversized jailor, who looked like a body builder slowly going to fat, met them. "Hey Mitch, your boy is waiting."

"Hey, Bill, how's he standing up?"

"Tanner? Shit, he's treating this likes it's a vacation."

"Yeah, I figured. Be too much to hope for that this place was softening him up."

"Naw, it's like old home week. Jersey Joe and Horsey are in; they got drunk and busted up that bar on Pantano."

"Heck and Winks? That place burned down years ago."

"Naw, that place up off Speedway."

They went back, stopping to check their guns with a deputy. They found Tanner sitting at the interview table, his feet up and his chair tipped back. "Enjoying yourself?" Mitch asked.

"Can't complain, food's not too bad."

"Good to hear," Mitch said, pulling a chair back and sitting across from Tanner's feet. "Okay, Tanner, let's cut the shit. You didn't kill Pyle."

Tanner shot them a rogue's grin. "Sure, I did. Shot that motherfucker right on his front porch. Felt pretty good too."

"How many times?"

"Fuck if I can remember," Tanner replied, grinning broadly. "I was flat out banging away. Probably all that was in the gun."

"Bullshit, Tanner, that GSR doesn't lie. You hadn't shot a gun recently."

"I was wearing gloves," Tanner replied smugly.

Mitch was already shaking his head. "Doesn't work that way, Tanner. There woulda still been traces on your arms and clothes."

Tanner yawned mightily. "Maybe your boy fucked up the test."

Mitch glanced at Tanner's boots and decided to run a bluff. "We found some tracks. Wanna bet they don't match up to those boots."

Tanner jerked the feet off the table, sitting up straight. He scowled at Mitch, knowing he messed up. "Bet whatever," he growled.

Mitch laughed. "That's why you pulled them boots outta sight so fast.

Tanner laughed back. "Hell man, my back's hurting." He shook his head and slapped the table. "Damn, Mitch we're getting older. This tough guy bullshit is getting hard to keep up."

"You're right, Tanner we're getting older. How long we known each other?"

"A few years," Tanner agreed, cocking his head as he thought about it. "Damn, getting up on fifteen years. I still remember when I first met your sorry ass."

"That big party out by Picture Rocks."

"Suzie Dafranis," they both said at the same time.

Tanner looked up at the ceiling. "I saw her a couple months ago. Her husband is some kind of broker. He came in to buy a bike. Bought a Vulcan."

"Let me guess, she weighs about three hundred pounds now."

"No way, she still looks like she could do a spread for Penthouse."

"Aw crap, you're killing me," Mitch groaned.

"You ever get with that?"

"No, you?"

Tanner shook his head and laughed. "While we were punching each other, that guy she married moved in."

Mitch glanced at Geena. "Me and Tanner met at some kegger; we were both going after the same girl."

"Suzy Defranis," Geena said somewhat amused.

"She was something."

Mitch hitched his chair a little closer, leaning across the table. "Look Tanner, we go way back. You know me. I won't fuck you. You're covering for somebody. Tell me who it is."

"You're dreaming, Mitch. I killed that mother fucker. I tell you what, I ain't lost a minute's sleep about it either. That prick deserved what he got."

"No doubt about that. That's why you should tell me who really did it."

"I did it man. How many times I gotta say it? I already signed the confession."

"Why?" Mitch demanded.

"Cause, I killed him."

"No, why did you kill him?"

"He cut up a friend of mine."

"Who?"

"A girl Jersey Joe was running, named Gracie."

"Oh yeah," Mitch said, not believing a word of the story. "What was her full name?"

"How the hell should I know?" Tanner shot back. "She came in the bar looking for work. She had a nice rack and could carry a tray of drinks without falling on her ass. What else did we need to know?"

Joe and Horsey owned a building where they ran an unlicensed bar. The Deacons called it a clubhouse to get around the liquor laws, but it was a bar. The kind of place where you could get twenty types of beer, a good stiff drink in a fairly clean glass, a good game of pool and your ass kicked all in the same night. You could place a bet on everything from the NFL, to a skeet shooting match down at Patagonia. And if you asked just right you could get a woman for an hour.

"She wanted a job and you didn't get her full name?" Mitch said, letting his doubt show through his tone.

Tanner grinned and looked at Geena like he was daring her to take offense. "Wasn't that kind of job? Like I said, she had a cute ass and nice tits; that was all we cared about."

"So, if I were to pull Jersey Joe in here, he'd verify all that?"

Tanner shot them a big lop-sided grin. "Sure, he's upstairs, bring him down."

"You say she was your friend and you don't know her last name?" Mitch demanded, letting a little attitude creep in his voice as he leaned a little closer. "I find that hard to believe."

"If I ever knew her last name, I forgot it."

"Forgot?" Mitch sneered. "Really? And she was a good friend?"

Tanner snorted. "Shit man, I heard you dated that gal who worked for the school down in Corona De for over two months and never did remember her last name."

"Shit I'm a cop," Mitch protested, smiling a little in spite of himself. Damn it, he always liked Tanner. "Only took me two days to remember her name."

"Shit what did you do run her fingerprints?"

"No," Mitch denied. "Ran her plates," he admitted, with a laugh.

"And you want to give me shit about not knowing Gracie's last name," Tanner said shaking his head.

Mitch shook his head. "You're pretty smug. But the GSR doesn't lie."

Tanner rolled his eyes and made a dismissive gesture with a flick of his wrist. "Whatever."

Geena cleared her throat. "Tanner, you look like a man who enjoys his freedom. Do you want to spend the rest of your life in a cage?" Geena asked. "Maybe you think you can pull a rabbit out of the hat, but it isn't going to happen. That confession you signed is going to bring you down." She hitched her chair closer, leaning in. "The thing is, your confession sours the milk on this entire case. Anybody we try to bring to trial their lawyer is going to put you and your confession up in front of the jury and they'd walk."

"That's right," Mitch said, picking up on her angle. "We know you are trying to protect someone. Just give us what happened and you can be outta here."

Tanner leaned back in his chair, crossing his arms across his chest. "Mitch, forget about it. That mother fucker Pyle is gone and that's all that matters." Deliberately, Tanner hitched his chair around and stared at the back wall.

They were done. They had fired their best bullets and Tanner had taken them all. They were done.

After Tanner was taken away, Mitch leaned back in his chair, blowing out a big sigh. "Well, shit, I blew that."

"I don't know," Geena said, offer a note of encouragement. "We have made some progress."

"Really? I don't see it," Mitch grunted, pushing out of his chair. "What did we accomplish?"

"Well, we have established that Jackson Pyle did meet with the Senator. We know that Tanner didn't kill Pyle. We know he's covering for someone. And we know Tanner's pretty good at making up stories."

"Hell, I already knew that," Mitch said, heading for the door. "Where does that get us?"

Geena frowned as they walked down the hall. "I don't know." She gave Mitch a little nudge. "We also learned that you date women and can't remember their last names."

Mitch grinned at her. "You just said it yourself, Tanner is pretty good at making up bullshit."

Geena snorted, rolling her eyes as they edged up to the counter. "You get anything out of Tanner?" Bill asked, passing their guns over.

"Less than nothing," Mitch grunted, wanting to punch his fist through the wall. Damn it. There was a thread running through all of this, Mitch could almost see it. He was wandering away, when Bill's voice stopped him. "What did you say?"

Bill shrugged. "I just said, I was working the tank the night they brought that Justin Carter feller in."

"Jacob Carter," Geena corrected.

"Oh yeah, I forgot."

"Anything stand out to you?" Mitch asked. "Anything we can use to track the fucker?"

"The whole thing stands out to me." Bill paused, rubbing his chin. "I don't know if there is anything there that will help you, but that cat was different."

"How so?"

"His whole attitude." Bill scratched his chin casting his eyes up at the ceiling. "You know I moved out here from Minnesota?"

"Yeah, I remember that," Mitch said. He didn't, but he wanted to hear what Bill had to say.

"Well, back then I was working at the jail in St Paul. We'd get these cold spells; it would roll in outta Canada." Bill shivered a little at the memory. "We'd get a week or so when the highs would be five above or maybe five below and the lows would be thirty-five to forty below."

"That's gotta suck," Mitch commented, wondering where this was going.

"Oh yeah," Bill agreed, bobbing his head. "Anyway, we'd get these cold snaps and the crime rate would sky rocket. Nothing big, mind you, just petty stuff, shoplifting, public drunkenness, that kinda thing."

"Homeless guys getting busted so they'd have a warm place to wait it out," Mitch said finally catching on.

"Yep," Bill replied bobbing his head some more. "These guys would get thrown in the tank and believe me, they were happy to be there. I got that exact same vibe off Carter." Bill ran a meaty hand along the side of his face. "I remember thinking at the time that Carter looked like a man who was exactly where he wanted to be."

"Huh," Mitch grunted, digesting the information. "We always thought that his getting arrested was part of the message to Brody."

"Seems like a lot to go through, but bet you're right," Bill said, as Geena wandered down the hall towards the vending machines.

"These guys don't seem to miss a trick," Mitch agreed. "Did Carter make any friends here?"

"You mean somebody who might be hiding him?" Bill asked and Mitch nodded. "Not that I seen. The others in the tank left him alone. He was wearing a big; don't fuck with me sign, if you know what I mean."

Mitch nodded absently. He'd seen it. Some people just put off a 'stay back vibe'. Carter could be one of those people.

"I could put together a list of everybody who was in the tank that night, give you some names to check out," Bill offered.

"That would be good," Mitch said, edging down the hall. "If you get time you might write down everything you remember about that night. You never know what might help."

"Sure," Bill agreed, following Mitch down the hall. "You best get that young lady something to eat before she does something stupid and buys one of the offerings from that machine."

"Nothing good in there?"

"Nothing good for you," Bill grunted patting his sizable stomach. "I weighed an even two hundred when they put that damn thing in."

Mitch laughed as they came up to Geena, who was studying the racks of snacks like a college student the night before finals.

"Don't eat anything from there. You'll wind up looking like Bill."

"Oh," Geena said, turning from the machine, her face starting to turn pink.

"And we sure don't want you looking like Bill," Mitch added as Geena's face turned bright red and she shuffled her feet.

"Hey bite me, I could look like you if I owned a blow dryer and a makeup kit," Bill said.

"Shit, in your dreams."

"Yeah, you're right," Bill said, holding the door open. "I'm way too manly to pull off that over the top gay look. Seems to work for you, though."

"See you jerk off," Mitch said laughing as he went out the door.

"Next time asshole," Bill shot back and winked at Geena. "Watch yourself around this prick."

"I have a gun," Geena said, flashing a smile.

Bill nodded approvingly. "Keep it handy, you'll likely need it."

Geena laugh shaking her head as they headed across the parking lot. "I have to hand it to you, Mitchell. You certainly have a way with people."

"I do what I can."

"No, I'm serious. People respond to you, they like you," Geena said, standing back as Mitch opened the car door for her. "Why, is still the mystery."

Mitch crossed behind the car, sliding in the front seat. "How about you Special Agent Dixon? Do you like me?"

Geena laughed, a merry sound which filled up the car. "Not really, but I'm a psychiatrist. I've been trained to spot and see through every kind of bullshit."

"You're too kind," Mitch grunted, starting the car. "You hungry?"

"Starved. You got any good Chinese out here?"

Mitch grinned, slamming the car in gear. "I know just the place."

They drove in silence, both lost in their own thoughts. Geena looked out the window as the city flashed by. "So, where do we go from here?"

"I was thinking we could get some take out and go back to my place."

"Aw jeez Mitchell, that was awful," Geena said, laughing. "I keep hearing that you are this smooth ladies' man, but that was the most unromantic pick up line that I've heard in a long time."

"Hey, I meant we could go back to my place to eat and talk about the case," Mitch protested.

"Sure, you did, Romeo." Geena chuckled, and then turned serious. "Where do we go from here? What is our next move?"

"I was thinking about that." Mitch glanced sideways at her. "There is something that ties all of these things together. We got Tucson sleeze balls and back east sleeze balls. What brings them together?"

"Money," Geena said quickly. "It's usually money."

"I bet your right," Mitch agreed. "Anyway, I was thinking we put all the names we have through the box. Run them through every data base we can think of and see what shakes out."

"Not bad, but how does that help us find Angie Brody?"

"I don't know, but it has to help. Do you know somebody at the Bureau that would run a computer search for us? Somebody that would keep it quiet?"

"There's this guy. He's a friend, but he's made a few advances. I think he would do me a favor, if I asked him just right."

"Would he keep it quiet? Keep it off the books? Maybe bend a few rules if necessary?"

Now, Geena smiled, a coy, little smirk. "If he thought I might sleep with him, I think he would jump off a bridge."

"Well hell, let's hope it doesn't come to that," Mitch said, grabbing his phone and holding it out. "Lay it on thick."

"Do you realize what time it is back there?"

"He's probably watching porno, dreaming of you."

"I'm not quite sure I want to interrupt that," Geena said, but she took the phone and punched in the numbers.

"Oh my, the plot thickens. The lady has his number."

Geena waved frantically, as Mitch heard the phone ring. After a few rings a man answered.

"Todd, its Geena. Look I'm sorry to call so late. Did I wake you?"

"No, I just got in. Are you still out west?"

"Yes. Todd, I know we are friends and it looks like that might become something more and I don't want to endanger that."

"But you're going to."

"Maybe. I'm going to ask you for a favor. If you say no, that's cool. I will understand. But if you could do it, I would be so grateful."

Mitch raised an eyebrow at that. His estimation of her just went up a notch. She'd manipulated this Todd beautifully. He was fairly well backed into a corner, and she's promised him nothing.

"Will it get me in trouble?" Todd asked a hint of wariness in his voice.

"It might. I need you to run a computer search."

"That's no problem." The wariness right out front now.

"But I need you to keep it quiet and off the books."

"Why?"

"When you see the names, you'll know why it's important to keep it under wraps and off the record."

"Don't give the names over the phone. I'm on a cell. Email them to me. Use an encrypted account. What exactly am I looking for?"

"I'll send you a group of names; see if you can link them in any way. I'll give you another name, separate. We need a complete financial work up on him. We've taken a look, and some things don't add up." She looked at Mitch and mouthed, *Brody.*

Mitch nodded, it was a good idea, but he could hear the agent on the other end of the line protest. "We? What do you mean we?"

"I'm working with a local out here, Detective John Mitchell. He's got his people doing the same search, but I know they won't be as good as you. You'll find something they might miss. I really need you on this one."

"I don't like the fact that the locals down there might know what I'm doing. Can they be trusted?"

"I think so. Only Mitchell knows I called you and he doesn't know who you are." Geena paused, lowering her voice a notch. "Todd this is important. There is a young lady out here who will be killed if we can't find her in time. We need this from you. You are the best at unraveling the financial stuff. We need the best."

For a long second only the faint hum of static came over the line. He's going to say no, Mitch thought, but then a long sigh came across the phone. "Okay, I'll head in now and get started."

"Let me know the minute you find anything."

"Send the names. I'll get back to you."

"They will be in your inbox as soon as you get to the office." Geena started to close down the phone, but stopped. "Todd be very careful."

She closed the phone, passing it to Mitch. "I'm gonna be fighting him off for weeks."

"You laid it on pretty thick. The way you said you would be grateful almost aroused me."

"Boy you don't give up," Geena said, smiling. "Where's this food I keep hearing about?"

"Right here," Mitch said, swinging into a parking lot and pulling up in front of a building that looked to Geena like it could fall down any minute. Or more precisely, it looked like a taller building had already collapsed, and the rubble was being used as a restaurant.

"This is the place?" she asked, wrinkling her nose.

"Best in town."

"Best in town, or did you pick this place since they don't appear to have any seating and we will have to go back to your place?"

"Like you said, I'm smooth," Mitch said, showing her his best grin. "What do you want?"

"Beef and broccoli, fried rice and low mien."

"Holy crap, you can eat all that?"

"Hey I'm hungry and the leftovers are good."

"Okay, I'll go get the food, then we can go to my house and you can send your email from there."

Geena started to point out that she could send the email on her phone, but let it go. As Mitch ordered she sent the email to Todd. She was just finishing when Mitch slid into the car handing her a grease soaked bag that smelled delicious. Geena took a long breath, the odors making her mouth water. "How far is it to your house, this smells so good I may not make it."

"Just a few minutes," Mitch promised.

True to his word, Mitch pulled into his driveway a few minutes later. Geena took stock of the place and was surprised. "This is a very nice place, Mitchell. I'm impressed."

"Thanks, I like it," Mitch said, a little embarrassed. Women were always saying that when they first saw his house, and he never knew how to respond.

"You live in this huge house all by yourself?"

"Hey I'm a big boy," Mitch protested, leading her inside.

Inside, Geena was once again impressed. The place was reasonable clean and very tastefully furnished. "Very nice, where's the plates?"

"Uh, over there," Mitch said, pointing to a very nice china cabinet. "You want to eat first or send that email?"

"I already sent it." Geena held up her phone, looking through the frosted doors of the china cabinet. Inside were six mismatched cups, four plates of varying sizes and patterns and several automotive filters. "Filters?" she asked holding one up.

"Seemed like a good place to keep them."

Shaking her head, Geena grabbed two plates.

"You want a beer?" Mitch called his head stuck in the fridge.

"Do you have wine?"

Mitch had pulled back from the fridge and now poked his head back in, looking desperately for a bottle of wine even though he was fairly certain there wasn't one. "Uh, no, sorry. No wine."

"That's okay, a beer will be fine."

Mitch twisted the tops off the beers, flipping the lids in the direction of the trashcan. "Damn, let's eat," he said watching as Geena unloaded the sack.

They talked about the case, kicking ideas back and forth, but coming up with nothing new. They were rinsing the dishes in the sink, standing shoulder to shoulder, when Geena leaned in a little. "I can't get over this house," she said. "There's more to you than meets the eye. I thought you were just a player, but this is a house to raise a family in."

Mitch shrugged feeling a pang of guilt. He didn't have the heart to tell her he just bought this house because he needed a place to live and this house was going dirt cheap. He fully expected to sell it in a few years and make a bundle. "I poured some concrete and put in a basketball court in the back," he blurted out. He'd put in the court because he enjoyed shooting hoops, but when he was finishing the concrete, a picture had come creeping into mind. A hazy vision of him and a boy, shooting hoops in the evening. It had been a warm thought on a cool winter day.

"Thinking of boys?" Geena asked a teasing note in her voice, her hand resting lightly on his chest. "What about a little girl."

"Aw man, I don't know." Mitch ran a hand through his hair. "What if I messed up? I've seen what happens to girls when they don't have a good dad."

Geena patted him lightly. "I have a feeling you would do fine," she said as her phone rang. "Sorry," she said, stepping back, her face flushed as she fumbled for the phone.

"I'll give you a minute," Mitch said, feeling a little flushed himself. "I'm going up to the bathroom. There's one down the hall if you need."

Geena nodded, working her phone.

"Geena, that you?" Todd asked, and Geena was ready to ask him who he expected since he had called her phone, but then she recognized the stress in his voice. Even a little out of breath.

"Yes, it's me. What did you find out?"

"Your guy Mitchell, he's dirty. And he's tied in with that dude Brody!"

Geena frowned, she found that hard to believe. Mitch didn't seem the type, plus he was worried about Angie

Brody, Geena could see it wearing on him. "Are you sure about that?" she asked, checking to see that Mitch was still in the bathroom. "I don't get that vibe off him. He doesn't seem desperate enough."

Geena could almost picture Todd dropping his shoulders and shaking his head, a habit he had when he was forced to explain things, that he felt were perfectly obvious. "Here's what I have. Mitchell bought his home from a Combined Homes LLC. Combined is owned by Flowing Wells Builders which is Brody. Hence Mitchell bought his home from Brody."

"Okay, I see that, but from what I gather, Brody is the biggest builder in this area. Mitchell might not even have known who he was buying the house from."

"Maybe," Todd admitted, grudgingly. "But Mitchell got his house way too cheap. He paid three seventy-five for his house. The next cheapest house in that development sold for four fifty."

"Maybe he bought after the crash?"

"No, he bought six months earlier, right at the height of the bubble."

"Huh," Geena grunted feeling a series of conflicting emotions tear through her.

"Before you ask, I pulled up all the records. They built four different models in that development. Mitchell's is the biggest and he has a pool. Cheapest that model with a pool went was five twenty-five."

Geena remained silent, trying to think, but Todd had more. "I looked at his mortgage. His payment is a little over two thousand. Pretty steep for a one income household."

"Okay," Geena said, a heavy feeling settling down on her. "Is there anything else?"

"I don't know, I'm just getting started. There's a lot of dummy companies to sift through."

"Okay, keep at it, and keep me posted," Geena said as Mitch returned.

"That your guy in DC?"

"Yes, he's just getting going. So far all he has come up with is the stuff we already knew He's trying to track down some of the companies. Tracing the ownerships is going to take some time."

"I figured," Mitch grunted, and began to pace.

As Mitch paced, Geena looked around the house. She ran her finger along the countertop. Granite. She turned checking out the appliances. Stainless steel. French doors on the frig. High end across the board.

"That means something," Mitch decided, scooping up a putter as he paced. "The fact that they've gone to so much trouble to hide the ownership. That says they are up to something."

"Well, we thought that from the beginning," Geena said, studying the dining table Mitch was leaning against. Geena wasn't sure of the brand, but she would think the table would cost at least five thousand.

She glanced into the living room. An Ethan Allen couch and love seat surrounded a crusty recliner. "I'm impressed, Mitchell, this house is very nicely decorated."

Mitch glanced around as if seeing the furnishings for the first time. "Aw, this crap? It came with the house."

Geena couldn't help but laugh. "That's an Ethan Allen. High dollar stuff."

Mitch shrugged, then putted a ball off the claw foot of the couch. "Yeah, well try sitting on the son of a bitch for a whole ball game. By the seventh inning stretch, your back will feel like you've been pouring concrete all day. I've been thinking of hauling it to the dump."

Geena shot him a look. "Are you kidding? This is a nice couch; it goes well with the house. Get rid of that ratty, old recliner and it would be perfect."

"Oh hell, no! That chair is the only comfortable thing I have." Mitch studied her, rubbing his chin. "No shit though, that crap is worth some money?"

"Yes."

"Huh." Mitch grunted wandering the room and looking at the furniture like he was seeing it for the first time. "Maybe I could sell it, make a few bucks. I've been looking at a couple of black leather reclining couches. Might have to think about that."

Geena took a drink of her beer, studying Mitch over the top of the bottle. He seemed sincere. Of course, that could be a cover. He might very well know what the furnishings were worth. "I would keep them. This is such a nice house and the furnishings compliment it perfectly."

"Aw, I don't know," Mitch said, kicking the foot of the couch. He grinned at her, cocking his head slightly towards the stairs. "But if you like the house, I could give you the whole tour."

"Easy, lover boy," Geena said, laughing a little. "Maybe another time. It's getting late. I had better be going."

"Sure," Mitch said with an easy, gracious smile. "I'll drive you."

"It's late; I can just call a cab."

"It's not that late. I don't mind driving you."

"No, get some rest. I can put the cab on my travel expense."

"Are you sure? You sure you want to stick it to the tax payers?"

"As far as we are in debt, what's a few more bucks."

"If you're sure you can live with the guilt."

She smiled, patting his hand. "I'll be fine."

Mitch called for the cab and they sat on his front step looking at the shadow of Pusch Ridge in the moonlight, splitting a beer. "It is beautiful here," Geena said her voice soft as the night. "Even the air tastes good. I can see why you love it here."

"It does grow on you," Mitch said, feeling a pang as the cab rounded the corner.

"That looks like my ride," Geena said, rising gracefully to her feet.

Not quite touching, they walked together down to the curb. Mitch opened the door for her holding it wide as she got in. "See you in the morning."

"Good night."

Mitch walked to the front of the car showing his badge to the driver. "Make sure she gets there safe," he said, slipping the driver a twenty.

Geena leaned back in the seat, thinking about what Todd had said. There was no doubt that Mitch had one hell of a nice place, but the question was, had he done anything wrong to get it. Her instincts said that Mitch couldn't be dirty, but her track record with men wasn't that great. Derek, the last guy she had dated seriously turned out to be a total prick.

Geena looked back and she could see Mitch standing at the curb, watching her drive away. It seemed thoughtful that he watched instead of just going back inside. And the thing with badging the cabbie, that was sweet.

She had watched him. He cared about people. Would a man like that be dirty?

Geena didn't think so. But then again, who ever knew.

Mitch watched as Geena's cab drove away. He sighed, wishing she would have stayed. He'd certainly let her know he wanted her to stay. He thought she wanted to, but at the last minute she pulled away.

Feeling a sense of melancholy descend over him, he trudged up the driveway. Halfway, he stopped, looking back, hoping to see the cab coming back, that she might have changed her mind.

But the street was empty. She was gone.

Damn.

"You strike out lover boy?"

Mitch jumped his hand darting for his gun. "Jesus! Frankie, you almost gave me a heart attack," Mitch shouted as Frankie O'Hara stepped into the light. "What the hell are you doing here?"

"Bringing you these," she said, holding up two boxes of cigars. "And checking to see if you been holding up your end. You got some names for me to call."

"Yeah, I've been handing them out."

"Are you going to invite me in?"

"Sure," Mitch said, taking a last glance down the empty street. "You want a beer?" he asked opening the door for her.

"That would be nice," Frankie said, dropping the cigars on the table. "Nice place."

"Yeah, I guess," Mitch grunted, grabbing two beers from the fridge. Sliding one across the counter to Frankie, he pulled out his phone. "You ready?"

"Yeah," Frankie said, taking a quick hit from her beer, then pulling her own cell. "Lay them on me."

Mitch gave her the names and numbers, sipping his beer while she typed them in her phone.

"Damn, Mitch you did good," she said when they were finished. She walked to the couch, taking a seat, leaning back in the cushions. "So, are all these guys uptight lawyer types?'

"Yeah," Mitch said, trying not to stare at her cleavage, but it was hard. "This won't be like selling a dime bag to some skate boarder. You've got to be low key here. You might want to get some different clothes before you go see these guys."

"You don't like the way I'm dressed?" she asked. Smiling wickedly, she climbed from the couch and did a small turn.

Mitch swallowed hard, and then took a quick jolt from his beer. She was wearing a little, skin tight, black tank top that didn't quite come down to meet a pair of very short, very tight denim shorts. "Hard to argue with that," he croaked, then took another hit from his beer.

Moving like a dancer, she slid up close to him, wrapping her arms around him. She nibbled on his ear, then whispered softly. "Cause if you don't like them, you could probably talk me out of them."

Mitch held her close, feeling her body press against him. For a second he was tempted to sweep her upstairs into his bedroom, but then Geena popped into his mind. "Frankie, I can't."

"What?" Frankie said, and Mitch could see the fire blazing in her eyes.

"Frankie, we're partners, now. That's never good to mix business with pleasure."

"Fuck you!" she snapped the fire in her eyes was an inferno now. "I see how it is. You son of a bitch! I don't have fancy clothes like miss prissy tits who just left so I'm not good enough for you!"

Mitch stepped back shocked at the ferocity of her words and even more shocked by the tears welling in her eyes. "Aw shit, Frankie, I'm sorry," he said reaching out to her.

She slapped away his hand with one arm and savagely wiped at the tears with the other. "Get away from me."

"Frankie, don't. Let me explain."

"Fuck you, Mitch! I get it. I don't have the right clothes. I'm just some lowly bar chick not good enough for you." She stormed to the door, throwing it open. "I'm not what you think. I haven't slept with a man in a long time. Almost two years. I thought you…, aw fuck you!"

She ran down the driveway, jerking the door shut behind her hard enough to shake the whole house.

For a second, Mitch stood frozen in shock, and then he sprang after her. "Frankie wait," he called, but she was already climbing on her bike. With a last hateful look back, she fired up the bike and roared away.

Feeling like a total ass, Mitch sank down sitting on his porch. "Shit," he muttered softly, feeling like a total ass. Frankie O'Hara. Damn.

He sat on the step, listening to the roar of her bike. He sat there for several minutes after the roar faded into the dark.

Geena's Hotel Room Tucson AZ June 17th 2018
Sunday Early Morning

Geena woke slowly, consciousness drifting up on her. For a second, she imagined that she was back in her own bed. She pulled the covers up and felt the roughness of the cheap motel comforter, and knew she wasn't home. She opened her eyes, squinting against the sliver of light which streamed in through the crack in the curtains.

It was late, she knew that, but what time she wasn't sure. Leaning over, she picked her purse off the floor.

A part of her wished she would have stayed with Mitch last night. He'd made it clear that he wanted her to. Her purse resting on her stomach, she closed her eyes. He was an exciting man. Very handsome, almost to the point of being pretty, but he had a strong masculine side. Underneath that easy-going exterior was a streak of roughness.

Geena sighed; the moment had come and gone. It was better this way. Falling in bed with a man she just met wasn't her style. Besides she had to work with Mitch. Pulling her purse to her chin, Geena was digging for her cell, when it rang. Mitch, she thought pulling it out. No number showed on the screen, just a note that the call was blocked. Hmm, she thought, sliding the phone app open.

"Geena! Geena, are you there? Are you there?"

"Todd, slow down. I'm here."

"Geena, you can't trust that guy Mitchell. Get away from him. He can't be trusted," Todd said, almost to the point of babbling.

"Todd, what are you talking about? Slow down and take a breath. Why can't I trust Mitchell?"

"I found out he's getting regular payoffs. Once a month from two sources. One of them is a property management company. That has to be Brody."

"What? What are you talking about?"

She could hear Todd actually take a deep breath. "Not over the phone," he said in a much calmer tone. "I'm at the airport right now. I will be out there in few hours. I'll check into the Holiday Inn closest to the airport. I'll call you and give you the room number. Meet me there."

"Okay, I will meet you there. Todd, what is this all about?"

"Somebody broke into my apartment this morning."

"What? What happened?"

"I finished the search like you asked, and you won't believe what I found out. I was waiting to call you but I couldn't sleep, so I went out for a paper and some coffee. When I got back there were two men searching my apartment. When they saw me, one of them came after me."

"Oh, my God, Todd are you okay?"

"Yes, I think so. I lost him in the park."

"What were they looking for?"

"I don't know, but I think they were looking for anything I had from my search last night. One of them was going through my desktop."

"Who did you tell what you were doing?"

"No one," Toddy said firmly. "The only people who knew what I was doing, was you and I and of course that guy Mitchell. You can't trust him. He's involved."

"What are you talking about? He's the lead investigator on the case. What do you mean he's involved?"

"I mean he's dirty and he's tied into this. I'll show you what I have when I get there. As soon as I get checked in I will text you the room number."

"Okay," Geena replied somewhat reluctantly. "I will be there."

"And Geena, stay away from Mitchell. He's dirty and he's dangerous."

CHAPTER EIGHT

Mitch's House Tucson AZ June 17th 2018 Sunday Early Morning

Mitch was dead asleep when the phone woke him. The phone rang four times before it even began to penetrate his alcohol induced stupor. Last night, after Frankie stormed out, Mitch feeling like a total piece of shit had hit the Jack Daniels. Hit it hard. And now Jack was hitting back. And damn, Jack did pack a punch.

The fifth ring was like a jack hammer drilling into his brain. The sixth produced a groan. After the seventh, he grabbed wildly for the phone, knocking it to the floor. On the eighth he managed to pick it up. It took two more rings for Mitch's eyes to focus enough to allow him to operate the slider and answer the phone.

"Damn it Ollie, this shit is getting old," he snarled.

Ollie chuckled, a long, dry, rolling sound. "I bet. I heard you and the FBI lady were out pretty late last night."

"Yeah? Fuck you. Who told you that?"

Ollie chuckled again, obviously enjoying himself. "I got my sources. Tell her good morning for me."

"Blow me, you old fart. She ain't here. Besides, there is nothing going on between us, we were working last night."

Ollie snorted. "You might have been working. Working on getting her into bed. But I am glad to hear that she has enough class not to fall for any of your tired old lines."

"Is there a reason you are waking me for like the tenth morning in a row, or do you have a burning desire to be back on foot patrol?"

"Shit, you're getting to be a grouchy cuss. You gotta learn to embrace each new day, like I do. Realize every new day is a gift, a fresh chance to better serve the residents of this fine community."

"Kiss my ass!"

"You might want to kiss my ass when you hear what I got for you."

Something in Ollie's tone sliced through the haze in Mitch's brain and his hangover vanished like fog in a high wind. "Angie Brody? You found her?" he croaked hopefully.

"No, not her," Ollie said, regretfully. "But maybe Carter."

"Carter?"

"Yeah, maybe. I just got a call from Monte. Last night, patrol picked up a guy fitting Carter's description during a failed home invasion. He had duct tape, a rope, a knife and condoms with him."

"No shit? They print him yet?"

"Naw, he's at St Joe's getting patched up right now."

Mitch sat up in bed, rubbing the side of his face. "St Joe's? Was he shot?"

"Dunno. That's all I got. They are patching him up, be about an hour, then we can talk to him. I was gonna hit the shower, then head over there."

"I'll meet you there."

Rolling out of bed, Mitch stumbled into the bathroom. He swallowed four ibuprofens dry, and then staggered down to the kitchen. He drained a Coke in two long drinks and started to feel more human.

Grabbing another Coke and his cell, he headed back upstairs. On the way he noticed the boxes of cigars resting on the counter and stopped dead in his tracks. He frowned at the cigars. Damn.

Frankie.

Mitch glanced at the cell in his hand. He should call her. Of course, she wouldn't be up yet. He should wait. Call her this afternoon. That's what he would do. Call her later.

Knowing he was putting it off, he punched in Geena's number. "Mitch?" she said, and she sounded weird to him.

Probably still half asleep he decided. No way she could've known about the fiasco with Frankie. "Ugh, yeah, look we may have a line on Carter."

"Carter," she barked, and Mitch could hear the excitement charging through her. "What exactly do you have?"

"We may have him," Mitch said, feeling his own excitement drill through his hangover. He quickly repeated what Ollie had told him.

"That certainly sounds like Carter," Geena replied slowly, her doubt near the surface. "All except for the part of him getting caught, that doesn't seem right. I would like to go see him to be sure."

"I'm heading over there; I'll pick you up in half an hour."

Fifty minutes later, Mitch roared into the parking lot of St Joe's hospital. He heard Geena squeal as they slid to a stop at the front door. He heard a roar, and saw Ollie round the corner, the suspension on his old truck sagging sideways. Ollie screeched to a halt behind them.

Ollie raised an eyebrow as Geena slid out of the Mustang. "Well, well. Ain't this cozy?" he asked with a sly grin.

"You hear anything?" Mitch asked, ignoring the leering from the older man.

"I just heard that it was a home invasion, attempted rape and the description sorta fits Carter."

"Shit. Could we get that lucky?" Mitch wondered.

Ollie shrugged, "Who deserves it more?"

Ollie was joking but Geena answered seriously. "Maybe," she said. "If Carter is holding Angie Brody, but can't touch her, that might put him under pressure. Pressure like you or I couldn't even begin to imagine. He might have had to go seek out another victim. He is usually very careful, but maybe this time, he acted out on impulse. Unable to control himself."

"Let's find out," Mitch said. He was hopeful, but the more he thought about it, the more he was finding it hard to get too excited. Getting taking down by some Joe Schmoe homeowner wasn't in the picture he was building of Jacob Carter.

Jerry met them at the front door of the hospital, a wide grin splitting his face. The look of joy on his face sent a jolt of pleasure surging through Mitch. Maybe they had caught Carter. Still smiling, Jerry shook his head. "Cool your jets, it wasn't him. Wasn't Carter."

"Fuck," Ollie said softly.

"What happened? Who did they get?"

Jerry was openly grinning now, almost laughing. "Well, we go one Elliot Campbell, serial killer wanna be."

"Want to be?"

"Yeah, seems like he'd been studying up on how to be a serial killer. They found books and shit at his apartment."

"Books? What kind of books?" Mitch asked.

"Books on famous serial killers, on locks, knives, that kind of thing. Some medical type books. Kinda like a serial killer starter kit was what they said."

Mitch glanced over at Geena. "Is that the way they start?"

"It can be. They start by reading and fantasizing. For some that is enough. But then there is always those who decide to take the next step."

"How does that happen?" Ollie asked.

"Different ways. Sometimes it's something traumatic that happens in their life. We call that a stressor. Sometimes it's a particular victim. They see someone and can't get them out of their mind, then they act."

Jerry was openly laughing now. "Well that's what happened here. Our boy Elliot, he reads some books all about this shit. Then he spots a little honey with big tits and bang he's in love." Jerry laughed outright, slapping his leg. "Elliot, now he takes some pictures of our girl, follows her some getting his balls up, then he moves in."

Jerry was turning red from holding back his laughter. "You will never guess who he got a crush on?" Snickering, he glanced around the tiny group and got only scowls in return. "Rachael Cooper!"

"You gotta be shitting me? Rachael Cooper?" Mitch asked, laughing a little himself.

"Oh, I shit you not," Jerry said, managing a solemn look before laughing again. "Now you know why he's in the hospital."

"What?" Geena asked a note of frustration in her voice. "Who is this Rachael Cooper? What is she like the ugliest woman ever?"

"Oh hell no!" Ollie said. "That woman could give a woody to rag doll."

"So, what am I missing?"

"She's married to Randy Cooper and Randy is a very bad man," Jerry supplied, still chortling.

"Bad like criminal?"

"No," Mitch said, shaking his head. "Bad like, don't fuck with him."

"Yeah if you made a list of the top ten people in town not to fuck with, Randy would be the top two or three all by himself," Ollie supplied.

"What is he huge?"

"Naw, he's kinda small, five eight something like that, maybe one sixty. He started boxing golden gloves when he was like seven. Won a bunch of tournaments. In high school he wrestled. Was state champion two or three times. Then he got into Karate, Taekwondo or something like that. Now he does that ultimate fighting in his spare time. I hear he's gonna get a shot at the title in his weight class." Mitch looked at Jerry. "So, what exactly happened?"

"Well our boy Elliot, he bumps into Rachael, and gets his dick up. Looks like from pictures he took of her he had followed her around for a few days. Then last night he gets his nerve up and breaks in to her house. He cracks Randy with this tee ball bat. Course he's a pussy and doesn't hit hard enough to take Randy out. Just pisses him off."

"Oh shit," Ollie grunted.

"Yeah, oh shit." Jerry agreed. "Randy came off that bed and opened up a twelve pack of whup ass on that boy. When the units got there, Elliot was under the bed, hanging on for dear life, and Randy was trying to pull him out."

"How bad is he hurt?" Mitch asked.

Jerry shrugged as if the question was totally irrelevant. "Not seriously, he'll be sore for a good while, but he'll live."

"So, nothing for us then?"

"I don't see how," Jerry replied. "Unless Agent Dixon wants to talk to him."

"Actually, I would," Geena said. "It will be interesting to talk to a serial killer so early in his development."

"He's not really a killer yet," Ollie said, scratching his chin.

"Of course," Geena replied shortly.

"No, no, I didn't mean to offend. What I was wondering, will he become one? I mean he'll get a few years for this, but when he gets out will he start killing? He may be a pussy now, but give him a few years in the joint and that might be a different story."

"I don't know," Geena said, feeling a little sorry for snapping at Ollie. "That's why I would like to talk to him. He may have got a small taste of it and it's a part of him now."

"Or maybe that ass whupping might have knocked some sense into him?" Ollie asked.

"That's what I would like to figure out."

Ollie put his arm around Geena's shoulders and gave her an awkward hug. "You got a tough job, missy. I didn't mean nothing by what I said. I'm sorry."

Geena smiled up at him, sliding her arm around him and returning the hug. "Thanks."

His face red, Ollie glanced around the group. "Well, shit, this was a big bust." He grinned at Mitch. "Sorry I got you out of bed, boss."

"Yeah," Mitch grunted. "What have you got going?"

"I'm gonna try and run down that Cal. I can't find him and I want to have a chat with him. Something weird about that dude."

Mitch nodded. "You find him, haul his ass in."

"That's what I figured," he said, ambling towards his truck.

"Take Parker with you," Mitch shouted and Ollie waved back "What have you got?" Mitch said looking at Jerry.

"If it's alright I was going to head back home. Carey has some stuff she needs to do; she wants me to watch the kids. I was thinking I could come in this afternoon, work late."

Mitch nodded. "Sounds good." As Jerry walked away Mitch turned to Geena. "You want to talk to this guy?"

"I do. Do you want to come up?"

"Naw, I was thinking I might go back home, take a shower, then run over to Tanner's. The warrant is still good, and it was late when they finished up. I was thinking I might do a walk through. I can come back and pick you up."

"You know a shower does sound good," Geena said, thinking quickly. She wanted to get some time to herself to call Todd. "I can call Hertz and have a car delivered here. I need to get one anyway. Then I can grab a shower and meet you back at your office later today."

"Sure, sounds good," Mitch said, sensing she wanted to get away from him for a while but not sure why. "We'll hook back up later. Make them give you a car with GPS."

"I will," she promised, laughing, but liking the feeling that he was concerned. As he walked to his car, she felt a flash of guilt, being deceptive in getting rid of him. Oh well, it had to be done. She waved as he drove away, and then walking to the hospital, dug out her phone. She called Todd's number and it went straight to voice mail. "Huh," she said, drawing a strange look from a nurse coming out of the building. Could Todd already be on the plane? Geena glanced at her watch, just after nine. He shouldn't be on the plane yet. Concerned, she slid the phone back into her purse.

Still feeling a twinge of betrayal, she glanced back over her shoulder, as Mitch roared out of the hospital parking lot.

Mitch left the hospital, heading home. Maybe a quick shower and something to eat, then go over to Tanner's.

Mitch wasn't sure what he expected to find, but he couldn't think of anything else to do. Maybe Geena's guy in DC would come up with something for them to chase.

Once home, he fell into his bed, sleeping until ten-thirty. When he woke this time, his hangover was at a manageable level, and after a hot shower, he felt almost human. Grabbing another Coke, he headed out the door.

Tanner had a place south of Mitch's just off Flowing Wells Street. It was a quiet older neighborhood, slowly sliding down. Mitch was surprised when he pulled up to Tanner's house. It was a neat little bungalow with new looking siding. A for sale sign in the front yard.

Mitch signed his initials on the door seal, before cutting it and letting himself in. The place was neat and smelled pleasantly of tobacco, and good food, with maybe a hint of motor oil. Mitch quickly cruised the house, not sure what he was looking for.

He found several things which surprised him. First was the kitchen. Tanner had quite the collection of pots and pans, as well as various appliances. Some Mitch wasn't sure what they did. Mitch glanced at the stove and shook his head. What he knew about cook stoves could be listed on a sticky note, with room to spare, but just looking at the monster in Tanner's kitchen, Mitch knew it was one serious stove. Tanner a cook? Mitch never would have guessed.

Nothing else really stood out. Fact was, the place looked downright homey. Mitch could see the woman's touch here and there. The curtains in the kitchen, the towels hanging in the bathroom. It made Mitch sad, when he realized it had likely been Kathy who picked them out.

The place had the requisite big screen TV, and giant stereo. The furnishings while old looked well cared for. The basement was unfinished, but a bench had been built along the far wall. A very nice reloading kit was set up on the bench. A gun case stood open, its contents removed. Mitch looked at the various tools and vices on the bench and realized that Tanner was obviously an amateur gunsmith.

Mitch realized his characterization of Tanner had been all wrong. Mitch had always seen Tanner as a big man, who got by on brute strength. Mitch had always known Tanner was smart, but never guessed he was a craftsman.

Taking his time, Mitch went back through the place but it soon became apparent that if Tanner had anything to hide, he didn't keep it here.

Which made sense. This was one of the first places anyone would look. Funny how that thought never seemed to occur to most people. Mitch pursed his lips, if a guy especially a guy like Tanner was going to hide something at his house, he'd likely keep it in the garage.

Mitch opened the door to the garage and stopped short. On the far side of the garage was a 1963 Corvette Stingray with the split rear window. Mitch stared at the car, feeling a little wave of jealousy. The '63 split window was every collector's dream. Mitch walked around the car looking at it from all angles. The car was in rough shape, it reminded Mitch of a pair of panty hose being worn for a second day. But still it was a 63 'vette.

Unable to resist, Mitch opened the hood for a glance at the motor, but it was gone. Glancing around Mitch saw a tarp draped over something by the bench. Crossing the garage, Mitch pulled back the tarp and saw the block. It was just an empty block, the moving parts gone, but the motor had been cleaned to the point that it almost shined. One corner of the bench under an old beach towel stood the pistons. Like the block they had been scrubbed within an inch of their lives. The crank was there but no heads. Probably sent off to get the valves done Mitch figured, carefully replacing the towel.

Turning to leave, Mitch ran his hand over the scuffed fiberglass fender, maybe he should let Tanner go to jail for the rest of his life and then buy the car from him cheap.

Grinning at that thought, Mitch shut off the lights, retracing his steps through the house. He hadn't found anything, but that had always been a long shot. But because of the car, Mitch didn't feel the trip was wasted.

Mitch was still thinking of the 'vette, as he walked in to the station. Tanner was just getting started and had a lot of work ahead of him, but damn, looked like a lot of fun. Rebuilding the motor was some of the best work.

Mitch was jolted out of his thoughts by a loud voice calling him. "Hey, Mitch holdup a minute."

Mitch stopped, turning to see Pete McElroy and young Neal. "Nice job on finding confirmation of Inez Perry's story." Mitch stopped, sensing they had something for him. "You guys pick up something else?" he asked waiting on the two patrolmen.

"Oh yeah," Neal said, excitement radiating off him like heat waves rising off an asphalt parking lot.

"Maybe," Pete said, shooting a look at his young partner. "We found out that Pyle was at a bar that night."

"Huh," Mitch grunted, deciding what that meant. "Are you sure?"

"Pretty sure, bartender and two waitresses picked him out of the photo lineup. He was there until closing."

"Okay," Mitch said, stilling thinking. "He alone?"

"Yep," McElroy said. "Came in alone and left alone."

"They know him there?"

Pete shook his head. "No, they picked him outta the six-pack easy enough, but they all agreed, he wasn't a regular."

Neal nodded eagerly. "They remembered him because he asked for a booth, said he was meeting someone, but nobody ever showed."

Mitch frowned. "And he left alone?"

"That's what they all said."

"Shit," Mitch said, thinking about the time frames and trying to make it work out in his head. "What bar was it?"

"That little hole in the wall place up off Twenty-second and Kolb," McElroy answered.

"Shit that's a ways from his house. How did you stumble on that?"

"It was Pete," Neal answered, elbowing his partner. "He said you can tell a lot about a person by looking in their local bar, talking to the people he drinks with. So, we kept looking for Pyle's bar?"

"And this was it?"

Neal glanced at his partner, who nodded. Neal stepped eagerly forward. "No, we don't think so. The people in the bar said, that Pyle hadn't ever been in before that night. We looked around some more, but never did find his bar. We," Neal said, waving his hand between himself and his partner, but Mitch knew, this was mostly Pete's thinking. "We think that he mostly did his drinking at home alone."

"That sound like Pyle," Mitch admitted, then asked. "Where the fuck did he pick up the girl?"

"Maybe she met him at his house? He said he was meeting someone at the bar, maybe she was running late?" Neal suggested.

"No car at Pyle's place. She didn't drive there," Mitch reminded.

"Oh yeah," Neal said, dejected.

"He left the bar at closing, that doesn't give him a lot of time to pick up the girl get her to his house and kill her," Pete observed. "What was it around five when he bought it? That's seems short to me."

"Might be a problem," Mitch said, his mind buzzing as he wandered away. "Good job guys, write up a report on it. Give it to Wade to put in the book."

He was still thinking about it as he entered the squad room. The bar closed at two and three hours later Pyle is killed. In that short amount of time Pyle somehow located Tamera Schroeder, got her to his house and killed her. Pete was right. Didn't seem like enough time.

Maybe Braxton was paying Pyle off and Schroeder was delivering the payment? Maybe but where was her car? She didn't fly to his house. Pyle had told the bartender that he was expecting to meet somebody, could that have been Schroeder? Maybe, they met outside in the parking lot and she left the car at the bar?

If she was just delivering a payoff, why go with him to his house? Maybe he forced her? How would he do that? Pull a gun? Physically over power her? Risky, in the parking lot at the bar's closing. People leaving the bar, heading home. They needed to check out the bar, get statements and see if her car was abandoned in the lot. Check with the cab companies. She could have taken a cab to the bar. But from where?

It was all running through Mitch's brain, when he noticed Wade Nichols on the phone at his desk, waving frantically. "You are positive about that? No chance you are wrong?"

Wade listened intently, then hung up, grinning up at Mitch.

"What was that all about?" Mitch asked.

"The nipples in Pyle's freezer, we found out where they came from."

Mitch frowned. "What do you mean? Where they came from?"

"Hollywood would be my guess," Wade said, smiling broadly.

"Hookers?"

Wade grinned. "Naw, man, the movies. They're fakes."

"Shit. Fakes?" Mitch said, taking a seat. "What the fuck? Fake titties?"

"Nipples anyway," Wade said, unable to keep the grin off his face.

"Are you sure about this?" Mitch asked, even though he had no doubts. Wade and Mickey wouldn't make that kind of mistake. He was just talking while he thought.

"Oh yeah, they were fakes alright. Thawed and out of that freezer bag, they didn't even look all that real."

"What were they made of?"

"Dunno, some kind of cellulous," Wade said. "So where does that lead us? Was Pyle a killer?"

"I guess not," Mitch answered, his words coming out slowly, but his mind whirling like a washer on spin cycle. "I don't think he killed Tamera Schroeder either."

Wade leaned back in his chair, looking cynically up at Mitch. "Oh yeah, what do you know?"

"We have witnesses that put Pyle in a bar several blocks away. He was there until closing."

"Is it solid? He was there?"

"We need to check it out, but I think so."

Wade leaned back in his chair, rubbing his chin. "Not a lot of time to find that girl, get her loaded up and kill her," he said, then sat up straight, slapping his desk. "Aw shit!"

"What?"

"Hang on," Wade said, pawing at the papers on his desk. Finally, he found what he looking for, scanning the page intently.

"What have you got?"

"This," Wade said, shaking the paper in front of Mitch. "Print out of Pyle's Visa charges. Shit how did I miss this? I knew there was something off with it." He said handing the paper to Mitch.

"What am I looking for?"

"The last item. He made a purchase at the Wal-Mart on Speedway at three forty-six that morning."

"Oh man," Mitch said. "So, he left the bar and went to Wal-Mart and was there for maybe an hour. Cuts the time even more."

"Makes it unlikely he picked up the girl outside the bar."

"You don't go shopping with a girl tied up in your trunk," Mitch agreed. "What did he buy?"

"This MP3," Wade said holding up the music player.

"I still say that is a weird purchase, especially for almost four in the morning," Mitch observed.

"Maybe he had the girl and he needed some music to set the mood," Wade joked.

"Yeah right," Mitch grunted. "What else you got?"

"Still going through it all, but nothing else jumps out."

"Okay keep after it, and if you get time see about getting the book caught up."

Courthouse Tucson AZ June 17th 2018 Sunday Morning

Feeling like she was betraying Mitch and trying not to slink, Geena entered the courthouse through the back door. She took a quick look around, half-expecting to see Mitch.

"Special Agent Dixon!" Judge Sanderson called, waving from the door of his office. "Come on back." He ducked back into his office without waiting to see if she was coming or not.

Smiling a little, she adjusted the strap of her purse over her shoulder and hurried after him. "You want coffee?" he barked as she entered the office.

"Please."

The judge handed her a cup and waved a hand at the tray beside the coffee machine. "You want any of that crap, help yourself," he said gruffly, carrying his cup around his desk.

Geena had to smile again. The old bastard was prickly as one of the cactus they had out here, but she couldn't help but like him. "Thank you, sir," she said, stirring her coffee. "And thank you for seeing me on a Sunday."

"I got an hour before church services." He smiled at her. "So, you got an hour."

"Thank you, sir."

"Don't sir me, in here it's just Harlan. Understand?"

"Yes, sir... Harlan."

"Sit yourself down," he barked waving her to a chair. "Now that all the niceties are done, tell me what I can do you for."

Geena paused, stirring her coffee while she collected her thoughts. "I need to ask you some questions about Detective John Mitchell."

The judge raised an eyebrow at the use of Mitch's formal name and title. He studied the young woman in front of him. Funny, they'd seemed pretty chummy yesterday. Something must have happened. And all of a sudden, the judge had an idea what might have precipitated the change. He threw a hard look at her, making a tisking sound and shaking his head. "You didn't give him your virtue?"

Geena felt herself turn red and had to suppress a giggle. "No, sir. We are just working together. Nothing more."

"Could do worse," the judge grunted gruffly, then cut his eyes up to the ceiling. "Oh, Lord, you didn't give him money for one of his hair-brained schemes, did you?"

"No," Geena said, hitching her chair a little closer. "But that is what I came to talk to you about."

The judge frowned picking up his glasses. "Johnnie's investments?" he mused, twirling the glasses by the earpiece. "Look, don't let all the razzing we give him fool you, some of them are pretty good. My wife put some of her mad money in one of them and got a pretty good return," The judge dropped his glasses on the desk blotter, took a quick glance around, leaning forward. "I got a couple of grand in his emu farm," he admitted, not quite whispering.

"You?" Geena asked, surprised at the thought.

The judge grinned sheepishly. "The prospectus looked good. The damn things are supposed to be good for you." The judge grunted a laugh that seemed to force its way past his lips. "You'd be surprised what them damn yuppies will eat and even more surprised what they will pay for it. Give me a good old fashioned fried chicken any time, but these freaks say chicken's too greasy." The judge shook his head, as if that was the craziest thing he ever heard.

"I like chicken as well," Geena said, sharing his smile. "But back to Detective Mitchell."

"Sure," the judge said, nodding. "Well, financially most of them are pretty sound; they're just so off the wall. I mean big birds, selling steaks out of the back of a pickup and those miniature horses?"

Geena frowned, thinking it over. "Then, he's not really bilking people?"

"Naw," the judge said, waving his hand. "Mostly folks make a little or at least break even. I know of a couple of times when folks took losses that Johnnie made up out of his own pocket." The judge laughed a little. "Don't be fooled by all the nonsense we give him, Johnnie has a damn good portfolio."

"So why all the crazy stuff?"

"Johnnie's got an active mind, always was turning. Besides he only puts his poker winnings in the really crazy stuff."

"Poker?"

"Oh yeah, Johnnie's always playing, does those online tournaments. Plays in three or four games around town," the judge said almost with a father's pride. "He's a lucky bastard too," he added muttering under his breath."

"You like him?" Geena accused.

"Aw, I've known Johnnie since he was a sprout. His dad was a lawyer and Johnnie was always hanging around this place. Always bouncing some kind of ball out in the hall. Pain in the ass." The judge leaned back in his chair, studying Geena. "So why all the questions about Johnnie." He raised his eyebrows at her, wagging them a couple of times. "You shopping for a husband?"

"No, no," Geena said, blushing.

"Probably could do worse."

"No doubt," Geena said, hitching her chair closer. "I was wanting to ask you about his house."

The judge scowled, leaning back a little farther lacing his fingers behind his head. "Maybe you better tell me what is going on here."

"I called a colleague had him check out some names. Well, while he was checking, he found some things, and thinks Mitch might be dirty."

"Well now, I don't know who your buddy back east is, but if he thinks Mitch is a dirty cop, then he's an addle-brained moron."

"He's actually pretty good at what he does. He thinks Mitch got his house from Brody and that he got it way too cheap."

The judge groaned. "Hell yes he did! Way too cheap. Lucky little shit."

"How did that happen? Our take on it is that he got his house a hundred thousand too cheap."

"At least a hundred." The judge scowled across the desk. "Maybe more than that," he grumbled.

"Now, you see our reason for concern?"

The judge nodded gravely. "You said he got his house from Brody?" he asked and Geena nodded. "Damn it to hell, that means I did too." The judge swore under his breath. "And I paid full price!"

"Hence our problem," Geena said, spreading her hands.

Still fuming, the judge leaned back in his chair. "Do you know anything about land development?"

"No not really."

"Well if you're a developer like Brody the first thing you do when starting a new development is form a new company. Then once the last house is sold you disband that company."

"Why do that?" Geena asked, frowning as she tried to follow the logic.

"A couple of reasons. First of all, once the last house is sold you can turn all the maintenance of the public areas to the HOA. In some cases, that's when you can turn the maintenance of the infrastructure, streets and such to the city or county. But the main thing is once you disband the company you don't have to mess with any warranties on the houses. And if a house falls down, or the sidewalks settle? Can't be sued either. Hard to go after a company that doesn't exist anymore."

"Ah, so I take it Mitch bought the last house?"

"Yup. I put him on to it too. Told him to make a low-ball offer and he might just get it. Well he made a ridiculously low offer. Course they turned it down. I think they expected Johnnie to come back with another better offer, but he didn't. He waited a month, and then resubmitted his original offer. They hadn't even had a sniff on the place, so after another month, they took it."

"Then there never was anything wrong with the deal?" Geena said feeling some relief.

"Nope, just like I said, he's lucky."

"Okay," Geena said, compartmentalizing that bit of information and moving on. "There is one more thing. Mitch is receiving two monthly payments that we are concerned about."

"Payments?"

"Yes," Geena said, glancing down at her notes. "One from Pima Properties and...."

The judge's barking laugh cut her off. "Let me guess; one from Masters and Solders?"

Geena nodded, as the judge continued. "The one from Pima is for two rental houses Mitch owns. And before you and your guy think there's something wrong, let me tell you how he got them. His dad owned the first one for years. John Sr. signed it over to Mitch when he retired. Mitch took out a loan on it and bought the other one. Bought after the crash, got the house dirt cheap and an interest rate of practically nothing. The rent on one pays the mortgage and he stuffs the rest in his pocket. The other one, the payment from Masters and Solders is rent from his dad's old law offices. Mitch rents it out to another firm."

"Masters and Solders," Geena said, a light going off in her head.

"You got it missy."

"So, Mitch basically gets his house payment from those properties?" Geena said doing some math in her head.

"Yeah, the little smart ass is raking it in with both hands." The judge peered over his glasses at her. "Is that all your super sleuth found on Mitch's finances?"

"That was it," Geena answered, feeling a wave of relief wash over her. A part of her brain was amused at the fact that it was so important to her that Mitch was clean.

"Well like I said, your fellow back east is about as sharp as a marble," the judge grumbled.

"He missed something? There is more?"

The judge laughed, a loud, cackling sound, which Geena was sure could be heard in every corner of the building. "Your guy didn't find the taco truck?" he asked leaning across the desk.

"Taco truck?"

"Oh yeah, Mitch makes a pretty penny off this taco truck."

"What is a taco truck?"

"You know, roach coach is what they are called. A mobile restaurant. Taco truck."

Geena raised an eyebrow. "Mitch owns one of them?"

"Part of one." The judge leaned back in his chair, clasping his hands over his head. "Couple of years ago, there was this Mexican guy and he got in trouble with the local drug runners down in Mexico. He saw something he shouldn't have. Being no dummy, he grabs his family and high tails it over the border. Rolls into Tucson in the middle of the night."

The judge got up, refilling his cup. He held the pot out to Geena, who shook her head. "Our guy finds himself a job up here and lays low for a couple of weeks." The judge dropped back into his chair. "And after a couple of weeks, he starts to feel safe. He thinks they have likely forgot about him and sneaks back across the border to get some of their stuff."

"And they were waiting and killed him?"

"You know it," the judge replied dryly. "So now we got this lady with four little kids. She's living in this clap trap down in a bad part of town, and even though the place is nothing but a dump, she can't make the rent. Can't go back to Mexico either."

"They would kill her just in case her husband told her what he saw."

"In a heartbeat. Kill the whole family. The bastards!"

Geena smiled. The judge's outrage was genuine. He cared about people. "Then what?"

"Somehow Mitch hears about it. Probably through some social worker he was trying to make time with. Anyway, he hears about it and he pays the rent on the clap trap for a few months. See Mitch knows everybody in three counties. And he just happens to know this old guy with a roach coach who wants to retire, so Johnnie buys the thing and gives it to her in exchange for ten percent of the profit."

Geena smiled liking the story. "That was nice of him."

The judge snorted. "Lucky little bastard," he grumbled. "Turns out this gal is like the Mexican Rachael Ray, one hell of a cook and built like Dolly Parton. This gal starts out making her tacos and the like and before long she is raking in money hand over fist. Mitch told me he clears about one hundred and fifty a week from the deal."

"Karma." Geena said.

The judge snorted again, shaking his head. "More like blind ass luck."

Tucson Police Headquarters Tucson AZ June 17th 2018 Sunday Afternoon

Mitch was reading all the paper on the case, trying to get a sense of how everything that had happened tied together. They were losing focus on Angie Brody, he could feel it. The thing was, they had nothing to work on. No place to push.

Mitch leaned back in his chair, closing his eyes reviewing the case from the start.

Several things were obvious. The killing of Pyle, that had to be a black mail thing. Pyle stumbled onto their little scheme and he tried to shake them down. Okay, that made sense, nice and linear. But, why kill Schroeder? Why make

Pyle look like a serial killer? They had to know that the nipples would be sent to the lab and would be found to be fake.

Schroeder worked for the Senator, maybe she found out something she wasn't supposed to and they had to get rid of her. But why put the nipples in the freezer? That seemed to be a miss-step. Sure, they cast Pyle as a serial, but they had to know it wouldn't hold up. So why do it?

And why would Tanner be willing to go to jail for killing Pyle? Mitch was positive that Tanner was nowhere around when Pyle was killed. But Inez Perry, her description fit Tanner to a tee. How did that happen? Could she have been paid off?'

Mitch sighed getting a Coke from the tiny fridge beside his desk. None of that helped them find Angie. The problem was she could be anywhere. Mitch had half the city watching for her and Carter but so far nobody had seen anything.

Brody was the key. He seemed to be in the center of everything. He had to have an idea where Angie might be.

It was time to push the man. So far, they had pussy-footed around Brody because his daughter was missing. Maybe now was the time to get a little rough with the asshole. Mitch called Brody's cell and got voice mail. Mitch tried his home and office but got nothing except instructions to leave a message at the beep.

Huh? Brody's daughter was missing, he should be right by the phone in case her abductors called with demands. Course maybe, he had caller ID, probably did, but still he should be desperate for news. He would take a call from the cops. In fact, Brody should be calling them every five minutes, not ducking them.

That thought crept into Mitch's brain like a thief through an unlocked door. It did seem like Brody was ducking them. But why? For what possible reason?

Mitch was thinking of Brody when his cell buzzed. He glanced at the screen seeing a call had come in while he was trying to reach Brody and now he had a message waiting.

Geena's seemed to spring from the speaker "Mitch! Something terrible has happened. I need you!" she said, her voice sounding strained, almost on the verge of tears.

Airport Holliday Inn Tucson AZ June 18th 2018
Sunday Afternoon

Just after three in the afternoon when Geena pulled into the parking lot of the Holiday Inn on Tucson Boulevard. Dropping the car in the parking lot, she checked her cell. Todd had texted her his room number. Feeling slightly ridicules, she slipped in the side door and up to his floor.

Wandering the hall for a few minutes she found his room. Glancing down the deserted hall, she rapped sharply on the door. After a few seconds, she rapped again, calling out this time. "Todd, it's me, Geena."

When no answer came from the room, Geena checked the number on her phone, assuring herself that she was at the right room before knocking again. This time she knocked several times, pounding the door until her knuckles stung. "Todd, its Geena open up," she called rattling the door knob.

Beginning to worry, Geena looked around and spotted a maid at the end of the hall. "I'm an FBI agent," she said, flashing her credentials. "I need you to open that room."

A worried frown sprang to the woman's face. "I am not supposed to," she worried.

Geena shook her badge in the woman's face. "I don't care. You can open the door, or I can take you in and we can make a call to ICE."

The woman wrung her hands, the pained look on her face turning to anguish. Geena felt a quick stab of guilt. "Look," she said softly. "I am a federal agent, I am supposed to meet someone in that room and I am afraid something terrible might have happened. Open the door and I will say I picked the lock," Geena offered, ignoring the fact that she didn't have the slightest idea how to pick a lock.

Still wringing her hands, the maid simply stared at Geena. Becoming frustrated, Geena stamped her foot on the carpet. "Open the God damn door!"

Geena's shrill cry startled the woman into motion. Fumbling with the keycard, she finally managed to get the card into the slot. "Okay, please step back," Geena said, pulling down on the handle. She felt it click and as the door started to open, Geena felt a pause. "Stand back please," she said, waving the maid back. With her other hand, Geena pulled her gun, a small snub-nose .38 pistol.

Feeling slightly silly and very scared; Geena pushed the door open with her toe. "Todd," she called softly. As the door swung open, she could see the foot of the bed with two bare feet sticking up. "Todd," she repeated hopefully, but then the smell hit her.

Geena hadn't really ever been a cop and in all her years as an agent she'd never really been in the field, but still she recognized the smell of blood and death.

"Go call 911!" Geena shouted turning to the maid. "And I need you to get the manager up here."

Even as the maid scurried away, Geena began to second guess her decision to call 911 and TPD. It'd probably be Mitch and his crew they sent. She liked Mitch, but could she trust him?

Maybe she should call the Tucson Field Office. Have them send a team of agents over. Before she did, she knew she should verify it was Todd. Swallowing hard, she edged into the room careful not to touch anything.

As she passed the bathroom, Geena used the muzzle of her pistol to push the door open all the way. After a quick glance to make sure the restroom was empty, she moved on into the hotel room. Todd lay on the bed, his eyes open, staring glossily at the ceiling. A blue-black bullet hole punctured the skin on his forehead.

Feeling bile rising in her throat, Geena swept the room with her pistol. The patio door and curtains were open. Geena backed out of the room; she slipped the pistol in her purse. Pursing her lips, Geena fingered her cell phone. After a second she pulled the cell out. First, she called Mitch. The call went directly to voicemail. "Mitch! Something terrible has happened. I need you!" Realizing she probably sounded like a lunatic, Geena took a dep breath and smoothed down her emotions. "Mitch, this is Geena. Call me back. I'm at the Holiday Inn. I got a call to meet Todd here. When I got here, he was dead. Call me."

Geena felt a slight pang of guilt, but Mitch didn't need to know when she'd talked to Todd. Punching up her phone book, she paged through until she found Doug Dockett's cell numbers. Docket was the special agent in charge of the Tucson Office. Doug picked up on the first ring.

"Doug this is Geena. I need some help."

"Sure, Geena, I got the email that I was to extend any assistance you might need. I hadn't heard from you."

"Sorry about that," Geena said quickly. "This case has been moving fast."

"No problem," Dockett said, his tone saying otherwise. "Now what can I do for you?"

"I need a crime scene team at the Airport Holiday Inn." Geena could hear the hesitation in his voice. "I've got a dead agent in a room here."

"One of mine?"

"No, no, sorry" Geena said quickly. "Todd Holland, an agent from Washington."

"Washington? What was he doing here? Was he working with you?"

"He wasn't really working for me, I had asked him to run some computer searches. He called today to say he was coming out. I was to meet him at the hotel, but when I arrived, he was dead."

"Is TPD on the scene yet?"

"No but they're on the way."

"Perhaps we should let them handle it."

"No, Todd was one of ours."

"Precisely why we should let TPD handle it. We have a conflict of interest."

"Maybe, but I want us to run our own investigation."

"You don't trust TPD?"

"That's a bit strong, but they were the only ones who knew Agent Holland was working for me."

"Okay, I'll send a crew over, they should be there within the hour."

"Thank you, Doug," Geena said. "Perhaps we shouldn't tell TPD why we are paralleling their investigation."

"You don't trust them?"

"I don't know, and that's the problem."

Geena hung up, pacing the hall. Dockett was going to be a problem, she thought. She'd met his type before. Ambitious and self-serving. Always looking to take advantage.

Thinking about that, she opened her phone, scrolling through the phone book once again. She called Mark Winter. Mark was an old friend; he'd been in the business forever. He'd been Geena's first partner and seemed to know everyone.

"Geena, how are you?" Winter said, picking up after the first ring.

Geena smiled. Winter had a voice that sounded like gravel sliding across a wood floor, but it was good to hear. "Good, and you?"

"I'm good, but you didn't call for that. Nobody ever calls to chat anymore. What can I do for you?"

"Do you know an agent named Doug Dockett?"

"Hmmm," Winter said, sounding like he was filing concrete. "Yeah, seems like I met him once. Blow dried little prick."

"Never met him but sounds like him." Geena said. "What I need to know is, can I trust him?"

"Absolutely," Winter said immediately. "You can trust him to do what benefits him."

"Great, that's all I need."

"Hang in there, Kiddo; you got one thing going for you."

"Yeah, what's that?"

"You scare the hell outta most people."

"I don't know if that's going to be enough."

"Hey if you need help....."

"I can call you?"

"Hell no! Call a fireman."

Geena twiddled with her phone. A part of her wanted to go back in that room and another part of her wanted to run away. The trouble was, she didn't know what to do.

Mitch had been right, she wasn't a cop. She didn't know if she should go down to start interviewing people, or stay and guard the room. In the end, she stayed like a bump on a log. She was in the hall, leaning against the wall, when the hotel manager rounded the corner.

Geena could tell the manager was mad from her stride. She was a tall woman, pretty enough, but slender and hard looking. "What is the meaning of this?"

Something in her voice grated on Geena's last nerve. "A man was murdered here tonight."

If Geena was expecting shock or sympathy, she wasn't going to get it. The woman looked like she'd bit into a sour pickle. "How long is all of this going to take?"

"As long as it takes." Geena snapped. "We'll need to interview your staff and probably see any surveillance video that you might have."

The pickle just got a little more sour. "I don't know about that. Do you have a warrant?"

"I can get one," Geena replied, as Mitch rounded the corner from the elevator. "I can have a warrant here in less than an hour."

Pickle face crossed her arms, tapping her foot on the carpet. "I will need a warrant."

"I doubt if a warrant can be obtained that fast," Mitch said, popping a stick of gum into his mouth. "My guess is it will be more like 9 or 10 in the morning."

Mitch offered the pack to the two ladies, who both looked mad enough to bite a nail in two. Mitch gave them his best grin. "Of course, we'll have to seal this entire floor until then. No one in or out."

Mitch let it hang in the air, then shrugged, "But, maybe the agent knows a judge and a warrant could be arranged more quickly? Aw hell, why argue? Might be better to just seal this floor until morning."

The manager ground her teeth for a second, and then managed a grim, little nod. "Okay, what do you need?"

"We need to talk to all your staff, especially the ones who might have been on this floor."

"How long will it take?"

Mitch shrugged, glancing at Geena. "It takes as long as it takes," she snapped. "Depends on what is to be found."

"Okay, I'll line up the staff."

After she left, Mitch looked over at Geena. "Sorry to butt in, just seemed like you needed some help."

"Thank you," Geena replied, but it would have taken a very generous soul to say that she sounded grateful for Mitch's help.

It had to be the weirdest crime scene that Mitch had ever been to. Two distinct groups of people swarming about the room, being overly polite to each other, and being very obvious about staying out of each other's way.

Mitch watched long enough to see that there wasn't anything of note come out of the room. Whoever had killed Todd Holland had been very careful. It seemed to Mitch that the killer had been careful, but he had also been good at this.

The shooter had waited in the room for Holland. It looked like the killer had tied Holland to the bed, perhaps to question Holland? At some point he shot Holland and simply walked away. Very simple, very brutal and very effective, a text book killing.

Mitch squatted down in the hallway watching the work. Who did that point to? His first thought was Carter. But maybe not.

Both the FBI and Tucson Police had been passing out pictures of Carter but no one remembered seeing him here. The hotel had cameras, and right now the FBI was looking through the videos. So far, Carter couldn't be placed at the scene. Mitch hated to turn that part over to the Bureau, but he had to admit, they had people that had seen Carter. It only made sense that they review the tapes. And they said Carter hadn't been here.

If not Carter. Who?

Mitch remembered what Geena had said about the people who Braxton might have working for her. The coldness of the killing looked professional.

CHAPTER NINE

Mitch's House Tucson AZ June 17th Sunday 2018 Evening

Mitch prowled his house, trying to place things in order. The case was getting bulky and out of hand. He had several legal pads sitting on his breakfast bar. On one he had written the names of all the players. Quite a diverse group.

On another pad he had listed all the things about the case he knew to be true. And on the third pad, he listed all the things he suspected.

Once he was done making his lists, Mitch began to pace. He'd circle the kitchen, carrying a putter. He'd stop in the family room and putt a few balls, then look at his lists. After three laps he paused. "Fuck," he growled, his voice echoing in the empty house.

They were basing a lot on suppositions. Suppose they were wrong somewhere down the line? They could be chasing down a dead-end trail. It worried him that he was locking in on one direction.

Think damn it!

What was he missing? Angie Brody could be running out of time. In fact, absolutely was running out of time. In the back of his head, Mitch could almost hear the clock winding down on her life. That was assuming she was a hostage and not a willing participant in all of this.

Mitch stopped to consider that. In the end, he decided, it really didn't matter. One way or another they had to find her. There was something missing from his lists, Mitch realized. There was something or someone who tied this all together. He looked at the list of characters. How does such a diverse list get mixed up together? Locals, people from the east coast, builders, bikers, lawyers and politicians. Shit it sounded like a bad country song.

Mitch made a couple of laps around the bar, putted a few balls, then came back to look at the lists. "Aw, hell," he muttered. Using his finger, he read the names again. "Fuck, Kathy. What have you done?"

Kathy Reynolds worked in finance.   Brody was in development. He should be strapped, over extended, but he wasn't. Where was his money coming from? Could Kathy be sliding him some money under the table? If she was, how to establish that?

Mitch putted a few balls. Kathy was a liberal. Could she be hooked in with Braxton? That was possible. Mitch remembered Kathy being politically active. It was one of the things they had fought about. Leaning the putter over his shoulder, Mitch started circling again. Fuck this was crazy. He knew her. Kathy wouldn't get mixed up with anything illegal. Certainly nothing as raw as the taking of Angie Brody.

Still Kathy being mixed up in this would explain Tanner's attitude. He would cover for her. He might not like doing it, but he would.

Naw, it was crazy. There had to be some other explanation. Mitch was lining up a putt when his home phone rang. Tossing the putter on the couch, he crossed to the phone. "Mitch, its Parker. Mickey just got a hit on the print from Pyle's. The one he lifted off the shell casing. You'll never guess."

"Shit, Kathy Reynolds."

"God damn it! Mickey said he wouldn't call you."

"He didn't. I was just looking over some stuff, wondering if she might be involved."

"Well, it's a tie back to Tanner," Carly said, still in a huff.

"Maybe not. He didn't do it."

"Man, you aren't thinking she did it herself."

"No. Especially not if Inez Perry is right about what she saw. I'm not sure what I'm thinking." Mitch tucked the phone under his chin, as he rummaged in the frig for a beer. "It's enough to get a warrant. Get one for her house, office, car and phones."

"We're on it. Hartek is already drawing them up now."

"Good. Let's serve her, get her rattled. See if she starts talking."

"We were thinking of doing it tonight."

"Good. Can't make bail until morning."

"You want us to take her in?"

Mitch twisted the top off his beer, dropping the lid on the counter. "I don't know," he said, then took a long pull. "Sometimes it really freaks people out to see their house being searched. On the other hand, the thought of jail would really put Kathy over the edge."

"So which way do you want to play it?"

"Play it by ear. If he's free, take Ollie with you guys, he's got a good feel for these things. Maybe take a few uniforms. Do the whole show. Light up the neighborhood."

Holding the phone, Mitch let his mind wander. While they dated, Kathy had been mixed up in politics. Could she be high enough on the political food chain to actually know Braxton? Mitch tapped the phone in his hand, and then stabbed the buttons to dial Wade Nichols. "Hey, boss," Wade answered after the first ring. "What's up?"

"I need a little information. I know you keep up on things politically."

"Got to. Besides, politics is way more fun than sports these days."

"If I was thinking someone was mixed up in high level politics in the Democratic Party, how would I check that out?"

Wade laughed, a deep ringing chuckle. "Hell, you are talking about Kathy Reynolds."

"You know something about her that I don't?"

"Yeah, I know she was in Charlotte for the last convention. I heard she's the head of fund raising here in Arizona for Braxton's campaign."

"No shit?" Mitch said, lapping around the bar. "Think she knows Braxton?"

"Dunno. I guess it's possible though, hell maybe even likely. She might not know her well, but she's probably met Braxton at some thousand dollar a plate fund raiser."

"How do you know this shit?"

"I read something besides a car magazine. You should try picking up a newspaper sometime."

"When they put a hot blonde in a thong laying across the hood of a '72 Firebird on the cover of a newspaper, then maybe I'll read one," Mitch shot back, hanging up before Wade could get in a retort.

After hanging up Mitch resumed his pacing. After a few minutes, he called Geena. She answered after the first ring, and Mitch could tell, she was a woman with something on her mind. "I've been doing some thinking, and to be honest; I'm seeing some holes in our theory."

"You think we are wrong?" Mitch asked. He purposely didn't mention the developments with Kathy. He wanted to hear what Geena was thinking without corrupting it.

"No, not wrong necessarily," Geena said hurriedly. "What I meant is there are gaps in what we know. There's something missing. Lynch pin. That's the word I'm looking for. We don't have the lynch pin. The thing that brings it all together."

"You sound like a woman with an idea."

"You're not going to like it."

"There's a lot I don't like. Spill it."

"Kathy Reynolds," Geena said, then hurriedly explained. "She could be the one thing that brings this all together. She has got to know Brody. She's practically living with Tannenbaum. It's a stretch, but she could know some of the people on the other end."

"Not so much of a stretch as you might think."

"I see that you've already been thinking of her. What do you know that I don't?"

"Well, I know she's heavily into the Democratic politics. I made a few calls. She's more active and higher up than I knew. She was a delegate to the Democratic National Convention. Now she's basically running the fund raising for Braxton here in Arizona."

"Doesn't necessarily follow that she knows Braxton personally."

"But it's a link."

"Shit, you know something else. You've been holding out."

"Print on that shell casing at Pyle's was hers. My guys are heading over there right now."

"So, you do think that she's the center of this whole thing?"

"I don't know. Doesn't really sound like Kathy."

"She's not ambitious?"

"Oh hell no. She's ambitious and then some. What I meant is she is way too straight-laced for something like this. We used to fight about that."   Mitch took a sip from his beer, kicking a golf ball across the floor. "See, I do a little investing on the side. Kind of a hobby. Some of the deals I've been in, might not always pass muster with the FCC."

Geena chuckled. "I've heard. I was warned to stay away from your investments."

"Fuck, who told you that?"

Geena laughed. "Who didn't?"

Mitch felt a little flash of anger surge through him, but managed to smooth it down. "The thing is, Kathy wouldn't go for any of it. She was way too uptight."

"I'd say she's loosened up. She's dating that biker."

"Yeah, that shocked the hell outta me."

Geena laughed again. "Damn, Mitchell, you've got a big blind spot where this woman is concerned. Did you ever think she might not want to risk her million-dollar deals with Brody to invest in cheap steaks and big birds?"

Mitch sat on a bar stool, leaning his elbows on the counter. "Yeah, well maybe."

"So, where do we go from here?"

"I'm thinking of kicking Tanner loose."

"Really?"

"I was thinking, we could make another run at him tonight. Hit him with this thing involving Kathy, see what that shakes outta him."

"Then just let him go?"

"Yup. Course, I was thinking we could follow him. See what moves he makes. We've got his cell. I can get a couple of our tech guys working on it. We can track his calls. Pirating the signal is what he called it."

"Do you have a warrant for that?"

"Not really."

"You wouldn't be able to use anything he says in court."

"He'll be careful. He won't really say anything on a cell we can use, but we can see who he calls. "

"Probably won't use his cell for that anyway," Geena said.

"Maybe not, but the thing is, I noticed at his house he didn't have anything but two cordless phones. My guys say we can listen into those as well."

"He had a hard line at his shop."

"Yeah, if he uses that, we're fucked. I'll arrange for two uniforms to give him a ride to his house. I'm hoping he won't wait to make the call. I want to see who he contacts first."

"Any insight on who that might be?" Geena asked.

"Not a fucking clue. That's why I want to know. Who knows, he might call Jacob Carter."

"Fat chance of that."

"Yeah, but you never know."

"You're right, so let's go jack him up."

"I'll swing by and pick you up in half an hour."

Mitch hung up, turning on the coffee maker. While the coffee brewed, he dug through his cabinets for some snacks, finally settling for some crackers and jerky. After thinking for a second, he tossed some water and a couple of beers into a cooler. Once the coffee was brewed, he poured it into a thermos.

Just in case, he grabbed a jacket on his way out. In the garage, he hesitated. Tanner knew the Trooper and he would sure as hell spot the Mustang. Frowning, Mitch slid into the Mustang. Punching the garage door opener, Mitch dug out his phone. He dialed Geena while he waited for the garage door to roll open. "Geena, its Mitch. Did you ever pick up a rental car?"

"Yes, I got it this afternoon."

"What kind?"

"Ford Focus."

"Perfect. I was thinking, maybe we could take it. Tanner knows my vehicles and he could spot one of our unmarked cars a mile away.'

"Sure, we can take my car."

Mitch hung up, enjoying driving for a minute. Who would Tanner call? One of his crew? Maybe, but Mitch knew most of those guys. While he could easily buy that they killed somebody in the heat of the moment, but to do it cold the way Jackson Pyle was taken out? Seemed a little out there for them. Besides they all had long hair. And if Inez Perry was to be believed, the killer had short, spikey hair and that was Tanner. Chappy Miers could do it, but he had long black hair and a beard.

Who then?

Mitch was still wondering about it when he swung into the motel parking lot. He parked the Mustang at the far edge of the lot and was just locking it up when he saw Geena come out of the side door. "Hey," he called, grabbing the cooler and his coat. "That was good timing."

"Not really," Geena replied with a smile dancing on her lips. "I had the window open, trying to catch a breeze and I heard you get off the Interstate." She held up a set of keys. "Since this is your town and you know where we are going, you mind driving?"

"Sure," Mitch said, snagging the keys out of the air. He fired up the Focus liking the stereo and surprised at the snap the little car had. He was just swinging up on the interstate when his cell went off. "Hey, Mitch, it's Parker."

"How's it going over there?"

"It's going. We found a nine mil in her house. Box of ammo. Federals, same brand as over at Pyle's. My guess is the ammo will test out as the same batch that killed Pyle, and this is the murder weapon."

"What the fuck, she ain't that stupid. How'd she react when you found it?"

"It was weird. She wasn't shocked that it was there, but she was a little surprised. No that isn't right. She just stared at the gun, then asked for a lawyer."

"Shit I was hoping it wouldn't come to that."

"She's on the phone with the lawyer right now. What do you want us to do?"

"Place her under arrest. Tell her to have her lawyer meet her down at holding. Have the uniforms take her in, and then you finish your search."

"Are you sure you want to do that?"

"Do it."

"Mitch did you know? Reynolds. She has a kid."

Mitch frowned. "I didn't know."

"What do we do with the kid? Reynolds got any family we can call?"

"No, her parents live back east. Connecticut, I think. Shit, ask Kathy if there is anyone she can call. If not call Social Services."

Mitch hung up the phone, glancing over at Geena. "What do you think?"

"Could be that Tanner gave her the gun and she was supposed to get rid of it."

Mitch shook his head. "Not Tanner, he didn't do it. But somebody either gave it to her, or somebody put it there for us to find."

"Something really good to bump Tannenbaum with. I wonder if the kid is his? Might be another card to play," Geena said.

"Yeah, shit." Mitch rubbed the stubble on his cheeks. "Man, I hate it when kids get involved."

Tanner was waiting in an interrogation room when they got to the jail. He looked relaxed and at ease. "Damn, he almost looks like jail agrees with him," Geena observed, as they looked through the glass.

"Does doesn't it?" Mitch grunted. It was true; Tanner was sitting relaxed, and very comfortable in his surroundings. "Let's go."

"Mitch, you know the rules, you can't be questioning me without my lawyer here," Tanner taunted, a smug look on his face.

"Sure we can," Mitch said, showing a wide grin of his own. He slid into a seat, watching the look of concern flicker in Tanner's eyes.

It was gone quickly, the smug look back on his face. "Why is that?"

"Cause we're dropping all charges. We just have a few questions, and then you are free to go."

"What the fuck is this shit, Mitch?" Tanner demanded, and then quickly relaxed. "Ah, I see you want to fuck around and play games." He wagged a finger at them. "Won't work ol' buddy."

"Nope, no games, Tanner," Mitch said, taking the chair across from Tanner. "We got a new suspect."

"Yeah, and who might that be?"

"Kathy, they're bringing her in right now."

Geena was watching Tanner, trying to read his emotions. She saw anger flash across his face and for a moment, she thought he might jump across the table and strangle Mitch. Then she saw him smooth down his anger, and though it was forced, the smile managed to crawl back on his face. "Shit Mitch, that the best you can come up with?"

"Not playing with you man, it's true. We found her print on one of the shell casings from Pyle's house."

Geena was still watching Tanner. His face gave nothing away that she could see. Instead he laughed, a barking sound. He waved a meaty hand at them as if to brush their words away. "Hell, I dropped the box of shells when I was loading the clips." He shrugged his heavy shoulders. "She helped me pick them up."

"Good try, Tanner, but there's more." Now Geena thought she could sense wariness in the big man. He doesn't know what is coming, she thought. "When we went to search her place, we found a Ruger nine mil and box of shells. Wanna bet they are the ones that did Pyle?"

"Fuck you, Mitch, she was just holding it for me. I told her to get rid of it." Amazingly, Tanner managed a laugh. "Hell, you know her. Damn woman is tighter than a rusted nut. She knew I paid three hundred for the gun, so she wouldn't throw it out."

Mitch smiled shaking his head. "Doesn't work. You told us you dumped it in that pond over off Sarnoff."

"Shit, Mitch, you're the cops, you think I would tell you the truth? I was just lying so Kath would have time to get rid of the gun."

"Did you tell her to dump it in that pond?"

"Fuck no, I ain't stupid. I wouldn't tell you the same place I told her. What would it look like if you guys showed up while she was pitching it? I told her to toss it in the water canal up off Avra Valley."

Geena had to admire the performance. Tanner was doing pretty well. He was a lot smarter than she would have believed. Tanner was wary, but he thought he had everything that Mitch could throw at him covered. But Mitch was setting a trap that the biker couldn't possibly see coming. "How did she get the gun?"

"After I shot that fucker, I went to her house. I gave her the gun."

"You were in your Jeep when we got to the shop. Was the Jeep what you used to do the killing?"

Tanner grinned impishly, thinking he saw the trap coming. "Fuck no, I was on my bike. I went up to Kathy's and got my Jeep."

"You're Jeep was at Kathy's?"

"Yeah, I've been pretty much living there. I left the bike in her garage, then took my Jeep down to the shop."

"Sorry, man, it doesn't work. You didn't have the time."

"What the fuck you talking about. I'd been at the shop for hours when you came?"

"Yeah, but I forgot to tell you. We have your ass on video a few minutes after the shooting. Way down on Valencia."

"So what, I had to meet a guy. He owed me some money. I swung by there, before I went up to Kathy's"

"Who was the guy?"

"Jersey Joe. I sold him a motor for a sixty-eight Firebird."

"The thing is. They have video out in the parking lot. You were in your Jeep."

Tanner didn't show any emotion, he just clammed up. He was smart enough to know he'd been caught in the lie. He didn't make it worse by denying it. Mitch placed his hands on the table, leaning into Tanner. "Look, man, I don't think Kathy did this. But the gun was at her house. We know you didn't kill Pyle. She was hiding it for someone else. I think you know who it was."

Tanner crossed his arms, and leaned back in his chair. He showed no emotion, but Geena could see tiny movements of his eyes. He's thinking, looking for a way out, she thought. She decided to try and give it to him. "Look, Tanner. I met Kathy the other day at your shop. I liked her. I want to help her. She can't handle a night in jail. We both know that."

Tanner shrugged trying to look unconcerned, but his movement was tense and stiff. "Look man, we had no choice," Mitch said. "She's on her way in here right now. Tell us who the shooter is and you can both go home tonight." Mitch let a little iron creep into his tone. "If not, we will book her tonight and she can spend the night in here."

Tanner ignored the threat, looking curiously at Mitch. "No shit, you found the gun at her house?" Tanner asked and Mitch nodded. "Damn it. I told her to get rid of it." Tanner groaned leaning forward, blowing out a big sigh. "Okay, hard-ass here's how it went down. See Kathy helped me just a little. I was trying to keep her out of trouble."

Mitch shot a quick glance at Geena. "What do you mean Kathy helped you?"

"I mean killing that fucker Jackson Pyle. I shot him and I had Kathy meet me over in the parking lot of that golf course. Can't remember the name."

"Fred Enke," Mitch supplied.

"Yeah, that's the one. Figures you would know. Fag sport if you ask me, but I guess you like playing." Tanner grinned at Mitch, and then shrugged when Mitch didn't take the bait. "So, Kathy brings down the Jeep. The gun was in my saddlebag on the bike. She took it. I told her to dump the gun. I took the jeep, went over to that Circle K. I knew about the cameras. Figured showing up in the Jeep would give me some kind of an alibi that I could pull out later."

"And Kathy rode your bike home?" Mitch asked, disbelieve sounding in his voice. "She can ride?"

"Yup, she's getting to be a good rider. Still wasn't quite sure I could trust her on my bike, but I guess she did okay."

"Okay, if you went to all that trouble to set up an alibi, why did you confess when we came in?"

Tanner brightened like a man just handed a free beer. "Oh hell, man, with you on the case, being super cop with this big promotion, your own little goon squad and all, hell, I knew I was done, so I just gave up." Tanner plastered the smug grin on his face again

"Still doesn't work. You didn't have any GSR."

"I was wearing gloves and my leathers."

"Nope, witness said the man on the bike wore a sleeveless vest."

Tanner crossed his arms, leaning back. "Your witness sucks."

Mitch leaned back in his chair, and for a minute there was silence. Geena had marveled watching the two exchange verbal volleys, like two fighters trading punches. "Tanner, do you want Kathy to spend the night in jail?" Geena asked softly. "We know you didn't kill Pyle. You were trying to protect her. You want to help her now, give us the name."

"Sorry, don't know what you are talking about?"

Mitch pushed back his chair. "Okay, I guess Kathy can be our guest for the night. I'll go get the paperwork started to get you out of here."

"You prick, Mitch. You don't have to bust her."

"Hey the offer stands. Give us a name and you both go home tonight."

"Screw, you. Man, you are one cold fucker." Tanner shook his head, then glanced sideways at Mitch. "What about Josie?"

"Josie?"

"Josie, the kid. You know...aw fuck me." Tanner cocked his head, looking quizzically at Mitch. "You don't know?"

"That she had a kid? I didn't know until tonight."

"What's going to happen to the kid?"

"Social Services has her."

Tanner chuckled, without humor. He shook his head. "Shit if this wasn't so tragic it would be funny as hell."

"What the hell are you talking about?"

"I'm talking about the kid, Josie. She's your kid man. You didn't know?"

"Fuck off, Tanner, I ain't buying it."

Tanner shook his head. "No way dude, I'm serious. I wouldn't lie about that."

"Yeah, right." Mitch pushed back his chair standing slowly up. "Last chance?" Mitch waited a beat but Tanner simply crossed his arms and looked up at the ceiling. Mitch shook his head and blew out a sigh. "Alright, I'll go get it started to get you out of here."

"Man, he is good," Geena said, once the door closed behind them. "What about the bit about the girl being your daughter?"

Mitch shrugged. "Shit, you heard him. He can come up with a story pretty fast. He's just trying to shake me."

"Okay now what?"

"Now, we go forward. I say we kick him out. He's going to be feeling a lot of pressure. I bet he makes a call pretty quick. We see who he calls then go from there."

"What about Reynolds? Let her sit overnight?"

Mitch nodded. "Hopefully by morning we'll have something else to hit her with." Mitch punched on his phone and called Parker. "Hey, it's Mitch you guys about finished up there?"

"Yeah, you want us to run at Reynolds?"

"Get her booked, then have a go, but don't tell her anything. Why I called, is Tanner's motorcycle there? In the garage?"

"There's a bike in the garage. It's registered to Roscoe Tannenbaum. I guess it's his."

"Harley, black with the skeleton playing cards on the gas tank?"

"Yeah that's it. Oh, Mitch, I checked, the gun it's registered to her."

"Hmm, I didn't expect that. Okay go ahead and finish up over there."

Parker hesitated for a long second. "Um, what about the kid?"

"Social Services been there yet?"

"Yeah, they showed up a few minutes ago."

"Who was it?"

"Doris Kieffer."

"Okay, Doris is good."

"Mitch, ah, well Reynolds claimed the kid was yours. And Mitch, I got to say, the kid, she looks a lot like you."

Mitch took a step back, a weird feeling sweeping over him. He stood there gripping the phone for a long time. "Mitch, you still there?"

"Yeah,"

"What do you want us to do after we get her booked?"

"Call it a night I guess."

"I was working on that victims list. I'd like to finish that tonight."

"Sure, go ahead," Mitch replied, dully.

"Jerry was thinking we should get Mickey or Linda Fang out and have them do some quick testing on the gun. Be nice to nail down that it is the gun."

"Alright, do that."

"Hey, Mitch, congratulations on the kid."

"Huh? Yeah, sure. Carly, did Doris leave a number with you?"

"Yes, I've got a card. You want the number?"

"Give it to me," Mitch said, pulling out his notebook and taking down the number. "Thanks, Carly."

Geena was looking at Mitch funny. "What was that about? They find something else?"

"Kathy told them the kid is mine."

"Is she?"

"Shit, I don't know. Maybe, I guess."

Mitch ran a hand through his hair, turning a slow circle. "I guess I need to make a call."

Geena nodded slowly. "You want a moment?"

"Naw, I'm good."

She watched him dial the phone and her estimation of him jumped up a notch. He looked a little set back on his heels, but not totally freaked out. Other than a few nervous passes through his hair, he looked fairly calm and composed.

With a thoughtful look on his face, his hands were steady as he dialed and his voice calm when he answered Doris Kiefer's greeting. "Doris, its Mitch. Sorry to get you out tonight."

"It's all part of the job," Doris said with good humor, a laugh bubbling just under the surface. "Bet this night has your panties in a bunch."

Mitch laughed with genuine humor. "It's been different I'll say that. So, what's going on?"

"Kathy Reynolds filed paperwork with the state, naming you as the father of her child. You should have gotten something in the mail."

"I haven't been checking my mail the last few days."

"Yeah, I bet. I've been following the case in the paper. You going to find that girl?"

"We're working on it," Mitch replied. "Judge Sanderson said I was supposed to be in his court on Monday, but wouldn't tell me why. I guess it was about this?"

Doris laughed merrily. "Yes. Usually we would handle the preliminary things out of our office, but the judge took special interest in this one."

"Old bastard."

"He likes you."

"Did Kathy say anything about why she is doing this now? Why she didn't tell me about it when the kid was born?"

"I guess she knew she was heading for trouble and wanted to make sure Josie was cared for. As for why she didn't tell you earlier, you'll have to ask her that."

Mitch leaned back against the wall, taking in what Doris just said. The cop part of him filed away what he heard. Categorizing it with what he already knew, and stacking it up against his theories. Apparently, Kathy knew trouble was coming. Knew far enough back to start the process to make sure the kid was taken care of.

Mitch felt a weird sense of disconnect. While his mind worked through the information, another part of him, far in the distance realized, he was a part of this. This was his life; his daughter this woman was so calmly speaking of. A part of him was already accepting the fact. Already realizing that his life was about to change.

Still, a part of it didn't seem real. Mitch had pried into and discussed other people's lives so many times, that now this seemed like it was happening to someone else. It was weird. The cop in him brushed all that aside and took over. "When did she start the proceeding?"

"I don't have my records in front of me, but I think it was about a week ago."

Mitch frowned. That was before Angie Brody was taken. Whatever triggered Kathy to do this, it hadn't been Angie. Another thought occurred to him. "A week? Isn't that a pretty short lead time for something like this?"

"No, not for this. All that is going to happen on Monday is the judge will inform you that you have been named as Josie's father. If you contest it, he will order a paternity test. If you agree that Josie is your daughter, the judge will set up temporary orders."

"How long does it take to get back the results of the test?"

"Couple of days, usually."

"Can I go ahead and get it done? Before Monday?"

"Sure. I don't know if the results will be back by then, but we can try."

"Okay. Let's do the test."

Doris let a silence hang between them. "Are you sure?"

"I'm sure," Mitch said firmly. "What do I do from my end?"

"You go tomorrow and give a DNA sample. There's a lab we use in those medical buildings south of Northwest Hospital." Mitch wrote down the exact address and was about to hang up when her voice stopped him. "You should definitely get the test, but I can tell you right now; Josie is your kid."

"What? Why would you say that?" Mitch fumbled, surprised at the flash which shot through him. A quick, sharp thrill.

"Because she is you and I mean to a tee. When I was explaining to her about the foster family and how much fun this adventure was going to be, she cocked her head and looked at me. Just like you do. Then she gave me that same skeptical look I've seen from you. I swear, it was just like talking to you."

"Thanks," Mitch replied, his head whirling as he hung up the phone.

"You okay?" Geena asked, touching his arm.

Mitch shook his head quickly. "Yeah, I'm fine," he grunted. "Let's go. I'm having one of our uniforms give Tanner a ride home. I want to be there and set up when they get there."

Mitch drove the rental car, weaving silently through traffic. "So, is that your daughter?" Geena asked after a few minutes.

Mitch shrugged. "Maybe, I guess so," he said, slipping into the turning lane to pass a car, then sweeping back into the left lane. "Her name is Josie."

"Pretty name. What do you think about being a dad?"

"Truthfully, scares the shit outta me. I've seen way too many kids in trouble because their parents fucked them up. What if I do that to her?"

Geena laughed. "You won't."

"What makes you so sure about that?"

"Because you are already worried about it. As long as you care about the kid, she will be alright."

"I hope so," Mitch said flipping a U-turn and parking. "That is Tanner's place there," he said pointing to a cute little house with a neatly landscaped yard and a for sale sign. "He's cleaned the place up over the last few years."

"Got a for sale sign. Getting it ready to sale," Geena commented, and then quickly regretted it, as she realized what the sign meant.

"Yeah, guess he was going to move in with Kathy."

Mitch pulled out his phone, calling the techs. "He's on his way. We're set up down the street a couple of houses."

"Yeah, we saw you park. We got a good lock on his phones and we stuck a tracker on his jeep and bike."

"Good," Mitch grunted.

They sat in silence, Mitch brooding. "They tell me you are some kind of athlete."

Mitch laughed ruefully. "I used to think so."

"What sport did you play?"

"Basketball and baseball. Mostly baseball."

"And you played professionally?"

Mitch laughed again. "I guess you could say that. We got paid, but it sure wasn't much."

"I thought baseball players made a lot of money."

"If you're in the majors, oh yeah, but not in the minors. I never made it out of the minors."

"What level did you play at?"

Double A mostly. Both years I got called up to Triple A for a few weeks."

"Then you quit?" she asked, and Mitch nodded. "Why? It seems like you were so close."

"Not really," Mitch said, his mind drifting back. He was looking at the house, but he was seeing a freshly mowed field. He could almost smell baseball, the grass, the pine tar, old leather and sweat. "I knew I was never gonna make it."

"Couldn't hit a curve?"

"Hey you're holding out on me. You know something of the game."

"Not really. Long time ago I dated a man who was a big fan. He was always saying this guy or that guy would be a good player but he couldn't hit a curve."

Mitch nodded absently. "That is a common affliction. Most guys who get to that level can hit the fastball. It's the off-speed and the breaking stuff that trips them up."

"So how about you? Could you hit the curve?"

"Yeah, I could, and I could handle the gas. I had a little trouble when they started mixing them up, but I was a good hitter."

"So why didn't you make it?

Mitch scowled, it seemed important to make her understand. "I was a good all-around player. I could hit and I could run, but I wasn't great at any of them."

Mitch paused, taking a sip from his coffee. "To make it in the bigs, you gotta be great at something. I wasn't quite fast enough to be a speed player. I had a little power but not enough to be considered a power hitter, and I wasn't quite good enough in the field to be a defensive specialist."

Even in the dark of the car, Mitch could sense her frown. "I don't understand. Isn't that what they want? Good all-around players?"

"Not really,' Mitch said. "You see, I was an outfielder. I could play center, but I was a step slow. They want guys who can really cover the ground out there. Plus, a centerfielder needs to steal bases."

"You couldn't do that?"

"If I got a really good jump, I could, but sometimes you have to be able to flat out run the throw. I couldn't quite do that."

"So, don't play centerfield."

"At the corners, I was very good defensively, but defense is not what they want at the corners. They want power from those spots. I didn't have enough power."

"So, you gave up?"

"More like I saw the writing on the wall. I was never going to make it in baseball."

"So how did you end up a cop?"

"After baseball, that's always what I wanted. What about you? How did you end up in the Bureau?"

"As you know, I started out in DC as a cop, but I hated it. So, I moved to the DA Office as a prosecutor." Geena laughed. "Man, I was going to change the world. You see I was tired of seeing all these bleeding hearts taking the side of the criminals. You see these movies, and the criminal is always just some miss-guided soul. He was really a good person, and its society's fault he's in trouble. What a crock. I was going to change that."

"What happened? Why did you quit that and join the Bureau?"

"I was like you I wasn't good enough. Wanting to do a job, doesn't mean one should. It was the case with Van

Zandt and Carter. We should have been able to put Carter away, but I blew it. So, I went back to school, I had gotten my BS in Physiology, before I switched to law. I went back got my Masters, then went to work for the Bureau. In the mean time I've been working on my Doctorate."

"Why did you switch from Psych to law in the first place?"

"I decided instead of helping people, I wanted to put assholes away."

"You were the victim of a crime?" Mitch asked quietly.

Geena shook her head. "I wasn't. Summer after my junior year in college, I was out with a couple of friends. There was this big party at this lake in Virginia. We were going up there. We stopped to pick up some wine. My friends went in the liquor store, but I had to pee, so I walked across the street to a gas station. While they were in there, two men came in to rob the place."

Geena sniffled then took a drink from her coffee. "I don't know exactly what happened, but they shot the clerk and one of my friends. They took Lisa with them. They beat her, raped her, and then threw her out of a van while they were going down the express way. She lived for a couple of years, but she was paralyzed from the neck down."

"They ever catch them?"

"Yeah, a couple of weeks later. They got life. Not necessarily mind you, because of what they did, but because they had so many priors. You know the bitch of it. They had a parole hearing this spring. They didn't get out this time, but they'll have another one next spring. I'll go again, but they'll eventually get out. If not this year, then next. Sooner or later it will happen."

"Yeah, I know. What's it been about ten years?"

"About that."

"Ten years ain't bad for this day and age."

"That pisses me off. Everyone says that," Geena snapped. "They killed three people that day, and they'll end up out in ten years."

"Yeah, but what can you do?" Mitch said, looking at the house.

"I'll tell you what I've thought about doing. I've thought about getting my gun and waiting outside the prison the day they are released!" Geena stopped, and then laughed. "I shouldn't have said that. It's crazy, I know, but I think about it a lot. Is that crazy?"

"No," Mitch said, still staring at the house. What was Tanner waiting on? "A few years ago, while I was still on patrol they bust two guys. These two had done a home invasion on this old lady. Raped her and killed her. Olshan and his partner, Wade Nichols they bust the guys a few days later. Stupid fucks were trying to fence her jewelry. Now one of the guys, Homer Patterson, he was a bad dude. He'd been doing these types of home invasions for a while. Other guy, I forget his name, Joe I think. Well Joe had mugged this lady at an ATM a couple of days before. Didn't hurt her, just took the money. Thing was, she was the wife of a big wig here in town. So, the DA was hot to put Joe away. They offered Homer a deal to roll over on him. And Homer being the asshole he was took the deal."

Mitch laughed, shaking his head. "Man, I guess Ollie went nuts; I heard he turned over the DA's desk threatened to kick his ass. Didn't matter though, the deal went down. Joe, he got fifteen to life, he's still inside. Homer gets out in a little less than four years."

Mitch poured himself another cup of coffee, looking up at the house. "When Homer gets out, I had just made Detective. There was three of us, went through the academy together, made Detective at the same time, me, Jerry Hartek and this guy Tim Harris. I was partnered with

Olshan, Tim Harris was with Wade Nichols and Hartek was with this old timer, Herm Sosa."

"When Homer got out, we all had a meeting at this bar. The older guys they just knew Homer was going to get right back into those home invasions. He'd been doing it for years. So, we decided to watch him. We split it up so one pair of us was on him all the time. Sure enough, in about a week, Hartek and Sosa spot him at this ritzy, over fifty community on the north side. He was slinking around, checking out the houses. Well, next day, me and Ollie saw him buying a gun."

"Few days later, on a Saturday, he's back up north, and we're watching him. He's got his eye on this one house. Old lady living alone, pretty well off. We figure he's just waiting until dark." Mitch closed his eyes, feeling the memory. "Man, it was one of those hot summer days, we almost died, waiting in those cars. Anyway, about eight, sun's just starting to set, so Herm and Jerry head down to this store. From the pay phone, they call in a prowler."

"Call comes over the radio a few minutes later. Ollie gets on and says we're all up there. He tells them we had been playing golf at this course right there and we can check it out. Course that was all bullshit, we're looking right at the guy the whole time. Few minutes later, Homer goes around to the back of the house. The lady had a fence, just a little two-foot-high wire thing, but it would have been enough to bust him for trespassing, but we waited."

"He goes up to the back door and busts out a window pane on the door. That's when we yell for him to freeze. Instead, he makes a move. Ollie, Wade and I all fire. Three shots to the chest. Any one of them would have killed him."

"Harris didn't fire?"

"Nope, he froze and by now he's freaking. Claiming Homer was going to surrender to us and we flat executed him."

"Did you?"

Mitch shrugged. "I don't know. He made a move. Looked like he was going for the gun. He had a gun. Good enough for me."

Mitch glanced back up at house, but couldn't see Tanner inside. "Harris convinced Sosa that we flat executed the guy. Said Ollie and I shoulda busted him that day when he bought the gun."

"What happened?"

"Shooting board took about five minutes to declare it a good shoot." Mitch chuckled a dry, hard laugh. "Course nobody asked golf course if we had actually been there. That mighta changed things. As it was, we all ended up getting medals. That lady we saved, she still comes down every year on each of our birthdays with a big tub of homemade cookies. Course after that they had to re-arrange the partners. Jerry got put with Wade Nichols. Harris was teamed with Herm."

"Guess it all turned out."

"Oh, but the story doesn't end there," Mitch said, digging out the crackers. He offered some to Geena, who took a roll.

"Thanks, I'm starving. I was going to order room service when you called."

"Sorry about that. There's jerky in the bag."

"No thanks. I'm good with the crackers. You were saying the story didn't end there."

"Oh yeah. Well about three months later. Harris is still bitching about the shooting, and Herm is feeling down. Herm was way too nice of a man to be a cop. I swear, that guy could go to domestic, where the husband had smacked around the wife and she'd come back at him with a butcher knife, and in ten minutes, Herm would have them ready to renew their vows." Mitch laughed pleasantly at the memory. He could still picture Herm's kindly, wrinkled face.

But, as he thought about what happened next, Mitch's face darkened. "Anyway, about three months later, we've got this crazy illegal jacking cars and driving them down to Mexico. Now this guy is a meth freak and he's always flying. He's beat a couple of people bad, put two in intensive care. He hasn't at that point killed anyone, but everybody knew it's just a matter of time. I mean this guy is outta control. If he don't crack up one of the cars running down to the border, or if the meth doesn't get him, it's just a matter of time before he kills someone. He ran over a lady. Shot at a couple of guys who tried to help her, so we knew he was carrying. It was whispered around, if he was spotted not to even try to take him in, just put him down. Well, Herm and Harris got a call, someone spotted him down off of Cardinal and Valencia. They go down there and run right into him. He's trying to pull this guy out of a beamer, but the guy doesn't want to give it up. They yelled at him and he turned. They hesitated and he didn't. He killed poor Herm right there in the street. Rumor has it that Harris turned and ran. But anyway, the guy got away. State guy named Logan took him out a few days later."

"What happened to Harris?"

Mitch laughed, and this time the sound wasn't that pleasant. "Being a bureaucracy, what do you think happened?"

"They promoted him."

"Yup. Word was out he ran, leaving his partner. Wasn't anyone gonna work with him after that. In the end, they took him off the street, put him in administration. He's the adjutant to the chief now. The chief can't stand him, but is stuck with him."

"You and him patch things up?"

"Nope" Mitch said with a note of satisfaction, "He really hates my guts. When the new chief formed my unit, Harris thought it should go to him. Shoulda gone to Ollie or Wade Nichols, but they didn't want it and recommended me."

"What about Jerry Hartek? He didn't want it?"

"Maybe, at one time but not now. He's got two sets of twins, year and a half apart, poor guy. Spends all his time with his kids."

Mitch's voice trailed off and Geena could tell he was thinking about Josie. "What about Wade Nichols? Whatever happened to him?"

"He's still on the force. He's on my team, just out on a medical leave."

"Was he shot?"

"Naw," Mitch replied laughing again. "Blew out a knee. Damndest thing too. 'Bout a month ago, they were having this Christmas in the summer thing. All the stores doing what they do for Christmas having these ridicules bargains but you have to be there at like five in the morning and then they only have one or two. Wade wanted to get this laptop for like two hundred bucks or some such price. He's there when they open and there's a crowd waiting for the doors to open. There's these two ladies, both of them there for a fifty-inch, curved screen 4k TV. They open the door and the stampede heads back to electronics. These two ladies get back to electronics and there's only one TV. They start arguing and a fight breaks out."

Mitch was out and out laughing now. "Wade steps in to break it up. Now these were both large ladies, and as Wade steps up they go down. Bang, they roll into him, taking his knee out. While they are on the ground, one of them decides Wade is trying to cop a feel and smacks him right in the face." Mitch laughed, snorting a little. "Broke his nose."

They laughed for a while, then settled back into watching the house. "I don't think he is going to make a call," Geena said after a while.

"Shit, I thought he would do something," Mitch grumbled. He dug out his phone, fumbled through phonebook for a number. Finding Howard Jones' number, he pressed send. "Make sure he didn't have a spare phone," Mitch told Geena while the phone rang. "Jonesy, hey its Mitch sorry to wake you man, but when you guys did the search on Tanner you didn't come across any cell phones? In the house especially?"

"No, Mitch, we didn't see any. We were kinda watching for something like that since we had the warrant to check his phones."

"Okay, thanks, buddy. Go back to sleep."

"What were you expecting Tanner to do?" Geena asked.

"I was expecting him to call someone to come pick him up." Mitch pounded the steering wheel. "Hell, maybe he don't know who to call. Maybe this is Kathy's deal all the way."

"So where does that leave us? Maybe the Pyle thing isn't even tied in with Angie Brody."

Mitch shook his head. "This isn't New York or LA. This is Tucson. We don't have big conspiracies here, much less more than one. But what ties a biker gang, a psycho reporter a presidential candidate and a shady developer together?

"Don't forget about Van Zandt and Carter."

"Oh yeah, can't forget about them two assholes. And then there's Kathy. So, what brings this all together?"

"Van Zandt and Carter were already together. It's easy to tie them to Braxton. As a congresswoman she would be well acquainted with Van Zandt. Like you said

Kathy probably knows Brody, may even do business with him, and she is the link to the biker gang."

"And Pyle stumbled onto something, tries to blackmail Braxton and they kill him."

"Exactly," Geena said.

"Well, hell we got it all figured out," Mitch grunted. "The thing is, I have no idea what it all means."

Mitch looked up at Tanner's house. They were talking in circles, going over the same ground. While Mitch knew there was value in that, he was tired of it. He was ready to do something. Since Tanner wasn't moving, Mitch just didn't know what.

"I have no idea," Geena said, cutting across his thoughts. "It's obvious that Todd found something. Let's do the same thing. Let's put all the names through the box. See if the computer can find any matches. Maybe find something that ties all of these folks together."

"Sure, I can get Parker started on that tonight. She was gonna stay late and work the book. I can pull her off that and have her work on this. At least she can establish whether Kathy and Brody do any legitimate deals together."

Mitch pulled out his phone, stabbing Parker's number. I'm gonna wear this thing out," he grumbled waiting for the call to go through. "Hey it's Mitch. You still at the office?"

"Yeah, I was just getting started on the book."

"Okay, push that aside for now. I want you to run through everyone connected with this case. See what matches you can find. Do everyone. Even the witnesses, victims, anybody whose name has come up. Any new names that come out of that search, run them. Do all the companies as well. Van Zandt's law firm, Kathy's firm, anything else you can think of. Then do known associates for everybody." Mitch rubbed his chin, thinking of Pyle. "Check that against violent crime victims."

"Sure, I'll get started right away."

"How'd it go with Kathy?"

"Didn't. Lawyer put the muzzle on her. She's gonna spend the night."

"Okay, thanks."

Mitch tossed the phone on the dash, then glanced over at Geena. "Damn, why hasn't he called?"

"Maybe this is Kathy's deal. Maybe he doesn't know who to call."

"Maybe" Mitch said with a shrug. That didn't sound right. "He has to contact somebody."

"Maybe he's afraid you got a tap on him and he wants to do a face to face."

"Got to be a quick call to set that up. That's what I was expecting. Something like the parts you ordered are in. Kind of coded messages." Mitch stopped short. A dark scowl crept on to his face. "Aw, kiss my ass! I'm so stupid!"

"What?"

"Message" Mitch said. "He didn't need to make a phone call! He coulda sent an email."

Geena laughed, shaking her head. "They said you do that."

"Do what?"

"Make jumps like that. Just figure things out. But you are right, we should have thought of that. Email is a coming thing with criminals. Hard to trace or track."

"Damn, I should have thought of that."

"Where does that leave us?"

"Don't know, but I say let's go get a drink."

Mitch picked up his phone, calling the tech guys. "Hey I think this is a bust, we're gonna take off."

"Sure, we might hang for another hour or so, just to be sure."

Mitch laughed. "You need some OT?"

"My anniversary is coming up. Wife wants to go somewhere nice."

"Okay give it another hour or so. If he moves or anything happens, give me a call."

"Will do."

Mitch killed his phone, glancing sideways at Geena. "So how about that drink?"

"You got any wine at your place?"

CHAPTER TEN

Mitch's House Tucson AZ June 18th 2018 Monday
Early Morning

Mitch lay awake staring up at the ceiling. He could hear Geena breathing heavily, not quite snoring, but in a deep sleep. She lay on her stomach, her face turned to him, her dark hair falling across her eyes. Mitch idly rubbed her back, thinking.

Damn. He was going to be a dad! Mitch had been so busy with the case, chasing around town, that he hadn't had time to stop and think about it. Now lying in the dark, it crept into his mind.

A part of him was excited beyond belief. He could close his eyes and picture it. He and Josie in the park, at the sandbox, him pushing her on the swings. He smiled, seeing himself hocking candy bars like Ray Jimenez. Damn, he could actually see himself enjoying it.

They could go to Cold Stone for ice cream. Just him and Josie. Josie that was a pretty name. Maybe not the name he would have chosen, but still a nice name.

Disneyland!

Hell yes. They had to go to Disneyland. He'd get some Mickey Mouse ears and they could ride the tea cups. Have to get a camera. A good one. One that took video.

Mitch felt a feeling of warmth rush over him. He was going to be a dad! Hell, maybe he already was a dad.

Man. What a feeling.

Course, what if he wasn't a good dad? Crap, what made him think he could even be a dad? Hell, he drank, smoked cigars. He gambled and chased around half the night. That sure didn't sound like a dad.

Dads were supposed to fix bikes, put on training wheels, and kiss scraped knees. Dads chased boys away and told you to eat your vegetables. How the fuck did you cook broccoli anyway? Shit, he would have to get a cookbook. Oh crap, he'd have to get some pots and pans. Real silverware, maybe a crockpot. A skillet. Have to have a skillet to make pancakes. He could make the bunny pancakes. Kids liked pancakes, didn't they? What the hell did kids eat?

Oh man, what if she didn't like him? A cold sweat broke across Mitch's chest. What if he couldn't do this? What if she didn't think he was a good dad?

Staring blindly at the ceiling, he mentally made a list of his faults and shortcomings. All the reasons why someone, especially a little girl wouldn't like him.

Pretty long fucking list too.

Really sweating now, Mitch slipped out of bed. Padding softly down the hall, he went into the kitchen and dug a diet coke out of the frig. Mitch had never really thought about it, but the prospect of being a dad was kind of frightening. Way worse than facing down some crazed maniac with a gun. All of a sudden, that seemed like child's play.

Already, he was letting her down. She was in a house with strangers, her tiny world turned upside down. Mitch felt an aching for her. Poor girl. She had to be wondering what had happened to the world she had known. It cut into Mitch with a searing pain to think he had been the cause of it.

No, that wasn't right. He hadn't been the cause of this. He had just done what he had to do. What his duty demanded that he do. It was her mom and Tanner who were doing this. If they would just come clean with what they knew, Mitch could have Kathy out in an hour.

Even telling himself that and knowing it was true, didn't help Mitch with the guilt he was feeling. He kept picturing that little girl, his little girl, sitting in a strange house, trying to hold back the tears. Maybe he should go to her.

Earlier in the day, Mitch had talked to Doris Kiefer, and she had suggested that it would be best if Mitch stay away until the results from the DNA test were back. If it turned out that Mitch wasn't the father, it would only further confuse the girl. Best for Mitch to hold back until they knew for sure.

Doris had assured Mitch that the foster family Josie was staying with was very good. They took in kids like this all the time, and knew how to handle it. How to make the kids feel at ease. They had helped many kids through tough times, and they would help Josie. Still Mitch's heart ached for his daughter.

He should get her a teddy bear. Damn right. A girl should have a teddy bear, something to hold close and make her feel safe.

Taking his coke with him, Mitch crossed to the bar and his laptop. Pulling up the internet, he did a search on teddy bears. Damn there were a lot of people selling teddy bears.

Among the myriad of sights, he found one that guaranteed next day delivery. Scrolling through the list of bears, Mitch picked a fuzzy red one with white hearts. After giving his credit card information, a screen popped up asking him what he wanted on the card.

Aw man, Mitch looked up at the ceiling, what to say? Looking forward to seeing you, well that just didn't seem to cut it. Mitch wasn't even sure that was true. A part of him dearly wanted to rush over there scoop her up in his arms and never let go. But another part of him was scared to death. Suppose she was disappointed in him. Mitch picked up the picture of Josie that Doris Kiefer had given him. God, she was beautiful. Funny how something so small and angelic could also be so terrifying.

A lump came to Mitch's throat. She looked so small and helpless. Suppose something happened to her?

Looking out his patio door at the stars, Mitch wondered what he would do if Josie were ever kidnapped like Angie Brody. He hadn't even met his daughter and the thought of something bad happening to her brought a wave of fear and a cold sweat to his body. What would he do?

One thing was certain, tonight he couldn't help his daughter, but he could help another man's daughter. He could find Angie Brody and bring her home.

Pushing his thoughts of Josie from his mind, Mitch tried to concentrate on the case. What was he missing? Where was Angie Brody?

Shit, somehow Jackson Pyle had managed to unravel it. Mitch leaned back in his chair. Intellectually Jackson Pyle had been a short, half step ahead of an orangutan. If Pyle figured this out, Mitch should be able to. He just had to concentrate. So, what had Pyle learned?

Judging from the brochures for new stuff at Pyle's house, he had gotten paid off once or was expecting too. But Braxton, or more likely Van Zandt knew it wouldn't end there. Knew it would never end. Once Pyle blew through what he had gotten from them, he would be back time and again. Or he might just go ahead and publish the story. Knowing all of this, they had simply done away with Pyle. Where Tanner fit in; Mitch wasn't sure. Mitch frowned at the wall. Tanner was the hitch in the story.

Still it was through Pyle that he would break this thing. Tanner was an unknown in this game. Better to stick with Pyle. Maybe he should see what Pyle had been writing about.

Back at the computer, Mitch clicked on the internet. After a few minutes of poking around, Mitch found the newspaper's website. Darby Lewis' picture adorned the homepage, along with a list of his recent stories. It was clear that Darby was the star here.

Mitch leaned back in his chair. Pyle was second rate at best. The newspaper itself was barely second rate. And even at a little paper like this, Pyle was the bottom tier. So how did he, Jackson Pyle get an audience with the likes of Braxton? Really, only one viable answer to that. Somehow, he turned up some good dirt on the Senator. Maybe he wrote about it?

It took five minutes' worth of searching to find Jackson Pyle's picture. While Darby Lewis' picture looked professionally done, Pyle's looked like it had been taken on a cheap cellphone in an alley. Mitch studied the picture. Didn't even really look like Pyle. Scrolling down the page, Mitch found a list of Pyle's stories. Car wrecks and bar fights seemed to be Pyle's stock and trade. Next to the bottom, Mitch saw a story about a suicide in a seedy motel.

Curious, Mitch pulled up the story. Halfway through the story, Mitch's curiosity became a full-blown itch. Skimming, Mitch quickly read the rest. "Motherfucker," he muttered after finishing.

Stabbing the print button, Mitch printed a hard copy of the article. Rereading the story as it came off the printer; Mitch saw the two detectives assigned to the case were Jones and Jenkins. Mitch picked up his pencil, tapping it rapidly. Now, that was real interesting. Picking up his phone, Mitch called dispatch.

"Tucson Police Department." He heard after the second ring.

"Monte, that you?"

"Mitch, what the hell are you doing up and about? It ain't even five yet."

"Hey, we detectives are on twenty-four seven, three hundred sixty-five," Mitch protested. "We're not like you uniforms. What are you guys working, like half days now?"

Mitch leaned back in his chair, grinning as he listened to a torrent of profanity and several slurs against his heritage and sexual orientation. Finally, Monte Simms ran out of steam. "What the hell do you want?' he growled.

"I need to pick your brain."

"Pretty slim pickings."

"I bet. Do you remember a DOA suicide at King's Court about a week ago?"

"Is that the case that Jonesy and Jenks caught? That the one you mean?"

"Yeah that's the one."

"Don't remember too much about the details. I did hear some talk around the shop that Jenks was sure pissed at Jackson Pyle over that case."

A tingling charge shot through Mitch. "Oh, yeah," Mitch said, trying to sound casual. "What was Pyle doing?"

"Just your usual reporter shit. Butting in, trying make more out of it than was there. Like I said, usual reporter shit." Monte laughed, a cackling sound. "I heard he was floating some kind of conspiracy crap. Making out like it was the crime of the century and he was going to be the next Woodward and Bernstein for cracking it."

"Fucking reporters," Mitch said with a laugh. "They got more imagination than most of the TV writers."

"Ain't that the truth? Can't believe a damn thing you read in the paper no more."

"You got that right," Mitch agreed, trying to finesse the information he wanted. "Do you happen to remember how the call came in?"

"Hmm, 911 anonymous, I think."

"I'd like to hear the tape," Mitch said, knowing that all 911 calls were taped.

"You got it," Monte agreed cheerfully. "I get a spare minute, I'll round it up."

"Thanks, Monte," Mitch said, then tried to casually slip in. "Hey, do you happen to remember how Jonsey and Jenks caught the case? Were they the crew in the barrel?"

"Naw, but it was early in the morning when the call came in, they were already here, so they took it," Monte said, then paused. "Aw shit, you think there was something wrong with the way they got the case."

"Maybe," Mitch admitted grudgingly. "Tell me, are they in the habit of coming in early?"

"Fuck no, that was an all-time first," Monte said, and Mitch could hear him drumming his pen. "Well maybe Jonsey would show up fifteen minutes or so early, but that fucking Jenkins ain't never been early in his whole life. He usually drags in here about eight-fifteen, then grabs the paper and heads straight to the shitter."

"You think maybe they were in early waiting on the call?"

Monte took his time with the answer and Mitch didn't pressure him. They both knew the significance of what Monte would say. Monte blew out a long sigh. "You know, Jenkins came up front a couple of times while they were waiting. At the time I thought he was scoping for doughnuts, but now?" Monte hesitated for a long second. "Shit, Mitch, I don't know."

"Okay, fair enough, but let me ask you. Did you ask them to take the call, or did they volunteer?"

"Jenks was up front when the call came through, he made the offer."

"Okay."

"Fuck it, Mitch. They knew the call was coming."

"I think you are right. They knew and were waiting."

"What are you going to do about it?"

Mitch rubbed his hand over his face. Good fucking question. "I don't exactly know, but for now, let's keep quiet about this."

"Shit, Mitch, I'm gonna try and forget that we ever had this conversation," Monte replied reverently.

"Don't forget too much. I may need a statement from you at some point. I may have to get a warrant and go after their phones."

Fuck me, you don't think the silly bastards would be stupid enough to use their own phones?"

"Maybe, you never know."

"Yeah, you know cops would do that. Cops never think anyone will come looking at them."

Mitch hung up, leaning back in his chair. Things were moving. That was the important part. Information was coming in. Now to start connecting some of the points of information. Mitch clasped his hands behind his head, closing his eyes.

Would it have been Brody who made contact with Jones and Jenkins? Probably. They wouldn't have trusted someone from back east. Of course, there was Tanner and Chappy Miers. Where did they fit in?

Mitch tossed the pencil away in disgust. He was really right back to where he started. More questions than answers. Jonesy and Jenks would both know Chappy and Tanner, but would they trust them?

Of course, the question was, which way did that street run? Did Chappy and Tanner bring Jones and Jenkins in, or was it the other way around? Mitch could see it happening both ways. If Jones and Jenkins were involved from the beginning, they might use Tanner and his crew for muscle. But on the other hand, if Tanner and Chappy needed a couple of crooked cops to push through a suicide, they would know who to call.

First thing Mitch had to do was talk to IA. Scratch that, he needed to talk directly to the chief. Maybe bring in Geena on this. Let the FBI investigate Jenks and Jones.

A part of Mitch wanted to grab Jonesy. Pull him out of bed and work him over. Of the two, Jonesy would be the one to crack and talk. By now, Jonesy would already be feeing the guilt.

Glancing at the clock, Mitch saw that it was almost five. After a second's hesitation, he dialed the chief's number. The phone only rang twice, before the chief answered, his voice clear and awake. "Chief, this is Mitch. Sorry to call so early, but I really need to speak to you."

"What's going on?" the chief asked concern leaking into his voice. "Has someone else died?"

"No, sir."

"Well thank God for that."

"You might want to save your thank Gods. This isn't good news."

"No?"

"No, sir. Not at all."

"Okay," the chief said, with a sigh. "What's going on?'

"I really don't want to say over the phone. I think we should meet in person."

"Okay, I have some time this afternoon. Why don't you come by the office around two?"

"Sir, I don't think this is something we should talk about in your office. I'd just as soon no one knew we talked. I was hoping to meet with you this morning, before you go into the office."

The chief sighed again. "Alright, give a half hour. Let's meet at I-Hop on Cortaro Farms. If I'm not there, order me the Western Omelet and coffee."

"Thank you, sir."

After hanging up, Mitch headed back to the bedroom. At the door, he paused, looking in at her. Her dark hair was spread across the pillow. In her sleep the serious expression had melted away.

He placed a hand on her shoulder. She moaned, rolling away from him. Leaning in close, Mitch shook her shoulder, and blew lightly into her ear. She moaned again, waving a hand in front of her ear. Grinning, Mitch blew in her ear, and this time her eyes fluttered uncertainly. "What is it?"

"I have to go out for a while."

"What time is it?"

"Five. I should be back by six-thirty. Make yourself at home. I'll start some coffee if you want it later."

"Bring me back a bagel."

"Sure," Mitch agreed, kissing her on the cheek. "Go back to sleep."

"Don't worry."

Mitch made the coffee, then gathered up his laptop. With a last look in on Geena, he headed to his meeting. He was first to I-Hop and had ordered and was tapping on his laptop when the chief slid into the booth. "Did you sweep the place for bugs?' the chief, asked with a smile.

"Maybe I should have," Mitch replied sourly. "This is some serious shit."

"Okay, let me get a jolt of coffee before you start pissing on my day."

Mitch scowled, while the chief poured himself a cup of coffee. Normally Mitch liked the chief's sense of humor and his positive outlook. Today was different. Seeing the frown, the chief waved his cup at Mitch. "Okay, run it down for me."

"We got two dirty cops."

The chief slammed his cup down. "Aw, fuck. Are you sure?"

"About ninety percent."

"Who?" the chief demanded.

"Let me lay it out for you. See what you think first."

"Christ, Mitch, just tell me."

"No. Look, Chief this is freaking me out. Man, if I accuse these guys and I'm wrong? You don't want to be involved in that."

The chief raised his hands in surrender. "Okay, lay it out for me, and I'll drink my coffee."

"Few days ago, there was a suicide at the King's Court." Mitch glanced at the chief, who shrugged. "Flea bag motel just north of downtown. Call came in early in the morning that there was a body in one of the rooms.""

"Hardly shocking news."

"Oh, but it gets better," Mitch assured. He spun the; laptop to the chief. "This is the guy." The chief looked at the picture of a smiling man in an expensive suit. "That is one William Joseph Forsyth. Lawyer from DC."

"I take it, not the type you'd expect to be staying at the King," the chief observed.

"Exactly," Mitch agreed. "The thing is, this got cleared as a suicide in less than a day. They waited for the autopsy to make it official, but it was already written off."

"What did the autopsy say?"

"Guy died of a gunshot wound to the head. The injury was consistent with a self-inflected wound. Forsyth had GSR on his hands. Toxicology said he was swimming in booze. More than three times the legal limit. He'd also taken several pain killers, for which he had a prescription for."

"Okay, sounds like a text book suicide."

"Does, doesn't it?" Mitch said with a nasty grin. "Question is, why does a guy come all the way to Tucson from DC just to off himself?"

"Maybe he didn't come here for that, maybe it was the heat that pushed him over the edge."

"Yeah, that's it," Mitch grumped. "But I'll bet you breakfast, that firm he worked for was tied to either Van Zandt or Braxton."

"You know that for sure?" the chief asked growing serious.

"No, I haven't got that far along. But his address is suburban DC, be one helluva coincidence if he wasn't connected up with all this stuff."

"You're right, now you mentioned two dirty cops, how exactly do they tie in?"

Mitch frowned as the waitress brought their plates. "You fellas need anything else?"

"No, thanks," Mitch replied shortly.

The chief shot Mitch a hard look, then smiled up at the waitress. "No thank you, this looks delicious," he said mildly. He waited until she walked away. "Tell me about the cops."

"Okay," Mitch said, playing with his eggs. "The two detectives who caught the case, I think they were paid to make sure it went down as a suicide."

Mitch deliberately didn't mention their names. If the chief wanted the names, he could get them easy enough. If he wanted to distance himself from the mess, he could simply choose not to find out who the cops were and let Mitch handle it. "These two, they weren't the crew in the barrel."

The chief was splashing salsa on his eggs, he stopped raising an eyebrow. "If it wasn't' their turn in the rotation, how did they manage to be assigned the case?"

"Well, now, that's the story," Mitch said, pushing his plate away. "See, the call came in early in the morning. Normally would have went to the crew that was up. Shoulda went to the crew that was up, but our boys were in early, Johnny on the spot. Being such great guys, they volunteered to take it."

The chief chewed his food deliberately, swallowing before answering. "Did they now? Perhaps we should have a little ceremony. Give them a commendation."

"Yeah, that would be good."

"So, do these guys make a habit of coming in early?"

"First time anyone can remember. The watch sergeant said one of them kept coming up front. At the time, the sergeant thought he was just grazing for doughnuts. But he was right there when the call came in and offered to take it."

"Johnnie on the spot?" the chief commented and Mitch nodded. "Is this all you got?" he asked and got the same nod. "Damn, that's pretty thin."

"It's paper fucking thin."

The chief wiped his mouth carefully with a napkin and pushed his plate away. "Okay, Mitch, say I believe you. Where do we go from here?"

"That depends. Do you believe they are guilty?"

"I do."

Mitch nodded. "Alright, as I see it we can do one of two things. We can pull them in and put them in the box. See if they want to cut a deal."

"They're cops. I doubt with what we have you could break them down."

"You're right, I think. Not with what we got. So, we look at them. Pull their phone records, look at their bank records, and we go back over the case. We need to find what they covered up. Give us a lot of leverage if we can show it was murder."

"You think it was murder, then?"

"Doesn't make any sense to cover it up otherwise."

The chief nodded. "That's right. Can we prove it wasn't a suicide?"

Mitch frowned toying with his water glass. "I don't know, I haven't looked at the file yet, but they have had several days to nail things down. Might be hard to make a case."

"Do you want to get IA involved?"

Mitch shook his head firmly. "I don't, not at this time, but I do want to look at any files they might have on these guys."

"Haffner isn't going to like that."

"I don't give a shit what he likes," Mitch said quietly. "For all we know, these guys are innocent. I'd like to keep it quiet."

"That's probably best for now. But I want to know their names."

"Are you sure? You can stay out of it. Might be best if you put some distance between yourself and this."

"No, I want to know."

"Jones and Jenkins."

The chief nodded, not giving away what he was thinking. "What's your impression of them? Could they do this?"

Mitch shrugged. "Of the two, Jones is the best investigator. He's not great, but he's steady and he's thorough. Works at it."

"And Jenkins?"

"He mainly rides on Jones coat tails. Likes to throw his weight around. He's a bully when you get right down to it. If you ask me, that's why he became a cop."

"What does that tell us? Could they have done this?"

"When I stop to think about it, Jenkins doesn't really surprise me to learn he is mixed up in something like this. Seems to be always looking for an easy way to do things. Jones on the other hand, I always thought he was straight."

"I can talk to Haffner. I can tell him I want to see the files on all the detectives."

"That will get out pretty fast," Mitch observed.

"I'll lean on Haffner, but you are right. It will get out, but not as quick as you asking for two files. Can you get by a few days without the files?"

Mitch frowned, twirling his water glass. As an investigator, he hated putting off looking at evidence. But to be realistic, he didn't expect to find much in the files. The chief was right as well. Once Haffner was contacted, it would be a matter of days before word got out.

Once it was out, it would be a matter of hours before Jones and Jenkins heard about it. If they were guilty, they would be warned. Slowly, Mitch nodded. "You're right. We should hold off on that, but I want to surveil them."

"You got it. Don't worry about the overtime."

"I was also thinking we should tap their phones and wire their houses and cars."

"Be tough to get a warrant with what you got, but it's a good idea."

Mitch nodded receiving the message. Do it whether he got a warrant or not. Mitch swirled his water, choosing his next words carefully. "You know the FBI agent I have been liaising with?"

The chief chuckled dryly. "Liaising is an interesting word. I heard she spent the night at your place."

"Shit! How did you know that?"

"I have my sources," the chief said, laughing at the look on Mitch's face. "Relax, I called your house to let you know I was running later than I had said. She answered the phone. I wasn't sure it was her until I saw the look on your face just now."

"Shit, for a minute there, I thought you were having me followed."

"Don't worry," the chief said, laughing. "What were you going to ask me?"

"Geena. I wanted to bring her in on this."

The chief ran his thumb under his chin. "Do you think that is wise? Or are you thinking with your dick?"

"Maybe, but my dick is pretty smart." Mitch smiled. "She's pretty good, and there are some things the bureau can check, that wouldn't get back to Jones and Jenkins."

"I don't know. Damn, I hate to lose control of the information."

"If they are guilty, it's going to get out sooner or later. Bringing in the Bureau could be a good move, PR wise. And if they are innocent, hopefully it won't ever come out we were looking at them."

"What happens if the Bureau leaks it out before then?"

"I'm hoping they won't. Geena has good reason to keep it quiet."

"And what might that be?"

"That FBI agent that was killed out by the airport was a good friend of hers. She asked him to run some things for us and he ended up dead. She's taking it personal."

"No doubt," the chief said. "If she runs an investigation through the Bureau aren't you afraid it will get back to Van Zandt? Obviously, the man has sources inside the FBI." All of a sudden, a slow smile broke across the chief's face. He slapped the table. "Hells bells! Mitch, you are one sneaky son of a bitch. You want it to get back to Van Zandt that we know about Jones and Jenkins."

Mitch shrugged, playing with his water glass again. "If Van Zandt tries to warn them, with the taps and the wires in place, we should hear about it."

"What if he decides to cut them loose?"

Mitch shrugged again and took a drink. "What do we have to lose?"

"Alright, bring her in, but it's up to you to keep her in line. I don't want the FBI big-footing our investigation. This is going to get out about Jones and Jenkins, but we want to control it. Have it come out on our terms. If these guys are innocent we have to establish that early on."

"You got it," Mitch said and started to rise.

The chief motioned for him to sit back down. "I need to ask you about your relationship with this Reynolds chick."

"Shit, that was years ago. There's nothing between us now."

"Except a daughter."

"You heard about that?"

"Like I said, I have my sources." The chief smiled warmly. "Your daughter. When do you meet her?"

"Sometime in the next few days. "

"When do I get to meet her?"

Mitch smiled uncomfortably. "Uh, anytime I guess," he replied, not sure what to say.

The chief laughed. "Boy, you are in for an eye-opening experience." The chief laughed again, shaking his head. "Is this going to be a problem for you? Becoming a dad and trying to run a case like this is going to be a lot to juggle."

"I can handle it," Mitch said, shortly.

"I bet you can." The chief leaned back his face serious as he studied the younger man. Mitch could see it in his eyes as the older man made his decision. "By rights though, I should pull you off this case."

"Bullshit," Mitch said flatly.

Unruffled, the chief pulled a piece of toast from Mitch's plate and nibbled on the corner. "You have a clear conflict of interest, with Reynolds, and now with getting your daughter, what's her name?"

"Josie."

"Very nice," the chief replied, nodding approvingly. "But by rights, I should get someone else to run the investigation."

"You can't do that, sir. It would take too long to get a replacement up to speed."

"I know." The chief shifted in his chair, dropping the piece of toast onto his plate. "Mitch, you are by far the best investigator on the force. We need your best effort on this."

"I'm doing everything I can think of."

"Okay, keep doing it. But remember, if this thing blows up on us, people are going to be pointing the finger of blame at you and me."

"Like I said, I am doing everything I can think to do. We are running hard on every lead that comes in. We'll pull this guy in a few days."

"I'm sure you will. Just let me know if you need anything from my end."

"The files are the only thing for now. When the time comes to look at them, I was thinking we might want to bring the union rep in on it. He ain't gonna be on our side, but it'd be nice if he wasn't against us."

The chief laughed. "I keep forgetting how new you are to administration. The minute you became a supervisor, you became an asshole. Forget about getting any help from the union. Time comes we need to involve them, I will handle that."

"Sure. What about Brody? It may come down to seeing what we can squeeze out of his fat ass."

The chief took the last sip from his coffee, then carefully wiped his mouth with the napkin. "Fuck him. For all I care, you can haul the bastard out in the desert and beat him black and blue with a rubber hose."

"And Van Zandt? I mean, as far as I can tell, all of this leads right back to him."

"Van Zandt, huh?" The chief frowned, looking like he had bitten into a lemon. "He's a powerful man. It would take some finesse. Couldn't go in there yelling and screaming with him."

Mitch smiled. "Actually, that was exactly what I was thinking. Kick down his door, maybe break a few things on his desk."

"Do you think that would be wise?"

Mitch shrugged. "I don't know. Part of me says stay away from the man, but I keep thinking maybe I should brace him. See if I could rattle him a little. I bet in his whole life, nobody ever slapped his ass against the wall."

"Do that and he might end up owning the whole city. Let's think about that. For all we know, cops have been slapping him against walls his whole life."

Toying with the salt shaker, Mitch nodded reluctantly. "You're right. We don't know enough about the man. We need to ramp up and get some back ground on the man. I'm just running out of people and hours in the day."

"You need more people, take them. Whoever you want. Overtime isn't a problem. Let's just get this finished. Bring that girl home."

Mitch nodded rising to leave, when the chief laid a hand on his arm. "Oh and, Mitch, don't forget about your daughter. She's going to need you. Spend some time with her."

Carl Braxton's Apartment Upper West Side New York NY June 18th 2018 Monday Morning

There are moments in a person's life, a single moment that changes everything. It changes everything they are and everything they will be. For most people, they don't even recognize those moments when they are happening. But they happen all the time; days that redefine an entire life.

Carl Braxton was having one of those days. At the time, he certainly didn't realize it. Had no clue that this day would change his life forever. It all started simply enough. He was eating breakfast in his New York apartment. He wasn't alone, a young lady sprawled on the couch, scrolling through her phone.

She was naked, but even so Carl wished she would go. He cleared his throat, trying a gentle nudge to get her started moving. "I'm just having bagels for breakfast, since I need to go into the office early this morning." A lie, he was planning to head up to his cabin in New Hampshire. "You want one?" he asked, holding out a bagel.

The girl, Braxton thought her name might be Zoey, barely looked up. "No, I'm good," she replied, showing absolutely no signs of leaving.

Braxton cursed under his breath, searching for a way to get her out of the apartment. Sweating a little, he checked his watch. The housekeeper was due any time, and Braxton had a feeling that the old shrew reported back to Jillian everything that went on.

For a second, Braxton thought of Tamera. She should be settled in the new place in San Diego. With Van Zandt's help, he'd gotten her into a nice little house close to the beach in La Jolla. In time, Braxton would purchase the house for her. A new Ford Escape, registered in her name should already be in the driveway. Van Zandt was handling it all, and said he could keep it quiet, but Braxton couldn't help but wonder what this was going to cost him. In the grand scheme of things, Braxton wondered how far he could trust Van Zandt. Boy now there was a question. Braxton knew that Van Zandt was a snake, but Braxton felt safe as long as their interests were intertwined, but after that, he better watch himself.

"Huh, that is so weird."

Carl grunted, jerked out of his thoughts by Zoey's words. "What did you say?" he asked, hoping she was asking for a cab.

"I just got the weirdest text."

"What was that?" Braxton asked, thinking he couldn't possibly care less about the answer.

"It says, *Tamera Schroeder is dead, she was killed Saturday night.*" Zoey made face. "Is that not the creepiest thing?"

For a second, Carl froze, his skin clammy and bile rising up his throat. He felt trapped and thought he could actually see the walls closing in on him. "That is strange," he said, sounding like a bad actor reading from a cue card. "Who's it from," he croaked, having trouble breathing.

"Oh, I don't know," Zoey replied, her breasts jiggling as she shrugged. "Who cares? Some creeper."

"Do you even know a Tamera Schroeder?"

"Oh, as if."

Carl felt a pounding in his chest, and the walls felt like they might crush him. Fuckin' Van Zandt! He knew all along that he shouldn't trust the prick. Van Zandt must have texted her. Wait. How could he even know about Zoey? Braxton just met her last night.

Drawing in a ragged breath, Braxton glanced wildly about. Was the apartment bugged? He stared at Zoey who was paying him no attention. Could she be a plant? In a flash, Braxton remembered Van Zandt bragging about how he had put a girl next to Brody to watch him and report back. Could Zoey be doing that?

In a flash, he knew she was!

"Get up, get dressed!" he shouted, "You've got to go."

"What? We haven't even had breakfast," she protested, pouting. "You said we could go shopping."

"I said get your ass dressed!" Braxton roared, bounding across the room. He grabbed her wrist, dragging her off the couch and slinging her across the room.

She bounced off the wall, and into his arms. He slapped her face, then shoved her in the direction of the bedroom. "Get your shit and get your ass out of here!" he screamed, spittle flying from his mouth.

Rubbing the red spot on her cheek, Zoey opened her mouth like she might say something, but Braxton took a step towards her. With a small bleat, she scurried into the bedroom.

His heart racing and his palms sweating, Braxton stumbled to the liquor cabinet. "Fuck me," he growled, grabbing a bottle of scotch. He took a quick pull from the bottle, then a deep breath. As the shaking subsided, he started to think. Just how fucked was he?

Tamera had been pregnant. Of course, the father of her baby would be the natural suspect in her death. Braxton scrubbed the side of his face with a meaty palm. Could they pull DNA from a fetus? Oh hell, for sure they could. If they could pull DNA from a single hair, then certainly they could get it from an unborn fetus.

But would they? Well, that answer was as plain as a turd in the punchbowl. He'd said it himself, the father would be a prime suspect. The police would do everything they could to identify the father. Including getting samples from everyone who they might suspect being the father. They could very well ask him for a sample.

Would they have reason to look at him? They had been careful. As far as Braxton knew no one knew about the affair. He hadn't been around the campaign for a few weeks and definitely not while they had been in Arizona.

He should be clear.

Still he should stay away from the campaign. He had been planning to go to the cabin for a week or so, that was a good idea. Let things die down. If he gave the cops no reason to look at him, he would be okay. And in six months or so there would be a dozen new murders for them to worry about. Braxton took another small snort from the scotch and replaced the bottle. He began to breathe a little easier. It was going to be alright.

The smile which was starting to grow on his face froze when a horrible thought jumped into his mind.

Somebody knew!

Somebody sent that text to Zoey. Shit, it had to be Van Zandt. Braxton stared blankly at the wall. Oh shit, where was his head? Of course, Van Zandt knew about the affair. Braxton had practically told him everything when he asked for Van Zandt's help to get Tamera out of town. If it suited him, Van Zandt would make sure everyone knew. Braxton looked wildly about, almost expecting the cops to break down his door any second.

Braxton felt a heavy sorrow crushing down upon him. It wasn't fair. He was a good person. But he would go to jail. He hadn't killed her. It wasn't fair. Braxton pounded his fist into the wall, it wasn't right.

Fucking Van Zandt.

On impulse, he grabbed his phone. He was dialing, when he saw Zoey slinking along the wall towards the door.

With a roar, Braxton surged to his feet. To do what, he had no idea. A rage was boiling through him, almost obscuring his vision. He might have slapped her, or he might beat her to death.

What he might have done, never happened as Van Zandt's condescending voice spewed from the cell phone. "What?"

Braxton stopped, shaking his head, like an animal that has been hit. In his rage he forgot he had called. As he hesitated, Zoey scampered from the apartment. Braxton stopped in the center of the room, bowing his head like a bull about to charge. "Braxton, what do you want?"

Immediately upon hearing Van Zandt's voice, Braxton's anger switched from Zoey to Van Zandt. "You killed her. You son of a bitch!"

"No, you did," came the mocking answer.

"What?"

This time Van Zandt openly laughed. "You killed her when you knocked her up, or when you couldn't control her."

"You killed her," Braxton hissed.

"Me?" Van Zandt asked, feigning innocence. "I never even met the lady. I would have no reason to kill her. You on the other hand. You knocked her up, so maybe you killed her." Van Zandt chuckled, obviously enjoying himself. "Could have been your wife I guess. Now she had a motive!"

"You rotten cocksucker!" Braxton screamed, and had Van Zandt been in the room, he would have beaten him to death. "You can forget that deal in Arizona. I will personally make sure it never goes through."

Van Zandt considered asking how Braxton thought he could actually do such a thing, but then thought the better of it. "Don't worry, you and your wife are safe. For now. Right now, the police think they know who killed Miss Schroeder." In an instant, Van Zandt's voice changed. His tone went from friendly to something hard, with an ugly edge. "One phone call could change that."

"What do you mean?" Braxton stammered.

"They think the reporter Jackson Pyle was a serial killer and he killed Miss Schroeder." Van Zandt paused. "And at this time, your wife knows nothing about her being pregnant."

"I see no need for her to know that."

"I agree," Van Zandt said heartily, but then the nasty voice was right back. "And as long as you and I understand each other she won't." Van Zandt left the threat unsaid, but it hung in the air.

"What do you want me to do?" Braxton asked his anger gone, replied by a greasy, nervous feeling.

"Do?" Van Zandt sneered. "What I want you to do is keep you dick in your pants, suck it up and you and your bitch wife to hold up your end!"

Van Zandt killed the connection, tossing the phone on the table. He stared thoughtfully at the phone. It was a prepaid, but after that conversation it had better go away. He picked it up, crossing to the sink. At the sink, he ran a bowl full of water and dropped the phone into it.

A smile broke across his face, as he watched the phone sink. He'd only been half truthful with Braxton. From his sources inside the Tucson Police Department, he knew the cops were thinking that Jackson Pyle killed Tamera Schroeder.

Van Zandt smiled again, very pleased with himself. As long as the cops thought the reporter had been a serial killer, they would look no farther to find her killer. They wouldn't even wonder why she had been killed. A motive was not needed. She was an attractive female, for a serial killer that would be enough.

But.

But if they were at all competent, and Van Zandt's information told him they were. Then they would soon find out the nipples were fakes.

Once that happened, the police would reassess, they would start looking for a motive. The pregnancy would lead the police right to the Braxtons. Van Zandt smiled. From the beginning, he always knew, he had too many partners.

CHAPTER ELEVEN

Northwest Tucson AZ June 18th 2018 Monday Morning

Heading home, Mitch called the office, catching Jerry. "Hey, man, what do you have going? You real busy this morning?"

"Not yet, just getting here. I was fixing coffee."

"Good. I want you to pull the file on a suicide over at King's Court Motel bout a week back. Guy was from DC, so I just want to make sure he wasn't involved in all of this. Take a look at it, but keep it quiet."

Hartek laughed. "Don't want to ruffle any feathers?"

"You got it. Anybody else in?"

"Wade is here. He's still fussing over Pyle's shit."

"Has he got anything?"

"Naw, just something bothering him. You know how he gets, fussy as an old widder woman."

"Alright, have him, take a look too."

Jerry turned serious, catching the intensity in Mitch's tone. "You got it, boss," he said, hesitating a little. "What are we looking for?"

Mitch hesitated a little himself. It wasn't that he didn't trust Jerry and Wade; he didn't want to contaminate their investigation. "I'm not sure," Mitch said finally. "Look it over. It just seems strange to me that a guy would come all the way from DC to kill himself. Be one helluva coincidence with all we got going on right now."

"That is weird," Jerry acknowledged, and Mitch could almost hear him thinking. "So just read through the file?"

"If it looks okay to you guys, then that should do it. I don't know, it just strikes me as odd that with all this Brody stuff tying back to DC and now this? A dead body from DC?" Mitch swung into his driveway. "Just give it the once over. That should do it." Mitch hesitated, shutting off the car. "Oh, and I may be a little late getting in. I have to stop for a DNA test."

"Good luck with that." Jerry hesitated a beat. "However, you want it to turn out."

"Yeah."

Mitch entered the house, smelling the coffee all the way out in the garage. Tromping through the kitchen, he saw Geena curled up on the couch looking particularly sexy in one of his old shirts. She was sipping a cup of coffee, reading the paper.

"I hope you don't mind, I helped myself to your paper."

Mitch shrugged. "Ain't my paper. It's the judge's. He'll flat have your ass when he finds out."

"Ha!" Geena shot back. "I think the judge likes me, he'll just blame you."

Mitch swore under his breath, knowing she was right. Damn it, he'd hear about that damn newspaper for the next six months.

"I thought you abandoned me," she accused.

"Sorry about that, I had to meet with the chief," Mitch said, holding up the bag he carried. "I brought food."

"Einstein's, you're forgiven then." Geena said, coming off the couch. "He called here," she said, rummaging through the bag.

"Yeah so he said."

"What were you meeting with him about?" she asked, pulling the spread from the bag.

"Cops," Mitch grunted. "Dirty cops. I have a couple of guys I may want your people to check out."

Geena looked up from spreading cream cheese on a bagel. "Does this have anything to do with what happened to Todd?"

Mitch nodded grimly. "Sure. It's all connected."

"I take it these cops are some of yours?" she asked and Mitch nodded. "You realize that if we open an investigation, it might get back to Van Zandt? Look what happened to Todd."

Mitch didn't answer, crunching angrily on his bagel. Geena tossed her bagel on the counter, carefully licking her fingers. Taking a napkin from the bag, she cocked her head studying Mitch as she dried her hands. "So you have thought about that? You want it to get back to Van Zandt." She frowned at him. "Do you think that is wise? You could be putting them in danger."

"I know," Mitch replied quietly. "I have thought about it." Frustrated, Mitch tossed his bagel away. "Damn it, I am not going to feel guilty about this. They are grown men, if they chose to get involved with this, then that's their own bad luck."

Geena cocked her head, studying Mitch. "What exactly is going on here? What did these guys do?"

Still angry, Mitch tersely laid it out for her. She listened carefully taking it all in, showing nothing of what she might be thinking. When he finished, she leaned back. "What exactly do you need from me?"

"I was hoping you could have someone run their bank accounts. See if they've been paid, maybe we can trace the money backwards."

"I wouldn't hold my breath on that. Van Zandt didn't get to where he is by not knowing how to cover his tracks."

"Yeah, I know, but we have to look. Pull their phone records; see who they have been talking to. I'm thinking that they were either brought in by Tanner, or they brought him in."

"I take it you want this run through the office in Quantico?"

Mitch nodded. "That's seems to be where the leak is. The work can be done from here, but run it through your office."

"What about surveillance? You want us to handle that?"

Mitch blew out a sigh, letting the Bureau handle that would certainly make it easier. If Jones and Jenkins turned out to be innocent, it would give him some deniability. And he was running out of people. "No, we should handle that," he finally decided.

"You sure, the Bureau has some of the best people at that."

"Maybe, but I don't want Van Zandt to know we are watching them."

"Are you sure? We've seen how Van Zandt deals with encumbrances. You'd be putting them out there in harm's way."

"I know. I'll brief the surveillance teams of the threat." He smiled wryly at Geena's skeptical look. "Believe me I want to keep those guys alive."

"That would be good. They might be the first link back to Van Zandt. Maybe the only link."

"I know. I'm hoping that if Van Zandt makes a run at them, it might piss them off enough to roll over on him."

Geena shrugged, not quite blowing it off. "Might work."

"Tell me about Van Zandt."

Geena shrugged slowly. "I don't really know him. I met him on the Salters' case of course, but I've only spoke with him a couple of times since."

Mitch smiled, shaking his head. "But you've been looking at him over all these years. Sure you want Carter, but what about Van Zandt? He's absolutely the big fish in all of this. I gotta think you've looked him over, at least a little."

Geena nodded, dusting crumbs from her fingers. "He's not a big man, but you do get a sense of power from him. He is very neat, very precise, in everything he does."

"What about the trials? Defending the murderers? Why even bother with that? Can't pay that much."

"Personally, I think they are a test of some type."

"Testing himself as a lawyer? Or living vicariously through the men he defends?"

"Who really knows? Around the office we have people who lean both ways. Before you ask, I think he gets his jollies defending these guys. I think he enjoys hearing about their crimes. I think it gets him hot thinking he is a part of it. Of course he absolutely thrills at vanquishing other lawyers in the courtroom."

"So, how long is that going to be enough? These guys usually accelerate. How long will coaching from the sidelines be enough? How long before he wants to get in the game for real?"

"Who's to say he has remained on the sidelines?"

Mitch raised an eyebrow. "So, you think he has killed?"

"Maybe, but how does that help us if we can't prove it?"

"I'm not sure," Mitch said, pacing back and forth. "The thing is the case is spider webbing on us. The investigation is fragmenting as well. We need some focus. We need to find a center to this whole thing."

"And you think Van Zandt is the center?"

"I do. There's the good Senator of course, but I get the impression Van Zandt is using her as well. Besides we nail Van Zandt, we'll get Senator Braxton as well. Van Zandt is the key," Mitch grunted, still pacing. "We need to run down the little things, they all tie in, but we need to start focusing some resources on Van Zandt."

"He'll feel it," Geena warned. "As soon as we start any kind of investigation into him, he'll know about it."

"That's okay," Mitch decided. "Might even be good. The guy strikes me as a plotter and a planner. He doesn't seem to make many mistakes. Maybe, if we could move him off his plan, get him to reacting to us for a change, he might just step in the shit."

"Does that help Angie Brody?"

"Maybe," Mitch grunted. "If he starts feeling some pressure he might let her go or at least keep her alive."

Geena shrugged, noncommittally. "Might work. What do you have in mind?"

"Well we are looking at Jones and Jenkins, that's a place to start." Mitch stopped pacing. "For now, maybe we pull in everything we can on him without him feeling it, and go from there."

"Go where?"

"Don't know, but maybe after we study him a bit, we'll know," Mitch resumed his pacing, idly rubbing his chin. "I'll have some of my guys do the initial work up on him. We know he has sources in the Bureau, but we should be alright if we run it through my office."

Geena laughed, shaking her head. "Are you crazy? He has two of your guys on the payroll right now. He'll know the second you do as much as a Google search."

"They ain't my guys," Mitch grumped, but she was right. He'd gotten himself worked up and forgotten about Jones and Jenkins. Damn it, they might have to hold back on Van Zandt.

"How are we going to find Carter? And Angie?"

"I don't know, Carter seems to be dug in pretty tight." Mitch picked up his putter, tapping it against his shoe. The thing is if he's staying with some scumbag, chances are we'll know that particular scumbag. Tucson's small enough that we know most of the assholes."

"Most but not all. He could be with someone you've never heard of."

"You're right about that but anybody we don't know we can run though the box. Won't be that many names."

Geena frowned. "Knowing Carter, he might have done a home invasion. We should consider that."

"You're right that is a possibility, but again if we narrow the search area that is something that can be checked." Mitch felt a cold hand on his spine as he considered what it would mean if Carter had actually done a home invasion. He certainly wouldn't keep the residents alive, easier just to kill them. But of course, that brought its own set of problems, folks not showing up for work, or missing appointments, those sorts of things got noticed. "Probably not a home invasion," Mitch decided, feeling a wave of relief wash over him. "Too many problems with that."

"Neighbors watching," Geena agreed, nodding. "That is a relief."

"Yeah." Mitch sat down across from her, pouring his cup full of coffee. "I think he probably rented a place. He had time to set that up in advance."

"With Van Zandt's money he could have bought something."

Mitch nodded absently. "Could have, we should look at that."

"Alright, you convinced me. What's the first step?"

"We need to meet. Your guy here in Tucson and I'll ring the chief. We divvy up the work load, setup the ground rules and get a liaison between us so we can share info."

"Who do you want at the meeting?"

"For now, just you and Dockett. You trust him?"

"I trust him to do what's best for himself first and for the bureau next, but he's not a leak. He's too tight-assed and up tight to even consider doing anything out of bounds."

Mitch nodded along as she spoke. That was his take on Dockett as well. "You must have crossed paths with him," Geena observed. "What do you think?"

"We never saw eye to eye," Mitch admitted. "I always kinda figured him for a bit of a weasel, but he is loyal to the Bureau."

"From what I hear, that's Dockett."

"Okay, just the two of you and me and the chief for now. I'd like to keep this contained for a few days."

"What about your two guys? Do we get started on them?"

"If you know somebody to call go ahead. I'd like to get that going right away."

"I'll make the call on the way, if you'll drop me off at the field office."

They walked into the garage, then Mitch stopped cold, Geena bumping into him. "What?" she asked.

Mitch just shook his head, holding up his hand. "Shit," he muttered, slowly walking around the car. "Damn it, I'm missing something."

"What are you missing?"

"I don't know," Mitch said, unable to shake the feeling that he was missing something. "Something you said," he added.

"What did I say?" Geena asked.

"Man, I can't place it. You said something important and I missed it," Mitch grumbled opening the door of the Mustang.

"Give it some time, it will come to you."

"Maybe," Mitch grumbled, his mind racing, the key poised in his hand. "Screw it," he said slapping the key in the ignition and starting the car. He backed out of the garage, the feeling that he was missing something nagging at his mind.

They both worked the cell phones while they drove. Mitch called Ollie and told him to pick up Brody.

"What if he don't want to come?"

"I don't even want you to ask. Just through his ass on the ground, cuff him and read him his rights. Tell him he's under arrest then hold him until I get there."

"Okay." Mitch could almost hear Ollie grin over the phone. "Did I tell you we were having trouble with the phone down at the station?"

"No, what seems to be the trouble?"

"Can't get an outside line. Might be a few hours for he can get a call out to his lawyer."

"Well, shit, that's a tough break. Don't see anything we can do about it though."

"Nope, not a damn thing."

Mitch smiled, then changed his mind. "I tell you what, send some uniforms out to mark him but hold off picking him up for a while."

"Unies? I take it, you want him to see them?"

"Yep, let him know he's being watched."

"We can do that. When do you want him?"

"If you don't hear from me pick him up at four."

Mitch closed the phone with a snap. "Brody, we're gonna try and shake something out of him."

"Can't hurt anything," Geena said. "Our people are ready to see if they can take a quick peek at Jenkins' and Jones' bank accounts. They are going for a federal warrant now."

Mitch frowned, not sure he liked that. "They're cops. It won't be in their Wells Fargo checking. It'll be subtle."

"I know," Geena said with a weary smile. "These guys have done this a few times."

"Yeah, I know," Mitch apologized with a sheepish smile. "I'm just getting cranked up."

"You nervous?"

"A little, lots riding on the next few days."

"I didn't mean that. I meant the impending arrival of you daughter."

Mitch felt a quick butterfly jump in his stomach. "Aw shit, why did you have to mention that? I've been trying to not to think about it."

"So, you are nervous?"

"Nervous? No. I'm scared shitless."

Geena laughed, a pleasant, merry sound. "Don't worry, you'll do fine. I have a feeling you'll be a great dad."

"Aw, Christ, I don't know."

"Is your chief going to make the meeting?"

"Yeah, I just talked to him. He'll be there."

"Good, because to be truthful, I don't know if I could get Dockett there otherwise. Half the office thinks you are involved in this and Dockett is one of the half."

Mitch laughed. "Don't worry. Just get him there."

They rode a few blocks in silence. "Do you think that it's a coincidence, or do you think they actually planned it out?"

"What do you mean?"

"The fact that it looks like you could be involved. If things had worked out a little differently, we might right now seriously be working you as a suspect."

Mitch shrugged. "Could just be coincidence."

"I hope so. It scares me to think they might be that smart and that good at manipulating us."

Mitch grunted, sliding the car to a stop in front of the FBI offices. "Don't worry about it. We're gonna nail these bastards."

Mitch dropped Geena off, and headed to the clinic. He was almost to the clinic when his phone rang, erupting with a ring tone he hadn't heard in a long time. Even though he hadn't heard it in a long time, he still recognized it immediately. Oh shit, Mitch thought looking warily at the phone. Kathy Reynolds.

Mitch glanced at the clock in the stereo of the Mustang. She must have made bail in record time for a Monday morning. She must have a good lawyer, Mitch thought, then changed his mind. More than likely it was Tanner. Tanner would know the system inside and out.

For a second, Mitch was tempted to let it go to voice mail, he had enough on his plate today. The last thing he needed was Kathy ragging on him. And as he remembered, she was pretty good at it. With a sigh he picked up the phone, no use putting it off, he'd be thinking about it all day.

"Hey, Kathy."

"Don't hey me you son of a bitch," she snapped.

"I see a night in jail hasn't sweetened your disposition any," Mitch commented.

"You're an asshole," she hissed, and if contempt was poison, her tone would have been lethal. "They won't let me go pick up Josie, or even see her. I suppose that is your doing?"

"I'm sorry about that. And your wrong, that's all Social Services, they said it would be less confusing for Josie if you weren't popping in and out. I didn't have anything to do with that."

"Bullshit, you arrested me!" she accused. "How could you do that to the mother of your daughter?"

"First of all, getting arrested that was all on you. I don't know what you are mixed up in, but it is crashing down. You need to look at make yourself a deal." Mitch paused, hoping she might give him something he could use. "As for the other, I didn't even know I had a daughter. If she's even mine?"

"Yes, she's yours," Kathy said, in a milder tone.

Mitch felt a jumble of emotions rush over him. Anger, fear, pride and love collided in his mind but Mitch also felt hurt. "Why didn't you tell me? Was that why we split?"

She laughed a bittersweet sound. "Ha, that is just like you to forget why we broke up. We broke up partly because we didn't believe in the same things, but mostly because we were both too busy to sustain a healthy relationship."

"Oh," Mitch grunted, swinging into the parking lot of the clinic as some of it came back to him. She'd be pissed that he was out all night chasing a case, and he would get mad when she was gone for several days with some political thing. "Still, why didn't you tell me about Josie?"

"I don't know," Kathy said, her voice so hushed, Mitch could barely hear it, but he heard the sob that followed. "I didn't know how to at first and I was afraid you would be upset. I just kept putting it off, then after a while, I thought, what's the use?"

"Gee thanks," Mitch said unable to keep the sarcasm out of his voice, as he eased into a parking spot. "Why did you do it now? Because you were heading for trouble?" Mitch demanded.

"Maybe."

"Maybe my ass," Mitch grunted, killing the motor and feeling the heat immediately begin to build in the car. "Kathy, you need to tell me exactly what is going on here."

"There's nothing going on!" she shouted.

"Kathy don't bullshit me. We are very close to putting this together. Once we do we won't need you, and there will be no deal for you. When that happens, you are going to go down hard."

"It was just supposed to be an ordinary business deal. Nobody was supposed to get hurt."

"But people are getting hurt." Mitch paused, hoping she would tell him something. Kathy wasn't a callous person by nature. "If you know something you need to tell me. They are going to kill that girl."

"There's nothing for me to tell!" she cried, real anguish in her voice.

Mitch hesitated, trying to figure out if the anguish was from the fact that she was in trouble or that her silence might contribute to the death of a young lady. "Mitch, if I knew one single thing about that girl being kidnapped, I would tell you in a heartbeat. Tanner and I aren't involved in any of that."

"Bullshit," Mitch said, bluntly. "Tanner confessed to a murder he didn't commit, and the gun that was used was found in your house, and it was in fact your gun. Your prints were on the shells picked up at the murder scene. You're in it up to your eyeballs."

"Damn it, Mitch. My dad bought me that gun years ago, when I moved to Arizona. He insisted that I have a gun if I was going to live alone. I honestly hadn't seen it or thought of it in years. I still can't believe that it was used to kill that poor man."

"Well it was, no doubt about it," Mitch said rolling down the window. "Kathy, did Tanner know about the gun?" Mitch asked, letting some bad cop creep into his voice.

Mitch could almost feel her anger flash over the cell phone. "No," she said in a tone that would have burned spines off a cactus. "He did not. That gun has been in a shoe box in my closet since the day my dad bought it and he left to go back to Connecticut."

"Was it loaded?"

"Yes, my dad made me load it before he left. That's how my prints got on the shells!" she cried excitement edging out her other emotions.

"You're saying somebody stole your gun, used it to murder Jackson Pyle and then put it back?" Mitch asked, letting her see his skepticism.

"That's exactly what I am saying. That's the only way it could have happened."

"You better hope not," Mitch informed her.

"Why's that?"

"Because you will never get a jury to buy that. If it comes down to a jury believing that story, you will be going to jail."

"Oh no," she whispered.

"Yeah," Mitch told her. "You and Tanner need to come in. Make a deal."

"I will talk to him."

"Don't wait too long." Mitch said, and killed the phone, wanting the last word. Give her something to think about.

For a second Mitch stared at the phone wondering how this changed things. He had no doubt that somebody took the gun and put it back for the cops to find. Tanner?

Not likely, Mitch decided, getting out of the car. Tanner might take the gun but he would have no reason to put it back and he'd have every reason to see it gone forever.

Who then?

The question was still on his mind as he pushed through the door of the clinic, feeling a blast of cold air wash over him. "Can I help you?" the severe looking woman behind the counter barked her tone indicating she had no interest in being helpful.

"I'm here for a DNA test."

"Court ordered?"

"It will be," Mitch answered wondering what that had to do with anything.

"Fill these out," she snapped, slapping a clipboard on the counter and then making a show of ignoring him.

Fighting the impulse to flip her the bird, Mitch carried the clipboard to the waiting room. After filling out the required paperwork, he waited for ten minutes, more nervous than he could believe. In that ten minutes he changed his mind several times about which way he wanted it to go. It shocked him that there was a big part of him that wanted it to be true. A daughter! Wasn't that something?

Another part of him, the cop part, said this was crazy. A bit past crazy. In fact, crazy was way back in the rearview mirror. He couldn't possibly take care of a kid. His job kept him out all night many nights. What to do then? Wasn't like he could take her along.

In his mind, he argued the point back and forth and he was no closer to the answer when they called his name. He jumped at the sound, feeling like a ten year old about to get some shots.

"So how does this work?" he asked the cute nurse as they walked back to the examination room.

"We take a sample from you, and then compare it to a sample from your daughter."

"Does it hurt?"

The nurse laughed. "Don't worry tough guy, I think you will survive. It's painless."

"I was thinking of my daughter. She's been through a lot these last few days." Mitch said defensively.

"Sure you were," she said, punching his arm. "But don't worry, it really is painless. But anyway, your daughter already gave her sample, her mom brought her in last week." She smiled at Mitch. "You have a lovely daughter. If you are as brave as her, I will give you a lollipop."

"I'll want cherry," Mitch said, grinning from ear to ear.

FBI Field Office Tucson AZ June 18th 2018 Monday Morning

Geena watched as Mitch roared away. She sighed, then turned to face the music. Dockett was going to throw a shit fit. Walking up to the office, she wondered how Mitch would handle things. He'd take the initiative. Which is what she should do.

She wasn't under Dockett's command structure; she didn't have to follow his orders. She needed to take control of this confrontation.

At the door, she paused, taking a deep breath. Blowing it out she shoved opened the door and blew into the office. Dockett was leaning over an agent's desk. He straightened. "Agent Dixon where have you been? You've got...."

"Never mind where I've been." Geena snapped, cutting him off and liking the feeling. "Right now, I need a cup of coffee then I need to see you in your office." Geena crossed to a small rolling table and poured herself a cup. Stirring it with her finger, she turned back to the room. "I'm going to meet with Special Agent Dockett for about fifteen minutes, and then I'm going to need reports on Agent Holland's murder. I want updates on the scene, a prelim on the autopsy and a report on what we know from the hotel. I don't want reports on what we knew an hour ago I want complete up to date intelligence. So, if you need to make phone calls I suggest you get to it." Geena took her finger out of the hot coffee and licked it off. "Any questions?" Seeing there were none. She pointed her still smarting finger at Dockett's office. "Let's go."

For a second she thought he would refuse. He glared at her then finally gave a quick jerk down on his vest, and spun on his heel, taking a couple of quick steps to his office.

"Agent Dixon, I must protest your attitude."

"No you must not. What you must do is sit there and listen." Geena snapped back. "I am not part of your command. This case is being run out of Quantico and I am the agent in charge. Do you understand?"

Geena waited until he managed a meager nod. "Good, now I called you in because I needed a team at the crime scene, but this is still my case, and if you have a problem with that let me know right now. I can have a team flown out here today and you and your guys can go back to watching the border for Poncho Villa. Do we have a problem?"

"No ma'am. No problem."

"Good." Geena said. "But one thing you should know, this thing is big and it involves some heavy hitters. We screw this up and we'll all end up checking congressmen's dogs for tics. You and your team up for it?"

Dockett didn't flinch, meeting her gaze steadily. "I've got a good team. We are more than up to the task."

Geena smiled. "I do believe you are right. Okay, I was out of line, barking at your team. I apologize. That won't happen again. You run them, but we need to get what information we can from Agent Holland's murder quickly.

"Am I hearing you correctly? We are moving on from that? Finding Agent Holland's killer is not the main thrust of this investigation?"

"That's correct." Geena said crisply, feeling a hollow ache in her chest. "Believe me, I want the man who killed Todd. He was a friend of mine. But I also want the man who ordered it done.

"Do you have any leads on that?"

"Yes, but we don't have time right now. I do want to hear your people's report, later today you and I have a meeting with Detective Mitchell and the Chief of Police."

Geena nodded as Dockett frowned. "I realize you are going to this meeting a little behind, but that's to be expected. I'll fill you in as much as I can," she offered.

"What about Mitchell? I have a strong feeling that he might be involved in all of this."

"I don't think so."

"But there is substantial evidence to suggest he is."

"I know, but I've worked with the man for several days." Dockett shrugged, ready to concede to her authority, when she gave a curt nod. "You are right, though. My instincts aside, we should pursue this. How do you feel about putting one person on Mitchell?"

"I would certainly feel more comfortable with that. I think perhaps two or three would be better."

"Noted, but let's stick to one for now. You and I can reassess that at our daily meeting."

Dockett was taking notes. "Fair enough." he said without looking up from his writing. "Now about this meeting with TPD? What is the purpose of this meeting?"

"I want to set up an inter-agency task force. There are some aspects of this case; they can handle better than us."

"Are you talking about complete sharing of information?"

"Yes, it won't work otherwise." Geena smiled. "Of course, for now we won't share that that we are investigating Mitchell."

Dockett almost smiled. "Of course not."

"Alright, shall we go hear some reports?"

"Of course."

"After you."

Dockett stepped out of his office. "Okay people what have we got? Miller, anything on the room?"

Miller a burly red-head with a crew cut stood up. He looked like a dim-wit but Geena noticed he moved with the grace of an athlete. "Not much there, sir. A massive amount of prints, which was to be expected. Preliminary reports aren't promising.

Dockett nodded like he'd been expecting that, which Geena realized he probably had been. "Anything else?"

"Maybe," Miller said, glancing at his partner. "There was a chair moved in the room. We could tell by the marks in the carpet that it usually sat by the bed and facing the door. It had been moved to the other side of the bed, not visible from the door. We took a sample of something from the arm."

"Blood?" Dockett asked, a trace of excitement creeping in.

"No, sir. I think it was gun oil." Miller moved to an easel with a drawing of the hotel room. "If I may sir?" he asked and Dockett nodded quietly. "We feel confident in assuming the shooter was in the room first. He pulled the chair to here." Miller marked the spot on the easel with a laser pointer. "This way he is hidden from the door by the bathroom wall. While he waits he rests the gun on the arm of the chair. Then when Agent Holland comes in the killer forces him to lie on the bed where at some point he shoots him."

"He was killed on the bed then?"

"Yes sir, no doubt about that."

"Okay, good report."

"Wait, that's not all." Miller said, a hint of a smile playing on his lips. "We pulled some fibers off the chair. Looks like off a jacket of some kind." Now the smile burst into bloom. "And Marcy found hair on the carpet behind the chair."

Dockett smiled as well. "Very good work, both of you. We need to run the DNA against the data base."

"Doug, if I may." Geena said cutting in. She waited until Dockett gave her a quick, firm nod, then looked to Agent Miller. "You might want to run it against Jacob Simon Carter. I know he's in the system. He's our number one suspect in this."

"Did you say Justin Carter?" another agent asked.

A look of irritation flashed across Dockett's face. "Agent Ferris, we'll get to your report in a second. Miller anything else?"

"No, sir."

"Okay, Agent Ferris, please proceed with your report."

"Okay, the room where the murder took place was rented by Agent Holland. Caller ID confirms it was his cell phone used to make the reservation. Nothing out of the ordinary about his checking in."

"Okay, what were you going to say earlier?"

"Well the room next door was rented by a Justin Carter." Ferris looked expectantly at Geena. "Does that mean anything?"

"It does," Geena replied. "Justin Carter is an alias Jacob Carter has used several times since coming to Tucson." Geena paced a couple of steps thinking it over. "He rented the room next door?"

"Yes ma'am. The room was rented but as far as we can tell, it was never used."

"Anything come from that room?"

"Not yet, but the room is still sealed. Didn't really look like anyone even went in."

"Did you get a description of Carter?" Geena asked.

It was Ferris' turn to smile. "Better than that, we've got a picture." Ferris picked up a photo from her desk. "We were able to pull it from hotel's security video."

"She handed the photo to Geena who glanced at it. "That's not Jacob Carter." Geena looked back at the surly face in the photo. It looked oddly familiar, but at least two decades older than Carter. "Anybody recognize?" Geena looked around the room, but no one ventured a guess.

"Okay, anything else from the hotel?"

"Nothing out of the ordinary."

The report on the condition of Todd Holland's body brought nothing new. After the reports, Geena and Dockett retreated to his office. "We need to get an ID off this picture. Jacob Carter is at the center of his whole thing. He's hiding out somewhere here in Tucson. Maybe with this man."

"We need to find this man." Dockett said, nodding firmly. "You are right, I think he can lead us to Carter."

"Okay, your people did very good work, but we have more to do." Geena smiled grimly. "Let's get on it."

Tucson Police Station Tucson AZ June 18th 2018
Monday Morning

"What have we got on Forsyth? Was it suicide?"

"No," Jerry replied, then hesitated, looking around the group gathered around his desk. He shrugged, his eyes sliding back to Mitch. "I mean that's what my gut tells me, but I can't prove it."

"There's something really wrong with it, or you just got gas?" Ollie asked.

Jerry cocked his head pursing his lips. "The gun," he decided. "I got a big problem with the gun?"

"Gun don't fit?" Mitch asked, still sucking on his cherry lollipop. He pulled it from his mouth and pointed it at Jerry. "Why?'

"After I first read it, my first thought was; where did the gun come from. Guy flies into town and a few hours later he scores a piece? I mean, can't fly with a gun, so obviously he got it after he landed here. How the fuck does that happen?"

"Knew somebody," Wade commented, easing his leg up on the desk.

"Maybe, but I don't know how. He was from Minnesota, Wisconsin, some place like that. Went back east to go to school and stayed."

"Lots of people move here from back east," Wade pointed out. "He could have an old college buddy living here."

Mitch glanced over at the older man. "You think he's wrong?"

"Nope," Wade said. "The kid's right; there's something wrong. I'm just pointing out where we may be reading this wrong. We went into this thinking maybe it might be murder after all. Might be messing us all up."

"What about that?" Mitch asked, shooting a look at Jerry.

"Sure, there's that. I mean it would be the opposite of what Jonsey and Jenks did. They showed up; saw a bullet to the temple, contact burns around the wound, a note, pills, and the booze. Hell, you see all that and you're already about eighty percent there. Calling it a suicide I mean."

"What did they miss?" Mitch asked quietly.

"The gun," Jerry said and everybody else nodded.

Mitch leaned back. "We need to track the gun?"

Jerry smiled, but Mitch caught the under tones of worry in the smile. Jerry held up a sheet of paper. "Already did. I just got this. It's his gun, Forsyth's."

Mitch frowned, understanding Jerry's worry. Did that help or hurt. "Hell, if it was his gun, maybe he drove?"

Jerry was already shaking his head. "Not according to TSA. He bought a ticket, flew to Denver, then here. They say he boarded the flight, and before you ask, they have no record of him checking a gun," Jerry replied.

"Okay, forget the gun for a second, was there anything else"

Jerry shrugged. "There's just a lot of weirdness. His wallet was missing for one, and then why fly all the way to Tucson, just to eat a bullet?"

"Frequent flier miles, maybe he wanted to use them up," Ollie grunted.

"Maybe a bitch. Followed her out here and she blew him off for good. Sent him over the edge," Wade suggested.

"No mention of a girl in the note," Jerry countered. "Seems to me if you're gonna do it over a girl, you'd want her to know. Make her feel guilty."

"And there is the note. I don't like the note, in general," Wade said. "Usually, like Jerry said, they try to put the finger on somebody, or it's short and sweet. This thing kinda rambled. Been my experience when they ramble, they don't finish the job."

"Cry for help," Carly put in.

Wade snapped his fingers, pointing at her. "Right you are, girly. They leave a long note, it's a cry for help, they really do it and the note is basically goodbye. And don't forget, the note was written on a laptop. Who does that? You write a suicide note, that's personal. You don't do it on a machine."

"Then there's the computer," Jerry said. "It's been cleaned."

Mitch frowned, tossing the sucker stick towards the trash. "What do you mean, cleaned?"

Jerry gave a shrug, waving a hand at Wade. "Ask the expert."

"It was completely cleaned of all its history. Programs looked like they did when it was brand new. No music, photos, hell, he hadn't even played one game of FreeCell."

"Maybe it was new," Ollie suggested.

Wade was already shaking his head. "Didn't look it. Case had a few scratches, keys showed signs of wear. This machine had been used. Probably used a lot, but well cared for. I think somebody was worried about what might be pulled out of the computer, so they cleaned it."

"But can't you still retrieve it?" Carly asked. "I've always heard that you can't really erase computer data."

"You can if you change out the memory and the hard drive," Wade answered.

"Was that what was done here?" Mitch asked.

Wade shrugged. "Looks that way."

"Wouldn't that take a long time?" Carly wondered.

"Not if you knew what you were doing," Wade said, shaking his head. "I think the killer bought a brand new computer, same model as Forsyth's. After he does Forsyth, our guy just switches out the parts, then types in the note."

"How sure are you about that?" Mitch asked quietly.

"About eighty-five percent. I found that a lot of the programs were free trials, like you get with a new computer."

"Maybe just left over from when he bought it?"

"Naw, even the operating system is a free trial. Besides, all them free trials woulda been expired by now. They ain't, they're still active."

"Maybe we should think about searching Forsyth's house back in DC," Ollie said, glancing across at Mitch. "You think, maybe Geena could put us in touch with somebody to do the search?"

"Good idea. I'll talk to her about it," Mitch said, already thinking about Len Dykes. "Okay what can we do with this?"

"We were going to take the computer to Mickey, see if he could take it apart and find any prints."

"Guy was good," Ollie grunted. "Ten bucks said he wore gloves and you don't find dick."

"Probably," Wade admitted. "But we can tell if the parts was switched. They'll be the only clean thing inside that computer. Computers, especially laptops get real nasty inside, more than you can believe."

"How about the components that were switched?" Carly asked. "Do they carry ID numbers, could we track them back to where they were sold?"

Everybody looked to Wade who shrugged. "Fuck if I know, but we could ask."

"Do that," Mitch said, then reconsidered. "But if it gets too time consuming, drop it." He looked at Wade. "If you're up to it, I want you to keep after this and keep looking at Pyle. The rest of us can get back to finding Angie Brody."

"Uh, Mitch," Jerry said, hesitantly. "There is one more thing about Forsyth."

"Yeah, what?"

Jerry looked around the room like a school kid about to be jumped by the class bully. "Aw shit," he said, then met Mitch's gaze. "Do you think Jonesy and Jenks fucked up or...or do you think it's possible that they tanked the thing?"

Now it was Mitch's turn to glance around. He got up and closed the door. "Okay, I believe that Jones and Jenkins worked it so they would draw the case and then they swept it under the rug."

"You may be right," Jerry said quickly, relief sounding in his voice. "Remember when I said that the wallet was missing and they ID'd him from fingerprints?" he asked and everyone nodded, as Jerry dug through the report. "Here's the notation," he said, holding up the report so they could all see. "Now look at this, Jenkins refers to the victim as Forsyth here when he is listing the personal items found at the motel. A good twelve hours before the ID was made."

"Don't mean shit," Ollie said. "Jenks was always lazy. He coulda been typing the reports days later. Knowing Jenks, he probably was."

"Nope," Jerry said, gaining confidence. "He did it on one of the station computers, it's time stamped. Like I said, twelve hours before he got the prints back."

"Fuckin' Jenkins," Ollie swore.

"Coulda gotten the name off the motel registry," Wade offered.

"Nope," Jerry countered shaking his head. "Forsyth checked in under the name Clay Kershaw."

Wade scowled, grabbing his Dbacks hat off his desk and jerking it down on his head. "Fucking Dodgers fan. Deserved what he got."

"The computer. Or maybe the note," Carly suggested. "Maybe the name came from one of them."

"Computer was clean," Ollie reminded.

"Note wasn't signed either," Jerry supplied.

"Wallet is missing?" Wade wondered, scratching the wiry stubble on his cheeks. He shot a quick glance at Mitch. "You think this guy had a shit load of cash in his wallet and Jenkins and Jones took it?"

"The missing wallet is problematic," Carly said quietly.

"You're right," Mitch said, picking up on what she was thinking. "If it was indeed murder, where is the wallet? Makes no sense that it is gone. It just creates questions, and the last thing Jones and Jenkins would want is questions."

"That cuts both ways as well," Carly continued. "If it is suicide then why is the wallet gone?"

"Maybe he was feeling generous at the end and gave it away," Wade suggested.

"No," Mitch decided. "He might give away the money, but he would keep the ID."

"A person committing suicide would want to be identified?" Carly offered.

"I would think so," Mitch replied. "I got to say the wallet being gone bothers me."

"Boss, I have an idea why the wallet is gone," Jerry offered.

"What is that?" Mitch asked, making a rolling motion with his hand.

"Let me ask you something first?" Jerry offered and Mitch nodded. "How did you come to find out about this suicide?"

"I was thinking about Jackson Pyle and that he must have gotten some good dirt on the Senator to get a couple of interview sessions with her. So I looked up what he had been writing about. A couple of his last stories were about this case."

Jerry smiled, nodding his head like a man bobbing for apples. "One of those stories happened to mention Forsyth was from DC and so you had me check it out."

"Aw shit," Mitch muttered seeing where Jerry was headed. "That's right."

"If you hadn't been looking into Pyle, or if someone else would have written the stories they would have gotten away with it." Jerry leaned back in his chair looking very proud of himself.

"Shit, got away with what?" Ollie growled. "What am I missing?"

"Beats the hell outta me," Jerry replied with a wide smile. "But you can bet Forsyth somehow connects back to Brody and Van Zandt."

"How can you be sure?" Carly asked. "Because the wallet is missing."

"Sure, for whatever reason they needed to get rid of Forsyth, but they knew if it got out that he was from DC we'd connect it up to Brody and Van Zandt. So they took the wallet and ID."

Mitch nodded feeling a little sad. "They knew a couple of days was all they needed to keep his name out of it. After a day or so, nobody would be talking about a suicide over at Kings Court." Mitch glanced at Jerry. "Like you said, if I hadn't been checking into Pyle's stories it would have went right under the radar." Mitch shook his head. "Fuckin' Jackson Pyle, if it hadn't been for him." Mitch stopped. "Man I think maybe Jackson called him out as Forsyth before the ID was made."

"You sure about that?" Wade asked.

"Yeah, I think so," Mitch said, replaying the timeline in his head.

"Does that mean Jackson Pyle was working with them?" Carly wondered.

"I don't know," Mitch said thinking about it. "From the tone of his articles, I don't think so. bHe was suggesting there was more to it than a simple suicide."

"And apparently there was," Carly observed.

"Apparently," Mitch agreed, but still not wanting to believe two cops he knew and had worked with would sell out.

"You say Jenks was keeping the paperwork caught up?" Ollie demanded looking at Jerry, who nodded. "That alone tells me this was something special. I've worked around that asshole for twenty some years and the brass has always been on his ass about not keeping his paperwork current. Guy was always behind. If he was keeping the book up to date that tells me they wanted this to go away quick and clean."

"Shit, maybe now the gun does makes sense," Wade said.

"Sure, you fake a suicide, makes some sense to use the guy's own gun," Jerry agreed.

Mitch felt a sinking feeling settle in his stomach. Jones and Jenkins. They'd fucking done it. He blew out a sigh, pacing the room. His gaze settled on Wade." Okay you stay with this. Nail down everything you can just keep it quiet. Keep after Pyle too. He figured out enough to run a blackmail on Braxton. The rest of us have to stay focused on Angie Brody. Anything new on that?"

Carly raised her hand slowly. "Maybe, I'm not sure." She glanced down at her notes, even though Mitch was pretty sure she knew exactly what they said. "I ran all the names of everyone involved through the box, seeing if there was any matches. Then I ran them against victims of crime, looking for something that might tie back to Jackson Pyle and I got a weird hit."

Mitch nodded, feeling a tingle race up his back. This was something. "What did you get?"

"I got one hit that fit that criteria. A biker from San Diego named Henry Flores. He came up twice, once as a victim and once again as a known associate of Chappy Miers. Flores and Miers were arrested at the same time out in San Diego a few weeks back. No charges were filed, so I called out there."

Carly looked down at her notes again. "I spoke to the lead detective, a John Hernandez. He said his group was working off a tip when they busted them. Hernandez had heard that two bike gangs were setting up a pipeline to bring drugs up from Mexico, through Arizona and then out to Cali. Hernandez told me they received a tip that a huge buy was supposed to go down."

"So what happened with the case? Ollie asked, hitching his chair closer. "Why did the charges get kicked?"

"Hernandez and his guys couldn't hold their mud and they jumped the gun. They thought it was going to be a major exchange but it wasn't. It was just a meet and greet, setting things up. Chappy had brought some samples, but there wasn't enough to get them on possession with intent to sell, so it was busted down to mere possession. DA didn't want to mess with it, so it got kicked."

"Interesting, but how does that tie to us?" Mitch asked.

"Like I said, when I crossed the list against victims of crimes, Henry Flores came up again. He and three others were killed a couple of days ago, close to the border, just south of Aravaca."

"Hmm, no shit?" Mitch mused, glancing about the room. "Ideas?"

Hartek shrugged. "Sam Logan told us he was looking into a new drug pipeline coming through here. Sounds like the old bastard knew what he talking about, but I don't see how it cuts into our case."

"Probably right," Mitch agreed. "I'll run it by Sam, see what he knows. Okay anything else?" He glanced around and got a few head shakes. "Alright, let's run with what we got."

As the group broke up, Mitch retreated to his office to call Len Dykes. He was scrolling through his address book when Ollie lumbered into the office a sour expression riding on his face. Scowling mightily, Ollie dropped into a chair, propping his feet on Mitch's desk. He unwrapped a piece of gum, tossing the wrapper in the direction of the trash can, missing it by a mile.

"Shit, just make yourself at home."

"Aw fuck you. I'm starting to get pissed," Ollie said, smacking on the gum like it was the sole source of his misery.

Mitch grinned at the older man. "You're always pissed."

"Bite me. This is different. Damn it, Mitch, I am starting to like this Brody girl."

"Oh yeah?" Mitch said, placing his phone on the desk.

"Yeah. There is more to her than your normal co-ed hottie. This girl might be the daughter of a total scumbag, but there is something real about her."

"Tell me about her."

"She's kinda funky. Did you know she sings?"

"I knew she was dating this drummer, but I didn't know she could sing."

Ollie chuckled. "I didn't say she could sing, I said she did sing. She ain't very good, but she gets up there. She takes food to a shelter, helps out down there pretty regular. And all the while pulling a double major at the university."

"So let's find her," Mitch said, leaning back. "What am I missing? Why haven't we found her?"

"Might not find her," Ollie said, his voice raw. "I can't help but think she's already dead."

"I don't think so. I think she is still alive," Wade said, grimacing as he eased into a chair beside Ollie.

"You doing alright?" Ollie asked.

"I'm fine, just not used to being up and around this much."

"You need to take some more time?" Mitch asked.

"Naw, Doc has been telling me to use it more."

"Lazy fucker," Ollie giving Wade a shove.

"Hey, why get up when I can have a pretty young barmaid bring me my beer?"

"What did you mean when you said you thought she was still alive? What makes you so sure?" Mitch asked cutting across their banter.

"If you think about it, if we are reading this at all right, they have no reason to kill her. They are using her as leverage to get Brody to fall in line. They kill her, then they lose the leverage. Even if Brody isn't giving in yet, still no reason to kill her."

Mitch scowled, rubbing his chine. "Shit maybe we should just go ahead and drag Brody in and find out what they want."

"Might be a problem with that," Ollie said, rubbing the side of his face with a heavy hand. "That's what I came in here to tell you."

"What's that?" Mitch demanded, not liking where this was going.

"I sent a squad out to his house like you said. They just called in, he ain't there."

"You had them go to the door?" Mitch asked.

"Yup, had them take some coffee. After talking to you I figured we wanted him to know we were watching," Ollie said, sporting a rogue's grin, but then he sobered. "When he wasn't there, I had those guys stay and set on the house, see if he comes back and I sent another car to his construction site."

"Let me guess," Wade requested. "No one there either."

"Nope. Harrison from the building department was there. He told the uniforms that Brody had scheduled an inspection for eight this morning, but hadn't showed. His so-called foreman, that Cal Pierson, he wasn't around neither"

"Alright let's see if we can find him. Drag his ass in here in cuffs when you do," Mitch said, scratching his chin.

"I'm going to call Geena's cop friend in DC and see if he can get a search done on Forsyth's house."

As they filed out, Mitch picked up his phone, bringing up Detective Dykes' number. "Detective Mitchell!" Dykes' voice boomed through the phone after just one ring. "What can I do for you today?"

"How do you know I want something?" Mitch asked, smiling.

"Hell, nobody ever calls a cop, not unless they want something," Dykes said, then added with a chuckle. "Especially other cops."

"Well shit, I guess you got me there," Mitch admitted sharing Dykes' laugh. "I was wondering if you might have time to do a search for me?"

"Hell, I ain't got time to wipe my ass," Dykes said with a heavy sigh. "What have you got?"

Mitch smiled, he could hear the curiosity underneath all of Dykes' belly-aching. "We have an apparent suicide here. The thing is, the guy was from your neck of the woods."

"Oh yeah, I caught the fact that you said apparent. You thinking that it might not be what it seems?"

"There are some things that don't add up," Mitch replied, not wanting to get into it too deep. He didn't want to kick Jones and Jenkins under the bus just yet. "The main thing that has me wondering, is did the dead guy work for Van Zandt?"

"Well fuck, that does make it interesting, doesn't it. And you got that little creep Carter out there sneaking around."

"So, you can see why we are a little skeptical about it being a suicide."

San Xavier Mission Tucson AZ June 18th 2018
Monday Morning

Sam Logan sat at one of the outdoor tables at the mission, eating an Indian Taco. Though not Catholic, Sam loved this old place. He and Maureen came here often, the peacefulness helped to calm the buzzing in his brain. They would walk around gaze in wonder at buildings which were constructed hundreds of years before either of them was born.

They would hold hands, light a candle and talk to the silversmith's in the plaza. Sam liked talking to the smith's, they were men who still valued the old ways. More often than not, he would end up buying Maureen a ring or some other trinket. And always before they left, they would share an Indian Taco.

Today Sam felt almost serene, his brain more tranquil. He didn't know if it was this place, or the fact that he felt like he was once again doing some good. Whatever it was, today Sam was at peace. He felt like he could actually concentrate today and not have his thoughts flying around his head like ping-pong balls in a dryer.

He saw Dave and Ted lumbering across the parking lot, and one look was all it took to tell him that they were not at peace. Far from it.

Dave's face was red as a sunset, and the scowl riding on Ted's face could have stopped a charging bull. "Fellas," Sam grunted.

"Don't fellas us," Ted said, a little huffy.

Dave tipped his head at the Indian Taco in front of Sam. "Where did you get that?"

"That little shop over there," Sam said pointing with his elbow.

"Huh, might have to get me one. Are they good?"

"The best." Whatever else Sam might have said was cut off by Ted's grunting.

"Can we get down to business?" he demanded.

"Alright," Sam said, pushing his plate with the rest of the taco to Dave. "Help yourself." Sam turned his gaze to Ted. "You fellers seem to have a bug up your butts this morning."

"Damn right," Ted fumed. "You can't be going off and doing shit like that by yourself."

Sam nodded. "You're right, I should have talked to you boys first. I was afraid you might try and talk me out of it, and it had to get done. I owed it to those two kids."

"It ain't that, it's you going off by yourself with no backup." Ted managed a smile. "Not that we care what happens to your wrinkled ass, but if they would have gotten on top of you, we'd all go down. We have to be more careful."

"What he said," Dave mumbled around a mouthful of taco.

"Sorry, it won't happen again," Sam replied and glanced at the parking lot. "I guess the others aren't coming?"

"No," Ted snapped, his anger flaring back up.

Dave shook his head sadly. "Aw don't blame them, they didn't really think we were going to actually kill people."

"Why the hell not?" Ted demanded. "We sat right there and talked about it."

"Talking is different from doing," Sam said, mildly. "Questions is, what are they going to do now?"

"They aren't going to turn us in, if that's what you are thinking?" Dave asked and Sam nodded grimly. "They won't, but they do want out. They all got too much to lose if we get caught."

"Which we will eventually," Sam said, as his phone begin to ring. "Mitch," he grunted looking at the screen.

"What's he want?" Ted wondered, as the phone rang again.

"Be careful what you say to him," Dave warned as Sam picked up the phone. "That Mitch is a right sharp cookie."

"Yeah, yeah," Sam grunted, waving away their concerns. "What the hell do you want?" he growled as greeting.

"Damn them tacos are good," Dave commented as Sam stepped away from the table. "Might have to get me one."

"Get one?" Ted asked. "You just ate most of one."

"It was mighty tasty," Dave agreed, his eyes drifting to the little shop that sold them. "A full one though, that would just about hit the spot."

"Damn, man, you're going to drop dead one of these days, you don't stop eating like that."

"Everybody's got to go sometime," Dave agreed mildly, as Sam came back to the table. "What did Mitch want?"

"He wants me to take him out to the desert to look at the crime scene."

"You mean the place where you killed those fellers?" Dave asked.

"Shit do you think he knows you did it?" Ted wondered. "He knows what we've been doing?"

"Maybe he's got an idea about that," Sam said slowly. "He's called me more in the last week than in the last year."

"Shit," Ted growled. "Did he give you a reason why he wants to go out there?"

"Yeah," Sam said, rubbing his face and staring at the church. "He said, he thought that those killings might be tied up with the Angie Brody disappearance."

"Shit. They're not, right?"

Tucson AZ June 18th 2018 Monday Morning

Mitch left the headquarters, racing across town to pick up Sam Logan. The old man was sitting on the curb holding two cups of Starbucks. "Figured you'd want some of this pussy coffee" he said sliding into the car.

"Thanks." Mitch said taking the cup.

"Damn stuff was almost ten bucks." grumbled Sam.

"Yeah, but you have to admit it's better than the free cup at the station house."

"Yeah, but for the amount of money they charge the least they could do is put a shot of Jack in."

"Well if you would have invested in my projects you wouldn't be worrying about money."

"Yeah, I heard you got some money for my wife," Sam said, almost grumbling. "You can just give it to me."

"Ha! Fat chance of that."

"What you don't trust me?"

"No even a little," Mitch shot back.

Sam swore under his breath. "Ungrateful little prick," he fumed. "Here I am helping you out and this is the way you treat me."

"Damn right," Mitch replied. "Maureen would kill me if I gave the money to you.
You tell me you would give it to her, but I know better. I know it'd go right into your elk hunting fund. I heard you drew a license up in Colorado this year."

"Was gonna invite you along, but now you can kiss my ass!"

Mitch laughed. "How's the best way to go, out west on Ajo or go south down the interstate?"

"Time wise doesn't matter much, but the cell coverage is better on the interstate. Better stay on the interstate, case this hunk of junk breaks down, we can call for a tow."

Mitch laughed, punching the accelerator to the floor. The car leapt forward, sitting them both back in the seat. "Better hang on, old man." Mitch said.

"Shit, my wife has a Kia that will blow the doors off this rust bucket."

"My ass." Mitch grunted, letting off the gas. "So what's the scoop on this deal on this thing in the desert?"

"Shit, I'm not sure." Sam swirled the coffee in the cup, then took a swig. "On the first look it's real easy to say just a bunch of druggies."

"What do you see on second look?"

"Maybe it was a bunch of druggies, or maybe it was made to look that way." Sam went back to swirling his coffee. "You know I was in the Marines.

"You a jarhead? Yeah, I buy that."

"Fuck you, buddy. Anyway, I did some training as a sniper."

"What does that mean?"

"It means, I recognized something at the crime scene."

Mitch frowned across at the older man. "What do you mean you recognized something? Was this done by some professional?"

Sam was swirling his coffee again. "No, shit, maybe, hell, I'm not sure." More swirling, Mitch concentrated on his driving letting Sam think. "The thing is the shots weren't all that hard, but they weren't easy either."

"So, you say it would....wait, what are you saying?"

"I guess it wouldn't take a pro, but not any Joe off the street could do it. And it'd take a cold fucker to take those shots." Sam cocked his head staring up at the headliner. "But it wasn't just the shots, the way it was laid out, that was text book."

"So, it was a pro."

"Could be, or could be somebody who read a book."

"So where does that leave us?"

Sam finished his coffee and tossed the cup out the window. Damn, he hated lying to Mitch. But he did it anyway. "Fuck if I know. It's been bugging the shit outta me. If we got some pro knocking off drug dealers there's gonna be a war for sure."

"Take some assholes off the street," Mitch offered.

"Yeah, but always ends up with the wrong people getting killed."

"It's good for the arrest sheets."

"Yeah, screw you, whistle dick, be serious," Sam growled.

"I know, but what are you gonna do? If it's a drug war it'll play out in the end."   Mitch hesitated. He liked Logan and trusted him without fault. Over the years, they had worked together and shared information, but he wasn't sure he wanted to draw Sam into this mess.

Sam sensed the hesitation. "Look, Mitch, I know you got something heavy going down with this Angie Brody thing. You don't want to let me in, that's cool. It's your ass on the line, after all." Sam looked Mitch dead in the eye. "But if you need my help, I'll do what I can."

Mitch swung into the left lane letting the car unwind. "Shit I know that, Sam. The problem is this thing is getting big. You might be better off staying out. Some big names are involved. The kind of people that can flat ruin your career."

"Fuck'um. I'm sixty-six years old. I put twenty and change in the corps and I'm getting close to twenty-five with the state. I can pull out anytime, leave them sucking on it."

"These are people that could fuck up your retirement."

Silence settled over the car, then Sam grinned. "Like I said. Fuck'um. I can always get on driving a trash truck. Hell, maybe I could be one of them male prostitutes, you know, a gigolo."

Mitch laughed. "Good work if you can get it."

"Hell yes," Sam said, grinning, then turned serious. "How does my puny little drug murder out in BFE tie into those types of people you are talking about? Seems like a stretch to me."

"Could be," Mitch admitted. "You know Jackson Pyle?"

"Wormy piece of shit. Heard he got hisself blown away."

"Yeah, well we think he was blackmailing Jillian Braxton."

"Jackson Pyle?" Sam asked, almost sounding like he had a new found respect for Pyle. "Blackmail? No shit? What did he have on her? Think she was a rug muncher?"

Mitch shrugged. "I don't know, but he was granted at least two private interviews with her."

"Think they found out what he knew, and then had him killed?"

"Who knows? There was a dead girl in his bed. She was a staffer for the Senator. It was set up to look like Pyle was a serial. We found evidence of other killings."

"Doesn't surprise me. I always got a weird vibe off Pyle. I got no problem seeing him as a serial."

"Turns out he wasn't though. It was just a setup."

"No shit, was it a good one?"

"Not really."

"Huh, what do you mean?"

Mitch glanced sideways at the older man. "Well, everybody said the same thing you just said, that they weren't overly surprised to hear Pyle was a pervert and a killer."

"So, they knew Pyle." Sam declared.

"Somebody did," Mitch said, scratching his chin. "The thing is the rest of their set up sucked. I mean it looked solid at first, especially if you knew Pyle but it came apart pretty fast."

"Huh, guess maybe they only needed or wanted it to last a short time," Sam grunted. "So how does this tie to my thing?"

"Roscoe Tannenbaum copped to killing Pyle."

"And?"

"And your dead guys were in business with Chappy."

"And Chappy and Tanner have always been tight." Sam rubbed his face. "Damn, that is one long, rough, dirt road to travel just to connect up with my murders."

"It is," Mitch agreed, letting Sam think it through.

Sam had a habit of rubbing his face when he thought and the way he was working it over now, he wouldn't have to shave for a week. "How'd it go down with Pyle?"

"Early morning, he opened his front door and ate a full chip. Neighbor heard the shots, and then a motorcycle tearing away. Gave a pretty good description of Tanner. When we went to Tanner he up and confessed."

"He's good for it?"

"Nope," Mitch said, swinging onto the off ramp. "No GSR, and Tanner is on a security camera miles away at the time."

"So why confess?" Sam demanded, then answered his own question. "Shit he's covering for somebody. He damn sure knows he's on that camera. When it goes to trial, he can pull that out and walk, shooting you the bird all the way out the door. And now, you'll play hell trying to hook anyone else up for it."

"I know, I already cut Tanner loose. Not that it matters much, like you said, even if we run down who really pulled the trigger, it's gonna be hard to get any kind of a conviction. A jury is going to have a hard time seeing Pyle as a victim."

Logan laughed harshly. "Yeah, good luck with that one. You'd have to have some damn good dirt on a DA just to get them to even think about filing those charges.

"I know, I don't really give a shit about Pyle. What worries me is Tanner and Chappy Miers, they've always been tight. Now we got this thing out here."

"Still not sure how it ties into what you got going?" Sam said, being very careful with what he said. Damn, Mitch was a smart boy and he had a good crew. Of course, they knew Chappy and Tanner had run together for years. And now, somehow, they had already linked Chappy to Flores. He best be careful around Mitch. "What makes you so sure these two things are connected?" Sam asked, figuring he might as well find out how screwed he really was.

"Bout a month back Chappy and your dead guy Flores were arrested together out in Cali. Supposed to be a big drug deal but the cops out there couldn't hold their wad and jumped it early. Went in too fast and the drugs weren't there."

"Hell, maybe, Chappy was working on a new NAFTA accord for Braxton." Logan said with a snorting laugh.

"Shit, Sam, I'm serious here."

"I know you are." Sam looked across at Mitch, his face hard. "How long have we known each other?"

"I dunno, ten years maybe, probably longer."

"A long time." Sam agreed. "I'm gonna say something and I don't want you to take it the wrong way."

"You're talking about Kathy."

Sam nodded. "So, you knew about that. Well I'd say if Tanner is mixed up with something like this I'd say you need to look no further than Kathy."

"Probably," Mitch admitted. "I just don't know how to come at her."

"Bust her," Sam said. "Better yet, let me do it. After a night in lock up, I bet she'll talk."

"Well," Mitch said, for some reason he felt reluctant to say he'd put the mother of his child in jail.

"Aw fuck me. You still got a thing for her." Sam said. "Your dick is gonna get you in trouble."

"Naw, that's not it. We picked her up last night. She already lawyered up."

Sam laughed a hard, barking chuckle. "Was she pissed?"

"Steamed," Mitch said, then laughed. He shook his head at the absurdity of the whole situation "You don't know the half of it. She has a daughter. Turns out it might be mine." Mitch let out a long sigh. "Probably is."

Sam laughed pounding the dash. "Damn boy, you are truly fucked." He cackled then suddenly pointed. "Take that track. This is the way Flores came in." Logan pointed ahead. "The whole thing went down in the crossroad. Flores was parked here."

Mitch stopped in the same spot, as Sam pointed to their right. "The Mexicans came from the west then parked in front of us here."

Mitch tried to picture the scene. "Where was the shooter?"

Logan pointed to the southwest. "Up there. Nice little nest up there."

"How did it go down?"

"Flores showed up first, him and some biker named Brantley. They waited on the Mexicans. First shots took out the leader, a guy calling himself Sanchez. Flores made a run for the truck. Stupid fuck Brantley tried to stand and fight. Ignorant prick only had a shotgun."

"Any idea what was taken?"

"Cash, dope." Sam said, shrugging. "Word on the street is over a million in cash and a butt load of dope. Some new kind of designer coke."

"Any of it show up?"

"Not yet" Sam squatted in the shade, watching Mitch. "So how does this tie in with what you got?"

"I don't know," Mitch replied, shaking his head. "Why would someone like Jillian Braxton get tied up with Chappy Miers?"

"Muscle." Sam said simply.

"Yeah maybe. You might be right. But then we still have to tie Chappy to this shit." Mitch walked a long circle. "So what happened here that has you bothered."

Sam sat down. He took off his hat, frowning into the distance. How to spin this? "I would say the way this was done," Sam said slowly. "There's a definite military feel to it, but then the guy made some mistakes. Seems to me it might be some nut, who's read a lot of those stupid military magazines. The thing is, this guy looked through the scope and took the shots, not just everyone can do that. Makes me wonder how long before he likes killing. Maybe, he already likes it."

"You think we're gonna see this guy in a tower with a rifle?"

Sam shrugged. "That's the thought that's keeping me up nights." Sam walked over to a spot. "This is where Flores got it. The shooter let him get close to the truck."

Mitch looked at the ground, but could see no evidence that a human being had lost their life on this spot. The thirsty desert had already drank in any blood that was spilt and the wind had done the rest. "Cold fucker then?"

"Ice fucking cold."

"Look I got a meeting with the chief and the Feds. You want in on that?"

Sam took out a cigarette and looked at it. "If you need my help sure, I'll be there." Sam rolled the cigarette in his fingers. "I just don't know what I can add to what you're already doing. I'm not sure this cuts into your thing. I think Chappy is just trying to branch out."

"Maybe, but there's Brody. He's getting cash from somewhere. We can't find out where. Thought he might have taken on a partner."

"Shit," Sam said, and spat in the dust. "Probably Kathy," he grunted, while he tried to think. Mitch was putting this together faster than he thought.

Mitch nodded heading back to the car. "You're right. I'm just not sure where it's going."

Sam frowned, deciding he had to slow Mitch down a little. Give him something else to think of. "Be careful buddy, there's some talk going around."

Mitch stopped at the hood of the car. "What kind of talk? Who's talking?"

"That whistle dick Tim Harris for one, he's been saying you're in over your head. That you should never have gotten the job in the first place."

"Fuck him; he's been talking forever."

"Yeah, but the difference is, people are starting to listen."

"Come on, man, nobody buys into his bullshit."

"They are starting to." Sam flipped the cigarette away without lighting it. "Just watch your step. If you need some help just let me know."

"Sure, I don't know what you could do."

"Look, Mitch, you need to start getting some distance from this thing. Start delegating some of this. You got some people you can trust?"

"Shit, Sam, I'm not selling any of my people down the river. If it goes bad I'll take the heat."

"Aw hell, I'm not talking about that. Just get some distance for yourself."

Mitch started the car considering what Sam was saying. "I think we got a couple of guys involved."

"Your guys?"

"No, straight homicide."

"How involved are they?"

"I don't know. I think they were just rushing a homicide through getting it ruled a suicide. That was it."

"You sure about that?"

"Pretty sure. I'd say at least seventy-five percent sure."

"Oh crap, if they did that, you can bet your ass they did other stuff. You need to pin some of it down."

"I've got the Feds checking them out."

Sam took a quick step back. "Fuck me, the feds? Are you crazy?"

Mitch shrugged, a small smile leaking onto his face. "The Feds got themselves a leak. A direct leak to Van Zandt."

Sam took out another smoke, cocking his head at Mitch. He shook a gnarled finger at Mitch. "You are a smart fuck. I keep forgetting that." He cracked a nasty smile. "You realize you could get them silly bastards killed.

Mitch frowned, a worried look creeping on his face. "I know, I'm going to put people on them.

"You're really worried about them?"

"Like you said, I could get them killed."

"Shit man, I wouldn't waste two seconds worrying about those smucks. They climbed up on this horse themselves, let them deal with it."

"I don't know. The suicide was pretty convincing. They might not have realized what they were getting into."

"Probably did." Sam said, without much feeling. "You know, they knew the risks they were taking when they put their dicks in this particular light socket."

"You keep saying that. Won't make it any easier to live with it if something happens to them."

Sam shrugged. "So, what's your plan?"

"I'm hoping if Van Zandt makes a move against them it'll be something we can trace back to him."

"Not likely."

"Worth a shot though. "Mitch replied, considering Sam's point. "But, however it shakes out, if he makes a move against those guys, I'm hoping to use that to break them, get them talking. Use what they know to work backwards."

"What about the girl who's missing? You think she's dead?"

"No, not yet." Mitch looked over at Sam. "Between you and me, Angie Brody might be involved."

Sam whistled. "No shit. That something really you know or you just got a wild hair up your ass?"

"I was looking at her Facebook page today. She's friends with Kathy Reynolds."

"Facebook?" Sam howled slapping the side of his face. "You're on the Facebook? Geeez, why don't we pull into one of these truck stops and see if we can buy you a set of balls. Wouldn't even have to be full-sized ones. We could get some tiny fuckers out of the bargain bin. Get you a man card." Sam sent a scathing look at Mitch. "Fucking Facebook."

"Hey it's a link from Angie Brody to Kathy."

"And you were fucking her."

"Not for a long time," Mitch protested. "I hadn't even seen Kathy for years."

"But you have a daughter with her." Sam shook his head staring out the window. "Jesus, Mitch, anything in a skirt walking around Tucson that you didn't screw."

"Your wife, but I'm hoping to cure that this weekend."

Sam frowned, hanging his head a little. "Guess you've been busy and hadn't heard. Maureen left me. Walked out 'bout a month ago."

Mitch felt his face burn as he fumbled for words. "Aw shit, Sam. Man I'm sorry."

While Mitch searched for words, Sam let out a snicker. "You asshole." Mitch exploded

Sam slapped his knee. "You should see your face."

"Fuck off. Man, I was concerned."

"Aw shit, lighten up. You're getting to be a tight ass."

CHAPTER TWELVE

Arizona State Patrol Headquarters Tucson AZ June 15th 2015 Monday Afternoon

Mitch dropped Sam off. Idly singing with the music, he drove slowly back to his office. Somewhere, in the back of his mind, a stray thought was pecking at his brain. A little voice telling him something wasn't right with the scene in the desert.

So where did this figure in with everything else? On the surface, it seemed to be your run of the mill drug murder. After all, drug murders weren't all that uncommon. Drugs tended to bring out the worst in people. And drugs meant money. Mounds of money. Money certainly brought out the worst in people. Frustrated, Mitch shook his head, he was probably making too much of this. Chances were that the Columbian Cartel got wind of what Chappy and his partners were up to and took steps.

The fact that Chappy and Tanner went way back didn't mean that Chappy was involved with Angie Brody's kidnapping. It could be simply one of those weird coincidences that came up all the time. Every case Mitch had ever worked, had one little detail that didn't seem to fit, or could never be fully explained.

Still something about the murders, bothered Mitch. Coasting up to the light, Mitch tried to put his finger on what was bothering him. It was the manner in which the killings were carried out, he decided. To precise, too planned. Sam Logan was right, the killings had a military feel to them. Drug murders tended to be wild affairs, creating blood soaked, chaotic, crime scenes. Mitch had once worked a drug murder where only one person had been killed and another wounded, and in that one, tiny scene they had picked up well over a hundred spent shell casings.

But, this scene? Four people dead, and no shell casings? The scene wasn't bloody at all and there were no bullet scars on the rocks to indicate the shooter had sprayed gunfire wildly. This scene screamed cold precision to Mitch. Somebody had sat on that ridge and efficiently murdered four people, then coolly collected his brass, along with the money and the drugs.

Sam Logan was right to be concerned. One man had calmly taken on four. What kind of man would do that? Mitch tapped the gearshift. Certainly, one who was supremely confident in his abilities. And apparently with good reason. He fired eleven shots with no misses. At that range, that was impressive.

To Mitch, this sounded more like the type of operation that Braxton and Van Zandt might orchestrate than a Cartel hit. Not that Cartels didn't have a stable of killers, because they certainly did, but those men preferred to hose down the entire area with automatic gunfire. This was different. Eleven shots, no misses. That said something.

Wait.

Mitch scowled at the windshield, idly pounding his palm against the steering wheel. How did Sam know how many shots were fired? Mitch glanced at the case file in the passenger's seat. Was there something in the report that told Sam that? Crap come to think of it how did Sam know it was only one man on the ridge? Made more sense that it was two or maybe even three. Why would Sam assume only one shooter? Maybe ballistics were already back and that report said only one weapon.

As Mitch eased in to the station parking lot, a nasty thought snuck into the back of his mind. Could Sam be mixed up in this shit? Sam had been acting a little strange since that young couple had bought it out in the desert. Mitch laughed a little at the thought. He shook his head. Mitch shook his head as he parked the Mustang. Hells bells, this was Sam Logan. Sam was a straight arrow and true blue all the way through.

Checking his watch, Mitch saw he had a few minutes before his meeting. Cutting through the back of the station, Mitch hurried to his office. "Where is everybody?" he asked seeing only Wade Nichols.

Wade looked up from the device he was tinkering with. "Jerry took that laptop down to Mickey. Carly was around here and Ollie is still out beating the bushes for Brody."

"Shit, you think he skipped?"

Wade scowled. "If he did, I'd shoot the fucker myself."

"Yeah," Mitch agreed. "What you doing?"

"Trying to solve a mystery," Wade replied holding up an MP3 player.

"I can solve that one for you." Mitch smiled, pointing to the MP3 player. "That's an I-Pod."

Wade shook his head, making a tisking sound, and wagging his finger at Mitch. "You poor, dense, illiterate bastard. This is not an I-Pod; it is in fact a MP3 player. I-Pod, as everyone knows, is only a brand name."

"Okay smartass, so it is a MP3 player, big deal I have one."

"Just one?" Wade asked, a crafty look playing across his face.

Mitch shrugged. "Sure, why would I need two?"

"Yeah, why?" Wade replied holding the MP3 higher. He shook it at Mitch. "Now take this little fucker, it's cheap, holds about ninety songs and will run you about twenty-five bucks."

"Was that the one that Pyle bought the night he was killed?"

"Nope," Wade grunted, pulling another MP3 from an open drawer in his desk. "This is the one he bought. Now, it is an I-Pod, holds about three thousand songs and cost hundred and fifty bucks."

"Okay makes sense, he has an old crappy one, it gets full, so now that he is coming into money, he goes and gets another. He's got some cash now, so he goes high end. No real mystery there."

"You might think that but you would again be wrong." Wade picked up the first MP3, waggling it at Mitch. "It ain't near full, in fact just one song on it."

Mitch made a face. "Oh yeah? What's on it?"

Wade smiled. "*What You Give*."

Mitch nodded. "Tesla, circa nineteen-eighty-eight, good song. Killer intro and awesome guitar work, Frankie Hannah, and Tommy Skeogh at their best."

"Very good, 'cept that it didn't come out until the early nineties." Wade casually picked up the other MP3. "So, we gotta wonder, why go out in the middle of the night to buy another one?"

"If he was supposed to be meeting a girl, maybe a gift," Mitch said, then frowned scratching his chin. "Shit by the time he bought the MP3, he had to know he was being stood up, so why buy a gift for her?" Mitch could feel a tiny tingle race down his back, all of a sudden, he had a good idea where this was going.

"That was my thinking, but I checked anyway. I was curious to see what kind of songs a sleaze bucket like Jackson Pyle would give to a girl. Again, only one song."

"*What You Give,*" Mitch offered.

Wade nodded. "So that got me to thinking, and I couldn't remember seeing any CDs at Pyle's house."

Mitch frowned, trying to picture Jackson Pyle's house. "You know; I think you are right. I don't remember any CDs."

"Good, cause there weren't any. I know, I ran back over there to be sure. Guy had a few DVDs and some porn, but no music. No stereo either. In the whole house he had one clock radio, in the bedroom. Wasn't even set to a station. Just static."

"So, he wasn't a music buff," Mitch said, nodding, feeling the tingle of anticipation kick up a notch. Finally, maybe they were going to see what Jackson Pyle had on Senator Braxton.

"I looked on his laptop, he had a couple of programs to download music, but they hadn't even been activated." Wade held up his hand. "But, there was one complete album burned to his computer. Wanna guess which one?"

"Tesla." Mitch closed his eyes trying to remember all the Tesla albums. "*Bust a Nut*?"

"Oh, so close but again, so wrong," Wade said obviously enjoying himself. "*Psychotic Supper. Now* I looked at the inventory of his desk from the search warrant. One CD was listed, *Psychotic Supper,* want to guess what was the third single from that very album?"

"*What You Give,*" they said at the same time.

"Yup, topped out at number seven a year later in ninety-two," Wade added. "So anyway, I decided to give the song a listen."

"It wouldn't play," Mitch offered.

"You know it, every other song from the album on the computer played, but not that one. I even went down to evidence and got the CD, it plays all the way through just fine."

"What about on the MP3s? Does the song play on them?"

Wade snapped his fingers and pointed at Mitch. "Nope. Not on the laptop, or either of the MP3s," he said nodding. "See, I figure he saved his dirt on the Senator in the usual places, zip drives and maybe an email for the Senator's goons to find, then he stashed a couple of copies disguised as songs on these MP3s. I'm thinking he was probably planning to add a ton of regular songs later so this file wouldn't stick out."

"Makes sense, so what does the file say."

"Which brings us around to the mystery," Wade said with a grimace. "Little fucker used an encryption program to save it."

"Can you still get past it?"

Wade rubbed his curly hair. "Shit Mitch, I don't know. These things are supposed to be impossible to crack. Now, I found an encryption program on his computer. I guess that's what he used, so I picked up a copy of that program today. If I can figure out his password, I should be able to get in."

Mitch stood up pushing the chair away. "Do whatever you have to. We need that file. We can do another search of his house and office if you think he might have written down the password."

"Maybe, but I doubt if he would do that. He wouldn't want Braxton's storm troopers to find it. Mostly people will just use a number they can remember. Sometimes they get cute with combining address numbers with birthdays or phone numbers. Something like that."

"What about using a credit card number as the password?" Mitch asked. "The number is on the card and you carry the card with you."

Wade shrugged. "Maybe. I hadn't thought about it, but it is worth trying."

"Drop everything else you are doing. Do whatever you have to do to get into that file." Mitch had started to turn away, then stopped. "You say the files on the two MP3 players are exactly the same?"

Wade shrugged. "Sure, far as I can tell. File sizes are exactly the same."

"Okay, give me one. I have a meeting with the chief and the feds in about ten minutes. I'll give one to the feds, see what they can do with it."

"You bringing in the feds?"

"Yeah, we can use the resources."

"Good idea, give them this one," Wade said, holding out the cheaper MP3. "I heard the government made all these encryption programmers put in a back door in all their programs. If that is true, and not just some urban myth bullshit, the feds may be able to skip around the password and go in the back door."

"That would be good, the quicker the better," Mitch said, taking the MP3. "But let's keep it quiet that we have an extra I-Pod."

"Don't want to piss off your lady friend?"

"Not that, I'm just thinking there is always a chance that this MP3 might disappear once it gets into their hands."

"You got a nasty suspicious streak," Wade observed.

"Comes from being around assholes like you all day," Mitch said, waving at Carly as she came into their offices. He held out the plain, yellow file. "Hey take a look at this. See if anything stands out to you."

"What is it?"

"Sam Logan's case file from that shooting out in the desert. Look it over. See if anything jumps out at you. Maybe give that detective in San Diego a call, see if we can tie these guys to anyone besides Chappy."

"Okay," Carly said slowly. "What are you thinking?"

Mitch smiled, handing her the file. "I already know what I think. I want to know what you think."

Carly didn't return the smile and in fact, made a face at his back as he walked away. Still scowling, she opened the file, turned the first page and felt a charge surge through her veins. "Holy shit!" she exclaimed, forgetting to use her inside voice.

Mitch who was several steps down the hall, spun around and rushed back into the office. "What is it?"

Carly held up a picture of one of the victims. "This one, the one that Sam Logan is referring to as Calvin Ramsey. That's that fucker, Cal Pierson!" she said, shaking the picture at Mitch.

"Huh?" Mitch grunted, wondering what that meant.

"Pierson, that the guy that was sheep-dogging Brody?" Wade asked, and Carly nodded vigorously. Wade glanced up at Mitch. "Well we know now why Brody took off."

"What does that tell us?" Mitch asked, looking at the two detectives who both shrugged. "Alright, let's nail it down. Make sure it's him. Find out who he really is."

Arizona State Police Headquarters Tucson AZ June 18th 2018 Monday Afternoon

Sam watched Mitch drive away, cursing under his breath. Damn, that kid was smart. Not only smart, but he had a damn good crew. Sam could feel the pressure mounting. It was only a matter of time. Mitch and his guys would put this thing together pretty soon. He had a couple of days at the most.

Sam swore again. He'd thought for sure the baby thing would slow Mitch down at least a little. It would have freaked out most guys, but not Mitch, he didn't even seem to miss a stride. Sam chuckled again, damn little prick.

It was funny when you thought about it. For a week, Sam had been racking his brain for a way to point Mitch at Kathy. Sam knew if she was pressed, Kathy would spring the kid on Mitch. Sam laughed a little. He had even called Kathy and talked a little tough cop talk to her. He'd hoped that explaining that she was headed for trouble, might make her run to Mitch and dump the kid on him. But crap that hadn't worked. She hadn't budged. Sam shook his head, marveling about the way things worked out sometimes. Here he was trying to figure a way to get Mitch to go after Kathy and then the next thing he heard was that Mitch had busted her.

And sure, as hell, she had told Mitch about the kid. But even with all that, Mitch was still coming full steam ahead. Sam shook his head, he needed to act fast. Sam was under no illusions, they would catch up to him sooner or later. He just wanted to make sure it was later.

Instead of walking inside, Sam went around the corner. There was a small courtyard. A quiet place with trees a little patch of grass and in one corner a little bench. Back in his smoking days Sam had spent many an hour sitting on that bench smoking and thinking.

After the accident he had come here and set for hours. Now he sat, twiddling a cigarette in his fingers. Something about smoking always seemed to smooth out his thoughts and help him think. Right now, he needed to think. His little band of avengers was becoming too focused with their efforts, Sam could feel it. It would make them all too easy to track.

For years an idea had tickled the back of Sam's mind. Just the faintest hint of an idea that every once in a while would wander in from the farthest reaches of his brain. Sam would pull it out and mull over it. But it was always more of a daydream than anything to be seriously reckoned with.

That had all changed that one terrible night. Now at times, it felt like it happened years ago and at other times it was a raw, fresh wound. But it had galvanized a resolve in Sam. He was sick and tired of what wasn't right. It wasn't right that his son and daughter-in-law lay in cold graves, while a psycho like Carter still drew a breath.

It wasn't right that his grandchild never got a chance at life, while two dirty cops profited from letting a murderer go free. It sure wasn't right that politicians like Braxton got rich selling themselves and the oath of their office to a piece of crap like Van Zandt.

Mostly it wasn't right that a pretty young newlywed, with the heart and determination of a tiger, was dead at the hands of animals that should have been put down years ago. Something about her death tortured Sam. If he stopped to think about it he would realize that the couple reminded him of his son and daughter-in-law. A drunk driver killed his Sammy and his wife, and because he could afford the best lawyer in the state, that asshole walked away practically scot free. When Sam saw that poor, young couple lying lifeless on the rocks, something in him turned.

Like a wounded animal, Sam had lashed out. He had turned that hazy notion into action, but he still didn't have a plan. Not a real one. He and his little group had muddled around and took some assholes outta the gene pool. He had stopped a drug connection from starting up. Sam smiled at that. He was under no illusion, someone new would move to take their place, but if he was still alive and able, Sam would deal with them as well.

Now was the time, Sam knew, he should back off. Let Mitch handle the rest of this mess. Sam smiled and shook his head. Damn, he liked that boy. And Mitch was smart, with Ollie and Wade they would have this thing sewed up by the end of the week. They would find that girl, get that prick Carter.

Sam frowned, hell yes; he should back out of it, just fade away. Right now, Sam figured he could still walk away. Mitch might figure out it was Sam behind that rifle in the desert. Probably would, but wouldn't be able to do anything with it. Might not even want to at that point. But Sam knew if he kept pushing things, Mitch would figure it all out. He would eventually come up with some real evidence against Sam. And for a guy that could deal a polar bear out his fur, that damn Mitch had a surprising streak of morality.

Even while the logical side of his brain was saying walk away, the fiery side was saying 'HELL NO'! This had to be finished his way. Finish it while he still had time.

Sam had no doubts; Mitch would run these mutts down. But in the end if the big players did any time it wouldn't be much and real soon they would be back out doing what assholes did.

And of course, there was that prick Van Zandt.

Sam had done some research on Van Zandt. The guy might be a grade-A psycho, but he was also a top-notch lawyer. Mitch might put them in jail, but they wouldn't stay there. Not with endless resources and a cunning lawyer like Van Zandt on their side.

And Carter? No way that little prick deserved to live. If Carter did any time it would be in some cushy sanatorium, being waited on hand and foot. Actually, treated like some kind of rock star. Sam had seen it before, for some reason there was a certain group of people that simply revered these killers. To them, Carter would be royalty.

Sam spat onto the rocks. He simply couldn't abide by that. A small grin stole onto his face. Before, he had been muddling around, but now, he had a real plan. Sam almost laughed at himself. He'd known what he was going to do before he sat down on the bench. Hell, he knew even before he got out of Mitch's car.

But Sam was a careful man and even though he knew what had to be done, he had to talk it through with himself. Argue it back and forth in his own mind. But now, that he had hashed it all out, he was all action. First, he called Dave.

"Yeah," Dave greeted him.

"I think you and the other boys should take cover," Sam said. "Things are about to get sticky."

"We don't mind sticky."

"You might mind this."

The pause was so long that Sam pulled his phone away from his ear and look to make sure he hadn't accidentally cut Dave off. Sam had a habit of bumping the power button with his thumb, which irritated him to no end.

But not this time, he could see Dave's number blinking and the timer counting away. "What did you do this time?" Sam heard Dave's gravelly voice as well as if he had the phone pressed to his ear.

"It's not what I've done; it's what I'm fixing to do."

"Aw shit," Dave grunted. "Why are you cutting the rest of us out? Me and Ted, we signed up to see this through."

"I know you did, and I've been proud to serve with each of you. Hell, them others too. You be sure and tell the others I said that."

Dave snorted. "Fuck that; tell them your own self. We are still with you."

"No," Sam said, feeling the warm wave of comradeship wash over him. "You're a good troop for saying so, but you don't want this on your soul."

"What the hell are you talking about?"

"Two dirty cops. I'm going to settle things with them."

"Oh." There was a silence for a long second. "Oh, shit."

"Yeah," Sam said dryly. "They won't ever let us walk away from it after that. Besides, Mitch and his boys are on this. They aren't more than a day or so from putting it all together."

"Shit, don't mean nothing. We are all still willing to help."

"I know," Sam said, a lump in his throat. "You boys carry on after I'm gone."

There was a long silence, and then Dave said gruffly, "Take care, jarhead."

"You too, tinhead," Sam replied, but he'd already killed the connection.

Looking off into the distance, Sam held the phone in his hand for a second, then hit Maureen's number. "What we talked about, it's started," Sam said.

He heard her sharp intake of breath. "Okay," she said her voice heavy. "Are we still on for dinner tonight?"

He thought about it, then nodded to himself. "I think so. If not let's meet in a couple weeks at that place, the one we talked about."

Years ago, they had spent a week out near Truth or Consequences, New Mexico, and had loved it. Ever since, they'd talked about going back but never had. "If I don't see you tonight, I will be there," she whispered.

"Love you," Sam said, having trouble forcing the words past the lump in his throat.

After talking with Maureen, Sam was tempted to call it off. Sam sat unmoving, his head bowed. He felt a great tearing inside his chest as he realized his time with the love of his life was coming to a close. Sam was sorely tempted to chuck the whole thing.

But he did not. Sam had grown up doing the hard thing, and now he wavered, but did not falter. Instead he opened the prepaid phone he had taken off Flores. In the phone's memory were several calls from a person marked

Chap. Sam punched that number up, firing up a cigarette as he listened to it ring.

"Hey, asshole, you want your drugs back?"

Tucson Police Station Tucson AZ June 18th 2018
Monday Afternoon

Mitch frowned as Harris trailed the chief into the conference room. A part of him knew that Harris had every right to be here, but it still pissed him off. The chief caught Mitch's scowl and shot a frown back. "Take it easy," the chief whispered in Mitch his ear as he took a seat.

Mitch nodded slightly. He was in a hurry to get the meeting going. Even though the meeting had been Mitch's idea, now it seemed like a waste of time.

Now, they had leads to run.

Mitch chafed as they waited for Geena and Dockett to arrive. A thousand thoughts were whirling in his mind. He was still trying to put all the information in its proper place, when the chief spoke quietly. "Have you made any progress on the Jones and Jenkins situation?"

Mitch frowned and flicked a hard glance at Harris, who grinned smugly. "Oh yes, I know your little secret."

"Tim," this chief said mildly, but there was a hint of steel just under the surface of his tone. He held Harris' eyes for a second, then glanced at Mitch. "Well?"

"They're guilty," Mitch grunted, seething inside.

Harris snorted and rolled his eyes. "I seriously doubt that." Harris turned towards the chief. "Sir, I have worked with both of them. Jones and Jenkins are good men. Good officers. That fact is simply not in question. What we should be questioning is Detective Mitchell's own character." Harris spread his hands and turned a sneer at Mitch. "I think it is rather obvious that Detective Mitchell has mismanaged this case from its inception. Painfully obvious. Now, he is off on some wild goose chase, trying to smear the good name of two brother officers in order to divert attention away from his own failings."

"Noted." The chief nodded and with a bemused expression, he made a flipping motion with his hand as if he were sending back cold soup. He glanced across at Mitch. "Okay, Mitch, explain why you are sure they are guilty."

"Yeah, uh sure," Mitch said, fumbling for his first thought. "First, let's look at the case itself."

"You mean the suicide?" Harris sneered.

"It was murder, but yeah, that's the case," Mitch said. "At a glance, you read the report and you see booze, pills, a note, cheap hotel and shot to the head with powder burns?"

"Text book suicide," Harris said.

"Text book, now, that's a good word," Mitch said, pausing as he saw Geena and Dockett enter the room.

"Please, continue," Geena said, as she and Dockett took their seats.

Mitch nodded curtly. "I had a couple of my guys take a second look at the suicide, and after reading the report they saw several things that didn't quite add up."

"Such as?" The chief asked.

"First, the guy was from DC, with no apparent ties to Arizona. Seems like a stretch that he would fly all the way out here just to kill himself."

Harris rolled his eyes a little. "Are you kidding?" Harris looked o the chief. "That's an anomaly. Nothing else. Certainly not something you would use to ruin the career of two good cops."

"Of course. There's more," Mitch said, very much enjoying the feeling that he was about to lower the boom on Harris. "The guy shot himself. He didn't hang himself or OD on the pills. He shot himself! He gets off a plane and in only a couple of hours somehow scores a gun, then checks into a motel and shoots himself?"

Harris shrugged. "Another anomaly, not enough to outweigh the other evidence. Could be any number of plausible explanations for it," Harris said, a shadow of a doubt creeping into his voice now. "Could have bought it at a pawn shop."

"He didn't," Mitch said, glaring at Harris. "It was his own gun. He didn't fly with it; so how did it get here?"

Harris squirmed. "Like I said could be any number of explanations for how he got his gun here."

"Name one." Mitch enjoyed watching Harris squirm for a second, then moved on. "Wanna venture a guess who Forsyth worked for?" Mitch paused a beat, but no one offered up a guess. "Perry Van Zandt."

"So?" Harris replied with a sneer.

"Perry Van Zandt is Jacob Carter's boss," Geena answered.

Mitch grinned over at Harris, who for once didn't have anything to say. Crossing his arms, he simply glared at Mitch. Mitch shot him a smile, then continued. "Let's look at the other issues with the case. For instance, why was his computer cleaned?"

"Cleaned?" Dockett said perking up like a hunting dog catching a scent. "We could send it to our lab, they could...," Dockett stopped as Mitch shook his head.

"Sorry, I should've been more precise. When I said cleaned, I meant somebody actually swapped out the memory cards and hard drive."

"Huh," Dockett grunted and Mitch could see him processing the information. Dockett gave a little nod as he came to a conclusion. "They knew him well enough to know what brand and model of laptop he used. Had it ready before hand."

"Yeah," Mitch agreed, his estimation of Dockett going up a notch. "But the main thing is the cops themselves made one big mistake. They called the victim by name in a report written twelve hours before they were able to ID him."

"Aw...," Dockett said softly, pausing where most cops Mitch knew would have added an expletive. "This is firm? No chance of a mistake?"

"Nope," Mitch replied. "Report was typed up on a computer at the station and was time-stamped hours before the victim was identified."

Dockett frowned. "The victim wasn't identified at the scene?"

"Nope," Mitch said, shaking his head. "They never did find his wallet or ID. He checked in the hotel under an alias. ID came out of DC on a print check."

"And you want us to check into your guys? Jones and Jenkins?" Geena asked. Mitch nodded smiling Geena wasn't about to let Dockett get ahead of her in this meeting. She planted her gaze squarely on the chief. "And you are okay with this? You are requesting the Bureau to investigate two of your own?"

The chief didn't flinch, he met her gaze and nodded slowly. "I wouldn't go quite so far as to say it's a formal request to investigate. More like a favor." The chief smiled, letting his gaze travel between the two agents. "I would like to be appraised daily of any progress you make. I don't want to read anything in the paper that I don't already know."

"That's reasonable," Dockett said crisply. "Any leads on the girl?"

"A few," Mitch said, giving a quick outline of what they knew, while Harris passed out copies of the file. Mitch noticed that Harris had kept a copy for himself, which didn't set well but Mitch let it pass.

He would deal with Harris later.

"And Brody is in the wind?" Dockett asked. Mitch nodded and noticed that Dockett was already making notes on his copy of the file.

"We were planning to pick Brody up this morning, squeeze him a while, then drag his ass to this meeting, but...." Mitch shrugged and spread his hands. "He's gone."

"You think Brody ran and is hiding?" Geena asked cocking her head. "Or did they pick him up and are right now pounding his nuts flat with a tire iron?"

Mitch shrugged. "I'd say fifty-fifty, either way."

"But Brody is involved?" Dockett asked.

"At some level, he has to be," Mitch said, hesitating a second. In principle it seemed wrong to share with the Feds, but he needed their help. "There's a good chance that Carter has Brody, or better chance that he may be running. Or...." Mitch paused trying to think how to phrase his next idea.

"There is another possibility?" Geena demanded, not quite snapping Mitch's head off.

"Yeah, something just came up a few minutes ago," Mitch said.

"What was that?" the chief asked.

"Let me explain," Mitch answered trying to round up his thoughts. "Okay, we knew Brody got a boatload of cash from somewhere. We can find evidence of him spending a ton of money. More than he can possibly have. We found the spending but, we couldn't find any record of how the money came in, so we are pretty sure it came in under the table." Mitch paused, looking around to see that everyone was following along. "We were exploring the possibility that he got the cash from the Deacons and Chappy Miers."

"The money would have passed through Kathy Reynolds because of her affiliation with Roscoe Tannenbaum?" Geena offered.

"Exactly," Mitch replied, nodding his head.

"How would that work?" Dockett asked, without looking up from his note-taking.

Mitch glanced at the chief who had come over from the private sector and had worked many years in finance. "I'm thinking that Brody sold the Deacons some property. Brody buys a cheap piece of land, slaps a crappy steel building on it and then sells it to one of the Deacons' front companies as a factory for a small fortune."

"That sounds about right," the chief replied, nodding slowly. "I would be very surprised if it wasn't something very similar to what you just described. I would assume when it comes time to repay the money, the front company would then be paid by Brody's construction company for goods and services they never provided."

"That's what we think," Mitch agreed. "We know Chappy and maybe Tanner has been working a deal with a Deacons chapter out of Cali to bring drugs across the border. The plan seemed to be; Chappy's guys bring it across here, then mule it out to Cali. We think this is probably where a lot of Brody's seed money came from."

"The group from California?" Geena asked, already nodding.

"Why is that?" Dockett asked.

"Brody got a new foreman a couple of weeks back, a guy named Pierson, we just found out a few minutes ago that this Pierson was a Deacon, and a member of that same Cali chapter."

"There to watch Brody," Geena said nodding. "And their money."

"Yup," Mitch said. "The thing is Pierson turned up dead along with his boss and a couple of Mexicans. We figured with Pierson gone, maybe Brody saw a chance to run and took it, or more likely Chappy has him stashed somewhere."

"Any chance these guys getting killed is somehow connected to Angie Brody?" Dockett asked, again without looking up from his note-taking.

"Man, your guess is as good as mine," Mitch said. "It might be or it might simply be the Cartel taking care of business. It could be Van Zandt, Braxton and Carter. My guess is that they need Brody for a little bit but wouldn't be crazy about his partners. Maybe they saw a chance to thin them out."

There was silence around the table as they thought that over. Mitch shook his head, getting back to the business at hand. "Did your guys get anything out of the hotel room that we missed?"

"Not really," Dockett said, and quickly gave a recap of what they found, which was exactly what Mitch's crew came up with. "We did get a photo off the hotel security camera of this man," Dockett said sliding a photo to Mitch. "Using the name Justin Carter, this man paid for the room next door, but as far as we could tell never entered it."

Mitch picked up the picture and felt a chill. It was like opening a super cold freezer on a blistering hot day, a wave of coldness rolled over him, enveloping his entire body. "Fuck me," Mitch said under his breath.

"You know him?" Geena and Dockett asked almost harmonizing.

Mitch didn't answer, he simply stared at the photo and nodded, the chill on his body getting colder.

Speedway Blvd Tucson AZ June 18th 2018 Monday Late Afternoon

Sam took the last curve, climbing to the top of Gates Pass. The sun was high in the sky, glaring off the windshield of the Cherokee he had stolen. Sam had spent many years patrolling southern Arizona, and he was a man who valued a clean windshield. This one was not only dirty, but it was pitted beyond belief. Fighting the glare and cursing under his breath, he swung off Speedway and into the empty parking lot just west of the pass.

On some days or early in the morning, the parking lot might be full of fools on bicycles. But not now. Today the temps had climbed to a blistering one fifteen and even as evening rushed in, it was still one twelve. That tended to keep even the worst of the idiots inside.

Sam smiled, feeling his lips cracking. Damn, getting too old to be traipsing around the desert. Sam leaned the seat back, rolling the window down. He was tempted to close his eyes, but didn't. He knew he would go to sleep. He waited, looking up at the stained headliner of the Jeep. How in the hell did someone manage to stain a fabric over their head? He frowned, still puzzling over it ten minutes later when he heard them.

He heard the pipes of the bikes rattle as they slowed on Kinney Road, then he heard the bikes rev back up as they came up Speedway. Tired to the bone, Sam crawled out of the jeep, and immediately the heat beat down on him. His feet dragging, Sam went to the back of the Cherokee. He knew the weariness he felt wasn't real. He wasn't tired from what he had done, but rather from what he was about to do. He didn't want to do it. It didn't set right, but Sam knew it had to be done.

Pushing such thoughts from his mind, he hauled the two large canvass bags out of the Cherokee, dropping them on the asphalt. He placed one bag closer to where Chappy and Dell would be standing.

He squatted beside the canvass duffle bags, unzipping them to reveal the white powder in gallon-sized freezer bags. The duffle bag that was closer to where the bikers would be, Sam spread open wide, invitingly wide he hoped. Only one freezer bag had drugs in it, the rest were filled with talcum powder. The one freezer bag containing the drugs he placed in the center on top, hopefully saying, pick me, pick me. Sam was praying that if they sampled a bag it would be that one. While Sam was willing to get rid of a few assholes, he wasn't about to turn a shitload of drugs loose on the streets. The real drugs were safely hidden in his garage while he figured out what to do with them.

Wondering idly what would happen if they sampled any of the other bags, Sam watched as Dell and Chappy Miers roared into the parking lot. They circled the lot, and then screeched to a halt in front of him. "Nice hair," he commented as Chappy swung off his bike.

Chappy grinned, a sheepish grin, running a hand over his close-cropped blonde hair. "Takes a little getting used to," he said ruefully. "Feels a little faggy."

"Yeah, you look like a fucking fag," his brother Dell said, shoving him.

Ignoring Dell, Chappy gestured to the stacks of powder-filled clear plastic bags. "That it?" he asked, taking a step forward and licking his lips.

"That's it," Sam said, tossing the special bag to Chappy.

Chappy held up the bag, looking at it lovingly. He grinned down at Sam. "Man this is the shit. Cheaper than coke, and safer than crack. Better high than any of them."

"No shit?" Sam said, he didn't really care.

"Ain't no shit," Chappy said, turning the bag in his hand. He nodded his head at the two gym bags. "Is that all of it?"

"More than we talked about. I think Flores was holding out on you." Sam rose slowly up to his feet, dusting the knees of his jeans. "Just goes to show you can't trust anyone."

If Sam expected Chappy to be upset to learn that his partner might not have been completely truthful, then the old trooper was in for a big disappointment. Chappy merely shrugged, licking his lips as he stared at the bags of drugs. "Guess you sorta did me a favor then, taking him out."

"Glad you see it that way," Sam said grimly. "I got a job for you." He handed two pictures to Chappy.

Chappy took the pictures, looking them over closely. "Are you shitting me?" he asked staring at the two faces. He passed the two photos to his brother. "These are cops."

"I know."

"No fucking way!" Dell shouted, blowing spit halfway across the parking lot. "We don't do cops."

"Too late," Sam said simply. "I already called them and told them that you have the drugs. Mighta let it slip that you two capped those fuckers out in the desert. They seemed to buy it. My guess is they are gonna be waiting on you when you get home." He gave them a daring smile. Sam had called no one, but these assholes didn't know that.

Dell Miers bared his teeth in a low growl, and pulled a chrome-plated revolver from his belt. "You stupid old fuck! What makes you think we won't kill you right here and now?"

Sam took a small step forward, raising his shirt to show a Smith and Wesson pistol. "You can try. Ain't gonna change a thing. Those cops are still going to be waiting on you." Sam shook out a cigarette and lit it. "There's a lot more drugs there than we discussed. You can cut it once, and you'll get a couple of mil easy."

Dell shook his head. "Be hard to move around here, now."

Sam smiled wolfishly. "Our deal was that you wouldn't move it around here at all. Remember that, shit head? Carry it out to Cali." He glanced at Chappy. "Let me know when you want to move the stuff and I'll make sure you got an open road, no cops."

Chappy nodded, slowly. "Okay old man, we'll do your dirty work, but it'll cost you another five hundred grand."

"Sorry," Sam said, with a slow shake of his head. "Don't have it."

"Bullshit, I know you took almost a mil off them Mex's when you took down these drugs."

"Okay," Sam said, he'd been expecting them to ask for more. "I don't want these bodies turning up for a few days. Lose the bodies good."

"What about the money?"

"Meet you after it's done. Out at Texas Canyon. West bound side."

"Alright, we will do it today." Chappy grinned, shaking a finger at the older man. "You fuck us around and those two dead cops are gonna turn up in the middle of Foothills Mall."

Sam waited until the bikers loaded the fake drugs and roared away. As they turned out on Speedway and disappeared, Sam let out a barking laugh. Part of it was humor, but mostly he was laughing out of relief. He'd been sure they would sample some of the drugs. Leaning back against the jeep he lit another smoke. He breathed deep, enjoying the feel of the smoke in his lungs. He'd bought this pack two days ago, the first pack in twenty years. He took another drag, feeling a twinge of guilt. Fuck it. Either way he'd be dead before long anyway might as well enjoy the ride. Sam thought about what the doctors had said. Hell, in six months he'd be better off dead.

Sam didn't waste a second thought on the cops. Fuck'em, they sold out. They deserved whatever they got.

Tucson Police Station Tucson AZ June 18th 2018
Monday Late Afternoon

With a flick of his wrist, Mitch sent the picture skittering across the table. "Fucking Jenkins," he said.

The picture showed Jenkins at the front counter of the hotel, the rat-faced look of a guilty man riding on his face as he leaned against the counter. "Doesn't prove anything," Harris protested weakly. "He could have been there chasing a lead on another case."

Mitch snorted, rolling his eyes at the ceiling. "Doubtful," the chief said, cutting off what Mitch was going to say. "But we need to quietly pull his case files and see if he had a reason to be there." He shot a hard glance at Harris. "We need to do that right now."

Mitch nodded absently, his mind leaping ahead. "How did he pay for the room?"

Dockett was already shaking his head. "Visa, registered to a Justin Carter. Card went through without a hitch, so probably not stolen."

"That says to me that Jenkins at least is working with Carter. We know Carter had a fake ID, good enough not to draw any suspicion when he was arrested here last week. Want to bet that he had credit cards to go with the ID and gave one to Jenkins to use?" Geena asked, and got no takers.

"Do you think Jenkins actually killed Agent Holland?" the chief asked quietly.

"Jenkins!" Geena exploded, slapping the table. "Doug, let me see our file."

Dockett passed her the file. "What are you looking for?" he asked as she tore through the paperwork.

"This!" she said the savage grin of satisfaction on her face. She tapped the file, then turned it so everyone could see. On the page she was indicating, there was two lists of names. "These are every print lifted from the scene. This list belongs to cops or agents." She tapped the paper again

"Jenkins is third on that list. I knew I'd seen that name before."

"So what?" Harris said, waving hand. "It's maybe a little unprofessional, but it happens. Cops leave their prints at the scene. That's why we keep the second list."

Ignoring Harris, Mitch tore through his own file. Towards the back, he found a copy of the sign in roster for the crime scene. "He didn't sign in."

"Huh?" Harris grunted. "Probably forgot. It happens."

"He wasn't there!" Mitch snapped, weary of Harris. "It was a small scene; we were tripping over each other. If he was there I woulda seen him." Mitch waved the log under Harris' nose. "He never signed in! He wasn't fucking there!"

Harris picked up the photo, holding it up for Dockett and Geena. "Did you see him there?"

Mitch snorted and swore under his breath but loud enough for everyone in the room to hear. "They brought the picture to us. I expect they would have mentioned it if they had recognized him from the crime scene." The 'you dumbass' he added was almost under his breath.

Ignoring Mitch's blistering rant, Dockett looked dutifully at the photo and shook his head. "He wasn't there. Not that I saw," Barnes said, glancing at Geena who shook her head.

"Well, shit, this is a mess" the chief said disgustedly. "What do we do now?"

"I say we picked them up now," Mitch said.

"That will certainly get back to Van Zandt," Geena warned. "I still like your idea of watching them. Do we really want to show our hand now?"

"Can't be helped," Mitch said. "Who knows, that might even do some good. Maybe spook Van Zandt a little." Mitch turned slightly, speaking directly to the chief. "Look, ain't no way we're coming out of this without a little shit on our shoes, but it will go down better if it looks like we were on top of it."

"I agree," the chief said nodding. "We pick them up, then what?"

"Then we sweat them. We hit them with everything we've got, and then we offer them a deal."

"A deal?" The chief asked raising an eyebrow.

"Maybe they know where Angie Brody is? We've got to think about that. And if not? Well, as much as I would like to see these two dumb fuckers go down, its Carter, Van Zandt and Braxton we really want," Mitch said. "If they rollover, maybe, we got a shot at Van Zandt, and maybe we find Angie Brody."

"I don't know them, but do you honestly think they will roll?" Dockett asked.

"If we spook them, Jenkins will," Mitch decided. "When it comes right down to it, he'll even sellout Jones to save himself."

"But do we have enough to spook them?" Geena wondered.

"Maybe, this picture and Jenkins' prints at the scene sure helps," Mitch said, sliding his glance over to the agents. "It would help if you guys could pull something out of there financials."

"We have a couple of people already looking into it. If there is something there they will find it," Dockett assured them.

"Well for now, we have the picture and we have Jenkins' print at the scene. We have them using the vic's name before he was ever ID'd."

"Is that enough?"

"Enough to get a warrant. I say, we pick them up and then we tear them apart. We go through their places, their cars, anything we can find. If we can find the gun or a match to the shells to Agent Holland's murder, we got them."

"You think Jenkins actually pulled the trigger on Agent Holland?" Geena's voice was quiet and calm, but Mitch could sense something sinister under the surface.

"Maybe, or probably Carter, but either way Jenkins was right there. The print proves that." Mitch glanced at Dockett. "Where did they pick up his print?"

Dockett retrieved the file from Geena. "Off the underside of the chair arm," he said after consulting the file.

"How did you pull a print off of cloth on a chair arm?" Harris asked.

"The chair was padded, but the arm was varnished wood," Dockett answered, then glanced at Mitch. "Do you want my men to pick them up?"

"I appreciate the offer," Mitch said and he did. It was always hard for cops to arrest other cops, especially ones they had worked with. But in this case, Mitch had an ulterior motive. "I'm thinking, I may want to perp walk them right into the station, or at least be able to threaten them with it. I want to try and shake them up."

Mitch took out his phone, glancing sideways at the chief. "You okay with this?"

The chief made a disdainful gesture as if warding away evil. "Do it."

Mitch nodded grimly as he placed the call to Wade. "Hey boss," Wade answered cheerfully.

"Any word from Ollie and Carly?" Mitch asked.

"Silencio."

"Alright, I need you and Jerry to go pick up Jenkins and Jones."

"Okaaay," Wade said drawing the word out. "Are you sure?"

"Yes, and take a couple uniforms with you. Call me when it's done."

"You got it boss."

"You okay with this?" Mitch asked, picking up on Wade's tone.

"Naw, not really, I hate busting cops. But don't worry we'll get'er done."

"Call me when you have them," Mitch said, killing the connection.

"What about the thing out in the desert by Arivaca?" Geena asked. "Is that somehow involved with all this?"

Mitch shrugged. "Maybe, on the edge of things. We think Brody needed some cash to hold up his end of this thing. So, to raise cash he threw in with Chappy Miers. We think the drugs were a way for Brody to raise cash."

"Or maybe it was Kathy Reynolds," Geena said softly. "She's involved in this and she's definitely involved with Tanner. You told me that Chappy and Tanner are old friends. It seems to me that Kathy might be the connection there."

"Maybe," Mitch admitted. For some reason even now, he found it hard to admit that she might be involved.

"How does any of this get us closer to Angie Brody?" Harris asked.

"That's the million-dollar question," the chief said, indicating he would like an answer.

"Maybe it doesn't. Maybe we're already too late." Mitch sighed shaking his head. "We need to start preparing ourselves for the fact that she may already be gone."

"Because Brody is missing," Geena said her voice soft.

"Yeah, either Brody saw his chance and took off and he's in the wind, or he gave them what they wanted and they got rid of all the witnesses."

"Or?" The chief prodded gently.

"Or Brody wasn't giving them anything so they snatched him up so they could make the fucker watch while they cut her fingers off," Mitch said, feeling down all of a sudden as he considered that very possibility.

His words brought a deathly silence to the room. "Let's hope that it hasn't come to that," the chief said softly.

"Amen," Dockett agreed.

"I don't think that it has, it could be that Brody took off," Mitch said. "But I'm thinking more likely that Chappy has him somewhere. Seems apparent that the Deacons had that guy Pierson watching Brody because they thought he would either take off or cave in to Van Zandt. Just because Pierson was going to that meet doesn't mean they would just turn Brody loose."

"So maybe all that nonsense out in the desert does tie in with the Brody case?" the chief said, more talking to himself than the rest of the table. "Where do we go from here?"

"We keep pushing," Mitch said immediately. "We go after Jones and Jenkins hard."

"We'll do the financial investigation on them. What else can we do?" Dockett wanted to know.

Mitch cocked his head, smiling a tight smile. "We could say fuck a bunch of being subtle. Your guys could get in the computer, crawl up everybody's ass, especially Van Zandt and Braxton, see what you can find out."

Dockett nodded slowly. "Sure, we can do that. It will certainly ruffle some feathers."

"Maybe it's time for that."

Dockett glanced at Geena who nodded. "Alright we can do that, I will get my people started on the warrants," he said, making a note. "Anything else we can help with?"

"There's this," Mitch said, sliding the MP3 across the table.

Geena picked it up, glanced at it, and then passed it to Dockett. "That come from Pyle?" Geena asked, a hint of irritation creeping into her voice.

"Yeah, I just got it," Mitch said, nodding to her. "You might have your guys look at *What You Give*."

"What is that?" Dockett asked.

"A song," the chief said. "Old school Tesla. Great tune, I have it on mine."

"Why look at that one?" Geena asked.

"For one thing, it's the only song on there, but mainly because it's encrypted."

"You think it's the dirt Pyle had on the Senator?" Geena asked.

"We are hoping." Mitch smiled. "We hear that the government has a back door built into all those encryption programs and you guys can walk right in and access any file you want."

"We will look at it," Dockett replied, giving nothing away. "Is there anything else we can do?"

Mitch smiled a little to himself. No way was Dockett going to admit whether or not the feds might have a back door into private programs. "You are more than welcome to look for Angie Brody and Carter."

"No," Dockett said, not taking the bait. "We'll stick with this." Dockett cleared his throat and carefully closed the file. He looked closely at Mitch, then gave a small nod. "Detective Mitchell, in the past, we may not have always seen eye to eye but for what it's worth I think that you have done everything that could have been done to try and save that girl." Dockett paused, looking straight across the table at Mitch. "You won't hear any criticism from me."

For a second, Mitch sat stunned. He would have been less surprised if Dockett had reached across the table and slapped him. He nodded gravely at the other man. "Thanks, man," Mitch said, unable to find any other words.

Silence settled on the room, as everybody began folding up notepads and slipping cell phones in their pockets. The silence was broken by Mitch's cell breaking into song. Mitch glanced at the screen, even though he knew from the song, *Sam I Am* by Sammy Hagar, that it was Wade Nichols calling. "That was quick," he muttered, as he opened the connection. "You find them?"

"Sitting right out in front of Jenkins house," Wade said, his voice sounding funny. "Mitch, they're both dead. Shot gun blast to the head."

CHAPTER THIRTEEN

Jenkin's House Tucson AZ June 18th 2018 Monday Evening

Mitch and Geena pulled up to the crime scene, parking on the shoulder of the road. "Nice place," Geena commented, as Mitch killed the motor. She glanced slyly across at Mitch. "Tucson PD got any openings? I might want to transfer out here; you guys seem to make out pretty well. You all certainly have nice houses."

"Yeah," Mitch grunted, looking at the house. Set several feet lower than the road the house was a large sprawling brick ranch. A wide concrete driveway led down to a three-car garage. The backyard was fenced by a cinderblock wall, but through a wrought iron gate, Mitch could see the gleaming reflection of a pool. "It is a nice place. Real nice."

They got out, walking on the edge of the road to Jones' car. Wade Nichols broke away from the crowd of cops, hobbling back to them. "Hey, boss," he said, sounding grim.

"What have we got?"

"You mean other than two dead cops?" he asked, and Mitch nodded grimly. Wade shrugged. "Beats the hell out of me. Whole thing seems weird."

"Shit," Mitch said. "Can nothing about this be simple?"

Wade cocked his head towards the car. "Well, the killing itself was pretty straight forward and fairly simple. Jones and Jenkins were parked up here; somebody came up behind them, and bam, bam." Wade gestured to an empty shotgun shell against the rear tire of the car. "Twelve gauge, two shots double ought buck. End of story."

"So, they knew the killer?" Mitch asked, trying to see in his mind how it might have gone down.

Wade gave a curt nod. "Hard to think otherwise. Neither one had drawn their weapon."

Mitch looked in the car and couldn't help flinching. After all, he had known these men, worked with them. Jones was the worst, most of his face was gone, spread across the dash and windshield. Jenkins wasn't as bad. The shot had spread some, catching him in the chest and in the neck.

Mitch heard Geena catch her breath. "Gruesome," she said softly.

"It is nasty, but I doubt if they felt much," Wade said.

"You are right, looks pretty simple to me," Mitch said. "Jones is dropping Jenkins off. He stops out here on the street, so he doesn't have to back up out of the driveway. Somebody is following them and pulls up either behind them or may be right beside them. If it was like that the shooter wouldn't even have had to get out of the car."

"Mickey thought the shooter was standing here," Wade said, moving forward to stand just behind the driver's door. "Shot Jones from here, then stepped forward a step and took out Jenkins."

"Okay, I buy that," Mitch said, nodding. "Still seems pretty straightforward. Either this was always planned or

Van Zandt got wind that we were on to these guys and had them killed."

"Hey boss," Jerry called stepping from the brush on the other side of the road.

"What you got?"

"Some brass, another shotgun shell there," He said gesturing to a spot in the ditch directly across from the car. "Saw that shell and then came back here and found a bunch of footprints and some tire tracks."

"Tire Tracks?" Wade wondered, looking doubtfully at the brush. "Is there room for a car back there?"

"Nope," Jerry replied. "Motorcycles. Looks like a couple of guys waited back there out of sight. They waited until Jones and Jenkins pulled up, then stepped out and did them."

"Mitch," Geena said, quietly. Mitch glanced at her raising an eyebrow. "This is very similar to what happened to Detective Harley, Len Dykes partner."

"Oh yeah," Mitch said, digesting the fact. "How so?"

"Detective Harley was sitting in a car and somebody walked out of an alley, came up on the car from behind and shot him."

"No woofin'?" Wade said a little wonderment in his tone. "Same deal, shotgun and everything?"

"No. Harley was killed with a pistol, but aside from the differences in the weapon, the killings are very similar."

"Could still be the same guy," Wade said nodding at Mitch. "Makes some sense. For one guy a pistol is okay, but for two armed cops you're gonna want a shotgun."

"Wouldn't have to be as fine," Mitch agreed. "With the shotgun, just put the gun in the window and pulled the trigger."

"Then it could be the same guy, working off a pattern," Wade observed, glancing across at Geena. "Could be that little pecker wood Carter?"

"Maybe." Geena nodded curtly. "DC police always thought it was Carter who killed Harley, but they could never prove it. And they certainly tried. They finally decided Carter must have had an accomplice who actually did the shooting."

"Makes sense, that he has a helper here," Wade said. "After all, he's got that gal to look after. He'd need someone to look after her while he came here to deal with these boys."

"Wasn't Carter," Mitch decided, shaking his head. "No way, they woulda ever let him get this close."

"I dunno, after all, these whistle dicks were working for Carter, or at least Van Zandt," Wade pointed out.

"Still wouldn't have trusted him," Mitch argued, shaking his head. "If they didn't know before, they knew by now what kind of a psycho this Carter is. I can't see them trusting him."

"Might be right, but the shooter would have been out of sight back in the brush. If he timed it right, he could have gotten right on them before they even knew anyone was close," Wade pointed out. "Who are you thinking?"

"The biker, Roscoe Tannenbaum?" Geena wondered.

"I don't know," Mitch, said rubbing his chin. "I don't see Tanner for this, I'm thinking Chappy Miers."

"Could be someone else, someone we haven't even seen yet," Geena agreed, nodding slightly. "We have suspected all along that Carter probably has someone local helping him."

"Yeah, maybe the fucker that did the shooting out in the desert. Could be anyone once you stop and think about it. If you are going to shot someone sitting in a car, this is how you would do it. If these guys were dirty on Forsyth, who knows what other crap they done," Mitch said thinking it over. "But either way this seems pretty straightforward, where's the weird shit you were talking about?"

"Over here," Wade said jerking his head to where Jerry and Mickey were bagging evidence. "Remember how Sam Logan said those Mexicans that got killed were bringing in some new kind of drug?"

"Yeah," Mitch said, getting a weird feeling about where this was going.

"Hey Mickey, show Mitch and Geena the stash."

Mickey pulled out an evidence bag from his kit, holding it up for Mitch to see. "Found it under the driver's seat."

"Huh," Mitch grunted studying the bag. "What is it? You think it's the stuff they were dealing out in the desert?"

Mickey gave a little shrug. "Not sure, but it could be." He glanced at Mitch and Geena. "I worked that case in the desert; we pulled a trace sample out of the trunk on the Mexicans' car."

"And this is the same stuff?" Geena asked.

"I'm not sure. It could be. This stuff is something new, I haven't seen it before," Mickey said.

"But it's the same stuff as in the Mexicans car?" Wade demanded.

Mickey nodded shortly "I think so. Pretty close anyway."

"How the hell can you tell that just by looking at it?"

"It's a crystalline formation." Mickey held up a jeweler's eyepiece. "The crystal formula is very similar. This isn't powerful enough to be sure. I'll have to get back to the lab before we know for certain."

"All right," Mitch said slowly. "What do you think, though?"

"Same shit. Maybe not the same batch, but it's the same mixture," Mickey said bluntly.

"Will you be able to tell if it came from the same batch as that out in the desert?" Geena asked.

Mickey cocked his head. "I'm not sure. I don't know enough about it." He pursed his lips, cocking his head. "Without doing a chemical analysis, even then probably couldn't say with any certainty that it came from the same batch. Might be able to say it didn't."

"Why is that?" Jerry asked, looking up from bagging evidence alongside the car.

"If it's basically the same substance but with some differences, then it wouldn't be from the same run. But if it's very close to identical it would be hard to say. If I knew more about the manufacturing process, maybe."

"If it came from the same batch, wouldn't it be identical?" Wade asked.

"Not necessarily," Mickey said. "Think of making cookies. Even if you stirred them very well they all wouldn't come out with the same number of chocolate chips. And this sample is small and what we pulled out of the car in the desert was trace samples, the limited quantities makes it harder to be sure."

"Then, we can't be sure if it was the same batch or not?" Geena asked.

"What are you thinking?" Mitch asked looking across at her. She was frowning biting on her lower lip, a habit she had when she didn't agree with what was being said.

"I don't know," she said, still biting her lip as she shrugged. "I'm wondering how this fits?" She waved her hand at the scene. "Was this an ongoing operation or something new?"

"We were thinking Brody might be getting money from somebody," Jerry said, glancing at Wade. "Maybe a dealer."

Geena nodded. "So, could this be a way to get the dealer out of the picture?"

"Man," Mitch said running a hand through his hair. "I'm looking at the drugs and thinking they were a plant."

"Isn't much there," Wade agreed. "Not a lot to have if they were dealing but they might have been using."

"Good point," Mitch said nodding to Mickey. "We'll need a tox screen."

"Maybe, Jones and Jenkins ripped off the drugs," Jerry suggested, nodding at the car. "Could be they did the hit out in the desert. Maybe, they were supposed to turn the drugs over to someone after the hit and they held some back."

"That'd sure get you killed," Wade said dryly. "I can't see that, though. From what you said, the shooter out there was set up in some rocks?" he asked and Mitch nodded. "I guarantee you that wasn't Jenkins, that guy would get blue in the face getting out of his chair. He didn't scramble up in no rocks."

"Yeah, you're right about that," Jerry agreed, then glanced at Mitch. "The sixty-four dollar question is, do the drugs tie in with Angie Brody?"

"Man, I don't know, could be though. Brody was getting cash from somewhere. Drugs would be one way," Mitch said heavily. "We need to search their houses, cars, the whole bit." Mitch looked around. "Where's Ollie and Carly?"

"Running something down. Something to do with Brody, I think," Jerry said.

"Ollie had an idea about something," Wade said, he rolled his eyes a little. "You know how he gets."

Mitch nodded. "All right, let's get started on the warrants. Who wants to go back?"

"No need," Wade said, grinning. "Check this out."

He led them back to his car. He picked up a small plastic device. "Mobile hotspot," he said, holding it up and turning it on. He placed it on the hood, and dug got a battered laptop. "I worked on this when I was off."

Powering up the laptop, he opened a new word file. "This is a warrant template that I put together." He quickly typed in their relevant info. "See when it's an easy warrant, like these, we don't need a lot of probable cause. Just fill in the blanks, type in a quick narrative and just like that you're done."

Finishing the tapping, Wade pulled up another program. "With this, I can send it directly to a judge's email in the court house."

Wade hit enter then glanced over at Jerry, who was just getting off his phone. Jerry nodded to Wade. "I called Judge Stubbins' clerk. He'll be watching for the email. We should be good to go in about fifteen."

Wade grinned snapping his fingers. "There ya have it. We can have a squad pick them up, and we're good to go"

"Nice," Mitch said nodding. "That'd be hard to do on a complicated warrant. But it is slick." Mitch gestured down at the house. "I'm going to go down and look around."

"You want us to go to Jonesy's?" Wade asked, motioning between himself and Jerry.

Mitch nodded. "Yeah, you might want to stop by and pick up the warrant for his house. Be sure to give a copy to his wife. If we find anything that ties to Van Zandt, I don't want it to be challenged in court."

"You got it, boss," Wade said, then hesitated. "I don't think Karen will be there. I heard she left him a couple months back."

"Huh, I hadn't heard that," Mitch said, realizing that since he became a supervisor, he was no longer in the gossip loop. "Alright, go ahead and pick the warrants up. If Karen isn't there, be sure to leave a copy at the house. I'll try and get an address for her and get her a copy." Mitch ran a hand through his hair. "Shit, I guess I'll have to do the notification as well. Dammit. I hate this. I was afraid of this."

"Don't beat yourself up, boss," Wade said. "They were big boys and they knew what they were getting into. They had been around the block; they had to know there was a good chance it was always going to end this way."

"Maybe," Mitch admitted. "Doesn't make it feel any better. I still kinda feel like I set them up for this."

"Shit happens," Wade said bluntly. "You want us to run the warrants for Jenkins' place back here to you?"

"Naw, I'll get one of the uniforms to go get it."

"Might want to wait until you get the warrant in hand before you go in there," Wade suggested, slyly.

Mitch frowned, they had every right to search the murder scene, but calling the house part of the murder scene was a stretch and maybe a bit beyond. Mitch kicked the dirt beside the road not liking the wait, but knowing Wade was right. Entering the house before the warrant was here was a gray area. Of course, Mitch could always claim he was checking to see if there were more victims inside, but since he knew Jenkins lived alone that would be shaky. Best to do this by the book. If this ever came to trial, they would be dealing with Van Zandt, not some fresh out of law school public defender.

Best to wait.

"Yeah, you're right," Mitch decided, looking around for a uniform to send for the warrant. As he looked, he saw Saul Driscoll jogging down the road, his equipment flapping as he ran. "I can get Saul to go," Mitch said then frowned. At first, he hadn't thought anything about Saul jogging, the man ran everywhere. A man of mixed races, Saul was a workout fanatic. He organized flag football, softball and basketball leagues in the department and was always hitting Mitch up to do a 5K run.

To see Saul running was no surprise, but something about the way he was running made Mitch take notice.

Mitch stepped away from the others, waving at Saul "Hey man."

"Hey Mitch," Saul said, not even the least bit out of breath. "I might have something for you."

"Well fuck, that would be nice," Mitch said waving at the others. "These pricks haven't come up with a damn thing."

"Out of shape," Saul said seriously, as he grinned elbowing Wade. "When was the last time you qualified on the mile run, old man?"

Wade snorted. "Shit, you see me running, and you'll know two things. One something real fucking big is chasing me and two I'm all outta bullets. See, son, that's way they give us guns. So we don't have to run."

"Yeah, what if it's a server coming at you with a paternity suit? You gonna shoot him?" Saul asked grinning. Then all of a sudden, the grin slid off his face, replaced by a red glow. He glanced at Mitch. "Aw crap, I'm sorry about that Mitch. I heard about your daughter."

"Don't worry about it."

Saul nodded, still a little red in the face. "Hope she don't look like you."

"You got that right," Wade said, giving Saul a nudge.

"Bite me," Mitch said. "You said you had something for me?"

Saul nodded. "Uh, I heard you're looking at Tanner. I was up the road and I talked to a guy, Sheppard Lynch."

"Sheppard Lynch?" Wade asked. "No shit?"

"Yeah, that's his real name, I checked," Saul said. "Anyway, Sheppard was coming home and he met two guys on bikes hauling ass, they almost run him off the road."

"What time was that?"

"A little after six," Saul said. "Sheppard said the car was parked here when he came by but he didn't notice who was in it."

"Nice, anything else?"

"He didn't notice the trail rider, just that he was a big guy, but the dude in the lead was a big guy was short, spikey, blonde hair."

"Shit, fucking Tanner," Wade said.

"That's what I thought," Saul agreed and nodding his head.

"No, not Tanner," Mitch said shaking his head. "That's the mistake we made at Jackson Pyle's house."

"Maybe you're right," Jerry agreed. "I heard that description and I was sure it was Tanner."

"Wasn't though. It was somebody else," Mitch said.

"Pretty well thought out though," Jerry said. "You hear that description and Tanner just pops into your head big as life."

"You know it," Mitch said nodding. "Which house is Sheppard in?"

"Third one up on the left." Saul answered.

"You got somebody who could run grab a warrant for us?"

"Sure, me and Ken can go. We are finishing up with the canvas now."

"Don't run, take the car," Wade advised.

Saul made a face, turning away from them to call his partner Ken Sizemore to come pick him up.

"So, you are going to wait for the warrant?" Wade asked, sounding a little nervous.

"Yes, mother, I will wait!" Mitch snapped.

"Don't worry, I will keep him out of the house until we get the warrant" Geena said.

"Bet you get a shit load of porn in there," Saul said waiting on his partner.

"Oh yeah," Mitch said, then thought about it. "You know something?"

"Naw, not really," Saul said, giving a little shrug. "Jasmine didn't like him. Said he was a perv."

Mitch nodded thinking it over. Women had a sense about these things and they weren't often wrong. "How's Jasmine doing?"

"Good. She's finally got her shop going," Saul said and ran a hand over his own closely cropped hair. "You're getting a little shaggy; you ought to go see her."

"Yeah, maybe," Mitch said, as Saul jumped into the car. Mitch watched the patrol car speed away, then glanced over at Geena. "You want to take a ride? Go talk to a Sheppard Lynch?"

William Forsyth's Apartment Washington DC June 18th 2018 Monday Night

Van Zandt was always proud of himself, but now he felt especially good. The deal in Arizona might be headed down the toilet, but no matter, in time it would be back. All things considered, it was an excellent idea. Wait a few years, let the dust and stink settle and then bring it back.

The important thing was that Van Zandt himself wouldn't go down with it. Carter of course would have to go, but then that had always been inevitable. Carter was too volatile, drew too much attention. From the beginning, Van Zandt had always known this day would come.

In a way, Van Zandt was sorry to let Carter go. If Van Zandt were able to have feelings for another human being, Carter would have been that person. Van Zandt often imagined if he had a son, that son would be a lot like Carter.

If Van Zandt had feelings, he might miss Carter. But he didn't, so Van Zandt only felt pride in himself, for having foreseen this day. And of course, having planned for it.

A year earlier, Van Zandt had hosted a party for all his employees and associates. A distasteful affair at this dreadful lakeside cabin. They had golfed, canoed on the lake, and shot at floating targets. Van Zandt had insisted they all shoot. As they shot, Van Zandt gathered up the empty shells, meticulously cataloging who had handled what shells.

Quite pleased with himself, Van Zandt grinned savagely. He had the gun that killed the fat cop, Harley, and he had an empty shell fired from that very gun with Forsyth's print on it. Before leaving home, Van Zandt had placed the spent shell in the gun. Van Zandt chuckled. Even if they found a video of him shooting the fat cop, they wouldn't be able to convict him. All the other evidence would point to Forsyth.

All that remained to do was plant the gun in Forsyth's apartment.

Van Zandt took a deep breath. He could actually feel his pulse quicken. This was the tricky part. The part that was going to take balls.

Van Zandt had balls.

More than that, he had brains. He had thought this all out. Forsyth lived in a security building. To enter from the front entrance, one had to sign in with a guard, but if that person had a keycard, they could enter from the parking garage. Van Zandt had a keycard. He checked his watch, nine-thirty, perfect. The timing was important he thought. He wanted to be late enough to reduce the chances of running into a cavalcade of people, but early enough that anyone he did encounter wouldn't be alarmed seeing a stranger and take notice.

Van Zandt picked up his briefcase containing the pistol and stepped from his car. The briefcase was important. It painted him as a businessman, not someone to be feared. Slamming the door, Van Zandt stepped away from his car. He knew, the secret of this was not to slink. People noticed any furtive movement. But if one acted like they belonged somewhere, then most people would naturally assume they did.

But a forceful walk was important as well. For years, Van Zandt had practiced his walk; he used it in front of the jury. It was the bold walk of a quarterback coming up to the line. But it wasn't the walk of Peyton Manning scanning the defense for a weakness to exploit. No, it was the walk of Tom Brady coming up to the line looking coolly straight ahead with the attitude that he was going to do what he wanted and the defense could just fuck off. Which, in Van Zandt's' opinion was why Manning won games and Brady won championships.

Using the Brady walk, Van Zandt strode through the parking lot. He nodded to a young couple heading out for the evening. He walked straight to the elevator, not worrying about cameras. He knew they were there, but he also knew they weren't working. They had been destroyed the night before. He had paid handsomely to ensure that.

Using Forsyth's key, he opened the door to the elevator vestibule, waiting impatiently. As he rode up to Forsyth's floor, he kept his head tilted down, just in case there was a camera in the elevator. Van Zandt's information, gleaned from the county as-built records said there wasn't one, but he wasn't about to look. He once heard of an idiot criminal looking for the camera and finding it. The idiot had been so proud of himself for disabling the camera, not realizing how good of a picture he gave to the cops while he looked. Taking no chances, Van Zandt kept his head down, and waited patiently as the elevator carried him upward.

When the car stopped and the doors opened, he strode directly to Forsyth's apartment. He used the key, breezing straight through the door as if he owned the place.

Once inside, he pulled on a pair of surgeon's gloves and looked around for a place to hide the gun. Best not get too fancy, he decided. He was after all depending on the intelligence of the cops. If he hid it too well, they might not even find it. Keep it simple, he decided. Sock drawer would be best.

He dropped the gun in the drawer, wrinkling his nose as he pulled Forsyth's spare socks over it. Feeling disgusted, and shuddering a little, he turned away. Even with the gloves, he didn't like touching another man's clothes.

In the living room, he stopped, studying the pictures on the faux fireplace mantle. Van Zandt allowed himself a small smile, this room was exactly as he knew it would be. Tacky. Insipid pictures of mundane people lined the tasteless, fake mantle.

Van Zandt pulled out the two framed photos from his briefcase. They were two pictures of Forsyth and Carter together. The first was real, taken by Van Zandt himself at the shooting party. The second was faked, photo-shopped together by a guy that Van Zandt knew. It looked perfect to the naked eye, but Van Zandt assumed it wouldn't holdup to close scrutiny. He also assumed it would never have to. Who would ever think to check it out?

Van Zandt looked around. That should do it. It was subtle but the pictures tied Carter and Forsyth together. Van Zandt had read many studies on the subject and he knew a subtle message to the brain was the hardest to erase. The cops would see the pictures of Carter and Forsyth and the pair would be forever linked in their minds.

Most pleased with himself, Van Zandt let himself out of the apartment, taking a quick second to wipe the door knob. He walked to the elevator already thinking of the bottle of wine he had chilling at home. He was also thinking of a woman. Not one woman in particular, just a woman. Even though he was calm on the outside, adrenaline was surging through his veins, creating a hot need deep in his belly. A savage smile crept onto his face. There was a service he could call. For a price, they would send over a girl.

Van Zandt was lost in thought, as he approached the elevator. The door slid open and a woman bustled out, slamming into Van Zandt. "Oh, pardon me," he said reflexively.

"Oh, no, it was me," she said flashing him a stunning smile. She cast a glance up at him. "Hey, I haven't seen you before. Are you new to the building?"

"No, just delivering some paperwork to a colleague," Van Zandt said, hoping to get out quickly.

"To Mister Forsyth?" she said in a deep voice and putting an obviously fake serious look on her face. "He is such a stick in the mud. So serious all the time."

"You should see him around the office," Van Zandt said offering his best smile.

"I bet," she agreed, nodding furiously.

Van Zandt looked at her and felt a hunger explode inside him. The excitement of the evening, stirred something inside him. Like an animal waking up, Van Zandt could feel the predator inside him begin to stir. "I was just about to get a late dinner, perhaps you would like to join me?"

She shot him a dazzling smile. "I just might...,"

"Van Zandt," Van Zandt said, extending his hand. "Perry Van Zandt."

She hesitated for the smallest second, but seeing his manicured hands, the tasteful, leather briefcase and obviously expensive suit, she nodded slightly. "Well Perry Van Zandt, what exactly did you have in mind?" she asked, hooking her arm in his.

"A magnificent evening."

Runway Bar Tucson AZ June 18th 2018 Monday Night Late

Ollie sat a table in the rear of the bar. He sipped a beer, glancing from time to time down at the stack of computer printouts on the table. He swore once under his breath.

His cell phone sat on the table beside the printouts. He glanced at the phone, like it was a snake and might bite him. He knew he was going to have to make the call sooner or later. "Aw, fuck it," he growled snatching up the phone. Squinting, he slowly punched in Mitch's number. Ollie knew about speed dial, but he preferred doing things the hard way, the old way. "Hey, boss, we gotta talk," he said when Mitch answered.

"What's up?" Mitch asked, recognizing the serious note in Ollie's voice.

Ollie reached for his beer, but he didn't drink, instead he veered off the subject. "You find anything at Jones' or Jenkins' houses?"

"Not a fucking thing," Mitch griped, still mad about it, and at the same time wondering why he was pissed. He hadn't really expected to find anything. They were cops, they would know better than to keep any damning evidence at their homes.

"Didn't figure you would," Ollie replied. He traced wet circles on the table with the bottom of his beer. He knew what he had to do, but the knowing didn't make it any easier.

"You need something?" Mitch asked, picking up on Ollie's mood. Something was eating at his old friend. "You okay?"

"I'm having a beer out a Chloe's Runway. Why don't you come and join me?"

"You got something on your mind, old man?"

"I might have. Buy you a beer."

"Damn, this must be important if you are buying," Mitch said, but Ollie didn't take the bait. "Okay, I'm on my way order me a Coors Light."

A half hour later, when Mitch pushed through the front door of the bar, Ollie was still setting at his table, a bucket of ice with four beers in front of him. Sidling up to the table, Mitch pulled up a chair, noting the sour look on the older man's face. "Man, you look like somebody's been pissing in your cheerios."

"Yeah," Ollie said, finishing his beer in a long gulp. He pointed the empty bottle at Mitch. "Maybe somebody has, and maybe a fucker we both know."

Mitch raised an eyebrow. "Oh yeah?" he asked and Ollie nodded sourly but didn't elaborate. "Well shit," Mitch grunted and fished a couple of beers out of the bucket. "Geena is coming over later. Is that okay?" Mitch asked, twisting the caps off and passing a beer to Ollie.

"Sure," Ollie muttered, taking the beer.

"Alright, I'm here, what's up?"

Ollie was back to tracing circles on the table with his bottle. Taking a quick drink, he sat the beer aside, and tossed Mitch the top print out. "Take a look at that." Mitch was scanning the list of names, when Ollie spoke. "Second one up from the bottom."

Mitch found the name Ollie referred to, frowning at it. He tapped the list. "What is this?"

"List of people connected with the case who also contributed money to Braxton's campaign."

"No shit?" Mitch grunted, almost laughing. "Are you sure about this?"

Ollie nodded taking a hit from his beer. "Yup."

"Damn, Sam Logan a closet Democrat? I never would have believed it." Mitch tossed the printout back to Ollie. "It's surprising, but it doesn't mean anything. Shit, knowing

Sam he tried to do an online contribution and gave to the wrong person. Or maybe, Maureen did it just to piss him off."

Ollie didn't even crack the hint of a smile. Instead, he slid more paper across the table. "Check this one out."

Mitch took the second printout a list of names with one circled in black ink. "Sam Logan? What the fuck is this?"

"Contacts from Kathy Reynolds' phone."

"Okay." Mitch frowned, staring steadily at Ollie. "I take it, there is more."

Ollie nodded silently passing another printout over. "A call from Tanner's phone went to that number." Another printout followed. "And a handful of calls from that same number back and forth to Chappy's cell."

"How do you know Chappy's number?"

Ollie smiled an evil grin. "Shit we had Tanner's cell downstairs for a couple of days. Somebody might have copied his contact list."

Mitch nodded; he should have seen that one. "What else?" he asked seeing other calls on the printout circled.

Ollie smiled, a tight grin almost a grimace. "Those that are circled are calls to and from that Cal Pierson."

"Humph," Mitch grunted He tapped the number on the top of the printout. "And that is Sam's cell phone number?"

"Nope," Ollie said. "That is a cheap prepaid, it was bought at a Kroger store in Cali. Sam has Sprint. He and his wife have consecutive numbers, and that ain't either of them."

"A burner, then," Mitch agreed. "So how did you tie it to Sam?"

"I'm not sure that I did." Ollie reached out a hand, stirring through the printouts. "Just that it's the number Kathy Reynolds had listed in her contacts file as Sam Logan."

"But if it is Sam, he has been talking to Tanner and Kathy, plus Chappy and that guy Pierson?"

Ollie nodded, picking up his Coors Light. "If it is Sam."

"Thin." Mitch frowned, trying to think it through. "Have you checked it out?"

"You mean called the number to see if Sam answers? No, I have not. I wasn't sure we wanted to do that." Ollie finished his beer, shoving the bottle away. "You believe it? "

"That Sam is mixed up in all of this?" Mitch asked more to himself than Ollie. "Fuck, I don't know." Mitch picked at the label on his beer bottle. He didn't want to believe it, but in the back of his mind, he was thinking about the doubts he had entertained earlier. But Sam Logan? It was just plain crazy. "There has to be another explanation. I can't see Sam in any of this. What's your feeling?"

Ollie gave a shrug. "I don't know. Sam was always a little tightly wound. Your typical jarhead."

Mitch smiled. He knew Ollie had been in the Army. "Personally, I can't see it. It isn't Sam's style." Mitch glanced across the table at his old friend. "Really? You buy it? Sam dirty?"

"He's in trouble," Ollie said quietly. "I pulled his credit report. He's way over extended."

Mitch laughed, feeling uncomfortable. "You? You pulled his credit report?"

Ollie shrugged, slipping a fresh beer out of the bucket. "I know my way around a computer," he said with a touch of defensiveness creeping into his tone.

"Yeah, right. You might and I stress might know how to pull up a porno sight."

Ollie laughed, twisting the top off the beer. "Naw, I keep getting tangled up in all those gay porn sights you got saved. But you're right, Parksey pulled it. But the fact remains, Sam is underwater bad. Question is; what do we do now?"

Mitch ran a hand through his hair. "Aw, man, I don't know. I say we keep it quiet for now."

Ollie nodded. "I already told Parker to forget about it."

"Jerry know?"

"Yeah, he and Wade were in there. Wade is coming by later."

Almost on cue, Wade Nichols approached the table, his flip-flops making slapping sounds on the floor. He was sipping a rum drink with the tiny umbrella from the drink poking out of the pocket of a very, loud Hawaiian shirt.

"So, Sam Logan, huh?" he said dropping into a chair.

"We were just talking about it. What do you think?"

Wade scratched his head of bushy curls, glancing back and forth between them. "I know you guys both like the dude, but yeah, I can see it."

Ollie looked curiously at Nichols. "Really, I always saw Sam as a straight as fuck arrow. Way too gung ho to get mixed up in murky shit like this."

Wade shrugged, taking a sip from his drink. "Yeah, I know, but I keep thinking back to that day when Herm Sosa got killed, and Sam put down that sorry fucker Estaban. I always got the feeling he kinda liked it."

"Shit I was jumping for joy when he put that sorry piece of shit in the ground," Ollie shot back.

Wade nodded. "Yeah so was I, but we were tight with Herm. Sam barely knew Herman." Wade shrugged again. "I don't know, all I am saying is, I got a weird vibe from him that day. He was carrying that rifle around and he had this cold look, but inside, I think he was a little hot. I think he kinda enjoyed it. The killing part." Wade took a sip from his drink sitting the glass carefully on the table. "I also heard something else about that day."

Mitch frowned liking none of this. "What did you hear?"

"I heard that it wasn't just luck that Sam ran into Estaban out at Mission Mine that day. I heard Sam got a tip and knew that Estaban was going to be there. There was a whisper that Sam had the mine staked out and when Estaban drove up, he took him out. That's why he used that big rifle."

Ollie snorted. "Who the hell cares? Estaban was nothing but trouble. Fucker was always flying on some kind of shit. If Sam hadn't taken him down, somebody woulda got hurt."

"Somebody did," Mitch said quietly, holding up his beer. "To Herman."

Together they solemnly raised their drinks. "To Herm." Most people would have felt the need to say something else, but the three of them took a quick drink in silence, each of them remembering the kindly old cop. It was Ollie who broke the silence with a harsh barking laugh. "Herman. I was thinking of the time that hooker hit him with her purse."

"Shit yes," Wade replied, slapping his knee. "She had a fifth of Calvert in the purse, almost broke his nose."

"Sure bled like it was broke," Ollie agreed.

"So, what do we do?" Mitch asked after a moment of silence. He tapped the paper. "Do we call the number, if Sam answers hang up?"

"No way," Nichols said flatly. "If he's involved, and sees your number on the caller ID. He will know we are onto him."

"Call it from the bar phone, if he answers hang up," Mitch suggested. "If the number comes up on the ID, he won't think it's us."

"That ain't a bad idea," Ollie said, heaving himself up out of the chair. "Give me that printout, I'll go make the call."

"How's the knee?" Mitch asked, as Ollie lumbered up to the bar.

"Hurts some, but a helluva lot less than my last divorce."

Mitch laughed. "You never learn. Always thinking with your dick."

"Yeah, blow me," Wade laughed holding up his glass. "This helps some."

"With your knee or your dick?"

Wade chuckled finishing his drink in one long swallow. "Hey buy a few more of these and you might find out."

"Yeah right," Mitch laughed raising his hand and catching the eye of the waitress and making a circling motion. "You still okay coming in like this and helping out? It ain't getting in the way of your therapy? I don't want them bitches from HR crawling up my ass."

Wade smirked a sly little smile. "I been cleared for light duty for bout a week or so, but I said, fuck it. I figured you'd stick me in dispatch, and the fish were biting down at Rocky Point so I stayed."

"I'm hurt that you would think I would put you in dispatch," Mitch said, knowing that all cops respected the people who worked in dispatch, but wanted no part of the job themselves.

Wade shot Mitch a skeptical look. "You actually gonna sit there and with a straight face say you wouldn't have stuck me down there?"

"Naw," Mitch answered with a grin. "Harris is looking for someone to help him with getting that inter-departmental response system in place. You could have helped him with that."

Wade made a face. "You know some bosses start out nice and slowly grow into being assholes, but I think you have a natural born talent for it."

"Maybe," Mitch admitted. "But I work at it too."

"Got a message," Ollie said. "Phone's outta juice."

"Maybe if it's pre-paid, he just run out of minutes," Wade offered.

"Ditched it," Mitch said. "Too much going on. He wouldn't want it with him."

"Where does that leave us now?" Wade wondered.

Mitch glanced sideways at the older man. "You ready to come back to work full time, maybe even do some overtime?"

"Yeah, fuck it. You need me. What do you want me to do?"

"Take a hard look at Sam. See if you can tie him to Brody and Kathy." Mitch toyed with his bottle. "I was thinking I might go talk to him. See if I can get a read."

Ollie was already shaking his head. "No way. Logan's an old dog. He'll smell it if you come around asking questions. Best to just stay away from him."

"Hell, I've already been talking to him. He's already offered to help. I was thinking of bringing him in."

"Bringing who in?" Geena stopped in her tracks, knowing by the way all three men stopped talking and were staring up at her that she had interrupted something. "Oh, I'm sorry. I shouldn't have come. Jerry and Carly said you were all meeting here for a drink." Geena was babbling and shut up suddenly, looking from Mitch to his two detectives. "I'm sorry, I didn't mean to interrupt."

Mitch smiled at her, pulling back a stool. "It's all good; have a seat."

"Are you sure? It seemed like you guys were into something serious."

"Just this fucking case," Ollie said, snagging a beer out of the bucket. He twisted off the top, tossed that at Wade, and passed the bottle to her. "Here you go."

"Hell, I would rather talk to you than either one of these crusty bastards," Wade said, giving her a smile.

Geena gave them a tentative smile. "Well, as long as I am not intruding."

"We were talking about Sam Logan," Mitch said.

"The state cop?" Geena asked, with the tiniest of frowns. Now she understood their clannish attitude. "You think he is involved in all of this?"

"Not this, per se," Mitch said, choosing his words carefully.

"But you are looking at him?" Geena asked, taking a stool by Mitch and leaning casually into his space. "He's dirty?"

"Aw, well," Mitch stammered, catching the quick look that passed between Wade and Ollie. They knew he and Geena had been together. He was fumbling for the words when he saw Hartek and Parker approaching. "Hey guys."

"See you started without us," Jerry said, as he and Carly came up to the table.

"Shit your just in time," Wade said, a crafty smile on his face.

"Yeah, I'm just in time to buy the next round," Jerry groaned, helping Mitch drag two tables together.

"And they said, you would never be a good detective," Wade boomed, clapping his partner on the back.

"Yeah; detect this," Jerry said, showing Wade his middle finger. He got the waitress' eye and motioned for another round.

"Some detective, Mitch just ordered a round," Ollie said, laughing as he dug an elbow into Wade's ribs.

"Well, shit we'll have plenty, then" Jerry said, sourly.

"Is that the stuff we worked on?" Carly asked sliding into a chair. "Did you tell Mitch what we found?"

"Working on it," Ollie grunted, but Mitch could see a little note of pride in Ollie's gruff voice. "Alright, check this out," he said, picking a paper out of the pile and pushing it across at Mitch. "Look at the dates, that phone Sam is using was bought and activated back in March, but no calls to Kathy until Tanner gets arrested."

"Calling because he can't get a hold of Tanner," Jerry offered. "Trying to find out how to get in touch with Tanner?"

"Nope," Carly said shaking her head. "Look at the call times. Fifty-three minutes first call and twenty-seven the next call. They were discussing something."

"Huh," Mitch grunted, thinking it through. "So, say Sam is involved. What do you think, providing protection for the drugs going from here west?"

"That would be my guess," Wade said, sipping his drink. "In his position, Sam would be able to give them an open road all the way to Cali. No worries getting their drugs to San Diego."

"Makes sense," Ollie agreed. "They got the border in Cali shut tighter than a librarian's thighs, and we are wide open here. They breeze it across the border here and mule it out to Cali."

"Pretty neat set up when you stop and think about it," Wade said, looking around the table. "The Mexicans provide the drugs, Chappy and his merry little band provide the transportation, and that cat Flores does the selling. Slick."

Mitch nodded, a few of the tumblers in his mind clicking into place. "And you say Sam is broke?"

"Not just broke," Ollie said grimly. "He's drowning."

Mitch nodded, his mind racing. "Okay, so he's broke and needs money," Mitch stopped, being strapped for cash did not fit the image he had of Sam Logan. "Shit, I've known Sam for years and he is tighter than Scrooge McDuck. He might not have the first dollar he ever made, but I guarantee you he can tell you where he spent that dollar, what he bought and how much change he got back. So, tell me: why is he so broke?"

"Cancer," Ollie said, in a tone that would have sent a shiver down an undertaker's back. "I thought about that. If he or Maureen were sick, that would explain why they are so broke. Nothing blows through money quicker than doctor bills."

"Aw shit, that's too bad," Wade agreed.

"You think that is right?" Carly asked.

Wade patted his knee brace. "Believe me, I know. Even if you got decent insurance, them docs will bleed you dry."

"Hah old man, go peddle your pity party somewhere else, I ain't buying you no more drinks," Jerry said, breaking the grim mood.

Mitch grinned weakly, still feeling a little queasy inside at the thought of either Sam or Maureen being sick. He pushed that aside and tried to think about the problem at hand. "Sam is dead broke and as a way to get well, he throws in with Chappy, and Flores?" Mitch paused, getting a few tentative nods. "But I know Sam Logan. He truly hates drugs, so you can bet he never had any notions of letting those drugs hit the streets."

"Aw crap, so that thing out in the desert, that was Sam," Wade agreed. "Shit, looking back we probably shoulda seen that."

"Yeah, maybe," Mitch grunted. "So now he has the drugs...." Mitch stopped, a physical bolt of pain shooting through him. "Aw, man," he said softly.

"What?" several voices asked at once.

"Aw fuck me," Mitch muttered. All of a sudden it felt like dawn was breaking. Mitch had a flash of one of those time lapse photos of the sun coming up where the light raced across the landscape, pushing back the darkness and revealing all the details of the land. But now, it was the sun coming up on the case, pushing back the shadows of what they didn't know. Slowly, Mitch could see the whole picture, the trouble was he didn't like what he saw. Mitch hung his head. "Jones and Jenkins, man I fucking killed them."

"Aw knock that shit off," Ollie said gruffly, pointing a finger across the table at Mitch. "Quit being a pussy about this. No way Van Zandt could have reacted this fast."

"No not Van Zandt."

"You mean Sam Logan," Geena said softly.

"Yep," Mitch said, tapping the sheet. "Look at this, Sam called Chappy right after I dropped him off. Man, I told him we what we were thinking about Jones and Jenkins. Check out the time. He had to have made the call within five minutes of me dropping him off." As Mitch talked, the light shining on the case spread out a little farther. All of a sudden, a picture slammed into focus in Mitch's mind. "Shit! Think of this." Mitch pointed at the group with his beer. "What would Chappy look like if he shaved the beard, butched his hair short and dyed it platinum blonde?"

"Damn, from a little ways out, he would be a dead nuts ringer for Tanner," Ollie said.

"Have any of you actually seen Chappy since he got back?" Mitch asked and got a series of head shakes.

"So Chappy killed Jones and Jenkins," Jerry said, a note of doubt creeping into his voice. Mitch heard what he said, but was also struck with how he had said Jones and Jenkins, being formal instead of calling them Jonsey and Jenks as they had been called for years. Thinking back, Mitch realized he had earlier done the same thing, and wondered if it was because they were dead, or because they had been dirty. "Why would Chappy do that?" Jerry asked, cutting across Mitch's thoughts.

"Sam had their drugs," Mitch said. "I'm betting he is the one who took down that deal out in the desert."

"Used the drugs to get Chappy to go after Jones and Jenkins?" Ollie said, rubbing his chin.

"But why would Sam want them dead?" Carly asked.

"Who the hell cares," Wade said. "Done us a big favor, either way."

"That is true," Mitch said realizing the implications. "Now the chief can announce they were killed in the line of duty. No need to air our dirty laundry in public. No one has to know the rest."

Ollie scowled, glaring at Mitch. "Shit you would be okay with that?"

Mitch nodded. "If they went out in the line of duty, then Karen would get Jones' bennies. If it ever got out they were dirty, she wouldn't get dick. I don't give a shit about them, but Karen deserves to be taken care of."

"Okay, yeah, you're right," Ollie said grudgingly. "Still kinda burns my ass a little."

"Doesn't matter," Wade decided. "Too many people already know about it, and one person in particular. It's going to get out."

"Harris," Mitch said grimly.

"Yup," Wade said nodding. "He won't be able to keep from spilling the beans on them. It's just in his nature. In the end Karen won't get dick from the city."

"I hope those two silly bastards got a lot of money," Jerry said. "Hopefully Jones has some stashed back for her."

"Won't matter," Geena said quietly. "The money is a link back to Van Zandt. We have to keep looking for it. She won't be allowed to keep it."

"Shit and that kills any chance of Karen getting Jones' bennies," Ollie groaned.

"What if the chief said they were working undercover?" Carly asked shyly.

For a second the table was quiet, then Wade let out a long laugh slapping the table. "Hell yes, might work," he said grinning. He shot a look at Mitch. "You think he will do it?"

Mitch shrugged reaching for his phone. "Maybe, he seems to be a standup guy." Mitch started to dial, then stopped.

"Aren't you gonna call?" Ollie demanded.

"Oh hell, it's almost mid-night. Don't really think I want to wake him up to ask a favor?"

Mitch was still holding his phone when it rang. "Oh shit," he muttered, as every phone at the table began to ring.

I-10 Benson AZ June 19th 20185 Tuesday after Midnight

Sam drove to the east, out of Tucson following the interstate as it dropped down into Benson. Sam had ditched the Cherokee and was now driving his own personal truck. It was an eighty-six Ford. It was old with a bench seat, but Sam liked it.

He felt a twinge of guilt over driving the truck. If anyone he knew saw it, they might recognize the truck. Sam scowled at the windshield, knowing he shouldn't be in the truck.

But hell, he just couldn't stand driving that Jeep any longer. That pitted windshield would drive a nun to drink, and Sam had ridden bucking horses that gave a smoother ride. Besides he was nearing the end of this anyway, Sam was under no illusions. If he were still alive by this time next week, it'd take a miracle. And Sam figured God had better things to do than save his sorry ass. So, he drove the truck, his truck. Sam loved that truck. It was the only vehicle he had ever bought that was brand new. He'd bought it in eighty-seven, a hold over, but still brand new when he drove it off the lot. Sam dearly loved that truck.

And truthfully, he didn't really give a fuck.

Coasting through Benson, he lit the cigar that Mitch gave him. Sam had never really done cigars, but damn, these were good. A man could get used to them.

Mitch.

Sam smiled. Fucking Mitch. Damn it, he liked that boy. The thought sort of surprised Sam. He'd known Mitch for years. And on the surface, Mitch was everything that Sam despised. Mitch was definitely a smart ass, and if you weren't real careful, that boy would deal you out of your last pair of skivvies. And with that hair, crap, he had more hair than a hyena. Mitch was in Sam's book, a hippie. Sam took a puff on the cigar, shaking his head.

Of course, Mitch might deal you out of your last dollar, but if you needed anything, Mitch would be the first one there to help, and if you needed it, he would give you his last dollar. Made him alright in Sam's book.

Sam savored another puff, wondering if Mitch caught up with him, if he would give Sam a break. Like maybe one of those two-hour head starts like they were always doing in the movies. Sam laughed, almost choking on the cigar. Not likely. When it came right down to the nut cutting, that damn Mitch had a streak of decency in him a mile wide.

Well, screw it, Sam thought. It wasn't all bad; he was puffing on a damn fine stogie. He had a longneck Coors Light to sip on, and the rest of a sixer in the cooler. And he had a job to do. What more could a man ask for? Didn't matter that it was a hard job, Sam was happy, rolling across the desert in the middle of the night. It made no sense, but he was happy. He might be dead in a few days, but he was happy tonight. Shit, he had the world by the tail.

He'd just had a great dinner with his wife, and she'd even paid. After dinner, they drove out to Reddington Pass and walked under the stars. They'd held hands talked about the good old days. Remembered old friends, and thanked God for the life they had led.

Afterwards, they drove home, lit candles, drank wine and made love. Sam had held the woman he'd loved for most of his life. He'd been so contented that he hadn't wanted to get up. But in the end, he done it.

It had been hard, but he done it. His whole life, Sam had been doing the hard thing. He'd done the hard thing as a boy growing up on a farm in central Arizona. He'd gotten up before dawn to feed livestock. He'd done the hard thing in the Corps, serving in Viet Nam and again in Kuwait.

A man did the hard thing. That's what made him a man.

The thing that was riding heavy on Sam's mind was the hard thing wasn't always the most honorable thing. Of course, it hadn't always been that way. Sam blamed it on the times, and the wimpy liberals who seemed to be everywhere these days.

Sam wasn't necessarily proud of what he was doing, but he felt like it had to be done. What bothered him was he was deceiving some good cops. But Sam was not going to leave his wife in a bind. That woman was a saint, and she deserved better.

Money, in the end, it always came down to money.

With a heavy heart, Sam pulled out of Benson, pulling the hill to Texas Canyon. He passed the rest stop on the eastbound side, continuing on to the next exit. The infamous *Thing* exit. Sam smiled as he crossed the interstate and headed back west. Many years ago, they had stopped and paid their dollar to see the *Thing*. Sam chuckled, if he died tonight, at least he could always say he saw the *Thing*.

Sam pulled into the rest stop, checking his watch. Almost two, he was almost an hour early. The rest stop was divided into two sections, one for the big rigs and one for autos. The side for the trucks was full, but the lot for cars was almost empty.

A couple of vehicles were parked at the far end. They were dark and quiet, obviously spending the night. Sam picked the first parking stall the farthest from the bathrooms. He smiled, noting that he would be directly underneath the light. Sam had been pulling into these stops for the better part of twenty-five years and he knew if he parked directly under the light, the truck would look innocent and well lit. But in reality, the cab would be dark, the light shining on the roof but not inside. Sam backed in so if he had to leave fast he could.

The cigar clenched between his teeth, Sam got out of the truck, stretching the kinks out of his back. From the passenger's seat, Sam grabbed a thirty-pound bag of dog food he had picked up at Fry's. He placed the bag upright in the seat. Next, he took a gallon jug of water purchased at the same time as the dog food. Stepping around to the front of the truck, he poured the water out. As the water gurgled out of the jug, splashing onto the dirt, Sam had a brief moment of introspection. It bothered him a little that he had known just how to do this. Seemed like an honest man woulda had to think harder about it.

Guess a lifetime of dealing with these assholes was finally paying off. Sam took the empty jug and taped it to the headrest. He pulled an old Diamondbacks cap on the jug, then backed away, nodding to himself. Not too bad, if he did say so his own damn self. The dog food leant bulk to the deception, giving the vague hint of a shoulder. The jug was sorta the shape and size of a man's head. But it was the cap that sold the whole thing. In this light no one even think that it wasn't a man sitting in the truck waiting.

Unless they hit the cab with the headlights.

Sam puffed on his cigar, thinking about it. Chances were they would cross in front of the truck and come up on driver's side. Since he was in the first stall, there was a curb next to his truck on the passenger's side. They wouldn't park on that side. They might circle the lot, checking things out but probably not. They wouldn't want to draw any extra attention to themselves.

In the end he decided they would be cautious, but not overly so. They wouldn't be afraid of Sam. To them he was just an old man, and they were badass bikers. Of course, they were dangerous men, Sam best be careful or they would be staking his hide. Sam looked the rest stop over, seeing the angles and setting up his ambush in his mind.

There was a Palo Verde tree directly across from his truck. If he stood beside the tree, in the shadows, he would be virtually invisible. He would have a clear shot no matter where they stopped. Also, if their attention was directed at the truck, Sam would be behind them. Unconsciously nodding his head, Sam walked around the truck to the right side. The truck was a single cab with a bench seat and behind the seat, Sam had a gun case mounted. The case had been fashioned and welded in years ago by an old man who claimed to have worked on cars for bootleggers back in the days of prohibition. Sam didn't know if he believed all of that, but the old man had certainly built Sam one helluva nice gun case. It meant the seat couldn't be moved, but that bothered Sam not in the least. Nothing pissed him off more than some peckerwood messing with his seat adjustment.

Sam leaned the seat forward and opened the case, surveying it's contents, even though he knew down to the last bullet what was in there. There was a nice Savage twenty-two rifle. Sam frowned, these boys were some big hosses, it might take a bullet with a bit more whump than a twenty-two to bring them down. And if they happened to have some kind of armor?

Not the twenty-two then. A lever action thirty-thirty? Naw lever action was too slow. Sam reached down and touched a Colt .223 semi-auto carbine. He smiled patting the rifle. Sam had two thirty round clips, that would get the job done.

It was what liberals might call an assault rifle. Dumbasses! Sam snorted, didn't matter what it looked like, it was a rifle pure and simple, no better or worse than the man behind it.

Sam frowned; he would be shooting towards the trucks parked on the other side of the rest stop. The .223 round could easily penetrate the sleeper of one of those trucks, killing or injuring somebody inside.

A part of Sam was saying fuck it, go ahead, setup by the tree, and get the job done. It was such a perfect ambush spot. But in reality, it wasn't perfect. Sam knew if a stray bullet from his rifle hurt or killed one of those truckers, he would never forgive himself.

Regretfully, he let go of the .223.

He picked up the Remington 11-87 12-gauge pump. Truly his favorite gun. The Remington was a Father's Day gift from his son. The last gift he had from his son. They had planned to go hunting last fall, sadly when hunting season rolled around, Sammy was dead.

He pulled out the shotgun. Even with the thirty-inch barrel and a full choke, it was a short-range weapon. Using a quarter to remove the modified choke that was in the gun, Sam once again studied the layout. The Palo Verde tree was too far from his truck.

Maybe if he took them while they were still on their bikes? Thinking about it, Sam dug a full choke out of a tray in the gun locker. Hell yeah. Sam grinned around his cigar, as he screwed in the tighter choke; he knew what he was going to do. He sat his cooler with five beers left in the back of the truck. From the gun locker he took out a Colt M1911. Sam had another one at home, almost the mirror image, but this pistol was special, this one had belonged to his daddy, issued to him before the old man shipped out to fight the Japanese in the South Pacific.

Even though he knew the mag was full, Sam hit the release dropping the clip in his left hand. After a quick look at the clip, he slapped it back in the weapon. Working the slide, he jacked a round in the chamber. Dropping out the clip, he replaced that shell in the clip, and slapped the mag home. Setting the safety, he stuck the weapon behind his belt.

Sam crawled up in the back of the truck, leaning his back against the cab. Puffing on the cigar, he pulled a fresh beer from the cooler. He knew he should put the stogie out, there was a tiny chance they might smell it. Fuck'em, Sam decided, it was a damn fine cigar. He might not have long left on this earth and he was gonna damn well enjoy what little he had left.

He took a sip from the beer, looking up at the stars. A clear night and he could see a thousand stars. He saw the red light on an aircraft heading south, probably a chopper bound for Fort Huachuca.

Sam closed his eyes. In a small way this was just like an early morning hunt. Even with the Interstate a few yards away, there was a stillness to the night. And just the slightest nip in the air. Sam sat his beer in the bed of the truck, thinking about all the hunts he had been on over the years. He ran a hand over the shotgun, caressing its smoothness, and thinking about the one hunt that never happened. A melancholy feeling settled over him. Dammit to hell, a man shouldn't outlive his children.

Sam wondered how many nights like this he had left. Nights when he could still remember the good times. Sam remembered his son's first elk hunting trip to Colorado. At a place called Sleepy Cat. An early snow storm had kept them in camp for several days, but on the last day, the sun broke out, and they went out. Just before noon, little Sammy had gotten his elk.

It was one of Sam's favorite memories. He could close his eyes and smell the wood smoke from the fire, the smell of damp, clothing and gear. Five grown men and two boys snowed in for days, eating canned chili and drinking cheap beer and even cheaper whiskey. Telling stories, mostly lies, and lighting farts. Sam smiled, he could almost close his eyes and see Sammy's shinning face as he sat around that campfire, listening to the stories. It pained Sam to think that soon he might lose this memory along with countless others.

At first it was faint, only a distance hum, but Sam's ear caught it. Calmly he took a last long pull from his cigar. His hands steady, he stubbed out the cigar on his boot, and tossed it onto the asphalt. By now the sounds was louder, the bikes growling as they came up the hill. Sam smiled around the neck of his beer bottle as he watched the bikes roar past the rest area.

With one last sip, he set the beer aside and slid down in the truck bed. He couldn't see, but it didn't matter, the sound of the bikes told him all he needed to know. He heard the pipes rattle as they slowed and took the same exit Sam had taken earlier. They revved back up, crossing over the interstate, and then the bikes bellowed as they really leaned into it heading down the ramp.

Coming for him. Sam had no doubts but what they meant to do was kill him. Which he supposed was only fair; since he damn sure meant to kill them. In a few minutes they'd see.

As the motorcycles roared back in his direction, Sam felt a greasy feeling deep in his guts and a dryness in his throat. Sam had felt these feelings many times over the years, and he ignored them now. Instead, he closed his eyes, concentrating solely on the sound of the bikes.

Stupid fucks.

If they would have ghosted up to the rest stop in a normal vehicle, they could have had the upper hand. But not now, those motorcycles were telling Sam all he needed to know. He could tell when they slowed and turned off the interstate. They were still slowing as they came into the rest area.

Sam waited until it sounded like the bikes were almost on top of him, and then he rolled onto one knee, bringing the shotgun to his shoulder, the muzzle right by the passenger's door. Even as the gun touched his shoulder, the massive body of Dell Miers seemed to fill Sam's sight picture. Sam pulled the trigger, watching as the blast knocked Dell backwards off the bike.

Sam knew this wasn't the case. The blast might have slowed Dell, but even if all fifteen pellets from the three-inch shell hit him, they wouldn't drive him backwards. Mostly it was Dell jerking backwards away from the ball of fire that streaked from the end of the gun. That and the momentum of the motorcycle driving out from underneath him. Either way, Dell flipped backwards off the bike and hit the asphalt with a dull thud.

Sam saw this, a part of his brain registering it, even while he swung the gun at Chappy. Already Chappy was twisting the throttle, leaning forward over the bike as Sam pulled the trigger again. Sam saw Chappy flinch, but he knew he had been a little behind with the shot.

Pointing the shotgun to the sky, Sam jumped to the other side of the truck, bringing the gun back down, squeezing off a shot when Chappy appeared on the other side of the truck. Chappy had been expecting the shot, because he jerked the bike hard to the right, still hard on the throttle. Sam couldn't tell if it was his shot or the fact that Chappy tried such a radical maneuver under full throttle, but the back tire of the bike spun out, dumping Chappy hard to the ground.

Quick as any pro athlete, Chappy came to his feet, sprinting for the rocks several yards away. This time Sam took his time, holding his aim low. The shotgun blast swept the legs out from under Chappy spilling him hard to the ground.

Adrenaline surging through his veins like high voltage, Sam vaulted from the truck, sprinting around Chappy's bike. He could see the biker struggling to sit up as he drew an old Desert Eagle pistol from his belt. Curious. A Desert Eagle, they had been all the rage back in the day, but Sam hadn't seen one in years.

Sam stomped down on Chappy's wrist, pinning his hand and gun to the pavement. "You ain't dead yet?" Sam grunted out of breath.

Chappy grinned, revealing bloody teeth. "Not even close," he declared, but Sam wasn't quite sure. He could see where one of the sixty-grain pellets had torn through Chappy's neck. At least two had penetrated the biker's massive bicep, and by the way the arm was hanging, Sam would bet the bone was broken. The biker's leather chaps were shredded and his legs were pouring blood. It was clear; Chappy wasn't going to be walking for a while.

Sam heard shouts and threw a quick glance over his shoulder. He could see several of the truckers, in various states of dress and undress running across the pea gravel field, which separated the two lots. "Shit," Sam growled under his breath.

"Looks like I'm saved," Chappy said.

"Shut up," Sam said, and drove the butt of the shotgun into the side of Chappy's head. The biker flopped over and was dead still. For a second, Sam feared he might have killed Chappy, but then he heard a snort and frothy bubbles blew from around Chappy's lips. Not that it mattered, Sam had no intention of letting the biker ever see the sun again.

Forgetting about Chappy, Sam turned to greet the truckers. Damn fools, Sam swore under his breath. Last thing he needed was a bunch of busybodies butting in. Painfully aware that the shotgun was as empty as a politician's soul, Sam angled the Remington in their general direction. "Hold up there, fellas," he said mildly.

As one, they skidded to a stop. One of them, a bare-chested fella with a motorcycle tattooed across his massive belly, waved a hand between Dell and Chappy's bodies. "You killed them!" he shouted.

"Not yet," Sam said grimly, thinking that feller's belly might have been flat when the tattoo was done, but that motorcycle had grown a sidecar over the years. The fella was breathing real hard and every time he took a breath, it looked like the motorcycle was trying to pop a wheelie. Had Sam been in a better mood, he might have found it entertaining, but probably not. "They ain't dead yet," he grunted showing them his badge. "Sam Logan, with the state police. I'm going to need you boys to help me."

"How so?" motorcycle belly demanded, the bike still doing jump-starts as he struggled to catch his breath.

"Like I said, they ain't dead yet, and I need to get these boys back to the hospital in Benson." Sam reached down and took the Desert Eagle from Chappy's limp hand. "I reckon you fellas been hearing about that girl that was kidnapped down here few days back?"

"Heard about it on the radio couple of days back when I was heading to Houston," a three-hundred-pound man in a Katie Perry tee shirt with no sleeves said, nodding his head. "Didn't hear anything today. I was kinda hoping they found her."

"Not yet," Sam said, shaking his head. "But I aim to tonight."

Katie Perry tipped his head to Chappy's lifeless form. "These the assholes that did it?"

"Yup," Sam replied, gravely nodding his head. "I'd be obliged if you boys would help get them in the back of the truck. I want to get them over to Benson to the hospital. Truthfully, I don't give a shit if they die or not, but I need to find out where that girl is before they die."

"Probably shouldn't have walloped that dude with the shotgun then," a whip thin man pointed out.

Sam grinned, nodding as he tried to put on his best aw shucks, good ol' boy face. "Danged if you ain't right about that. But you know how them damned doctors are, I probably won't get a chance again. Wanted to show him who is boss." Sam clapped his hand. "So, how bouts we get these boys loaded so I can get them into town?"

Sam stood back and watched as they carried Chappy to the back of the truck and wrestled him into the back. "I think this asshole is dead," Katie Perry said as they struggled to lift Dell.

"Probably, but I will let the doc decide that," Sam said, closing the tailgate after they managed to get Dell's massive body in the truck.

"How do we know you are really a cop?" motorcycle belly wheezed, the bike on his belly jumping up and down like a wild horse on the end of a short rope.

Sam took the last four beers from his cooler, giving them each one and keeping one for himself. He slid into his truck, giving them a wry grin. "Don't reckon you do," he said placing the Desert Eagle on the seat beside him, and his 1911 on the dash. "It occurs to me that a smart man might want to write down my tag number as I leave," he advised, dropping the truck into gear. "Thanks, boys," he said taking a sip of Coors Light as he rolled away from them.

Sam eased out onto the Interstate, thinking that probably everyone in the rest stop had already called 911.

Sam wasn't overly worried. He had a head start and he knew every highway, every dirt road, and every goat trail in southern Arizona. They'd play hell catching him

Sam took another long pull from the Coors Light. And if they did? Well fuck it everybody had to go sometime.

CHAPTER FOURTEEN

Interstate 10 Outskirts of Town Tucson AZ June 19th 2018 Tuesday Before Dawn

The city felt quiet, like a slumbering giant as they rolled back into town. Mitch and Geena sat shoulder to shoulder in the back of Jerry's Expedition. They sat quietly, their shoulders touching, but it wasn't the easy peace between two people who were comfortable with each other. Instead it was the awkward silence of two strangers who had fallen into bed and were now feeling uncomfortable about it.

Geena yawned and leaned her head on Mitch's shoulder. "I think I am going to go back to my hotel room. I need a shower." She stuck out her tongue. "I feel like the floor of a subway car," she said patting his chest. "Maybe I can catch a few hours' sleep."

"Sure," Mitch replied, trying not to sound too relieved. "I think I am going to go back to the office. See if I can figure out a few things."

"Wow, you're not tired?"

"Exhausted," Mitch said, shrugging heavily. "I just don't think that I could sleep. I'm hoping something will come to me. I keep feeling like I am missing something."

"Well, good luck with that. I plan on being asleep twenty seconds after my head hits the pillow."

"Good luck with that," Mitch said with a small chuckle. "You want a ride?"

Geena smiled, patting his arm. "You are sweet, but I have the rental car."

"Sounds good," Mitch replied as Jerry swung his rig into the bar parking lot. He stopped behind their cars, looking back over his shoulder at Mitch. "What time you want us back in, boss?"

Mitch shrugged thinking about it. "Anybody got anything to run with?"

"I'd like to take another whack at that I-Pod," Wade said.

"We need to find Brody," Ollie growled, his voice reminding Mitch of junkyard dog.

"You're right about that," Mitch agreed, glancing at his watch. "It's just after three. Everybody go home; get a few hours and be back by ten. Ollie, you and Carly can go find Brody. Grab his ass and drag him in here. Jerry, you stay after Forsyth, get whatever there is to get. Wade, crack that I-Pod."

Wade nodded, throwing a quick look at Geena. "Let me know if your people get anything out of that other MP3."

"I will," Geena promised working her way out of the Expedition. She glanced around, waiting for Mitch to climb out of the vehicle. "Is this alright?" she whispered, leaning close to Mitch. "That I go to the hotel?"

"Sure," Mitch said, a little too quick.

"Are we okay?" Geena asked as they drifted towards her rental car.

"Yeah, just tired," Mitch said, avoiding the real question, she was asking. "You good to drive? Not too tired?" he asked, opening the door for her. She flashed a tired smile and nodded. "Sleep well," he said leaning in for a quick kiss.

Geena slid in the car, looking up at Mitch. "You should get some rest as well," Geena instructed.

"Yes dear," Mitch said, smiling as he closed the door. Mitch sighed, watching her drive away, feeling guilty that he was glad to see her go.

As he turned away, Mitch saw Ollie leaning against the fender of the Mustang, anger radiating off him like heat waves from a desert highway. "What's up?" Mitch asked, sensing the older man had something on his mind.

Ollie scowled, pushing away from the car. "What the fuck are you doing?" he demanded, a bit of an ugly edge to his tone.

"Whoa, man," Mitch said, holding out his hands. "What's eating your ass?"

Ollie gestured at Geena's retreating car. "What are you doing? She's a nice lady."

"Shit, no argument there," Mitch conceded, a little taken back by Ollie's tone.

Ollie stepped in close. "You're fucking her," he hissed, poking Mitch in the chest. "You need to get your shit together. Grow your ass up."

Mitch leaned back against the car. "Ollie, what's going on with you?"

"It's not me," he hissed, jerking his head towards the shadows. "You got a visitor." Ollie held Mitch's gaze with a hot stare, then jabbed him in the chest again. "Do the right thing, dickhead."

"Mitch," A voice called from the shadows as Ollie stomped away. "Is it okay?"

"Sure," Mitch replied, trying to place the voice.

"I have something for you," Frankie O'Hara said, easing from the shadows.

Mitch had started around the car to meet her, but stopped dead in his tracks as she emerged from the darkness. "Frankie, holy shit! You look fantastic," he exclaimed.

It was true, she looked dynamite. She was wearing a crisp, white button up shirt. Over the top she wore a woman's dark gray blazer and tight, black pants. "Thank you," she murmured, turning away a little, and maybe blushing just a touch.

"Frankie, what are you doing here? It's late."

"I know, I'm sorry," she whispered. "I wanted to thank you."

"Frankie, forget it. You don't owe me a damn thing. Listen, I was an asshole the other night," Mitch blew out a sigh. "I've been feeling bad about it. I should have called you and apologized. I meant to. I just…."

Frankie shook her head, "No, you were trying to help me and I didn't want to hear it." She slid forward, moving like a dancer and touching his arm lightly. "Oh man, you were so right. I went to that first place that bank or whatever it was and the minute I walked in I felt like crap." She laughed a little, covering her embarrassment. "Nobody said anything, but they were looking down their noses at me. I realized right then that you were right and I needed to get a new image."

Mitch smiled, suddenly aware of how close she was standing. He felt a trickle of sweat roll down his back, which had nothing to do with the ninety-five-degree temperatures. "That's great, Frankie. You sure look great," Mitch stammered.

"Thank you." She smiled, plucking at his sleeve. "I also have something for you. When I went to see that fucking

Joe to collect for the cigars he lost to you, I saw that asshole Chappy."

"Be careful around him," Mitch warned, feeling a wave of genuine concern.

"You know it," she said and managed to slide a half step closer. "Don't worry. I have a two shot Derringer that I always keep close."

"Good girl," Mitch said, nodding wondering where she could hide a paperclip, much less a pistol. "I had heard that Chappy was back, but thanks for the heads up."

"No, no," Frankie said hurriedly. "I figured that you already knew he was back. But I had heard that you were looking at Tanner for killing some reporter."

An idea of where she was heading sprang into Mitch's mind. "We were," he said. "But we know now that it wasn't Tanner."

"It was Chappy!" Frankie spat out, leaving no doubt how she felt about Chappy. "Like I said, I saw him. He cut his hair and dyed it blonde! From a block away, he easily could pass for Tanner."

Mitch smiled, liking the confirmation of his own ideas. He gave Frankie a quick business-like hug. "Thank you," he said. "We were wondering how all that might have gone down. A wit gave a spot-on description of Tanner."

"It was Chappy!" Frankie said, almost beaming. "Did I do good? Did I help?"

"Hell, yes you did."

Frankie smiled her whole face lighting up. "Will you go arrest Chappy now?"

Mitch scowled, mad at himself. "I don't know. I think I screwed up by arresting Tanner. Makes it hard to go after anyone else now."

"That sucks."

"Yeah," Mitch grunted sourly. Shaking his head, he grinned at her. "Really? You actually have a gun on you?"

Mitch asked, leaning back and looking her over. "I can't imagine where you might have it, and I've been trained to spot concealed weapons."

"It's there," she said, stepping back, spreading her arms and doing a little turn. "But only a strip search would find it."

Mitch groaned, putting an arm around her shoulders. "Aw man, your killing me."

"Yeah," she whispered, sliding her arms around him.

The coolness of the night long gone, Mitch felt a flush on his face and sweat run down his back. "Damn it's late, have you been waiting on me?"

"Not long," Frankie replied, her head against his chest. "I thought about calling you, but I wanted to tell you in person." It might have been the poor lighting in the parking lot, but Mitch actually thought she blushed. "And I wanted you to see my new clothes."

"Very nice. You look fantastic," Mitch said. "Shit, did you ride your bike? Can I give you a ride?"

"No," Frankie said, shaking her head. "I did a rental. That was another reason I wanted to talk to you, I think I need a car. Could you help me get a good one?"

"Sure," Mitch agreed. "Give me a week or so to finish up this case."

"Ok," Frankie said, nodding slowly. "I can deal with the rental that long." She made a face. "My brother suggested that I get a Prius."

"Hope you kicked his ass," Mitch replied, thinking he never even knew she had a brother.

"Kicked him right in the balls."

"Good for you," Mitch said. "I can't see you in a car though."

Frankie shook her head, a grimace springing to her face. "Got me some skirts, they don't work so well on the bike."

A vision of Frankie in a skirt exploded across Mitch's brain, as sweat rolled down his back. In his mind the skirt was black, form fitting, and of course very short. "Shit," he muttered. "So, a car, huh?" he asked, trying to get the conversation back on safer ground.

"Maybe not a car. I was thinking of something with a few more balls." She looked up at him, her eyes seeming very large in the moonlight. "What do you think of a Jeep Cherokee?"

"Good rigs," Mitch conceded. "Go anywhere, except past a gas station."

Perry Van Zandt's Home Great Falls Virginia June 19th 2018 Tuesday Pre-Dawn

Idling quietly along, Van Zandt swung around his house, pulling the Jag into the garage. He felt better once the car was safely inside. Not that any of his neighbors were very close or that they were even early risers but he didn't want to take a chance on being seen. After all, most of them had gardeners. This time of the year, the landscapers sometimes showed up very early trying to beat the heat. The last thing he wanted to explain was why he was just coming home at this hour.

He stabbed the button closing the garage door, feeling a roaring in his veins. He'd heard an expression somewhere about wire in the blood, but this didn't feel like that. Not at all. It felt like raw jet fuel burning in his blood, pumping out pure power.

But while his body felt to be invincible and on fire, his mind had the blissful, peaceful, almost sleepy feeling of sexual release. A part of him, the pussy part wanted to grab a bottle of wine, draw a nice bath and while away the day. But another part of him, the animal part, cried out to hunt.

Van Zandt had always known he had the animal inside of him. A beast that wanted to run free and pillage. For years he had controlled the beast, with an iron will, and a steadfast refusal to feed the animal.

That had all changed the night he killed the fat cop. At the time, Van Zandt hadn't thought it much of an experience. More like taking out the trash. A problem taken care, nothing more. But now, looking back, he realized, that had been the start of something. However small, the animal had gotten a taste of blood. Van Zandt poured himself a drink. Not the wine or scotch of a civilized lawyer, but a straight whiskey. The raw drink of a hunter. Tasting the whiskey, he smiled, a predator's grin.

Last night, the beast had gotten more than a taste. The animal had gorged himself. Now Van Zandt knew, the animal would never again be satisfied to sit in the corner of his mind. The animal was running, roaring through his bloodstream, like a hot drug. Demanding and addictive.

Van Zandt fired down the whiskey, liking the fiery burn. For a second he closed his eyes, picturing her. Begging, willing to do anything to save her pitiful life. In the end she'd done everything he demanded. Van Zandt smiled wolfishly, his mind replaying her last moments on this earth. He could see it so clearly. Her face contorted, as he chocked the life out of her. He could feel her life force leaving as he came inside her.

Van Zandt poured a fresh drink. Already the animal demanded a fresh victim. Van Zandt sipped the whiskey thinking about it. There was a girl in the shop where he bought coffee. He unconsciously rubbed his groin, fresh-faced and trusting. She was perfect.

Not now, but soon. Very soon.

The practical side of Van Zandt, the lawyer side took over. He had work today. Things needed to get done. He needed to completely isolate himself from the mess in

Arizona. Van Zandt had already made moves to shift the blame to Carter and the Braxtons, but still he needed to stay on top of it.

Plus, he had some work to do here. A woman had died in this very house. Van Zandt frowned, that had been most foolish. Now he must make sure to eradicate any sign that she had ever been here.

Van Zandt glanced down at his wrist, the deep scratches. The lawyer part of him worried about that. Suppose when he cleaned her hands he missed something? Some scrap of skin, blood or DNA?

The beast said fuck it. They would never catch him. But the lawyer worried, the lawyer whispered, be careful. With a sigh, he gave into the lawyer. He set the whiskey aside and headed upstairs to clean. His whole bedroom would need to be sanitized. Every sign that she had been in the house must be erased.

He glanced at the raw wounds on his wrist. He should treat them. But he wouldn't. The pain from the scratches was a delicious reminder. He grinned down at them.

Some souvenirs were worth keeping.

Tucson Police Department Tucson AZ June 19th 2018 Tuesday Early Morning

It was like fishing with the wrong kind of bait. Mitch could see all the facts of the case swirling through his mind like fish in a pond, but for the life of him, he couldn't reel one in that made any sense. Any way he laid out the facts, they just didn't add up.

Maybe that was it. Maybe they weren't supposed to make sense?

Mitch leaned back in his chair staring up at the ceiling. First thing he noticed was someone had drawn a small fist with middle finger extended in the middle of his ceiling. Mitch shook his head. He worked with children.

Mitch yawned and rubbed the back of his neck. Damn, he was tired. Maybe he should have gone home last night. At the time, he hadn't felt much like sleep, but now the long hours were grinding down upon him.

Still shaking his head, Mitch brought his mind back to the case. He was here to think, so best get to it. He knew so much, why didn't any of it make sense? How did Sam Logan fit into this? What was he doing? And what of Perry Van Zandt?

Shit, Van Zandt was a lawyer, which automatically meant that half of everything he said was pure bullshit. Could he be throwing out stuff just to confuse things? The fake nipples, they made absolutely no sense, Van Zandt was a lawyer, he would have to know that they would be found out as fakes and in rather short order. Made no sense to plant them. Hell, maybe they weren't planted. Maybe they were just something Pyle had.

Mitch stopped to consider that. Suppose the nipples were just something that Jackson Pyle had picked up somewhere? Mitch snorted a barking laugh. Wouldn't that be a bite in the ass if they turned out to be some cheap ass souvenir that Pyle picked up years ago on a trip to Hollywood?

So, forget about them, Mitch decided. He should throw out everything that seemed to make no sense. Figure it was just coincidence or the lawyer in Van Zandt confusing things, clouding the issue, because that is just what lawyers did.

Mitch could remember a case where a man had been murdered in his living room while watching a Coyotes' game on television. He'd been beaten to death with a softball bat. Mickey had lifted a set of prints from the bat. A neighbor picked the owner of those prints from a lineup as the man he saw leaving the house. But because the coroner put time of death at eight in the evening, and the neighbor said it was around nine when he saw the man running from the house, he walked.

So, Mitch knew it didn't take much to establish reasonable doubt, and Van Zandt would certainly know that. Mitch frowned. But still why the nipples? They were so easily found out? Mitch grunted, scratching his jaw. Maybe Van Zandt only needed the story to hold up a short time?

Mitch was trying to follow that string, when his phone rang. The string broken, Mitch cursed, as he picked up the phone. Still muttering, Mitch checked the screen on his phone. Huh? Len Dykes.

Mitch glanced at the clock. Damn, it was way late. Mitch felt his pulse jump. If it was way late in Tucson, then damn straight it was late in DC. In fact, it was so late, it was early. This was something.

"You got something?" he asked, almost shouting into the phone.

"Slow down cowboy," Dykes said with a rumbling chuckle. "We got something, not sure what it is that we do have. Probably a dose of the clap."

"Well shit," Mitch said, trying to read what Dykes was telling him.

"Exactly," Dykes grunted.

"So, what exactly, do you have there?"

"We have the gun that killed my partner, Harley. Picked it up in Forsyth's apartment."

"Huh?" Mitch sat up a little straighter. "Well shit, that sounds good."

"Naw, it's all bullshit," Dykes replied. "The gun was an old snub-nose, real piece of shit. Right under the hammer, we found an empty casing with your guy Forsyth's print on it."

"Wow, you got ballistics and prints ran and back so soon?"

Dykes chuckled. "I threatened to kick everyone's ass if they didn't get it done."

"And that worked?"

"Probably not. I think mostly, they all liked Harley."

"Sounds like a helluva nice guy," Mitch offered.

Again, Len Dykes chuckled. "You might say that, but you'd be wrong as hell. Harley was mean and cranky, didn't shower as often as you might like and he complained all damn day long. He was a pain in the ass was what he was." There was a long pause. "And damn it, I still miss him."

"I bet you do," Mitch replied. "What are you thinking? Is Forsyth good for your partner's murder?"

There was a pause as Dykes thought it over. "No, I don't suppose so."

Mitch nodded even though they were a thousand miles apart and no chance that Dykes saw the gesture. "You might be right. Cold-blooded cop killer doesn't seem to fit with the picture we're building of Forsyth. Seems like he was running scared when he hit Tucson."

"Cop killer doesn't really fit with what we are picking up here," Dykes agreed.

"Okay, what else do you have?"

"We found the gun and then some other stuff to tie Forsyth back to Carter," Dykes admitted. "But when you look at it hard, it is all stuff that could be easily planted."

"And you think it was planted?"

"Probably," Dykes rumbled. "I'm thinking about the one thing we didn't find."

"The shield," Mitch said, recalling that the killer had taken Detective Harley's badge.

"Yup," Dykes agreed. "That's your trophy right there. That's the one thing the killer would want to keep close."

"Cop killer doesn't strike me as the type to commit suicide," Mitch said, thinking out loud.

"Nope, me neither." There was a long pause. "I don't mean to offend, but is there any chance you boys have yourselves a leak out there?"

"Almost certainly," Mitch replied. "Probably the FBI as well. A direct leak back to Van Zandt."

"I figured as much. I think Van Zandt was probably the one that killed Harley. I figured he hung onto the gun all these years and planted it at Forsyth's."

"Any reason to think that? I mean other than Van Zandt being the exact type of asshole that would do such a thing?"

"Ain't that enough?" Dykes said with a laugh. "We do have a couple of things."

"Anything good?" Mitch asked hopefully.

"Nothing concrete, but a couple of little things. First thing that bothers me, is the gun. Who shoots a cop then tosses the gun in his sock drawer for years? Doesn't even clean it or punch out the empty shell? This guy Forsyth, he wasn't rich, but he sure had some money and this was a cheap, piece of shit Saturday night special. Why even keep it? Drop it in the river, it's gone and can't never come back on you. If you want, buy another one for a few hundred bucks."

"You're right, seems hinky that he hung onto it," Mitch said, thinking about it. "Seen weirder things though."

"Yeah me too, but I can't figure why anyone would keep it. Unless of course they had a reason to."

"Like planting it on someone years later," Mitch agreed. "Now that does sound like Van Zandt. He strikes me as a man who plans way ahead."

"One thing he didn't plan on though, we pulled one print off the gun itself. Wanna guess whose?"

"Aw shit, Van Zandt." Mitch said. "He did it then. He killed your guy Harley."

"Maybe, but the print wasn't from shooting the gun. It wasn't on the grip; it was a thumb print on the barrel."

"Like you could get from putting a spent shell into one of the cylinders?" Mitch said, trying to picture it in his mind. "Or maybe shoving it into a sock drawer?"

"That's what I am thinking," Dykes agreed. "But the main thing is, one of Forsyth's neighbors went missing last night and was found dead this morning. That's why I was asking if you had a leak. The timing seems too neat."

"You think Van Zandt got wind that we were looking at Forsyth and went to plant the gun?"

"That was what I was thinking, and the neighbor spotted him."

"Aw shit," Mitch said, feeling a wave of guilt. He had set all of this in motion. "Young lady?"

"You know it. Joggers found her about an hour ago, dumped just off a trail."

"You gonna catch the case?"

"Naw, I doubt it, but I know the guys that got it, they'll represent her right." Dykes paused. "But I am heading out there in a few minutes. I want to check up on things. Let you know what I find."

"Do that," Mitch grunted, hanging up.

Perry Van Zandt's Home Great Falls Virginia June 19th 2018 Tuesday Morning

Casper McCaully looked across the car at Len Dykes. "Just what are we doing here, boss?"

Len wasn't his boss, and especially not on this case. This was Casper's case, he was the lead detective. The tittle and the fact that he was out here at the suspect's residence were just the respect he paid to the older detective.

Len flicked a quick glance at Casper, and wondered as he often did if McCaully's parents had named him Casper because he looked the part or if he had simply grown into the name. With curly hair so blonde it was almost white, pale skin and a roly-poly build, McCaully could play the role of Casper the ghost without make up.

"We can't be here," McCaully warned.

"I know," Len said, then smiled at the younger man. "Relax, dad, we're just looking."

"Looking? Looking at what? What are you hoping to find?"

"I don't know," Len said, through tight lips, he was still fuming over the fact that his search warrant had been denied. It had been denied in record time, in fact. Len could feel his blood pressure rising as he thought about it. Fucking lawyers, they sure stuck together.

"Come on, man. Let's get out of here. Staring at his house won't do any good, it'll just piss you off."

"Oh yeah?" Len demanded stabbing a finger at the house, as an ancient Ford Taurus inched up the driveway. "How about that?"

"What have you got in mind?" Casper asked cautiously.

"Let's talk to her," Len said, as the Taurus crawled past them, the woman driving was holding a cell phone to her ear. Probably telling a husband or friend that she was getting off early, Len thought as he cut a tight U-turn. "Pretty early for the maid to be leaving?" Len commented, feeling the rush of the hunt.

Casper pursed his lips. "Shit, you think she's leaving because he already cleaned up?"

"If you just raped and killed someone, that's not something you leave for the maid to clean up."

"Give her some space," Casper advised. "Let her get down the road. No use letting Van Zandt know we talked to her."

A part of Len wanted to argue. A part of him wanted Van Zandt to see them talking to the maid. He wanted the lawyer to wonder what she was telling them. Maybe rattle the asshole a little. "We don't need to bring trouble down on her," Casper said almost like he was reading Len's mind. "She didn't do anything."

Len swore softly under his breath, knowing Casper was right. "Okay," he grunted, his fingers resting on the switch that would light up the flashers as he followed her. Once they were clear of Van Zandt's house, he flipped on the lights.

Len felt a little bad, he could almost feel her apprehension as she hesitantly pulled to the curb. Without needing to speak, they both got out of the car, walking slowly to the driver's window. She lowered the window as they approached. "Yes," she said hopefully.

"Do you work for Perry Van Zandt?" Len asked, leaning in a little as Casper hung back, standing so his coat gapped open, letting her see his holstered weapon.

"Si," she said, her eyes fixated on Casper's gun. Tearing her eyes from the gun she looked up at Len, and nervously added. "I mean yes, I clean for Mister Van Zandt."

"What's your name?" Len asked trying to establish a friendly rapport.

"Juanita LaRosa."

"You done already, Juanita?" Casper asked, his voice rough as the asphalt on the Jersey Turnpike. He made a point of looking at his watch. "Seems awful early."

"Si, I never leave this early," she said, looking back and forth between the two detectives, her eyes begging for mercy.

"What is different about today," McCaully pressed.

"I do not know. Mister van Zandt was already washing the bedding when I got there. I think perhaps he had an accident."

"And, you say he was already cleaning when you got to work?" Casper demanded.

She nodded vigorously. "Si," she said as McCaully snorted and spun away in disgust.

Len placed a hand on her shoulder, trying to sound friendly. "Mister Van Zandt make a habit of letting you go home early?"

A trace of fear shinning in her dark eyes, she shook her head slowly, her whole attitude begging for forgiveness. "No, this has never happened before. This is why I think maybe he make pee in the bed."

Casper edged back in front of Len. "You were on the phone when we saw you. Who were you talking to?"

"My mother. She is sick." Juanita looked hopefully at the two detectives. "I was hoping to take her some lunch."

Len nodded, reaching into his pocket. "Of course," he said with a gentle smile. He pulled out a money clip and peeled off a twenty. "Take her some pie. Pie makes everything better."

Juanita took the money with a smile. "Thank you," she said, and kissed Len's hand.

Embarrassed Len motioned for her to move along. He watched her drive away, clenching his teeth, as a slow rage brewed deep in his belly.

Len's shoulders were hunched with anger, when he heard Casper chuckling. "I want some pie too."

"Fuck you, asshole," Len growled, stomping back to the car as Casper laughed out loud.

Tucson Police Department Tucson AZ June 19th 2018
Tuesday Early Morning

She walked into the station and every eye swung to her. She was used to the attention, but still she craved it. Monte Simms heard her coming, and glanced up with a bored eye. He quickly did a double take, struck by her dazzling beauty.

"Can I help you?" he asked, sitting up a little straighter, swatting a few stray crumbs from his uniform.

She flashed a smile which could have melted an iceberg. "I hope so," she said, as Monte beamed. "I am looking for Detective John Mitchell."

"I am afraid Detective Mitchell is very busy. Can you tell me what this is about?"

"Of course," she purred, but a coldness flashed across her face, like the sun dipping behind the clouds. This was a woman used to getting her way without any questions. "I'm Jennifer Brody."

"Oh, okay," Monte said. "I will walk you back to his unit." Monte heaved himself out of his chair. There was a part of his brain screaming that she probably wasn't to be trusted, but none the less, Monte found himself standing a little straighter and trying to suck in his gut. "Come with me," he invited, wishing there was a way she could lead the way. Although he couldn't see it, Monte had the feeling that she had an ass that would make a Picasso look like pig shit.

"I'm not sure if Mitch is in," Monte said, unable to stop himself from looking back and damned if she didn't have a rack that would make even a Rocky Mountain elk jealous. "But I am certain some of his team is around. Don't worry ma'am, we will get you taken care of," Monte added, thinking he would like to take care of her all right. You betcha. Give her the old high, hard one.

"Well I was hoping to speak with Detective Mitchell, but perhaps someone from his team will do," she said, her tone becoming terse.

"Here we are," Monte said, holding the door open wide, and smiling to himself as she breezed past him. With one eye on her ass, he motioned across the empty squad room to Mitch's open door. "Hey, Mitch, you got a visitor."

A bit of a perplexed frown on his face, Mitch stepped to the door of his office, shooting a quick look at Monte. "This is Jennifer Brody," Monte said, making motion between them. "Miz Brody, Detective John Mitchell."

"Missus Brody," Mitch said, nodding to her and thinking it was odd that this was the first time he was actually meeting her. She certainly hadn't been out front playing the grief-stricken parent. Interesting. "What can I do for you?" he asked, stepping back into his office and motioning for her to follow.

Jennifer Brody tried to appear distraught, but she was certainly no actress. The look of pain she plastered across her face came off as more of a pout, while the tremble in her voice and the quiver in her lips was obviously manufactured. "It's my husband," she said dabbing at tears that weren't there. "I'm afraid something has happened to him."

"Huh?" Mitch grunted, noting that she hadn't asked about Angie. "Why do you think that?"

More dabbing at her cheeks, which were so dry that it didn't even smear her makeup. "He didn't come home last night and now I cannot reach him on his cell! I just know something terrible has happened."

Mitch leaned back against the wall behind his desk, crossing his arms across his chest. Her words were wrong. Not at all natural, it was as if someone had written them down for her to say. She paused obviously expecting Mitch to say something at this point. Instead, Mitch studied her, wondering what the real reason was for her visit to his office. She glanced quickly at Monte, who was engrossed with staring at her ass to even notice.

Jennifer Brody brought her gaze back at Mitch, she pulled at her hair, clearly flustered. And if she was a poor actress, she truly sucked at improvisation. "Uh, can you help me?" she finally stammered.

"Help you with what?" Mitch demanded, throwing the ball right back into her court.

"Well finding my husband of course!"

Mitch pasted his best perplexed look on his face. "Ma'am there isn't anything we can do. Your husband is an adult. If he wants to stay out all night and not answer his cell, well that is certainly within his rights." Mitch let a severe look slide onto his face. "I simply don't have the time to go looking for a grown man who didn't come home last night. We are using all of our available resources looking for Angie. You wouldn't want us to pull people back from trying to rescue Angie?"

Mitch paused, watching her face. He could actually see a trace of anguish on her beautiful face, but Mitch suspected that it wasn't for Angie, or even Brody for that matter. Mitch had a feeling she was anguished because this conversation wasn't going the way it was supposed to.

It struck Mitch that she had come or been sent here to get something. But what? Information? Probably. Mitch decided to see if he could rattle her cage a little. "You do want us to find your step-daughter? Don't you?"

"Well yes, of course," she stammered, twisting her hands together. She started to say something, then stopped suddenly. Like the sun emerging from behind a cloud, her face lit up. The frown lines crossing her face smoothed and the tiniest hint of a smile winked across her lips. "I do want to help Angie," she purred and slid into a chair. A move which Mitch figured was calculated, she leaned forward, flashing her cleavage. "I really do want to help."

No longer hypnotized by her ass Monte woke up and gave Mitch a little wave and a wink. "Do you think you could help us find Angie?" Mitch asked as Monte retreated across the squad room.

"Yes. I think can." Jennifer said, becoming excited. Mitch took a seat, knowing this would encourage her to keep talking. "I know those awful men who took Angie wanted my husband to sign some of his properties over to them." Jennifer leaned forward another notch, giving a small waggle of her shoulders. She placed her hands on top of Mitch's and let loose a thousand-watt smile. "If I could just get control of Brad's things, I could give them what they want, and then they would let Angie go."

"You mean like a power of attorney?"

The wattage on the smile soared to blinding levels. "Yes, exactly that! Can you arrange that? If only I had control of Brad's things, I could end all of this."

Mitch extracted his hands from under hers and leaned back in his chair, clasping his hands behind his head. His first thought that jumped into his mind was, could this woman possibly be that stupid? The next thought was; how could he be that stupid? They knew nothing about this woman, and she might be involved right up to her petty little eyeballs.

Mitch shook his head. "I'm afraid I don't have the authority to grant you anything like that," Mitch said, watching a frown slide down her face, pushing the smile off her chin. "But I take it you have been talking to the men who have Angie?"

She shook her head, her eyebrows scrunching together. "No, I haven't spoken to them…, I mean we haven't spoken to them."

"Then how do you know what they want?"

"Huh?" Jenifer Brody grunted. All her life Jenifer Brody had relied upon her looks, and a flashing smile. It was obvious, that any kind of thinking was perhaps a struggle, but thinking quickly on her feet was something that was simply beyond her grasp.

Mitch almost felt sorry for her, but he still fired another accusation at her. "You said that they wanted some of your husband's property," Mitch reminded, letting a little wolf creep into his tone.

"Yes," she said, nodding slowly. "If I could get control of Brad's things, then I could give them what they want."

Right then, Mitch knew, Brad Brody was dead, and his lovely wife had a hand in killing him. "How do you know that? How do you know what they want?"

"I ugh." She wrung her hands, looking past Mitch, which told him that she was thinking. It also told him that the next words to pass her lips would be a lie.

"Brad told me," she said, her voice hopeful.

"He's been talking to the kidnappers?" Mitch demanded. "The last time we spoke, he expressed to me that he had no contact with them."

Her frown deepened, causing furrows in her forehead. "I don't know, maybe he lied," she said. "Or maybe they just called him." She placed her hand over mouth in an exaggerated look of horror. "Oh no, do you think he got the call yesterday and that is why he's missing. That he went to meet them?"

"Maybe." Mitch shrugged, wanting to keep her talking. It was obvious that she had something on her mind.

The worried look on her face, blossomed into a full-fledged catastrophe. Her hand flew to her mouth and she shook her head. "I heard about a shooting at a rest stop on I-10 last night. A place called Texas Canyon. Was that Brad?" she asked, and even managed to inject a little hitch in her voice. "He's dead, isn't he?"

Mitch leaned back in his chair, clasping his hands behind his head his mind racing. For all her theatrics, Mitch thought this might be the very thing she came to ask about.

There was a definite uptick in her intensity all of a sudden. That might be fear for a loved one, but Mitch seriously doubted if she were capable of such emotions.

"There was a shooting last night. I can't say much, except to say your husband was not among the victims," Mitch informed her, watch her reaction closely. Instead of sweeping relief that a loved one was safe, her intensity jacked up a notch.

She leaned forward, hugging herself. "Who was killed," she asked, reminding Mitch of a junkie asking for a fix.

"I'm afraid, that I cannot release that information until all family members have been notified."

"Please," she whispered.

"I can't, sorry."

She put a pouty look on her face and nodded. "I understand," she purred. "It's just that I am so worried about Brad. He never stays out all night."

Mitch managed to keep a straight face, and even eke out a meager sympathetic nod of his head. He wasn't buying any of this. From what he had heard, Brody was notorious for staying out to all hours and chasing everything in a skirt. "I am sorry," Mitch said gravely. "Like I said, all I can tell you is that from eyewitness' descriptions; your husband was not among those at the rest stop."

"But people were killed?" she asked a catch in her voice, that was real this time.

"We think so," Mitch said, "The killer took the bodies with him so we can't be sure."

"Do you know who they were?" she asked, that junkie desperation bubbling back to the surface again.

"We have a good idea," Mitch allowed quietly. "But as I say we cannot release that information until the identity of the victims have been verified and the notifications are completed."

Jennifer Brody slapped the top of Mitch's desk. "I do not accept that," she said, fire snapping in her eyes. "Perhaps I should contact my lawyer."

Mitch gave her his most innocent smile. "Maybe you should, maybe you could talk to him about your husband's assets."

She branded Mitch with a scathing look. "I believe I will speak to him about your behavior as well. I must say, I find you attitude infuriating."

Mitch smiled leaning back in his chair. "That is certainly your right," he said, motioning her away with a flip of his hand.

As she stalked across the squad room, Mitch snatched up his phone. He was pounding numbers in the keypad as Jerry Hartek sauntered in, looking back admiringly at the backside of Jennifer Brody. Mitch dropped the phone back in the cradle and as Jennifer disappeared around the corner, Jerry hurried into his office.

He smiled at Mitch. "Man, how would you like to bite that on the ass and get lockjaw?" he asked, sporting a huge grin. "Maybe, get dragged for a couple of blocks?"

"Yeah," Mitch grunted. "I have a job for you."

"Shit, I hope it's tailing her," Jerry grinned, waggling his eyebrows.

"Actually, that's exactly what it is," Mitch replied. "That's Jennifer Brody. I want you to follow her. See where she goes and who she talks to."

"Oh man, I love you," Jerry said, leaning in to give Mitch a hug. "You are such a good boss. I don't care what Ollie and Wade say."

"Yeah, go," Mitch said, shoving him away. "I'll see if I can get Monte to hold her up a little so you can get in position to pick her up as she leaves."

"That will help," Jerry said, turning to leave. "Do we know what she drives?"

"No, but I got ten bucks that says it's a Subaru." Mitch shook his head, "I guess you will just have to catch her as she comes out." As Jerry hurried out the door, Mitch snatched up his phone, stabbing in Monte's extension number. "Hey can you hold up Jennifer Brody for me? I need to ask her a question."

"Will do," Monte agreed, then added cheerfully. "Hell, I'll tackle her and hold her down if I have to."

"Well shit, let's hope that it doesn't come to that," Mitch said with a chuckle.

Mitch hung his phone, taking his time. He wanted to give Jerry plenty of time to get into position. Mitch shook his head, as he stood up. Damn, Jennifer Brody. Could she really be involved? Mitch knew the answer to that before the question even popped into his head. Of course, she could. In fact, it wasn't at all uncommon for a step-parent to try and get rid of the kid. Happened all the time, especially if a large estate were involved.

Mitch pursed his lips. Jennifer Brody and Chappy Miers? Unlikely, but…. She sure had been interested in what went down at Texas Canyon last night. Mitch had the feeling that was the whole reason for her visit was simply to ask about the shooting. Chappy and Jennifer Brody? They seemed like an odd pair, but the same thing could be said for Kathy and Tanner.

Taking his time and mulling it over, Mitch sauntered down to Monte's broom closet-sized office. As he walked, his pace slowed, Mitch's mind was racing. Could he possibly get a warrant for her phones? Try as he might, Mitch could find nothing to use as probable cause for such a warrant. Early on, Parker had taken a quick look at Jennifer, but Brody had her sign a pre-nup. If they divorced, she wouldn't get much. Brody had a will that backed up the pre-nup, if he died, she still got nothing. Except for the fact that she might not be bright enough to realize that, there was no real motive for her to go after Angie. Of course, maybe Jennifer thought if Angie were out of the way, maybe Brody would change his will. Leave everything to her.

Mitch shook his head, man as a motive, that was thin as mosquito piss. Certainly not enough to get a warrant to look at Jennifer Brody's phone.

As Mitch walked a better idea crept into his mind. Smiling, Mitch picked up the pace. Now all he needed was her phone number.

Jennifer was waiting, leaning against Monte's counter. She let loose a smile, sure that she was going to finally get what she wanted. "Mitch," she purred, taking his hand in hers.

"Miz Brody," Mitch acknowledged, pulling his hand from her grasp. "I was just realizing that I do not have your cell number."

The beautiful, china doll smile froze on her lips. "What?" she sputtered.

"Your cell phone number," Mitch replied. "You know so I can get in touch with you if we hear anything about Angie, or of course if your husband turns up."

"What about the other thing?" Angie asked, absently pulling a business card from her tiny purse. "Are you going to help me with that?"

Mitch took the card, glancing down at it. The card proclaimed her to be a beauty consultant, which he figured was the only thing she was even remotely qualified to be. "I'm sorry, ma'am, as I said, I can't help you with that," Mitch said, then a wicked thought occurred to him. "But you should go over to the courthouse and talk to Judge Sanderson. He would be the one that could help you gain control of your husband's holdings. Ask for him. Judge Harlan Sanderson. He can help."

Jennifer Brody unleashed a smile which would have melted the polar ice cap. "Thank you so much, Detective

Mitchell," she said, taking his hands and giving him a small peck on the cheek. "Thank you both," she added, shinning some of the smile on Monte, before practically bolting towards the door.

"What gives?" Monte asked. "You know the judge can't do anything for her. He ever finds out you sent her over there, he will have your ass on a stick."

"Paying the old fucker back for this morning," Mitch said grimly.

"Ooh yeah, the paternity thing," Monte said with a nod. "I heard of that. How did that turn out?"

"Not much happened, the judge just ordered me to get the DNA test, which I already did, so we should know maybe today or tomorrow."

"Well good luck." Monte stood up and held out his hand. "I don't know how you want this to turn out, but I'm hoping you are around tomorrow passing out cigars."

"Thanks," Mitch took the hand feeling embarrassed, but also pleased to his core. "Crap, the sun is up, what are you still doing here anyway?"

Monte shrugged his face a little red. "Dennis had a chiropractor appointment, so I am covering for him until noon."

"You're a good man, Monte," Mitch replied, turning to go.

"When you find out about the kid, and you are passing out cigars, remember I know you have a stash of Cubans, don't come in here trying to peddle off some old Swisher Sweets."

Mitch laughed, waving a hand. "You got it old man," he said hurrying down the hall, pulling out his cell phone as he walked. At his desk Mitch began to have second thoughts. Really, Mitch couldn't see a down side to it. But still he hesitated.

Should he really make the call?

He was still thinking about it, when Geena breezed into the office carrying two cups of coffee. "Whatcha doing?" she asked, holding out a cup.

Mitch took the cup, looking her over. She seemed okay. "Thinking about making a call," he said holding up the phone. "Thinking of calling Sam Logan."

"Huh?" Geena grunted raising an eyebrow. "Do you really think that is wise?"

"Not sure, but he has something I want."

"Tell me about it," Geena said, dropping into a chair.

"Jennifer Brody was just here."

Geena took a sip. "Fishing for information?" she asked, her upper lip puckering into a frown. It was a habit Mitch noticed she had when thinking.

"I think so," Mitch agreed. "I also think Brody might be dead and she maybe had a hand in it."

"Not surprising," Geena decided. "So, what did the good widow want to know?"

"Well first thing, she reported her husband missing. I figure, she thinks that will cover her ass when he turns up dead. Then she made a half-assed play to get her hands on his holdings."

Geena's frown was in full bloom. "You think she threw in with the bikers?"

"Damn, very good," Mitch said, impressed with how quick she followed that string. "She asked about the shooting at Texas Canyon last night. She claimed that she was worried about her husband being one of the victims, but I think she was worried about Chappy."

"You think she and Chappy were sleeping together?" Geena asked raising an eyebrow.

"Maybe," Mitch grunted. "I sure got that impression. She kept pressing me for the names of the victims, even after I told her that Brody wasn't among them. She was definitely concerned about someone. I figured Chappy."

"And Sam Logan has Chappy Miers."

"Or hopefully at least his phone," Mitch agreed, tasting the coffee. "I'd like to see if Chappy and the good Miz Brody have been talking, or better yet, texting."

"You think Logan will give you that information?"

"Only one way to find out for sure," Mitch said, shrugging. "Whatever Sam is doing or what he has become, he was once a damn good cop. I think he will help."

Geena matched Mitch's shrug. "What the hell, give him a call."

Mitch nodded, dialing the number of the burner phone Sam had, placing his phone on speaker, so Geena could follow the conversation. "Bet he doesn't answer," Geena predicted.

"He will," Mitch predicted, as they heard the phone ring. "Blocked my number and I'm betting his curiosity will get the better of him."

Geena pursed her lips, and shrugged. "We will see," she said, shaking her head.

She was still shaking her head, when a gruff voice leapt from the phone. "Yeah, what?" it said.

"Hey, old man, I need a favor," Mitch said, a grin spread across his face as he tried to envision Sam's reaction.

The first reaction was dead silence, then a low, rumbling chuckle. "What the hell do you want, you little prick?" Somehow despite the content of his words, Sam sounded almost glad to hear from Mitch.

"Like I said, a favor and maybe some advice."

"You want some advice? Well get a damn haircut and listen to some Johnny Cash."

Mitch laughed, winking across the desk at Geena. "I'd rather listen to Chappy Miers. I'm guessing you have him?"

"Fraid not. Only person listening to Chappy is Saint Peter." Sam chuckled dryly. "Bet that is one interesting conversation."

"You kill him?"

"Reckon I did, but then I figure you already know that," Sam replied. "I got those fellas to help me load him and Dell. Dell was already gone, but Chappy was still breathing, but by the time we got to where I was going he had passed on. Not that anyone will ever miss him."

"Where did you dump the bodies?"

There was a long silence as Sam thought it over. "Not yet. One day soon, I will tell you, but not just yet. I still got a few things to do first." Sam waited a beat then asked. "Is that all you needed?"

"No," Mitch replied, still trying to wrap his head around the changes in Sam Logan. "I wanted to see Chappy's phone."

"I'm looking at it right now," Sam said, sounding pleased with himself. "Doesn't seem like much. Just your regular burner."

"I was wondering who he has been talking with, or maybe texting with," Mitch said hopefully.

"Weeeel let's see," Sam said, obviously enjoying himself very much.

"I saw where you made a contribution to Jillian Braxton. Have you lost your mind?"

Sam laughed a little. "Damn bitch suckered me. Did it slicker than a riverboat card shark too."

"What happened?" Mitch asked, suppressing a laugh.

"Went on her website. Wanted to do a little research on her, I saw a place where for a minimal contribution I could get a bio on her."

"What did you learn?"

"That a fool and his money are soon parted," Sam grumbled. "Alright, I guess this phone fired up. Let's see what he's been up to. He's had two calls on this particular phone." Sam laughed with genuine humor. "What do you know, both from me."

"Are you the new drug kingpin of southern Arizona?" Mitch asked, his mind racing.

"Hell no, dumbass! I'm retired."

"I forgot," Mitch said. "How about texts?"

"Hang on," Sam grumbled. "Nary a one."

"Are you sure he knows how to work the phone?" Geena whispered.

She whispered, but Sam's old ears were keen enough to catch her words. "Bite me, missy. I can work any phone ever made! I can work the old ones that you had to crank to make their own juice all the way up to the new blueberries."

Geena held up her new Samsung Galaxy. "Blackberry?" she whispered.

"Sam," Mitch said, but the line was dead. Mitch glanced at Geena, a realization dawning on them both.

"Chappy got a new phone!" they said together.

Mitch nodded, pounding his fist on the desk. "We need to find the old one."

Perry Van Zandt's Office Washington DC June 19th 2018 Tuesday Early Afternoon

Len Dykes walked into Perry Van Zandt's office, his back creaking, feeling the effects of a long day. Van Zandt's office wasn't at all what he expected. He'd been expecting plush opulence on a grand scale. What he found was cold, hard glass and chrome.

Probably Art Deco or some such shit Len thought and shook his head. Still seemed like pretentious crap to him. Not impressed he crossed the marble floor to a severe looking woman seated behind an even more severe glass desk. The desk was almost entirely bare, a slick, black tablet the only adornment on its spotless surface.

"May I help you?" the woman asked, her tone indicating she would like to do anything but help.

"Detective Len Dykes," he said, even though he had already given this information to the girl in the outer office. He pulled back his jacket, revealing the badge clipped to his belt. "I would like to see Mister Van Zandt."

She shook her head. "I'm sorry, that would not be possible, Mister Van Zandt is very busy today. If you would like to schedule an appointment, I can probably get you in sometime next week."

Len Dykes had been polite so far, but his patience was long gone. He took a step forward, gesturing to a door behind her desk. "No, I don't want to make an appointment. I want to speak with Van Zandt. If I have to kick down that door and haul his ass downtown, I will." Len paused, smoothing down his anger, and continuing in a calmer tone. "But I don't want to do that. I suggest that you do what you have to do to get his ass out here." Setting a stubborn look firmly on his face, Len crossed his arms across his chest and spread his feet.

A look of pure disgust sprouting onto her face, the secretary made a clucking sound as she picked up the tablet. She caressed its surface, and after the appropriate number of strokes, Van Zandt's voice sprang from it. "Yes."

"A policeman is here to see you."

There was a pause, then the door swung open with an audible click. "Send him in."

Len Dykes smiled to himself, he was on the right track. If Van Zandt knew nothing about this, he would have shined Len on, but the fact that he was meeting with Len said a lot. Len thought about how he would do this. Van Zandt was a lawyer, and as such would know that he shouldn't talk to the cops. Len allowed himself the tiniest of smiles. Van Zandt would talk because even though he knew it wasn't wise, he also thought he was smarter than Len.

As a lawyer, Van Zandt would know that his best option was to say nothing. But as a smart-ass, he might try to taunt Len. If he could keep switching things around, Van Zandt might let something slip. Len knew from countless interrogations that just the smallest slip would provide the crack he needed to get inside the web of lies and tear them down.

Harley had been the master at that. Being naturally quarrelsome, Harley would get under a suspect's skin, get an argument going. Without even meaning too, the suspect would blurt something out, and Harley would have his crack. His way in.

All of this flashed through Len's brain, as he crossed to Van Zandt's office. The interior office sported the same cold, hard décor as the outer office. Sheik, was what it was supposed to be, Len thought. Van Zandt was seated behind a larger version of the secretary's desk. Like hers, his desk was almost empty, a folder with several documents and a pen was in front of him, while a stubby glass with a brown liquid sat at Van Zandt's elbow. Behind Van Zandt on a long glass shelf, Len could see a blacked-out laptop. That meant either the laptop was shut down, or Van Zandt had killed it before opening the door. Interesting.

Van Zandt didn't bother getting up, he simply leaned back in his chair, a look of curiosity on his face. "Detective Dykes, isn't it?" he asked, and Len nodded curtly. "Do you care to explain why you are here? Threatening my staff? Interrupting my very busy day with your ridicules demands?"

Van Zandt hadn't offered a chair, but that was okay with Len. For now, he preferred to stand. He liked having the power position, towering over the lawyer. Len knew, subtle advantages like that could significantly influence an interview. Len leaned forward, being the aggressor. "Woman was killed last night. Her body dumped off a trail in Rock Creek Park."

Van Zandt shrugged, but he leaned away a fraction of an inch. "And you naturally assumed I would want to know this information?" he asked, his tone biting.

Len paused thinking how to play this. "Oh, I think you already knew all about that." Len met Van Zandt's gaze with a bit of a smile. "What I really want to know is, where were you last night?"

Van Zandt smiled, spreading his hands. "At home. Alone I'm afraid."

"You get those scratches home alone?" Len countered, nodding his head at Van Zandt's wrist.

Where most suspects Len had encountered would have instinctively tried to hide the wounds, Van Zandt held his hand up showing them off. "As a matter of fact, I did. I was doing some gardening. I was pulling out some dead rose bushes and an old trestle."

Len nodded, thinking maybe, he had a break. "So, if I was to go out to your place, I would find a broken-up trestle?"

Van Zandt broke into a dazzling smile. "Of course you would, if you had a warrant that is."

"I could get one."

Van Zandt's smile blossomed into a full-blown laugh. He wagged a finger at Len. "I don't think so, Detective. Not with what you have."

"We'll see," Len replied, feeling that he was losing the interview. He tried to switch tracts. "I spoke with your housekeeper today. Funny thing, she was getting off early. She said she was off early because you changed your own sheets, did your own laundry this morning. Wanna explain why you did that?"

"No," Van Zandt replied simply.

Len paused, knowing this was when most suspects would feel the need to say more. But not Van Zandt, he simply stared up at Len.

"I know about the gun you planted at Forsyth's house."

"What gun? Detective, I have no idea what you are talking about."

"Really?" Len said mildly, letting some doubt creep into his voice. He watched Van Zandt, hoping the silence might prompt him to fill the void. While he waited, Len studied the lawyer. He was certainly smug, convinced he was smarter than Len. Smarter than everyone. They'd see about that. "You don't remember a thirty-eight caliber revolver that you placed in Forsyth's sock drawer?"

Van Zandt leaned back, clasping his hands behind his head. "Detective Dykes, you certainly have a vivid imagination."

"I didn't imagine your thumb print on the gun."

Years ago, Len had taken his kids to the zoo and he saw a lizard do a double blink sort of thing. Right then, Van Zandt reminded Len of that lizard. A flash of surprise, then something ugly and rabid flicked the lawyer's gray eyes, but all of it gone in a heartbeat.

Len leaned in, hoping for a knockout. "That's right smart guy, you were careless and you left your thumb print on the barrel," Len taunted, hoping to get a rise out of the lawyer.

The smile was back on Van Zandt's face, but now instead of smug and taunting, it looked forced and frozen. But then the frozen look melted, and Van Zandt's face lit up, like the sun coming from behind the clouds. "Are you talking about some cheap, piece of shit Saturday Night Special? Barrel all pitted up?"

Len pursed his lips, not liking where this was heading. "That's the one. You remember it now?"

"I do," Van Zandt said heartily, the smug look once again plastered firmly on his face. "About a year or so ago, we had a company retreat. Dreadful thing really. One of those things designed to bring a staff together as a team."

Len watched realizing why Van Zandt was such a good lawyer. The man could spin a lie and make it sound perfectly believable. Probably because he mixed a little truth in with the lies. "At this retreat we had some targets and everyone was shooting," Van Zandt continued. "Forsyth brought out this crappy revolver. It was a total piece of shit, but he claimed it was a family heirloom, belonged to Uncle Fester back in the Civil War or some such nonsense. Just to please him, I fired it a couple of times."

"Bullshit," Len stated bluntly. "I'd be willing to bet my left nut that you ain't never once in your life done something just to please another."

Van Zandt clapped his hands, laughing a little. "Very perceptive, Detective. You're right, normally I wouldn't have bothered, but some of the partners had pushed for this retreat. They were convinced that it would promote a more efficient and harmonious office."

Van Zandt, paused almost daring Len to contradict him. "So now Detective, tell me this woman, she was shot from this gun?"

"No, she was strangled. Raped and strangled."

Looking perplexed, Van Zandt shook his head. "What does all of this gun talk have to do with the young lady getting killed?"

"You tell me."

"Detective, I am sure I don't know. If you wish to discuss this further, you will have to divulge more details."

"This woman who was killed, she lived just down the hall from Forsyth. It seems she was abducted from the building. She was raped and killed, her body dumped along a jogging trail. What do you know about that?"

"I know exactly what you just told me. Nothing more."

"We have a witness who saw a man matching your description entering that apartment complex last night."

Unconcerned, Van Zandt reached for the glass on his desk. "I'm sure you do."

"We also have your car on a traffic camera not far from the apartment building." Len stopped, giving Van Zandt a second to respond. For his part, Van Zandt coolly sipped his whiskey, eyeing Dykes the way a cottonmouth stares at a mouse. "You want to tell me what you were doing over there last night?"

Van Zandt took another sip from his drink. Whiskey, he was acquiring quite the taste for it. He smiled up at Dykes and carefully set the glass on the coaster. Outwardly, Van Zandt remained calm, but inwardly he was seething, as he realized he had made mistakes. He never should have used his own car.

"Mister Van Zandt, do you want to tell me what you were doing in that part of town last night? Was this before or after your gardening accident?" Len demanded.

Van Zandt didn't answer. He knew, this is where most people made their mistake. Thinking they had to answer a cop's question. He had already made enough mistakes, and was not going to compound them now.

Len felt like he had landed a heavy body blow, and decided to try for another. "We ran ballistics on the thirty-eight. Turns out, it was the gun that killed my partner Ed Harley. You remember him?"

"A disgusting slob," Van Zandt said, back to taunting Len. "Are you suggesting that Forsyth killed your partner? Personally, I don't see it. Forsyth wasn't the type."

"I agree. I think you did it."

Van Zandt shrugged, a condescending gesture. "Good luck trying to prove that."

A wave of embarrassment sweeping over him, Len stared down at the marble floor which probably cost more than he made in a year. Damn it, this wasn't right. He knew this asshole killed his partner. Killed that girl to, and who knew how many others. Len had come here hoping to get something from Van Zandt that he could use to nail him. So far, he hadn't even mused the lawyer's hair. He pointed a shaky hand at the lawyer. "I think you killed Harley and you planted the gun at Forsyth's. And I think you killed that girl last night."

A tiny smirk crawled onto Van Zandt's face. "Like I said Detective, you have a vivid imagination."

"I don't think so."

Van Zandt openly laughed, as Len felt the burn of embarrassment. Van Zandt shook a finger at Len. "If you had anything on me, we wouldn't be having this conversation here, we would be talking in an interrogation room downtown."

"That can be arranged," Len said through clenched teeth, fighting the impulse to leap across the desk and beat the smug lawyer to death. Had it occurred to Len that he had a gun, he might well have pulled it out and killed Van Zandt. Instead he settled for an empty threat. "I'll be back, count on it."

Van Zandt laughed again, waving a hand at Len "Good day, Detective."

Mitch's Home Tucson AZ   June 19th 2018 Tuesday Evening

Mitch picked up the phone on the second ring. "Yeah, Jerry."

"Well, I've followed the good Miz Brody all afternoon. She's home now and looks like she's buttoned in for the night. You want me to hang around a while?"

"I'm not sure. Did she go anywhere of note?"

"Now, that is a real good question," Jerry said cheerfully. "She went and got her nails done, then to some other place for a facial and finally for a massage."

"Sounds normal enough," Mitch commented, but he could tell from Jerry's tone, that he had something on his mind. "If you were to ask me, I would have guessed that was exactly how she spent her days."

"True, true, but the thing is, every place she visited was on the south end of town."

"Huh, long ways from home," Mitch grunted, trying to think why she might be on the south end of town. "Her card said she was business consultant, maybe she was doing business."

"No shit, she had a business card?" Jerry said, like that was the strangest thing he ever heard of. He laughed a little. "Tell you what it's a good thing you sent me, 'cause I noticed something those others might have missed."

"And what might that have been," Mitch said.

"I noticed that she kept driving by the Deacons'' clubhouse."

"She go inside?"

"Nope, she just kept driving by. She'd go by and then circle around by the Triple T, then drive by again. It was like following some teenage girl or something. She'd drive by a couple of times and then give up and go to one of those beauty parlors, but then she'd be back."

"Do you think she was doing all that to shake a tail?" Mitch asked.

"From the cops? Nope, like I said, she was just like a teenager chasing a boy. I think she was looking for one of the Deacons, if you can fucking believe that."

"Chappy Miers, I think."

"No shit, that mutt!" Jerry exploded, then laughed. "Well, I guess she likes bad boys. You want me to hang out here for a while?"

"I don't know," Mitch said, wondering what good it would do. "What's your feeling? Is she going anywhere?"

"I don't think so. Course she might have a visitor."

"You'll wait a long time before Chappy shows up."

"She might get in the pool," Jerry said, and even over the phone, Mitch could tell he was wagging his eyebrows. "Seriously though, it's not too far to my house, I could run home and have dinner with my family then come back. See if she is up to anything?"

"Sounds good, but are you sure you want to leave, she struck me as a skinny dipper," Mitch said mainly torment Jerry.

"Aw man, you think?" Jerry asked thinking it over. "Damn if you think I need to, I could hang out a bit."

Mitch laughed. "Go home, spend some time with your kids. If you want sneak back over later and see what she's up to that'll be good."

Yawning, Mitch crossed to the frig grabbing a beer. In the end, he and Geena had decided it to be a fool's errand chasing after Chappy's old phone. If the biker got a new phone, it was because he thought somebody might be onto the old one. No reason to keep it around.

They'd spent the day reading all of the paper on the case, looking for something, anything they might have missed. At the end of the day, all Mitch had to show for it was a dull ache behind his eyes. He and Geena had parted awkwardly at the end of the day, with some mumbling about dinner.

On impulse, Mitch turned on the TV. Braxton was giving a speech tonight, speaking from ASU campus. Mitch frowned. The good Senator seemed to be spending a lot of time in Arizona. While an important state to win, Arizona had voted Republican in every Presidential election, going back all the way to the days of Barry Goldwater.

So why was Braxton spending so much time and energy here? And in the summer no less. Most folks avoided Southern Arizona in the summer time. The Democratic Convention was well over a year away and Braxton was already the presumed candidate. She didn't need Arizona to gain the nomination, and she wasn't going to carry it in the general election, so why spend so much time here?

Mitch smiled grimly. There was only one answer to that.

She wasn't here for her political career.

Mitch groaned. Shit I am so dumb, he thought.

Braxton was here to keep an eye on whatever it was that Van Zandt had going. Thinking it over, Mitch wandered around his living room. So, was it that her presence was required, or was she the only one that Van Zandt trusted. Or hell, maybe she didn't trust Van Zandt? Mitch frowned, unconsciously rubbing his chin. Which way did that particular street run.

Mitch leaned back in his chair, he was tired and his brain was like mush. He had all these stray thoughts about the case, running through his mind, but none of them seemed to mesh. Bored, Mitch picked up his mail. He was thumbing through the letters when one caught his eye and made his heart stop. The report from the lab. His heart racing but his hands steady, Mitch opened the letter. He pulled out the report and laid it in his lap, all of a sudden scared of what it might say. Finally, he took a pull from his beer and picked up the report from the lab. The first couple of pages just detailed collection procedures and chain of custody of the samples. The third page was where it got down to business. It was full of scientific bullshit, about markers and probabilities, but the bottom line was that Josie was his daughter.

He turned the paper in his hands, staring at it in pure amazement. Such a small thing. Only a piece of paper, but Mitch realized, it would have a tremendous impact on his life. He had a daughter. Hot damn! His eyes misty, Mitch stared across the living room, not seeing it as it was, but seeing it with a little girl playing. Toys on the couch and a tricycle on the floor.

With a sigh, Mitch forced his mind back to the case. They knew so much, why couldn't he put it together? Idly sipping a beer, Mitch opened the back slider letting a little desert air in. The pool worried him, suppose Josie fell in? He should put in some grass. A kid needed grass.

Unable to concentrate, Mitch grabbed the report, heading next door. He was reading the paper again when the door opened. "Hi, Mitch," Elizabeth Sanderson said opening the door wide. "How are you holding up?" she asked with a kindly smile and a pat on the shoulder. "Are you excited at the prospect of being a daddy?"

Mitch grinned, despite himself and held up the paper. "Guess it's more than a prospect now."

"Oh my, I've been praying for this," she said, wrapping Mitch up in a fierce hug. "You're going to do great," she whispered.

Mitch shrugged, trying to be nonchalant about it. "I hope so."

"You'll do fine," she said, patting his shoulder. "And if you ever need a baby sitter all you have to do is ask."

"Thank you, I am going to hold you to that," Mitch said, giving her a quick hug. "Is the old tight wad in?"

"Downstairs," she replied.

"Can you believe this heartless bitch?" the judge said, hardly looking up from Braxton on the television as Mitch came in the den. "What can I do for you, Johnny?"

"I got this," Mitch said, handing the judge the report from the clinic. "Says I am the father," Mitch said, feeling a warm feeling wash over him. "What happens now?"

"Gimme that," the judge growled, ignoring the glasses setting on top of his head, and digging on an end table for another pair. Slapping the glasses on his face, he still held the paper at arm's length, mumbling as he read. "Huh," he grunted, scowled up at Mitch, then went back to reading. "We will go ahead with the court date tomorrow and I will set temporary orders."

"What does that mean?"

"I understand the girl's mother has some legal issues?" The judge glanced over his glasses and Mitch nodded. "I will listen to both of you, but likely I will grant you temporary custody until she can sort out her troubles. Then we will meet again and I will set down the permanent orders."

"Okay, when do I pick her up?"

"After court tomorrow. Well maybe, Doris at social services may want a physical for the child. I'll let you know," the judge said handing the paper back and turning his attention to the television. "What a bitch," he grumbled waving at the television as Jillian Braxton screeched into the microphone.

"As President I promise to rebuild our crumbling infrastructure. And I think there is no better place to start than right here in the great state of Arizona."

She paused to let the crowd respond, as a smattering of applause drifted through the television speakers, Mitch felt a cold shiver creep along his spine. Not for her speech, he didn't find it the least bit inspiring, but for the realization that she was about to let the cat out of the bag.

In an offhand way, Mitch heard the judge muttering, but the words didn't penetrate. Mitch felt like he was being sucked into a tunnel and the only thing he could see was Jillian Braxton. Her face looking like someone had taken mud and plastered features on a basketball, the Senator resumed her caterwauling.

"I am proud to announce that plans are under way to build a new airport here in southern Arizona. A huge new facility near the town of Coolidge. A state of the art complex that would service both the Phoenix and Tucson metro areas. In fact, all of Southern Arizona. "

"Shit," Mitch muttered, as Braxton prattled on about a commuter railroad between the two cities which would service the new airport. His mind racing, Mitch headed to the stairs. "I got to go," he muttered, not even seeing the astonished looks on the Sandersons' faces.

A fucking airport, that's what this is all about. Shit how much money could be made off that? Billions, Mitch decided. Certainly enough that it would be worth the occasional dead body.

That's why they were buying up all that land out in the desert. What didn't get folded into the airport grounds, would be sold off to developers. There would be warehouses and rental car places close in, and then hotels and restaurants farther out, and….

Oh shit!

A thought clicked into Mitch's brain like a bullet in the firing chamber. Cursing under his breath, Mitch sprinted for his house. He was digging for his cell, when *Sam I Am* sprang from its speaker, signaling a call from Wade Nichols. "Yeah, Wade," he said practically yelling in his eagerness to tell someone his idea.

"I did it, boss! I fuckin did it!" Wade shouted every bit as cranked up as Mitch.

"What did you do?" Mitch asked, momentarily forgetting his own news.

"Cracked it! Cracked that fucking I-Pod!"

"No shit! How?"

"Password was staring me in the face the whole time. Name of the band, name of the song and time of the song. I plugged in Tesla, *What You Give*, 4:21, no caps and no spaces and the fucker opened up like the legs on a two-dollar hooker." Wade sucked in a long, ragged breath which sounded like a passing tornado over the phone's speaker. "Mitch, I found out what this is all about!"

"Airport. Out near Coolidge."

"Aw shit," Wade said, his excitement deflating like a pricked balloon. "Damn it, the feds beat me to it."

"Nope," Mitch replied smugly, jerking open his front door and hurrying inside. "You beat those fuckers hands down. I was just listening to a speech by Braxton."

"That bitch!"

"Yeah. But she was talking about building this airport out in the middle of nowhere, and then it hit me; that's what this is all about."

"Well shit, you guessed right," Wade said, some of his earlier enthusiasm starting to bubble back to the surface. "It's all there, man. Somehow, Pyle got hold of a file from Forsyth. Forsyth was either looking to turn it in to the authorities, or he knew he was in trouble and was trying to protect himself, but either way, it's all laid out. They did the same thing in Denver."

"Denver? They got a new airport in Denver?"

"Yeah, about twenty years ago. You probably don't remember because at that time you were still running around in short pants with both hands around your wiener."

"Shit I still do that."

Wade barked out a laughed. "Yeah, I forgot. You're a golfer."

Mitch smiled looking for keys "So what happened here?"

"Well Forsyth had a buddy Jared Morris. They were the main ones doing the leg work, putting this deal together for Van Zandt. Well they cooked up this little scheme with Brody and Kathy to make a little cash on the side. Just like we thought, they snatched up a few parcels that were essential to the airport."

Mitch was nodding along with the story. "So, we were real close to being right. Brody had land that Van Zandt needed." Mitch picked up the Mustang keys from the bar and frowned. "Still why didn't the deal get done? I mean, it would have been in everyone's interest to do so. What was the real hold up? Van Zandt trying to be a hard ass?"

"Maybe, Forsyth didn't seem to understand it himself. He blames Brody for getting greedy and holding out, but I think maybe you were right from the start. When Brody needed cash, he brought in Chappy and his band of goons, and that fucked everything up."

Thinking he might need the four-wheel drive before the night was over, Mitch dropped the Mustang keys and grabbed the keys for the Trooper. "Chappy and Flores got greedy and forced Brody to hold out for more and after a time Van Zandt figured it was easier just to kill them."

"Probably, or Van Zandt took it personal and was always planning on killing them," Wade agreed. "Well shit, I guess we got it all figured out. Now we just have to find Angie Brody."

"I think I have."

"No woofin'?" Wade exclaimed. "Where?"

"Think about it, if you're Van Zandt and you just bought a whole bunch of property out in the sticks. Where would you stash a hostage?"

A second of silence, then Mitch heard a long sigh. "Aw shit, how did we not see that?"

"Head in our ass," Mitch said, stepping down into the garage. "Where are you? You at the office."

"Sitting right at my desk. You want me to call everybody in?"

"Yeah," Mitch said, feeling the adrenaline surge. "I'll stop and grab Geena then I'm on my way in. If you get time round up all the plats and maps we have of that area."

"You got it. We going to find that girl?"

"Yes, we are."

Mitch opened the garage door, surprised to see Geena crossing his yard. She was carrying a bottle of wine and some kind of meat and cheese platter. Seeing Mitch, she changed direction, heading for the garage.

"I was just coming to see you," she said, her face turning a bit red. "I was thinking we might have a proper date." She stopped seeing the look on Mitch's face. "We aren't going to, are we?"

"No, not tonight anyway," Mitch said reaching out and taking the wine and platter from her. "Jump in, we are going to get Angie Brody," He added setting the food in the back seat. Mitch jumped in the Trooper as Geena hurried around to the passenger's side, jerking open the door. "You know where she is?"

"Maybe the area," Mitch admitted, waiting as Geena crawled into the Trooper. He dropped the Trooper in reverse the second her door closed. "All this time and we missed it."

"How so?" Geena jerked her head towards the back seat. "That meat should really be in the frig."

"To hell with that." Mitch backed out into the street and stabbed the garage door controller. "Think about it, Van Zandt bought a crap load of property out in the country. Secluded places."

"And you think he is holding Angie at one of these places?" Geena asked. "Makes sense," she decided, answering her own question. "I take it some of these places will have houses on them?"

"Probably most of them. We need to start checking them out." The door closed, Mitch glanced up the street. He saw a motorcycle sitting against the curb a half a block up the street. It was dark, but Mitch could make out the tiny figure sitting on the bike.

Aw crap, Frankie. Mitch hesitated, staring up the street at the dark figure.

"Is everything alright?"

Mitch glanced over at Geena and shook his head to clear the stray thoughts. Tonight, he needed focus. "Yeah, I just had something pop into my head," he said, dropping the Trooper into gear. "If he sees us coming for him, what will he do?"

Mitch didn't elaborate on who he meant, he didn't have to. "That depends on how far he has disseminated. But if he sees us, he will lash out."

"At Angie?" Mitch asked, looking in the mirror as he drove down the street, but the bike didn't move.

"At anybody," Geena replied gravely. "But yes, especially at Angie."

"How do we prevent that?"

Geena paused for a long second. "I don't know." She looked out the window at the darkness. "I don't know if we can."

CHAPTER FIFTEEN

Mitch's Office Tucson AZ June 19th 2018 Tuesday Night

"Land, that's what this is all about?"

"Yup," Mitch said, nodding his head. "They did the same thing over twenty years ago in Denver. Van Zandt buys up all the land around the area where the new airport is going to be, then Braxton pushes it through Congress, getting those big federal dollars into the pot, and then they clean up selling the land to the airport authority."

"Aw man, I don't know," Ollie said doubtfully. "I mean, sure you can make some cash from the land sale, but how much? A few mil?"

"Maybe several million," Wade supplied.

"Yeah maybe, but how many ways does that get chopped up?" Ollie pointed out. "Brody and Cathy Reynolds for sure get some, and how about that little prick, Carter? And you can bet the good Senator got a cut."

"Sure, but a lot of the Senator's share could have come in political clout," Wade said. "She's running for

President, Van Zandt would be a big help in that, and if Kathy and Brody could deliver her Arizona? And I would say maybe that is the cause of the problem here, Brody didn't like his cut and is trying to weasel into more."

"Probably," Mitch agreed with a short nod. "Doesn't matter though, the big end of the money would come later," Mitch said. "In Denver, part of the deal was that Van Zandt ended up with the property where the old airport was."

"Shit, the property where Sky Harbor was would be worth a fortune," Wade said, whistling softly. "To say nothing of the airport property down here in Tucson." Wade looked to the ceiling and seemed to be doing calculations in his head. "Man, now, we are talking some serious money."

Mitch nodded. "Yeah, I did some checking, they are still developing the old airport area in Denver, twenty some years later and they are still raking it in," Mitch said, "Then, there is all the building contracts. Just think of how much concrete would be poured on a thing like this?"

"And Brody just bought a concrete company and batch plant," Wade agreed.

"Wouldn't just be the airport, there will be car rentals, hotels, probably some warehouses as well," Mitch said. "According to Braxton there will be a light rail connecting Phoenix and Tucson going through the airport complex."

"Shit that don't sound half bad," Wade said.

Maybe," Mitch grunted. "But it's all dirty."

"Yeah and I bet you a dollar against a dog turd that we can't hook Van Zandt into any of it," Ollie grumbled.

"Maybe not," Mitch said, with a tight, evil smile. "But we can tear it down."

"How do we use this to find Angie Brody?" Carly asked.

"We look at the property records. Van Zandt bought a lot of property," Mitch answered.

"You think she is out there?" Ollie asked quietly.

"Sure," Mitch said, with a shrug. "Some of those places would be pretty isolated, the perfect place to keep a hostage."

"Ok, it's worth a look" Ollie agreed with a slow nod. "So..., what is the plan?"

"We pull all the records. Make lists of all the places that have been sold recently, and we go check them out."

"Just us?" Wade said, glancing sideways at Ollie.

Mitch frowned, knowing what they were thinking. "Yeah," he said slowly. "I think so."

The two older detectives exchanged a long look. "Damn it man, are you sure? If she really is out there, we should bring in some help. That girl is running out of time," Ollie grumbled.

"I know, I know," Mitch said, running his hand through his hair, already starting to second guess himself. "I'm thinking about what Geena said; that if Carter feels cornered he might simply up and kill Angie."

Every eye in the room swung to Geena. She nodded curtly. "That is a very real possibility. If he feels cornered, he will lash out. He certainly won't surrender peacefully."

" Good ol' boy huh? Gonna go down shooting?" Ollie commented, looking sideways at Geena.

"Maybe," Geena answered. "He will put up a fight, but in the end, I think he will surrender. He will want the spotlight of a trial. When he lashes out, I suspect that will be directed at Angie."

"What if we did the opposite?" Wade wondered, rubbing his jaw. "What if we flooded the area with cars? As many as we can get. Bring them in with lights blazing, sirens going. He'd see it coming and I'd bet he will try to slip away.

You just know he has something planned for that very thing. A way out."

"I'm afraid he might slit her throat on his way out the back door," Mitch worried.

Again, every eye shuffled to Geena. "That would be a very distinct possibility. If cornered I am worried that he might do something truly horrible to her just for the shock value."

"Aw fuck you know he would," Ollie said, gruffly. "So, we go in dark and quiet and do what?"

"Look for the vehicles, the little Nissan, maybe the van," Jerry offered.

"You got it," Mitch agreed. "And I want everyone in vests, we take no chances tonight."

"What do we do when we find him?" Carly asked.

"Pull back and call the rest of us, then we will decide. If we have to, we go in at that point. Hopefully we can set up and watch the place and catch him moving. If we have to, we just call in the cavalry." Mitch glanced over at Wade. "Your knee up for this?"

"Fuck yes!"

"Okay, let's get the lists going. I want you and Jerry together. Ollie and Carly are together and me and Geena."

"How do you want to work it?" Jerry asked, looking at the lists.

"Let's do a leap frog pattern," Mitch said. "We can keep in closer contact that way."

While the lists were being compiled, Mitch wandered down to dispatch. He tip-toed up to Monte's desk, then slapped his hand down on the counter, laughing as the older man jumped a foot in the air. "Hey Monte, how's it hanging dude?"

"Shit, Mitch are you still here? I thought you crawled home and turned into a big turd after the sun went down."

"Ha! Your wife doesn't think so," Mitch shot back, taking a mini-Snickers from the bowl on Monte's desk. "She really likes snuggling up to a real man."

"Aw crap, now I know you're absolutely lying. You see, I am totally convinced that my old lady is a lesbian," Monte snorted, waving a hand at himself. "I mean, seriously, how else could you explain her turning down this on a nightly basis?"

"Shit, I got no answer for that," Mitch said, laughing. "Except that she may finally be developing some good taste."

"Bite me, dickweed," Monte grumbled. "Did you come over here for a specific reason, or is it just my day to have to put up with you and your bullshit?"

"You got a contact with Pinal County Sheriffs?"

Monte raised an eyebrow and cocked his head sideways. "I do, I know a couple of guys up there. I bowl in a weekend league with the night dispatcher, Joe Bachler. Good man." Monte leaned back in his chair. "What have you got going, cowboy?"

Mitch quickly laid out the plan. Monte nodded, leaning forward and spinning an old-fashioned rolodex. "You want me to have Joe send you a couple of cars?"

"Maybe," Mitch said thinking it over. "Tell you what. Give him a call and brief him on the situation. See what kind of assets he has for tonight. Right now, we want to take it slow."

Monte nodded, writing a number on a sticky note. "You afraid that if Carter spots cops rolling up on him he will kill the girl?"

"That is the consensus," Mitch said. "I'm hoping we can locate them and then pull back, get a plan going. Right now, I'm thinking, get Swat in there about dawn. Hopefully catch him sleeping. Take his ass down."

"Sounds good," Monte said, handing Mitch the sticky note. "That's Joe's cell. Call him when you get out there. I'll call him now and give him a heads up."

"Sounds good," Mitch agreed taking another Snickers.

"Shit asshole, help yourself, be sure to take all my candy. Maybe, you want me to buy you lunch or what?" Monte bellowed, snatching the bowl off the counter, but not before Mitch snagged another candy bar. "Jack off," Monte grumbled, placing the candy out of Mitch's reach.

"Hot damn, you sure are getting to be a grouchy bitch. Or is it just that time of month?" Mitch asked, grinning at the older man and popping one of the candy bars in his mouth as Monte shot him the bird. "No shit you bowl?"

"Yup a two-ten average," Monte said, a note of pride shining in his voice.

"Well hell, that explains why your wife is looking for a real man," Mitch said, grinning at the older man. "You should take up golf."

"Blow me," Monte said. "You know what the hardest part of golfing is?" Monte waited a beat and when Mitch didn't answer he cackled. "Telling you folks that you are gay!" Monte leaned back in his chair slapping his thigh.

"Yeah, bite me, fat boy," Mitch said, shaking the last mini-Snickers at the older man before turning away and heading back to his office.

Monte grinned and shot him the bird. "Hey Mitch, you guys be careful out there tonight."

Arizona Countryside South East of Coolidge AZ June 19th 2018 Tuesday Late Night

Mitch eased the car slowly down the narrow blacktop road. It was one of those gorgeous nights in the desert, so crisp and cool. And it was dark, so dark that the night seemed to eat up the light from their head lights. When he thought they were close, Mitch killed the lights. The darkness fell upon them, like a giant hand had tossed a blanket over the Trooper.

Mitch glanced sourly at the pitch, black sky. "Wish these clouds would roll out of here," he grumbled, struggling to see the road without the benefit of headlights. "A little light would be nice."

Geena nodded absently, staring at the GPS on her phone. "The driveway should be right in front of us," she decided.

"Okay," Mitch grunted easing the Trooper off the edge of the road. Not wanting to use the brakes, Mitch killed the engine and let the Trooper coast to a halt. In the silence of the night, the tires crunching on the gravel shoulder sounded like a battle raging. A little moonlight was escaping around the clouds, and they could see the house, a quarter mile off the main road. It looked like a lurking shadow, something out of a bad dream. "We can walk from here," he said, digging out the flashlights.

"How do we work this?"

"We can walk in, and start by looking for cars. You can bet Carter has a car here."

"He might try to stash it a few miles away, keep it hidden. He's got to know we are looking for the Nisan."

"Naw," Mitch said, mulling it over. "He'd for sure want to keep his wheels close, just in case he has to bug out in a hurry. But you are right, he might have the Nisan stashed somewhere, and have a car here we haven't seen." Mitch shot her a little grin. "That's why I took this place to search, according to the plat, it has a barn."

"To hide the car and van," Geena said, nodding.

"Yup," Mitch said, flipping the switch to kill the dome light. They crawled out of the truck, easing the doors shut as quietly as they could. At the rear of the Trooper, Mitch opened the back of the truck, pausing, to take in the night air. "It's so beautiful here at night," Geena said, echoing Mitch's own thoughts. She took the vest that Mitch handed. "It smells so clean."

"Nights like this make you want to go camping and never come back," Mitch said, shrugging into his own vest. Mitch picked up the shotgun, resisting the temptation to check it and make sure it was loaded. He had loaded it himself back at the station, but a part of him still wanted to double check the weapon. "Ready?" he asked, as he closed up the Trooper. He caught Geena's quick intake of breath, and barely saw her nod.

"No need in being sneaky," Mitch said, walking down the middle of the driveway. "I doubt if they could see us from the house," Mitch said, pulling out his phone. Cupping the phone to hide the light, he sent a text to Wade and Ollie.

He immediately received a reply from Wade, confirming he and Jerry were going into their first house. A few seconds later, a message from Carly, letting him know they were also at the first house on their list.

Mitch chuckled, sliding the phone into his pocket. "Ollie won't text. He made Carly do it."

A hundred feet from the house, Mitch stopped short, a nasty thought crossing his mind. "Did you see something?" Geena hissed.

"Naw, I was just thinking, motion sensor lights."

"You think Carter would use them?"

"I would," Mitch replied grimly. "Anybody gets close to the house and they come on. We'd be standing right in the light."

"So, we circle around," Geena said, nodding along. "Which way, do you think?"

Mitch shrugged trying to see through the gloom. At first, he couldn't see much, but slowly a darker shape caught his eye. 'Is that the barn?" he asked, pointing to the left of the house.

Geena squinted, nodding slowly. "I think so."

"Let's go that way. We can use the building for cover as we close in on the house," Mitch decided, leading the way.

Walking on the road had been relatively easy, but circling around proved to be much more difficult. In the poor light the ground looked reasonably flat, but the gloom hid all sorts of subtle variances. Stumbling along, Mitch cursed the ground, with every trip or slip. Carrying the shotgun, didn't help, nor did the fact that Geena was holding onto the back of his vest for balance.

Fighting the loose rocks and the uneven ground, Mitch struggled around and up to the back corner of the barn. To his surprise, it wasn't an old wooden barn but a metal garage. There was one window on the back side, but it was so dirty and scarred that in the dark, Mitch couldn't see in. Geena touched his arm, holding up her flashlight. For a second, Mitch was tempted, but then shook his head, not willing to risk the light.

Leading the way, they circled, keeping the building between them and the house. A huge garage door dominated the front of the building, the side that faced the house and the driveway. A smaller, walk through door was on the side they were creeping down.

Mitch tried the small door and was not surprised to find it locked. "Locked," he hissed at Geena. He'd have to come back and pick the lock, but first he wanted to get a look at the house. Stacking the shotgun against the garage, he peeked around the building at the back of the house.

The house was fifty feet away a small orange tree between the house and garage. The house was dark, but Mitch could see a flickering dull blue light through the open door. Television, Mitch thought, and as bright flicker flashed across the doorway, Mitch saw that the door had an old-fashioned screen door. Unconsciously, Mitch smiled. He hadn't seen one of those screen doors in years.

He looked over his shoulder to tell Geena he was closing in, but she was hunched over the door knob working on the lock. Mitch frowned, might be best to wait and see what was in the garage. But he didn't want to wait. This was the place he could feel it.

Carter was here!

Mitch glided up to the small tree. Hugging the tree, Mitch studied the house. The screen door had no latch, but they usually had a hook on the inside. If it wasn't hooked, he could slip into the house and maybe sneak up on Carter. If it was locked, he could back off and help Geena search the garage. He was about to move up again when he heard a sound from the house.

Suddenly a man appeared at the screen door. Mitch squinted, trying to see if it were Carter. Having never seen the man in person, Mitch couldn't tell in the low light. The one thing that Mitch could tell, was the man was packing. Mitch couldn't see the gun, but from the way the man stood, Mitch knew he had a pistol stashed behind his right hip.

Carter!

Evidently Carter had heard something, because he pushed open the screen door and stepped out onto the porch. Mitch smiled as Carter's hand strayed to his right hip. He was packing. Whatever had alerted Carter it wasn't Mitch and Geena, as he stared down the driveway.

Carter reached back, flicking an unseen switch. A scorching light seemed to spring from the ground, lighting the entire front of the house and driveway in a harsh white light. For a long time, Carter stood staring, his hand on his hip.

Satisfied that nothing was out there, Carter flicked off the light, turning back towards the house. As soon as Carter's back was turned, Mitch sprang forward. He didn't think about it, he just reacted. Mitch covered the twenty feet to the porch in three long bounds.

Carter sensed danger and tried to turn. His hand was on the pistol, when Mitch crashed into him. Mitch drove Carter through the screen door and across the room. Mitch wrapped his arms around Carter, keeping him from pulling the pistol as they crashed into the far wall.

Carter took the brunt of the impact, the wind leaving his lungs in a heavy grunt. Before Carter could recover, Mitch drove his elbow into Carter's face three times. Feeling Carter go a bit limp, Mitch slammed the smaller man to the floor. While Carter was stunned, Mitch jerked the gun from Carter's waistband and tossed it across the room. He punched Carter in the stomach, then flipped him on his back. Using his knee for leverage, Mitch pulled Carter's arms behind him, reaching for his cuffs.

Mitch snapped the cuffs on Carter, feeling a sense of satisfaction washing over him. The feeling was short lived as he thought of Angie Brody. He wasn't done until she was safe. Feeling a wave of anger like he had never experienced, Mitch drug Carter to his feet, slamming him against the wall hard enough to cave in the plaster.

"Where's the girl?" he asked, resisting the impulse to punt Carter in the nuts.

Carter tried to shrug with the cuffs on. "Who?"

Mitch took a step forward, baring his teeth. "You know who." Carter smiled at him, but remained silent. With a viscous sweep of his leg, Mitch kicked Carter's feet out from underneath him, knocking him to the floor. "Angie Brody. Where is she?"

Rolling into a sitting position, Carter smiled, crossing his legs and leaning back against the wall. "Don't know what you're talking about."

"Step aside, Mitch. I'll find out where she's at."

Mitch glanced over his shoulder, seeing Sam Logan standing in the doorway. Sam had a few days' growth on his cheeks and a wild look in his eyes. In his right hand, he carried an old fashioned forty-four revolver. "Step aside, I'll handle this," he growled.

"I can't do that."

"I wasn't asking," Sam said flatly, cocking the revolver. "Lay down your piece and step away from that little cocksucker."

"Oh hell, Sam, you're not going to shoot me," Mitch said, but all of a sudden, he wasn't so sure. There was something different about Sam, the man had a wild hunted look to him. Mitch wasn't sure what he might do.

"No, you're right, I wouldn't shoot you." Sam Logan grinned, an ugly, tight smile. "But I can sure as hell shoot that wormy piece of shit." Sam leveled the pistol at Carter and fired.

Mitch jumped, seeing the bullet tear through Carter's left leg. Carter screamed drawing the leg to him. "You fucker!" he screamed as blood began to ooze between his fingers.

"Shut up pussie," Sam growled, his eyes never leaving Mitch. "Lay down your piece."

"Sam, what the hell are you doing?" Mitch asked looking past Sam for Geena.

"We need to find that girl," Sam said, smiling wickedly at Carter. "This little asshole is going to tell us where she is. The only question is how many holes I have to put into him before he does." To punctuate his threat, Sam fired another shot into Carter's leg.

"Jesus Sam! What the hell are you doing?" Mitch screamed as Carter groaned, slumping back against the wall.

"I'm finding that gal," Logan said grimly. "Now, lay down your gun or I will put another hole in Junior here."

"Okay," Mitch said nodding, seeing a shadow behind Logan. "Easy," Mitch said, moving slowly. Trying to hold Sam's attention, Mitch pulled his own gun holding it between his thumb and forefinger, showing it to Sam. "Here it is."

"Put it down and kick it over to me."

His eyes never leaving Sam, Mitch slowly bent down, placing the gun on the floor. "Damn it, Sam what have you done?" he asked kicking the gun across the floor.

Sam smiled, taking his left hand off the revolver and wagging a finger at Mitch. "Don't try and distract me." He cocked his head to the side, smiling a little. "Missy, you can either shoot me or come and join us."

Geena edged into the room her gun leveled at Logan. "Drop your weapon Mister Logan."

"I don't think so, missy," Sam chuckled. "Now either shoot or lay down your weapon."

Geena didn't respond, she just flicked a questioning glance at Mitch. "Do what he says." Mitch advised.

Her face grim, Geena cocked her pistol. "Shoot him or put my gun down?"

Mitch smiled at Sam's double take. "Whichever."

Sam chuckled with very little humor. "Go ahead and shoot, might save us all a lot of trouble," he said, his voice a harsh whisper. "Probably would."

Geena shifted her feet, adjusted her grip on her gun, and took a hesitant step forward. Sam blew out a sigh, pulling the hammer back on his pistol. "Either shoot me or put your gun down. Do it now or I will put another bullet in this little piece of shit."

"God damn it! Shoot that old fucker!" Carter screamed his face red and twisted in pain.

"I thought I told you to keep your mouth shut," Sam said, a mean streak riding in his voice. "You, missy, put your gun down."

"Mitch?" Geena asked, her gun waving, but still covering Sam.

Mitch locked eyes with the older man. "We don't have to do it this way."

Sam grinned. "Don't worry, I got myself a plan."

Mitch hesitated, and then nodded to Geena. "Okay, put it down."

"Fuck me," Carter groaned as Geena lowered the hammer and placed the gun on the floor.

"Shut up!" Sam snapped, waving with his gun. "Get over there with your boyfriend." Sam stepped back as Geena crossed in front of him. He grinned, picking up her gun. "Berretta nine, serious shit," he grunted and picked up Mitch's gun. "A Sig? Would it hurt you to buy American?"

Mitch shrugged. "I like it."

"Yeah, you would. Gay bastard."

Mitch cocked his head at Geena's gun. "Like Berretta is American. Why ain't you giving her shit?"

"She's cuter than you." Sam sat on the arm of the thread-bare couch, turning his attention to Carter. "Alright whistle dick, I'm gonna ask you a question and you damn well better answer."

"Fuck you, you shot me!"

Sam chuckled, sounding entirely pleased with himself. "Oh shit, you ain't hurt, I just nicked you a little," Sam said. He tilted his head, studying Carter intently. "I thought you was supposed to be a bad boy, killed all these folks, you kinda seem like a pussy to me."

Carter glared up at him clutching his leg. "Got nothing to say, huh?" Sam smiled down at the younger man. "This is how it's gonna go. I'm gonna ask you a question; you answer right and I'll let Mitch call you an ambulance. You don't?" Sam shrugged, still grinning. "Well in that case, I will shoot you someplace that really hurts."

Sam flipped open the cylinder of the revolver, calmly punched out the two spent shells. "Where is she?" he asked as he slowly slid in two fresh bullets. Sam flipped the cylinder shut with a flick of his wrist, looked up and fired. The bullet smashed into Carter's shoulder, slamming him screaming against the wall.

Carter screamed again, cursing wildly.

A wicked smile danced merrily on Sam's weathered face. "That one hurt a little bit, didn't it?" He cocked his head, studying the wound. "Smashed collarbone," he decided. "Bet it'll take a team of surgeons to fix."

Sam leveled the gun at Carter's crotch. "You think that smashed shoulder hurt, wait till I blow your little dick off."

"She's in the barn!"

Sam shook his head, cocking the pistol. "Nope, I already checked in there."

"No, no, please" Carter wailed, shrinking back against the wall. He sucked in a huge gulping breath, sounding like a drowning man coming up for air. "There's a cellar, it's under the tool bench."

"You better not be lying to me numb nuts." Sam hissed. "If she ain't there I'm gonna come back and shoot you in the nuts and let you bleed out."

Sam shot a sly smile to Mitch. "See how easy that was? Now let's go get that gal."

"What about him?" Geena asked, pointing to Carter, who had curled into a whimpering ball.

Sam laughed gleefully. "He ain't going anywhere."

"We should get him some help," she maintained.

"He'll be fine," Sam predicted looking curiously at Geena. "Would it really bother you if he died?"

Geena shifted her feet, but then she met Sam's gaze. "No," she said quietly. "Not really."

Sam's face split in a grin. "Me neither. How 'bout you, Mitch?"

"Fuck him. Let's go get Angie."

They pushed through the back door and out onto the porch. Mitch grabbed Sam's arm. "Sam, what the hell are you doing?"

"Finding the girl. Setting things right."

"Shit that's not what I mean. That shooting out by the border, that was you," Mitch accused.

Sam cackled a little laugh. "Yep, sure was. I kinda knew you'd figure it out sooner or later."

"Why?"

"You remember those two kids that got killed over by the border"

"Yeah," Mitch grunted as they approached the garage.

"That was Henry Flores and his goons that killed them. You know why they were killed?"

"No."

"Not because those kids were bad or because they were doing drugs or shit like that. They were just out hiking, on their honeymoon, seeing the sights and they saw something they shouldn't have. That's what got them killed."

Sam waited while Mitch slid the door open. "Lights are to your right." Sam sighed. "The thing is Flores would have gotten away with it. I couldn't abide by that. So, I took steps."

"Jesus Sam. You flat out murdered them."

Sam nodded grimly. "Yeah, fuck'em. They deserved it."

Mitch glanced over at his old friend, something had changed. Sam had always been a hard man, but now there was something else. A hard edge of something, desperation maybe. "Sam, what is going on with you? This kind of shit isn't you."

Sam ignored Mitch as they walked into the garage. "Missy, why don't you stand here with me. Mitch, you see if you can open that cellar."

"Damn it, Sam," Mitch started.

"Don't lecture me, son," Sam barked, his voice rough. "Let's find that girl," he added in a tone that on most people would have sounded harsh, but from Sam, it almost sounded kindly.

Mitch stared at the man who he had known for so many years. Mitch was a poker player, and he could read when somebody was putting on the old stone face. Sam was definitely hiding something. "Shit, are you dying, Sam?" Mitch blurted out.

The question staggered Sam, almost like a physical blow. The old man stopped, righting himself and squaring his shoulders. "Oh hell, everybody dies," he said, a sloppy smile slipping on to his face. "But let's make sure today ain't the day for that Angie gal."

Mitch stared at the old man, feeling a wave of sadness. After a second, Mitch nodded. "Alright, let's do it," he said, turning to the bench. Mitch tugged on the bench, but it felt solid. Dropping to one knee he looked underneath spying a small handle.

"Whatcha see?" Sam called.

Ignoring him, Mitch twisted the handle and pulled on the bench. Moving easily, the bench rotated away from the wall, revealing a set of stairs. Shit," Mitch grunted, looking down the stairs at a formidable steel door. "Looks like a cell," Mitch said, starting down the stairs.

"Mitch," Sam called, his voice hard and cold as marble tile. "Give me your phone before you go down there."

Mitch hesitated, then passed his phone back to Sam. "You too," Sam grunted, holding his hand out to Geena.

After Sam had both phones, he nodded towards the cellar. "Go get that girl," he said, shooing Geena towards the stairs. "I'll call Ollie in five minutes to come get you."

Mitch hesitated, then nodded grimly. Mitch went down the steep stairs, instinctively reaching for his pistol, which wasn't there. At the bottom of the stairs was a tiny landing and the huge, steel door. A simple sliding bar secured the door, clear evidence that the door was designed to hold someone in rather than keep them out. Mitch could feel Geena press up against him as he grabbed the bar. Surprisingly it slid back easily and the door swung open.

"Is she there?" Sam whispered, like he was afraid to raise his voice.

Mitch ignored him, pushing the door all the way open. A tiny light in the center of the room was fighting a losing battle to beat back the darkness. The room was small perhaps fifteen feet across, but even so the light struggled to reach the corners. In one corner, Mitch could make out a toilet and sink. Huddled on a blanket in the far corner and surrounded by gallon jugs of water and boxes of crackers was a small figure.

The figure was so still that Mitch feared she might be dead. "Angie," he called softly, almost afraid to raise his voice.

"Yes," she croaked, clearing her throat. "Help me." She reached out a wavering hand, "Please."

"Police, ma'am. We are here to help," Mitch said. "Are you okay?"

"Maybe," she said pulling herself up a little straighter. "I think so," she added, her voice getting stronger.

Geena pushed past Mitch, kneeling beside the girl. "You are not injured? He didn't hurt you?"

"No. He put me down here, then came back later with all the water, crackers and tuna pouches. Then he never came back." Angie swiped at a tear rolling down her cheek. "I was afraid that no one would ever come. How long have I been here?"

"Ten days," Mitch said, feeling as helpless as he had ever felt in his life.

"Mitch," Sam called from the top of the stairs. "I'm leaving. I will call Ollie and have him come get you."

"Sam do not do this," Mitch said softly. "Give it up, man. Whatever it is, we can work this out."

Sam laughed, a bitter sound. "Not this." He threw Mitch a tight salute. "Take care of her. I'll send your boys right over."

With that, Sam closed the door. Mitch heard the bar slide into place but still he tried it. Just as he knew it would, the door held fast, not even budging an inch. His hand on the knob, Mitch felt the quick, greasy feel of panic run through his guts, they were locked in. Trapped!

The smartass part of his brain laughed at his quick panic. That girl had been locked down her for days, and he was shitting himself after a couple of seconds.

"Did he leave us?" Angie asked, her voice sounding as forlorn as a foghorn in the darkness.

"He's just going for help," Mitch said, hoping desperately that it was true.

"Why did he lock the door?"

"It's a long story," Mitch said, smiling down at her. "Are you sure you're okay?"

The beginnings of a smile tugged at her lips. "I think so," she said, her tone suggesting she might still be trying to convince herself of that fact.

"Are you sure?" Geena said, softly rubbing Angie's arm. "He didn't hurt you?"

"No like I said, I woke up down here. He only came back down here once with the food and water. After that, I never saw anyone." She glanced up, the lost look of an orphan on her face. "How long did you say have I been down here?" she whispered as if she were afraid of the answer.

"Ten days," Mitch said, feeling a quick stab of guilt.

"Wow, ten days," she said almost in wonderment. "I had no idea. It seemed like months." She bit her lip, hesitating. "My dad, is he okay?"

"We don't know," Mitch admitted. "He seems to have gone missing. He hasn't been seen for the last couple of days."

"Is he...." Angie squared her shoulders against the concrete wall. "Is he dead?"

Mitch hesitated. He knew, he should be preparing her for the likelihood that her father was gone, but he just couldn't bring himself to crush her hopes.

"Ma'am, I will be honest with you, your father is missing. But we have no reason to believe he is dead. It is our theory that they need him alive." Mitch didn't add what he was thinking. They needed Braxton, right up until he gave them what they wanted. Mitch paused, feeling a little bit guilty for what he was about to do. He was going to use her plain and simple. He didn't like doing it, but he was going to. "In fact, the only reason we have to believe that your father is even missing is because your step-mother said he didn't come home. Any reason why she would lie?"

A quick, distasteful look sprang to Angie's face. The look hung on her lips as she chose her words carefully. "Not really, Jennifer has never given me a single reason to distrust her."

"But you do," Mitch said, smiling as he took her hand. "Don't worry I don't trust her either."

Angie nodded very slowly, a wooden expression on her face. Mitch had seen that look many times over the years. It was the look someone gave a cop when they were told a loved one wouldn't be coming home. "He's dead, isn't he?"

Rubbing her hand, Mitch paused for a beat, which he knew gave it away. "There's always hope."

Angie nodded again, but she wasn't agreeing with Mitch's words. She knew.

Feeling like crap, Mitch gave her hand a final pat. "I'm going to see if I can get us out of here."

"Are we stuck down here?" Angie asked, a quiver in her voice and a single tear squeezing out of her left eye.

"No, no," Mitch assured, watching as the tear cut a clean swath down her dirty face. "He is going to tell the other cops we are here."

"Why would he lock us down here?"

Mitch hesitated, thought about lying, but decided she could handle the truth. "He wants to kill Jacob Carter, and he doesn't want to be interrupted."

Angie cocked her head, then nodded grimly. "Good."

Mitch smiled, turning away. This girl had grit. She'd be alright. Mitch turned to the door, leaning his shoulder into it, but it was firm. Using a pocket knife, Mitch was picking around the edges of the door, trying to slide the bar when he heard voices.

Pulling the knife back and folding it Mitch stepped back. After a few seconds, the door swung open and Ollie's smiling face beamed down at them. "What are you doing? Taking a break?'

"Bite me, old man," Mitch growled. "Any sign of Sam or Carter?"

Ollie shook his head. "The others are looking, but they're long gone." Ollie looked past Mitch, nodding his head at Angie. "Sam said on the phone that she was doing okay?"

Mitch's eyes followed Ollie's pointing a finger to Angie who was talking quietly to Geena. "Seems to be for now. Time will tell."

"Your right about that. This kind of stuff has a way of creeping up on you later," Ollie agreed. "I called an ambulance for her anyway."

"Good deal, did you call Pinal County."

"Wade did, they are sending a half-dozen cars this way looking for them. They've already got a couple of road blocks set up."

"What do you want to bet that they don't find them?" Mitch asked, feeling a grin pushing at his lips wanting to burst across his face.

"Oh hell, no bet," Ollie grumped. "They are looking on the main roads. I bet Sam's easing down some goat trail. They won't even get a whiff of him."

"Yeah," Mitch grumped, wondering why it bothered him. He sure didn't give two cents about Carter. He turned to the women. "We have an ambulance coming. They will check you out."

"Thank you. Can I wait outside?" Angie Brody managed a small woeful smile. "I think I have spent enough time down in this hole. I want to see the sun." She paused, then smiled again. "It's night, isn't it? I can tell by your face."

"Yes, ma'am it is."

She shrugged. "Doesn't matter, I still want to go out. If somebody could help me up."

Grumpy, frumpy Ollie stepped forward with the grace of a dancer, and with a move that somehow reminded Mitch of a bull fighter, extended a hand down to her. "Ma'am, allow me," he offered. "I have been reading up on you and I must say it is one of the greatest honors of my life to finally meet you."

A gracious smile blossomed across her face. "Thank you, sir," she replied, taking his hand.

Ollie helped her to her feet, and for a second, she stood spraddle legged like a new born colt. She pushed away their hands. "I want to do this on my own," she told them. "When I woke up down here, I made myself a promise that no matter what, I would walk out of here."

"He didn't hurt you?" Ollie asked, his voice, sounding like a hurt animal.

"No," Angie said with an uncertain smile. "Not in the way you think." All of a sudden, Angie stood up straight and threw her shoulders back. "You know what, he didn't hurt me at all," she said, tottering towards the stairs, somehow reminding Mitch of a drunk trying to pass a roadside sobriety test.

At the stairs, she looked back and flashed a crocked smile. "I'm good."

CHAPTER SIXTEEN

**Starbucks Coffee Shop Washington DC June 20th
2018 Wednesday Morning**

Perry Van Zandt accepted the coffee, flashing his best smile. With his perfect tan, two-hundred-dollar haircut and laser-whitened teeth, it was a nice smile. A nice smile if you were willing to overlook the complete lack of warmth in his eyes.

"Thank you, Courtney," he said, slipping a hundred-dollar bill into the tip jars as only a rich person could. He did it casually, naturally, not making a big deal of it, but somehow making sure she saw the bill's denomination. With the flair of a Vegas dealer, he snapped out a business card, letting her see it. "I was thinking we should go to dinner Friday night. I was thinking sometime around eight," he said, then casually tucked the card into the top of her bra. "That's my car service, call them when you are ready, they will come pick you up."

"What's the restaurant?"

"Per Se, in Manhattan. The car will take you to the airport. Dress nice." Van Zandt gave her a small salute with his coffee cup and strode boldly from the coffee shop. It never entered his mind that she might refuse.

Courtney Grissom pulled the card from her bra, looking at it for a long minute. It occurred to her to toss it in the trashcan at her feet. But she didn't. With a smile she tucked it back in her bra, pushing it a little farther down.

FBI Field Office Tucson AZ June 20th 2018 Wednesday Mid-morning

The room had the feel of an arena just before a big event. A sense of anticipation, an almost electric charge that something big was about to happen. Mitch leaned back in his chair, watching, feeling apart from the whole procedure. And in a way, he really didn't care. His part, what he could do was done.

The room might have an electric feel to it, but it wasn't his room, and they weren't his troops. They were Geena's. They were at the FBI Field Office, and they were waiting on a warrant. Geena had gotten a heads up from a colleague that a warrant was coming down. A warrant for the immediate arrest of Jillian Braxton.

It was a federal court and the warrant would be federal, served by federal agents. Any charges filed would also be filed by the United States Government. A stranger in this office, Mitch felt a peculiar detachment from the whole process. It was his case and he was here as a courtesy, but from here on out, big brother was running the show.

That was okay with Mitch. First of all, he was genuinely happy for Geena. Besides Mitch was ready to move on. The case had crashed from a red-hot high when they found Angie Brody alive, to a frozen, glacial log jam. Sam Logan had disappeared with Carter. Everyone was looking for them, but Mitch knew if anyone ever saw Jacob

Carter again, it would be nothing but a pile of bleached bones.

They were looking for Brody as well, but he was flat out gone. It seemed like everyone in the city had an opinion and they were split right down the middle. Half thinking Brody had blown town, and the other half convinced he was dead. Ollie had taken the hunt personally, and was vowing to find the man one way or the other.

For his part, Mitch was pretty sure Brody was dead. He had definitely gotten that feeling when talking to Jennifer Brody, and looking back, it made sense that if Chappy was doing the wife that he would get rid of Brody. If Brody didn't have a will, then she would get it all. And even if Brody had a will leaving all of his assets to Angie, it would be void if Angie died first. In that case the entire estate would go to Jennifer, and under Chappy's control.

It was a good plan, but like Carter and Brody, Chappy was probably decomposing somewhere in the desert. Mitch knew from experience that one day, some hiker would stumble upon their bones. And that would be that.

The rest of it would grind its way through the federal system. This is what the feds really excelled at, grinding things down into a fine dust. Whatever happened, Braxton would be finished in politics. Probably her or her husband would do a little time. It wouldn't be much, and it would be in a federal resort prison. Mitch's bet was it would be him that did time. The word he was getting was that they were both ready to roll over on each other, but Mitch knew she would not be the one to go down. It might be sexier to go after a sitting Senator, but it was a dream come true to have one in your back pocket. Give her the break, and they owned her.

Of course, it wouldn't be his decision either way.

Right now, there was a lot of bluster about going after Van Zandt, but Mitch knew it wouldn't come to much of anything. The Feds would puff out their chests and make a few threats, but that would be the end of it. Through all of this, Van Zandt had been one step ahead of everyone, and he still was.

Van Zandt had effectively insulated himself. Already Dykes was hearing rumors out of Quantico that Van Zandt was whispering to the Feds, offering to roll over on everyone. By the time the dust settled, they would let him do it. It wasn't right. Hell, it wasn't even in the same zip code as right, but Mitch understood it. Hell, Stevie Wonder could see they weren't going to hang anything on Van Zandt.

The Feds wouldn't like it, but they would let Van Zandt skate and use him to go after the Braxton's. They would use Van Zandt to strengthen their case against the Braxton's, knowing Van Zandt he would probably end getting immunity.

It rankled Mitch to his core that Van Zandt was going to sail away from all of this unscathed, but he had them neatly boxed. For every argument of his guilt Van Zandt had an alibi or at least some credible deniability. It was sad that Van Zandt had ordered the deaths of William Forsyth and Jared Morris, and their involvement was what was going to make it possible for Van Zandt to walk away. He simply claimed that the two young men in his employ had been acting on their own. That he knew nothing of their actions.

No one was really buying it, but there was nothing to be done about it. If it ever went to trial, those two young men would give Van Zandt all the reasonable doubt he needed. No one could prove he knew anything about any of this.

In the end, the Feds would do what they did. Make a deal. They would accept Van Zandt's help to nail the Braxtons. Then the Braxtons would do their own deal and in a year from now it would all be forgotten. One of the

Braxtons might do a little time, but not much. In a couple of years, they'd probably be making millions on the lecture circuit.

Did he really want to be a part of that?

Not really, Mitch decided.

Even if he did push his way in, he'd be little more than a spectator. No thanks. Besides he had better things to do today. Mitch glanced at his phone, reading the text from Doris. She was looking at his house, making sure it was suitable for a child. The text was typical, short and to the point but somehow still managing to convey a cheerfulness. "It's all set. Your house passed. Nice place! If the judge sets temporary orders you can pick up Josie after her physical."

The thought of picking her up scared him to death. Maybe the judge would come to his senses and realize Mitch wasn't fit to be a single parent.

What if she didn't like him? What would he even say to her? These thoughts raced through his head, repeating like a broken record. Mitch tried to picture the first meeting with his daughter. What would he say to her? Even in his mind, he couldn't think of what to say to her. He had a feeling he was going to blow it. Sitting in an over air-conditioned Federal office, Mitch began to sweat. He could feel large drops rolling down his back. A daughter!

All of a sudden, something rolled over him like a wave of panic. Feeling like he was cornered, and unable to sit still, he jumped to his feet, crossing the room to where Geena was talking to two men in matching suits. "Hey, I'm gonna shove off."

She turned to Mitch, disappointment showing on her face. "Oh, don't go," she said, the disappointment quickly melting under the hot glow of her excitement. "These gentlemen were just telling me that the warrants are coming, even the one on the Senator."

"Nice," Mitch said, glancing at the two men. They were both alike, crew cut hair that had been whipped to attention, and suits so severe they would make a Brooks Brothers suit look like casual Friday. "Van Zandt?"

Blonde crew cut shook his head and black crew cut grunted, "No, not him."

"But we get the Senator," Geena quickly pointed out, her excitement bubbling over. "We're checking her schedule right now. I think she has a break next week." She stopped as Mitch was shaking his head. "What?"

"This is your arrest, but I wouldn't wait. This woman broke the law. She ordered people killed. Go get her. She doesn't deserve to be free."

Geena bit her lip, shuffling her feet. "I don't know, she is, after all, a sitting United States Senator. It seems prudent to do these things with a little decorum."

"Fuck that," Mitch stated flatly. "Fuck decorum. She ain't one bit better than some street corner dealer."

"I might have to get permission from Quantico," Geena said, wavering.

"Whatever," Mitch said with a shrug. "But I can tell you one thing, if I was Braxton's lawyer, I would make a lot of hay with the fact that you sat on the warrants."

"Yeah, maybe," Geena admitted, shifting her feet and pushing back her hair. "I've been advised to wait."

"By who," Mitch snorted. "Look, this is the type of bust that makes careers. You want to be out in front on this and you want to make a big splash. You do this right and you can write your own ticket."

"But this is as much your bust as mine. Probably even more. You should be the one out in front on it."

"No," Mitch said shaking his head. "This is a fed thing. One way or the other a fed is going to be out in front on it. If you hesitate, one of those pencil dicks from DC will swoop in and take all the credit."

Geena let loose a bright, bubbly smile. "I'm from DC," she reminded.

"Yeah, but I bet never in your life have you ever been referred to as a pencil dick."

A sneaky smile found its way on to her face. "Not to my face anyway." Geena pushed back her hair, shifting her feet again. "What are you suggesting?"

Mitch cocked his head, looking at the schedule in her hand. "There you go," he said tapping the schedule. "Tomorrow night. She is giving a speech in Miami. Go pick her up there."

"You mean grab her at her own event?"

"Why not?"

Geena frowned. "Are you sure?"

"Yup," Mitch advised with a firm nod. "Wait until she is on stage giving her speech and then hook her up. Drag her ass right off the stage."

"Really?"

"Yeah, really," Mitch maintained. "That will do two things, first, it will make your name. You will always be known as the bad ass who took down a sitting Senator."

A smile stole onto Geena's face, and she nodded slightly. "What else?"

"Well if you jerk her off the stage, it will go viral. The media won't like it, they kiss Braxton's ass every chance they get, but in the end, they'll have to show it. That will convince a big part of the country that she is guilty. Seeing somebody dragged off in cuffs is a powerful picture. It will help drive home the point that she is guilty."

" My superiors are advising me to wait," Geena worried.

"Of course, they are," Mitch said nodding. "They assume there will be a deal to be made."

"A deal where Braxton skates?"

"More than likely. She is no good to them behind bars. If a deal can be reached that keeps her out of jail and in the Senate, they own her. A United States Senator in your pocket could be a powerful thing to own. You can bet somebody is already thinking about that."

"If the arrest goes down nice and quiet, then there is room for them to maneuver." Geena glanced at Mitch who nodded. "But if we hook her up in the open, with some fanfare?"

"No room for shit," Mitch said nodding.

"Come with me," Geena said, grabbing his arm. "We will take that bitch down and then go celebrate."

Mitch shook his head. "I can't. I have to go over to HR and get Josie signed up on my insurance." Mitch took a deep breath. "Then I got court and then I get to pick her up."

Geena smiled. "Your whole face just lit up

Tucson Municipal Court Tucson AZ June 20th 2018
Wednesday Afternoon

Mitch walked out of the courtroom his head buzzing. There was no denying it now, he was a father. All this time he half thought it was a joke, or that at least someone would come to their senses. But it was done now. The judge had just awarded him temporary, full custody. In a few hours, he would pick up his daughter and his life would change forever. And change for the better he suspected.

"Mitch."

Still in a daze, Mitch barely heard his name, and it didn't penetrate his fog until a hand grabbed his shoulder. "Hey, Mitch." Mitch turned to see Tanner and Kathy. "Whoa dude, you sure got that deer in the headlights look. Are you okay?" Tanner asked, almost laughing.

"Yeah, sure," Mitch replied, not at all sure about anything. He glanced at Kathy. "I'm sorry about all of this."

Kathy shifted her feet and tucked her hair behind her ear, a clear indication she was furious. Reading the sign, both Mitch and Tanner took a step back, sharing a quick glance and a smile.

"What's up with you two?" Kathy snapped.

"Sorry," they both said at once then laughed.

"What!"

Mitch and Tanner exchanged another look, but it was Tanner that spoke. "We both know the signs when you are about ready to blow your stack," he said with a smile. "Just remember, babe, its Mitch your mad at. He's a rotten son of a bitch."

"You're both rotten sons of bitches!" Her face red, Kathy stomped her foot again. She shook her head at the two men. "Let's go to the cafeteria, I want some coffee."

They walked down the hallway in silence, each lost in their own thoughts. "Are you going to take my daughter?" Kathy blurted out all of a sudden.

"You mean our daughter?" Mitch snapped, then immediately regretted it. "I'm sorry," he said, then regretted that.

"You're sorry," Kathy snapped. "Well that's just peachy."

"Hey, let's keep it clean," Tanner said, pointing at the cafeteria. "Let's get that coffee."

"Where do we go from here?" Kathy asked, as they sat down.

"First of all, I don't hear anything about me trying to take Josie." Mitch pointed his finger across the table at the pair, unconsciously letting his tough cop voice out. "You guys brought this on yourselves. You broke the law and all I did was my job. Whatever happens now is on you two."

Kathy hung her head, and whispered in a small voice. "Okay."

"Mitch, it wasn't Kathy, that was all me," Tanner said. "Kathy was just helping me out. Chappy said if I helped him one last time, I could get out of the Deacons."

"Help him kill Jackson Pyle?"

"Yes, that was all me, Kathy had nothing to do with it," Tanner said, repeating himself. "How do we get her out of this?"

"The gun is a problem," Mitch said. "It was her gun that killed Pyle, and her prints were on the shells at the scene."

"Hell, you know she didn't kill him," Tanner said.

"But we also know she brought Chappy Miers and the Deacons to Brody and into Van Zandt's airport scheme. It looks like maybe she was helping get rid of a problem, when she helped Chappy murder Pyle."

"You can't believe that," Kathy said, almost like she was afraid he'd say he did.

"No, I don't but I'm not a jury, and I'm not District Attorney Conners." Mitch shook his head, trying to make them understand. "You see if you guys had come clean that first night, I could have helped you, but now it's out of my hands. Look at it from the DA's point of view, we had a very high-profile crime here in Tucson and there's no one left to charge. Carter and Chappy both missing. Brody is gone, maybe dead. The two crooked cops are dead, and nobody from the DA to my chief wants to shed any more light on those two. That just leaves Van Zandt, Braxton and you. If they get charged it will be federal charges. That only leaves you for Fred Conners to charge."

"What do you suggest?"

"Get a lawyer first."

"We hired Terry Milton, the guy you recommended," Tanner said and glanced slyly at Mitch. "You say nobody wants to deal with the dead cops. Maybe we could use that."

"That might work," Mitch said with a shrug. "It's worth a try. I could have the chief reach out to Conners, maybe whisper in his ear that it would be in everyone's best interest if this all just went away."

"Would that work?" Kathy asked, a raw desperate sound to her voice.

"Maybe, especially if you were willing to plead out. Agree to something like obstruction and agree to a few years' probation and a fine."

"What kind of fine?"

"Twenty, thirty grand. Something like that."

"I could swing that," Tanner said, closing his eyes and blowing out a sigh.

"Are you going to try and take Josie away?" Kathy asked, her voice suggesting that she might not want to hear the answer.

"No," Mitch said, as Kathy's whole face sagged in relief. 'When you get clear of the charges, we can work something out."

"Thank you," Kathy said. "Can I see her?"

"Sure," Mitch said, nodding. "Maybe you could go see her before I pick her up. I've taken a few days off, I'd like to use that time to get to know her a little. After that, you can see her when your schedule allows."

Kathy closed her eyes, touching Mitch's hand. "Thank you," she whispered.

Len Dykes House Washington DC June 20th 2018
Wednesday Afternoon

A thunderous scowl riding on his face, Len Dykes sat in his beat-up lawn chair, quietly sipping a beer and staring at the clouds building in the west. Len was angry, furious in fact, but not at the approaching storm. Len was angry at the situation, and he was angry at himself. Another woman was dead, and he could do nothing about it. Not one blasted thing.

Len took a small sip of his beer. Damn it to hell, he was supposed to be able to do something about this kinda shit. He was supposed to be able to make a difference. A flash of anger washed over him. Cursing, he hurled the half full can out into the yard. As it sputtered and spewed foam across his yard, a sheepish grin stole on his face. He'd have to pick that up, or his wife would have his ass.

Smoothing his temper, he opened the small refrigerator on his porch and grabbed another beer. He opened the can, taking a sip, but it tasted like ashes in his mouth. He carefully set the can on the small table beside his chair. Tipping his head back, Len closed his eyes. It wasn't supposed to be like this. Len could feel the guilt crushing down upon him. He'd failed that girl today, and he'd failed Harley.

Len had met with one of the Assistant District Attorneys earlier that afternoon. The attorney, Jerry Janson was very good, and Len had been hopeful he might convince Janson to file on Van Zandt. In the end, Len had been almost begging, but to no avail, Janson wouldn't budge. Sitting on his front porch, Len didn't want to admit it, but he knew, Janson had been right not to file. A public defender straight out of law school would be able to knock down what they had on Van Zandt.

But damn! That meant Van Zandt was going to walk. Again!

Len felt the impulse to throw the new beer into the yard, but instead took a long pull from the can. He'd failed. Failed them all. Len finished his beer in one long drink. An idea growing in his mind, Len snagged another beer from the frig, thinking it over. Aw what the hell? What was the worst that could happen?

On impulse, he pulled out his phone, painfully scrolling through the numbers. When he came to the one he was looking for, Len hesitated. He looked at the clouds for a long second, then stabbed the button. A storm was brewing. In more ways than one.

"Yeah, Mitchell."

"Arizona," Len said, feeling better already. "How's things out there in the desert?"

"Hot," Mitch grunted glad for a break from insurance forms. "What can I do for you?"

"You can tell me you got something on Van Zandt."

"Shit nothing," Mitch admitted. "Carter is gone, and I don't think he is coming back." Mitch waited a long beat then added. "Ever."

Len took another taste of his beer. "You sure about that? He seems to be one shifty white boy."

"Shifty don't last long against a pissed off marine." Mitch leaned back in his chair. "Someday some hiker will stumble across his bones, but otherwise he ain't never coming back."

Len nodded absently, taking a sip of his beer. Earlier, the beer had tasted sour, but now, suddenly it was sugar sweet and a peace settled over him as Len made up his mind. "Your buddy, that state trooper, he finish Carter?"

"Yeah," Mitch grunted, frowning as he picked up the change in the older man's tone. In a flash, Mitch knew what that meant. "Don't," he cautioned.

"Got to," Len stated. "For Harley." Len finished the beer in one long pull, smacking his lips. "And for that girl today. And all the others."

"Others? What do you mean?" Mitch asked. "You mean Forsyth? What others?"

Len chuckled, sounding like a new man, or maybe a man saved. "Forsyth? I forgot about him. But yeah, for him too. I was talking about all them girls."

Mitch felt a bolt of fear shoot straight through him. "Women?" he croaked. "You found more bodies?"

"No, but we will," Len admitted. He paused, trying to put into words what he was just beginning to realize. "That fuck has changed, man. I think he is losing it. I think we are going to start seeing bodies. Lots of them. I think he is just getting started."

"You think doing that chick last night changed him?"

"Or brought him around to what he always was," Len answered still thinking about it. "You shoulda seen that fucker yesterday. He was setting there smiling at me with this wild look, and firing down straight whiskey. He had these big scratches on his arms. Wasn't even trying to hide them."

"Hot damn, that's something there. Was there skin under her fingernails?"

"Nope," Len replied. "Her hands had been washed and under her nails was cleaner than a nun's mind."

"Huh," Mitch grunted, trying to see an angle. "Well, that in itself tells us something."

"Tells us that Van Zandt is smarter than your normal pervert."

"And we already knew that," Mitch agreed, his mind churning. "Shit, he's taunting us, letting you see the scratches."

"What I figured," Len grunted. "I figure he's also letting us know he's just getting started."

"If he is already losing control, means we'll get him."

"Eventually," Dykes agreed. "How many are going to die before then?"

"Yeah," Mitch grumped, knowing Dykes was right. There would be bodies. "What are you thinking?" Mitch asked quietly.

"I don't know," Len said grudgingly. "But we can't wait too long. This mutt needs to be put down!"

Bruce's Grant Street Pawn Shop Tucson AZ June 20th 2018 Wednesday Evening

Ollie walked into the pawn shop, nodding to Bruce, who was reading the paper. Bruce returned the nod and pretended to go back to reading his paper, but he was in fact watch Ollie like a hawk.

Oscar Olshan, Bruce thought. This can't be good.

Bruce had known Ollie for years, and he knew Ollie didn't mess around. If he was in here, he had a reason. Bruce snapped his gum, he had an idea what that reason might be.

For his part, Ollie circled the store slowly. Seemed that Bruce was overstocked on house-building tools. Ollie could see ten framing nail guns and a half dozen pancake air compressors. Several power miter box saws, and a stack of cordless tools. Looking out the back door to where Bruce kept the vehicles, Ollie saw a Ford truck he recognized.

Ollie smiled, he could still see on the door where a sign had once graced the door. If he were a betting man, Ollie would bet that sign used to say Brody Construction.

Nodding to himself, Ollie headed back to the front. He was halfway to the counter, when Bruce quit pretending and dropped the paper. "See anything you like?" he asked hopefully.

"I saw a lot of tools, more than you usually have."

"No, not really," Bruce said slowly. "Tools is a big seller. We try to stay fully stocked."

Ollie laughed harshly and leaned against the counter. "Don't bullshit me," he warned, his tone deadly. "I ain't got the time nor the patience."

"Yes sir," Bruce said, swallowing his gum.

"I'm betting a man came in here in the last few days and unloaded a whole boatload of those tools."

"Maybe," Bruce admitted cautiously. "We got folks in here all the time."

"I'm betting this guy had way more tools than your normal customer, and I'm betting his name was Brad Brody."

Bruce nodded slowly. "There was a guy like that, didn't get his name."

Ollie carefully placed both hands on the counter and leaned in to Bruce a little. "Really, 'cause I'm betting this guy also sold you that Ford out back."

"Well shit, if you knew all that why didn't you just say so," Bruce whined digging out a stick of gum. "Yeah, his name was Brody."

"This him?" Ollie asked, laying a picture of Brody on the counter.

"Yeah, that's him. What else you want to know?"

"How much did you give him?"

"A bit over thirty grand."

Ollie shook his head. "For that truck and all them tools?"

"That was all I had, and he wasn't haggling," Bruce replied with a shrug. "They weren't stolen, were they?"

"No, I suppose they were his to sell," Ollie grunted taking the picture.

Ollie stepped out in the street barely noticing the heat that washed over him. So, Brody was raising cash? This was the fourth pawn shop that Brody had hit. Ollie figured Brody had raised close to two hundred thousand. Running money.

Ollie rubbed his chin unconsciously, as he wished for a cigarette. Brody was running, he'd need a new ID. "Gotcha, asshole," Ollie muttered. He smiled, hurrying to his car. He knew just who to call.

CHAPTER SEVENTEEN

Dade County Events Center Miami FL June 21th 2018
Thursday Night

Geena drove up to the event center, leaving her car running with the red light flashing on the dash. Feeling her heart pounding in her chest, she climbed from the car. Taking a deep breath, she pulled her jacket down. She was thrilled beyond words; this was the kind of bust that made careers. Or broke them, if she messed it up.

A part of her wished that Mitch was here, but deep down, she knew he had been right to stay behind. This was her bust to make. And of course, Mitch had Josie to think of. Sink or swim, this was her operation. Another deep breath and a quick check to make sure she had cuffs. It had been years since she had actually carried a set of handcuffs, but she had grabbed a set for tonight. She wanted to be the one to snap them around Jillian Braxton's scrawny wrists.

It had been Mitch's idea to get Braxton at the campaign event, and at the time it seemed like a great idea to Geena. But now it seemed a little out there. While no doubt it would make a spectacular arrest, as long as everything went well. It would be an equally spectacular failure if things went south. Now it seemed that quietly picking up Braxton at her hotel tomorrow would be better.

The thing was Geena had already picked up a team from the Miami office and they were here. Realistically, there was no backing down now. She had set this up and no one in the Bureau would ever take her seriously if she were to back out now.

Giving her jacket another jerk, she turned to the six men climbing from the three cars that had followed her from the Miami field office. To a man, they wore properly, somber, even grim expressions, but Geena could feel the excitement boiling off of them, like heat waves off asphalt. "Gentlemen," she said, struggling to keep the excitement out of her voice. "Are we ready?"

"Yes, ma'am," they replied in unison.

"Alright, let's do this." Geena blew out a sigh, feeling her palms sweat. "You all know what your assignments are?"

Nods and another chorus of "Yes ma'am."

"Okay, then" Geena said, a little surprised at how calm she sounded. It was hard to remain calm when her heart felt like it was about to leap from her chest. Leading her little band, they marched up to a metal door marked stage entrance.

As they approached, a tall, serious man stepped out of the shadows. Geena smiled grimly. She hadn't been able to see the man in the dark, but she knew he would be there. "I'm sorry, you can't come this way," he said in a tone that suggested he wasn't the least bit sorry.

He wore a black wind breaker that simply said security, but Geena assumed he was Secret Service. "FBI," she said curtly, holding up her credentials for him to see. "We are here to arrest Senator Braxton."

It could have been a flicker in the poor lighting, but Geena swore she saw a look of shock leap across the agent's face. If it was ever there, it disappeared quickly, replaced by the impassive look that Geena suspected this man wore all the time, even while making love.

He glanced at her credentials, then nodded. "Of course," he replied, his tone neutral, as if she had asked for a table at Denny's. "I will need to contact my supervisor."

"Of course," Geena replied, making a flipping motion with her hand.

"Thank you." He turned his back, speaking softly in to his left sleeve, while his right hand held an ear piece in place. Geena couldn't make out what he was saying, but she didn't have to, she could almost guess word for word what he was telling his boss. After a few seconds, he turned back. "Miss Vigil is on her way."

"Thank you," Geena said, giving him a nod.

They stood silently waiting on Agent Vigil. It was an uncomfortable silence, but no one made a move to break the silence. People in any other profession might have made an attempt at small talk, but they did not. The Bureau and the Secret Service weren't exactly enemies but they didn't socialize and they certainly didn't engage in idle chit chat.

Geena found herself studying her own credentials when the door swung open and a small, neat woman stepped outside. Like her subordinate, she wore all black, a severe pant suit, and she sported an even more severe hairstyle. Despite the haircut and the somber expression, she had a pleasant, almost friendly face. "Special Agent Geena Dixon," Geena offered, extending her hand.

"Crystal Vigil," she replied, accepting the hand.

"We are here to take the Senator into custody," Geena informed her. "We have a warrant."

"I will need to see that."

Of course," Geena replied. She had been expecting the request and had a copy ready.

Without a word, Agent Vigil took the warrant reading it carefully. As she read the tiniest of smiles tugged at the corners of her mouth. Which told Geena that the good Senator wasn't popular with her security detail. "Okay," Agent Vigil said slowly. "Are you going to do it as soon as the rally ends?" she asked, holding out the warrant.

"Keep it, it's your copy," Geena replied, then grinned wickedly. "I wasn't thinking of waiting. We have a properly authorized warrant and we are going to go in there and place her under arrest."

Like lightening, this time the smile that flashed across Crystal Vigils face was there and gone in a split second. "What do you need from us?"

"Just keep the crowd back."

"We can do that, give me five minutes to inform my team."

Geena nodded, but Agent Vigil had already turned away, talking into her sleeve just as her subordinate had done. Geena turned to her own detail, feeling hot adrenaline rush through her like boiling acid. "Are you ready, gentlemen?" she asked, wondering if this was how an elite athlete felt before a big event. She got a round of nods and grunts, which she was learning was what passed for a gab fest with these guys. "Okay then," she said as Agent Vigil returned. "Let's get it done."

"I will accompany you onto the stage," Agent Vigil said, then flashed the quick, charming smile. "If that is acceptable?"

"Fine by me." Geena said, pushing through the door. They trooped through a snake's nest of cables to another door. They could plainly hear Senator Braxton's screeching, and Geena knew that door led to the stage.

An agent stood in front of the door, arms folded, showing no sign of moving, but a small nod from Vigil and the man stepped aside, opening the door wide.

Braxton was hitting her stride in the speech. She was screaming at the crowd like a woman possessed. As Geena, Agent Vigil and Geena's detail walked on to the stage, Braxton's words stumbled to a ragged halt. "What is the meaning of this?" she demanded, but her tone was subdued, almost hushed.

She knows what's coming,,Geena thought, stepping up to her. "Senator Braxton, I am placing you under arrest," Geena said formally. Her words seemed to leap from her mouth, picked up by the microphone they echoed around the room.

"What? Who are you?" Braxton screeched. "What is the meaning of this?" she repeated.

"FBI ma'am," Geena replied, and quickly spun the older woman around. The podium mike picked up Geena's words throwing them to farthest reaches of the building. "You are being charged with four counts of murder, and two counts of conspiracy to commit murder." It had been decided to charge the Senator with the deaths of Jackson Pyle and Tamera Schroder, as well as Forsyth and Jared Morris the two men who had worked for Van Zandt. They might not all stick but that was for the Attorney General to decide. Pushing her up against the podium, Geena pulled Braxton's right hand behind her back. "You are also charged with racketeering, obstruction of justice and kidnapping."

Geena fastened the first cuff, then pulled Braxton's left hand behind her back, hooking it into the cuffs. "You can't do this" Braxton screamed, kicking the podium. "I am going to be the next President! You can't fucking do this!"

"It's done," Geena said, grabbing Braxton by the arm and dragging her back. Screaming insults and profanity at the top of her voice, Braxton tried to pull away. She kicked at Geena, fighting to get away.

Geena glanced over her shoulder, nodding to the agents. Immediately, two men sprang forward, gabbing Senator Braxton by each arm.

She immediately went limp and would have fallen to the floor if they hadn't been holding her arms. Old hands at this, the agents didn't even try to stand her back up, they simply dragged her across the stage. Screaming profanities and beating her heels against the stage, the Senator went with them.

Geena turned back to the crowd who almost to a person was staring open-mouthed at the spectacle on the stage. They were staring at her and Geena felt like she should say something. Make some kind of announcement, but she didn't have any idea what she should say. Finally, she flashed two fingers at the crowd and shouted. "Peace out." Which to her surprise produced a huge roar from the crowd.

With that, Geena hurried after her guys. Backstage they had stood Braxton up and one of them was reading the Senator her rights. "Do you understand these rights that I just explained to you?

"Fuck you flat foot!" Braxton said, spiting at the agent. "You cocksuckers will never work again!"

"She understands," Geena said. "Let's get her out of here."

"Yes, ma'am," the agent replied crisply, nodding to Geena.

While they marched Braxton to the car, Geena turned to Agent Vigil. "Thank you for your help."

Agent Vigil took her hand, with a curt nod. "My pleasure," she said, then added. "We are at the Holiday Inn."

"Me too," Geena replied.

"I figured, Government and all," Agent Vigil said, nodding. "If you and your team want to come by, we will be in the bar. My group would love to buy your team a drink."

"Sounds good," Geena said, nodding. "Might be a couple of hours. We have to get her settled in county lockup for the night."

"We will be a while shutting this down as well."

Geena glanced at her watch. "Eleven then?"

Law Offices of Milner and Jefferson New York NY
June 22nd 2018 Friday Late Evening

Carl Braxton left his lawyer's office staggering across the parking garage. His feelings and emotions were a jumble. They had just watched the arrest of his wife. Even though he knew it was coming, it had been surreal to watch. It filled him with sadness, but somewhere within that sadness was a tiny vein of glee.

On one hand, he was going to miss his wife, but on the other hand he was finally free. Free from her nagging and complaining. Free from escorting her to all those God-awful fund raisers. Gave him a bit of a woody just thinking of it.

Still he was sad. They'd been together forever, and in his own way, Carl Braxton loved his wife. Trouble was, he loved a lot of women. Yes, he would miss her, but he would get through it.

And now, he was free!

Braxton frowned, well mostly free. He would of course still have to testify. However, his lawyer assured him if he testified against Jillian, any charges he would face would be minimal. The kind of charges that could be taken care of by paying a fine.

It meant that Jillian would certainly have to do some time. But it wouldn't be hard time. Her time would be served in a cushy Federal resort prison. She would do a little time, but she would survive and he would be free. Carl decided, he could live with that.

As Braxton approached his Range Rover, he frowned. This was a night to celebrate. He should call the car service and arrange for a driver tonight. He could have someone from his staff drive the Range Rover home.

His wife might be going to jail, but for him, it was time to celebrate.

He was reaching for his phone, when a pleasant-faced, young man stepped around the Range Rover. "Are you Carl Braxton?" he asked, his voice mild almost friendly.

"Yes," Carl replied slowly, not sure if he should be concerned. "Who are you?"

The young man flashed a brilliant and disarming smile. Braxton was returning the smile when the young man hit him. The punch was fast, catching Braxton square in the mouth, breaking his teeth and knocking him to the ground. "Who are you?" Braxton mumbled, having trouble speaking around the blood and bits of teeth in his mouth.

The young man flashed the smile again, as he adjusted the brass knuckles on his right hand. "Jeff Schroeder," he said, grimly. But when Braxton showed no sign of recognition, he added. "I am Tamera's brother." He nudged Braxton with his toe. "You do remember Tamera? The woman you killed?"

Braxton put up his hand, like he was shading his eyes from the sun. "No, that wasn't me." He whimpered.

Growling from deep in his chest, Jeff dragged Braxton to his feet, pinning him against the Range Rover. Holding Braxton with his left hand, the young man began to pummel him. With the brass knuckles, each blow brought blood. The first broke Braxton's nose, splitting a gash along the bridge of his nose. Braxton tried feebly to protect himself, but Schroeder slapped Braxton's hands away and continued to rain blows on the older man.

Braxton's knees gave out and he slid down the Range Rover, leaving a bloody smear on the glistening paint. "No," he moaned, trying to crawl underneath the vehicle.

"Fuck you!" Schroeder growled, grabbing Braxton by the ankle and jerking him back. The young man kicked Braxton in the crotch as hard as he could. A whimpering bleat escaped past Braxton's lips, as he forgot crawling and tried to cover up.

Jeff stepped back breathing hard. That kick felt good, so he wound up and kicked Braxton again, breaking two of Braxton's fingers and rupturing his left testicle. Openly sobbing and too hurt to crawl, Braxton curled into a ball.

Jeff Schroeder jerked a Highpoint .40 caliber pistol from his waistband, racking the slide and pointing the weapon at Braxton. Crying, Braxton rolled away, trying to hide. "No," he moaned.

"Look at me!" Jeff shouted, stabbing at Braxton with the pistol.

"No, please, don't kill me," Braxton blubbered, covering his head with his arms and turning away.

Tears streaming down his face and his hands shaking violently, Jeff pointed the pistol in Braxton's direction. Using both hands, he tried to hold the weapon steady, willing his finger to pull the trigger.

"Please, I am begging you." Braxton sobbed, holding his hands like he was praying. "Don't kill me, please," he said the last word ending in a pathetic squeak.

Jeff tried to ignore him, concentrating on keeping the gun trained on Braxton. He tried to pull the trigger, every fiber in his body was screaming for him to pull the trigger, but he could not.

"Shit!" he screamed looking up at the ceiling. His body shaking Jeff heard the first siren. It sounded lonesome and far off, but Jeff knew it would be on him in minutes. Tucking the gun in his waistband, Jeff gave Braxton one last kick and turned away.

As he walked away, Jeff pulled a pad of sticky notes from his pocket. He tore the top one off and slapped it on the back window of Braxton's Range Rover. It said;

I KILLED TAMERA SCHROEDER

END OF THINGS

Dead Horse Bar, Douglas AZ June 23rd 2018 Thursday Afternoon

Detective Oscar Olshan stepped into the bar, stopping just inside the door to stretch his back and let his eyes adjust from the bright sunshine to the dim of the bar. There was a time when he could have walked right in with no need to let his eyes adjust. Of course, there was a time when he could spend more than a couple of hours in a car and not have his back kinking up like a cheap garden hose.

After his eyes became accustomed to the dim, Ollie saw there was only three other patrons in the bar. Two Mexican laborers eating a late lunch at a table and a lone, scruffy figure hunched over a beer at the bar.

While the bartender and the two diners stared openly at Ollie, the scruffy figured didn't bother to turn around, instead keeping his eyes on his beer. Ollie smiled grimly, knowing they had all already made him for a cop. Hobbling a little, Ollie nodded to the pair of eaters as he crossed to the bar. Satisfied that he wasn't there for them, they calmly returned to their meal.

"Coors light," Ollie said to the bartender, and took a seat beside the scruffy fellow. Ollie took out his badge and slid it down the bar, placing it beside the man's beer. "Brody."

"Are you here to take me back?"

"Yes, I am" Ollie replied, his tone indicating he would stand for no argument.

"I don't want any trouble in here," the bartender said, placing a small glass of beer in front of Ollie.

Ollie took the glass wondering if they taught that line at bartender's school or something. Seemed like every bartender in the world said it any time a cop came in. "Up to him," Ollie grunted jerking his head at Brody. Ollie tasted his beer, sat the glass on the bar then pinned the bartender with a cold stare. "And to you, but one way or another, he's coming with me."

"Whoa," the bartender said, straightening up and putting his hands up like they were playing stick'em up or something. "Like I said, no trouble, officer."

"Okay, why don't you go wash some glasses or something," Ollie said to the bartender, then turned to Brody. "Finish your beer, then we are leaving."

"I didn't do anything wrong," Brody complained.

"What about running off and leaving your daughter with those assholes?" Ollie growled.

"I didn't know what else to do, if I signed they were going to kill me," Brody wined, playing with his glass. "They were going to kill me!" he screamed.

"What do you think Van Zandt and that phsyco Carter were going to do to your girl?" Ollie growled, as an almost irresistible urge to smash Brody's face swept over him.

Brody sighed, grabbing Ollie's sleeve. "I heard you found her. Is she alright?"

"Yeah, no thanks to you."

Brody nodded quietly. "How did you find me?"

"I talked to Bruce at the pawn shop, he said you were hocking a lot of your stuff. Figured you were looking to buy fake IDs. So, I called my old buddy Timmy Frisco."

"He sold me out?" Brody asked like he couldn't believe it.

"Sure, who are you to him? He knew you couldn't hurt him, and if he pissed me off, he knew I'd be camped on his front door," Ollie said, suddenly tired. He finished his beer in one long drink and grabbed Brody by the arm. "Let's go asshole, time to face the music."

Mitch's House Tucson AZ June 23rd 2018 Thursday Late evening

Why didn't he call?

Mitch turned the phone in his hands, glancing down at his daughter as she played with her dolls. Despite his frustration, a smile crept onto his face. She was an absolute marvel, he decided.

Easily the most beautiful thing he had ever seen.

He delighted at the way she lined her dolls up, bossing them around. One got scolded for wearing the wrong outfit to play in, and immediately her clothes were changed. With the tone of a patient mother, Josie spoke to another one about a new hair style. Fascinated, Mitch watched her brush the dolls hair, then sit her back on the floor, picking up another doll. Sensing Mitch watching her, she glanced back. "Margret simply will not behave tonight," she said her tone dripping with exasperation.

"What are you going to do?" Mitch asked, amused. "Give her a spanking?"

"Not yet," Josie replied, her tone serious. "She's in time out." With that she placed the offending doll under the corner of the couch, wagging her finger at it. "You can just stay there until you learn to behave yourself."

Mitch was smiling broadly when his phone rang. The smile quickly faded as he saw the number flashing across the screen. "Shit," he muttered, rising to his feet and walking into the kitchen.

"You calling to give yourself up?" he demanded, glancing back to make sure Josie wasn't listening.

A dry chuckle rattled through the phone's speaker. "Not hardly," Sam Logan replied with genuine humor in his voice. "I was just at your house. That is a good-looking girl you got there. Mitch…," he started, then stopped. When he spoke again his voice had a ragged edge, like a rusty, old saw. "Kids are what it's all about. Remember that! You take good care of her. Don't let nothing happen to her. Keep her close, and you damn well better be there for her when she needs you."

"Yes sir, I will," Mitch said grimly, feeling a lump in his throat. "You were here?"

"I left something on your front porch."

"Oh, yeah," Mitch grunted, wondering if there might be a bloody corpse on his steps. "You're not talking about Jacob Carter?"

Sam laughed, a merry sound which was totally out of place for him. "Nope, that little prick is gone and he ain't coming back. This is something even better."

His mind racing, trying to figure out what might be on his porch, Mitch crossed to his front door. "We got the Senator. She is going down," he said.

"Saw that on the news," Sam replied. "You think in the end, she will actually do any time?"

"Maybe," Mitch replied, turning on the porch light and looking outside. A small old-fashioned duffle sat on the concrete step. "Her and her husband are busy throwing each other under the bus, I think they will both do a little time."

"Won't be much," Sam predicted as Mitch opened the door and stepped outside. "However, much time they get; it won't be enough."

"Somebody lit Braxton up in New York, kicked his ass pretty good from what I hear. That wasn't any of your doing?" Mitch asked, kneeling beside the bag.

"Nope, wish it was though. I'd say somebody needs to do the same thing to his bitch-ass wife."

"That'd be good, but it ain't gonna happen. Even so, she's done in politics. And we are looking at her and Braxton for Tamera Schroeder's death."

"That the gal that was found at Jackson Pyle's place?"

"Yeah," Mitch grunted, unzipping the bag. "She was pregnant, and it turns out that Braxton was the daddy."

"I still got a dollar that says neither one of them do any real time over it. Wouldn't be surprised if they manage to walk away clean. Write books about the whole thing. Make a shit pile of money."

"Not if I have anything to say about it," Mitch vowed, pulling open the bag. "Either way, she will never...," Mitch stopped in mid-thought, staring into the bag. "What the hell is this?"

"It ain't for you," Sam said, his voice scolding. "You just keep your mitts off it. It's for Jones' wife. What was her name?"

"Karen," Mitch answered, staring at the bag stuffed full of hundreds.

"Yeah, that's it, couldn't think of it to save my life," Sam replied. "Jonesy might have fucked up, but it ain't her fault. There's plenty of cash there. You see that she is taken care of."

"I will," Mitch promised, wondering how in the hell he might be able to do that.

"There's an envelope in the bag. That is for your gal."

"What is it?" Mitch asked, pulling the plain brown envelope from the bag.

"It's a college bond, takes fifteen more years for it to mature. Bought it when I heard I was going to be a grandpa, but then the accident." There was a long silence, and Mitch imagined that he could hear a sniffle. "I want your gal to have it. It should be good to go just about the time she needs it."

"Geez, Sam, I don't know what to say," Mitch stuttered, noticing that the bond would be worth twenty-five thousand when it matured.

"Don't say nothing, just promise me you will do what I asked with that money. I know Karen will end up getting screwed out of getting Jones' benefits because he was such a stupid prick. But you make sure she gets along," Sam said, grimly. "And promise me you will look in on Maureen every once in a while."

"I will, but where will you be?"

"Oh, I will be around."

"Sam, come back, turn yourself in," Mitch pleaded. "I will see you get a fair deal."

"Can't do it, I ain't done yet."

"Sam, you have to stop. What you are doing; it isn't right."

"Ha, like you wouldn't want to take out that whistle dick Van Zandt. All this shit that went down and he is the asshole behind it all. And you just know he's going to walk away from all of this scot free. Tell me that doesn't twist your skivvies in a knot and you wouldn't want just one clean shot at him?"

Mitch didn't answer with a wave of guilt crashing over him. "Ha! I thought so!" Sam gloated, then turned serious, his tone almost lethal. "Mitch, when it comes down to the nut cutting, don't be the one they send looking for me."

Parking Garage Perry Van Zandt's Office Washington DC
June 18th 2018 Thursday Night

Len Dykes crouched in the shadows. He shifted his feet, grimacing. He'd already been waiting a couple of hours and his old legs were starting to talk to him. And they weren't being very polite about it either. His knees felt like he must be kneeling in hot lava.

Getting old, Len mused, he placed a pillow from an old couch on the ground, resting his right knee on it. The pillow wasn't to kneel on, no, it had been brought for another purpose all together. But damn, it did help his aching knees.

Len tried to keep his mind blank. He purposely wasn't thinking about what he was about to do. Wasn't like he had any great plan anyway, he was just going to get it done. From years of investigating crimes, Len knew, when planning something like this, it was usually best to keep it simple. Less ways to screw up. Besides, if he thought about it very long or very hard, he probably wouldn't do it.

And this was something that damn sure needed to be done.

Keeping his mind on his aching knees and away from the task at hand, Len watched the metal door. That's where he would come from. Len knew it could happen fast, and he best be ready. He might get only one chance at this. Certainly, if he were seen, he would have to finish the job or forget about it.

Dykes was in a parking garage, kneeling in the shadow of a support column. Next to a Jeep Renegade. Len wrinkled his nose. Didn't matter how fancy the building was, or how snooty the cliental, these parking garages all smelled the same. Like someone pissed on an oil fire.

Len looked down at the gun in his hand. An old thirty-eight revolver, with a six-shot cylinder, and a four-inch barrel. Standard issue to recruits at the police academy going back to the beginning of time.

Len had one exactly like it, stuck in a closet somewhere, but this wasn't his gun. No, this was Harley's gun. Harley had carried it every day for nearly thirty years. A smile crept onto Len's tired face. That was Harley. The guy drove the same car for twenty years, wore the same damned suit and sat in the same battered recliner ever since Len had known him. And of course, carried the same firearm they issued him at the academy. Years ago, once he made plain clothes, Len had switched to an auto, but of course Harley had stuck with the old revolver.

Harley might have carried this gun every day, but he very rarely, if ever, shot it, Len couldn't even begin to remember the last time Harley went to the range to qualify. Somehow Harley had always managed to talk his way out of having to qualify. If Len had to guess, he'd reckon that a twelve pack of Coors Light was involved. Len smiled and shook his head staring down at the ancient weapon. Harley hadn't shot it much and he had cleaned it even less. Len shook his head ruefully; there had been potato chip crumbs between the cylinder and the frame.

Len had to smile, as he gripped the pistol and hoped to hell the damn thing would fire when the time came. That thought sorta snuck up on Len, but it gave him a quick, hard shiver. Hot damn, what if it didn't shoot? Len almost panicked. Crap, wouldn't that be a cluster fuck? If he jumped up screaming and pulling the trigger and nothing happened? He'd be like some john caught up in a vice sting, standing there with his dick in his hand, looking stupid as hell.

Shit, what would he do if the gun wouldn't fire?

Aw man, he'd better think of something. It was almost midnight, and it surely wouldn't be long now. Sweating, Len began to have doubts. Would it really shoot?

When he got the gun from Harley's effects, the bullets had been actually stuck in the cylinders. When he had pried them out, there had been mold growing on the lead.

He had vigorously cleaned and oiled the gun, and taken new bullets from his stash, but he had not test fired the gun. At the time it had not seemed wise, after all what if someone saw him on the range test firing an old thirty-eight? At the time, that seemed to be a huge risk.

Now it occurred to Len that it might have been a mistake to forgo the test firing. Of course, it was an old revolver, not much ever went wrong with them. Hell, if it didn't shoot, Len would just beat the fucker to death with it. He grinned a little. That might feel real good.

Len closed his eyes, his mind drifting back to better days. Softball games and barbeques. Ribs and cold beers under the stars. Hot, sweaty nights shooting hoops in the park. Len shook his head, Harley, the chubby white boy in those god awful Hawaiian shorts, who could play ball with any ghetto kid Len had ever known. Well, long as nobody was calling fouls too close.

With his eyes closed, Len felt like he could almost touch it. Almost feel the cool grass and smell the barbeque, taste the cold beer. He was jarred out of his memories by the soft click of the metal door closing. He jumped, gripping the gun and resisting the urge to peak around the Jeep. The sound of the door no matter how soft, told him what he needed to know. That was rich folks for you, they didn't like the loud clanging of steel doors slamming shut, so they installed cylinders to make them close softly.

No one ever thought that those slow-closing doors could let a lot of vermin in. Over the years, Len had seen it many times. Len had even considered doing something like that. Waiting in the garage until he could grab the door after someone came through. But in the end, he decided too many unknowns with that. He could burst into Van Zandt's office and find twenty people in there.

Keep it simple, stupid.

Rocking forward, and looking past the bumper of the Jeep Renegade, Len saw Van Zandt walking towards him. Somehow, Van Zandt managed to walk softly and with an economy of motion, but still exude a confident almost arrogant vibe. Probably served him well. Arrogant son of a bitch.

But it sure pissed Len right the hell off.

As Van Zandt approached his car, Len moved to stand up. Len had dreamed of this moment for days, picturing it in his mind. The thing was, in his mind he had always risen to his feet smoothly, confronting Van Zandt with the grace of Billy Dee Williams. In reality he lurched to his feet, staggering like Fred Sanford having the big one. He'd been kneeling too long and his old knees just couldn't take it. Staggering sideways and waving the pillow, he almost dropped the pistol, as he grabbed onto the Renegade for support.

A look of pure disgust sliding onto his face Van Zandt stared as Len regained his balance. "What do you want?" he demanded condescension practically dripping from his tone.

Len had dreamed about this moment, practiced what he would say, but now, nothing came to mind. He simply stared open-mouthed, breathing hard and blowing spit like a yard sprinkler. Van Zandt smiled and blew through his lips, a sound which signaled his disgust. He shook a finger at Dykes, and clicked his car remote. The locks popped with an audible chirp.

"Stop!" Len screamed his voice raw, and his shaking hand waving the old pistol frantically.

"Are you going to shot me?" Van Zandt demanded, practically sneering, as he opened the car door and tossed his briefcase inside. A contemptable sneer puckered Van Zandt's lips, and he shook his head in disgust. He spread his arms, giving Len a clear shot at his chest. After a second he dropped his arms. "I didn't think so," he said, moving to get in his car.

The clever words that Len had practiced deserted him, and he simply stared, the gun shaking in his hand, as huge tears rolled down his cheeks. "I said, stop!" he screamed, spit flying from his mouth.

"Why?" Van Zandt taunted, looking more amused than scared. He took a step forward, crowding Len. "What are you going to do?"

Sweating, crying and anger surging through him, Len felt like he was being electrocuted. "You killed, Harley!" he shouted, his whole body shaking.

Van Zandt snorted, poking Len in the chest. "Don't fuck with me," Van Zandt hissed, pushing Len back. "Same thing could happen to you, old man." Van Zandt smiled, an evil grin which would have sent shivers down the back of an undertaker. "I own you! I want you dead, and you are as good as gone. Just like your fat friend."

Suddenly tired of the whole thing, Len slammed the pillow against Van Zandt's chest. Growling fiercely, Len drove the smaller man back against the car. Jabbing the muzzle of the pistol deep into the pillow, Len squeezed the trigger. The pillow muffled the sound of the gun to the point that it didn't even sound like a shot.

Len barely heard it, he was fixated on Van Zandt's face. For a second, the smug look was frozen on Van Zandt's face. The smugness slowly melted into horror, as Van Zandt realized he had been shot.

For a second, Len savored the moment, but then when Van Zandt tried to speak, Len pulled the trigger a second and then a third time. He felt Van Zandt's body shudder as the bullets tore through it. Whatever Van Zandt was going to say died on his lips, as his face went slack and he slid away from Len, crashing hard against the cold concrete floor.

For a long second, Len stared down at Van Zandt, thinking he should feel something. The truth was, he really didn't. It was as if all the feelings had been wrung from his body. Len shuffled his feet, thinking there was something else he should do. He was tempted to spit on the body, but didn't.

In the end he simply walked away, his shoulders drooping. With each step though, he felt better, as if a weight was being lifted from him. A half a block from the parking garage, Len stopped to light one of the cigars Mitch had sent him.

With the air of a man out for a late-night stroll, Len walked towards his car. He'd parked a half mile away, just in case. He was six blocks away from the garage when he heard the first siren. Len stopped at the river, gazing into the water, which looked black as night. Looking to make sure no one was watching he tossed the pillow in the water, watching solemnly as the current swept it away.

A single tear rolling slowly down his face, he pulled out the gun. Wiping the gun with his shirttail, he started to whisper something, goodbye perhaps, but his throat locked and a racking sob was all that escaped. He held the gun for a second staring at the dark water. Swallowing hard, he threw the weapon out as far as he could.

Even as the gun was sinking to the bottom of the river, Len was walking away. He pulled out a cheap cellphone as he walked to his car, still several blocks away. He dialed the number the old-fashioned way, punching the numbers in from memory.

"It's done," he said, then tossed the phone in the water. Puffing on the cigar, he walked slowly to his car.

Josie Mitchell looked up from her dolls. "Who was that, Daddy?"

Over two thousand miles away, Mitch tossed his phone on the couch and sat down on the floor beside his daughter. "Nobody, sweetie," he said and kissed the top of her head.